A SOLDIER, A LOST GIRL
A PILOT, A FILMMAKER
AN ENIGMA, A MACHINA
A NOMAD, AN EMPRESS
AND THE WORLD AT ITS END.

THIS IS

I0665798

THE
MEMORY
OF BLUE SKY

A novel by J.M.Bardsley

In three parts:

THE ENGINEER'S DAUGHTER
THE LAST GUIDE
THE EMPRESS OF SHORAKAI

ORATANTO

Copyright © Text Joanna Bardsley 2015

Copyright © Cover illustration Joanna Bardsley 2015

The moral right of the author has been asserted.

ISBN: 978 0 9875137 0 0

www.jmbardsley.com

For my big brother Dan,
who ventured into the blue sky with me.
(and taught me how to whistle, tie my shoelaces,
and read the waves.)

Do you remember a blue sky? Not just blue, but wide as the eye can see blue, and deep, eternally deep. A vista at once calm and still, but free and full of dreams, so open, but somehow undeniably certain, and as much a part of the fullness of existence as breathing? Here there is no such sky, such a sky is long forgotten. This is a broken sky, a broken mantle covering a broken landscape. The earth is dying, it is in its last violent throes.

A few fragile islands of life remain despite the toxic steam draughts, constant tremors, new chasms and wasted deserts, but not for much longer. You don't need to be an expert to count the tremors, or see the ever more corrosive power of the recurrent ash clouds.

According to those who keep records it has been over two millennia since the main collapse, when the earth as it was known came to an end. Where people were separated from people, knowledge, progress and technology was lost and had to be regained, and many things that were never known when there was blue sky, that were never known before that time except as myth, things that should have remained hidden deep in stone and darkness were released, even before the ashes from that first great shift had settled and long before the molten rock that had escaped beyond those rifts had cooled.

Now, in 2319 post collapse, surviving colonies have regained and surpassed much of what was lost, but for the state of the world, which remains dire. All fear imminent and final disintegration of the inhabitable earth. Many of the outer remnants have already been lost, along with their cities and all the lives that dwelt in them, either consumed by the quakes or by the death that comes with the steam from the wastes. The end is coming, everyone knows it, but too long has the end been near, and the cities that survive remain superficially content as the people continue to be as they always have been, despite the convulsing earth; they are experts at surviving in this place. Wars are still fought, discoveries made, fortunes are still won and lost, and the media are hungry for stories as always, as information and distraction are commodities sought by a population constantly on edge.

One intrepid media crew begins an expedition hoping to document the vibrant cultures and peoples that inhabit the remaining islands of life before they are lost. Along the way they uncover stories of desperation and of hope, but their journey soon becomes more than anticipated as the crew struggle not only to film, but to survive. Connected to their journey is one man's quest to find his long-lost daughter, another man's desperation to hold together a fraying thread, and a people's desire to uncover a descendent from an old royal line in order to re-establish their nation's former strength to face what end comes.

This is their story.

Part 1: The Engineer's Daughter

CHAPTER 1:

Introducing: The Soldier, the Engineer, the Father: Jonathan Rebus Mark.
Location: Outpost P12, "The Urchin." Off the Island of Corrio, North Island States.

We begin at an insignificant little place, a desolate beacon standing silent out in the empty smog, the tiniest scrap of rock that ever formed part of this earth's fragmented crust. This precarious fragment remains in spite of everything that has befallen, spinning around just like the other defiant yet weary splinters that together turn and make their way around the sun.

From a distance when the clouds condense low to the ground, this scrap of rock doesn't look like part of the earth at all, but like a fallen satellite. Some have endearingly called it 'The Urchin' with reference to those spiny creatures that are found in the rare strands of remaining ocean – the spines, in this case, are formed from a great conglomeration of every kind and make of radio receiver and transmitter known to man, along with who knows what signal reading and relay instruments. However, for the purposes of distinguishing this particular rock from other such ones scattered in the far corners of this place, authorities have labelled this outpost P12.

There used to be a lighthouse here, when there were seas, when there were storms of winds and rain and cyclonic tempest, not of sand and rust and unbreathable air. P12 is still a lighthouse of sorts, a beacon. It collects information from the far corners, deciphers them, and sends any significant rumours to the ships and freighters, travellers, other outposts, and of course, back home to the relevant statisticians, media franchises, and government departments. Rumours, however, have been sparse for more than a few years now, from P12 in any case. One might have even thought P12 deserted but for the occasional relay of some necessary information about the state of volatility in one area or another, of weather and of wars.

As well as being this invaluable data resource P12 is a refuelling depot, but since the modern ships were far more fuel efficient, or ran on alternative energy which P12 had not been equipped to supply, they would often bypass P12 altogether. For the ships that do go by, P12 provides a sort of coast-guard function and somewhat reliable weather beacon. With such an intemperate and unpredictable frontier lying out from the North Islands, a good captain knows never to place too much credence on forecasts, especially if good winds are predicted, for the only kind of winds this place has are searing and tainted with a bitter salt at the best, and barely breathable. At worst, well, they don't list being a shipman as one of the most lethal occupations for nothing. Those winds could push you and the entire ship into the wastes without warning, where even breathing the air could kill you. So if the forecast from the mainland was good, no one believed it.

One man keeps watch over this fragment of rock and its conglomeration of decaying technology, an old soldier, and in his sparse communication he had never given an optimistic forecast, even if his array of instruments brought in fairly positive readings. He knows what it's like out there only too well. But now he sits alone day after day watching, listening and thinking. He sends out the odd, doomed weather balloon, or works at re-wiring a broken transmitter, or welding together a new brace to replace a rusted-out one. He keeps an eye on the old computers and the radios for signals, for information, and stirs himself into action on the rare occasion of a customer or passing enquiry, but mostly he watches the walls of black screens, watching the instruments, analysing, revising, updating the weather readings.

He taps his fingers, blanks out, rubs the dark folds around his eyes, sips from his cup that always seems to contain room-temperature tea, watches, listens, revises. And from time to time when the weather brought the opportunity he would look up at the stars, they always amaze him. P12 is, or was, on top of everything else, an astronomical station. It was put in place at the outset of the exploration revolution, some time after the war of the mines. It has a white domed observatory with a powerful telescope looking up through a gap in the Urchin's antennae. Although, it isn't quite so white as it used to be. Like everything else decay is inevitable, especially out here. He can't use it often in any case, as the atmosphere is usually too thick with cloud and dust to see much of anything.

It might be expected that here could only live the most eccentric or mad man obsessed by a passion for some particular branch of scientific enquiry which he can pursue here, largely undisturbed by others and with such an array of data and apparatus at his sole use, but the reality is the contrary. The man employed on the outpost of P12 is, by appearances, just an average, ordinary man doing his job, though he is built on a slightly more solid and larger scale than the rest. And like most average, ordinary men he gets tired, he gets bored, he eats and drinks what he shouldn't eat and drink, doesn't exercise as much as he should exercise, sleeps when he is tired, but generally does a fairly good job even though he isn't really enthused about it. It's not the most respected position either, most ordinary citizens probably aren't even aware of its existence, but for a man who neither cares nor thinks about it, it makes no difference. This is his chosen early retirement, to sit here day after day on below minimum wage. He'd rather be here than in the crowded cities, he had decided, he was weary of their stench and throng, and after all, someone had to be on P12 to relay to the ships the latest information about their destination, observe changes, update information and maintain the post.

It was at most times a nice quiet life, and the pay was near enough to make do with for a resourceful man like him, so he was content. But if anyone had been able to observe the man, they might have considered that he was in no way as content as he would have himself believe. First of all the man's fingers were tapping twice as fast and twice as often as usual, and when he wasn't tapping he would leave the observatory and take a turn around the Urchin, inspecting, or appearing to inspect, the receivers and transmitters, the landing bays, his lithop garden, which had sprung up entirely by itself in one corner of a deserted landing strip amongst the cracking asphalt, and everything else until there was nothing more to inspect, and going to great lengths to test the fuels for quality and make sure all were in good supply. All this was highly unusual. He had even done the regulation trial evacuation of the tower, to break up the monotony; he was supposed to do one every six months and this was the first time he'd done it in the years that he had been here. Any observer would have been intrigued, if not concerned by this behaviour.

The truth was that the soldier had begun to dream, which he had never in all his life till about a month ago, well, not dreams like this. These dreams were intense, real, gut-wrenching, heart pumping dreams which stayed with him in his waking hours. It was a strange thing, and terrifying, to a man who had considered being so affected by dreams proof of a weak mind. A doctor may have prescribed some mild sedative or anti-depressant, but drugs would have done nothing to cure him anyway and he knew it. Blue skies filled his dreams, blue as blue and eternally deep. No starry vista or shrouded desert could wrench his heart like that sky could. The first time he had seen anything close to it was in reality, in his youth, even though it was nothing like the full blue sky of his dreams, he had been struck with awe at such a sight - the fabled sky of Shorakai. It had taken his words away and filled his blood with a pulse that made every desire seem possible. Now it was just an illusion, haunting him at every hour. That blue blanket would be thrown off and he would be facing the black screens again and going through the monotonous readings.

The engineer's daughter would have been 21 this year. 21. That's 20 years he hadn't seen her face or heard her laugh. 20 of the longest years a man could live. Yesterday he'd been so young himself, yesterday he'd held a baby in his arms and smiled the irrepressible smile of a new father. Today he felt fifty, or older, and yet one might wonder if underneath that furrowed brow, heavy head and lifeless eyes a strong young man still lingered, waiting for the right moment to fight against the time and torture that had been dealt him.

He would wash his face to try to wake himself up, touch the picture of his wife and baby girl tucked into the corner of the mirror, kiss his big fingers and touch them to the photo again, let himself be torn again seeing her cute green eyes and button nose. His daughter is his last link with this place, this accursed earth, if he could have found her his life would not have seemed like such a waste. If he could, he would give his life if only he could know that she was somewhere out there and alright. When he thinks of her and her mother and how perfect it was for that moment, he can believe that life was a wonderful gift. This last month in all his dreams he dreams of her mother, her voice echoing across that wide blue sky of her country, calling him. So he tries to stay awake, for nothing is more painful than the memory of his beautiful wife, the shock of her death and his guilt over losing their daughter.

Perhaps mother and daughter are both together now, somewhere in the afterworld. It is a nice thought in some ways, but so terribly bitter as he is here, and he is alone. But he can't believe his precious child is there, for that he is her father has sustained him all these years, the last drop of hope the overtaking darkness could not quash. He believes that she has to be out there somewhere, but where? his mind asks over and over, if only he knew where! When it happened, when his daughter disappeared from the Universal City Port on Corrio, where he worked, neighbours and fellow workers had searched the streets with him, and the entire port. Though the bosses had refused to shut it down, they still had helped in the search, but she was never found. That was not long before her first birthday. He did not stop searching for fifteen years, he searched the world till he was utterly exhausted, and found himself here.

Tonight as he sat and held his head the rusty hands on the old clock turned over midnight. He looked up, and then took a tall bottle and a short glass from out the cupboard at his knees, filling it only enough for one sip. He held the glass up and looked from screen to screen, from the cloudy skies that hid uncertain stars to the feed from distant satellites and the camera footage of the docking bays on the Urchin itself.

'Happy birthday Ava my girl,' he toasted and quickly downed the draught, 'happy birthday.'

CHAPTER 2:

Introducing: The 'Gutter-Mouse', Laundry Worker & Amateur Photographer, Melissa.
Location: Junto-a-Mar ('alongside the sea') aka 'The Gutter', Island of Corrio, North Island
States.

'So, a toast to you Melis, here's to you for getting out of The Gutter in style girl. Don't forget me if you make your fortune chicka-babe.' The vivacious Katrina took a long sip, belched and giggled in a girly way that was far from the pin-up girl appearance she obviously aspired to convey, but this was her farewell to her dearest friend, little Melissa, who she loved and protected like she might a younger sister, or daughter, had there been more years between them. As it was they were nearly the same age, Kat just had the street smarts that Melissa lacked and Melissa had the conscience that Katrina lacked. Yet they were the best friends regardless, or even perhaps because they complemented each other's failings. Without Kat, Melissa was sure she'd end up in a scrape in no time, it's not like this city was safe for anyone, let alone a timid girl like she was. And Kat, though pushing Melissa to get out of this place, was sure she'd do something terribly wrong within a day of Melissa's departure and was already trying to formulate backup plans for various potential calamities.

But that wasn't yet, this was now, and Katrina was shouting Melis a hot chocolate, as despite all her friends protestations she still preferred that over coffee or liquor. And it wasn't just any hot chocolate, it was real chocolate, yes, *real* chocolate, which was so difficult to get these days, and with marshmallows and cream, at the best little café in Junto-a-Mar, which had cushioned chairs and bright painted tables and walls strewn with found artefacts and everything.

'I still can't believe I'm going, I can't believe I actually got the job,' Melissa went over it again. 'I'm sure they'll just throw me out when they see I really don't have any experience at all.'

'Come on girl, don't be so damned shy! I seen your skills, sure you don't got the language of the pros but you got the gift see.'

'The gift!' Melissa laughed.

'You're an artist girl, you know that, I know that, artist to the core.'

'Somehow I don't think the executives at TnTv are going to want a photographic impressionist. I'm sure they just want a simple shooter for the cut and paste.'

'Then why was they looking for you in the Expo de Arms hey?'

'I don't know. Even those pics were hidden away in a back corner of the exhibition, I'm surprised anyone saw them at all. I didn't have my stuff showing anywhere else, I mean I only just started taking pictures when I found that old Carrelli. It wasn't that long ago, and I didn't think those two shots I entered in the show really got much attention. I think I'm still in shock that anyone noticed, and that I got a call! I'm so nervous that I'll stuff this up.'

'You'll do fine girl. It could be worse, I mean, TnTv of all the stations! They're youthful, artsy, fun.'

'Extreme,' Melissa added as a downside.

Katrina was about to reply with a positive comeback, but something caught her attention. 'Oh no,' she gave Melis the *better watch out!* glance. 'Here we go.'

'Hiya girls,' a well-rounded and heavily made-up woman came up to the two girls and greeted them familiarly, having seen them from the street. 'Not like you two to waste your notes on this swishery. Janie noticed Melis was a bit too keen to take the break today. What's the occasion?' she asked, eyeing their drinks and taking a seat. She had an expression of mild interest on her face, but behind her eyes was a determination to get at the truth, something was up and she knew it. Melissa glanced at Kat. What should they do?

'Hey Sophia,' Kat welcomed, her bangles jangling around Sophia's neck as Kat embraced her warmly, 'yeah, I wanted to do something special, it's Melissa's birthday you know.'

The woman looked at her cunningly, 'You know I know it ain't. You know I know not even sweet Melis herself knows her birth date, unless, honey, you discovered something?'

The girls looked at each other for help, 'We decided to make it today,' Kat said.

Madam Sophia continued, 'I also know her room is empty, she's got all her gear in that bag there, and I have this goodbye letter.' She put it on the table. 'You going to explain this to me honey?' she asked. She was firm, but still friendly.

The girls looked at each other again. Melissa began, 'You weren't supposed to find it yet, I thought you'd be out till later.'

'What you want to go and leave for honey?' Sophia chided, 'You don't want to leave us do you? Us who looked after you all these years?'

'I got a call from this guy, I've been offered a job, a real job,' Melissa stammered, 'I thought what better way to get out of The Gutter, right?'

'*This guy?*' Madam Sophia raised an eyebrow, unimpressed.

'His name's Weston Alamo, you know, that famous documentary maker for TnTv, he said he'd seen some of my stuff and asked if I could send in my portfolio, said there might be a job there for me.'

'Doing what girl? Hey? Even if this guy is legit, you already got a job, and what do you know but what you learnt here?'

'I've been practising photography when I wasn't working. I was surprised at the offer too, but he said they used stills as well as motion, because TnTv has the news media arm and publishing company on top of all the television stuff they do, and anyway, he said they had an opening for someone like me,' she explained.

Madam Sophia chuckled, 'Oh honey, you're fooling yourself if you think you'll make good of it, if it's the real deal that is, which I very much doubt.'

'Why? What's so wrong about wanting a better life? About taking an opportunity like this, just handed to me on a plate almost. I don't want to work in that sweatshop, doing Sir's laundry forever!'

'No, no, and I don't blame you. It's just, well, sudden. You can't just walk away from him.'

'Well I'm going to,' Melissa replied, firm in her resolve to go.

'So this job's definite then, is it? I'll bet this guy's just making a fool of you or using you, mind my words honey.'

'No, it's serious, Mr Alamo should have hung up on me by all rights, I told him straight out I didn't have a folio, but he just said to send in whatever pics I had because they were really interested in my work. I ate nothing but barley broth and noodles for a week so I could get some more shots done and pay for the line time so I could send him the pictures. Now here I am, I'm getting out Sophia,' she said determinedly, 'I'm going!' Melissa's eyes sparkled, though her whole body was shaking.

'You are, are you?' Sophia mused, eyes on the envelope of the letter Melissa had left her, pushing the flap back and forth with her polished fingernails.

'*Sir* didn't send you did he?' Kat questioned, 'you can't stop her going Sophia, you know she's got to get out of here!'

'Yeah, I know,' Sophia relented quietly as she stood to go. She patted Melissa's shoulder warmly, and though she was obviously upset she said, 'Good on you honey, good luck.'

Melissa spontaneously sprang up and embraced the woman tightly, 'I'll miss you, you know.' Sophia just pursed her lips and patted Melissa's hair in a motherly way, nodded, then turned and rushed away before another word could be said.

Melissa sat again and sipped. The two girls were silent for a while then Melissa said nervously, 'I still don't think they'll keep me on though, then what will I do?'

'Well you got to give it a go, got to start somewhere, why not there, with the best?'

'Oh, I don't know about this.'

'How else are you gonna fly girl? I always knew you had wings, ever since Sir brought you here. You were so little, and beautiful - like an angel, I knew you weren't meant for this place. Get out of here while you got the go,' Katrina encouraged, then paused and scraped the rim of frothy chocolate from her glass and sucked it from her finger, thinking. 'You know it's gonna be desolation without you here sista,' she added.

'I wish you could come with,' Melissa said, 'I really do.'

'No, no you don't babe, you got an adventure to do by your own sweet self. One more minute here babe, that's all, can't let you miss your ride.'

'I don't want to go Kat,' Melissa shook her head, suddenly overcome by everything that lay before her. 'I've never been further than, than Universal City, this is big, if they keep me on I'll be going to the other side of the world like those crazy people you see on the adventure channel!'

'Melis, I hate to tell you, but you'll be one of those crazy peeps,' Katrina laughed.

'I can't go Kat,' Melissa said, then whispered, 'I don't want to go, you and all my friends are here, I don't know anyone else, I don't know anywhere else.'

'Settle babe, listen to yo'self,' Kat said, chuckling yet staying firm, 'you want to stay here? What? Mendin' clothes, doing the steam laundry for them toffs in the city? What? Packaging their cigs, re-labellin' Sir's back of the truck booze? Sortin' the pills? In this mess girl? Get out!'

'Yes I do,' Melissa hugged her friend, 'I do, I want to stay,' she cried.

'I don't think so, you know you don't want this, hey,' Kat squeezed little Melissa tight and said in her ear, 'come on, *I* gotta go back to Madam Sophia's and I *don't* want you to come with, I don't want you to end up in the top house like me. Sooner than you know you'll have grown up and you'll be even more beautiful and womanly. I don't never want to see you back there girl, you understand? You know the way it goes, she can't protect you from Sir anymore, you know he's had his eyes on you forever, and he don't never take no from no-one.' Kat pushed her out of their embrace and looked at her worried, and serious, 'So you gotta go, understand?'

Melissa nodded, then Kat laughed, 'Oh babe, you ain't never going to make it if your eyes run like this every time you say goodbye. Look at yo' face,' she wiped the dark lines of mascara and tears from off Melissa's cheeks. 'You know I'm not going to let you stay here to rot away like the rest of us empty souls.'

'No.'

'You go and make us proud. You know you'll be earning more in a week than I'd hope to rake up in a year babe.'

'If I last.'

'You *make* it last girl. Show 'em you can still find stars in The Gutter babe.' Katrina sighed, a tear trickling down her own cheek as she smiled sadly, then turned as she heard a familiar sound. 'Check it out, here's your ride.'

'Matthias?!' Melissa's face lit up with joy and surprise as a fine motorbike pulled up and waited by with a deep purr. 'I thought you were cabbing with me over to the station?' Melissa asked Kat.

'Nah girl, saying a lonely goodbye's a boy's job. Since you ain't got no fella I thought you might like the next best thing, right?' She didn't wink at Melissa, but she may as well have, Kat was the only one little Melissa had told about her one-time crush on this particular guy.

'One last ride for you Melis,' the rider smiled, a roughly good-looking young guy who handed her a helmet then went about strapping her small amount of gear to the back.

'Oh I love you Kat, thank you,' Melissa embraced her friend once again, 'I'll miss you so much, I won't never forget you, ever.'

'Never ever?'

'Never ever.'

'Go, go, go, can't be late babe. Don't let anyone hassle you now,' Kat pushed Melissa towards the bike. 'Love you. Get her there safely Matti,' she yelled after them, 'hell to pay if you don't!'

They were gone, goodbye was over. Kat returned easily to the bar, counting the coins left in her purse now that she'd paid for their treat. Boy was it an expensive place to go if ever there was one, but still, there was just enough here to order herself a small glass of the stuff she spoiled herself with, but as soon as she sipped it she clasped the charm that hung about her neck and stared blankly at the tinted window. Sir had just walked past, like a chill on the spine, then his footsteps became clear, those squeaky new shoes, then the swish of his pressed suit came much too close.

'How's my Kat?' he slid onto the chair which Melissa had only recently vacated. His voice sounding like the serpent's own in Katrina's ears. 'I've just seen Sophia,' he said. To her horror Kat noticed bruises just beginning to show colour on the man's knuckles. 'Where's my Melis?' he asked.

Kat watched this smartly dressed yet greasy individual as he watched her in turn, as if each was daring the other. The hostess brought Sir's usual drink.

'Kat?' he asked again and sipped, 'where is she?'

'How should I know,' she answered.

'Don't play fool with me girl, I know you too well. Where is my Melis?'

'She ain't yours,' Kat whispered.

'What did you say?'

'I said,' Kat's eyes widened, and she huffed in defiance, 'She ain't yours. She's gone.'

'You know you'll pay for this,' Sir said, but continued to sip casually as he pondered what step to take next, 'the both of you, you'll pay.'

'She's just one little girl Sir, let her go!'

'Just one little girl!' Sir curled his lips, leaning frightfully close and grabbing Katrina's wrist too tightly, 'You're right Kat, she's not mine, she belongs to someone who's paid me to keep her till they want her. Why do think she's not in the top house already! You've no idea what that one girl means for me! Who she belongs to! Where is she Katrina! Tell me!'

Kat shook her head, 'She doesn't belong to anyone! Please sir, let her go! Why is she so important? Oh, please let her go.'

'Where's she going Katrina? Tell me!'

'No. No I can't, Sir I can't do that, if you do anything to her there'll be no sunshine in the world, never again,' Kat protested.

Everyone in the café was silent, but trying not to turn towards the place where Katrina and Sir were. Sir lowered his voice further, 'Kat, my dear Kat, is that what you think of me? I would never harm Melis. Please tell me where she's going, it's for her own good Kat, you don't understand, just tell me, I don't want to have to hurt you.'

'No, of course you don't,' she dared, 'you'd lose too much money with me not looking sweet.'

'Kat, come on, there are people out there who will do far worse to Melis than you imagine I will, tell me Katrina, you will pay dearly if you don't!' he threatened.

'Better make it worth it then,' Kat laughed in her gravelly little way, though terrified of the man, she spilt his drink over his trousers as she picked up her bag and ran out. She should leave like little Melis, she thought, but where would she go? She'd just end up in another city, the same old situation, besides, where would she get the money for the ticket? She'd spent the last on these farewell drinks. Oh this place was going to be so desolate without her dear friend. But was Sir right? Would Melis be alright out there on her own?

~

Melissa thought the world of Matthias, he was a bit older than her, rough, bit of a charmer, well known about the place. He was something of a mechanic, but everyone knew there was more going on at that workshop than just fixing cars. Some cars would come in and other cars would go out, and some cars were never seen again. Others delivered packages and others picked them up. But none of that mattered to Melissa, she'd always looked up to him with the same admiration as one might look up to an older brother, even though he was Sir's nephew he wasn't like Sir at all. She savoured this ride into the train station, holding tight around Matti's chest and pressing her nose close against his jacket so she wouldn't forget just how he smelt. There was something strangely comforting about that strong scent of grease and leather, it made her feel like she was floating.

'Here we are butterfly,' his voice came so softly to her after the loud hum of the motorbike's engine had ceased. Her heart was swelling in her throat as she slowly came back to earth and let him go. 'Come on,' he said, picking up her things and heading down the steps to the underground platform. She had to stretch her shorter legs to keep up with him and not lose him in the crowd.

He checked the timetable on screen for when the train was due. 'It says four minutes, I'll wait with you,' he said, 'I might not see you again right?'

'I don't know,' she tried to be casual and gave him a faint smile, 'maybe, I hope.'

He studied the timetable again. 'You don't have to wait, you know,' she said, thinking he was bored, 'thanks for the ride, and everything.'

'No, no I don't mind, I want to, I mean, well Kat'll pound me if I don't see you safe away, and besides,' he stopped, seeing the train round the corner, 'oh, here it is.'

The long inter-city line pulled up with neat precision. It was strange to see the new high-speed aero-designed machine pull up at this old station, which had remained in a state of perpetual neglect since its construction when this place had been a thriving metropolis of its own, so many years ago. Melissa would be in the city in no time at all.

She was about to step on board when Matthias pulled her back suddenly, 'Melis, just wait, almost forgot, I've got something for you.' He pulled his hand out of his pocket and took hers. 'Just a little thing,' he explained, depositing the item and folding her fingers back over it.

'What is it?' she asked, very surprised.

'Just a little something to remember us by, it's nothing, really, or if you ever get in a spot it has some value, so you could sell it if you needed to.'

She carefully opened her fingers and peeked at it. 'Oh man! Matti, it's your crew's button! You can't give me this!'

'Just did. I love you butterfly. Good luck.'

'What?'

'Get on the train.'

'No, I didn't think you did, you never even looked at me like you did the other girls.'

'Exactly.'

'But,'

'Don't talk girl, go on or it'll go without you.'

'Let it, if I'd have known I'd never thought of going.'

'I know it, why'd you think I never said nothing,' then to himself angrily, 'shouldn'ta said nothing now,' he shook his head. 'I'm the opposite of innocent, and I ain't gonna change. I ain't right for you butterfly. Don't you ever come back, you know what I'm saying, not unless you're prepared to die here.'

'No,' Melissa cried and hung onto his coat sleeves, 'no, no, I'm staying.' More tears ran down and stained her cheek.

He bent, kissed her gallantly on her brow, and gave her hair a rub. 'No you ain't, you got a life beyond this place,' he said gently, 'you got a destiny girl, we all of us know it, you just got to go live it.' He stepped back, then she realised she was standing in the carriage and the door closed suddenly between them. She saw him say 'goodbye butterfly' as she banged the window.

'No! Matti!' she yelled, but he was sped away in a moment. The last thing she saw was Sir running up to the platform, yelling. Was he yelling for them to stop the train? Whatever it was it hadn't impressed Matthias who had turned quickly to Sir's surprise and knocked him flat with one hit, but then there were men all over Matthias.

No wonder people hated goodbyes, goodbyes were painful and horrible. She sank to the floor at the feet of other passengers and looked at the silver button he had given her. It was beautifully embossed with the mech-angel motif of Matthias's crew; a pair of wings, half machine and half real. It was such a small thing, but it was the pride of every self-respecting biker in The Gutter. Melissa polished it with her thumb, but then the train slowed suddenly as it came into the next stop and the button was flung across the floor.

Melissa struggled through the crowd after it, but before she could get it a man in uniform had discovered it and pocketed it. He saw her look of utter dismay, but the man just sniggered, 'Got a ticket Gutter-mouse?'

She put her hand in her pocket, the ticket was here somewhere, it had to be.

CHAPTER 3:

Introducing: The Producer, Weston Alamo, & The Captain, Orin Hardan.
Location: TnTv Tower, The Universal City, Island of Corrio, North Island States.

In an obscure office on the fifteenth floor of TnTv's headquarters in the metropolis, an office which also seemed to be a storage room for various artefacts, memorabilia, photographs, awards and various other items which could only fall into the category of garbage, TV's acclaimed documentary producer, director and presenter, Weston Alamo, was discussing the future with the captain he'd hired to take his team on a potentially dangerous tour of the southern extents of the remaining populations on earth.

The producer was a middle-aged man, older or younger depending on whether or not he had got out of bed in a state of confusion or was heading off on some exciting new project. Today was the former. He ran his hands through his dark, though fading, hair. He was looking older and that wasn't helped by the three day whiskers around his chin and the lost-ness of his gaze. In contrast his captain was pristine. Shirt, jacket, trousers, all ironed and pressed to an immaculate finish. How he kept them so clean and schmick was a mystery to the producer who couldn't keep a shirt clean above ten minutes, there was breakfast to eat and coffee to spill, ink, dirt, grease, dust, that's why he didn't wear particularly good clothes to work, or at home, or in fact on any occasion except perhaps with the exception of television awards nights. It was also why he liked bright pattern print shirts, like the one he was wearing today, with pictures of pineapples and palm trees all over it.

The producer sighed the sigh of a man who had just about given up. 'What to do Hardan?' Weston said. 'You know I'm not going any further than Satsuan without a guide. I can't keep Fisher on, he's far too chancy.'

'I agree, Fisher's not ideal,' Captain Hardan replied.

'You only saw how close a call it was coming in, the boy's a fool,' Weston said, while trying to unlock the top drawer of his desk.

'Just as well you found out before the crew's together and we're on the way.'

'Too true, what trouble we'd have been in it doesn't do to think on. Pity though, he seems to know how to deal with people, he could have been handy to have by.'

'Sure, he seems to have a deceptive charm, but we won't have the need for an amateur con-artist on this trip, in my opinion.'

'By no means, he'd be more trouble than he's worth, we just need a bit of diplomacy and nous, someone with an understanding of the south. Different peoples and different places, that's the whole topic Hardan, showing our viewers the places they'll never get to or dream of going to, places where our far flung ambassadors are kept on edge every day,' Weston laughed, 'and the places we don't send ambassadors. I've got to keep the team safe,' Weston continued as he searched in the drawer for some item or other, 'I just want them to be reliable. I can trust the photographers to do their jobs, I can trust you to get us around and take care of the ship, particular care since you know what lengths I went to to get her, at your recommendation.'

'The Blue Moon is exceptional, you must admit.'

'I do, the best I've had yet,' Weston agreed, while continuing to rummage through various cupboards and drawers around him, 'but is it too much to ask that I could just find a guide?'

'You're not going to find a guide in the drawer West,' Hardan laughed.

'What?' Weston's face screwed up, but then he understood, 'oh, no, of course not, I'm looking for these! Aha! There you are.' Weston pulled out two tiny metal things that looked like they belonged inside a clock or other mechanical device. Weston cleared a spot and put them proudly on his desk.

'What are they?' Hardan asked politely.

'Balance wheels.'

'What do they do?'

'You spin them,' Weston explained, very enthused about them. 'I've timed them, that one can go for over a minute without falling over.'

'You're procrastinating,' the captain laughed.

Weston sighed. 'Well do you want to make the call? I don't, but I'm not going to let my people go into the virtually unknown with *that* upstart.'

'Of course, you can't go without an experienced guide. That would indeed be reckless, but then again you are usually somewhat reckless so-'

'I'm not reckless,' Weston sounded like he really believed he wasn't.

'Let me rephrase,' the captain continued amiably, his was not a countenance that was easily shaken, nor was his mind easily consumed by unnecessary worry, which made him the ideal captain for Mr Alamo, 'you do have a tendency to dispense with certain precautions.'

'Yes, certain unnecessary precautions of course, everyone does, don't they? But we're going a long way from home, and doing such a, a monumental, doco-travel-tv-event thing, I can't risk anything. You've no idea how many executives are leaning in to make sure I realise the importance of this expedition. Filming the last fragments of earth and civilization before it disappears, in a way people here haven't seen, that's a big responsibility, and they add a little *pressure* every time they stick their heads in. They remind me how much I begged them for this opportunity and how much money they've already poured into the project though we haven't even lifted off the ground yet. Not to mention the extra finance we've managed to glean from the government and their pressure to use the funds how they'd like on top of all that. Ho, I'd like to see them out there risking their heads like we'll be doing,' Weston sighed, 'Boy oh boy. I really need a holiday and we haven't even got going.'

'Coffee?' Hardan asked.

'No thanks,' the producer shook his head as he lifted a cold, third full mug to the captain, 'I've already had too many today, you go ahead though. Honestly I don't know why I drink the stuff, I don't really like it that much, maybe it's just social convention? Or boredom? Or perhaps indecision. I don't know what to do about this guide. Where was I?'

'You need a holiday but we haven't even started the job yet.'

'That's right. The crew will be arriving today and tomorrow. It's all set except for the guide, I was so sure of young Fisher.'

'Knew how to con you too, that's the problem.'

'He sure pulls a good bluff, didn't even think to check his qualifications, course I didn't, he was such a confident kid you know, sounded like he really did know his stuff. Such a shame.'

'Plenty of people know the south to some degree, I'm sure you'll find someone in a few days.'

'But they really have to know their stuff. I don't know who else to call that I haven't called already, and it's got to be tomorrow Hardan, tomorrow or I will have to cancel the whole thing for the moment. And it can't just be anyone, it's got to be someone who really knows their way around, inside out. Co-pilot for you, someone who could take over if the worst happened, you know, not that it would but–'

'There's always that possibility, naturally,' Hardan replied in his usual soft, unworried way.

'Why does your calm irritate me? It irritates me Hardan, can't you get a little concerned? Here I am stressing like a dog who's trying to catch his tail, and you're like yep, yep, it's going to be fine, it's all good, all the time. It's not good Hardan, alright, this whole thing's falling apart a day before we're due to go and you're smiling.'

Hardan shrugged his shoulders, 'You don't have kids do you West?'

'Do I look like a goat? No. But what's that got to do with anything?'

Hardan just chuckled. Weston continued, 'I know one or two of the team has some reasonable flying experience, but Melissa's just a kid, purest intuition, but I'll bet she's never even been as far as Parahn, and this'll be her first real jaunt you know. Astrid sure could do it but I know she wouldn't want to and I don't want her to either, and she might have a lot of academic knowledge but she's never been really far south, as far as I know, so co-pilot sure, but she wouldn't do for a guide. Tarku, well, who knows about Tarku, he knows the south a bit sure, and I reckon he knows how to do a nice turn in a standard Avero, but I'm hiring him to be a photographer, not a guide or a pilot, and this is the Moon, Hardan, my Blue Moon. You've no idea what I had to do to get the station to agree on spending so much on a mere vehicle.'

'She's worth it though.'

'I won't ever say she isn't,' Weston replied, wide eyed and grinning. 'Who was she designed by again? Some famous designer wasn't it?'

'Mm, you just mentioned one of his other designs, it's D'Avero, Luca D'Avero, he did racing vehicles and motorbikes as well as vessels like the Blue Moon that can navigate the difficult divides and get through volcanic ash cloud and all of that.'

'Ah yes, that's right.'

'Have you thought of John Mark for the guide?' the captain suggested.

'What?'

'You know, John Mark, the soldier, the engineer.'

'Yeah, I *know* who he is, I did a doco on him way back, but is he still around the place?'

'Don't reckon he'd be in the city, but he's got to be around somewhere. He'd sure know the deep like no-one else.'

'He would, he would. Not much fun though is he?'

'He seemed like a nice enough fellow to me.'

'So how do you know him?'

'Saved my life once.'

'Really?' Weston raised his brow, 'Wow.'

'Yeah, over in Salamonde, my first co-pilot position. John was a passenger on the cargo flight when the captain went cataleptic, you know, like he couldn't move or do anything. I was out of my depth, and what with that and the shock of it, well, it would have been too late if it hadn't been for John. Ooh, here we are.' The machine was finished so Hardan took himself a mug of coffee and proceeded to fill it with sugar as he continued. 'Just when I was in a panic with all the lights and what have you flashing at me -'

'*You* were in a panic?'

'Yeah,' Hardan said slowly, as he remembered.

'That's hard to believe,' Weston chuckled, 'Hardan in a panic, sorry, I can't picture it.'

Hardan just raised his eyebrows and shrugged his shoulders as he smiled and emptied another sachet of sugar into his coffee.

'Apologies Hardan, do go on.'

'As I was saying, something about John wasn't it?'

'The cataleptic captain to be precise, and your panic.'

'Ah yes, and the captain not responding at all, then John came into the cabin and casually pointed out a few tricks to me to pull the bulky thing round, saved us all. Of course the ship needed a bit of beating back into shape afterwards, not to mention a fair amount of new panelling at great expense, but what's that when we all could have met our end right then.'

'Sure is a story, I didn't know that one. Should have told me, I'd have put it in the doco. John was so, I don't know, reserved or something, you can't talk to him, I mean, have a conversation, you know. I could only ever get one word syllables out of him, and all the time I felt like he was interrogating me. Strange sort of man,' Weston observed, then watched Hardan put yet another sachet of sugar into the cup and wondered whether or not he should advise his stout friend to go easy as he didn't want to have to find another captain too, but Hardan picked up the spoon and began to stir it so Weston refrained, and looked with some thoughts of disgust at his own mug of long-cold coffee, pushing it aside.

'You just went about it wrong,' Hardan supplied. 'John didn't want any attention, all he cares about is his little girl, and you were making a series about heroes of the exploration revolution. All those things he did were only because he was searching for his girl, it's true. I know you touched on it, but he wanted to say more and whenever he tried to bring it up you kept on with the questions about his exploits and the trouble he got into here and there. Watch it again West, you'll see where you went wrong.'

'Should've told me back then.'

'Wasn't working with you back then.'

'True. So, John Mark you reckon.'

'He's different when you're not trying to get something out of him. Does seem the silent type though, was pretty solid back in the day too, could be handy in a tight spot.'

'So you've kept in touch over the years?'

'No, just that day, yep, saved my life, had a few drinks together, he gave me some pointers, asked me to keep an eye out for his daughter, then we went our separate ways.'

'Yet you know so much about him?'

'Well -'

'Can't think I could spend weeks in the same ship as him though, better find someone else.'

'Ain't no one better in my opinion,' Hardan said as he sipped.

'Supposing you're right, and supposing I can't find anyone else, where am I supposed to find the engineer anyway?'

'Have you checked the listings?' Hardan asked as he gently extracted a glazed roll from a brown paper bag.

'No.'

'Be worth checking the listings.'

'A man like that's not going to be in the listings, he moves around too much, and yet,' Weston paused as he accessed the database from his computer. 'Would you believe there's a John Rebus Mark on P12. Where is P12 Hardy, isn't it one of those outposts on the edge of the great divide?'

'Mm. That's interesting.'

'Yeah, what's a man like him doing out there?'

'No I mean look how they put the apricot in the roll like that, nifty, don't you think?'

Weston blinked, 'Sure, the cafeteria must be having an artistic revolution.'

'Should do a story on it,' Hardan mused as he enjoyed the sweet confection, chuckling to himself. Making Weston believe he was a touch dim-witted was one of his favourite past-times. He continued his fun, 'Hey, I just had an idea for this trip we're doing, you could call the documentary, 'Once in a Blue Moon.''

Weston sighed as he picked up the phone to make the call. Hardan was a great guy, he really was, but it had only been two hours and already this expedition was getting tedious.

The engineer of their conversation, whom Weston thought was far too great to be resident on lonely P12, or any other similar locale, was leaning back on his chair, lapsing in and out of another surreal dream, something inside him tense and angry under the mask of sleep; he could never get to her but he could never let her go. There was a noise intruding, his eyes slowly opened. There was a blinking light, it was the phone. Now if there was one thing the engineer hated more than reporters it was telephones, and the only reason he answered it was because it was part of his job.

'P12,' he answered gruffly as he checked the time.

'Is that John Mark?' Weston steeled himself

'And you are?'

'John great to hear your voice it's Weston Alamo from TnTv. How have you been? I hear it's getting hot out there, is it really any hotter than usual? And what have you been doing with yourself these days anyway?'

'What do you want Alamo?'

'Well if you're keen to get to the point it's fine by me. Listen, I was just wondering, we have this ah trip coming up, it's ah in the south you know, doing a documentary on-'

'Alamo,' John bit in sharply, 'I assume you're not just calling to check on the weather?'

'The point, right, I-I'm looking for a guide for the trip, you fit the bill John, would you consider-'

'No thanks.'

'But it pays great, your forte, John? John, are you there? John? Oh that's just great.'

Weston put the phone down. 'What are you laughing at?' the producer questioned his captain, 'Think you could convince the hulk do you?

Orin Hardan chuckled. 'I must leave you West,' Hardan said, rising, 'I've a big day ahead getting all the supplies together and loaded.'

'What if I have to cancel?'

'Orh, you'll think of something I'm sure.'

'I hope I don't fail your optimism,' Weston laughed then sighed, and spun the balance wheel again.

CHAPTER 4:

Introducing: The enigma, the Akaia, the Photojournalist & Videographer, Tarku.
Location: TnTv tower, Universal City.

Later the harassed producer looked up as a bag and helmet were thrown on the floor and a young man took the seat where Hardan had been a short while ago. This young man, with dark sunglasses, a jagged dark fringe, and attire just as dark, had not walked through the corridors of TnTv without attracting some attention because of who he was. But no one who knew who he was, or more acutely, what he was, not even the boldest of journalist's, had had the courage to say a word to him. A few had taken a step towards him thinking they might, but none had gone further after seeing the boy's grim countenance.

'Tarku?!' Weston blinked as he leaned back and looked the arrival over. 'You surprised me, as usual, so I guess that means you didn't surprise me. Hehe, ah.' Weston gave up and gave himself an imaginary kick in the backside. You just shouldn't joke with Tarku if he wasn't in the mood, he reminded himself, but who could ever tell if the kid was in the mood?

He was only of average height and build, this boy, and Weston had previously observed he had the bearing of a stray dog; he was always wary, and, the producer had discovered, rather unpredictable. Weston often thought he had a certain presence, but it was something he couldn't explain. Tarku's silent attitude, and his withdrawn yet defiant demeanour, led some to think him untrustworthy and led many to suppose him somewhat of a snob, but Weston knew otherwise, and he took the boy's hand and shook it warmly.

'Aren't you hot in all that gear?' Weston commented, as Tarku was dressed as he most often was, with near knee-high motorcycle racing boots that tread as quietly as their owner spoke, fingerless motorcycle gloves and a jacket zipped right up to the jaw.

Tarku ignored the question, 'You said you had some forms for me to sign before we go?' he said, explaining his presence in Weston's office.

'That's right,' Weston found the file on his notebook and slid it across for Tarku to initial. 'You know, the usual stuff. Indemnity, publishing rights, all that.'

'Sure,' Tarku looked at him darkly with the faintest trace of a sarcastic grin, but he didn't care to read the form, just signed it and handed it back.

'So you trust us then?' Weston chuckled.

'No, just don't care. We go tomorrow right?'

'Sure thing,' Weston lied, smiling.

'I'll set myself down in the ship now if you don't mind,' Tarku said, standing and picking up his gear.

'If you want to waste a day holed up it's none of my worry. Hardy's still loading up. Did I tell you we got a new ship? It's the Blue Moon, she's docked in our usual spot upstairs.'

Why is he so down? Weston wondered to himself. It didn't take him long to remember. They were discussing the fate of people like Tarku, those known as

Akaia, in parliament this week, and as coarsely as if they had been kids discussing the ways of killing a toad, with the odd faint voice of someone's little sister, or parliamentary backbencher in this case, saying, 'No, no that's so cruel,' but being otherwise powerless to do anything about it. It was a ghastly side of politics Weston didn't want to think about, and neither did the majority of the millions that lived in the Universal City or in the rest of the north islands, and as the majority weren't affected by whatever the outcome there was very little outcry. In complete truth, the majority really did want to see Tarku's kind gone, or at the very least locked away or segregated somewhere they could be forgotten. Whether or not the people currently arguing over the proposed new laws would admit it, Akaia were a constant reminder of how broken the world was, and a reminder of the fear that lay in the deep places, so close below every island. This alone made them enemies of any nation seeking to remain optimistic and at ease, even besides the violent and cold-blooded reputation of Akaia in general, which was the basis for the latest discussions.

Weston knew there wasn't anything he could say to make Tarku feel any better, so he didn't try. The producer would have loved some company to distract him or help him, but not such company as was going to add a burden this heavy to his spirit. Part of him really did worry for Tarku, but it was like an itch, and Weston wished it wasn't there.

'You don't want to stay for coffee?' he asked, hoping Tarku wouldn't say yes.

'No,' Tarku replied.

'Pastry?' Weston pressed, 'Fresh today, Hardy left them, they've got apricots. Go on,' he shook the bag, 'take one, you don't see apricots very often.'

The young man didn't even look at the extravagant confections, 'West, if they were real apricots they would have cost 50 bucks apiece, more likely you're eating some sort of re-constituted algae that's been bleached, dyed and flavoured. Enjoy your pastry. I'll see you tomorrow,' Tarku dismissed himself and strolled away down the hall.

'Killjoy!' Weston muttered, taking another sweet pastry and bitting into it. 'Tastes like apricot to me,' he said to himself, coming to the conclusion that he liked apricots and that his captain was a decent sort for purchasing these, but then he put it down and stepped out after the boy, thinking he should at the very least ask Tarku if he was alright, but Weston tripped, knocking the pastry. He went to catch it but smeared its sticky sweetness across his shirt and arm in the process. A few curses, but the pastry now safe again in his hands, Weston continued, but by the time he got to the door Tarku was gone.

'Astrid better not be depressed I tell you or it'll be a dismal trip,' Weston observed, going back to his desk as he licked his fingers, 'and I still have to find us a guide.'

~

Introducing: The Machina, the Photojournalist, the translator, Astrid.
Location: Quantum Corporation facility, Universal City.

Astrid was Weston's name for the Machina series 20M model A* id. Machinas, or Mechs as they're informally known, were expensive pieces of equipment, designed to have far greater sensory perception than the average person, and also be an animate interface between the real world and the digital world. They combined the warmth of human interaction with the calculated precision of machines and the depth of readily accessible knowledge of a computer database. Originally Machinas were used in covert espionage operations before the war, then in the war itself, even on the front line, mostly to give timely calculations and advice where needed. After the war they found many uses for the Mechs, in medical, corporate and government roles.

Depending on which eminent professor you talked to, Astrid, and machinas in general, could be classed as human or robot. A machina definitely looked like a real live person on the outside, but tests would show they were not exactly what they seemed on the inside. And while some would argue they had free will to a degree, and choice, others would argue that yes, but, their purpose was pre-determined and they were not born, but put together for this purpose, and they had no self-determination, or will; they were given orders and obeyed orders, there were no questions, no emotion except if the task required it, hence: robot.

But the proponents arguing that machinas were no more than robots must not have known Astrid. Astrid was an exception to the rule and no one's puppet. She'd been around long enough to understand how the world worked and knew exactly who she was, how to be happy, and how to be angry, and everything there was to be in being human, despite the efforts of Q-Corporation's expert manipulative psychologists.

So, Astrid regarded herself as Weston regarded her, as 100% human, just with a whole lot of annoying, though sometimes handy, cybernetic implants, which gave the powers that be enough excuse to label her a robot, but ultimately no more than a legalised slave.

Astrid woke up in the same fog that she usually did after weeks in stasis, as the gases exchanged around her in this sterile drawer that was her home and prison. As she regained normal temperature and movement once again the drawer slid open and she began to pull the monitoring cords away from her body. The vault room was no friendlier than the drawer itself, it was devoid of life and colour, it was all cold steel, concrete and machines. She got herself up quickly, slid the drawer back in and locked it. She opened the locker underneath and pulled on her cargo pants, jacket and boots, and packed the rest of her gear in a duffel. She checked for the latest data-set on her computer subsystem, for any tasking, but there was nothing new there. 'What have they done now?' she asked herself. But a technician entered at that moment, red from running down the corridors.

'Sorry Astrid, running late, there's been a lot happening,' the young technician puffed, handing her a data drive.

'I was wondering what was going on,' she smiled, taking the drive and holding it to download its contents. 'You know I'd rather you did this while I was out though,' Astrid scolded, though smiling. 'I hate feeling like a computer.'

'I know, but I also know how much you hate the vault so I gave the go ahead for your release as soon as we got the request. You can blame the guys who do up the packages for the delay in getting that.'

'Alright. I'll thank you and blame them. So,' she analysed the new data.

'Is it working? Are you good to go?'

'Are you telling me you didn't even get me out to see the premier league final!' she hit him on the shoulder in a friendly way, 'Universal City finally beat Parahn, and how! 46-17! Oh I wish I had been there!'

The young tech grinned, 'Well, at least the latest data-set's working. Oh, also, the heads want me to remind you to take better care of yourself this time you're out.'

Astrid laughed, 'Take care of myself? What do they care?'

The tech grinned, 'You know what they mean. No new tattoos, no new piercings, stay out of trouble and stick to your brief. Just tell me you'll try.'

'Alright, I'll try,' Astrid said, 'but you better get onto them about getting my optics updated, I've been waiting for months.'

'I'll get onto it.'

'Is this how it starts sonny?' she asked seriously.

'How what starts?'

'End of the line? Is this how it happens? Do they just stop doing upgrades until we're obsolete?'

'What are you talking about Astrid?'

'J series was retired recently weren't they? There's not many letters between J and M. Do you know how long I have?'

'J series is much older Astrid, they were the first real Machinas. M series is far more advanced.'

'We're not much different, really,' Astrid said, but put on a smile.

'So you know where you're going? Everything's alright?' the young tech asked, his brow knotting.

'Are you worried about me sonny?'

'I ah,' he looked aside, 'yes.'

'Don't be, I couldn't be happier right now, it looks like I'm going abroad. I've got a few new languages here, maps and general information from the south and far south, building and ship schematics, flight paths-'

'You're not suppose to tell me.'

'Hey, don't fret, I'm not sent on anything top-secret anymore. This is nothing, this is just fun.'

'TnTv?'

'Yes. I'm so relieved it's not for another government agency again.'

'I've never understood why TnTv need a machina?' the tech said.

Astrid laughed and rubbed his head roughly, 'It's a dangerous world out there sonny, they need every edge they can get,' she said walking towards the exit.

'There's still the pre-op check to run before you go,' he said.

'Oh I think we can skip that one this time,' she said, 'just get yourself and your key-card over here and let me out of this prison.'

His brow knotted, 'Astrid, you know I want to, but it'd be my job on the line if anyone knew I went around protocol.'

Astrid held her hand up to the door and laughed. She was so, so earthy, even her voice was rough, it was hard to believe she was actually a Machina 20M. She looked like she belonged out in the open, selling fruit at a market place somewhere or on a ship with the wind in her dreadlocks, not standing here in these slick labs.

'I don't need your key-card sonny, you should know that by now, I was just being polite,' she laughed, as she sent the same signal as his keycard to the card reader and the door opened. 'I'll see you when I get back.'

The young tech waved a helpless goodbye, 'I could call security to stop you!' he called after her.

'I know, but you won't,' she chuckled and kept going.

'No, I won't,' he sighed, all the techs loved Astrid. 'They couldn't stop you anyway.'

CHAPTER 5:

Introducing: The traveller and his way, Scott Thomas and Kyu.
Location: Above the Universal City.

After searching too long and fearing that she'd lost her ticket, Melissa finally put her fingers on the stray paper and handed it to the unimpressed ticketer.

'Can I have my button back now,' she put out her hand.

The ticketer just smirked, 'Finders keepers Gutter Mouse,' and continued on his rounds.

It wasn't a good start to the journey. For a moment Melissa indulged a feeling of helplessness and desperation, but then she pulled up her spirit and went after the uniformed thief.

By the time the inter-city line pulled up at Universal City Central, she had the button back in her possession, and stepped out of the train smiling at her success. Growing up in The Gutter she had not gone without picking up a little of certain delicate street arts, such as pick-pocketing. She had made sure to stay out of that man's way for the rest of the journey and arrival. Now she stood transfixed as the crowds of so many diverse and wonderful peoples sped around her. The odd Tamashani, Shorakaian, Salamondan or representative of a people she had never before seen or heard of, and of course people from all over the five regions that made the North Island States. It was not since her childhood that she had ventured to the core of the Universal City, and the consequences of that one escapade were enough to ensure she had never tried it again, until now.

The train had pulled into its central stop below ground. As she disembarked Melissa was caught up in the crowds as the swarms of emerging passengers went this way and that, and when the crowd thinned enough for her to try to gain her bearings she found herself in a bright arcade full of everything you could want to buy at prices Melissa thought no one on earth could afford – and she had thought the boutique coffee shop in Junto-a-Mar was expensive! Melissa, making her way, was soon too scared to even glance at the beautiful things, not only because of the prices but because of the down the nose looks she was getting from various persons whom she could only assume were there to arrest you if you so much as breathed on any item.

Melissa began to feel somewhat suffocated and she hurried to find a map. After a few anxious minutes which seemed terribly long she was finally out of the glitzy spread into the gritty streets above. This was more like it, she breathed. She followed other pedestrians this way and that, dodging the treacherous traffic in crowds to be safer, but when she thought she'd found the place she needed to be it would turn out that it was an entirely different street to the one she'd been expecting, so she would look for a map and try again. This strategy failed miserably however and she was obliged to find a friendly looking face in the window of a friendly looking, deliciously smelling, but rather empty café.

'Excuse me,' she asked hesitantly, 'hi, I was wondering-'

The plump man at the counter, who wore an apron of an undeterminable colour and held a cleaning cloth which was suffering under his slow but heavy waxing motion, sighed with a smile. 'Go on honey, you may as well, take the stairs at the back,' he motioned with his thumb, 'then take the elevator to the roof, it'll get you a better view than everyone else.'

'But I-'

'Go on, go on with you, I won't charge you,' he laughed genially, 'don't worry your pretty head about that.'

He was nice, sure, but Melissa didn't understand what he was talking about. 'I just wanted to know where TnTv Tower was,' she explained, 'do you know?'

'Oh, sure, it's not a block away, we often have their shirts in here of a lunch-time,' but he stopped his cleaning and asked her, 'but don't you know what's going on?'

'What do you mean?'

The chef clicked his tongue, thinking that this young girl must indeed be very focussed on finding TnTv Tower not to have noticed the shadow creeping across the street, not to notice the change in the behaviour of the people around her as they all ran for better vantages, as the cars and pedal-taxis stopped in the street and the people got out to stare up into the sky.

'There's a Kyu above our roof,' he explained, 'where do you think all my customers are?' He motioned to all the half-touched meals around, and laughed, 'even my staff have run out to see.'

'A Kyu?!' she repeated. It was unbelievable.

'You know, a Kyu, one of those giant mantas, go and have a look.'

'Really?!' she was amazed, 'here in the city?'

The good-natured cook nodded at her surprise, 'Yes, it's right above us now, so you better get up there, this could be your once in a lifetime opportunity.'

Melissa now noticed the chaos in the street, the chef was right, and the excitement caught her. She ran out the back as he directed, found the lift, and appeared out of the door at the top to find that she did indeed have the best view, along with a few others she found herself directly below a giant Kyu.

The Kyu was like a massive manta-ray but of the sky and not just the sea. Its wide wings flowed gently but their movement was felt by those below as the air twisted about in reply. The giant Kyu came lower and lower to the rooftop and many rushed out of its shadow and back into the building. Others stared across from the balconies of adjacent buildings. Melissa was in awe, and contrary to everyone else her awe made her draw closer, stepping slowly forward as she gazed.

The Kyu's wingspan must be more than 50 metres across and far greater in length, at least double that or more with the length of its tail. It was so close now and Melissa was nearly alone on the roof, she felt as if she might almost be able to touch the strange skin. The creature called out in a long and deep note that Melissa felt go all the way through her as if her very bones were strings being played by the Kyu's voice. Then her attention was caught by a curious slit, almost like a mouth, in the Kyu's underside. She noticed it widening and to her very great surprise a man's head appeared out of it upside down, he was looking about him and saw her standing there.

'Hey, hullo,' he yelled out, 'can you take this,' he handed out a case. She ran over and took it from him, then another bag and another. Then he jumped out of the opening and as soon as he had it closed up so tightly it was hardly visible. He patted the skin firmly, said a quiet word and then the Kyu moved away.

It was then Melissa noticed the bright blue letters boldly shining though the smog, there was TnTv Tower at last, it could be no more than a block away.

The young man fixed his shirt and pulled his cotton bandana back into place around his neck then he picked up his bags, taking the last one from Melissa. 'Thanks for that,' he said, 'always handy to have a friendly hand to help unload. What's your name anyway?' Melissa didn't answer, but stood stunned as she continued to watch the Kyu as it flew further away. 'I'm Scott, I'll have to call you Shortie will I? Come on Shortie, I'll shout you lunch, what will it be?'

'Sorry?' Melissa came back to earth, looking up at Scott finally. He was just like any north islander, it was hard to believe he'd just jumped out of the massive ray.

'Lunch, a little thank you, my shout, what would you like?'

'Lunch? I didn't do anything. No I, I have to get to TnTv.'

'It just so happens that so do I.'

'Really?'

'Yep,' he nodded, 'really. In fact I asked Kyu to drop me there, but she dropped me here instead, so she obviously thought I needed a bowl of Carlo's renowned chilli dumplings,' then more quietly, 'or something else that was here.' Melissa didn't notice his momentary scrutiny of her.

'Is it *your* Kyu?' she asked, 'Wow! I've never seen one before, well, I mean apart from on the television. It's so amazing.'

'More like she owns me Shortie, and stands to figure you haven't seen one before because Kyus don't like coming this far north, and she's brave to come I tell you. She doesn't like it but what can I do? A man has to call home now and again.' They reached the lift, 'After you.'

They journeyed back down to the café, Melissa looking up at this stranger, thoughts rushing through her head, an array of questions for which she could not find the words to articulate, and the more she looked the more she began to think that he wasn't quite so ordinary after all. Clean cut blonde hair, fresh face, neat attire, responsible attitude, and good manners, and a distinct Universal-City-upper-class accent, no, not so ordinary after all.

'So, what's your reason for going to TnTv?' he asked.

'I um, I'm starting work. I'm supposed to be meeting a man there right now to go over everything before I start, but I'm probably late already,' she stammered, 'and I can't be late, I can't lose this job.'

'Ah I see. Are you going into journalism?' he asked politely.

'No, oh no I couldn't do that, I'm not nearly pushy enough, I'd much rather be behind the camera.'

'Ah,' Scott nodded his head, 'you're a photographer.'

'Well, not really, but that's the job yeah.'

'Sometimes photographers have to be pushy in that line of work too you know. It wouldn't be Weston Alamo you had to see now would it?' he smiled. 'It's just that I've got to get some footage to him before he goes off tomorrow. Save me a bit of time if you could take it with you when you go.'

'Oh. Ok, I guess I could, if you could tell me exactly the best way to get there, I keep managing to go the wrong way.'

'Actually I better do it, don't worry, I was just being lazy, but I suppose I really should see him as well. Here,' he said, 'sit down and have a bite to eat and then we can walk up there together, and if Weston's in a fluff about you being late I'll take all the heat, but trust me, I don't think Weston will even realise what day today is, so I don't think he'll be too concerned about what the time is when you turn up.'

Scott pulled out a chair for her and after she'd thought about it, 'I suppose, if we're not too long, thank you,' she said at last and gratefully sat down and put her head on her hands.

'You still haven't told me your name yet Shortie?' he asked, and she couldn't resist his coaxing smile.

She smiled back, 'Sorry, it's Melissa.'

'Melissa,' he nodded. 'First time in the Metropolis? The Megalopolis?' he laughed, 'it's all a bit overwhelming isn't it?'

'Kind of,' she said, 'is it that obvious?'

Scott leaned forward a little and lowered his voice, 'Forgive me if I'm too bold,' Melissa was about to laugh but she saw just in time that he was completely serious, 'but I have to ask you, do you have any Shorakaian heritage?'

'I wouldn't know, I never knew my parents,' she replied honestly, shaking her head, then laughed, 'why?'

'Oh, it's nothing. Just something about you, I can't place it,' he saw she was looking confused. 'Forget I said anything, it's nothing, really.' My stupid mouth, he thought, but he had to ask, there really was a quality about her that made something in his mind tick over, an old picture or an old thought that his mind couldn't quite bring out of storage to compare, yet, but it would come to him sooner or later, it always did.

Carlo the cook brought steaming, wonderfully aromatic dishes to the table, and tired as she was Melissa could not refuse, despite the picture of Kat in her head reminding her not to get into situations like this with people you've only just met. But how else did one make friends, Melissa thought, when there wasn't time to get to know them slowly?

After a while Melissa looked up from her plate, 'Did you just mean it as a compliment?'

'What's that?'

'Well, they say the people of Shorakai are the most beautiful people on earth, don't they? Not that I think I'm – sorry,' Melissa laughed, 'that came out all wrong.'

'Oh, no I didn't it mean like that, not that you're not, well,' Scott was nearly blushing himself, looking at his food, then he turned to her grinning. The two of them laughed. 'I was in earnest, and meant nothing untoward,' he said, 'but yes, they do say that, and the most beautiful language, and the most breathtaking cities you've ever seen, and the clearest, bluest sky there is in the world.'

'Have you been there? To Shorakai?' Melissa asked, her eyes sparkling, very much intrigued.

'Often, yes,' his look of mild concern faded away and he became very animated. 'Shorakai is one of those places that seems pulled out of legend, like it was never supposed to be part of this world. It's magical. The people are secretive in their way and not that open to outsiders, but they are good people, with an art and culture all their own. They have the most remarkable aquatecture on Shorakai, you must go there one day if you get the chance.'

'Aquatecture?'

'Ah, structures, buildings, architecture, but with water as a significant element of the design.'

'Oh.'

'It's so beautiful, and extraordinarily clever, pictures don't do it justice. Even if you just go to the gardens in Merouin or Rinau it would be enough, let alone seeing the whole of Shorakai.'

'I can see you love it there.'

'Yes, it's Kyu's favourite place too, can't keep her away. If she's a mind to go to Shorakai it doesn't matter what plans I have.'

'It must be so much fun, being able to go anywhere.'

'Oh, not fun, no, more like, like exhilaration, that's it, but it's all Kyu, she's an amazing creature, and such a friend, I love her more than life, and what I mean by that is I couldn't live without her now, we've been friends too long to be apart. The places we go,' he stopped and closed his eyes and moved his hand through the air, 'are just indescribable.'

'Wow. What's it like, inside?'

Scott laughed, 'Everyone asks that. The general opinion is that it would be hot and acrid, and dark, but it's nothing of the sort. To tell you the truth the air inside her chest is much better than the air everyone is breathing here because it's been filtered, and generally it's cool even if it's hot outside, her hide's so thick it's not a worry. Once we even went through a massive fire storm in ruins on the rim of where the Panyanae Ocean used to reach to, a complete wasteland now,' Scott looked aside at the memory, and said softly, 'but I felt as safe as eagle's eggs. It might get a little dark, but I tell you the darkness is worth it.' He lowered his voice again, it was something he loved very much, something so special, his eyes widened and he leaned closer to Melissa as he explained, 'She's got her own lighting system in-built, it's incredible, it's like phosphorescent, no, I don't know, you know like those glowing things in caves or the little organisms in water that make it shimmer even when there's no light, she's got something like that in all her exposed cartilage. That's it, bioluminescence, it's so amazingly beautiful.'

Melissa had little idea of what he was talking about, but it sounded so otherworldly and wonderful, and his honest passion made her like him.

'How did you come to know Kyu?' she asked.

He finished another chilli dumpling then answered her, 'I was nineteen, hitchhiking back from Salamondé. I got a lift with a group of entertainers heading to Tamashan, but there was a siderolite monsoon, totally unexpected, we were caught in a shower of magma and ash. The pilots were blinded, the ship was hit, and it was a pretty old ship, she couldn't take it and we went down. I've no idea where it was we went down, but I found myself alive, found a way out of the wreck, the only one not supposed to be on the ship, the only one who made it off. When I woke up and came out of the daze of it I found myself surrounded by kyus, but they weren't alive. I was so sick, the whole place was just a mass graveyard of their giant carcasses, rotting away. Some were just bone. Daylight never really came to that place. I think it was a sinking island, slowly crumbling into the depths below with every tremor, it was so, oh, just thinking about it,' Scott shivered. It was one nightmare he wanted to forget. 'Anyway, I found her there,' Scott continued, 'I'd given up trying to find a way out, soon I even lost my bearing of where the ship went down. I sat down to die, and then a sigh moved the body I was leaning against.'

Above the city Kyu sighed as she had then, the note penetrating through to them. Scott looked up and smiled, 'We made it out of that place together.'

'Wow.'

'Ah, you'll have to excuse me Melissa,' Scott pulled out his phone, 'Seems I've got a call coming in, could be important.'

'Scott Thomas,' he answered.

'Hey, get your gangly self over here, I know you're in town. How's it going? I have to talk to you,' Weston began.

'Hi Weston,' Scott shot a knowing grin at Melissa while thinking that for a man who's supposed to be as good as Weston was he still didn't know how to begin a conversation. 'Yeah, listen, I'll be over soon,' Scott said, 'Melissa too, she might be a bit late but I'm sure that won't matter to you, will it?' Scott got up, stretched, and strolled down to the back of the café.

Weston started, 'Melissa?'

'Sorry West, she was there when I landed, couldn't help myself, I had to ask her to lunch. She needs a chaperone West, she's completely out of her depth,' Scott sighed, tilting his head wistfully, and letting his shoulders fall a little, 'and so absolutely lovely.'

'Who are you talking about?'

'Melissa, that pretty young thing you hired. The photographer.'

'Oh that Melissa, now I know who you're talking about, I'd completely forgotten. So she's there with you now?'

'Yeah. Where'd you find her West?'

'I didn't, it was my major Tarku who found her, and in some remote corner of the city too. I agreed with his assessment of her skill, that she's got a blessed intuition, her work has soul. We had a competition, and I don't know how many interviews, but no one came up to scratch. It was just the same old stock stuff and shock stuff, and I'm getting over the crisp, soulless, propaganda style that students are taught to pump out these days. She's just the girl I need for this trip, new eyes, fresh approach.'

'Where did this Tarku find her?'

'Junto-a-Mar.'

'The Gutter!' Scott exclaimed, his eyes widening, 'poor kid.'

'Yeah, Tarku told me to go and check out this whack exposition they had on out there, hers was the only stuff in the place worth anything, showed real depth you know, I was impressed so I followed it up. I'm convinced she'll learn fast, and at least she don't speak da gutta funk.'

'Explains her clothes though, you might give her some credits to get some new gear, take it off my commission if you like.'

'That bad?'

'Nah, it's fine, just thinking she might need something a little, well, more, for the expedition you're planning. You know, sturdy boots, all weather gear, couple of warm jackets, cargos and what have you. A singlet, shorts and sandals aren't going to cut it.'

'Sure, I'll do something about it, just get over here Scott.'

'Alright, we'll be there soon.'

Scott sat down and thought as he finished the generous meal. 'Small world sometimes,' he commented, then smiled, 'Come on, Weston will have an apoplexy if I'm not there soon.'

~

'Scott! My boy! So good to see you, oh, excellent you could make it to see me before I go off again.' Weston took the young man's hand and shook it warmly, but his greedy eyes looked to the case that hung on Scott's shoulder. 'Did you bring it?'

'Would I have come if I hadn't?' Scott laughed and handed the producer the case, also informing the producer, 'Melissa's waiting in the hall.'

'Good, good, but one thing at a time,' Weston carefully opened the case as though it contained a rare treasure. The camera, lenses, mounts, hard-drives and other bits of expensive equipment he'd lent Scott were all there. He took the small drive, licking his lips, and plugged it carefully into his notebook.

'Play on projector,' he told it and sat back as one wall of his office lit up and the other lights dimmed. He pulled Scott down to another seat and they watched segments of the film Scott had collected.

'This is astounding,' Weston could not stop saying. Melissa too watched on from the shadow in the doorway in awe. Scott just smiled and watched Weston and looked back at Melissa. Neither noticed him, they were watching the flight of the Kyu, over untouched lands and places that still remained undiscovered, through mountain ranges and under them, through the decaying pillars that supported the remaining islands of life, such as the Universal City, and on through the toxic steam where barely a thing could be defined, and across deserts where the bones of long forgotten cities lay.

'These are great pictures Scott, outstanding. I'm going to send them straight through to the editor. I've got a proposal for you.'

'What's that?'

Weston lowered his voice, 'I need a guide for this trip, we leave tomorrow, do you think you could do it?'

'Maybe, in a small way, but I'm not really that knowledgeable about the south, only the major spots, you know, Satsuan and Rorona, Tamashan, Shorakai, Salamonde, Soamé, and you'll need someone with a bit more brawn than me if you're going to go anywhere near the Arc.'

'Nah, Tarku and Hardan can handle themselves with credit, so can Astrid, and you and I aren't without our skills either.'

'Weston, to be honest I'm already booked.'

'Really? By who?'

'Kyu.'

'Come on,' Weston mocked him, 'she won't miss you for a few weeks.'

'Promised I'd go with her down to Oconia, found myself a gig raising tuna. It's only short term of course, but it'll be a nice break for both of us, she loves the sea.'

'What sea!? Fishpond would be a more appropriate term I think!' Weston continued to protest, 'No Scott don't turn me down for tuna! Come on, I'm stretched, desperate, you know I even rang John Mark this morning.'

'John hey?'

'You know, the engineer. He used to work for your dad didn't he?'

'Yes.'

'Must have been hard to be around an intimidating hulk like him when you were so young too.'

Scott laughed, shook his head and said, 'No, he was more of a hero figure to me, he looked after our family as we toured Rorona and Satsuan, and wherever the government sent my father. I looked up to John, I still do. He would have been a good choice for your guide though so it's a shame he decided against it.'

'Yeah, are you sure you won't do it?' Weston asked.

Scott sat in thought, Weston grew hopeful, but Scott just muttered to himself, 'Amiana, that's it.' The name of John Mark was like a key in Scott's mind, and Scott recalled the picture that he knew would come, it came quite suddenly right then, much sooner than he'd expected, that thing, that something about Melissa. Scott looked back at her briefly but didn't say anything, only sat rubbing his chin in thought.

'John's dead wife?' Weston tried to follow Scott's train of thought, 'what's she got to do with anything?'

'Nothing, I just remembered. Where is John now West? Do you know?'

'Turns out he's been rotting out on P12 for a few years,' Weston continued.

'I wondered when he'd give up,' Scott said, 'he couldn't keep up that kind of pace forever. So he turned you down did he?'

'I didn't have a chance. Are you sure you won't consider it?' Weston pressed again.

'Quite sure.'

Weston moaned, but then something twinkled in his mischievous eyes, 'Say, Scott, are you planning to go soon?'

'This very same day, Kyu doesn't like the smog here, it's worse than the steam in the divide for her. Maybe I'll go see John on my way.'

'That's what I was going to suggest! Could you talk him over for us? If he has terms, tell him to name them, I'll deal with it. Could you do that for me?'

'No,' Scott grinned, 'but I could do it for John, it wouldn't be doing him any good to be stuck out there, and he'd be the right man for the job. P12 hey? It's a wonder I haven't seen him, then I guess it has been a while since we took that route.'

'No time to lose then,' Weston clapped his hands together. 'Off you go, I'll send you a copy of the documentary with your footage. It's brilliant Scott, absolutely brilliant. You know what,' Weston said with excitement, 'take the camera again, film what you like, anything, we'll buy it off you.'

'What about tuna?' Scott teased.

'Get out of here you rascal.'

'See ya.'

'Let me know how you go with John.'

'Yep,' Scott yelled back as he walked down the hall. He patted Melissa's shoulder as he passed, 'Later Melissa, nice meeting you.'

'You're not coming with us?' Melissa asked. 'I thought maybe you'd be coming?'

'Not I,' he smiled in a friendly way as he kept on walking down the hall and into the lift, 'look after yourself Shortie,' he said in a tone at once laughing yet serious, then he too was cut off from her.

CHAPTER 6:

'You may come in Miss Melissa,' she heard the producer behind her, and bit her lip. The truth was that Mr Weston Alamo scared her. Was it his position? His brashness? Her general distrust of men in positions of authority? Melissa took a deep breath and bravely entered the producer's office.

'Hi,' she smiled and shook his outstretched hand, 'it's ah, it's good to meet you. Thank you for taking me on.'

'Take a seat,' he said, smilingly oblivious to the angst Melissa was feeling.

'Thank you,' she put her bag down and sat, though her legs jittered up and down as half her will urged her to forget this and run back to the little 11th floor apartment with Kat and the others, looking out across the desert wastes that they said used to be oceans, years and years ago, watching the steam rise up in the distance and battening down before all the dust and dirt and hot air came sweeping across that wasteland and blasted the unfortunate suburb again. But Sir was there, and she had got this far, this could turn out to be a brilliant job, so the other half of her will made her stay. She breathed, trying to still the rush of things and gather the spent energy used up on getting out of the gutter and getting through the city. For a moment she looked back out the door after Scott, wishing he could have stayed, but as she breathed in she pulled herself together, and to her great relief she managed to smile.

'Right,' Weston began, 'before I can let you do any work for us there are a few forms I need you to sign. We need your basic details, address, phone number, what licences you possess. There's the insurance form, the standard TnTv contract, the contract for this expedition, et cetera. Once you're done with all that let me know and I'll answer any more questions you may have.' Weston smiled purposefully and slid her the notebook just as he had Tarku.

But unlike Tarku, Melissa took her time and after a moment was disrupting Weston from his work. 'Um, I'm sorry, but I can't fill this out very well,' she said, sounding a little distressed.

'What's the problem? If it's paragraph 13 in the insurance policy no one knows what that means.'

'No, well,' she said frustrated, 'I don't have a last name, at least, I-I might have one but I don't know what it is because I don't have a birth certificate or anything, I usually just make one up but this is important isn't it,'

'You don't even have an ID number?'

'I've never needed one. And I don't have an address, I've brought everything I own with me, and I can't go back,' she shook her head, 'I can't go back.'

'Stop, stop, don't fret honey,' Weston tried to encourage, 'let's see what other staff have put on their forms, some of them wouldn't be able to fill it all in either, I know that for a fact. I'll see what we've got on our records. Give me a moment,' he said, bringing up various records, 'I shouldn't be doing this you know.'

'Doing what?'

'All this stuff, dealing with new employees, forms, all this business, not my job at all, I've got far better things to be doing but, you see,' Weston confided, 'my secretary quit yesterday.'

'Oh, I'm sorry.'

'Yes, so am I.' Weston laughed, 'Serves me right though, I admit I was getting quite ah, agitated, to put it mildly, and I know it was no fault of hers. But anyway, nothing I can do about it now. No point getting a new girl in either, just for a couple of days.'

Weston looked at the screen, 'Well,' he said, flipping through the forms, 'she's just put her name in the place for the first name and left the other blank. He does have a PO Box for his address though, but I tell you what, you could put care of me, here, if you like.'

'Can I do that?'

'I don't see why not, and it would just be a temporary thing in any case.' Weston scratched his head. He wasn't sure he liked that idea entirely, but what could he do? His suggestion had come out of nowhere, without thought, pop. Scott was right, she was lovely in her way, and she was obviously distressed, Weston didn't like stress himself, and he didn't like seeing a young thing that should be happy in such a state.

'Thank you,' Melissa continued, 'oh, date of birth? I only know the year, not the day. What should I put?'

Weston looked at Tarku's form and suddenly realised that there were several things on it which young Melissa shouldn't see, raised both eyebrows at once but then tried to disguise his reaction, but made sure the screen was turned a little more away, 'ah just put the year in or make something up, I'm sure that will be fine.'

Weston got back into his work and Melissa got through the forms eventually, with several other questions to harass the poor man as he tried to work. There were a few uncertain points in the contract but these were brushed aside or explained simply by Weston, though he maintained that if she had any real doubts she should go through it with a solicitor because he was in no way qualified to tighten such wordy paragraphs, but in the end she had no real qualms in signing it.

After that he sent her away, telling her to get some rest and meet him back here tomorrow. 'Do you have any other questions honey?'

'Um, oh heaps, where are we going? What's our focus? What will I be expected to do? You know, all that.'

'Well, as I said to you originally this expedition's about documenting the cities and the people that survive in the south, getting a perspective on how things are out there, we're going all over the place, doing all sorts of things so just be ready for anything. You'll pick things up as you go.'

'Okay.'

'I'll have some more detailed information packages to give to everyone when we're on the way. Oh, almost forgot, here,' he handed her a TnTv employee account card, 'you'll find your first pay cheque already in the account, don't spend it all at once now, and ah make sure you get an all-weather jacket, or something similar, something warm, and trousers, tough trousers, and oh, don't forget to get some good shoes too, with thick soles, you'll need 'em. Scott would recommend Knowles's Warehouse but it's on the other side of Corrio so there's no time for that, and Nix's is just two blocks down, you should find something suitable there.'

'Wow, thank you,' was all she could say for a moment, then as what she had received dawned on her, 'ah, um, how much is on this?'

'I think about $650,' he said, shooing her out.

'Wow,' Melissa's jaw dropped, 'really? But I haven't even done anything yet!'

Weston just grinned and nodded as he closed her out of his office.

'Nice!' she smiled to herself. 'Here we go Melis, tomorrow, tomorrow. Wow. So much has happened already!'

The day before departure: Katrina v Sir.
Location: The Gutter

Katrina's face was full of tears and blended mascara, with bruises developing underneath. Her loose mouse-blond curls fell messily around her cheeks. Sophia was in hospital, Matthias had been imprisoned by Sir's lawmen, and the rest of the neighbourhood stayed out of the way as the crazed man's blood raged. Sir wanted to know where he could find her, his Melis. Matthias wouldn't tell the men Sir had sent to beat him, Sophia wouldn't say more than that Kat might know, none of the other girls knew anything and Kat wouldn't say a word, no matter how many bruises or threats Sir had inflicted on her. Sir knew Melis had caught the train, but he didn't know where she was headed, for all he knew she might have got off at the very next stop, and the much neglected and vandalised surveillance systems of the network couldn't help him either.

This afternoon the tainted rain clouds came in fast, and they came with a saturation of destructive elements from the restless divide. Sir locked Katrina out of the apartment building the girls rented from him. None would pity her for fear, so there she stood as the rain-drops started to fall. She stood at the door under the canopy which someone had neglected to take in with all the commotion going on. It would have to be replaced after this. More drops fell, warm in temperature, and a dirty rust in colour today, staining everything they touched once again. When the water evaporated it would leave a toxic dust on everything. Some large drops were worse than others, even as she watched Katrina saw the fibres in the canopy soak up some drops, then the material seemed to just melt away in that spot while other drops ran harmlessly over the side. She begged to be let back in as the drops grew larger and more often, as the wind picked up and found rubbish in corners and plucked it out, toyed with it, then swept it away, and doors started to shudder on their bolts. Katrina screamed and banged the door, seriously terrified of this rainstorm. She shielded her head with her arms as the canopy flagged and was suddenly torn away, its red fabric vanishing into the midst of the deluge and the steam up the road.

Then the rain found Katrina. She banged on the door till her voice was drowned by the downpour, then she squatted as tight as she could, back to the rain, face sheltered under her arms. The neighbourhood could see her there in her bright blue dress as they peered through the storm from behind their protecting windows and watched on with what seemed callous idleness, but no one had thought Sir could be so brutal as that, especially not to one of his favourites.

When he couldn't hear her anymore Sir opened the door a fraction. 'Where's Melis?' he asked, without a trace of emotion.

'Sir please,' Kat faced him, 'please let me in!'

'Tell me where she is!' he shouted back.

'I don't know!' Kat returned, 'Sir, please I don't know.'

'You forget I know when you're lying Kat!'

Kat tried to be brave as she stifled another cry at the pain, but she couldn't hold on any longer, 'Universal City,' Kat cried, 'she's gone to Universal City.'

'That's the truth?' he lifted her chin and demanded. Kat nodded. 'Where in the city? What's she doing there?'

'I don't know, I swear all I know is she's got a gig taking pictures for one of the big media companies. I swear that's all I know.'

He pulled her inside and closed the door on the pelting gale. 'Dear Kat, why'd you have to be so damned stubborn.'

The other girls were stunned at Katrina's condition. Her face was ok, she'd protected it, and mostly her chest and arms too, but her back was welting up, all red and sore; in places the skin and the blue dress seemed fused together. The bottoms of her feet, where she had stood in the water, were blistering in places, and on the back of her head some hair was discoloured, some had been lost. It must be one of the worst rains they'd had in ages. Sir took her up to her room and lay her gently on her stomach. They made her at ease, then let her be.

'Why'd you leave me here alone, Melis?' Kat cried, but then said to her friend, 'Don't you dare come back here girl, hope you're listening to me girl, don't you dare come back!' Semi-conscious Kat hoped and prayed that little Melis would have soon left the Universal City. 'I'm sorry Melis, I'm so sorry,' Kat whispered as she cried.

CHAPTER 7:

The day of departure: Melissa's Morning.
Location: Universal City

The morning came, bright and dazzling through the remnants of the cloud and the gathering smog. The impressive new sun was ablaze in all its fierceness across the sky, reflecting in the glass panelled towers, blinding those who dared to look upon it.

Melissa woke up slowly into the warm morning, gazing blissfully at the play of light on the sunburnt walls of her room in this three star hotel. She pommelled the pillows in excitement, sat up and let out a, 'Wooo!' She was leaving today, she couldn't contain herself. Then she lay back again and looked about her. She had not been sure about spending so much money on accommodation, but in the end gave in and was glad she had. From the narrow view of the city between the other rises, to the chocolate on her pillow, the soft, clean sheets, the little packaged soaps in the bathroom that would find their way into her bag, it was all superb. If this was a three star hotel, what were the five star hotels like?! Oh man! She wondered. She had never felt so spoilt and wonderful, and never thought she would ever feel this way again, or ever have this much money again.

It had taken all her courage to ask to stay here, but they were fine with her after they had checked that she was actually an employee at TnTv and yes, the TnTv account card was actually hers and not stolen property. They had given her a funny kind of look at first, but what did Kat always say? 'You don't gotta worry about what no one thinks of ya, you just be you and they'll see you're alright.' Melissa sighed, man oh man she missed her friend so much. She set her face determinedly and took a deep breath. She was going to be the best photographer TnTv had ever seen, then she'd make lots of money and get Kat and the rest of them out of the gutter for good. Why couldn't it be Kat who was leaving, she was the adventurous one. The idea of leaving the North Islands made Melissa feel a strange surging up inside of her every time she thought about it, like she was going to explode or faint or be sick. She switched the television on to distract her mind while she got ready for the day. They had so many more channels to watch here as well. Everything was so incredible.

"Good morning everyone and welcome to TnTv Today. We go where no other station dares, to bring you the freshest, most exciting news of the moment. In this bulletin, fires continue to burn uncontrollably in the north-west threatening many homes and businesses; senators continue to debate Echlin's proposed legislation which would effectively nullify the rights of the Akaia; but first Doug Evans brings you an exclusive live from holiday capital of the north, the exotic Lalapahue."

'News, who wants to listen to that, even if I am working for them,' Melissa flicked to a rival station as she did her hair.

"Yes well, the truth of it is Sam, that TnTv have won a lot more awards in the area of filming and such, particularly in the areas of conflict and adventure travel footage; they have become almost unbeatable at the Gerning Awards so I doubt we have any greater chance at the top honour this year than any other year. But the question I ask is at what expense does this come to TnTv? No one can deny that they often have the best, but the figures speak for themselves, one in three of their photojournalists died while on assignment last year, that's a risk we cannot ask our people to take." They went on, but Melissa didn't hear anything else they said, as the words repeated in her head - one in three!

Then the television picture shuddered, went fuzzy and blinked as Melissa heard that sound everyone here was getting used to, that drrr-grrr-drrr of a tremor rolling across the city. She felt it coming and hid under the dresser. The building swayed gently as the tremor passed on. A minor thing, but there would no doubt be a few cracked windows and power outages around.

Melissa turned off the television and went out to make some last minute purchases. Normally she would have thought nothing of what they were saying on the TV, but it was different now, she thought, she was one of them, she'd just signed up. Melissa tried to forget that she'd heard such a shocking statistic as that. One in three photojournalists had been killed while working for TnTv. Was that really true? Would she be the one in three? A lump was rising in her throat. She desperately hoped to be one of the other two. Had she thought about her safety? She was just getting away from The Gutter, it was a proper job. Thinking about it, well, she had never really felt safe in her entire life now, had she? What about with Matti? No, not even with Matti she had to admit, almost, but never quite had she felt completely safe, no, she wasn't even sure she would know what that would feel like, to feel completely safe, so she told herself it was nothing new. But one in three! She so wished she hadn't turned the television on at all.

The day of departure: Weston's Morning.
Location: His TnTv office

Weston had a bitterly unsuccessful morning trying to track down a guide worthy of the expedition. He toyed with the idea of going without one, surely with himself, Hardan, Astrid and Tarku, and some local guides here and there, they would deal tremendously; every one of them had unique skills that would get them through. Then there was that consideration if something did happen to one of them what would happen? They did need that extra person, and the insurance TnTv paid required there to be a professional guide. Weston decided once again, he would just have to postpone the trip till a suitable candidate could be found, that was all there was to it. He still had a few hours though, he thought, and groaned as he called the next unlikely person on the list as he played with the balance wheel on his desk, watching its shining rim spin and spin till it wobbled and fell. He screwed up his mouth and rubbed his brow, what was he going to do?

The day of departure: John Mark's Morning.
Location: P12

John Mark had just about tapped out his fingers on The Urchin, P12. He was now whittling away his fingernails with his teeth and staring at a spot in space. He couldn't concentrate on reading, yet watching anything seemed beside the point. Whether it was television, or trying to glimpse space through the telescope when the clouds thinned, it all seemed pointless, was pointless, he thought to himself, a pathetic waste of time.

Then the radio blipped, and a voice came through the fuzz, 'P12, P12 this is Vector, Vector, over.' The call came again as John reached for the microphone, clearer this time, 'P12, P12 this is Vector, Vector, over.'

'Vector this is P12, go ahead, over.'

'G'day John, still here hey.'

'Still here Vector, what can we do for you?'

'Ah, just come from Ethersea, heading to Tamashan via Satsuan, any updates for that sector?'

'No updates Vector, there's a bit of an extra updraft over the divide once you've passed us but nothing much more than usual, you should be right all the way, that is *if* your old wreck holds up,' he laughed.

'Oh don't you worry about her, she'll be right, thanks John. Send a note through to Satsuan for us, we should be there in two days or so depending on the weather and how the old girl handles it.'

'Righto, will do.'

'Thanks John, Vector out.'

'No worries Vector, P12 out.'

John shuffled around a bit and banged the screen in front of him to stop it flickering then sent through the relevant information. The radio blipped and fuzzed again. Voices, then a clear signal came. Another ship.

'P12 this is Archimedes, respond P12.'

'Archimedes, P12, go ahead.'

'We'll be passing by you in a few minutes.'

'Heading home?'

'Right you are P12, you can take us off your log.'

'You're early, did have you a good trip back?'

'Yeah P12, but anyone going back that way should be careful, it seems like it might be getting a little hot down there, and I'm not talking about the weather.'

'What, not Satsuan?'

'No, but when we passed through Tamashan there were rumours of Delevian warships being sighted further south, east of the route down to Salamondé, nothing certain though. Sorry I couldn't be of more help, but something was clearly up and we didn't want to stick around to find out what.'

'Thanks Archimedes, let's hope it's nothing. Safe journey home.'

'Till next time P12.'

'Archimedes is back. Warships in the far south,' John said to himself as he wrote in the log book. 'Shame. Ah, it'll come to nothing, always does.'

'Vector, Vector, this is P12, did you catch that? Over,' John tried to reach them, they were headed to Tamashan and should know.

'P12, this is Vector, yes thank you, received.'

Then John looked up knowingly as a great shudder ran over the observatory, and a gentle accent came to John Mark's headset. It was a busy day for once. A broad smile lit up his care-worn features as he heard the voice.

'P12 this is Scott Thomas with Kyu, over.'

'John Mark here Scott, what can I do for you? Over.'

'Good morning John, can we come in and rest for a bit?'

'Sure thing Scott, there's no other ships in the bay at the moment so take your pick'

'Thanks John, see you soon.'

'Right Scott, hi Kyu!'

Kyu replied with a sigh akin to that of a great whale and it echoed and reverberated around the hills and craters of P12 for many minutes, running up and down the antennae and causing them to shudder and disrupt the pictures on the screens in John's tower. The cry echoed around the whole place, turning back on itself, overlapping then running on, a song constructed by chance over the ground and its density and hollowness. John felt the cry, every note of it, which was far more than just an audible sound, it penetrated his body to the very threads of the fibres that made up his muscles. He shivered as the warmth of the cry dispersed and left, but then the echo returned through him, flowing like a hot tonic through all the extents of his flesh before radiating out and returning to the air. 'Wow,' John gasped. The retired engineer left his post and hurried down to the dock. 'Scott! My boy!'

'Mr Mark,' Scott greeted.

'I'll never get used to that!' John shook his head.

'Did she read you did she?' Scott laughed, 'found the deepest part of you, pulled you out, examined you and put you back again?'

'I'll say,' John smiled, hand over his heart, still shaking from Kyu's cry. 'Oh Scott, it's been such a long time, tell me what's happening back home.'

'So good to see you John,' Scott said, taking the man and embracing for a moment, 'Oh it's all the same really, constantly changing. How've you been anyway?' Scott asked.

'I'm doing fine,' John nodded.

'I worried about you when I heard you were out here, but you look well, not quite as much brawn as back in the day though!'

'No not quite,' John laughed, 'Scott and Kyu hey, who would have thought you'd turn up on my doorstep this morning? Still inseparable?'

'Of course.'

'How is Kyu?'

'Wonderful, wonderful. We had a particularly rough passage a while back but we made it to West Fall, recovered. I would have liked to get us through to

Shorakai, they've the best ways with Kyus as you know, but we were coming from the north and we couldn't have made it. It's all good now though.'

'I must say hello to your girl.'

'She was so pleased we were stopping here, she likes you John.'

'Just as well, I wouldn't want to be under one of her penetrating cries if she didn't, I think I might be dead otherwise. Does it feel the same for you when she calls?'

'Yes, doubly so when I'm inside, but it's a tonic to me, not an examination, though I have seen men truly quake under her cry.'

John Mark ran a strong hand along her side, 'Hi Kyu,' he yelled up.

She replied again in a high whistling sigh. They rubbed the tip of her nose and worked their way around her massive form. Kyu turned as they rubbed, putting the effort of their whole bodies into massaging her and she lapped it up, this simple bliss.

Scott turned to John as they massaged her. 'Would you travel again, if you had the opportunity?'

'No,' John said mildly, then thought about it, 'no, I think I'd stay here, suits me just fine.'

'I was afraid you'd say that.'

'Oh,' John put up his brows and laughed, 'why's that?'

'I, well,' Scott pursed his lips and hesitated for a moment, but continued bravely, 'I've got a job for you.'

'Hey?!' John laughed, 'you what?'

'It's on the new Blue Moon with TnTv. They're heading into the deep south. I thought you might jump at this, you could make use of the opportunity. I mean, you always said that's where you thought your daughter would be, in the south.'

'But I've been there, and I haven't found her.'

'But you'd have access to different places with money behind you, and a television crew. It would be a completely different situation.'

'If you think there's any hope of finding my girl alive 20 years after she went missing you've more hope than I have.'

'You could earn a better wage, maybe enough to fund your own team of investigators, you could go further afield. West said just name your price.'

'Alamo sent you? Listen Scott, I'm only getting older, I'd be of no use to Weston, there are plenty of young guns who would jump at this chance.'

'You know you could still do it,' Scott argued. 'West doesn't need a *young gun* or want one. He doesn't trust them, except me maybe, but I can't go, I don't have the knowledge you do. You've been all over and you know about things and that's more important than knowing the specifications of the latest craft. What you can offer is valuable and real, not a lot of insubstantial trivia West would get from a novice, I mean, Weston himself knows more than most of them in any case.'

John shook his head. 'It's not for me Scott, I've travelled enough to last ten lifetimes, and I'm tired, I'm just plain tired,' John sighed, 'and doubtless West'll want someone who can pilot a vessel too, and you should know I can't get a license anyway, not for a North Island ship. I've got a record for unauthorised use of a military ship.'

Scott had been going to back down, but in that last reply Scott could see that maybe there was a part of John that did really want to take the job, so Scott continued to press him.

'That would have been more than 15 years ago though wouldn't it? I'll stake you it's of no concern to Weston, I think he'd even manage to get you a licence he's so desperate.'

'No, I can't do it.'

'What about Ava? Five years ago you told me you still had hope, what happened?' Scott strained.

'Nothing, nothing happened, it just occurred to me that I was chasing ghosts the whole time. Everything I had held onto, it was only grasping at cobwebs. I only ever had a feeling in my gut, never proof of anything, and that feeling could have just been desperation, a hopeless cure to cover my guilt over losing her. I have no idea where she could be, I never did.'

'So what are you going to do, just sit here drowning yourself with regret? You didn't lose her John, you might tell yourself that, but she was taken and you know it! That's why you searched so hard.'

'But I turned my back! I lost her. Don't talk to me like you know anything about it. You weren't there!'

'I know you were a good father. I know the man you were when you were in my father's service before Ava was born, so I know that. And I know this isn't the place for a man like you.'

John gazed hopelessly at Scott, 'Why are you talking to me like this, about this, now? I've told the ships that pass of Ava, and they watch out for me. I've friends scattered around the furthest corners that know my situation. Do you think I don't think about her and her mother every day?'

'I'm sorry John, I-'

'Yeah. I tell you, it would take me a lifetime just to search the Universal City, let alone the whole of the south. You think I've given up, maybe I have, I'm not sure, but I don't think I can do it anymore. I can wait for an answer, but I can't go out there chasing it anymore.'

'John, I'm sorry, I didn't mean,' Scott turned away, then turned back again, 'you don't need to justify yourself to me, you're like an uncle, you know, I care about you. I'd no right to say any of that. I wouldn't have pressed you but Weston is in a tight spot, and you know if Kyu didn't think it was a good idea she wouldn't have let me come here.' The great creature whistled and sighed, 'and you know how she has an instinct about things. But if you're okay, I'll go, I want to let you know though, I didn't ask you to do it just for Weston's sake. Partly I asked you because, well, like I said, I thought you might get something out of it, but partly because I don't want Weston to have to call the expedition off, because he's just hired this kid who seems like she deserves a bit of a break, and well, he might cut her loose if he can't use her straight away. Seems to me he only got her as a cheap offsider for the trip, and there's something about her John, there's something,' Scott waved his hand, trying to think of the right words, 'I don't know, she's got a certain way about her, something I think she's completely unaware of, but she reminded me of your Amiana. And I didn't want to tell you this, I just wanted you to go and see for yourself without me saying anything, because I didn't want you to get your hopes up, but that something makes me wonder if she could even be your daughter.'

'Really!?'

'Her name's Melissa, she's an unusual sort of pretty for a north island girl, and like I said, there's that something. I asked her straight out, but she doesn't know anything of her parents or her past. The more I think about it, the more unlikely it seems that she could be, but I don't know, you should see her in person John, just go and see her.'

'Do you know where she's from?'

'From what I can pick up she's spent all her life in The Gutter.'

'I never looked that way. The ships at port where mostly heading southwards, and nothing that way, it was the international port I was at when she went missing, not domestic,' John thought, 'but a young girl shouldn't be going out there, not the south, not with TnTv-'

'Yeah, well, you haven't seen The Gutter lately have you? She's as good out of there as not, that's the way I see it. I just wanted to tell you to think about the job, you will always have my friendship and respect whatever you decide.'

'I'm at a loss,' John said, but then he almost laughed and shook his head, 'ha, I didn't really imagine that anyone would give me a thought outside of P12.'

'Don't you know that you're a hero among us northern nomads? We talk of your travels so often, for we meet folk from all over that have met you at some stage. If we say we're from the north so many ask if we know you, the big northerner. They speak of things that you did here and there, from upsetting human trafficking gangs in Flythsyge to the time you challenged the prince of Vahrna to a land race because you'd run out of money and transport and he had both.'

'We'll I didn't break them up but I gave them a pretty good thrashing, and as for the prince, he didn't have much money in any case, and his ship got me back to Soame sure enough but not without attracting all the wrong sort of attention along the way. He didn't tell me he was wanted for all sorts of things, I had a posse on my tail, he was likely right glad to be rid of that ship and go another way.'

'And,' Scott laughed, 'the story of you and Amiana has become a bit of a folk story too, the lowly northern soldier and the ambassador of Shorakai! I've heard so many different versions of it. That you found her in a red desert of all places is a common theme.'

'How vivid her blue eyes against the red earth and sky, how irrelevant were all the wonders of the silver city and everything else when she stood beside me,' John remembered, 'And you Scott, do you tell my story too?'

'Well, I have been known to,' Scott grinned.

'And do you embellish the tale, like they do?'

'What? No, the story is so incredible I need embellish nothing, and after all, I am one of those who was actually there so I have to tell my version with as much accuracy as possible.'

'Were you there?' John questioned.

'For a little while, on Rorona, the red plains of Rorona.'

John smiled as he thought back again, 'That's right, you were still just a boy.'

'It was the year you left my father's service.'

'Amiana was very much out of place there, but less out of place than I at that time. Do they still mourn her on Shorakai? I haven't been there for years. To be honest I'm afraid I would not be welcome there, I never really felt I was even when she was alive. The north islands and our people were still so new to the international community, they didn't know what to make of me, the rough northern soldier taking their ambassador for my wife.'

'There is a beautiful garden in the city Merouin, still grown in her honour.'

John nodded, 'You speak their tongue very well Scott, I'm surprised.'

'Kyu is a good teacher, though she cannot speak of course, she knows it well and corrects me when I make mistakes. I think before I found her she must have been with a rider from Shorakai.'

'You should be a diplomat like your father, not this drifter you make yourself out to be, you're a good man Scott and the government needs good men like you.'

'Oh no, I'd soon tire of it.'

'I don't blame you,' John said, then gazed at Kyu in wonder, 'She is something isn't she.'

'She's amazing, oh how she loves a good massage, don't you girl.' Scott was silent a moment, then turned to John seriously, 'So, will you go?'

John looked at Scott, so many years of heartache and loss behind his eyes, he shook his head, 'I don't know, Scott, I don't know.'

~

After Scott and Kyu had gone John paced, sat down, paced once more, sat again. Now amongst the assortment of radios, communication devices and manuals it was almost completely silent, apart from random clicks, beeps, distant hollow sounds and intermittent fuzz. The furrows were growing on the engineer's brow, his jaw was tight, his fists clenched one within the other, and his eyes, though staring at a screen, roamed his memory of the past, of the places on earth that were known to him. He thought of his lost girl.

'Ava,' he thought, 'if only I knew you were safe, if only I could see you. What should I do? Could you possibly be alive somewhere out there? Could you be this Melissa?'

'P12 this is DC20,' John jumped as the transmission disrupted his deliberation. It certainly was turning out to be an unusually busy morning. Someone must have given a fairly positive report on the state of the weather in the divide, but it wasn't him.

'P12 this is DC20 any updates for sector 70?'

'DC20 it's P12, better dodge sector 70 altogether, it's been hit and miss with the weather for the past week. I'd suggest 68 or 72, but it might be better to go through to Satsuan then get an update there to be sure. If the report's still unsure maybe go the long way round via Tamashan, but then again Archimedes reported possible unrest in the area, so take your pick.'

'Thanks P12.'

'No worries DC20, over and out.' John sighed, what should he do? Should he go? Scott had said not to get his hopes up, so it probably wasn't likely. Maybe it was better to let it go, no good getting involved, it would just cause trouble, this girl wouldn't be his daughter, would she? How could she be?

CHAPTER 8:

The day of departure: Sir's Morning.
Location: Junto-a-Mar to Universal City

Serace Garner, dubbed 'Sir' by his cronies and subordinates, made call after call, and eventually one struck gold. One of the busy receptionists at TnTv picked up the phone again, 'TnTv, how may I direct your call?'

'Yes ah, I'm trying to get in contact with a girl called Melissa, I believe she works there,' Sir requested.

'Melissa?'

'Yes, that's right, Melissa.'

'Do you have a family name sir?'

'I don't, I don't, but would you look for me love?' he smoothed, 'she'd be new. I need to get in contact with her, it's, it's very important.'

The receptionist thought it strange to have a first name request for someone who wasn't a presenter, and of whom she hadn't a request for previously but she did as was her practice. 'Of course sir, not a problem, one moment please,' she put him on hold and searched the employee list on the network, and there it was, Melissa, just the name Melissa, via Weston Alamo's office. There were no action notations on the file so she put him straight through.

The phone rang in West's office. He jumped, swore and knocked his spinning balance wheel off his desk.

'Haven't you any respect for my frayed nerves!' Weston protested to the phone as he reached for the wheel, simultaneously knocking his cold coffee over. 'Ah!' Then suddenly it occurred to him that it might be a guide ringing, having changed their mind and deciding to come. A guide! The producer clapped his hands and picked up the office phone, answering cheerily, 'Weston Alamo, at your service,' while he shook his coffee dripping fingers, wondering what to do with them and the small mess he'd created.

'*The* Weston Alamo?'

'Yes, and?'

'Ah, do excuse me, I was after Melissa.'

'Oh,' Weston sighed, what a let down.

'They must have put me on the wrong line, sorry, I'll try again.'

'No, no, you've got it right, she works for me. Who, who is this?' Weston wiped his fingers on his shorts then began taking off a shoe.

'Ah, her uncle. Can I speak to her?'

'Uncle hey? Well she's not actually here.' After looking around for a suitable receptacle and finding none Weston tipped the coffee that had spilt in his shoe back into his mug.

'When will she be in? I'll call back.'

'I don't know, sometime today, listen leave your number and I'll pass it on.'

'No, never mind, I'll ah, catch her another time.'

Weston put down the phone then stepped back to take a seat, his heel finding the sharp axis of the balance wheel. 'Aaaah! Blast it!' he yelled, sitting down and grabbing his foot. 'Blast it! blast it! blast it!' the producer almost cried. No guide, spilt coffee, no secretary, strange phone calls, oh, he was really getting to the end of himself.

The rain and storm at Junto-a-Mar had lasted well into the night and the rail network had been shut down till crews could inspect the tracks for damage. Sir had waited and waited for the first train of the morning as the roads were impassable, as it was, it just made the city at half twelve. Sir stepped off the train and made his way up to the street, promptly commandeering a pedal-taxi and shouting directions to TnTv.

~

After finding the store Weston had told her of and purchasing the items of clothing he had recommended despite the fact that they seemed to cost a terrible lot of money, Melissa walked into the lobby of TnTv tower again. It was so much bigger and grander and far more daunting than she had remembered it, but she'd had Scott's company yesterday. She was surprised at how many familiar personalities were coming and going, she was so nervous carrying her new purchases and wearing her ordinary old clothes in front of them. She felt the very street urchin they thought she was. She supposed she must have been too excited about her first pay cheque to notice all the TnTv favourites when she had left yesterday, although it had been rather later in the day, maybe they'd all gone home by then. She turned around to take it all in, the grand lobby, the people, the way she had come. But all trace of that joy then disappeared from her face, she stopped stiff, whispered, 'No, I don't believe it,' then turned and ran further into the building.

She was quite nervous as she navigated the hallways, dodging questioning looks and near apprehensions by security guards then sharing the lift up to the fifteenth floor with TnTv's intrepid weather man, who she discovered was actually quite a nice guy, unlike she had presumed. He maintained a friendly flow of conversation until she excused herself as the lift opened, to go and seek Weston. How could Sir know she was here? No, no, no! This wasn't happening! She wasn't going back!

She did not find Weston in good spirits however when she burst in on him and he sent her out to the corridor.

'Wait,' he apologised as he saw her face. 'What's the matter?' he asked, rubbing the four day old whiskers on his chin.

'There's a man following me, I'm not here if he asks,' she was shaking, 'I'm not here.'

'Alright honey,' Weston calmed, 'is he in the building?'

She nodded, 'I-I think so, he was.'

Picking up the phone to call security Weston asked, 'Do you know him? What's his name?'

'Sir.'

'Sir-?'

'Um, no, it's Garner, Serace Garner,' she stammered.

'Oh kid,' Weston's heavy brows creased, 'he doesn't call himself your uncle does he?'

She shrugged her shoulders, and shook her head, not sure why Weston would ask a question like that. 'I don't have an uncle.'

'Oh no. Does he sound kind of sharp, slur his esses a bit?'

'Yeah.'

'Oh kid, he phoned earlier, I'm so sorry, if you were here incognito I blew your cover for sure.'

'It's not your fault.'

Security finally answered the phone. 'Yeah, it's Weston Alamo, listen, I have reason to believe there's a dangerous man in the building, a Serace Garner.' Then to Melissa, 'What's he like honey?'

'Slim, about this much taller than me, dark hair – oh, it's going a little grey on the sides, he dresses neat.'

'That describes a third of our employees kid,' Weston sighed but passed the info to security. 'Slim, 170cm, dark hair a bit grey, neat. Yes it's important, don't you boys dare let anyone even slightly resembling that get up to this level. Thanks.' He put the phone down.

'Sorry kid, I haven't slept, might have been more alert otherwise.'

'No, well you didn't know.'

'What's this bloke done that's so bad? or is it you've done something? Is he a stalker or something?'

'No, he runs a…' she couldn't say it. 'He's a certain kind of businessman, you know, back of the truck stuff, anything, liquor, medicine, cigarettes, drugs,' Melissa looked down, 'people.' She swallowed and confessed, 'I've been his property as long as I can remember.'

West's brows went higher, his eyes startled. 'Melissa, you weren't – he didn't – make you-?'

Melissa laughed, 'Oh no, he has heaps of businesses, some are even legitimate, almost. I worked in the laundry or wherever, it wasn't like I was locked up or anything, well, only that one time, and he never made me-,' she grew serious, 'well, not yet, but Kat and Sophia reckoned- '

'Stop, stop, stop,' West held up his hand and put the other over his ear. 'That's enough, I don't need to know more than that. Don't you worry about him now, you just sit yourself over there and if he shows himself I'll show him how this producer can wield a weighty camera to more than one purpose.' Weston saw Melissa smile, 'Good, that's good,' he encouraged.

A guard approached a man fitting the description, heading for the lifts down a corridor right of the main entrance.

'Excuse me sir,' the guard halted him, 'may I see some ID please.'

'Sure, not a problem,' Serace Garner searched his pocket, he looked at the guard, smiled. 'Here we are.'

The guard read, 'Mr Harmon?'

'Yes.'

'What's your business here today Sir?'

A security officer came into Weston's office, nodded a greeting then brought up a screen of camera vision on Weston's computer. 'One of our officers is talking to a likely man now, is this him?'

'Melissa?' Weston turned the screen to her. She nodded.

'Right, thank you,' the officer left.

Moments later Serace Garner was escorted from TnTv Tower. He wasn't fazed, but went on his way to do some further plotting. At least now he knew where she was.

'Relieved?' Weston patted Melissa's shoulder.

'I just want to get out of here.'

Weston cringed, 'I'm afraid I've got some more bad news for you, it seems we might not be going after all, not for a while yet at least. Why don't you go and wait in the tea room till I know what's going on.'

'Can I do anything?' she worried, 'what's the problem?'

'No, don't you worry your pretty head. The tea room's just down the hall and to your right, you might find something to read or watch, and I'll let you know what's happening when I do.'

The day of departure: Melissa meets Astrid.
Location: TnTv employees lounge.

Melissa did as she was bid and went down to the staff kitchen and lounge. She was surprised to find it quite empty. Without looking for a refreshment or place to sit she strode straight across to the floor to ceiling windows that gave a great view of the city and the streets below. For quite some time she stood here just watching. Then looking around her she picked out a cosy lounge which faced that window and began to flip through all the magazines and books lying about. She picked out a book that caught her attention, only because Weston Alamo was one of the authors, and sat down to read it: The Unofficial Biography of Jonathan Rebus Mark, a man whose life was one that many could only dream of, a life in and out of danger, a life discovering more about the world, a life that led him to be considered one of the greatest adventurers and explorers of the time.

Melissa read on. She discovered that John was born here in the Universal City during the final and most productive years of the exploration revolution, when clear signals had at last been sent and received through the crazed atmosphere, beyond the cluster of isles here in the north. When vehicles had at last been developed that could withstand the corrosives and toxins of the divide that surrounded the North Islands and when the engineers and pilots worked together to come up with ways to navigate the unpredictable and hazardous steam and ash drafts. When visitors came from abroad and brought news of distant colonies, when the leaders ventured into these places and made treaties far and wide, discovering lands where trade could bring benefits on either side and bringing back knowledge and technology before unthought-of, and Melissa read of what began a decade of rapid change.

Two chapters in and the focus was back on the life of John Mark. Melissa read of his early days in the military, his time on an elite squad tasked to contain rogue Akaia, his choice to shift his career and complete his apprenticeship as a ships engineer. But after serving only a few years in this role his expertise led him to be employed in the service of the newly appointed ambassador to the southern nations and he was there when the ambassador represented the North Island States at the first International Summit since the north had discovered the rest of the world.

International travel, she read, was still new and held many dangers, 'It still does,' Melissa thought, and at the time of the summit the government had been warned of many tensions by their close allies in Satsuan and Shorakai. Ambassador Willam Thomas was keen to attend, as the North Island States had been particularly asked by the international body to do so. There was a picture here of the ambassador with his family, they were standing in front of their vessel, in the red desert, with the city of Rorona a distant backdrop. Melissa noticed a similarity to her new friend Scott and the ambassador, and wondered if he was related to this man in some way, but then she read the footnote - *Ambassador Willam Thomas, his wife Emily, and their son Scott.* 'No way, it is Scott! It must be!' she smiled.

John Mark was one of the group that accompanied this ambassador to the neutral protectorate of Rorona for the summit. His computing and engineering experience, along with his former military training made him a valuable asset to the team. But the ambassador returned disheartened by seeing the same flaws at the summit as he saw in the north's own political spheres, commenting that on the surface it seemed transparent but underneath lay the same selfish denial of truth, different rules for different peoples, and insatiable greed. But that was not all that disheartened the ambassador, he had not only lost his confidence in the new found international community, but he had also lost his most valuable team member, John Mark, the engineer. For amongst the envoys of other nations in Rorona at this time, one had stolen the engineer's heart.

On the opposite page there was a picture of the young Shorakaian envoy. Melissa could not help but laugh at the thought that Scott had asked her about Shorakaian being in her heritage. It was an ridiculous idea, look at this lady Amiana – she was the most unusually beautiful and refined young woman Melissa could ever remember seeing. She continued to read about the tragedy that met the fair couple only 12 months after their marriage. Amiana, as special envoy from Shorakai between the warring factions of Vahrna and Delevi, was assassinated and no one had ever been charged with her murder, and no party had claimed responsibility. On top of that, Melissa read, John returned to the North Islands in disbelief, with their young daughter Ava, where he took a position at the Universal City Port. Here countless interstate and international visitors passed every day, and it is from here that his daughter Ava disappeared, and her body had never been found.

'You must be Melissa?' Melissa suddenly looked up to see a hand outstretched to her. She took the hand and let the woman shake it firmly. 'I'm Astrid. West said I might find you here, seems we're going to be working together.'

'Oh, pleased to meet you.'

'Reading about John Mark I see?'

'Sorry? Oh, yeah, not much else worth looking at in here.'

'Oh, don't let them hear you say that, these magazines are all TnTv publications,' Astrid chuckled, taking a seat, then nodded seriously at the book, 'he's a good man.'

'Do you know him?' Melissa asked, much intrigued.

'By reputation. So, I can feel your nerves from here darling, what can we do to cure you I wonder?'

'I'll be alright once we get going,' Melissa said bravely.

'Yeah, of course you will darling.'

Melissa found herself wondering what kind of person Astrid was. It was hard to say how old she was. She had thick hair, matted in long dreads and held up in a twist of fabric. She had more piercings in her ears than Kat did. She wore a khaki jacket over a singlet and cargo pants and boots that made it look like she was ready for anything. But behind all that, Melissa thought, she seemed like a very gentle sort of person.

'So, what gear are you using?' Astrid asked, looking at Melissa with such bright, kind eyes.

Melissa was a little hesitant, 'Oh, I don't have anything much, just an old Carrelli.'

'Oh, what model?'

'Ah, it's a E380.'

Astrid smiled, 'Now don't you be ashamed of that darling. Sure it's an old giant, but the old Carrelli is a reliable machine. It might not interface with a lot of our new technology and she's heavier and what have you, but the Carrelli's, they just keep on going. Do you have it with you?'

'Yeah, I do,' Melissa took it out of her bag and handed it to Astrid.

'Mm, feel that,' Astrid took the old camera and closed her eyes, 'yep, it feels like something it does.' Then Astrid took a closer look, 'Decent glass, wow, heavy duty body, nice, that'll come in handy.'

'Yeah,' Melissa smiled with a little pride at Astrid's appraisal of her gear.

'Matter of fact I think I know this camera,' Astrid said as she studied it, 'where did you get it?'

'I um,' Melissa grew a little worried, 'actually I found it.'

'You found it?'

'Yeah, it was just sitting by the trash at the back of a friend's workshop. He didn't want it so I got it.'

'Ah. You know, I think I know who used to own this,' Astrid smiled, 'one of the best photographers I've ever met. He's a mad kid, don't know how he does it, he came out with photos like nothing anyone had done before. I don't think he's used a Carrelli for a while now but he made his mark with this camera, almost like he saw the world through different eyes to the rest of us, so like I said, it's nothing to be ashamed of just because the technology is old.'

'You really think this is his exact camera?'

'Fairly sure. I think I could even tell you where it got some of those scratches.'

'Wow. And, um, what do you use?'

Astrid chuckled, 'Me? The OptikaTe 1K.'

'Oh. I don't know that brand.'

'I'm afraid I can't exactly show it to you,' Astrid laughed, 'it's my right eye darling.'

'What do mean?'

'The camera is my right eye,' Astrid winked.

'No way! Are you serious! I heard of something like that being possible but I didn't think anyone would actually be that crazy! Sorry Astrid, I mean, that is-'

'Hahaha, don't stress darling, I am crazy, but there are times when it comes in handy, when you need to be inconspicuous, or need to have your hands free.'

'But can you see? Does it stuff with your normal eyesight?'

'Yes, and yes,' Astrid smiled, going to the fridge now and finding a cool drink, offering one to Melissa.

'So, do you know who else is coming on the trip?' Melissa asked her. 'I thought everyone would be here and we'd be on our way by now.'

'Well let's see. I know Hardy's around somewhere, he's the captain, and then there's Weston, who you know. There's us. Other than that I'm not sure yet. Don't you worry though, West always gets a good team together.'

Weston at that moment was actually pulling out his hair in complete frustration, it had been a long few days. Why couldn't he find a suitable candidate? It seems all his standbys were away, not available, otherwise employed or in some far flung hospital recovering from a recent job, or dead. Weston Alamo went into the bathroom, shaved slowly and washed his face, brushed his hair back into place, changed his shirt, then came to a decision. He began down the hallway preparing the right words with which to disappoint his girls. But Weston stopped suddenly as he neared the tea room, was that his phone? His eyebrows lifted high in hope, he listened more – without a doubt! it was his phone! He hurried back to his office.

'Weston Alamo,' he answered.

'I'll take the job.'

'John?'

'No.'

'Oh, Scott?'

'No, it's Jem Fisher. Come on Weston, please let me have this job, please, I need it and word is you can't get no-one else. I mean I heard you phoned Clancy and you'd never phone Clancy if you weren't desperate, come on man, I really need this job.'

'I told you no already. You're not qualified, you lied in your original application, you take too many risks.'

'I'm sorry West, come on, please, just till you can find someone else, you know, and only this side of the Arc I promise.'

'Ah.'

'I'll be careful, come on.'

'Um.'

'Weston, I'm on my knees, I'm begging you, I really want this job, I need this job.'

'Hm.'

'West?'

'If you can get here in ten minutes I'll take you on till Satsuan or until I can get someone better.'

'But I'm on the other side of the city!'

'Better get moving then Jem.'

'I'll be there.'

Weston wasn't exactly jubilant, but he was beginning to see the positive side of everything. Fisher wasn't what he wanted in a guide, but he didn't care anymore, he wanted to go and he wanted to go now, that's all. He'd had enough. Weston wanted to be out of this place doing what he loved, if he had to have Fisher on board to do that, well, he'd just have to have Fisher. Weston was sure Melissa had nowhere else to go and Astrid wouldn't want to go back either, he couldn't call this off or postpone it. He wouldn't. He hurried back down the hall to tell his girls.

'Get your things together and go up to the ship, give any larger bags you won't be needing straight up to Hardan and take the rest on board with you. Oh and make sure Tarku is about, and chase him up if he isn't. Well, up with you! Hurry!' Weston left them, running back to his office.

'Oh, so Tarku's coming, that's interesting,' Astrid said, 'he's the one I was telling you about, who used to own that Carrelli of yours.'

'Really? Do you think he'd mind that I have his camera?'

'Tarku? No, if you found it, he must have got rid of it somewhere along the way, I wouldn't worry about it.'

'I am so out of my league, wow! Tarku who's one of the best photographer's you know, and you, who's crazy enough to have a thing in your head and Weston Alamo who's produced some of the best shows on TnTv, what am *I* doing here?'

Astrid just laughed kindly, patted Melissa on the back and repeated what Kat had said, 'You got to start somewhere darling, why not with the best.' She picked up her gear and Melissa followed after her.

CHAPTER 9:

The day of departure: Garner meets Tarku.
Location: TnTv Tower.

Serace Garner put his phone away, glanced at his watch and looked around. Finally he spotted his men. They crossed the road to him and he filled them in on the situation.

'Right boys, Melissa's in the building. Man inside just informed me she won't be there much longer, they're flying out from the thirtieth floor dock, we'll intercept her there, but for all that's sacred don't you hurt her, got that boys, I just want to bring her home. You ready?' The two men nodded.

A back entrance was opened from the inside and a wad of cash placed in the pocket of a familiar guard. Garner and his men passed and headed on as the security officer had directed. They took a service lift to the thirtieth floor.

'There it is, the ship, he said it'd be the Blue Moon. Any moment they'll be coming through those doors to your right,' Garner nodded the direction and his men stood by and waited.

Captain Hardan had been called away to take possession of a particular carton which the couriers must have neglected to bring with the previous delivery, but the young man Tarku was there, lying idly, low and invisible in the ship's cabin. He raised his eyelids and lifted his head gradually as his instinct warned him. He saw three figures out in the dock, familiar perhaps? His face was grim. Something like a growl or a huff escaped his throat. He stood casually, shook the fringe out of his eyes then walked out, down the stairs of the Blue Moon to meet these men. Tarku noticed the security cameras on this level were stuck on a rotation of the other side of the dock. One of Garner's men noticed Tarku and he pointed his weapon towards him. Tarku nodded to Garner.

'Boss,' the man grunted. Garner turned, looking Tarku up and down.

'Do I know you?' Garner asked, his eyes narrowing.

'You may have seen me,' Tarku corrected lazily, 'but to see is not to know.'

'Ha. Yes I know you, you're the Akaia I saw at the garage the other day aren't you? Buying some old bike off Matthias. That's it.'

At the word, 'Akaia' Garner's two men became even more alert and focussed on Tarku's movements.

'A fine motorbike,' Tarku answered casually.

'I saw you at the station at Junto-a-Mar as well,' Garner pointed, 'at the same time Melissa left. I saw you in the footage we went over. You're not behind this, this escapade, are you?'

Tarku glared at Garner darkly, 'She's free now, let her be.'

Sir laughed, 'What do you want with her? I can hardly believe your intentions are any more admirable than mine. Do the right thing here, save yourself an injury, let me get the girl back, and I'll even throw in a reward fee for your time.' Garner stopped momentarily, seeing Tarku's grim and determined gaze only grow harder at his words, but he wouldn't leave it be, he accused, shaking his head, 'I know your kind, you're just as mercenary as I am! So how much do you want?'

Tarku almost lunged at Garner and ripped out his throat right then, but he held himself back and controlled his rage, only letting escape a gruff exhalation under his breath.

'Did Matthias put you up to this?' Garner continued, 'he's been besotted with the waif as long as I can remember, but we can come to some arrangement, leave her to me now, I'm warning you, stay out of this.'

'I don't think so,' Tarku answered strongly, 'she's no one's property.'

'That's where you're wrong. Don't push me boy,' the man said angrily, 'I will kill you if I have to.'

'Go ahead,' the boy challenged.

'Well, if you're keen,' Garner laughed, 'I'm sure no one will mind if I rid Corrio of another Akaia.'

Tarku just smiled and dared Garner, 'I'd like to see you try.'

Even as Serace accepted the dare and began to draw his pistol from the shoulder holster inside his suit Tarku slid over, tripping the nearest man, grabbing his silenced pistol, firing it at the other man, who had his weapon ready, then firing at Garner, who was still pulling out his own gun, kicking that man's weapon hand and grabbing his pistol as well, then aiming back at the man he'd tripped as that man tried to stand.

The boy stood still. The three men remained where they were, only winged, but not willing to move while this Akaia stood over them with their weapons now in hand.

Tarku stood over Garner, 'Why do you take this risk to get her back? She's just one girl.'

Garner laughed, a nervous hollowness in his voice, 'She's our little Melis.'

'What is she to you? Why do you want her?' Tarku pressed, his manner more threatening. Garner was not unaware of the danger of angering Akaia like Tarku, his soul shivered under Tarku's gaze. He was not an easy man to intimidate but Garner was sure the fury of this boy was palpable in the air around him, like a thickness in every breath, and he could see the fire ignite under the soulless grey of Tarku's eyes, and he knew enough about Akaia to know that was a dangerous sign. Tarku had almost choked him, the world was slipping into darkness around him, and Garner's fear was real.

'What is she to me?' Garner finally answered, though he could hardly speak, 'What she's worth, it's all about the gold boy, that's all. We've got a buyer coming for her soon, there's money in it for you boy if you'll take it,' Garner pleaded.

Tarku weighed the words, and the situation. He watched the floor number on the far lift get closer and closer; the rest of the crew would be here soon, including the girl. He asked one final question, 'Who's the buyer?'

'Don't have a name, don't have a face,' Garner answered, 'they're foreign, but the cash is real enough.'

Tarku pulled the man close, 'Well, you'll have to pay the deposit back, she's free now. Now get up, the stairs, get going, don't look back,' he ordered.

'She's better with us boy, you watch my words, they'll come after you. They're serious, I know that much. They'll take her, you won't be able to stop them.'

'If you or anyone comes after her you'll have to deal with me, and next time I won't be so lenient.'

Garner and his men held their wounds and hobbled to the exit. Once they were in the stairwell Tarku closed the door and locked it securely behind them. He closed his eyes and breathed in, he shook his head and breathed out, and when he opened his eyes there was no spark in them, they were cold flint again. He wiped the blood spatter quickly from the floor, and threw the rag, the guns and ammunition away, letting them sink into the collective sump pit of all the ships on this level, then climbed back on board the Blue Moon, lying down idly and closing his eyes just as the lift opened and Melissa and Astrid stepped out laughing.

Astrid looked around, she could smell the gunfire, the blood and the fear-laden sweat in the air, but nothing seemed out of place, she didn't know what to make of it. For a moment she touched the wall of the building, connecting with it. She observed the three men on the stairs and their injuries and she found the heartbeat of Tarku and noticed its speed. Something had happened here. She would ask Tarku about it later.

'Wow!' Melissa had to stop still to look up at the Blue Moon and take in its mad design. 'Is that our ship?'

'Yep, that's our ship,' Weston said proudly as he and Hardan exited the next lift.

'Designed by the great man Luca D'Avero himself,' Hardan added, 'isn't she beautiful.'

'Beautiful?' Weston laughed, 'I don't know that I'd agree with you there Hardan, but it certainly is an eccentric design and altogether the most exceptional ship you will find in the north.'

'That's so,' echoed their guide Jeremy Fisher, now arriving as well, still puffing from his mad dash across the city to get here. At once he got into the role of guide, giving them a whole lot of information that no one had asked for about the ship. 'Though D'Avero never revealed what the inspiration was for the design some hypothesise that he was inspired by the water beetle. And did you know, the original Blue Moon had been a horse transport,' he told them, 'as horses from Parahn are sought after throughout the world, near and far, for their sturdiness and heart. Its design was so successful, it had to be, as horses are very sensitive to travel, more so than people. And so to the smooth flight they added a comfortable interior and a few other things and there you have it, a great ship.'

The whole vessel sat balanced on two points either side of the craft, about two thirds of the way down the hull, so the entire front section of the ship seemed to hover above the ground, supported by nothing at all, but in fact it was able to be this way as the weight of the engines in the rear, along with some clever hydraulics, which counterbalanced it perfectly. There were of course supports that were also used when the ramp was down, but these weren't necessary most of the time, and their use was more for the peace of mind of uncertain travellers than for anything else.

The entrance ramp to the hold lowered from the underside between the two rear points, where Weston now entered with a few last minute additions to Hardy's neatly packed cargo. Stairs were available either side as well when needed, giving direct access to the front and rear cabins. There were wings that came out when necessary for stability and lift, but the entire design was such that when all the ramps and wings were drawn in it was all smooth, rounded lines. Inside was just as fine, the fit-out was as all good fit-outs should be, so good no one even took notice of it; it was simple, comfortable, and unobtrusive.

Everyone loaded on board and found a seat and soon the Blue Moon was away, Garner and his men could do nothing more than look up from the street below and watch it disappear out into the red, decaying, afternoon sky.

CHAPTER 10:

The Blue Moon is away.

Weston was in the cockpit standing behind Jem and Hardan. Hardan hadn't been that impressed to see the young man again but he had accepted it with the equanimity he did most everything, and he understood Weston's decision to have him was only a temporary measure. It wasn't that Jem wasn't good company but just that one couldn't always rely on his decisions, or that he had the expertise he said he had.

Every now and then one of Weston's loud guffaws would travel back into the cabin where Astrid and Melissa talked quietly of random things. Tarku remained asleep as they had found him when they boarded, cocooned behind his sunglasses, his neglected fringe, and his jacket collar.

It was fairly spacious at the moment, for all in all the forward cabin could seat twelve. Four seats facing each other just behind the cockpit, where Melissa and Astrid sat, and two rows of four seats facing the front, two either side of the walkway, where Tarku was seated in the furthest row from the cockpit, on the right, just in front of a small stowage compartment.

The forward cabin could be entered by an outer door, opposite the stowage that was behind Tarku, or by coming from the rear passage which went past the bunk area, in which there were six small bunks, and an emergency exit set into the roof complete with a pull down ladder. Further down the rear passage were kitchen facilities, and further, through another door, were the amenities which even had a modest shower and bathroom with water filtration and recirculation, and through yet another door you came to the rear cabin where there were a further four seats and various parachutes and masks and body suits and other safety equipment. From here you could open the safety exit, a double door set up, complete with an airlock and air-exchange system, and you could also access the engine via a narrow set of stairs set below a hidden hatch, and also, through an obvious hatch, you could access the cargo hold below from which you could also lower the main ramp to disembark. It was a very handy little ship, designed well for trips just as this.

Melissa looked around her, excitement and nervousness surging through her. She felt all shaky inside, so excited she almost felt ill with being so scared but so happy. What they were heading into was gradually creeping up on her and she was beginning to wonder if it had been a stroke of good fortune that had landed her the position or ill fate. She pondered the Mech-Angel button Matthias had given to her when her anxieties began to overtake her and remembered his words, 'Don't come back, not unless you want to die here.' Of course she didn't want to go back there, it was enough just to see Sir today to make her shudder, to make her realise she'd done the right thing in leaving The Gutter, even if this was perhaps a very extreme route to take to get out of there. Just as well for Weston and the security guards, she thought, but she wanted her friends, she didn't want to be lost out in some unknown corner without a soul she knew. There was nothing but to suck up her fears and get on with it, and try to be some company. But, Melissa thought, Weston, Tarku, Astrid, Jem, Hardan and her, that's six. One in three. From the report it was only reasonable to suppose that two of them would die. Melissa shook her head, it wasn't good to think like that, she told herself.

The first stop was P10, but it was just a quick stop, a last final check that everything onboard was doing what it should, and that the tanks were full and the electricals functioning well. Then the Blue Moon was really away, speeding low through the atmosphere as it entered the northernmost limits of the great divide. Hardan had Jem beside him in the cockpit and together they kept a careful eye on the instruments and the conditions outside. Many a ship still went down in this dangerous place because it was unpredictable and rarely gave warnings of its actions. After all, this was the great divide, the wall around the north that had separated it from the rest of the world for so long.

All but Tarku, who was still sleeping, crowded by the left-side windows for a better view as the ship now veered east and they could see back towards the North Islands. It was not that long ago in the history of the north after the collapse that it had been estimated by a symposium of scientists that there could be nothing beyond this place, beyond the north islands, that they and they alone were the last vestige of humanity left in all the world. Imagine what a stir took place when it was found that not only were the north islands not alone, but that they were in fact so insignificant in comparison to the technology, knowledge and size of many of these other surviving nations. Even now, over two-thousand years since that collapse, fragments of mankind are still being discovered, colonies that had survived in the harshest places since the world was redefined. The cartographers are kept busy updating the maps, and many expeditions are sent out to do soundings in the cavities under the immense platforms of remaining habitable crust that they call the islands.

Slowly a clearer picture is being formed of the earth, and it has the authorities concerned. It seems that at any moment, any city, any nation, could be swallowed by the convulsing earth, or by the tides of toxic air that continue across the surface. And not only could it happen at any moment, but there is much speculation as to why it has not already occurred. For as far as they can determine many islands that remain are held up by brittle platforms that are being slowly eaten away by the condensation of the toxic steam that gathers about and under the islands and runs back down the cliffs and columns to the unliveable stone deserts and molten wastes, and the earth itself moans and creaks and quakes relentlessly in the agony of its own slow death.

Though the ship sped it seemed to be hardly moving at all, their surroundings were so immense. No other ships could be seen through the steam, but every now and then Melissa thought perhaps she could see a flash of the fire down in the deep, but it was explained to her that what she had seen was more likely a lightning storm somewhere below them, or a burst of molten rock shot fresh from a restless and surging core.

'Now there,' Astrid pointed and quickly turned Melissa to look back out in the direction they had come. For the briefest of moments the cloud behind them had parted by some freak wind, and the view, however short, left Melissa speechless. They were a long way from the North Islands now, and P10 seemed no more than another urchin stranded in the desert, but from here, just for a second, the far mountains beyond the Universal City could be made out. But the thing that made Melissa gasp was that she also saw in that moment the precariousness of the island she called home. For as tall as mountains were above the crust, inverted mountains grew twice as tall underneath, the land simply fell away below the deserts and cities, eroding into the crumbling emptiness of the wastes. Everything she knew existed there, so uncertain.

Astrid gave the child a pat on her shoulder, 'It's different seeing it for yourself isn't it?'

'Wow. I saw some of Scott's film, it showed a lot like this, but I had no idea the North Islands were-'

'Don't scare the kid Astrid,' Weston admonished as the rest chuckled.

'You're not scared are you darling? Now you can feel safer out here knowing that where we come from is just as dangerous.'

'You have an inverted way of looking at things my dear,' Weston grinned at Astrid, then turned to Melissa, 'Here, Melissa, I haven't had the chance to properly introduce you to the captain, come, this is Orin Hardan, or Hardy to his friends, a man with catacombs of experience.'

'No, no, quite ordinary I am,' said Hardan, through the trim ginger beard that he sported at present which made him look quite distinguished. 'Pleased to meet you Melissa.'

'Oh and this is Jem Fisher, Jem, this is Melissa, but Melissa I don't want you to get to know Jem because he's a bad lad and I'm getting rid of him as soon as I can.'

Melissa was wide eyed and gasped at Weston's frank admission.

'Oh, thanks for good rap West,' Jem laughed, taking Melissa's hand and smiling mischievously as he shook it.

'Anyway, we'll leave them to do their job,' Weston ushered her back into the cabin.

Weston's large smile was sitting comfortably on his face. He was at peace now the expedition was underway, and he and Astrid glanced knowingly at each other as he walked back into the cabin and sat down. 'Oh, and of course Melissa, you've met Astrid, my Muse.' Astrid laughed at Weston's description of her. 'And I'd introduce you to Tarku but, as you can see –' Weston shrugged his shoulders and glanced back at him. Tarku was still asleep.

Weston handed out the information about the trip, about their destinations and other relevant data and gave the crew a little talk about what he wanted them to focus on, 'Ultimately there's three main areas of focus in each place we go to, we must film and research enough to have a good understanding and visual story of each people in terms of the region's culture, the region's beliefs, and the region's environment and how the people survive there. Our first stop will be Shorakai, so at least it will be relatively easy.'

'We're going to Shorakai first?! Really?' Melissa was amazed and very excited.

'Yes, well, it's a good place to begin settling into the expedition because it's a civilized place and the people are usually easy to communicate with, unlike many of the other places that are on our agenda,' Weston explained.

Things had been quiet and everyone settling into the feel of the flight and what lay ahead, when the gentle cruising of the ship faltered and the Blue Moon began to shudder. Weston looked into the cockpit at a yell from Hardan.

'I knew the run was too good so far, something had to happen, the divide's trying it's best to have us,' the captain grimaced. 'Secondary thrusters on?' Hardan asked Jem.

'Yeah, and the wing cheats,' Jem gritted his teeth as he concentrated on the readings and adjusted the controls. 'It's holding us, the divide'll have us down soon Hardan.'

'Not if I can help it. Reposition the rear-boosters in quad formation, bring the wing-cheats in close and turn them out.'

'Done. It's not helping, it's not helping!'

'Hold her steady now!' Hardan yelled to himself as well as Fisher, as the ship began to twist and spin, and the passengers made sure again that they were strapped in securely.

'I shouldn'ta begged West to come if I'm going to die already,' Jem spoke quickly as he worked, almost laughing though he gritted his teeth, 'she's caught Hardan! We'll be splintered soon!'

'Wait, wait, now bring the forward boosters online.'

'Done.'

'Shutdown the secondaries.'

'Done.'

'Come on, come on, come on,' Hardan urged his precious ship, but the winds were too unpredictable. 'It's playing with us,' Hardan gasped in utter disbelief as they were again thrust jarringly aside and back, no more than a leaf in a breeze. 'We can't get above it. I've lost control of her!'

'Full thrust?' Weston yelled forward.

'It's on full thrust, it's no use, we're caught in a channel! We can't pull out!' Hardan winced through his clenched jaw, though he continued to try to maintain some control over the ship.

Melissa couldn't help but feel more than just a little uneasy in her stomach and concentrated on a spot on the ceiling. Astrid pressed her own hand spread-out hard against the cockpit wall and concentrated on the floor. Weston, sitting opposite her, was over-worried and glanced at her from time to time. Tarku's head just dropped a little lower as he slept on. Hardan and Jem tried everything to stabilise the ship but the unpredictable divide was at its most temperamental, a sudden and strong channel had caught them and nothing they did made a difference.

'Wait, she's stabilizing,' Hardan breathed.

'How? What did you do?' asked Jem,

'I don't think I know.'

'But the gauges are still going off the scale.'

'Did you bring out the second cheats again?' Hardan asked Jem.

'No.'

'They're out, but it's not on auto,' Hardan checked, 'maybe something got knocked around. Now the thrusters are moving back into parallel, the cheats away. Look, the wings are retracting all the way! This is some quick thinking flying, and dangerous! Hold onto your chair Jem!'

Without the wings the winds could not push the little ship around so easily and at once the Blue Moon began to fall. The passengers did not feel much of the drag in the well protected cabin but in the cockpit lights were flashing and alarms going off and Jem and Hardan were helpless to do anything as the ship plummeted, as the flashes in the wastes below them grew ever closer through the haze, but then suddenly everything settled.

'Wings are coming out, she's pulled out of the channel! She's pulled up!' Jem exclaimed, 'primary cheats out, forward off, rear off, standard engines back online. The gauges are all showing green. Wow, I knew the Moon's were good, but I had no idea they had a mind of their own. That was incredible.'

'Aye, some angel's looking out for us that's for sure,' Hardan sighed, wiping his forehead.

Astrid grinned to herself as she heard the words, she wasn't called a Mech-Angel for nothing. Weston winked at her, for her being a mech, or more precisely, Machina 20M A*id, who could interface with technology and had the manuals and specifications of the Blue Moon and all D'Avero's craft in her head, along with much else, was their little secret.

Weston took a deep breath, 'So we're out of trouble?' he asked.

'Seems that way,' Jem answered, taking a seat with them as Hardan had it all under control now. Melissa breathed again too.

After a moment recovering, Weston noticed that Tarku had changed position. 'Tarku,' he spoke to the young man, sounding a little annoyed. Weston raised the great expressive mounds that were his eyebrows, 'Tarku,' he began again, his eyes telling he was just joking and not seriously annoyed. 'I've been wanting to introduce you to the rest of the crew, you scamp. Now I know you're awake so don't try to pretend you're not.'

Tarku's blank face crept into a reluctant smile, though he still faced straight ahead, up to his jaw in the collar of his black jacket, eyes still shielded by his glasses. Weston continued to berate him in a friendly manner, 'Come on, get up, I'll introduce you to the others.' Tarku sighed and stood up, following Weston the few steps to where the others sat.

'Astrid, you know her from a couple of years back. You remember Tarku, hey Astrid?'

'How could I not, smooth kid,' she shook his hand firmly.

'Dread head,' Tarku smiled back.

'Tease.'

'Activist.'

'You two,' Weston laughed, 'get on with it.'

'You haven't changed a bit Tarkars, glad to meet up with you again,' Astrid smiled, the boy nodded.

'This, Tarku,' Weston led him on, 'is Melissa, who we saw the work of down at that exhibition. This is her first big trip,' Weston went on, but Tarku wasn't listening, he just took in of her what he had not been able to glance at sidelong from behind his glasses, or in the reflection in the window. To him she seemed happier than when he'd last seen her, when he had waited to make sure she got onto the train at Junto-a-Mar safely, and he was glad of that. She was a short, sweet girl, currently exploring a military-chic fashion, and by appearances only a fraction younger than Tarku. She had a smooth, slightly olive complexion and her eyes were as close to green as hazel could be.

'And Melissa, this is Tarku, well, he's done a lot of work for us over the last few years,' Weston went on. Melissa studied Tarku as he had studied her, veiling her curiosity behind a generic smile and glances towards Weston. She had watched Tarku on and off while he slept, and he seemed no different to her now. He still wore his sunglasses, he still wore his blank face - his smile, if it came, always disappeared in the same moment. To Melissa, he came across as too lazy and self absorbed to even smile.

'Hi,' she said politely, ripping herself away from her consideration, she hadn't been listening to Weston either, but she realised that he'd stopped talking. Tarku nodded and gave her a disappearing smile. 'Too lazy even to say hi,' Melissa thought, 'or maybe he can see I'm from The Gutter,' she sighed inside, at once deflated by the thought.

'Tell her about your trip with the Li,' Weston prodded Tarku.

'I don't know,' Tarku sat down on the arm of a chair.

'Come on,' Astrid teased, 'I'd like to hear it again.'

'That's where he really made his mark in the profession Mel – is it ok to call you Mel?'

'Yeah, sure, um, but if you like they call me Melis back home. I'm used to that.'

'Melis it is. Come on Tarku,' Weston pressed.

'You can tell the story if you care to West, I haven't the desire,' Tarku said in dull monotone.

Who did this guy think he was? Melissa laughed inside, so snobbish, and oh so chill.

'Okay then, I will if you don't mind,' Weston continued cheerily as if he hadn't even noticed anything cold in Tarku's response. 'I know I wasn't there myself but I've seen the pictures you took,' Weston said enthusiastically and took up his story telling pose. 'He was working with this Li while covering the Duanuan migration. Every 10 years they say, these communal, giant gnat-like creatures make their way through the centre of Vahrna to the other side. You have to be a pretty obsessive, not to mention reckless, photographer to wait and catch them as they burst through. Well, anyway...' Weston continued the story and the others listened, amazed as always, while Tarku bent his head down and became distracted by a loose thread on his coat sleeve.

Anonymous poets say memories are like gems, sparkling beautiful things to lock up like treasures in your mind, to pull out and think on when you're feeling low or going through tough times. Tarku however, pondering this thought, prefers his own summation, that memories are like shrapnel. Like bullets, like old wounds that keep reminding you that they're still there. That itch and re-open and never quite heal. Some folk are blessed with a happy past, with memories of family, of friends and good times and good days, and it's not that Tarku does not have some small store of these kinds of memories but that they have been crowded out and overwritten with such memories as make his summation understandable, perhaps even a little less aggravated than it could be. So, memories being out of the question, but circumstance making it necessary for distraction, Tarku put his mind as completely and wholly as he could to that loose thread.

After Weston had finished he laughed and grabbed Tarku again, 'You didn't hear a word I just said did you?' Weston got a real grin out of Tarku, even be it a little dark.

'Oh and this is Jem Fisher,' Weston continued with the introductions, 'Jem, Tarku.'

Jem Fisher was a youngish man, average height, but very thin and awkward. He'd gingery-brown hair, including a rat-tail goatee, a lop-sided smile, and hollow, scratch-scarred cheeks. It was instantly apparent to the observer that he'd lived hard for a while, but even despite all that there was still a certain charm about his face, well, certainly Melissa and Astrid had come to that conclusion in any case. Tarku, however, took an instant disliking to the man.

Jem took Tarku's hand and shook it firmly. 'Oh man, I've wanted to meet you for so long, kid, your film on Delahar, oh, like wow! I've never been so inspired,' Jem praised, with genuine admiration.

'I'm glad,' Tarku said, though the reply was a little forced.

'And the captain, Tarku, you better come say hullo to Hardan.' Weston pulled Tarku through to a friendly reception, and the offer of coffee and glazed bun from dear Hardan. As the two were already known to each other the meeting was easy. Tarku declined the offer, but Hardan was pleased either way, so he said, as he would have more to himself that way. He chuckled, he did particularly like glazed buns from his favourite cafeteria, and he congratulated himself on his forethought at procuring quite a few for this journey, all safely stowed in the freezer in the cargo hold, and after that close call just now he might need an extra large coffee, or two for that matter.

'Tarku was saying the apricots would have to be made of reconstituted algae unless you spent 50 bucks apiece!' deplored Weston, 'Hardy what do you say to that?'

'Don't spoil my apricots!' Hardan laughed, 'I did not spend that much!'

'You don't really think they're algae do you Tarku?' Weston scoffed.

'No, but I'm not certain that they're apricots. You know what was left of the apricot production was recently lost to fire in the far north. The flowers had just come on the trees too. What was left of the canned supplies would now be worth their weight in gold.'

'I shall still hold these to be apricots, and let me believe what I will,' Hardan bit into another with great enjoyment, 'and I shall die a happy man.'

CHAPTER 11:

The ache behind the thread.

The worst of the divide being over, and the flying more comfortable, Hardan recommended that everyone take some rest, and to make them comply he dimmed the lights and continued to fly the ship smoothly along. Hardan's strategy did not fail. In the silence and the darkness everyone was soon finding a bunk, until only Astrid and Tarku were left in the cabin. Astrid had wanted to talk to Tarku alone, even apart from anything that may have happened before they had left the TnTv dock, she could sense all was not right with the Akaia, and she knew of the recent reports on Echlin's ruling. Finally it was possible to talk to him. She got up and sat on the seat opposite, looking at him seriously.

'Are you okay Tarkars? I mean, really?'

'Yeah, thanks,' he nodded, and threw her question back, 'You?'

'Yeah, I'm fine.' Astrid knew he was lying and wanted to say so much but after a moment of pondering the best words just said, 'You know if you need anything, if I can do anything-'

'You can't change what I am, and that is the root of the issue, is it not? There's nothing you can do Astrid. I fully expect Echlin's proposal to get through the senate. I am neither shocked, nor distraught, nor in need of your sympathy,' Tarku said, his voice was not harsh, but rather contemplative and almost sad, 'I have been through worse.'

'Well, when you need a friend, you know I'm here right.'

'Yeah, thanks Astrid. Though I might suggest you could find many a better friend than I.'

'But no one I'd rather have watching my back,' Astrid said earnestly. 'Well, I better go crash, I'll see ya. Oh, Tarku, did something happen before we arrived at the Blue Moon today?'

'Nothing you need to worry about.'

'Right.' Astrid went. Soon everyone was falling asleep. Tarku waited a while then he got up, he poked his head into the cockpit.

'Just a heads-up Hardan, if you see the airlock door alarm go off it's only me. I need some air.'

'Hey? Tarku we're still in the middle of the divide, it's toxic out there.'

'I know, that's the point,' Tarku answered grimly, 'don't worry, I'll make sure the airlock is secure before I open the outer door.' He patted Hardan's shoulder firmly, then made his way towards the back of the ship. He took off his jacket and his glasses, and went down the rear right side of the ship and out those doors, standing in a spot that wouldn't be too clear on the camera feed that Hardan could have seen in the cockpit, waiting until the seal was tight again before sliding the outer doors apart a fraction to allow the corrosive air in the divide to find him. He stood in the swirl of it as the ship sped on, he made himself stand there, even as it began to sting his eyes, even as his lungs began to be seared.

Though Weston tried to lie still for quite some time, he was too excited and had too many plans and thoughts to fall into the wraps of sleep. As he lay there he noticed Tarku's shadow go past and he thought he heard a door open and close but he thought nothing of it. It was only after so long of not being able to fall asleep when he decided to get up and fix himself some supper that Weston saw Tarku, coming back from the rear cabin. It was dark but Weston could hear the airlock door close tightly and begin flushing the space with filtered air and he wondered at it, but it still didn't click.

'Tarku I was just going to get some tea, would you like - ' Weston began, but he stopped. There was just enough light for him to see that Tarku's hair was dishevelled, his jacket was hung loosely over his shoulders and his eyes seemed to be bleeding around the edges, where blood had mixed with the boy's tears and stained his face.

'Tarku, are you alright?'

'For now,' the boy answered, his voice rough and barely audible.

'What happened?' Weston looked down to the rear cabin, then back to Tarku. 'What's wrong?' Weston pressed. Tarku didn't answer, but he was close now and Weston could suddenly smell it, that acrid reek. 'You've been out there haven't you? In the airlock! You opened the outer doors!' Weston whispered in hoarse surprise. 'Are you insane boy?! Those gases out there can kill a man! What are you doing to yourself?'

'Surviving,' Tarku answered with hardly a breath.

'What? By half killing yourself?!' Weston exclaimed.

Tarku ignored Weston, walking on, holding the wall to steady himself.

'You better wash down at least,' Weston said, trying to be helpful, and at last realising Tarku's state and taking the boy's shoulder to help him along.

'Trust me, that's what I plan to do,' Tarku took a deep breath with difficulty.

'Good. Do you need anything?'

'Just go Weston, get some sleep,' Tarku pushed Weston away and stumbled into the shower cubicle, fully clothed, sliding to the floor.

'How hot do you like it?' Weston asked, turning the taps on for him.

'I don't care, it's just water,' the last words seemed to disappear and Tarku's head rolled to the side.

Weston knelt and watched over him, 'Tarku, hey,' he hit the boy's cheek, 'come on, stay with me.' Tarku was so weak, Weston couldn't remember seeing the boy quite like this before. 'Tarku come on!' Weston shook him again.

The water ran over Tarku's face, soaked through his hair, washed the toxic air from his skin and clothes. He came to again shortly, to Weston's relief, and leant his head back on the cool wall and breathed, 'I've had a rough few days. Thanks for getting me through this afternoon.'

'What? I didn't do anything.'

'You didn't press me. You talked for me.'

'It's nothing. Come on, you're alright now aren't you?'

'Yeah, thanks West.'

'Don't thank me, you know I only do this for my own self interest, I'm not going into the south without my best videographer, but I'm not happy about this Tarkars, this is not a good way to start the expedition, you could have killed yourself, then what would I do?'

'I'm sorry West.'

'Yeah, well, I'm the one that hired you. You do something wrong it comes back to me, you understand. I'll go back and make sure you're not missed, we can't let the others see you like this.'

'There's no need to look at me as though you've seen a monster,' Tarku said darkly, painfully, though he almost smiled, 'I am not fallen that far yet.'

Weston was shame faced, he had not thought his fears would be so obvious. 'I don't know how you can keep going,' Weston shook his head, 'I couldn't live like this.'

'Like what?'

'I know what you're doing, you're almost killing yourself over and over so you don't- so you- to postpone the inevitable! So you don't lose hold of reality, so you don't forget you're still here and you're still part of the human race! So you don't go mad like the rest of them!'

'You can go back to your bunk West.'

'But am I right?' Weston challenged.

Tarku didn't answer for a time, he looked up at the acclaimed producer, who now stood there half saturated from the shower in his effort to help Tarku. The Akaia looked aside. 'I don't know how long I can keep doing this either,' he admitted, 'my time was up years ago.'

'Well, I know you've got more in you yet, so get up and see to yourself Tarkars. I'm relying on you, you know, and not just for your filming, ever since the first time you got my team out of a tricky situation I've known the value of having you on board, so you better get yourself together.'

Weston pulled the door closed and made his way to his bunk, sitting down and thinking over what he had just seen. He took a deep breath. He hoped he had said the right words, he hoped Tarku would forgive him for flinching; but who could know what Tarku was, what he was capable of, and not feel some amount of fear? Even as weak as Tarku had been, it had taken all Weston's willpower to stay with him and help him just now. Weston sighed, and tried to go to sleep again.

~

Tarku let the water wash over himself for a few long minutes, eventually he was able to stand, to hold on to the taps, then he was able to let go and stand on his own, then slowly take off his shirt, his singlet, his belt, his boots, his trousers, everything, and let the water run over him properly, over his tortured body. Even as he stood there his breathing became easier as his lungs recovered, his eyesight returned to normal, his blood was washed away and the damage done by the destructive elements outside lessened as he healed, relatively quickly like many Akaia.

He had stacked a change of clothes ready on the basin. He gave himself one last check in the mirror to make sure his body had recovered well enough, just a cursory glance, as he didn't like looking at himself too hard, at the intricate markings on his body that were slightly paler than the rest of his skin, that were not there by his choice and went far too deep to be erased. He pulled on a nice pair of denim jeans, grey shirt, and then sat by while his jacket went through the wash and dry cycle. Then he put on his jacket, zipped it up, making sure it was zipped all the way up, and pulled down the sleeves as far as they would go to cover those markings, then he checked his eyes; at present they were idle, but in his current state they could easily spark, so he put on his sunglasses again and styled his fringe low over them before returning to the forward cabin.

Everyone seemed asleep as he passed the bunks. Tarku didn't think he could sleep, he was actually feeling quite good now, as he always did when he'd recovered from near death, though he knew he'd pushed it a little further than he should have this time. He decided to go and see how Hardan was going, he stepped quietly into the cockpit and closed the door behind him.

'Oh, hi Tarku,' Hardan welcomed, 'You up for a roll and coffee now? I was about to go and get myself another.'

'Sure, why not,' Tarku accepted, 'maybe just a tea, no sugar, no milk.'

'Alright, won't be long. She's on auto, but call me if anything starts beeping,' Hardan grinned, patted the boy on the shoulder then headed to the kitchen to put together the provisions.

Tarku leaned back in the seat and smiled, he seemed very comfortable sitting at the controls. He checked the various dials and configurations and shook his head, 'Hardan, you can do better than this,' Tarku said to himself. He took the ship off auto and adjusted a few complicated settings as one who knew the Blue Moon inside out. 'There now, that's more efficient,' he popped it back on auto and then propped his head uninterestedly to one side as Hardan returned.

'There we are.'

'Thank you,' Tarku took the hot mug, leaned back and sipped, in a rare, totally relaxed moment.

'So, how's the bike going?' Hardan asked.

Tarku grinned wickedly, 'I bought another one. I couldn't help it, it's magnificent. You should see it.'

'Oh? What brand?'

'Well, it was one of the early Avero's, but they had drawn the original design from a vintage racer they dug up from years ago, but altered it to better suit more road conditions.'

'I think I know the bike, a very nice machine. Rare though. Does it go well?'

'Doesn't miss a beat.' Tarku took another sip. 'How's your family?'

'Great thanks. Yeah, the two lads were so hurt I was going away again, so was the missus, but Angie's too little to know what going away means. They'll be alright. Growing up so fast the lot of them. You know I didn't want to ask her, but I'm fearing Emma has another one on the way too,' Hardan chuckled and shook his head. 'Don't know how she does it. Amazing woman.'

'Well, if your suspicions are true, congratulations.'

'Thank you,' Hardan smiled then yawned.

'Go get some sleep captain, you know I've flown before, and like you said it's on auto.'

'Are you sure?'

'Yeah, I'll call you when we're getting close to Shorakai.'

'How'd you know I wasn't too keen on the idea of Jem being up here. Thanks Tarku, I really do need to get some sleep.'

'With all that coffee in you?' Tarku laughed.

'Bah! I can sleep no worries, that stuff doesn't affect me anymore, think I must be getting immune. Alright I'll see you when you wake me up.'

Hardan went past the snoring Weston and the others and pulled off his neat shoes, massaged his toes, let out a satisfied yawn, made himself comfortable on a bunk, pulled up the blanket and promptly fell asleep.

Tarku took the ship off auto again and picked up the speed, flying through the steam drafts and drifting cloud with an old pilot's ease, enjoying the silence of the night, the satisfying design of the controls at his fingers. At this rate it wouldn't be long till they were in the territory of Shorakai. After a while the boy heard quiet footsteps, then the door handle turn. One button the Blue Moon was on auto again. Jem Fisher entered, rubbing his eyes. 'Oh, hi Tarku,' Jem said surprised, 'I thought, Hardan?'

'On his bunk.'

'Oh.' Jem seemed like he may have been a little cut, 'He should have called me, I was supposed to swap with him a few hours ago. I can do this, you don't have to.'

'It's alright, I offered to watch the controls.'

'Oh. Well, I can take over if you like,' Jem suggested helpfully, 'it is part of my job after all.'

'Sure,' Tarku stood and vacated the captain's chair.

'Wow,' Fisher exclaimed as he took the seat and studied the positioning on the control panel, 'the Blue Moon's are great I know, but this is brilliant, even on auto we're almost at Shorakai already.'

'Oh, good. I'll leave you to it then,' Tarku said.

'Wait, Tarku, I have a question for you. My mates and I could never figure out where you were standing when you did that legendary section of film in Delahar.'

'Can't recall.'

'From what we could tell you would have had to have been standing so close to the outer limits in some of those scenes, the heat must have been intense.'

'Oh, the Kardha desert rally?'

'Yeah.'

'Ah, it was a while ago, but yeah it was full on,' Tarku answered, and left before Fisher had a chance to ask more questions. He went back and roused the captain.

'Fisher up front, Shorakai not far now.'

'Thank you,' Hardan whispered sleepily and sat up, rubbing his eyes.

Tarku went and took his usual seat, and his usual pose, the sleeping, uninterested boy in the back seat, just as a light was beginning to be seen in the sky. The others soon started to come around, and they were all wide awake by the time Shorakai came into view.

CHAPTER 12:

The View of Shorakai

It was a remarkably clear morning, and the view of Shorakai from afar was no more than a glint, like the sun on a fragment of mirror glass. But the closer the Blue Moon sped across the miles of salt encrusted hills and flats the more could be seen, the more the crew realised that this was going to be the most incredible place in the world. Below them stretching wide and now even ahead to the horizon was the greatest expanse of ocean that still existed, surpassing even the great lakes of Oconia. The crew watched the sea below, the deep water-filled hollow that had somehow survived the collapse - that had survived the heaving and splitting of the oceans floors and remained, a reminder of the largest oceans of earth's bright past, of the turbulent Aramah and the vast Panyanae.

Soon the cities of Shorakai could be seen ahead, rising out of the sea. Hardan headed towards the city called Rinau, to the main port. Everyone crowded to the windows to better view the city as they came in. In the north they call Rinau 'The City of Jewels' for the skill of the builders here, their skill with glass, and their aquatecture, as Scott referred to it. At first the city appeared almost as a cluster of fine reeds bestrewn with droplets of dew; structures that seemed precarious and random, but in reality were perfectly balanced along and within spanning curvatures, what seemed to be bamboo structures, having the look of fragility, but being able to withstand the severity of the tremors that continue across the land because of their strength and flexibility.

Then as they grew closer those buildings rising out of the sea and the verdure became clearer, some areas were like a collection of glass-blown bottles that mirrored more colours than there seemed to be in the world, some below were ancient sandstone buildings abutting narrow greenswards on one side and canals on the other. The crew could see now some evidence of destruction caused by the last great quake, but the city seemed largely unscathed. But Melissa didn't focus on the city for long, she was looking at the sky. For as the morning grew and the sky cleared further she could see it, the fabled blue sky of Shorakai. The ocean and sky reflected each another and the glass city reflected both, so although it was not so blue as in times past, it was dramatic nonetheless to those who knew a sky to be mostly grey, brown, or shades of amber and red.

'I hope everyone's been over the itinerary,' Weston disturbed the awe filled silence, 'there's a lot to do here, I don't want any delays or mishaps or we'll push back the rest of the trip, and we can't have that, we don't have the funding or the time, and we don't want to be anywhere near some of these places when summer comes around, it's just too hot.'

'So we have a week here?' Melissa spoke as she watched the city draw closer.

'Yes, one week. It's not long, but it will have to be long enough, there's an event in Arrojor next week we won't want to miss.'

'Have you ever been to Shorakai before Melissa?' asked Astrid.

'No, I haven't even been off Corrio before.'

'Do you know the story of Shorakai?'

'I don't think so, but I guess I may have seen something sometime.'

'The people here believe that Shorakai existed even before the collapse, which makes it one of the oldest nations and cultures on earth as most of the world's cities and governments that we're familiar with were established post-collapse. Their history books tell that Shorakai was a city hidden from the rest of the world, somehow maintained under the great Panyanae Ocean, but revealed during the collapse as the level of the ocean fell.'

'That's amazing. Is it true?'

'I don't know, we're talking about something that happened over two-thousand years ago, but no one who's been to Shorakai dismisses the story.'

The Blue Moon was met by an escort vessel as they grew closer to the city, and they were led into the port for processing. Hardan steered into their allocated space at the port, and the crew were requested to hand over their papers. Weston stepped down to talk with the officials, with Astrid following him to help translate. The producer was at pains to explain the reasons the crew were here, and that they were not asking for more than a few days, just as the paperwork TnTv had sent through weeks ago explained. While they waited for approval to stay the crew could not help but notice that so many others were here too, ships were crowding the port, but there was something of angst amongst the crowds, an evident fear and despair - many officials argued with pilots, many mothers pushed their children in front of them while weeping and pleading with the officials. It was a sad sight.

'What's happening?' Melissa asked as she watched the scene.

'They're refugees,' Jem answered, 'but there are too many for Shorakai to take. It's been like this for a long time. You'd like to think that something could be done but what can Shorakai do? Everyone wants to come here, but even if they opened the parks to put up tent camps, what then? There's just another few hundred going to come tomorrow, and tomorrow and the day after that.'

'So what's going to happen to them?'

'I don't know,' Jem shrugged his shoulders.

'Shorakai will take as many as they can, the most desperate of the women and children who can go no further, but most will be turned away,' Tarku explained without turning his head as he stood at a window watching Weston's progress with the officials, and watching the refugees and other arrivals in the background. The light was on his face, but it did nothing to soften his hard profile as he continued to answer her question. 'They will head to a camp on the rim of Panyanae from where they can still glimpse Shorakai, but they will soon find living there too difficult, not just because Shorakai discourages it, but because any place becomes hell when you can see but cannot have the heaven you seek. The refugees who leave here will head on to Oconia but they will be turned away, so they will head to Arrojor, but they will be turned away. Any that have enough fuel and haven't already been lost to the hazards of travel will then head to Soamé, which is the most absurd, as Soamé is already crumbling just because of the weight of bodies upon it, but by this time none here will care to factor that. The north is too far and too dangerous for most of their ships to go, they wouldn't make it through the divide. Heading south west is not much better, though some will try, though Satsuan and Rorona will not let them stay unless they have money, and only those born nomads know how to survive in the desert there. Further afield, some few may make it to Tamashan or Salamonde, some may think of Delevi but most are too afraid of the sovereign and his people so they won't even try, besides everyone knows that Delevi is about to be lost in any case and Vahrna has been mined and stripped to its core so there is no reason to go there. So they will head back to the Arc, braving the pirates that favour those routes, and facing all manner of hardship just for the slim hope of a spare metre of good earth to die upon.'

Melissa didn't know how to reply to that, Tarku had hardly spoken up till now, but she didn't have to reply as Weston ran up the stairs and became quite animated. He was gesturing but seemed unable to vocalise for the moment, but then it came out, 'Would you believe we have an official invitation to dine with Asmara Viléla!' Weston was met with blank stares from the crew, except for Astrid of course, who knew exactly who Weston was talking about.

'Her role is what would equate to our governor,' Astrid explained, coming in behind Weston.

'So, how'd you wrangle that?' Hardan asked.

'I don't know, it just happened,' Weston went on excitedly.

'What about them?' Tarku looked out the window to the refugees, 'are they coming to dine with Asmara Viléla?'

'Tarku why do you do that?' Weston sounded off at him, 'why do you see the bad in every good thing that happens?' Tarku held up a questioning eyebrow at the producer's words, Weston added quickly, 'I'm sorry, don't answer that. Just be happy, alright. This is a good thing.'

'Sure. What about your plan for no delays or mishaps?'

'What about it? This is exciting. And you're not saying you're not coming because you are, they've asked for the whole crew to attend,' Weston added, 'and you're going to be amiable.'

'But like Tarku says,' Melissa spoke up, her brow knotting with concern, 'how can we go and eat with the governor when these people are turned away even as we watch?'

Weston was about to say something, but Tarku spoke again, 'Actually I wasn't speaking of the refugee issue,' he explained, 'I was merely wondering why they would invite us as opposed to anyone else.'

'Oh,' Melissa looked back out the window, her opinion of Tarku sliding back to her first doubtful impression of him, 'isn't there something we can do? We could take some of them some food at least?'

'We're not on a mercy mission Melis,' Jem spoke up, 'you'd start a stampede. Feed one family and they'd all want something. Trust me, better to leave it be.'

73

'Like Jem says,' Weston added, 'focus on your job, that's the best thing you can do. As to why we're being asked to dine with Viléla, well, we're filming Shorakai, showing it off,' Weston said, as if it were as simple as that.

'That's my point. Why would they want more attention?' Tarku replied. 'They wouldn't, they are a quiet but clever people, already burdened by those seeking a better place. There must be another reason we're being asked to dine with the governor, don't you think?'

'I think it's no more than that we are from the north and they would get very few visitors from the north,' Astrid said, 'and Weston and TnTv are not without renown.'

'Perhaps,' Tarku thought, 'but is it really essential I come?'

'Yes, don't be a child. You'll dress the part too. No motorcycle gear, no gloves, no hoodie, and,' Weston pointed, 'no sunglasses!'

Tarku looked at his knuckles, thinking through the difficulties that may present for him, then asked, 'When is this thing?'

'In an hour. Oh, but there was one other thing, the official would like to have a word with you before we move on.'

'With me? Now?' Tarku questioned.

'Yes, with you, now,' Weston hurried him.

'Do you need me to translate?' Astrid offered.

'No, I know Shorakaian well enough.' Tarku stood up, neatened his jacket, then walked down the steps of the Blue Moon to talk with the official as requested, but he was soon back.

'You better go ahead Weston, they're taking me in for a formal chat,' Tarku grinned darkly.

'Oh. Right. Do you need me to say a few words?'

'No. I don't think it would help.'

'Alright. Well, we've got the go ahead to move into the city. Do you know the central port? The local one? They said it was near the gardens. Can you find us there when they're done with you?'

'Yeah, I'll do that, if it goes well. If it doesn't, come get me when we're leaving.'

'It can't be much, they did say they wanted all the crew at this dinner with the governor.'

'Well, we'll see.'

So as Hardan took the Blue Moon on, the crew watched Tarku being led away.

'Is he in trouble for something?' Melissa asked, 'was there an issue with his papers?'

'Didn't say honey, I'm sure it's nothing.'

On the way to the office the official turned to Tarku, 'It's been a little while Tarku, you keeping well?'

'As well as can be expected. How are you Keersi?'

'Well, very well. Apart from having to deal with so many refugees. You see them Tarku - double last month. This is how it's getting. With things as they are I fear it's only going to get worse.'

'Very likely.'

'Listen, Tarku, I've got new superiors and they're pretty tough so, just pretend like you don't know me once we're inside and I'll get you through this smooth as I can, alright.'

'Through what?'

'You won't like it, but just go with it.'

They walked in. Keersi ushered Tarku to a desk where another official was already waiting with Tarku's papers in hand. Keersi directed Tarku to sit down. He did.

'This passport is for Tarku Na Araka? This is you?' the other official began.

Tarku looked at Keersi with a little annoyance, wondering what the issue was, but he answered them, 'Yes.'

'You are Sansahme, or as de Nordan speak it, Akaia, yes?' the official asked with some concern.

'Yes,' answered Tarku.

'Problem is, Tarku,' the official broached the subject delicately, 'these papers are not authentic.'

'Of course not, none of my papers are,' Tarku replied and calmly explained, 'I haven't concerned myself with finding out what the law is here, but where I come from people like me can't have papers. The documents you have, though fake, are authentic in content. But I have been here before with the same papers, why bring it up now?'

'You see, Tarku,' the official took off his glasses and rubbed his eyes for a moment before continuing, 'there has been trouble and not just in de Norde.'

'Trouble?'

'Sansahme are, how shall we say, restless of late. Though the number of Sansahme are very few on Shorakai, and even less than once were, our government too has some concerns.'

'I see.'

The official put his glasses back on and looked over the papers again. 'We note that you've been here on prior occasions without incident, and we have no cause to take issue with you but in the light of the current circumstances we thought it best to let you know that we hope your visit is peaceful this time as well.'

'All being the same I'm sure it will be.'

'I'm glad to hear it, because I must advise you that if you are not enjoying a peaceful stay we will be quick to take action.'

'That's good to know. Thank you. If anything disturbs my peace I'll be sure to inform you.'

Keersi grinned slightly at Tarku's words as the other official handed Tarku back his papers, but the official remained serious. 'Also, I am obliged to ask that while you stay you wear this,' the official brought out a tracking bracelet, 'with respect, your wrist, please.'

Tarku looked aside with a distasteful scowl, but held out his arm without protest. It wasn't so much the thing in itself, for the device was as light and unobtrusive as it could be, it was just demeaning, no matter how many times he told himself the people of Shorakai had every right and reason to fear Akaia.

'Is that all?' he asked, now pushing the bracelet up under his sleeve.

'Yes,' the official said and motioned for Keersi to escort Tarku out.

Keersi continued less formally again as he ushered the Akaia along, 'Why not use fake details? I don't understand? It would be safer for you. I think the only reason they looked twice is because of the content, the forgery is of the highest quality, they wouldn't have noticed otherwise.'

Tarku glanced over the details on his papers as he put them away. The statistics of who he was, height, date of birth, eye colour, country of residence, birthplace. 'I had no wish to test you with false information, nor thought I, any need.'

'You can go on your way Tarku. If you get a chance you should come by the house one evening, Mila would be glad to see you.'

'I doubt I will be able to come, but thank you.' Tarku nodded then left the offices of the port authority, heading on to the central gardens to meet up with the crew.

CHAPTER 13:

The thread between.

The port at the central gardens was far friendlier than the main international. It was a domestic port reserved for local travellers and select visitors, a water port that lay below a few city rises and beside the gardens. From here many canals could also be accessed, and from the gardens gondolas could be hired to explore the city.

As the Blue Moon settled onto the surface of the water the crew were in awe at the towers that reached above them, and even down into the water below, the residences and workplaces of the people of Rinau. Here the Blue Moon revealed further evidences of being designed by a genius, the ship glided across the surface of the water alongside the local vessels, as easily as though it had been made with water travel as its primary function.

At the gardens the crew disembarked, stepping straight out of the door onto the dock. The gardens were informally neat; beside the stone paths that greeted their feet grew fine grasses and low green heath over which leaned trees, willow-like, with their trailing branches catching the slight breeze. One could easily believe, if one lived with these gardens as their outlook, that there was nothing wrong with the world at all.

After a moment to absorb the marvels of their surroundings, the crew returned to the ship and scrubbed up again and were looking very smart as they stood ready and waiting for the gondolas to take them to the formal dinner with the governor. Even Tarku had made his way back and was now in a suit, though he had the collar turned up defiantly and was fidgeting with the cufflinks and the top button on his shirt collar now and then, and still wore his sunglasses, and his fringe across his face.

'What was that about before?' asked Jem as they stood waiting for their escort to the dinner. The others also listened for his answer.

'Minor details,' evaded Tarku, making sure the tracking bracelet was tucked well up his sleeve.

Their escort arrived and they stepped onto the glass gondolas and began along the canal towards the buildings of parliament where the dinner was to be held. They hadn't gone far when Melissa, who had been watching the water and all that could be seen below them in wonder, had to sit back and hold her head.

Astrid sat by her and held her, 'What's the matter darling?'

'I don't feel so good. I've had a bit of a headache since we landed, I hoped it would pass, but now I'm feeling a little queasy too. I hope it's nothing.'

'Sounds like sea sickness,' Jem laughed, 'have you never been on the water Melis?'

'No I haven't, but I don't think that's it, really, surely I wouldn't get sea sick? My head's just throbbing, well it's coming and going in waves, oh I think I'm going to be sick,' Melissa held her throat, 'or maybe I'm not. Maybe I'm ok.'

'Will you be right to keep going?' Astrid asked, 'or do you want to go back?'

'I want to keep going, I don't want to miss this, I want to do my job,' Melissa said, determined to go on, but for the rest of the way had to look at her hands rather than into the water or out at the city.

Soon the gondolas came to the formal entrance. They were welcomed by the governor's personal aide, who spoke their language admirably, and she took them up the wide sandstone steps and into the buildings of parliament, down the long halls, with a continual running commentary about the various artefacts and historical images they passed along the way.

'This,' the aide stopped them before a large painting in a prominent place, 'is the last empress of Shorakai, Syratreya é Nuamoi.'

They looked at the impressive painting as directed. The lady, firm in countenance and stately of bearing, indeed an empress, was painted here in the traditional costume of Shorakai and holding a long staff, but this was no impassive, symbolic head of state who they looked upon, this was a woman who's very image conveyed such confidence, strength and determination, and warmth.

'She looks like a warrior,' whispered Melissa to Astrid.

'It has been over five hundred years since her reign came to an end,' the aide continued, 'all the governors whose portraits you see along these walls have ruled stewards since then.'

'Why is that? Did Empress Syratreya have no heirs?' Astrid asked politely, even though the answer was already in her computer subsystem.

'One,' the aide told them as they walked on, 'the empress had one child. This portrait is the child at the age of three.'

'Syraveia,' Tarku said her name, standing back to take the painting in. No one turned to him, which is a shame because if they had they would have seen a rare, true smile light his face, but the group all looked to the painting.

'Her eyes are so blue!' Melissa studied the artwork, still feeling not at all well but very interested at the same time and determined to go on, 'were they really that blue?'

'The royal line of Shorakai often possessed such colouring, shades of blue,' the aide noticed Melissa's hazel eyes as she added, 'and green.'

'Why did the child Syraveia not become empress after her mother?' Astrid asked.

'Unfortunately she was taken into seclusion soon after this, having been found to be marked Sansahme, to the despair of all.'

'Sansahme?' Melissa questioned.

'Akaia,' Jem repeated.

'And having been marked Sansahme it was deemed she could not rule,' the aide continued, 'so upon Syratreya's death the first governor was installed.'

'What happened to the daughter? To Syraveia?' asked Weston, looking down the wall, 'did she live? I don't see any other pictures of her.'

'According to the records she died within a few years of her seclusion. It is generally the way of the Sansahme to fall into decline before they reach adulthood, as you in the north must know,' the aide said as she beckoned them on, 'the human body and the human mind simply isn't built to cope with what they are forced to.'

Tarku remained standing at the picture as the others moved on. 'A few years in seclusion, that's a nice story isn't it Syra?' Tarku sighed, then followed after the others.

'Why not abolish the monarchical system altogether, if it has been so long and there are no heirs?' Weston asked. 'Or why not choose another line to continue on the tradition?'

'A good question. I will tell you why,' the aide began, 'the nation of Shorakai was established a long age ago, when our historians tell us the sky was still clear blue. Before the collapse, before the fragmentation and splitting of the earth, before the seas were lost and more than half mankind wiped out, before all of that. Before such things as the Mrukai, Tuxra, or the creeping death, or the mark of the Sansahme were even known, we were here. But without the line of our late empress, the line that began our nation, none of this would have been possible. None of this would exist. Therefore there are none on Shorakai who do not hope for the return of Syratreya's line. That do not hope for the slight chance that our records may be incorrect, that a descendant or relative has been overlooked. That somehow another in that line will return to hold Shorakai together through the times ahead, for there is no doubt that the terrible future that so far we have only imagined, is very near.'

'But how could any one person allay the further fragmentation and decay of the earth?' Astrid and Weston asked almost at once.

'Ah,' the aide said with an understanding smile, 'have you not heard the story of how Shorakai began?'

'I have heard the beautiful myth that is spoken,' Astrid said.

The aide smiled, 'Perhaps in the north you must believe that it is a myth because you have not seen enough to believe otherwise, but to us it is our history.'

'What is the story?' Melissa asked.

The aide checked the time, but obliged Melissa. She had been going to hurry them along but she stopped and pointed to the patterns that were repeated along the hallway, subtly in the embossed detailing. 'The story is all around us,' the aide said, 'telling of a river that flowed into the great Panyanae Ocean here, three-thousand years ago. It was a long and wide river whose tributaries were many and spread far across the land. This river was benevolent to those who lived upon its banks, sustaining them by the bounty of its waters, but as time passed destruction came from over the sea and over the land, right to its beloved people. The greed of men spilt refuse into its waters, and wars came because of that greed, causing the river to bleed into the Panyanae with the blood of those it loved.

'According to the story, the river stopped being passive at this violence, it could not sleep any longer. It is told that the river spoke to a boy from amongst these people, and it began to guide that boy; the heart of the river became his heart, and his heart became the river's. Through him the river led these people to safety, away from the war that had come to them. The strength of the river was his strength. The waters he used as he would, the river was his weapon, his defence. For many years they together kept their people safe, but war followed them. When the threats grew many and terrible the river knew its people would be lost if they could not escape that land, as the echoes of a coming army reverberated in its depths. So the river began a city beneath the ocean, a haven to which its beloved fled when they had no other choice, and this city, this oasis in the middle of the desert and waste, remains our haven even now. Those original survivors gave the boy all authority in the new city, as he was the particular one to whom the river spoke, and continued to speak from time to time. So you see why no mere governor will do, and you see why so many come to Shorakai. Though there is little hope that Syratreya's line will ever be re-made, many do still hope, and do still come here, having heard some rumour, thinking that the worst will be averted by one who has some power to sway the way things will be at the end.'

'That's a beautiful story,' Melissa whispered, still looking around at the art.

'Do you believe it's true?' Tarku asked of the aide, very seriously.

'I believe that laws of heaven and earth were broken to create our city, as it originally was below the waters, however it was done. I believe there is the slightest chance that Syratreya's line is not broken, but I do not live in hope of a descendant, I live in the reality of uncertainty. As to whether or not it would make a difference in the end, whether or not one person could again change the course of history, I don't know, though go out into the city, and you will find many who do, many who believe we would get through the end if a descendant could again speak with the river, as the boy once spoke.'

'But there is no river, is there?' queried Weston, 'not anymore.'

'Ah, but water is everywhere still, as steam, as vapour, as the few seas that are left. Even in you, Mr Alamo, and in all of us. And there are other rivers too, rivers of fire below us, angry, and churning within the earth. If anything can be done to save our present state, I believe there is only one way; any efforts of man would surely fail, it remains for the laws of heaven and earth to be broken once again, or there will be no doubt, we will all face our end. Now,' the aide checked the time again, 'let's move on, or we will keep the governor waiting.' They continued on, corridor after corridor.

'I don't know if I'd be able to find my way out of here,' Melissa spoke to Astrid as her head turned from one amazement to the next, 'but everything's so beautiful.'

'Yes, not too ornate or overdone but pure and real,' Astrid agreed, 'and the evidences of the folklore of Shorakai is everywhere, even in the nuances of the architecture, in the curves and design elements. See, memories of rivers and tribes. There is so much history here.'

'Oh, I recognise this picture,' Melissa said. She held her head as it throbbed terribly again, but she looked up, amazed that she knew anything of Shorakai at all, 'this photograph was in the book I'm reading, the book on John Mark.'

The aide hadn't been going to stop at these lesser figures of the Shorakaian parliament but she stopped at this one for Melissa. 'Yes, this is ambassador

Amiana Lailae Arin. It was a tragic day that we heard of her assassination while she was special envoy on a peacekeeping assignment some twenty years ago.'

'John Mark's wife,' nodded Weston to Astrid.

'She's so beautiful,' Melissa said, 'so regal looking.'

Tarku remained in front of the photograph for a moment again as the others walked on. 'And your eyes are still blue,' he whispered, smiling again though behind it his face was full of a weight of sadness. 'I miss you, I hope you're well.'

'Keep up Tarku, come on,' Weston yelled back.

'Well, here we are,' the aide led them at last to the governor's office. But Melissa held the wall as she lost her balance.

'Melissa!' Astrid grabbed her, 'Melissa, what's the matter?'

'I'm alright,' Melissa tried to stand up properly, 'I'm sorry, it's coming back in that wave again, my head's throbbing,'

Astrid touched her forehead, 'You've probably got a bad migraine darling, it was a long flight we've just had.'

'I'll be alright, I'm just tired I think.'

'I'll take her back to the ship,' Tarku offered. 'The rest of you can go ahead and enjoy the dinner.'

'No I'm ok,' Melissa protested, though they could see that her whole body cringed against the pain she was feeling.

'No you're not darling,' Astrid soothed, 'let Tarku take you back to the ship, lie down and make sure you drink some fluids. Are you sure Tarku? I can take her if you like.'

'No, I'll take her,' he said, 'you know I don't want to be here anyway.'

'There's some specialist re-hydration packs in the supplies, that might be an idea,' Astrid suggested.

'I'm alright, really,' Melissa said, but even saying it she had to lean against the wall again to keep herself steady.

'Our apologies to the governor,' Tarku said to the aide, then to his colleagues, 'I'll stay with her, we'll join you later if she's feeling better.' Tarku took Melissa's arm gently and put his own around her, 'Come on butterfly, you need to lie down,' he said, she didn't protest. He guided her out to a gondola, then from the gondola he carried her back on board the Blue Moon and saw that she was comfortable in her bunk before letting her be.

'I don't know what's wrong with me,' she said as Tarku went to go, 'I've never felt like this.'

'Like what?'

'My head feels like it's about to explode, I feel like I'm somewhere else, not on the ground, I don't like it. I feel all shaky inside but I think that's the pain.'

'Would you like a painkiller?'

'I took two before we left, it hasn't done anything at all. It's just getting worse.'

'They don't work for me either. Try to sleep, I'll bring you something else.'

Tarku soon returned with a cup of tea. 'Here,' he offered, 'you'll feel better, trust me.'

'Thank you.' Melissa sat up and took the mug. The warmth alone was a tonic, but it was more than that, she felt a calmness come over her at once. 'What kind of tea is this?' she asked, closing her eyes and putting her head back, breathing in, trying not to shake with the pain.

'It's a special blend,' Tarku evaded.

After she sipped some more she turned to Tarku, 'I bet you're glad I'm not feeling well.'

'Why would I be glad about that?'

'You had an excuse not be at the dinner. You didn't seem to want to go.'

Tarku grinned, but shook his head and answered seriously, 'It gives me no pleasure to see you unwell.'

'Why didn't you want to go to dinner?' she studied him, still sipping the hot tea.

'Are you sure you're sick?' Tarku laughed at her curiosity. 'Let's just say social gatherings are not my preferred environment.'

'I know what you mean,' she said, 'I can't believe I'm missing dinner with the governor though! I'm sure it's important, and I don't want to let Weston down. What a time to get the worst headache I've ever had.'

'You won't be missing much, and Weston's concern would be that you are well.'

Melissa was quiet for a moment, sipping the tea.

'Are you finished?' he asked after a while, ready to take the mug.

'Yeah. It's taken the edge off, I think I might just be able to sleep now, then hopefully I'll be ok.' He stood to go, but she called out as he reached the door, 'Tarku-'

'Yes?'

'Thank you.'

He nodded, then left.

CHAPTER 14:

A Shorakaian Girl, almost.

When the other four returned to the ship they found Tarku sitting at the kitchen bench reading. He held a hand up to quieten them as they entered, talking noisily about their time. 'She's finally sleeping guys, keep it down,' Tarku told them.

'Do you think it's just a migraine?' Weston enquired.

'Yes, most likely, the atmosphere here is quite different from Corrio, that's probably all it is,' Tarku said, then asked, 'so, how did the interrogation go?'

Weston laughed, 'The dinner was very lovely.'

'Best seafood I have ever tasted and will ever taste,' agreed Hardan, giving a big sigh and rubbing his stomach.

'The governor was congenial,' Weston added, 'you missed a very pleasant hour.'

'Congenial? Pleasant?' Tarku chuckled, 'was it really that bad?'

'Yeah it was a bit of a bore,' Fisher said, 'the food was amazing, but a little too high-end for me though.'

'The governor was very interested in all of us and what we were doing, and asked about you and Melissa too, and was sorry you couldn't make it. Oh, and our ambassador was also present at the meal, by the governor's invitation, and he was eager to catch up with us on all the happenings back home.'

'Then I'm glad I wasn't there,' Tarku said, and focussed back into his book.

'Actually Tarku,' Astrid took a seat and spoke quietly after the others had left the cabin, 'I think you may've been right, I think it might have been an interrogation, a very polite one.'

'What was their goal, do you think?' Tarku asked, though he didn't turn away from what he was reading.

'I really don't know, they were very careful not to stay on any topic over long.'

'So it could be nothing?'

'Yes, it could be nothing. Though they did ask more questions about you and Melissa than I thought necessary.'

'Did they?'

'They were probably just being polite.'

'Mm.'

'Tarku!' Weston came back in, 'Astrid can watch Melis for a bit now, get your gear and let's make a start.'

Tarku already had his gear good to go, so he put his book away and went out with Weston. Hardan conscripted Fisher to help with the routine ship maintenance, and Astrid went to check on Melissa.

Melissa's eyes opened after Astrid had been sitting there a little while.

'How are you feeling darling?' Astrid asked.

'Much better.'

'That's good.'

'Yeah, Tarku brought me some tea and I started feeling better straight away.'

'He gave you some of his tea?'

'Yes.'

'No wonder you're feeling better,' Astrid laughed, 'that stuff would make a dying man feel fine.'

'Oh, what's in it?'

'If you ever find out, let me know,' Astrid patted Melissa's knees, 'Now, are you up to getting out there? I've got some great locations picked out for us.'

'Yes, I think I'll be ok now. I really want to see this place.'

The two ladies stepped out amongst the diverse people of Shorakai. The people here were pale to dark skinned but mostly in the middle, a rich sun-kissed olive. They had a distinct way of dressing and adorning themselves, and way of walking. They weren't a tall people but they walked tall, proud shouldered and straight backed. Their eyes were bright, and as they spoke the native language their voices were effervescent, like water racing over stones. There were some here that almost looked like they could be from the north, until they opened their mouth and spoke.

'What was Governor Asmara like?' Melissa asked of Astrid.

'Well, I think she is much like the Lady Amiana, who you saw in the picture. She was very refined, but still warm at the same time.'

'Do you know a guy called Scott Thomas?' Melissa asked Astrid another question as she looked around at the people, and the dwellings in this area that were at ground level and appeared to be pressed sand constructions. 'Scott who has the Kyu?'

'I know of him, yes. Why do you ask?'

'I met him on my way to TnTv. He thought I might have some Shorakaian heritage, I don't think so though, it's too incredible to think that one of my parents might have come from here!'

'It would be a rare thing,' Astrid agreed, 'but not impossible. You would be about the age to have been born when more travel had begun between the north and the rest of the world.' Astrid looked Melissa over and a cheeky spark lit her eyes, 'There is something about you that looks almost a little Shorakaian, why don't we see if you could be?'

'What do you mean?' Melissa asked.

Astrid grinned, 'Come on,' she took Melissa along the street, from time to time asking a local a question in Shorakaian, pointing to Melissa and they would nod and think and point down the street as they gave an answer.

'What are you asking?' Melissa begged Astrid to tell her.

'You'll see. Here we are, I think.' Astrid checked the house number then hopped up the stairs and knocked. A young lady opened the door, babe in arm, and children behind her.

'Are you Marie, the costumer?' Astrid asked.

'Yes, I am Marie,' the lady spoke.

'I'm told you do makeup as well?'

'Yes, that's right.'

'We are travelling from Corrio in the North Island States, but I'm wondering if you could possibly make my friend up in the Shorakaian way? Do you have time now?'

'Yes, yes,' she laughed, 'if you don't mind a messy house. Come in, come in.'

Melissa found herself being sat down and studied by the curious children as the young lady prepared.

'So, traditional Shorakaian?' Marie asked, pulling out the case which contained all the tools of her trade.

'Just everyday Shorakaian,' Astrid nodded, 'like you.'

Marie sat in front of Melissa and held her face, touching her cheeks and holding her chin a moment. 'Mm,' she thought, but said nothing more, only began to lightly cleanse Melissa's skin.

Melissa laughed to Astrid, 'Here I was thinking you were going to get my blood or my dna tested or something!'

'Well, we could do that, but that would take a long time, and money, and this is much more fun,' Astrid chuckled.

It didn't take Marie long at all. 'There's not much to do, you are very easy,' she said to Melissa and Astrid translated. 'Your skin is light for us, but it is the tone of Shorakai, and your bone structure is very traditional. Very easy. Now all I have to do is the line of malachite,' she explained, 'this is an essential part of the Shorakai detail, and it's not for fashion, it's for necessity to make less the glare that hits the eye when the sun is out,' and with that she added the darkest green line along Melissa's lower eyelids and out to the side.

'Now stand up,' Marie instructed and began to measure Melissa, then spoke to one of the children who ran to another room at once. 'We will find you some more appropriate clothes,' she explained.

'Can I look?' Melissa asked.

'Not yet,' Astrid held the mirror away, 'wait till she's finished.'

Marie played a little with Melissa's hair, untying it and letting it fall naturally, and then the clothes were brought. Melissa was re-dressed right here to her embarrassment, but soon it was done.

'Well?' Melissa asked.

Astrid was smiling, so were Marie and the children there. 'Can she really not speak Shorakaian?' one of the children looked up at Melissa and asked. 'She could be Eljay's sister,' Marie agreed, folding her arms as she thought.

'Please can I see?' Melissa laughed.

They finally let Melissa see herself. 'I still look like me,' was the first thing she said, but as she stood back and let herself see the overall impression, she could see what the others saw, a Shorakaian girl, almost.

Astrid thanked and paid Marie, then took Melissa, 'Come on, we've got to film you presenting something done up like this.'

'What? Presenting?! We don't do that do we!? No I -' Melissa exclaimed.

'Sometimes we do, come on, I have the perfect place in mind. Don't worry, I'll give you an idea of what to say.'

'But, presenting? Me? I don't think I -'

'Darling, you'll be great,' Astrid encouraged, and led on. 'We'll send it through to editing before West sees it and he'll get a surprise. Come on, it'll be fun.'

In the evening the crew returned to the ship to regroup and have a meal before going out again. Melissa came into the cabin, still in full Shorakai costume and make-up, laughing about something with Astrid.

'Wow look at you!' Jem commented.

'What's with the outfit?' Weston said, taking his meal in hand and sitting down.

'I thought it would be fun,' Astrid winked at Melissa.

Tarku almost dropped his meal as he came out from the kitchen and saw her, but quickly covered, sat down and hurried a few mouthfuls, without joining in the conversations, then got up and left the ship.

'Tarku! What's with you?' Weston yelled after him. 'Where are you going? You and I are going to film the city lights tonight.'

'I'll meet up with you later,' Tarku called back.

'Blast it Tarkars! You can't just take off!' Weston shouted, but it did no good.

The Akaia strode through the central gardens and boarded a gondola. 'Merouin,' he directed the oarsman. Once in the area Tarku disembarked and walked to the gardens there, the gardens renowned all over the world for their quietly spectacular forms, a garden of water, light and naturally sculptured verdure, but that's not why he was here. In a sheltered corner, slightly overgrown, but blessed with delicate blooms now sweetly fragrant to welcome the evening, he found the memorial to Syraveia, daughter of Syratreya, the memorial built over four-hundred years ago for a monarch who wasn't dead, for a monarch they never gave the opportunity of rule because she was like him, an Akaia; a monarch they dismissed to expire as Akaia expire, but she lived through that fevered age, like Tarku, becoming almost ageless. Tarku walked on and came to the smaller and less visited remembrance of Lady Amiana and stood there under the moonlight, his face hard as he thought.

'I'm still waiting to hear back from you,' he said. 'Years Syra, it's been years. I found her, I planned, I got her out. Now she's here. What would you have me do? Will I tell them? You never had a great deal of love for those in charge here, but you respected them. You know the edge on which I am forced to live, you know I can't possibly protect her.' He shook his head and huffed, 'You have trusted me with too much. You should have told John, he's her father after all, doesn't he deserve to know? Shouldn't this be his responsibility? What should I do with her Syra? You asked me to look for the girl,' Tarku stressed, 'you didn't say what to do then! I couldn't leave her there any longer. I have been waiting for a reply to the words I sent you, but none have come.' Tarku worried, but tried to calm now, breathing deeply as the trees around him seemed to breathe, as the wind came through, and as the fountains nearby could be heard in their continuing flow. The memorial did not answer his questions. He sank to the grass, knees on the dew, 'I cannot hand her over to Shorakai, not yet, not without a word from you. Those who still have hope look for an heir, imagine the weight that would be on her shoulders, and so suddenly, but she is not the saviour they hope for, she's just a naive girl. I'll protect her, you know I will, as long as I can. I just need to hear from you!'

~

'So darling,' Astrid turned to Melissa and asked as they ate their quiet meal, 'tell me more about yourself.'

Melissa shrugged her shoulders, 'There's nothing to tell, really, I don't know.'

'Sure there is. What did you do before this?'

'Well, I worked in a kind of laundry, kind of place.'

'Oh, hard work I bet.'

'Yeah, sometimes.'

'And what about your free time, any hobbies, favourite pastimes? Apart from photography that is.'

'I didn't really have much time to spare, mostly when I had time off I just spent it hanging out with my friend Kat, or whoever else,' Melissa answered.

'Sounds like me. So you got a boy back home?' Astrid pried.

Melissa laughed, 'No, not me. I never had anything serious going, I've had some pretty protective people around me, they never let me get close to anyone, and it's a bit hard when it's so hard to tell who the nice guys are anyway.'

'Never been kissed darling?' Astrid teased.

Melissa blushed, but laughed, 'Well, -'

'I could help you with that,' Jem offered, as he sucked up the last dregs from his bowl.

Astrid hooted and Melissa's blush increased dramatically, 'No thanks,' she laughed.

'What's so funny?' he asked, but then he too broke into a grin.

'What about you Jem?' asked Astrid.

'What?'

'Anyone waiting for you back home?'

'Nah, not me. It's all too hard that game, although I had a real nice girl for a while but she up and left me, my fault, she told me the news but I told her I didn't want to be no father. But I mean really, what did she expect? Me, a dad? Can't even think it.'

'Oh Jem,' Astrid shook her head at his pathetic show.

'But seriously, I never intended to bring a kid into this world anyway, and really, who would? No offense Hardan, but you know what I'm saying,' he countered.

'Yes, I know what you're saying, indeed it was a hard decision for me to make,' Hardan admitted.

'So what about you Astrid? Anyone?' Jem continued.

Astrid grinned, 'Ah-'

'You're the type who'd have a guy strung to every one of your fingers I bet,' Jem figured, 'in all corners of the world too, and they probably don't know all the others exist.'

'No, no, I'm nothing like that,' Astrid laughed, 'give me one good man and I'll be happy, besides, I'm not such a looker that I could catch so many.'

Jem shook his head, 'It's not the looks, it's that indefinable quality that defines a good woman, trust me, I know, I've been around, and I'll be the first to tell you, you ain't that bad in the looks department either.'

Astrid gasped, and chuckled, 'Thanks Jem.'

'Anytime Astrid,' Jem said.

'So, do you have someone?' Melissa asked Astrid in her quiet, sincere way.

'Do I have someone? Well, nothing official, but yeah, there's someone, a lovable fool. And I know what Hardan will say,' Astrid turned to the pilot to avoid more talk about herself, 'Hardan has been in love with his wife for years.'

'I have,' Hardan smiled, 'Emma is my darling since forever and will be my darling forever yet.'

'You're lucky to have a love like that Hardan,' Astrid said.

'Indeed I am,' he agreed, 'indeed I am.'

'Come on you lot,' Weston came in and urged them, 'less chatting more filming. Fisher, Hardan, you guys can take the little Rinke and go get some random generic tourist film if you like.'

'What about you Alamo?' Jem asked.

'What about me?'

'Do you have anyone?'

'I do, I do, but we're not here to talk about that are we,' he headed out, Jem and Hardan following.

'And Tarku?' asked Melissa as she and Astrid left as well.

'I don't know, I don't think so,' Astrid said, picking up her gear and securing the ship behind them.

Soon they were all up and back out filming across Shorakai. Weston was positioning his cameras for a shoot near the central canal when Tarku caught him up.

'I guess you don't want to tell me why you went off before?' Weston asked.

'No I don't.'

'Didn't think you would. What about the meeting at the port? Go ok?'

Tarku merely raised his sleeve and let the producer see the tracking bracelet.

'I see,' Weston nodded, then looked back through his lens and continued to frame the shot.

'The city lights,' Tarku commented, 'a true mark of any truly wonderful city is how safe you feel walking the streets at night. It is a rare thing to feel as safe as one feels walking the streets of Shorakai.'

Weston gave Tarku a questioning glance, 'The way you can handle yourself I think I'd feel safe in the very armpits of Flythsyge.'

Tarku laughed at Weston's frankness. 'Don't count on me West, I am liable to let you down.'

'Yeah, I know, that's why it would have been good for an experienced guide to come as well. Anyhow, I assume you're here to work and not discuss security, hand me that extender there would you.' Tarku obliged. 'You're supposed to be filming,' Weston complained, 'and I'm supposed to be the one telling you what to film, not the one fiddling with the equipment.'

'You couldn't stand back and leave it to the rest of us if you tried!' Tarku laughed, but as he looked around for the best angles and the best spot to set up his gear, he sighed, 'There is a peace here I will be loath to once again leave behind.'

'It's when you talk like that I remember you're older than you look.'

'And yet you still call me 'boy'.'

'Well you're as moody as an adolescent sometimes you know! Would you prefer I call you gramps?'

'Definitely not,' Tarku laughed.

They filmed for some time, the reflections across the waterways, the sparkling city, the gardens illumined and quiet and the calm traffic of an enchanting people across these scenes in the night.

'Where do you have the girls filming tonight?' Tarku asked.

'First they had the moonlight markets, but they should be on their way to the amphitheatre in Saiuin by now.'

'And tomorrow?'

'The clear-water caves.'

'And us?'

'Obviously no one except Melissa reads the itineraries I so diligently put together,' Weston said in mock hurt.

'That's because your itineraries always change. Don't worry, Melissa will soon come to know this and stop reading them too.'

Weston couldn't help but laugh. 'Fine, we're doing sea-life and then wildlife, if we can find any, day after maybe the refugee camps on the far side, then the salt flats beyond, better us on that one than the girls.'

'Yeah, we'll come back plucked of every shred and shrivelled as sour plums if we're not careful.'

'Now Tarku I've been meaning to ask you, what do you think of the external cameras on the Blue Moon? Have you had a look at any of the footage? Pretty decent in my opinion.'

'I've watched some of the recordings of the flights out of Corrio and the north, yes, it's decent, especially seeing as it's being done mostly automatic.'

'Yeah, I had a few extra cameras installed so we wouldn't miss anything. Underneath front and rear, on the sides, and even on top. Saves us a lot. Tell you what it'll be interesting to watch that section coming through the divide again,'

Weston laughed, 'I don't know if I'll be ready to watch it until we're back home though.'

'And what made you hire this Fisher character?' Tarku asked after another silence. 'He doesn't seem of the same calibre you usually manage to hire. He might be ok in the end, but I don't know, he does seem careless, and somewhat irritating.'

'I was getting the impression you didn't think much of him. He's only temporary. I've sent out numerous requests and re-requests, no one free, no nothing back.' More quiet. 'I asked John Mark, you know, the engineer, he'd have been a good choice, but the man was, well, I think I got him at a bad time. Maybe I should ask him again?'

Tarku didn't want to meet John. 'That's your call,' he said.

'Maybe I'll leave it a few days then ask him again.'

Tarku focussed his lens again, 'Look at the water West.'

'What about it?'

'It's agitated,' Tarku's eyebrows pulled together in concern.

Just then the sirens sounded in the street, the warning of an imminent earthquake. While Weston picked up his gear and ran, Tarku stood a moment and watched the rippling of the water, then looked above at the glass constructions surrounding – the glass echoing the uneasiness of the water. Even as they ran toward the open gardens with the many citizens, the ground shuddered and heaved and the buildings began to sway.

'This isn't how I imagined our first day filming,' Weston complained as they set up the equipment again from the safer ground and proceeded to film the tremor. 'I've got plenty hours of tremor and quake footage, I don't need this!'

'But you've filmed Shorakai before too haven't you? There's always opportunity to catch something different.'

'Don't try to cheer me up Tarku, it won't work, I can be as stubborn as you you know.'

'I hope the girls are ok,' Tarku said, looking around at the shaking city, 'this will be no small quake. I should try to get to Saiuin.'

'Astrid's got good sense Tarkars, she'll keep herself and little Melis safe.'

~

Astrid and Melissa had stepped through the wide and unassuming entry to the partly-natural amphitheatre in the district of Saiuin and taken their seats in the round. The second act of the opera had just begun when they felt the first of the shudders run under their feet. They heard the alarms as well, and soon the attendants to the performance were ushering the crowds to areas that were thought to be more safe. They found themselves in the group that was directed to the centre of the open theatre, but even here the feeling was uneasy, as Tarku had said to Weston, so Astrid too became aware, this quake would rate high on the scale. She watched the higher tiers of seating, the tall columns all around, the mouldings and cornices that even now threatened to crack and shatter to the ground, the swaying of the lights that were strung around, soon to fall and possibly ignite whatever lay under them. The threat became reality and screams were heard, the storeys high curtains caught fire and the smoke plumed up and across the theatre, and even where the people stood in the clear, unroofed area, they were not safe but found debris shaken and flung in all directions.

The city may be a safer place than here, in the city the buildings were newer and made to stand such events to a greater degree, but this was an old area, the amphitheatre said to be a relic of the time when Shorakai was still a land hidden under the ocean, a time before such quakes were feared. Astrid held Melissa across her shoulders as they waited and hoped for the end of this torment. At some point in the chaos, as the authorities ushered groups to safer ground, the pair became separated. Astrid had been struck by some debris and Melissa found herself pulled along by hands she did not know, but then ripped away from those hands as the panicked crowd now pushed to gain safer ground. As Melissa was carried along, trying to look back and calling out for Astrid, trying to see some sign of her colleague, she found herself stepping onto a short bridge just as it gave way, collapsing with everyone into the canal below.

For a terrible moment in which time itself seemed paralysed, Melissa struggled amidst the bodies and the debris that had fallen down with her. The water was not fast flowing but it seemed to be churning with the panicked crowd and convulsing with motion caused by the rolling tremor. Melissa gulped for air but felt she was losing the struggle, she could see people above trying to help, but with every glimpse she took another mouthful of water. She had never learnt to swim, she had good instincts and kicked and used her arms but in that chaos she found herself soon under the blue waters, sinking fast and being pulled away by the converse swell below.

The next thing she knew she felt a firm hand at her shoulder and found herself collapsing onto timber boards, coughing up water and gasping for air. She looked around her, others were being pulled out of the water and lay all along the canal. She gasped in terror as a dwelling shattered and fell just the other side of the water as the massive earthquake continued across Shorakai. Astrid had caught up now and held her arm, 'I thought we'd lost you there for a second darling.'

'Astrid?' Melissa blinked, trying to regain some sense of the world around her, noticing the blood upon her colleague's shoulder.

'I'll be alright. You just take it easy, you were under for a long time.'

It wasn't until hours later that the crew were finally able to find and get to Melissa and Astrid. They were in a hospital in the Shorakaian capital, Astrid had been seen to and now she and the crew waited anxiously as Melissa came around.

'Here, you'll be thirsty,' Astrid sat on the bed and gave her some water.

'All good?' Weston asked. The crew all watched on from the end of the bed.

Melissa rubbed her head, 'I feel hazy.'

'Look out darling you're balance is off, you're leaning, straighten up or you'll fall off the bed.'

Melissa put a hand out to steady herself. 'Are we filming again soon? I just need a moment, I'll be ready.'

'Take your time Melissa, just be thankful you survived the quake and almost drowning,' Weston said kindly, 'Astrid only just made it through. The rest of us are a bit shaken and we've all minor cuts and bruises but amazingly we got through relatively unscathed.'

'That's right, I remember, you were hurt?! Are you alright?' Melissa turned to Astrid. She noticed the bandages around Astrid's shoulder now.

'Got caught with a bit of debris, but I'm alright,' Astrid smiled. 'Are you sure you're ok darling? You're coming across a little spacey.'

'No I'm good, I'm fine,' she blinked and rubbed her eyes. 'Is it the morning already? Aren't we filming the underwater ways today? I was so looking forward to it! Will they still be intact? Are we going?'

'We won't be diving, but if you're up for it we'll go see what we can,' Astrid smiled. 'The doctor will want to check you over before you leave and if everything's good, we'll go.'

As the crew waited to make sure Melissa was given the all clear, which Astrid knew she would be, they heard a murmur run through the crowded wards.

'What's going on?' Weston asked.

Tarku looked ahead, 'It's governor Asmara, visiting those injured in the quake.'

They watched the beloved governor make her way from ward to ward, as gracious and upright as any empress would be. Melissa hardly heard the words of her doctor as he gave her liberty to go, hardly heard his advice on how to manage her recovery from here, as Asmara Viléla herself arrived at her bedside.

'You must be the one they call Melissa,' the governor spoke, 'I'm glad to see you are recovering well. They say you are lucky to be alive, you were under the water for far too long.'

'You wouldn't know it,' Weston laughed, 'she's as plucky as a pluck is.'

Asmara smiled, 'Your employer told us much about you, he tells me your work holds remarkable light. I would be glad to see your work after this expedition, if you come through Shorakai again.'

'Thank you, very much! I'm sorry I missed your reception yesterday,' Melissa apologised, 'I wasn't feeling so good.'

'Yes, but now we meet so all is well.' The governor farewelled and moved on to see the next patient.

Apart from the fact that the underwater ways could not be explored to the extent that was usually available, the rest of their stay on Shorakai went off without incident. Weston was relieved that the crew were able to cover all the areas he wanted to cover, and thankful that they were able to leave only marginally later than his ideal time.

CHAPTER 15:

This is Arrojor.

Arrojor was a small island, east south east of the North Island States. An exciting destination for the adventurous traveller, or so Weston would get his narrator to say when they put this episode of the series together. But the truth was that Arrojor was a very rough place, it was one of the most mountainous places in the known world, its people tough and spirited. The beauty of it lay in the pristine lakes hidden in the high mountains – their screaming blue so vivid against the slate and the flaming colours the sky so often held. Though most of Arrojor was like the other islands, a desert, creeping into the liveable lands more and more, only on Arrojor the desert was of crumbling stone, not sweeping sands or red plains, but a vast and cavernous landscape of towering grey pillars that somehow supported life. Mountains that stretched out to the very edges of the island protected the inner regions of Arrojor from the severe elements which wreaked havoc on other islands, but it was a mostly lifeless, shattered landscape. Even the trees and grass here were grey, blending in with the rock so it was hard to distinguish what was living and what was dead.

When the Blue Moon neared even closer it became clear that this island was not the empty, lifeless place it seemed to be from afar. Even as Hardan received a call over the radio from the Arrojor control tower he realised things were much different to what he had expected. Ships of every make and size were lining up to be allowed entrance to the capital city, and by the look of them the majority weren't refugees. Hardan could only pull into the line and await his turn to take them through the checkpoint.

It remained quiet inside as they waited. At first Melissa was overawed, coming into Arrojor was like nothing she had ever experienced. The feel of the ship, the view of this unknown city from up high; a city tightly packed in the sharp valleys below, it was incredible. Soon she had her camera out and positioned tight up against the window, but she took only the fewest of shots. Then when they had been there so long, waiting to be given the right of entry, she grew contemplative, even sad, at the grey view. This place was so foreign and uncertain. She toyed with Matthias's button inside her pocket as she stared out the window at the bleak place, wondering how anyone could live here, then she remembered The Gutter. People could find a way to survive just about anywhere.

Astrid had her eyes closed smiling at some inner thought, a book half open in her hand. Hardan and Jem remained in the cockpit. Weston tapped his knees. He looked around. Twiddled his thumbs. He hated sitting still.

'So is this Arrojor?' Melissa asked Weston, looking at the itinerary he had given each of them.

'This is Arrojor.'

'Arrojor. Do they speak our language at all?'

Weston chuckled, 'No, very few would. They speak Rojdi, and probably the south-east standard. You'll find there aren't many people speak our northern lingo anywhere, the divide has seen that we're still largely cut off from the rest of the world.'

'And yet they continue to call our biggest city The Universal City,' Tarku added quietly through his sleeping pose.

Melissa stared at Tarku momentarily, surprised that he'd spoken, but then turned back to Weston, 'Do you speak Rojdi?'

'No, but Astrid does, and there are phrase books, so it's all good.'

'What's special about this place, I mean, why did we come here?'

'Well, it's on our way south and it's a very different kind of place, that's all,' Weston replied. 'Why don't we see if we can pick up a local station, you might learn a little more about it before we get in.'

Weston turned on the television screen, it sat hidden in the wall panel behind the cockpit, positioned so it could be visible to the whole cabin. At first only fuzz but then Weston got Astrid to have a go at finding a station and she found a popular Arrojori channel, which was halfway through the morning news broadcast. Of course it was in the local language but Astrid translated enough to give the crew an overview of the story.

While the others entertained themselves in this way Hardan tried to contact the tower numerous times to find out what the hold-up was. But after first getting that one individual who informed him that it may be a while before they could land, Hardan just kept getting a recorded message in Rojdi, and repeated in numerous of the southern languages, which told him the exact same thing; that there was a long wait as this was a peak period, a statement which one could easily deduce was true from the sheer number of ships of every kind converging here. Some of those ships were obviously far less patient than the Blue Moon, but they were dealt with fairly swiftly and heavily by the authorities so those impatient fools did themselves no favours, but at least they made the wait more interesting for everyone else.

Behind the continual running script across the screen about the standstill of the traffic along various routes and something to do with the hype of some upcoming race, there were several local incidents in the news, then other world news and developments, including some disturbing footage of another small island crumbling into the wastes, and others experiencing terrible tremors.

'How long will it be?' Melissa asked, looking away from the footage, 'how long do we have till the north islands just crumble away like that? How long does the rest of the world have?'

'Honey, no one can predict that,' Weston said, 'one guy reckoned last month would be the end, another reckons five years, another reckons twenty.'

Tarku looked up from his thread. 'Don't let it worry you,' he said, directing his statement at Melissa, as it was for her sake he said it, 'it may not come to pass.'

'You don't think the collapse is inevitable?' Astrid questioned him.

'I didn't say that,' he looked evasively aside, 'I said not to worry.'

'Yes, and that it may not come to pass. Even the experts agree that it is inevitable, we lose more species to extinction every day, and the wastes keep creeping in to the outer limits, in fact the world is in what you might call an accelerated state of decay,' Astrid went on.

Tarku didn't reply, this was why he never got into conversations. How could he give his reasons, when he knew he wouldn't be understood. Why let the girl live her life with that fear, when fearing such an end wouldn't stop anything? And if she was Syra's heir maybe she had a part to play yet, if the myths some still believed on Shorakai were true.

But then they all stopped talking anyway, as footage from the north was now on screen. There was a news report, a little unimportant appendage to the other news rushed over briefly by the reader.

'What is she saying? What's happening back home?' Weston asked.

Astrid hesitated for a second, but translated the newsreader's words, 'Today the government of the North Island States issued a ruling regarding the future of the Akaia in that region. In a statement Governor Echlin maintains that Akaia are too volatile to be left to move freely amongst the other citizens and after several state commissioned reports it has been decided for the protection of all, including themselves, that Akaia over the age of fifteen will now be automatically institutionalised or asked to leave the populated areas of the islands. Opponents to the legislation claim the new laws undo over a century of progress in the area of Akaia relations. No Akaia has made comment and so far things have remained peaceful in the region.'

Tarku rubbed his forehead and looked sadly back out the window. At least things had stayed calm. Weston glanced at him but didn't say anything.

'I've never even seen an Akaia,' Melissa commented. Weston noticed the slightest grin come across Tarku's bleak countenance at the innocent remark.

'No there aren't many of them,' Weston said, 'but chances are you probably have seen one and just not realised it, they're not all as inhuman or as violent as some would have us believe, and most would look to you like any other person on the street.'

Fisher came back into the cabin at this point and took a seat.

'Are they really as bad as the governor says? As bad as the reports?' Melissa asked, 'my friend Matthias mentioned a friend of his who's an Akaia, but I never met him myself.'

'What's this?' Fisher asked.

'Echlin just put through new restrictions on Akaia over 15 years of age,' Astrid explained.

'That's probably a good thing,' Fisher said.

'But you can't just apply one rule to their entire population,' Astrid remarked.

Melissa plucked up courage and asked her silent colleague, 'Tarku, what do you think?'

'About?'

'All that stuff, you know, about this law they just passed?'

Tarku answered seriously, 'Just be thankful you haven't met one yet.'

Weston was surprised by Tarku's answer and laughed inside, the boy certainly did have his own kind of humour. Melissa surprised Weston too, she had the beginnings of a journalist with all the questions she was asking.

'Have you?'

'Many.'

'Do you think they should be segregated like this?' Melissa pressed, trying to further sound Tarku out, and trying to understand the situation herself, because she really didn't know much about it.

Every trace of humour fell from Tarku's face as he thought, after a moment he replied darkly, 'They shouldn't even exist.'

So stunned by that statement, no one could say anything for a moment, but for Fisher who guffawed in amusement at Tarku's words. Weston wondered why the boy made people dislike him, but Weston knew he was an Akaia so it was humorous in some ways to him that Tarku should speak as he did of himself and the others like him, Astrid knew what Tarku was too, and Hardan, but Jem and Melissa had no idea so what he had said could seem the extreme of prejudice.

'What Tarku means is,' Weston tried to explain, 'is that Akaia are a consequence of the collapse, history tells us they didn't exist before that, they only appeared after that time, along with many things – along with the Mrukai, the creeping death, the tuxra, the Kyu, all those things.'

'Really? I don't understand, I thought Akaia were just a people group,' Melissa asked, quite confused.

'No,' Weston explained kindly, 'individual Akaia can come from any people group, they're not their own race so to speak, no one is born an Akaia. You heard what the aide said as she showed us the picture of empress's daughter at the age of three, in the hall on the way to dinner with the governor, she said Syraveia was taken into seclusion after being found to be marked Sansahme. That's what happens, very rarely, an infant is found with a mark, like a barely visible tattoo smaller than the palm of your hand, and that child grows to be an Akaia. For the most part they're like the rest of us, physically they're superior, they can have strength, speed or healing capabilities beyond our own, but something of their humanity seems broken. Generally speaking their capacity for compassion, love, empathy, fear, all of that is minimal, and most have fairly volatile temperaments, that's why they're seen as dangerous, and why most don't usually live into their thirties.'

'Ok. But if what you've said is all that's different they can't be more of an issue than the gangs back home,' Melissa went on, defending the Akaia despite the little she knew, 'so why make such a fuss when there's so few Akaia anyway?'

'I'll tell you why everyone's afraid of them,' Jem spoke up, 'I've been in a spot or two and I tell you, you don't want to get on the wrong side of an Akaia. They've got a destructive fire inside, and they're all crazy like they've got a death-wish, or like they've seen what's coming to us at the end of the world.'

'Fisher,' Weston interrupted, but Astrid spoke again before Weston could say anything.

'The ruling has very little to do with the Akaia, Melissa,' Astrid explained, 'Governor Echlin is just using the natural prejudice and fear of the north island community to boost his chances for success at the next election.'

'But that's so stupid.'

'It's politics darling, he wants to be seen to be getting things done,' Astrid answered.

'Not just politics,' Tarku spoke quietly as he stood up and walked towards the cockpit, weary of this conversation, 'Akaia are dangerous, and that's the truth. I may not agree with what Echlin is doing, but no policy, in their favour or otherwise, will change what they are. So I advise you Melissa, if you come across an Akaia, to keep your distance.' He stepped into the cockpit to join Hardan and closed the door behind him.

'Tarku's right,' Weston added.

Melissa watched the door a moment then turned back to the others, 'So there'll be Akaia in other places we're going, or are they just in the north and on Shorakai?'

'They're everywhere people are, though they're not always called Akaia, or Sansahme,' said Weston.

'Oo, I can tell you this one,' Jem said, sitting up, thinking to impress upon Weston that he was actually a knowledgeable guide, 'In Delahar the nickname for the Akaia is Amsgan, monsters, on Arrojor and the other isles of the near south they call them Sansahme, the soulless ones. In the east they call them Mugenno, which means nothingness. Further south, from Tamashan through to Salamonde, they are traditionally known as Sa'ar, meaning storm, although in recent years Sansahme has also been widely adopted in most areas. And did you know, on the north isle of Parahn they used to call them the Evaseri, destroyers, and in the far north they had other names for them, they thought the Akaia were harbingers of death and fury. Many Akaia were killed in the past because they were seen as ill-omens.'

Standing against the door on the other side Tarku heard all, though he tried to listen to Hardan's friendly conversation, he heard every one of Fisher's words, and though his face remained hard, the slightest gloss glistened his eyes.

'Why are they called all these things?' Melissa said, but kept talking before anyone could reply, such was her distress at what she could only see as grave injustice, 'I don't understand, on the one hand you guys say the Akaia are out there, and that I've probably seen them but just hadn't noticed because they're not much different to the rest of us, then on the other hand you say all this terrible stuff, but I've never seen anything like what you speak of, and I live in a pretty dark place. Surely they can't just lock people up like it seems the government is proposing, not when they haven't done anything wrong except to exist.'

'Oho no,' Jem laughed, 'trust me Melis, they're not people, well they were, but once they're around 15 like Echlin's talking about, they're not. You don't see them because they're usually gone by then, either killed, suicided or gone to live in the wastes, and if they're not gone, they've got good at hiding.'

'Jem, check with Hardy will you,' Weston interrupted again, 'I wanted to be getting on to our tour of Arrojor hours ago.'

Jem opened the door, Tarku quickly picked up the used mugs from the cockpit and pushed past Jem, heading back to the kitchen. Hardan spoke to the cabin, 'I've been watching the line, there are a few officials moving this way slowly, checking each ship. Some ships have been getting the go ahead into the city but not many.'

They watched as the official worked his way towards them, slowly up the line of ships, becoming animated now and again, obviously dealing with far from happy people. But within a fairly short time the official rode up to the Blue Moon on his scooter-like craft, with his face prepared for another argument. Captain Hardan turned the lever and released the hatch by the window, then slid open the small slot provided for such times as these.

'Papameni Capitan,' the official requested, hand out and waiting. Hardan handed him copies of the appropriate documents.

'De Nordan huh?' the official said, showing slight surprise, but otherwise just making notes in his book. 'So, du lingera jour on, oder jour aver?'

'Do you speak anything other than Rojdi?' Weston asked the official.

'Huh? Rojdi, ya.'

'Can you come do Rojdi Astrid?' Weston looked back into the cabin and asked.

'Sure, I love speaking Rojdi,' she laughed and stood up.

'You can speak Rojdi as well as Shorakaian?' Melissa asked Astrid in astonishment.

Astrid laughed and patted Melissa's shoulder as she passed. 'Languages are my forte darling.'

'Wait I can do it,' Fisher pulled on his rat-tail goatee and surveyed the scene. 'Let me have a go,' he pushed Weston aside, grinning, 'it's why you hired me after all, isn't it?'

'By all means, have a go.' Weston moved back to allow Fisher to talk with the official.

Fisher cleared his voice and began to speak. To the official Jem's words were at first a string of incoherent, random Rojdi words mixed with common expletives, then a few phrases that seemed to say 'to Arrojor, yes, we go to Arrojor, let us go to Arrojor.'

The official merely raised his eyebrows further and repeated, 'Ah-ano. You wait,' he managed to say. The official started to move on, but Weston and Fisher yelled out for him to stop with such urgency that he did, but he pointed to his watch.

'What did you say Fisher!' Weston reprimanded.

Tarku was chuckling at the whole scene, he really didn't have much respect for Fisher.

'Maybe I haven't got his dialect right,' Fisher shrugged his shoulders, 'Well, where's that dictionary, phrase-book thing?'

'Astrid save us will you!' Weston begged.

Astrid leaned over and spoke to the official quietly, in perfect Rojdi. 'Those guys are idiots,' she smiled, the official grinned in agreement, 'What's the problem?' Astrid asked him, 'what's the hold up?'

The official shook his head and shrugged, 'It's always like this for the Arrojor Grand Prix. I must admit it's busier than last year, far busier than any of us expected in any case, but I suppose there's a lot of hype this year because there are four big names in the race listed as definite starters.'

'It's quite important we get to Arrojor city soon,' Astrid said.

'I'm afraid everyone has to get to Arrojor urgently,' he shrugged, 'but unfortunately only those entering the Grand Prix, or those that have pre-purchased VIP tickets can go through at the moment, we just don't have the capacity to house so many vessels. I tell you what though, you could always go on to Larue, and find some sort of ground transport from there, you should be in good time for the main race in two days time.'

'What did he say?' Weston asked.

'Have you pre-purchased VIP tickets?'

'No. Why would I have pre-purchased-'

'I didn't think so. He says it's the only way to get through at the moment, or if you are in the grand prix, of course, then you can get in, or we could go to this other city and be back here in two days, but otherwise the whole place is packed.'

'Oh. Well, I knew the Grand Prix was on, it was on my itinerary, that's one reason I wanted to come here now, but I didn't think I read anything that said it was this big.'

Tarku spoke to the official, in Rojdi, 'I am entering the race, do you need to see my identification or anything?'

'Yes, but I just check it quickly, then I have to wave you on and they'll sort all that out at the other end.'

'It's just that I'm not sure they would have received my entry fee. I was hoping to be here earlier to see the race officials, but our departure from Corrio was delayed, and we had a hairy ride coming through the great divide, not to mention the interruptions we encountered on our way via Shorakai. Do you think that will be an issue?'

'Well, I am a fan of the motorcycle championships, and now I think of it you do look familiar, yes, yes,' the official became excited, a smile of realisation growing on his face. 'Have you raced here before? Or maybe at the Rorona Tourne?' the man asked.

'Well, I guess you may have seen my father, some years ago,' Tarku showed him one of his ID's.

The official looked at the ID and then at Tarku a few times, mouth open, then stammered 'Riyu Savah! I thought there was something about you! I thought you looked too young, but your father, yes that makes sense. Oh, your father was a most skilled racer. I'll be cheering for you, you better go on. Hurry now, the qualifying will be starting within the hour. Good luck.' The official waved them on.

'How'd you get him to let us through?' Weston asked Tarku, as he enjoyed the sensation of finally moving on at last.

'I just told him I was going in the race.'

'But you're not, seriously, you're not thinking -' Weston gulped, looking at the track below them, 'are you?'

'Why not?' Tarku replied, without any emotion, 'I'll get some good shots from out there in the midst of it.'

'But people die in this race! Have I told you before that you're insane?'

'I believe so.'

'But you can't just waltz up and enter this thing, surely.'

'Apparently I can.'

'Do you even have a bike?'

'The Avero's down in the hold.'

'What? Did you, Tarku, you didn't plan this all along did you?'

'No. I held it as an option. That's all. Quite a nice coincidence it turned out this way really.'

'Oh, for some I guess, for some!' Weston yelled after Tarku as the boy made his way down to the cargo hold to get his racing gear on and check on his bike. 'You're my lead cameraman Tarku! You can't just go off all that time racing!'

'You're the one that wanted to get in to Arrojor quickly,' Tarku's voice trailed up in reply.

'What's he doing?' Melissa asked Weston, not quite following what was going on.

'Oh, his job,' Weston sighed.

Melissa looked to Astrid, who explained, 'Tarku's just entered the Arrojor Grand Prix, from what I can pick up, it's a very dangerous and cut-throat motorcycle race around those mountains down there.'

Melissa looked at the grey peaks below them and swallowed, 'Why would he do that?'

Astrid laughed, 'To get us into Arrojor, today.'

It took Hardan another fifty minutes to get through all the checks and then they were finally allowed into the city and allocated a bay near to where the qualifying race was due to start. As soon as the ship touched the ground Tarku released the ramp and they heard the motorbike revving, then he was away, straight to the starting line, handing the race officials his papers even as they counted down to the gun. They waved him on, he was just in time, then all the riders were off.

CHAPTER 16:

A necessary irritation.

The other members of the Blue Moon stepped off far more sedately, stretching their legs and looking around. On the ground it was just like it had looked from the air – a grey landscape, though the people and all their activity made it vastly more colourful in the streets. Weston wanted to get to work straight away, pulling out large cameras and other gear and sorting out how he wanted to go about things.

'Hardan, can you stay here with the ship for now. Melissa, I want you to go and get some footage of the markets and whatever else takes your eye in that direction, Fisher I want you to go with Melissa, take the Rinke and get some shots yourself. Astrid and I will see if we can find a cultural translator, maybe do an overview of the city and the Grand Prix course and meet some of the riders and other important people. Put these on.' He handed them navy TnTv spray jackets. 'We are a known company, even out here, so it may help you get around. Also they have an inbuilt radio in the collar here,' Weston pointed out, 'so we can keep in contact at all times, which is important. It's not quite as civilized here as on Shorakai so keep alert. Those of you with phones will find they don't work so well out here either, likely not at all. For your use I also have maps,' he handed them out, 'and don't forget the phrase book and the list of what not to do while in Arrojor, which you all should have read already. It's all still fairly untested though so tread carefully, our government cannot help you out here if you put a foot wrong. Oh and one last thing, almost forgot.' Weston rummaged through his chaotic case of gear then pulled out a wad of cash. 'Local currency, well, currency that will be accepted here anyway.' Fisher's eyes lit up as Weston handed a little out to everyone. 'Always handy in a scrape, but don't flash it around. A little goes a long way here. So, I think that's everything, off you go.'

Melissa did as she was told and pulled on the jacket. She put the maps and everything in her pockets and picked up her camera.

'Can I help you with anything?' Jem asked smilingly, 'any gear I could carry?'

Melissa laughed and shook her head, 'I've only got the one camera.'

'Oh, ok,' Jem was surprised, 'so, you just do what you want and I'll follow yeah.'

'Alright. Weston said the markets, they're just over that way aren't they.'

'Yep. I'd say so.'

So Jem and Melissa headed off.

~

Captain Hardan was doing a standard check of the ship's exterior as Weston and Astrid prepared. Weston double checked that Hardan was not going to be coming back in at any time soon then pulled Astrid along to the back cabin.

'You're up to something, I know it,' Astrid grinned as Weston pulled her along, and she laughed in a way that Weston secretly loved, it was her sparkle as it were, even though the laugh was somewhat gruff.

'I've wanted to talk to you for days,' he said.

'Really?'

'Oh yeah.'

'Just talk?'

He grinned but continued with a tone that was trying to be positive but serious all at once. 'I couldn't think how to get you aside on Shorakai, and I couldn't get you out any sooner before we left either, you know, TnTv costs, Q Corp policy and all that. I wanted to come get you myself but, things, you know.'

'Thanks West, at least you got me out. I got the impression Q Corp didn't want you to have me this time.'

'Well, yeah, but having you on this trip is important to TnTv, and we do have a contract, though Q Corp would know about us that's for sure, I mean-'

'They sure do, I get a thorough going over and debriefing every time I go back there.'

'Don't you feel so degraded by that? I would. So intrusive, so -'

'I'm used to it,' Astrid dismissed, 'I guess I'm a valuable piece of equipment, even besides my age, and they're only going by the service manual.' She laughed at the face Weston pulled.

'Don't you start calling yourself a piece of equipment, that's what they've drilled into you, you're their slave, and they want you to know it, at the beck and call of-'

'You,' she smiled.

'Not yet,' he kissed her, 'but, by the end of this trip I'll have enough in the account to buy out TnTv's contract over you with Q Corp and then buy you off them in full, a hundred percent, you'd no longer belong to any of them.'

'You'll really buy me?'

'You bet I will.'

'Surely I'm not worth whatever it is they're charging.'

'I've been saving since I met you,' he held her face, 'I'm going to buy you and tear up the papers.'

She returned his kiss with double the passion.

'I was going to surprise you, but you know I'm no good at keeping secrets, especially not from you,' Weston said.

'I'm glad.'

'So, ah, thanks for getting the Blue Moon out of that tight spot back there in the divide.'

She grinned, 'How'd you know it was me?'

'I know you, just little things, your hand, your face, and the spec sheet from your agency. My Astrid,' Weston smiled and kissed her again. 'Oh, and I almost forgot,' Weston fumbled in his pocket as he got down on his knees in the tiny compartment, gazing up at his muse. 'I meant to do this before now but I never seem to get a chance, and I couldn't get you alone for all of Shorakai, it was the most frustrating thing.' He took her hand. 'Astrid, my darling, my Machina Angelic, will you consider this humble proposal,' he held out a carved stone box to her, flipping the lid open to reveal a magnificent and yet not overstated ring, that, together with his next words took her breath away.

'Will you, Machina series 20M, model A* id, whom I like to call Astrid, be my wife?'

Astrid stood stunned for a moment. She knew the man was in complete earnestness, and she loved him, she really did, his irritable temperament, his annoying habits and his loud shirts didn't worry her at all, but she found herself suddenly scared.

'West,' was all she could utter.

'Well?' Weston asked, worried at her long and stunned consideration. Then Astrid laughed casually.

'Of course I'll consider it,' she grinned.

'Is that all?' Weston said, deflated, 'no rapturous, gleeful acceptance?'

She couldn't remain impassive to that pathetic face of his that looked up at her trying to understand. So she showed her real self to him, sinking down to where he sat on the floor. 'But West I'm, I'm a mech, no matter how long or how much you love me, I'll always be a mech, do you realise that?'

'Yes, but-'

'What if I was decommissioned tomorrow?'

'What's up Astrid?'

'Would you still ask me the question if I was going to die tomorrow?'

'Absolutely! And I wouldn't let you say no.'

'I'm sorry West. You took me by surprise.'

'Did I?'

'Aha.' She took the ring and put it on slowly. She answered him, not believing how heavily her heart was beating inside. 'Wife is kind of a funny word isn't it.'

'Is it?'

'Mm, but Mrs Alamo sounds alright, I suppose.'

'Is that a yes?' Weston asked.

Astrid laughed, 'Yes.'

They laughed together, he was so far beyond happy, he pulled her into his embrace and kissed her again and again.

'Oy, you. We're supposed to be out there filming,' she reminded him, giggling as his whiskers found the tickly spot on her neck. 'You know I can't wear this ring though, or everyone will be asking questions.'

'I guess that might be so.'

'Would you hold onto it for me? It's still a yes, but I can't take it with me back to Q-corp. either. Save it till it's all settled.'

'I will.'

~

Fisher walked with Melissa along the crowded streets. He'd brought the Rinke again and was being a complete tourist filming just about everything. The people of Arrojor seemed to suit their surroundings very well. They were very dark or very pale, but always with a greyness in the tone of skin, and with black or silver-blonde hair, dark eyes or a pale blue. Melissa pointed out to Jem that most of the women wore long dresses and had longer hair than any she'd ever seen on anyone, flowing right down till it almost touched their sandals. Melissa felt quite out of place in her tight jeans and shoulder length hair, pushed up randomly into her cap. Even her slightly olive skin and her brown hair seemed out of place. Jem told her not to worry, mentioning his own gingery goatee, and continuing to look around at everything, unconcerned. Melissa took a little longer to settle into her work. It was so overwhelmingly different to the north, with wide, pedestrian cramped squares and narrow alleys stone-paved, earthen buildings that looked ancient but were crammed with technological inputs and outputs, transportation, communication, entertainment, et cetera. She tried to steady herself in the midst of the chaos by focussing on composing her shots.

The streets were so busy in preparation for the big event, the annual race. Crowds were gathering already and the markets were thronging with activity and noise. It wasn't hard to get an interesting picture, apart from the fact that there were so many distractions. The whole place was alive with aromas of herbs and baking bread, honey, sugared nuts and sizzling meats and the sounds of enjoyment, of haggling, of selling, of eating, of animals and vehicles, and the sights. Colour burst into the dull streets, people, clothes, stall covers, goods, and then at around 10.30am local time, the sun rose completely above the high peaks that surrounded. The grey hills became dazzling and the day warmed instantly. The lingering clouds above the land were banished and the sky held such a vivid brightness.

Fisher squinted his eyes tight, 'Wow.'

'Yeah,' Melissa agreed, turning around, looking up at the sky, breath taken away. 'How could you photograph that?' Melissa asked herself. Tomorrow, maybe, if she could find a good location, perhaps she could take a series of shots showing the rapid and vast change.

Fisher on the other hand, took momentary notice then was captivated by a passing vision, the Arrojori beauty eyed him too then turned down a narrow lane, disappearing.

'Hey Melis, I'll be back in a bit yeah.'

'Where are you going?'

'Just down this way, don't worry about me, you go ahead, I'll catch up with you later.'

Jem disappeared. Melissa waited for a few minutes and was a little concerned that Jem had so suddenly gone, but she could still see the building by which she was remembering the way back to the ship so she didn't feel too concerned. After a while she tried the radio on her jacket to reach him but there was no response, but she decided not to worry just yet as Jem could surely look after himself, and so she began taking photos again.

At first she stood in the general area where Jem had left her, then she began to go further and further away, though still keeping an eye out for him. She worried, but became distracted and didn't realise she was being carried along with the general flow of the crowd in distance and minutes, further and further away from the ship.

~

Tarku qualified for the Grand Prix easily. He had used his old papers, using the name that had stunned and excited the official earlier that morning. Many enthusiasts knew the name and were surprised to see it there, many guessing that this must be the son of the racer Riyu Savah who was still spoken of, and whose races were often replayed, even sixty years after having disappeared from the racing scene. They pointed the name out to each other and some cheered him on during the 40 minute trial, crowding around him and the other riders as they dismounted at the end of the race.

People had loved Riyu Savah because he was a bit of an enigma and a bit of a showman, he turned up at random races and usually won a placing, and he always had something for the crowd. They were already placing their bets on the big race and he was suddenly thrown into the mix, not a favourite, but with fairly respectable odds.

'Now that I did not know,' Weston said to Astrid, when they figured out that Tarku had been this Riyu Savah at one point in his long life, 'the kid's a champion racer!'

The Arrojor Grand Prix was very informal compared to big events in the North Islands, well, apart from the Delahar rally where just about anything was allowed. Here the crowd was not controlled, the lines, and even parts of the race were not marked. There was some few hundred metres that would be through the paved city streets, but most of the race would be around the peaks and the canyons, some of it would be packed gravel surface, but most of it was a rough and ready race if ever there was one.

When Tarku finished the post-qualifying rigmarole he spotted Astrid and Weston on a distant stand and began to make his way to them, riding slowly through the crowd of spectators. A little boy sat with him, proudly holding Tarku's helmet. The boy had been hanging around the racers and getting himself into trouble, so Tarku had let him have a ride. He had short black hair, a wiggly-toothed grin, and his nose dripped like a tap but it didn't seem to bother him, he just licked it away like most boys his age did when their mother's weren't watching. His hands and pants were dirty and his knees grazed, but he seemed very happy.

'Are you really the son of Riyu Savah?' the boy asked Tarku. Tarku didn't answer, he just smiled, it was too hard to explain that he had called himself Riyu Savah for a time all those years ago, and that it was him and no he hadn't aged much, and that was because he was an Akaia. No, Tarku wasn't going to go into it.

'My Granddad says you're the best racer,' the boy went on, 'but he doesn't think you're going to win.'

'Oh, why not?'

'He reckons you haven't raced for a long time and you've got an old bike which isn't really that well suited to this terrain, and you're not concentrating.'

Tarku laughed, it was all true. 'Wise man. Who's your granddad kid?'

'He's a mechanic, he always gets a lot of work this time of year.'

'Yeah, I bet he does.'

'He's working on Coban's bike with Dad at the moment. It has issues with the dual engine switch.'

'Oh right. Your Granddad's not Marcus Sabiani is he?'

'How did you know?'

'What? He's only the best mechanic on Arrojor, how could I not know him.'

'No, he's the oldest mechanic on Arrojor!' the boy laughed.

'I guess he must be getting old. What is he, seventy?'

'Eighty-two.'

'My time goes. We used to kick up such a lark,' Tarku remembered. Had it really been that long? The first time he'd met Marcus was when the mechanic had been twenty something, Tarku had looked twenty something, he still did. 'Tell him hi for me when you go back, and tell him I might be around to pay him a visit later.'

Tarku waved as Weston and Astrid made their way from a high tier down to where he'd come.

'These are my friends,' Tarku told Leon, 'Astrid and Weston. Guys, this is Leon, his Dad and Grandad are race mechanics. So, how have you guys been getting on so far?'

'We haven't done too well,' Weston explained, 'seems difficult to connect with the locals more than general conversation, but we got some nice takes of the crowd and the event here, other than that not much. Some nice takes of you though, but I don't understand why you were in the middle of the pack? Are you really the son of Riyu Savah?' Weston jibed, scratching his chin, 'if you are, I thought you'd have blitzed them all.'

'Oh you know your southern hemisphere racing history do you?' Tarku laughed.

'No, not really, Astrid just relayed the live playback to us here, and translated. You've got them talking that's for sure, but you didn't do as well as they wanted you to boy.'

'Yeah, well, not on this terrain, with this bike. She's an urban girl West, not used to all this scree.'

'Yeah but, Savah!' Weston pressed, repeating some of the commentary he'd heard, 'he got away with everything, even on the slopes.'

A glint lit Tarku's countenance, his momentary grin.

'What I don't get Tarku,' Weston continued, 'is how you were here then. I get that you are this Savah, but I don't get how you were here then, I mean that was well before travel out of the north became possible.'

Tarku's grin remained a moment longer, 'When you're designing aircraft, you need to test the prototypes.'

'What are you saying?!'

Tarku laughed.

'No wonder I couldn't find D'Avero for an interview when I was doing the series on heroes of the exploration revolution. Not even a picture! Had to go with the company men.'

Tarku spoke to the boy in Rojdi, 'Hey Leon, my friends need a cultural translator, do you know someone who can talk them through the history and way things are here? My friends can pay.'

'Sure, my mother's cousin is a teacher, they have the race week off. If he's not into his books I'm sure he'd like to make some extra money.'

'Go with Leon,' Tarku directed Weston, 'he knows an expert who can help you with Arrojori culture.'

'But you're here now, and you seem to know the way things are done here, you can do it,' Weston opposed.

Tarku shook his head.

'Orh, come on, why not?'

'That's not what I'm here to do, and my knowledge is only minimal in any case,' Tarku said simply, taking his helmet off the boy Leon. 'Oh, and there'll be a dinner for the riders and others tonight, I got you guys access,' he handed them a pass each, 'might see you there.' He revved loudly so he wouldn't hear their rapturous thankyous then sped off back to the ship.

Astrid and Weston followed behind little Leon as he led the way and beckoned them on and on through the crowded narrow byways.

'So, Melissa seems a nice girl. You think she'll do alright?' asked Astrid.

'I hope so. She still needs a bit of training up but the best way to learn is on the job I always say, but it's clear she understands lighting and that can be one of the hardest things to master. I'm glad I owed Tarku a favour and relented to his insistence to see that exposition, else I'd never have found her. What do you think of her?'

'Honest opinion? She's a little out of her depth, but only a little. I think she'll shine up pretty good.'

'Yeah, I think so.'

'And what's with this Fisher character? He seems a bit chancy.'

'My words exactly, and Tarku said the same thing to me on Shorakai, but you didn't want to have to go back to the facility did you? Melissa didn't want to go back to The Gutter, and I didn't want to be in the office any longer, I was losing my mind. Tarku and Hardan were already waiting as well. I didn't want to call it off. Jem was the only guide I could find ready to come south at the moment.'

'So he's a necessary irritation,' Astrid laughed.

'Precisely.'

'He'll wind Tarku up if he's not careful. Jem has no idea how close Tarku was to thrashing him today. West, I'm worried about Tarku,' Astrid said quietly as they continued along.

'So am I,' Weston replied.

'He's practically shut-down most of the time, that conversation just now was the easiest he's spoken to us the whole trip so far.'

'He's always been aloof. That's just Tarku.'

'But he's wound so tight at the moment. I think there's something hanging over his head, something big.'

'Wouldn't you be afraid if your people were being treated like his are? I worry about what's going to happen to him when we go back to the North Islands, if the government catch up to him he'll be locked up like the rest. I worry that what he is has finally caught up to him, and he's finding it hard to keep hiding.'

'That's all true, but I don't think that's what he's afraid of.'

'What do you think it is?'

'I would never have thought I'd ever say this but since meeting Tarku again I've been wondering about the connection between the Akaia and the Mrukai.'

'No,' Weston shook his head, thoroughly refuting all that Astrid's statement could infer, 'Come on Astrid! You're talking about folklore, myths that have perpetuated themselves by the sheer horror of the thing, like all good urban legends.'

'I want to ask him if it's true.'

'Astrid, come on, have you ever even seen a Mrukai?'

'Not in person, but I have a great deal of data about them, and why would they have a name for the creatures if they didn't exist? Why would there be a legend if there was not some truth behind it? I believe the data I have. There's definitely a connection.'

'Well, we all know Mrukai do actually exist, I've never seen one, but science has proved they are creatures that lived deep inside the earth that were released in the main collapse and for a time assaulted those first survivors, but they've retreated back to the caves and deep places of the earth and haven't been seen for generations.'

'That's not entirely true, they have been seen.'

'But that there's a connection between them and the Akaia?'

'We know that Akaia didn't exist before the collapse either, so there is a connection even in that, and there have been sightings from time to time. You've seen the pictures from the war years, it was an Akaia that brought an end to the war of the mines, a war that would have lasted years without intervention, you know that. No one speaks of it because it was too terrible to recount - but doubtless it was brought up at the governor's legislative review. We know the recounts of the soldiers who witnessed everything - though few were left there were enough to verify what happened, though I read their words were dismissed at the time; Mrukai came to the battlefield West, under darkness, working with the Akaia.'

'But that the Mrukai are behind the existence of the Akaia! Astrid!'

'You just don't want to believe it because it's too hard.'

'Yes, it is too hard - to even speculate that something as terrible and powerful as a Mrukai could impart something of its nature into the confined vessel of a man, of course it's too hard, it's unthinkable. Besides, how and why would they?'

'I want to ask Tarku what his opinion is, if he knows the origins of the Akaia, if he thinks it's true.'

'No, you'll do no such thing.'

'But I can feel something. I know he's trying not to show it, but he's afraid like no man should have to be afraid.'

Weston knew it too, he'd seen it all too recently in Tarku, but didn't want to admit it to himself yet, or to Astrid. Why else would Tarku bring himself to the point of near death? It was out of fear. 'The Akaia are the Akaia,' Weston continued to maintain, 'that's all there is to it. I don't want to know any more about them than I already do. If Tarku feels the need to share anything, he's a good kid, I'll listen, and I'll help if I need to, but I'm not asking him. I want him to stay on the expedition, this is hardly the beginning, and he's already proved to be very useful. I don't want him to get up and leave us because we're asking too many idiotic, unnecessary questions. The kid likes his privacy and I don't blame him.'

'I don't think he'd mind.'

'I do. You've seen him, sometimes he's as touchy as a princess.'

Astrid chuckled, 'Now, if he heard you say that!'

Weston smiled briefly but then shook his head in all seriousness, 'Astrid, I don't know what's up with him, but I get the feeling it's not easy being Tarku right now, so I'm just going to let him be.'

'Yeah, poor Tarku, and here I am feeling sorry at my own situation. At least I've got you to get me out.'

'Yeah,' Weston put his arm around her, 'you've got me.'

'Come, come,' Leon urged them, 'not far now.'

CHAPTER 17:

Never go anywhere alone, ever.

Tarku rode his beloved Avero up the ramp and then gave it a good clean and general check, considering the best way to mount a few cameras to it and his helmet.

'How was it?' Hardan greeted as he climbed down into the hold.

'She actually did better than I thought she would on the slate sections,' Tarku replied, pulling off his gear. 'So, this ship's got a welder stashed somewhere doesn't she? And drills and things?'

'Yep, for repairs on the fly. You need them?'

'Yeah, if I'm going to film this race I think a few bike cams will be the best way to go. One rear, one side, or maybe two. One at the front, or perhaps a helmet cam would be better than that. I'll have to think about that one.'

'Got the equipment? I mean, all the cameras and whatever else you need?'

'Should do. Posted a box of bits to TnTv a few weeks ago. Should be down here somewhere.' Tarku looked.

'I don't remember receiving or stowing such a box,' Hardan worried as he helped to search. 'It's not on the inventory.'

They searched but couldn't find the box. 'Ah. There were some decent shock-mounts in the box too,' Tarku sighed, 'and a glide cam.'

'West might have put it in somewhere.'

'Nah, more likely it was lost in the post. Never mind, I'll go check out what I can get in town. I saw Astrid and Weston over by the track, where's the rest of the crew?'

'West sent Fisher and Melissa to check out the markets and whatever else took their fancy.'

'Poor you, stuck sorting the ship.'

'No, no, it's all good, part of my job, I don't mind.'

'Well, hopefully I won't be long, see you soon.'

'Righto.'

'Oh and here,' Tarku handed Hardan a ticket, 'racers and company dinner tonight, thought you might like to sample the local haute cuisine.'

'You know me too well,' Hardan chuckled down in his belly, 'I will gladly come of course, thank you.'

It was already well after noon when Tarku left and when he returned it was almost dark. Weston, Astrid, Hardan and Fisher were all there waiting.

'Have you seen Melissa?' was the first thing anyone said.

'Why?' Tarku asked as he quickly put down the bits and pieces he'd purchased.

'Ask Fisher!' Weston glared at the careless guide, who stood there looking deflated and sporting a bruised eye.

'Oy! It wasn't my fault she wandered off,' Jem retorted, 'I got mugged by the way, not that anyone cares what happened to me!'

Tarku took in the situation, noticing the TnTv jackets, 'You didn't try the radio?' he asked.

'Of course I tried the radio!' Weston snapped, 'they're just not working.'

'I got ours working now though,' Astrid told Tarku and looked at him with genuine concern. 'We've got to find her Tarkars.'

Tarku took one of the jackets with a radio and pulled out the radio device clipping it to his own collar, not saying a word but looking around at the crew then disappearing down the ramp and out into the crowded evening streets on foot.

'Right,' Weston rallied, 'he's got the idea, Fisher you go after him, Astrid and I will take the highway round and work back from the other side of the city. Good luck.'

'I'll stay here then shall I?' Hardan asked, worried about Melissa but fingering the dinner ticket in his pocket with regret.

'Good idea,' Weston said, 'if she comes back you can let us know.'

Fisher had to speed up a bit from his usual swagger to keep up with Tarku, through the sweaty ship bays with drunken crews returning, lounging around drum fires, laughing, joking, telling tales, playing cards, boxing to pass the time, for the sport and for the gamblers. So many times did Fisher turn his head and wish to stop and play and try his hand against these foreigners, but Tarku kept on and so he followed.

'Hey wait up Tarku,' Fisher yelled, but this time when he turned back from being distracted he couldn't see Tarku at all, just a crowded market, dimly lit.

Having gladly lost Fisher Tarku put his head down and slipped into the shadows, then up to the rooftops, getting to the business of finding Melissa seriously.

'Can you pick up anything?' Weston squeezed the hand of his mech as they hopped off the taxi on the other side of the city centre and began making their way back. Astrid shook her head, 'Not in this crowd I'm afraid, well, of course there's lots I can tell you but I can't pick Melissa out, not unless we get fairly close to her. I hope she's alright. Poor darling.'

'I hope so too,' Weston sighed, 'I didn't think Fisher would be so stupid as to let this happen.'

They stopped to ask a passing official if he'd seen a northern girl, about so high, might be wearing a jacket like this one. No luck.

'Supposing she's okay,' Astrid said, 'she's a photographer right, so where would she be?'

'Snapping the street performers? Tracking some famous rider in some hot spot.'

'No,' Astrid shook her head, thinking. 'She's not that type West, I think she's the type sees details, and the big picture, you know, if you wanted to convey this whole atmosphere, the crowd, the anticipation, the warmth and colour of the moment where would you go?'

'I don't know, somewhere up high I guess, not too high though just a first or second floor, somewhere where I could see the whole strip but still get some close action.'

'You have to remember too, it's not that long since sunset really, and as we didn't set a time to meet back at the ship she may well have been capturing a particular moment. I think this whole area would have been rather vividly glowing just at sundown, I'd have wanted to capture it if I'd been here that's for sure.'

'I hope that's all that's happened,' Weston said, sounding pessimistic.

'I think we should check out that tower up ahead.'

Tarku was on the ship side of that particular tower, watching Melissa from a roof top. She was making her way through the dense throng with some difficulty. He had let the others know but there were obviously radio black-spots in this place, or perhaps Weston's equipment was intermittently faulty, whatever it was Tarku had not been able to alert the others. He watched Melissa pass his position then followed at a distance and to the side.

Then Tarku spotted what he had been afraid of. A group of men split up through the crowd, they had been following her, the beautiful young thing, and now that darkness was embracing the streets they decided it was time to move.

The nearest man was suddenly pulled up into the thick shadows by Tarku and temporarily incapacitated. There were definitely two others, now rounding in on Melissa, and a woman Tarku hadn't noticed before, old and bent, she stepped in front of the girl and distracted her, trying to sell her some jewels or scarves, but she was part of the set up, she must be. The second man fell where he walked, some few metres behind Melissa. Tarku moved on to the third man, he was almost at Melissa, he hadn't noticed that his friends weren't close about, he was about to touch her shoulder when Tarku grabbed him from behind, in a way no one around noticed, then pulled him over into another dark corner by an empty street stall that had sold out of all its skewered goat's meat and whatever else hours ago.

Only the old woman noticed that the men she worked for had disappeared and so she immediately stopped her selling and walked away. Melissa's steps quickened, the old lady had alarmed her, she didn't really want to buy anything, she just wanted to get back to the ship and out of all this, why did Jem leave her on her own! Was he alright? It had been okay during the day, but now Melissa was feeling a little worried, the darkness had come so suddenly.

Tarku held the third pursuer's head hard up against the stone wall, 'Who are you and what do you want with her?'

'Let me go, I don't know what you're talking about,' the man shook under Tarku's grasp and cringed.

'I think you do,' Tarku applied some pressure in strategic points. It was beyond painful.

'Alright, alright, it's de Nordan girl you mean, ha?'

'That's right.'

'If we'd known she was important we'd have let her be, I'm sorry man, she seemed to be alone.'

'You didn't answer me, what were you planning to do with her?'

'What do you think?' the man sniggered, though still under Tarku's painful grasp, 'crowd like this, all revved up, biggest race of the year.'

'Who do you work for?' Tarku pressed,

'Listen we have paid workers as well if you're interested.'

'Who sent you?'

The man didn't answer, only kept up his sell, 'Guy like you, hoo! All you need's a little touch up and you'd fetch a prime fee every time.' Tarku didn't have time for this, that was the last the man knew.

When Tarku looked around he'd lost sight of Melissa. A lump in his throat bigger than he could ever remember sat there and wouldn't move. He pushed through the uncaring crowd, desperately surveying the street, but the street soon diverged three ways, two of them would get you back to the ship. Which way was she!

The radio in his pocket blipped, Weston's voice came across. 'We've met up with Melis, she's fine, we're heading back to the ship now. Everyone read us?'

'I hear you,' Hardan replied, 'Fisher's here too.'

'Well done West,' Tarku said, 'you guys should head on to the dinner, if you're up for it, it should still be on, these things can last for hours. There's spare tickets in the front of my bag if Melissa and Fisher want to go along with you.'

'Thanks Tarku, I'd almost forgot, Leon's relative, the teacher, what's his name? Kyman, was going to meet us there.'

'Don't wait for me, there's something else I've got to attend to first,' Tarku said. He saw the little group ahead, Melissa held in between the safe arms of Weston and Astrid, but he saw someone else watching, someone in the dark, following, now turning away. Would that man Garner have the connections and the resources to take Melissa back even out here? Would the buyer Garner had warned about? Or was this something else? Tarku followed the figure for a while, long enough to discover he was from Vahrna and here with a group of travellers from the far south. Tarku stood in the dark, listening to the conversation of the group for a time, they spoke in the southern standard so Tarku could understand what was being said and it was all casual conversation, nothing about the girl, so Tarku breathed, maybe he was just imagining things. He made his way back to the ship, wishing he didn't have so many concerns of his own, wishing he knew the best way to keep her safe.

'So,' Weston asked Melissa, 'what happened?'

'We were worried sick about you darling,' Astrid held her around the shoulders as they walked back to the ship.

Melissa smiled gingerly, 'I'm sorry, I should have waited, Jem was so long, he disappeared and when he didn't catch up I tried the radio and when no one answered I just decided to go on myself. Is he alright?'

'Oh, he got mugged, but he's alright, but what's this? Are you saying he left you on the street alone?' Weston frowned.

'Yeah, but it was alright, I'm sorry he got mugged. Did he lose much?'

'They took all the currency I gave him this morning, and the video camera he was using.'

'Oh that's terrible! But this is such an amazing place, I didn't realise it was so late and then suddenly it was dark. Do you think I can come back tomorrow? I'd like to be here for the late sunrise, well not here but somewhere I can see here from, if that makes sense.'

'I'll come with you tomorrow darling,' Astrid offered.

'Really! That would be great.'

'Now, you're coming to the dinner right?'

'What dinner?'

'Drivers, racers, teams and friends, everyone pretty much. Little bit of a formal affair, should be good. Weston and I are hoping to meet some of the other racers, we've got a local coming along to explain things so it should be good.'

'Of course I'll come.'

'Do you have a formal dress honey?'

'Ah, no, not really. Well. I don't have to go. I'm quite tired anyway.'

'No, no,' Astrid shook her, 'you're coming. I've got a nice sari we can pin into something.'

'Are you sure? That would be really great, thank you.'

Everyone was just about to go off to the dinner when Tarku returned. He had hoped and expected that they would have left already. They were all well done up, Weston and Hardan looked smart in their suits, even Jem managed to scrub up fairly decently although his black eye was still very obvious. Astrid was glowing in a simple but very chic indigo-blue dress. Melissa, well, never had she looked so entrancing, one bare shoulder, her hair hanging down, her face soft and somehow glowing, such gentle eyes - she'd done them in the Shorakaian way again, and her dress, Astrid's sari, was perfect. They were laughing, Melissa was feeling beautiful for once in her life and starting to enjoy herself, but Tarku came up to her.

'Never go anywhere alone, ever,' Tarku said to her with such intense seriousness that he scared her, then he stalked onto the ship.

Melissa was obviously taken aback by Tarku's scold. She knew Kat would probably have said the same thing to her but he had no right.

'He's a bit like that sometimes,' Weston encouraged Melissa, 'but he's right though, it's not safe for you to be alone, that's why I sent Fisher with you,' Weston glared at Fisher significantly.

'Well, she's alright isn't she?' Fisher protested.

'Yes, but if she hadn't been it would be down to you, keep that in mind,' Weston spoke to Fisher straight, 'I'm paying you to do what I ask you to do, not what you feel like doing, so if you don't like that you can catch the next ride north.'

'Alright, I'm sorry I walked off for a bit and got mugged,' Jem replied, rolling his eyes, then apologised properly thinking of his job, 'seriously West, I am, Melis I'm sorry yeah, it won't happen again.'

'It's alright Jem,' Melissa smiled, 'it's no big deal, I'm just glad you're alright.'

The crew turned up to the dinner and found that there was a table reserved for them, 'I wonder if this cost Tarku much?' Astrid said to Weston aside. The evening was well underway but there was still a lot to follow. They were served various dishes, as was everyone, trays of plates were brought out and they could choose the ones they thought they'd like. It was an experience for them all, the local cuisine of Arrojor. Their cultural translator Kyman had met them at the door, as he was being paid he had waited patiently for them, and even he was enjoying himself very much, explaining the various dishes to them.

Many racers and fans had come to their table too, hoping to meet and talk to the young Savah. Some of the racers were known in the North Islands as well. There was the heavy but very slick Roderick Coban, the seductive but dangerous Mischa LeVanta, last year's winner Bastian Tantaras, and the deceptively nervous Ernst Garene, to name just a few of the big names, but Tarku had not turned up. It was however the perfect opportunity for Astrid and Weston to talk to the racers and as most of them were only too happy to pose, they shot a great many photos, and recorded a lot too. Fisher was just overawed to be in such company. Melissa was taking it all in, it was one awesome glittering night and she was happy to be there, in the background, sitting back and watching everything happen with wide eyes. Hardan was content to smile, make small conversation with her and sample all the dishes.

'How are you finding working for TnTv so far?' he asked her as he began to gnaw a lean but tasty pigeon thigh.

'It's been great,' she said, 'to be honest I didn't know what to expect, but it's amazing. I'm learning so much from Astrid, she's an awesome teacher.'

'Yep, it's a good crew West's put together I reckon, for the most part, and I reckon you've done yourself proud so far, so just keep going the way you're going and like West says, you'll have a good career ahead of you.'

'Thank you,'

'Here, pass me those fried things that we're not sure what they are,' Hardan pointed. Melissa handed him the plate. 'Kyman! What are these?' Hardan yelled to the other side of the table, it was certainly very loud with the music and the wealth of conversation that was going on in the hall.

Kyman yelled back, 'Asp, sliced in rounds of course, after being de-venomed and cleaned, then pickled for several months in salt water and sometimes with other herbs, and then fried. A delicacy from Koha mountain, where the riders circuit during the Grand Prix.'

'Snake? Let's give it a try,' Hardan did and was pleasantly surprised. 'Let's hope Tarku doesn't meet one of these that's still alive on his ride,' the captain chuckled. 'Would you like to try a piece?' Melissa looked at the strange meat and considered it. 'Go on, you only live once,' Hardan urged. Melissa took a small piece and held it, but wasn't sure about putting it in her mouth. Finally she did and found it a little rubbery, but nice to taste.

'Do you think it's strange that Tarku hasn't come to his own dinner?' Melissa asked.

'What, Tarku? No, Tarku's been a reserved sort of fellow as long as I've known him,' Hardan considered as he chewed another piece of fried pickled snake. 'Well, he has his moments when you see a bit of his other side come through, but those are few and far between.'

'How long have you known him?'

'Years, I suppose, on and off. As long as he's been doing work for TnTv.'

'Has he always been like he is?'

'What do you mean?'

'Well, I don't think I've known anyone that smiles as little as Tarku, and when he speaks it's usually abrupt, and he sleeps so much when we're travelling, when there's so much to see.'

'Yes, he's always been like that, but he does seem a bit more withdrawn this year I suppose.'

'But he's missing out on so much! I know on Shorakai he was glad to miss the governor's dinner, he said he doesn't like social gatherings, but still, there's more to it than that, he's missing out on the food, and the music, and when we're travelling he's missing so many sights that are so amazing I don't even know how to begin to describe them.'

'Well, I guess it's all old to him,' Hardan said.

'I could see Shorakai a hundred times and it wouldn't get old,' Melissa said contemplatively.

'No, you're right there,' Hardan agreed.

All the racers were called to be introduced on stage and receive their starting position, Riyu Savah was called, but he did not show.

'Hardan, do you feel that?' Melissa asked seriously, looking up at the hanging decorations, wondering if they were shaking or if she was imagining things.

'What?'

'I think that's a tremor starting.'

CHAPTER 18:

The truth behind the ache.

Tarku locked the ship up and sat in the quiet hold with the welder and his beloved Avero, carefully mounting tiny cameras on it, casing them with extra protection; it was going to be a rough ride the day after tomorrow. He was also altering his bike to suit the conditions better. It was one of the most relaxing things he found to do, it was focused, it was using his hands, it was working on something he loved. And since the ship was locked and he knew exactly where the crew was, and how long they were going to be, he'd stripped down to his jeans and singlet, which he would never do if others were present. For unlike other Akaia, who as Weston described possessed one tattoo often smaller than the palm of your hand, almost his entire body was covered with those pale, intricate tattoos. From his torso they were creeping up his neck, along his arms and even down his legs, almost to his feet. He was ashamed of them because they told of what he was, and they told of his connection to a world beyond the sight of men.

He had thought of going to the dinner tonight, but when it came to it he realised he'd never really planned to go anyway. The price he'd paid for the dinner was a small price to pay for some space and some peace. But he stopped what he was doing. His heart sank. Peace? For Tarku? There would never be peace for him. He felt it before it started, then heard the rumble of a distant quake, felt the tremor gently roll across the ground here in Arrojor. But this was no ordinary tremor, everything he was told him that something big was about to happen. A cry was wrung from him as his eyes ignited against his will, he looked up and knew a Mrukai surely coursed above the city now, in the thickness of the night beyond. Tarku could feel it, he didn't have to see it to know it came for him. The spanner dropped from his hand and he collapsed to his knees as he gasped and uttered the quiet plea of a man at his end, 'No more!' but his words were ignored. Through the darkness a call echoed, but it was unlike a Kyu's call that flowed around and through what it touched with some flexibility, this call was piercing and direct, and without sympathy. And as a Kyu's call could hold a man entranced or search his depths even until fibre and bone knew it was under inspection, this call too could change a man - from Tarku's skin ashes began to fall away as new lines burnt into place from within him. The lines kept burning further and further across his skin, another layer to his already much tattooed frame. Tarku yelled at the pain at first, but soon the torture was too much and his shoulders fell and he passed out, falling back onto the ship's floor amongst his tools.

The tremor that shook the mountains of Arrojor disrupted the party momentarily, none heard the Mrukai's call in that moment, and being that the tremor was overall relatively small the party continued, as soon as the shaking subsided, and the rest of the evening went on without any hitches. The crew returned very late, laughing and tired, surprised to find it mostly dark inside and locked up, as they expected to find Tarku. They called out and knocked and buzzed.

Tarku came around slowly, he cried out as he felt the new tattoos – all over his right shoulder and arm, and partly across his chest. He held himself for a moment, the pain was unbelievable and he could barely see this world for his sight was still stuck partially in that hazed place. He lifted himself up unsteadily. He felt so sick inside, not himself. Though pain seared through him he managed to stand, to stagger forward and grab his jacket. He managed to get to the keypad to let the front cabin stairs down for the crew, then he knocked the tools away from his motorbike, starting it. He had to get away from here, they couldn't see him like this, couldn't be near him like this, he was too volatile and he knew it.

The crew climbed aboard, Fisher, Melissa and Hardan going straight to the bunks to sleep.

'Where's the boy?' Weston asked Astrid, 'I want to thank him for a grand night.'

'And ask him why he wasn't there,' Astrid laughed, but she stopped suddenly, for even as she touched the ship to locate Tarku she could feel that something wasn't right, but then they heard the lower ramp open and though Weston jumped straight down to the hold he missed Tarku, just seeing the tail-light of his motorbike disappear out into the now empty darkness.

Weston saw Astrid's troubled face as she climbed down into the hold, 'What is it?' he asked.

'I don't know,' she shook her head.

'Does he have a radio with him?'

'No, it's here.'

'Oh. Well, the boy's his own man, he can look after himself. Best we get some sleep at least,' Weston reassured Astrid, but to no effect. She could sense the heaviness that still hung about, and she touched the floor where Tarku had been working. There was oil and grease from the motorbike, and there was some few spots of blood, and what looked like ash. She didn't know what to make of it. A shiver ran down her spine and she looked back out to the shadows, stepping slowly down the ramp after Tarku and looking around. Weston followed her but didn't speak, knowing she was trying to figure something out. She stood still and listened to the night. After trying to sense any irregularity all she could detect was a slight aberration in the flow of air, like something had been high up over the city but was now gone. She wondered at it, pulling her shawl tighter around her shoulders, taking a last look around, then climbing quickly back onto the Blue Moon.

Tarku rode and rode till he was far out of the city and in the middle of nowhere, he rode a deserted track till it petered into nothing and even then kept riding out, until he skidded and crashed on some rocks, out in the middle of a great waterless lake, out where no one lived because of the waste creeping in. He was thrown from his bike as he veered, tumbling across the sharp stones, but he pulled himself up and stumbled on further, one arm around the other in agony, till he collapsed to his knees and was sick. He shivered all over, clasping his arm tightly. He cried inside. He felt so heavy, aching, nauseas, weak. He couldn't stop the shaking. He didn't know what to do, in all his years he'd never felt a heaviness like this. His whole arm and that whole side of him stung, throbbed and ached so deep and unbearably, the pain speared inside him, spreading to his chest and to his heart, physically and psychologically. He could feel the lines of the new pattern upon him and he began to realise something - he'd seen this pattern before, he'd seen the pattern on another Akaia, that wasn't new, all his tattoos were once carried by other Akaia, but this was different, this was one he knew so well.

He ripped his jacket away to look, he thought he must be hallucinating with the pain, he did not want to believe it, he did know these lines, he recognized the roundel upon his right collarbone, the corner of which could just be seen if you looked closely at the picture of Amiana on Shorakai, and with horror he recognised the curves along his arm. 'Syra! No!' he cried, holding his arm.

At the realisation that he now carried his friend's tattoos as well, so many brief visions flashed before his eyes, her violent death, her final moments, their time so long ago, her smile. He soon sank to the stones, choked by pain, memories, and tears. 'Syra no!' For a long time he was locked in this state, in the conflicts of pain and fear and grief that crazed his mind, then at last he calmed enough to try to make a plan. He knew he couldn't return to the Blue Moon until he was stable and certain of himself, but he knew he needed help. Eventually he concluded there was only one other option. His old friend Marcus Sabiani.

The workshop of Leon's father and grandfather was still full and noisy even at this time of the morning, when the rest of the world was heavily asleep. It was always so over race week. Even Leon was there, but he'd fallen to sleep on a chair by the entry, near the cool of the night air. But Leon woke at the distinctive sound of Tarku's motorbike. The boy ran out to greet him, but Tarku stayed in the darkness and held the boy away, 'Will you call your grandfather for me Leon,'

Leon was a smart kid, and he knew something was wrong so he didn't hesitate but ran to find his grandfather. Soon the old man came out. 'Riyu?' he said, peering into the dim, and studying the face there, then he laughed and stepped out to embrace Tarku, 'My old friend, why don't you come in!'

'Marcus,' Tarku stayed where he was, leaning on his motorbike to stop from falling over, 'it's been a lifetime since you knew me.'

'Yes, it's been too long,' the old man agreed, 'but I'll bet you haven't changed. Come in, come in, I'll introduce you to my son and the rest of the crew, and you can tell us how you're going to pull off the big race.'

'Marcus,' Tarku stopped him, 'please, I need your help.'

'I see. Does the same trouble haunt you now as it did then? I haven't forgotten.'

'It multiplies every year my friend.'

'What do you need?'

'Somewhere quiet for a few hours where I won't be in anyone's way, a shower if there's water enough, and a friend who knows who I am.'

'Come, my office is free, and there's the bathroom out the back. Anything else you need you don't have to ask, what's mine is yours.'

Tarku took a step but fell again, Marcus tried to help him to stand, but the mechanic was an old man, it took some great effort on his part, but he did it at last, little Leon trying to help as well, coming forward despite his fear, and together they made the way inside.

'I'm sorry to come when you're so busy, and in this state,' Tarku apologised as they helped him into Sabiani's office.

'No need to make an apology to me.' Marcus directed the boy, 'Leon, find a cushion for Riyu, and bring him a cup of strong tea.'

Leon hurried to do as he was asked. Marcus showed Tarku to his office, and pointed the way to the bathroom. 'What can I do Tarku?'

'Kill me, Marcus,' Tarku replied in all seriousness as he sat down against the wall in the dimmest corner of the office.

'We tried that, remember,' the old man said, a grim grin on his face. 'Don't give up now Riyu, you always find a way, no matter what vehicle you're given, not matter what terrain. The race is almost over for me and you both, don't give in till you've won.'

'What is winning Marcus? I hardly know anymore.'

'Living, Tarku, living is winning,' Marcus tried to encourage.

Tarku held Marcus's arm a moment. The old man could see the trouble in Tarku's face, feel the shaking deep inside him. 'Do you remember Syra?' Tarku asked the old man.

Sabiani smiled, 'Yes, very well.'

'She was one of the few left who lived this life with dignity, she was almost as old as I am, I can see her death before my eyes replayed, and it feels like my own death. Syra dreamed of blue skies Marcus, she believed we had some higher purpose but not I, the blue sky I believed in was in her eyes, it should have been me, not her. Why her!'

'I have no answers Riyu. Here,' Leon brought the tea and Marcus helped Tarku lift the mug. 'Rest will do you good Riyu, just rest now,' Marcus said, and pulled down some more blinds to stop the garage lights coming in. 'Call me if you've any need. We're just finishing alterations on Coban's second bike so he can test it in the morning. He still hasn't decided which bike he wants to take.'

'Thank you Marcus. Again let me say I'm sorry for my state. One day I must sit and talk with you about all the old times again.'

'Yes, one day, but not today Riyu. It's alright, you just get yourself together.'

A while later, but still in the dark hours, Tarku sat up sweating. He shook, found reality, but still searched for breath as violently as if he had almost suffocated. He saw Leon sitting in the opposite corner of the office, watching him.

'What are you doing here?' Tarku asked as he lay back again, exhausted.

'Grandfather said to watch over you. Did you have a nightmare?'

'No.'

'It seemed like a nightmare.'

'True, but it was a memory.'

'Tell it to me.'

Tarku was silent.

'Are you Sansahme?' Leon asked, 'You can tell me, I can keep a secret.'

'You have seen enough to know I am.'

'What was the memory?'

Tarku looked at the ceiling. 'My friend was killed.'

'What was their name?'

'Her name was Syra.'

'Who killed her?'

Tarku looked at Leon a moment but didn't answer, instead he got up, 'I might see if the shower's working.'

He tested the shower, but there was not enough water pressure today. He stood at the basin and filled it, taking a cloth and beginning to clean the blood that had run from the deep scars, and clean the grazes and dirt from where he had skidded the bike out on the stones. But now he cried. They had executed her violently, so violently. He shook, and lost all his ability to breathe for a moment as he saw himself in the mirror there, saw his body as the blood washed away. He stared at his skin, his new tattoo. It had all healed now. It was clear, two definite patterns were now intertwined together all over his right shoulder and arm and inwards across his chest, towards his heart. The lines that had been hers had the faintest bluish tinge. 'Syra,' he said again, 'Why?!'

For an instant he saw her looking back at him in the mirror through his eyes, her brilliant blue eyes crying out, he put his hand up to her, 'Syra.'

'You carry almost all the world with you Tarku, now even my people,' her image said,

'You know I've never believed that Syra, don't ask me to believe that.'

'Don't give up now, you can't give up now.'

'Syra,' but he blinked and it was just him, his own eyes, 'Why!' he smashed the mirror, and cowered away. More tears fell. 'Pull yourself together Tarku!' he urged himself, but slid to the floor, shaking and overwhelmed as the full gravity of the situation fell on him. Syraveia was dead. The last in the royal line of Shorakai was now her daughter, Melissa. Melissa who he had to protect, Melissa who he found it hard to look at. Melissa, who he wanted to keep innocent of knowing anything about any of this as long as he could.

'Riyu?' old Marcus came in, having been called by Leon who'd heard the smash but had been too afraid to go in.

'I can't do it,' Tarku said.

'One thing at a time my friend,' Marcus found a footstool and sat, taking Tarku's hand and cleaning the new cuts. 'Remember, one thing at a time.'

'I'm sorry I came to you like this Marcus,' Tarku apologized. 'I don't know why I came and put you in this position again, I don't know why you always help me, you know what I am, why do you always help?'

'I know no man has been given an easy fate, but no one should have to bear the lot you've been given.'

Tarku was silent for a time, staring at the shards of mirror glass on the floor.

'Plus there's the fact you did save my life that time,' Marcus said, 'and the fact that you're my friend, and this is what friends do.'

'I only saved you because I almost killed you,' Tarku reminded the old man with a grim look.

'Yes. I know,' Marcus grinned.

'I'll pay for a new mirror,' said Tarku.

'It's alright, I never liked that mirror anyway, it tells me I have too many wrinkles,' Marcus joked, 'and not enough hair.'

Tarku's face lightened a little, but he said, 'Today I truly feel I am Sansahme.'

'We all feel empty when we lose a friend Riyu, there is nothing soulless about that.'

'The weight is so great Marcus, it shadows all that I am, every thought, every muscle and bone, I can barely stand under it.'

'Maybe you don't have to stand, there's another reason I've always looked out for you, I've got money put down on the race tomorrow, and it's on you, so don't let me down now. If you still want to, you can ride. Your bike out front doesn't look so good, but I still have your old one locked up here. If you can pull yourself together, I'll have it ready for you to ride in the grand prix.'

'You still have my old bike?' Tarku looked hopeful.

'I do. Every year for all these years I've cleaned, rust-proofed and polished your old girl, and taken her for a spin around the city.'

'Show me.'

Tarku followed Sabiani, and the old man brought out the machine from under its covers. Tarku touched the frame. He loved this bike, it was a machine he'd built from scratch, it could take just about anything you threw at it. The only reason he'd sold it was because he was going to give up his racing identity, but he really loved racing, and he really loved this bike. He and Syra had tried to outrun and outplay the Mrukai on this bike, almost died trying. Of course it was impossible from the start but there are some things that you just have to do anyway. It had ended in laughter, and then tears as their lives inevitably forced them in separate ways. If they had stayed together, they probably would have both met the same fate as Syra had now, Tarku understood that, but oh how he resented all that he was, but Marcus was right, he couldn't give up till he'd won.

'I still want to ride,' Tarku nodded.

CHAPTER 19:

The Arrojor Grand Prix.

That morning on Arrojor they heard the news, that little tremor they had felt last night was not so little after all. What they had felt was just the edge of a greater quake that had caused massive destruction throughout the south-east. Oconia had subsided, one small uninhabited isle had crumbled completely, and Shorakai had been shaken terribly again. The footage horrified the crew who had just come from there, and the news cast a cloud over the meet, but not for long. They had the stunts, short course and the junior races today. Tarku's little friend Leon was in it, he didn't place but he had lots of fun, and was filled with pride because Tarku had helped him shine his bike, and had come to watch him.

The crew from TnTv had a more relaxed day today. Astrid and Melissa did their thing, while Weston, Fisher and Hardan all went their separate ways. But when they were all together again later on, everyone was questioning where Tarku was and if they should be worried. Weston was not particularly concerned about Tarku and explained, 'When you've worked with him as much as I have,' he told them, 'nothing surprises me. He often disappears for a while, but he always comes back and with something to show for it too. Never an explanation though, mind you.'

When Tarku did not show up that night nor the next morning, Weston really did begin to worry, but it was mostly Astrid's doing, as she was certain Tarku had been greatly troubled the last time they'd seen him. If it weren't for Astrid, Weston wouldn't have been so concerned, well, Astrid and the fact that the Arrojor Grand Prix was in a few hours and there was still no sign of him. But then a package arrived. Just when Weston realised that not even Kyman, their cultural translator, nor any amount of currency, could manage to acquire decent tickets for them at this late stage, a courier turned up with a package addressed to himself, with the tickets enclosed, in positions near the finishing line where there would be good opportunity for unobstructed shots of the race and final sprint. 'The boy's a genius,' Weston dubbed, 'see Astrid, I told you he was alright.'

There were of course free, standing-only positions for spectators, but these were not the most exciting sections of track, and they would have been hot and sweltering and generally a tight squeeze if you wanted to see anything at all.

The crew had all taken their seats and they'd watched the pre-race hoo-ha with amazement, but a growing impatience to see the big race actually start. The riders were called out one by one, given an over-the-top introduction by the announcer and then took their places at the start. They were waiting for his name, waiting for Riyu Savah to be called, it was, and called again. Then there was a cheer as a distant figure headed towards the line. Weston looked through the telephoto lens he had with him. 'It's him!' he nudged Astrid in excitement, 'I told you didn't I, he always shows up!'

'Are you sure it's him?' Astrid teased, 'All I can see is a man in black racing gear on a bike.'

'It's him, yeah look, I saw his face.'

'Doesn't look like his bike though, does it?'

'No, you're right. But who else would be insane enough to wear black on a day like today? And there's that kid beside him, Leon.'

'Yes, that's Leon,' agreed Kyman. 'Ah, yes, and that bike, my great-uncle, Leon's grandfather, he bought it off Savah's father many years ago. Maybe Savah bought it back?'

Tarku had stopped to shake Leon's hand, then he sped on to take his place on the track. The riders looked so good, all of them, with their shiny bikes and their slick racing gear that wouldn't be shiny or slick for much longer. Then the race was underway, the riders off and out of sight in an instant.

'What's the kid doing!?' Weston yelled. Tarku remained where he was until the dust from the other riders had settled. He gave a great stretch, then motioned to the crowd, 'I think I'll give them one more minute.' He got a round of uproarious laughter, and somehow got the crowd giving him another countdown for the last five seconds, then he did a trick, waved goodbye and sped away.

'He is insane!' Weston laughed, then got to setting up his cameras for the next time the riders would come around.

The race went as races go, many crashed out, others passed each other numerous times, some did things that would have had them disqualified if they had been racing anywhere else, but the race went on. The race teams were kept busy changing tyres, patching or replacing damaged parts, and reviving their riders. Riyu Savah had not stopped once, he had no race team, only old Marcus, little Leon and some of the other juniors sitting by a can of fuel and some random spare parts. By saying they were his race crew he'd got them free entry to the riders area as well so they did this with pleasure. By the third lap he was tailing the leaders Coban and Tantaras, LeVanta was just behind him. The course went round the rocky Koha mountains, through vacant streams, gravel tracks, to the edge of Arrojor, the forgotten desert land and then up and down the range, on and through the city, then around again. An expert rider could do one lap in an hour, a novice or a rider with trouble along the way could take over three. There were more than thirty riders competing, after all, there was a fortune to win in prize money.

Halfway through the second lap Astrid realised that some of the footage they were seeing on the big screen came from cameras on Tarku's bike.

'I don't know how they do it,' Weston commented, 'my body couldn't take all that jolting and jarring. Man, I can hardly take it just watching.'

There were three laps in all, an enormous cheer went up as the leaders passed to begin the last lap. Tarku pulled in and as Leon and his friends looked after the fuel, Tarku and Marcus worked at strapping the exhaust which had been knocked about. He nodded thanks to Marcus, patted his little helpers on the head then waved to the crowd again, did a spin and was off. They really loved him, the cheer was huge.

Melissa rubbed her eyes and tried to focus her lens again. It had been a big week, and she was beginning to feel the tiredness fall upon her despite all this excitement, and what with the warmth and odours of the sweat and food, the encompassing noise from the stands and the track, she grew even more drowsy. She yawned as she went through her previous shots on the camera. Perhaps if Matthias had been racing she would have been more enthused, but soon she did look up, catching some of the excitement of the crowd, as the last lap went quicker than anticipated. The riders were seen coming into the city, vying for a place, all the big names bunching up even after such a long ride. All of them gained first place then lost it as they came in, nearer and nearer the finish. It was so close, even Melissa was on her feet now, holding her breath as Tarku let the other riders battle it out, as he hung back until the last minute, then began to gain on the others, weaving through and finding every advantage.

The crowd roared wildly as they called for their favourite rider. Leon and his friends were jumping up and down and shouting for Riyu with all they had as Tarku passed Garene, then swung wide and back leaving LeVanta in his dust, side by side he vied with Tantaras then pulled ahead, and at the last outsmarted Coban's false move and crossed the line in front. Leon and his friends danced, the crowd gave a massive cheer, Weston and Astrid hugged, the producer was grinning ear to ear, so was Hardan, and Fisher grabbed random people around him, yelling, 'I know that guy! I know that guy!' Even Melissa smiled, as she watched the happiness of the others, she was glad Tarku had won.

Officials came, they took their time setting up for the awards to be given, and various performers lined the track. Then a band marched out playing an unknown march, whatever it was it sounded grand and made your heart swell. Then the trophies were laid out, the presenters called up and the riders stood off to the side.

Weston elbowed Astrid again. 'Where is he?'

When first place was called, the boy Leon carried the helmet of Riyu Savah and went to accept the prize, while back in the quiet and now empty workshop, Tarku and Marcus Sabiani sat drinking strong tea, and laughing about the old days.

CHAPTER 20:

A quiet word with you please.

The crew had more days to film yet here on Arrojor, and Weston was thankful that the place had settled down somewhat. The team started working like it should have been, not swept up in the pace and hype of the race but focused on documenting the world and life of this jagged isle. Tarku was still absent, but Weston had received a note via Kyman, via Leon, that Tarku would be photographing a certain region but would return before the Blue Moon left for Rorona. Kyman took Tarku's gear to pass on to him as well.

'Blast him,' Weston cursed, 'I wanted him to come over to the stalactite caves to do a shoot. Kyman said they're worth a look.'

'Yeah, and I wanted to ask him how he won the race, I bet he switched some super booster on for the last section there,' Fisher said enthusiastically, admiring Tarku's apparent genius, 'cause he just shot through, don't you reckon West?'

'Boosters? No, not Tarku,' Weston shook his head then shrugged his shoulders, 'he's just that good.' Then Weston spoke to everyone, 'Alright, I want you all to get a good rest tonight, we've still got two days scheduled here and I'm not going till we've got enough to last six episodes. Got it? But from now on we stick together, remember, no one's to go off on their own,' Weston eyed Melissa and Fisher in particular, 'I don't want to lose anyone again. Right. Do I hear a 'yes Weston'?'

'Yes Weston,' Astrid chuckled, hitting his shoulder then walking past him to sit down.

Melissa smiled sheepishly. Fisher grinned, and Hardan patted Weston on the back then went off to the kitchen.

'Oh and Jem, a quiet word with you please,' Weston said.

Weston led Fisher back to the rear cabin and closed the door.

'Ok, what's this about?' Jem asked, sensing a restrained temper in Weston's voice.

'You know very well what this is about,' Weston whispered to him hoarsely, shaking his head, 'I don't want you on board after Satsuan, where you get off between here and there is your choice.'

'Orh! West, c'mon! I'll do better, this was just Arrojor! C'mon.'

'Hey, I only signed you up till Satsuan, I'm just letting you know I'm still of that position. You haven't proved yourself to be of any real value to this team. You've spent money provided to you for project costs on yourself, you lost little Melis in that crowd, and a camera, you've fooled around, you've pretended you know what you don't which could have seriously jeopardised this expedition, you got yourself beat up-'

'Well that wasn't my fault!'

'And then to top it off you steal money from me to gamble on the race and you lose it all!'

'How did you-? Well it wasn't my fault! The perfecta was a sure thing! A half a second between Coban and LeVanta, half a second West, that's it!'

'Listen, you're irresponsible and arrogant and it just isn't good enough. I'm not blaming you for everything, I knew you weren't up to the job but I hired you anyway, hoping you'd step up, so it's my fault when it comes down to it. A few more years maybe, when you've had some sense knocked into you, then you'll be a fine guide, but not how you're acting now.'

'Orh man, I really wanted to go on to Tamashan and Salamonde with you guys. It's like, a dream for me, you know, please don't kill it West.'

Weston guffawed, 'You don't expect me to crumple to that slobber do you?'

Jem sighed and shrugged his shoulders, 'It was worth a try. Can I try the 'I need the job for the money' tack now or would that be a waste of time?'

'Just give up Jem, be satisfied you got to see Shorakai,' Weston huffed then headed off to send John Mark another desperate request to be their guide after Satsuan. Weston knew that it was as Scott and Hardan said, there was no one better than John for the job.

On the last day Weston stopped in at a little local bar he had seen on previous excursions and had let himself come in as a final treat before they left this place. He sat himself down with a long drink and listened to the indecipherable local chatter as he munched the roasted chickpeas. Afterwards, as he was heading back towards the ship he felt a familiar presence behind him. He looked back. Tarku came up and strolled along with him.

'So, what happened to you?' Weston asked.

'What do you think happened?' Tarku returned quietly.

'I've no idea,' Weston replied.

'Good,' Tarku said.

'But,' Weston pried gently, 'Astrid looked like she'd seen a ghost after you took off and she doesn't believe in ghosts.'

'What do you imply?'

Weston didn't want to say, he screwed up his mouth, shrugged his shoulders and shook his head, as if to say nothing was implied, but he hoped Tarku would explain something. But Tarku said nothing more on the issue, only walked on in silence.

'Have you found a replacement for Fisher,' Tarku asked after a while, 'if he keeps going like he started he'll do more harm than good.'

'I know, I already told him he's gone as soon as I find a replacement, I keep trying.'

'Good.'

'I didn't want to ask you, and I guess I hadn't been sure, but from what I've seen you do now and in the past, you could do it you know, be the guide,' Weston proposed, 'what do you say?'

'No.'

'But you could do it, couldn't you? What I mean is, you do have the knowledge, the expertise.'

'To a point I suppose I do, but I don't really know the deep south, and like most I make a point of avoiding the Arc, unless it's absolutely necessary.'

'See, even the fact you know that much – come on, I'll give you another full wage on top of what you get already.'

'No.'

'Why not?'

Tarku thought, rubbing his forehead. He looked a little troubled and answered, 'I don't want the extra responsibility, I have too much as it is.'

'I could get another photographer in. You take it all far too seriously Tarkars.'

'Better than not seriously enough,' Tarku answered sharply in a direct reference to the errant Fisher.

Weston quickly followed after Tarku. 'Melissa's been going on great too by the way, well spotted that one.'

'Oh, good.'

'She's got the eye for it certainly, just like you said. I went through some of her best shots from Shorakai, really good, a lot of useable stuff, especially when it comes to making a book of the series, and Astrid started her off on the motion camera too, she's getting the hang of the little hand-held. And, I've been thinking she'd make a pretty face for the takes we need a presenter, well, she'd be a nice change for the viewer from me or just voiceovers now anyway.'

'I'm not sure putting her in front of the camera's the best idea,' Tarku said.

'Why not? She's shy but we'll make a pro of her yet.'

'Only if the world lasts long enough,' Tarku said with a crooked smile, not saying why he really thought she shouldn't be in the spotlight.

'Yeah,' Weston laughed, then sighed, 'yeah, so you heard the news of the tremors then.'

'Mm.'

'Well, the world just isn't allowed to implode just yet because I've still got half of it to put on film. But with the other thing Tarku, seriously,' Weston struggled to bring it up, but made himself say it, 'are you sure there's nothing I can help with?'

'No, thanks though. I was just losing my head, needed some space to sort things out.'

'And what happened to your Avero?'

Tarku grinned sheepishly, 'Crashed it out in the mountains beyond Arrojor. I managed to ride it back to the city but it's in a bad way, I left it with Leon's dad.'

'What will I tell the crew? They've all been going on, trying to guess where you went, why you went, and how you pulled off the race.'

'Tell them whatever you like,' Tarku smiled, putting his sunglasses on, 'When we're on the way, I'm going to go through this lot,' he held up the footage he'd taken the last few days, footage TnTv would need soon if they were to begin putting these episodes together. Tarku bounced up the stairs and into the cabin of the Blue Moon, though when he entered his face wore that blank, slightly aloof mask as usual, his detached manner followed and his shoulders hunched a little too. He gave a little nod as Astrid led a round of applause to honour his win, then took a seat.

Everyone was ready to go, Hardan began to lift the ship. Soon they were looking back at Arrojor wondering if they'd ever have a chance to come to this remarkable place again.

Once the flight had gained stability Tarku took his footage and sat by the screen and transmitters in the back cabin, which doubled as their temporary editing room. Here he went through his footage quietly and very focused.

'Is anyone else curious to see what he's filmed?' Astrid asked, 'I'm going to go have a stickybeak.'

Astrid went, and her rapturous wows soon had everyone following her down to the back, crowding into the cabin. They watched, mostly in silence but for the repeated sighs of 'oh wow', as it seemed a crime to speak while such beauty was visible. Mountains and lakes and such life as was unseen before by any of them. Where had Tarku filmed this? He had captured the other side of this harsh environment, not only the feared elements that defined this world, but the awe-inspiring majesty of the stone mountains that remained despite all that assailed them, the stillness of the aqua pools hidden deep in the hills, the fragility and beauty of the creatures and plants that still survived out there. Then the sections of the Grand Prix were seen, causing exclamations from all at different intervals, and then footage of family life on Arrojor, it was dinner at the Sabiani home, but Tarku stopped it there. He began making notes and preparing the files for Weston to send through when he sent the rest.

When the crew still stood there admiring the thumbnail pictures he had on screen Tarku turned around and looked at them, at first he didn't say anything, but then he turned back.

'Was there a queue to use the equipment? I can go if anyone else is in a hurry.'

'No, no,' Astrid said, 'we're done.' The others left him to it at last.

CHAPTER 21:

The Smouldering Engineer

Still out on the Urchin, P12, John Mark, the smouldering engineer, was having a hard time keeping up with the flood of news coming from the south east. So many islands had suffered in this last quake, the magnitude of which was greater than any other in recent years. Residents and governments were in panic, would the subsidence in certain regions stop here or would there be continual movement? Would the continuing encroachment of the wastes now speed up? Would other islands begin to break up? Would this scale of quakes continue now or would there be a lull for a time? Would their nations survive or would they be lost like so many in the past? Was this the end? The real beginning of the end? All these questions that had been asked before were asked again.

John shifted uneasily in his seat. Perhaps he should have accepted Weston's offer and been the guide for the television crew, at least then he'd be in the action and not just sitting here waiting for the end. Too late now. He rubbed his whiskers. He hoped Scott and Kyu were alright, he could imagine them helping to restore things down there in Oconia. He could go, John thought to himself, surely he could do more good somewhere else than sitting here. Apathy again proved stronger than his musings however, and he took another sip of his tea and fell asleep where he sat.

Later, John became aware of an alarm going off in the control room, 'What on earth could that be about?' He shook himself awake and rushed into the main room. One monitor lit up, but before John could see what had caused it another lit up then another and another. He pulled up the radar. Something was coming directly for P12 at phenomenal speed. Was it a ship? It was a ship! John followed her flight.

'Whoa! Where'd she come from? No, she's coming in too fast, she won't be able to stop soon enough.' John could see the ship from the window now, already smoking, and with flames in various sections. 'Come on, pilot her, pilot her, turn her round, no! She's going too fast pull her up! Oh no, it's the Vector! My word she's in a bad way! I'm coming guys, hold on!'

The tower shook as the Vector came down, John stumbled down the stairs. He ran out to the burning hull of the ship, it had overshot the runway, pulled through the net and the trip line and run into the hill which the tower on P12 was built. Out with the extinguisher he ran, keeping low and easing the hose to and fro. With his work and the automatic extinguishers the fire was soon down to a low simmer but the wreck remained hot and reeking. The smell of it permeated John's being, what memories it brought back to mind! He devoured the ship's flavour, that full and penetrating aroma of a flight at speed. Now it was before him again, oh, how he had missed this feeling, this feeling that now coursed through his veins and reminded him of the man he used to be. John wrenched the hatch of the Vector open. Were there any survivors? He entered the steaming cabin, crushed on all sides, with wires and other debris hanging from the ceiling, and strewn throughout.

A voice broke and wavered through the flickering darkness. 'Are you John?'

'Yes,' he looked about, 'yes I'm John.'

'I had to come,' the voice rasped weakly, 'I'm the only one of our crew left, the transmitters were shot out, they said to get back to here if I could and you would pass on the message. Everyone's dead.'

John found the voice, a young man, a ships apprentice, wounded severely. John held the boy's head up and grasped his hand, 'What happened?'

'Looks like the Delevian army is taking Tamashan, we didn't realise soon enough, we tried to get our cargo through but they stopped us, when we tried to turn back that's when we got hit.'

'Why now? Did you find out why? The Delevian have been at war with Vahrna but never Tamashan,' John said, more to himself than the boy.

'Mr John, Sir,' the boy's eyes gazed into his own, 'I've a letter the captain wrote, he said to give it to you,' as the boy spoke blood ran silently from the corner of his lips. He fumbled one-handed through his jacket and held a shaking hand out with the red and crumpled notes, 'will you send it home.' John pocketed it and nodded trying to calm the boy's painful shaking, 'and Mr John,' the boy pulled out his identity card, 'to my m-um and sister, a-and little brother. Tell em I'm sorry I can't make it home. Tell em I love em.'

'Nah, nah, you made it all the way here across the divide, you'll make it home yet son, you'll make it, stay with me!'

John took the ID card sadly from the boy, rubbing the blood off the tag and reading the name. Jaxon Adams. 16 years old. 'I will Jaxon, I'll tell them, just stay with me, Jaxon?' John held the boy, but the boy faded away and forgot this world. John quickly left the wreck, becoming aware of the sticky blood covering his fingers, hand and arm that wasn't his own, the blood of a mere child. What was the boy doing on a ship so old she rattled at the thought of travelling? It was dangerous enough to fly in a military cruiser. And south! What was he doing?

The Urchin seemed to become immensely empty all at once, so far from anywhere and anyone. John looked around, the soulless receivers, the decaying tower. John shook his head, took a deep breath and quickly went back to the tower. He washed his arms as best he could, steadied himself and made his way back up to the control room, immediately getting on the radio. He tried to get through to his contacts in Tamashan to find out what was going on. He tried the phone, the long range radio frequencies. Nothing. He tried again. He tried ships he knew should be in the area, he tried ground control, he tried the home numbers of friends he had there. Nothing. John tried contacting control on Satsuan, they had heard nothing, but soon came back saying they couldn't get onto any of the ships known to be heading to Tamashan either.

'This is an open broadcast from P12,' John began, he had to stop for a moment to collect himself, as his voice was shaking. 'The ship Vector has just returned from Tamashan, they were unable to get through. I report Vector was fired upon by battleships from Delevi, and crew advise Delevi attacks Tamashan. That's all the information I have. Out.'

There was radio silence for a time then the questions began coming in.

'As I said, I don't have more information, nor can I get through to anyone in Tamashan.'

Then the question came, 'How badly was the Vector hit?'

'No survivors. One crewman lived long enough to make it back and pass on the message, but died soon after.'

The phone rang, John picked it up. It was a reporter from TnTv. 'Can you shed any light on this John? Why this would have happened? What politics might be behind this attack?'

'I don't know,' he answered, 'Tamashan was supposed to be one of the most peaceful countries in the south. Now this! It doesn't make sense.'

'Vahrna was traditionally seen as the principal rival of Delevi, wasn't it?'

'Yes. Tamashan's always been very neutral.'

'Do you think it could have anything to do with the recently elected viceroy on Delevi?'

'I don't know anything about that.'

'Apparently the Sovereign and his government elected a woman of partly Vahrnan descent to rule under him and to be his representative, particularly in the districts where the population has a higher concentration of residents with Vahrnan heritage.'

'Why do you think that would have anything to do with Delevi attacking Tamashan?'

'Well, that may have drawn Vahrna and Delevi closer together, leaving Delevi at greater liberty to look elsewhere to pick its fights. What do you think?'

'I suppose, but I can see no reason for this, Tamashan is a far from hostile neighbour, besides it's hardly a neighbour, the distance between them is considerable, not to mention the gulfs of the Pireomerai and the Aliyr, which stand between them. It doesn't make sense. There's only one thing I can think of that does make sense,' John said, 'but it's just speculation, and I could be completely wrong, I hope I'm wrong, because if I'm right it sets an truly ugly precedent, not that it hasn't happened before to some degree, but not at this scale.'

'What are you thinking?'

'Delevi is, well, it's gone isn't it. They have a large population sitting in an area that's in a terrible state, they don't have long at all and they know it, and Vahrna is no better. Whereas Tamashan is relatively stable, and prosperous.'

'You're suggesting Delevi might be seeking to occupy Tamashan by force?'

'Yes, what do think of that theory?'

'I don't like it Mr Mark, but you could be right.'

The owner of the Vector phoned a while later, he told John that he'd arranged to send out some salvage men and a transport to bring the bodies home. The salvage men were there in a couple of hours, they were busy men but they didn't mess about. John watched the work, but then they went, and the Urchin was as empty and quiet as it ever was. They still had to collect the bodies from the wreck. The salvage men had hauled the crew out without ceremony and left them on the tarmac. John had had to find something to cover the bodies himself, and when he realised it was going to be a while before anyone turned up for them he made a stretcher and dragged the bodies one by one into the smallest room in the tower and turned the air-conditioning on as low as it would go, to try to preserve them a little. It seems undertakers were busy men too but they didn't get paid as much, and no one was going to steal their bounty so they didn't hurry, the families wanted their loved ones home, but arrangements had to be made, and fees paid. John placed Jaxon in last, the engineer's face was grim. Out of respect he put an old shirt over the boy's head and upper body, he didn't have any more sheets. John closed the door on the crew of the Vector.

Once again he climbed the stairs of the tower, weary but still somewhat in shock at what had happened and restless because of it. John sighed and set to work in the kitchen, deciding to make himself a proper dinner, but after looking in the pantry realised he didn't have the right ingredients to make himself a proper dinner after all. He got out a frozen meal and tipped its contents into a bowl to heat up. His fingers began to tap again while he waited, as he thought, as he made decisions and threw away decisions, all under the expressionless gaze of a bored man.

John took his bowl of, well, who knows what it was, and sat down to eat his dinner in the comfiest chair on P12. He put his drink on the table beside and turned the television on to divert his mind from the banality of the meal. It would be easy for any visitor to observe that this was a usual practice for the man, as the chair, though the comfiest, was also the most stained, and the rings from past drinks patterned the table beside. But John was looking forward to tonight, he'd once again turn on TnTv, to the documentary that had only aired a few episodes so far, and laugh at the seemingly intelligent, but ultimately flawed, overview of the south that the acclaimed Weston Alamo, or the editing team at TnTv, was thrusting on the world. The pictures were great, but the voiceover content, when it wasn't live filmed commentary, was laughable to one who knew the reality. Tonight it was an episode about the sea surrounding Shorakai. It turned out to be quite breathtaking, and there was nothing to laugh at in it at all, so John went to sleep feeling a little hard done by.

In the morning John was reluctant to get up, having slept little but dreamt much, but being an old soldier he did get up when the clock turned over 6am, even though he didn't feel like it. John washed his face, kissed his fingers and touched them to the photo of his wife and daughter just like he did every day, and made his way to the kitchen to fix himself a heavy brew, but passing the monitors noticed there was a communication waiting for him. He looked at the message eagerly, hoping it would be a communication from his friends on Tamashan, but it wasn't.

John, if you change your mind about being our guide, we hope to be on Rorona till the 30th, Satsuan till the 7th. Leaving for the deep south after that, as soon as we find a guide. Hope you decide to come. *All expenses paid, regular salary plus bonuses, spending money and future royalties. Weston Alamo.'*

The man was persistent. John scratched his head, took a deep breath and rubbed his face. Well, he didn't have to make a decision right away, he decided. But he did leave the message there, he didn't put it in the rubbish straight away like Weston's last communication. But right now John wanted to stay here and keep on top of this situation in Tamashan, and find out all he could. John tried to get through to Tamashan all morning. His good friend D'aoda was there with all his family, along with many other good folk, but John still couldn't get through. In the afternoon John tried to chase up the undertakers on when they'd get here for the bodies, but they just brushed him off with excuses and obscurities.

In the evening John talked to some fellow observers in Satsuan, which was closer to Tamashan, but they knew no more than him except to confirm that several ships were now in Satsuan having fled at the sight of the Delevian warships in Tamashani airspace.

So it was a fruitless day, apart from the fact that one of the lithops in his lithop garden had flowered, but this event remained unobserved.

Another day passed in similar fashion, perhaps it was even two or three days, as they all seemed to meld into one another in the state of mind John was in, when he sat down on the comfiest chair on P12, with his bowl of who knows what it was, and put his drink on the many ringed table and turned on the television again. He'd just got comfy, when he promptly stood up.

'Today we're in heart of Shorakai, in the gardens of Merouin,' Melissa began the presentation, as Astrid had directed her all those days ago.

'It can't be!' John gasped and held his head. This was Weston Alamo's extreme expedition to the south again, this was the girl Scott had spoken of, was Scott really right? Could it be Ava!? Had she been on before? Had he missed her? John fell to his knees in front of the television. She looked like a northerner, but also looked undeniably Shorakaian! 'No, it can't be.' His head was hazy, his mind a mess, he shook his head, 'She's not like Amiana. She couldn't be Ava,' he whispered, staring at her, 'but she's the right age.' His heart pounded, he ran and found the photo from the corner of his mirror, the photo of Amiana, Ava and him. He raced back and held it up to the television. Could it be possible? 'No. No.' He refused to believe it. He told himself it was his foggy mind, his blurry eyes, his lack of sleep, his own desperate need to find her. He looked at her again, 'No, there's nothing there,' he told himself, 'there's no similarity, no connection.' He couldn't bear that hope, but even so he went to the communications room and found Weston's message. He prepared to send a message back, but he couldn't do it, couldn't bring himself to make the decision yes or no. 'What if she's not Ava? What if she is?' he paced again, then sat, tapping his fingers. 'What have I got to lose?' he said at last. 'I have to see her in real life, in person.'

He sent a message through to Weston, *'Will meet up with you on Rorona. Wait for me there.'* Even as that message was sending John phoned his superiors. 'Get someone else out here as soon as you can, a replacement for me,' he demanded,

'I'm leaving.' John rushed around, packing his things, feeling strangely exhilarated, hopeful, worried too.

In the morning he phoned the undertakers again and berated them into sending a pick up that day. In a few hours the ship came out to pick up the bodies from the Vector and when it came he persuaded the pilot to take him with them. It didn't take long to load up. John stowed his gear then headed back for the North Islands with the dead, promptly disembarking as soon as they landed, heading straight for the main port where he used to work, hoping to get a ride to Rorona as soon as possible. It wasn't long before he found a berth, it was on a big freighter, he knew the captain.

CHAPTER 22:

Red Desert Sand

The Blue Moon had not long been in Rorona when they received the engineer's reply. It was Hardan who lifted his head, hearing a beep in the cockpit. He got up and came back holding a communiqué, 'They're cancelling the expedition,' he said grimly, holding back a grin, 'apparently the ratings just aren't stacking up.'

'What!?' Weston stood up and grabbed the paper, but as he read it he couldn't help giving a whoop, 'He's coming!' Weston shouted, 'John's agreed to be our guide!'

'This John?' Melissa held up the book she'd brought with her from the tea-room of the fifteenth floor of TnTv.

'Yes! Yes, that John, where'd you get that? I've been looking for that book for months. Never mind, he's coming!' Weston danced around in jubilation, first with Astrid then with Hardan, even with Jem till he realised that Jem was the one John was replacing. 'Oh, well, I am sorry Fisher, but like I said, you have to understand that the way you're going isn't good, you up your act a bit and I'll have no qualms about hiring you, but not until that day.'

'It's alright West, I've had fun while it lasted,' Jem laughed.

'When does he join us?' Tarku asked, being the most subdued of them all.

'Before we leave for Satsuan, so, two to five days time I suppose, depending on how he can manage to get here,' Weston answered.

Tarku picked up his gear, 'Well, I'll be off filming. If you want me you know how to reach me.'

'Tarku we just got here, it's the middle of the night.'

'And this is a desert. Catch the cool while you can West,' Tarku said and headed out.

'Aren't all the places we've been to partially deserts?' Melissa asked. 'I mean Shorakai wasn't but it was surrounded by desert.'

'Yeah but Rorona is really tough,' Jem told her, 'it has a reputation for being one of the harshest places liveable, with the temperature of the sand even reaching up to an unbearable 75 degrees Celsius during the day in the hotter months, which thankfully it isn't at the moment, but it will still be bad out there.'

'75 degrees?! How can anything survive?'

'Nothing much does, on the surface,' Jem said, 'the fun stuff in Rorona is indoors or underground, except in winter they do have the Rorona Tourne here which is awesome, kind of like the Grand Prix on Arrojor. It's a shame we came in while it was dark, oh, it'll knock you over, the city's awesome.'

'I saw the lights and the reflections as we came in,' Melissa said, 'even by those I was blown away.'

'It is incredible,' continued Jem, 'the thing is, the desert may be harsh, but the elements aren't as bad here as elsewhere in terms of toxicity, ultimately it's just heat you have to deal with, and the desert here is expansive, containing a wealth of bauxite and other minerals which they refine and use everywhere, the city is like this gleaming forest of pressed aluminium and other metals. You know Rorona is renowned for its striking architecture, although many experts put it behind the city-rises of Delevi and the aquatecture of Shorakai, but it is really practical because they use what they have here, and it's handy too because if you lose your way in the desert you just have to head towards the sparkle and you know you'll get back to the city, if you last long enough. The wealth from the ore here also makes Rorona one of the most politically stable places in the region, well, the ore, and that fact that even though Rorona is independent it's also sort of a protectorate of Satsuan, so it's like they have a big brother that no one wants to mess with.'

'Jem!' Weston laughed, 'I've just found your replacement and you come out with that! There is more to you after all!'

'Nah, that's all I got,' Jem chuckled, 'You learn a lot watching the races.'

'Well,' Weston sighed, 'I suppose Tarku is right about getting to work straight away. Anyone feel like going out for a bit before hitting the bunks?'

'I wouldn't mind going over the ship while the sun's away,' Hardan said, 'if you wouldn't mind I could use a hand Fisher.'

'Sure.'

'A little cool night air might be just the thing,' Astrid said. 'What do you say Melis? Fancy getting some red dust on your shoes tonight? Go see what we can see?'

'Sounds like a plan.'

So Hardan and Jem went about doing the checks while the others prepared to go out, but just as they were about to go Weston received a call.

'I better take this, it's the office, could be a while,' Weston told them, 'you guys go on.'

Weston went down to the editing room and picked up the call there.

'Hey West, it's Max, thanks for picking up, I'll put you through to the board, they want to talk to you.'

'Right, right, thanks Max,'

As he listened to the TnTv executives Weston spun his balance wheel and wondered if they were going to get to the point before it stopped spinning. It seemed the executives were going on about a whole lot of this and that which was neither here nor there, talking about what had been filmed so far and the response from viewers, and marketing and so on and so forth.

'Well, it's good it's going well, I thought it would, yes,' Weston agreed, 'it's a shame marketing revenues haven't been higher, but you know that will increase as the popularity of the show increases, just as you say it is with every episode, yes, of course we'll keep doing what we're doing, yes, yes I agree we should use the girl more, Astrid's idea that, I didn't know about it till after the fact, but it was a good plan, I was planning to use her more, yes. Tamashan? Yes, it was on our itinerary but I've been thinking of alternate routes seeing as this war and all ruined that. No, Tamashan isn't on our itinerary anymore. No, we won't be going to

Tamashan. What do you mean? I don't think you heard me, we won't be going anywhere near Tamashan, or Delevi for that matter. Oh I see. With all due respect ladies and gentlemen, that's not going to happen, I won't take my team into war. No, I don't think you do understand, you can sit there in your office with your double-shot of the best Salamondan bean, in your leather recliners, gazing like royalty over the city through that wide and impenetrable glass facade, but you can't sit there and tell me to take my team into a warzone! You people don't know a filter from a sensor, a Salamondan from a Soaméan! Nor would you know a vartle bug if it came along and hit you in the backside! Exactly! It's not a bug it's a type of transport they use on Soamé! Well you better care because they're dangerous to drive and they're powered by a certain type of gas which if handled incorrectly can go kaboom! No, I won't go. What? Oh. Bonuses? Well. I was hoping you wouldn't say that. If we did go it would be in a few days, I wouldn't go without the guide and he won't be here for a while. Yes, yes, I understand. Of course, of course. I'll let you know.' Weston put down the phone and put his head in his hands for quite some time, taking the team to the south was one thing, taking them into war was another.

~

Rorona City, they saw it clearly as the morning came. From the port the crew could see the blinding silver towers of the central city rising above the red brick dwellings of the outer suburbs, surrounded by wind-washed red desert sand stretching in every direction for as far as the eye could see. Sand which was much like pigment, making everything that was in it or touched it that deep burnt ochre red as well, but for the silver city which remained silver, the city that rose up like a sculptor's show of majestic metal forms. The crew would have to take an underground shuttle to get to the city, or hire vehicles to make the way over land, as the port lay a distance out for security.

Weston sat at breakfast, carefully cleaning his precious lenses as he chewed. His thoughts were still heavy this morning. How could the executives at TnTv ask him to take this team into a warzone? This is how people got killed. This is how to get a posthumous award at the Gernings next year. Bonuses wouldn't count for anything if they were dead.

'What's up with you?' Astrid asked him as she came in.

'What? Nothing,' Weston excused.

Astrid laughed, 'Good try West, but you know I can see through you.'

'Can you? X-ray vision? That's not on the spec sheet from your agency,' he joked as he chewed.

'You know what I mean,' she laughed.

'Yeah, well, it's nothing to worry on. I'll be good in a bit.'

The others were soon in the kitchen so any further pressing by Astrid was halted. She turned to Melissa, 'West has given us the ultimate job today, we've got the go-ahead to film inside the international conference hall.'

'That doesn't sound exciting,' Melissa laughed.

'Haven't you read your packet?' Weston admonished, with a grin.

'Mostly, but I didn't read the bit about the conference hall because I didn't think it would be interesting.'

Tarku smiled to himself at her comment and felt beholden to enlighten her on a choice fact that may not have been mentioned otherwise, 'It's where John, in the book you're reading, met Sy-' he almost slipped the old name, but saved, 'where John met Amiana. Well, actually, that's not exactly true, they really met right here at the port, but that is where they first truly understood each other.'

'Really, wow.'

'I thought that would interest you,' Tarku said quietly, almost to himself rather than her.

'The thing about the conference hall is that it's just incredible,' Astrid explained, 'how anyone built such a structure with the equipment at hand so long ago has baffled experts for years. The North Island States were first invited to participate in the summit here about 22 years ago, in 2297, that was years after the north had discovered the existence of colonies beyond the divide, and after they had at last welcomed us into the international community,' Astrid added, 'things have come such a long way since then, but the same issue will always remain - communication is the most vital key in serious talks, and that's why Rorona, and this conference hall particularly, will always be preferred by the international community. For you see, the hall hides within its design the most advanced interpreting technology in the world. Sit anywhere around the oval room, in any of the tiered seats, and you will hear everything said by the person in the centre in your own language, regardless of the language of the speaker.'

'How does it work?' Melissa asked.

Astrid shrugged, 'They won't reveal their technology.'

'Hundreds of tiny men under the floor, and some funky microphone setups,' laughed Jem.

'People have tried to find it and steal it, but they don't even know where to look, or what to steal. At the time John was here I believe there was a lectern or plinth in the centre, that was taken at one point and had to be replaced, but the translation never ceased. Usually only the dignitaries and ambassadors are allowed inside, so this is a rare opportunity for us. You should be excited,' Astrid encouraged.

'Well I am now,' Melissa nodded eagerly.

'Of course when John met Amiana here, they did not speak the same language,' Astrid explained, 'Amiana may have known some of our Nordan, as they call it, and John would have perhaps known a few phrases in the southern standard, but not enough for easy conversation, after all it was the first time the north had even been to an international meeting. So the story is she snuck him into the hall one night after the conference talks had ceased and they must have stayed all night, talking.'

'Yes, enough talking,' Weston stood, 'let's get out there. You girls to the city, Tarku and I are off to the underground cave network today. Right. Hardy, Jem, look after the Moon, we'll see you in a while I guess,' Weston farewelled, 'It better not quake while we're down there! I don't want to die underground! Fair shook the last time I was here.'

'Half the city's down there West, you'd think they'd have it shored up pretty well,' Tarku encouraged, 'Look at it this way, at least if the worst happened it'll save somebody's back not having to dig a hole to bury you later, or waste precious fuel to incinerate your remains.'

'Thanks for the positivity,' Weston shook his head.

'Anytime,' Tarku laughed.

Astrid and Melissa took the shuttle into the city, it was a much cleaner, safer and easier way to get there, and the shuttle was fairly regular so it wasn't long to wait and soon they were on and away with the other passengers, speeding along the tunnel. Meanwhile Weston and Tarku decided to arrange an overland vehicle and enter the underground city via the central hub. Weston was sure this would make the film far more interesting for viewers, and of course, Tarku took any chance to ride. So they packed their gear against the red dust, using only one camera strapped to the vehicle in a shock-mount to capture the ride in.

'I'm still not sure about getting on a vehicle you're going to be driving,' Weston said as he gingerly took his seat. 'Maybe I should drive?' Weston suggested. Tarku just laughed, pulled down his goggles and revved. The dust kicked up behind them as they sped in, sometimes they were lost in the cloud of a rider ahead and would have to wipe their goggles and the camera lens to see enough to keep going. When they reached the outskirts of the city they were confronted by a maze of makeshift dwellings – refugees from the various nomadic tribes that had at last been forced to the city by the severity of the elements in recent months. Passing these there were stalls of traders vying to sell over-priced oddities and essentials to newcomers, and idling riff-raff who had no better place to be, or could not afford to live along the more sheltered streets within or underground.

It was amongst this desperate chaos that they became aware of a commotion. A crowd was across the narrow road. Tarku and Weston had to stop as had some other few vehicles, questioning what was going on and if they could push through or if they should wait here until the hubbub quietened before trying. But then they realised what it was, they heard a certain word amongst the shouts, Weston looked at Tarku, and the Akaia became grim.

'You can hear what they're saying can't you?' Weston said to Tarku. 'I only know a little Roronan, but I know the word *Sansahme*, and I know the word *crazy*.'

'What do you want me to do about it?' Tarku replied, his expression blank.

'I've seen you deal with this before, you know how to deal with them, you might save some people some injury.'

'Since when do you care about that? You just want to get through,' Tarku huffed, 'you should film it and give Echlin more ammunition against his complainers on the Akaia ruling.' Tarku was reticent to act, but he knew if this went on the authorities would come and the outcome would not be desirable, so he dismounted and stalked through the crowd towards the commotion. Still covered in red powder dust from the ride in, Tarku made his way. He lifted his goggles and pushed through the rowdy spectators who stood by, watching the erratic violence and seeming insanity of a lone Sansahme in the street.

Tarku watched the young Roronan a moment, the boy could be no more than sixteen, and there was nothing in his appearance that was any different from any other boy, apart from his eyes and that one small tattoo, but he had already reached his end. The boy was looking around, but not looking at any individual in the crowd at all, only through them, he did not see them, but held a knife out thrashing it violently but without clear aim. Tarku could see the boy was just afraid, it was only when someone came too near that he would really lash out, but he was like a wounded animal in a corner, one wrong move and many could get hurt by his actions. The boy himself was already hurt from where others must have tried to stop him, or where he had fallen or hurt himself, blood was evident across his frame, and red dirt clung to his blood and sweat. Who knows how long he had been trying to make his way through the streets in this state.

Weston now pushed through behind Tarku. 'He is mad,' Weston observed.

'No. He can no longer see the world clearly, his mind has lost hold here but he can still feel this place, and every approach is like a danger, so of course he fights the shadows around to protect himself.'

'Have you been there?' Weston asked.

'I've been close, too many times,' Tarku answered.

'What are you going to do? Take him on?'

'He is not one that should be feared, he is one that should be pitied,' said Tarku, noticeably distressed by what he saw, 'but I'll give him something he can see and be sure of.'

Tarku's cold grey eyes lit up as he broke through the crowd, he yelled out to the boy, and the fear on the boy's face more than doubled and he tried to run, but tripped as Tarku neared. He quickly stood and thrashed his knife about madly and yelled in terror, but Tarku ducked near, grabbing the boy's arm and forcing the knife out of his hand. The crowd moved further away as Tarku wrestled the boy to the ground. Tarku held him down, knee on his chest and arm on his throat.

The crowd cheered and clapped at the show, but Tarku took no notice. He spoke to the boy in a language none there would have understood, he spoke firmly, 'Look to me boy, look to me! These shadows are not the fiends you fear, they are the people of Rorona.' The young Sansahme was gasping and terrified as his eyes focussed on Tarku.

'Boy, you're lost,' Tarku said simply.

The boy's breathing became more steady and the confusion and fear and aggression left his face, replaced with something like relief but also shame.

'Listen to me,' Tarku continued, 'you have to leave the city, are you prepared to go?'

'I can see you,' the boy spoke at last, 'I saw you when you called. Now I believe the many rumours amongst the Sansahme about you; you are Tarku Na Araka aren't you? You have to be. I can see - '

'I don't want to know what you see,' Tarku said shaking his head, aware of the crowd. 'Get up boy,' he commanded, 'be on your way.'

But the boy did not go, only knelt on the ground at Tarku's feet in a position of submission and respect. 'Don't send me away! I will surely die here or be killed. Let me stay by you. I will be in your army, just tell me what to do.'

Tarku grew sad, 'Get up boy. The desert is that way, if you don't want to hurt anyone else or bring shame to yourself I suggest you walk and keep walking,' Tarku pointed the way and then turned to go.

'Why don't you end it all?' the boy asked, 'don't make me do this, don't let me fall away again.'

'I can't help you boy, not for long,' Tarku said quietly. 'Rumours are many, truths are few.'

But the boy felt the knife there on the ground and picked it up, he ran and fell before Tarku again, desperately and looking up at him, 'But you can end this for me,' he pleaded and offered his knife up to Tarku. Though they still spoke in the rare language Tarku had begun in, the crowd knew what the boy asked of Tarku. He was afraid, he wanted to die, he wanted Tarku to take his life.

Tarku took the knife, but he folded it carefully and put it away. He stood the boy up then took him firmly by the shoulders and looked at him straight. 'This end is not the end you seek,' Tarku pressed him. 'Don't fear the end you know lies ahead but hold your head high. Do as I tell you now. Go to the end of the desert as your compass now decrees, and meet the fate that awaits you there. Hold your ground, don't give in until the last. Your going will ensure more days for many here, it will ensure your days have not been lived in vain.'

The boy's head bent low, he couldn't find the will to make a step that way.

'Here,' Tarku relented, putting the key to the hired vehicle in the boy's grasp. 'Take my ride, it will get you further faster. Remember the way things lie as I tell you, the desert lies ahead,' Tarku showed him, 'the shadows here are the people of Rorona, and the city, the shadows ahead and left are where the port lies, stay clear of there and head straight out. Take no notice of any other shadow that passes you until you reach the stony ground, that is the end of the desert, and the end of your journey. It may take you a few days.'

'And then?' the boy said, his jaw trembling with fear as he knew the answer, but trying to hold his head up proudly all the same.

'And then you can fight the fiends you fear, and find the end you seek.'

'I cannot pay you for this,' the boy shook his head as he accepted the key to the quad bike.

'I will cover the cost, do not concern yourself over it.'

The boy revved the engine. Tarku hauled his and Weston's gear off the back and onto his shoulders. They nodded to each other in understanding, then the boy was off.

Weston came up behind Tarku, 'Is he bringing that quad back?'

'No.'

'You're picking it up somewhere?'

'No. We won't see it again.'

'Do you know how much that will cost me?'

'I have a pretty good idea. But you wanted me to sort it out, so it's sorted.'

'I didn't mean give him our hired quad bike! But I suppose you did well to get that done with no one getting hurt, I should say congratulations.'

Tarku looked at Weston, then back to the dust in the boy's wake, 'I just sent him to his death West, I don't think that's something to be congratulated for.'

'What?!'

'What do you think waits for us out there?! An oasis? Green fields?'

'No, but, just the desert, but you can survive that.'

'Maybe I can, for a while, but he can't, he is no more a Sansahme than a boy with a gun is a soldier! And it's not the desert West, I sent him to the end of the desert, he would have got there eventually but I made his way sure, to the end of the island, where the desert meets the rifts of unmeasured depths, unmeasured darkness, and there he will begin to be consumed by the elements of this broken earth. He will forget that he was ever just a boy growing up in a silver city, and though he wants to die, he will fight what he finds there until he loses his life, all because that is his fate, one more lost so a few can others can live a moment longer.'

'Tarku, what are you talking about?'

The Akaia turned to Weston but only huffed then began walking on, Weston jogged after him, 'Tarku?'

'You wanted me to deal with it, so it's dealt with. I'll pay for the quad, you don't have to worry about that.'

'Tarku I - '

The Akaia let it out, 'Remind me not to come to you when I am near the end, I will need someone who can say to me, there is your end, go and face it. There may come a time when I will give you a gun as he gave the knife to me, and you may even pull the trigger, but it won't solve anything.'

'Tarku - what?'

'I'm sorry, but I didn't want to see that. That boy was afraid, but not as afraid as I am.'

Weston grew thoughtful, puzzling over Tarku's more over the top reaction than usual. He puzzled it out. 'Astrid thought something was eating you, that's what it is isn't it? You don't think you have long left to live, do you?'

'I'm not afraid of dying.'

'No, but like you said, you don't know how long you can keep going. You're afraid you'll end up like that kid, aren't you?'

'I didn't come on this expedition for a psychotherapy session West,' Tarku frowned at the producer, 'are we filming or are we filming?'

'We're filming.'

'Alright then.' Tarku strode on.

'There was one other thing,' Weston queried as he hurried after Tarku, 'why did he kneel down to you like that?'

'You would have to ask him,' Tarku evaded.

'Is it because you're ridiculously old?' Weston kept on, 'could he tell? Is it something of inside knowledge amongst the Akaia?'

'Weston!' Tarku yelled and glared at the producer.

'Ok, ok,' Weston laughed.

CHAPTER 23:

The vacant conference hall

'This is it,' Astrid breathed in the magnificence as they were let into the vacant conference hall to do their filming. 'This is the place where they host the gathering of folk from all over the known world to discuss issues ranging from poverty and social justice to regional conflicts to the impending end of the world.'

The silence of the grand room was almost touchable, their footsteps barely sounded as they walked down the many steps to the central floor. The further in they went the more they felt the awe of this place enveloping them. The intricacy of the design and detailing was astounding, the skill of the craftsmen who built it was immediately evident.

'Wow,' Melissa whispered as they walked in further. 'It would be impossible to capture this room in a picture, you couldn't possibly convey how it feels to stand here.' Melissa was drawn to the stone mosaic that covered the floor, kneeling down to touch it and study the complex design and the colours, the aqua like oxidized copper and the ochres like rust, all interspersed with streaks of silver reminiscent of the city outside.

'This is where the speaker stands.' Astrid took the centre, 'Right now I'm speaking Arrojori, what do you hear?'

'Northern,' Melissa laughed in amazement.

Astrid began to set a camera up to pan the room in a smooth circle, while Melissa looked for angles that struck her, but she kept being drawn to the centre, and stood there for some time, looking at the floor and then the ceiling and around. 'There's something about this place isn't there,' Melissa said at last, 'almost like it's living.'

'Living?'

'Well, not alive and breathing, but like it's part of the earth somehow. Look at the main lines in the ceiling, to me they look like trees, you see the main line splits and splits again and again into smaller parts, until they wrap around the skylights, like a tree and branches, and the mosaic on the floor mirrors it.'

'So do the carvings on the main pillars around the room, which, if I'm not mistaken, are made from bone, or rather, hard cartilage, if I were to be precise.'

'Bone? Really?' Melissa went to one and touched it. 'But these pillars are huge! It couldn't be bone? What animal could get this big?'

'Only two I can think of.'

'What are they?'

'The Kyu and the Mrukai, but I'm not sure the Mrukai have bones like this.'

'Oh. Do you think this really is Kyu bone?'

'Well, we couldn't know without taking a sample for testing, but that would be my guess, we're probably standing in the centre of a Kyu's rib cage.'

'Wow.' Melissa took some close-ups of the carvings here. 'That's one thing I don't understand,' she said.

'What's that darling?'

'Well, they say all these terrible things happened when the earth broke, and things came out of the earth that were scary and dangerous, but West included the kyu in the list, and Kyu seems really wonderful.'

'Kyus are different,' Astrid said. 'You said you had met Scott Thomas? Did he talk much about his kyu?'

'A little.'

'Did he tell you that they are symbiotic creatures?'

'No. I don't know what that means.'

'Symbiosis is the close association of two different types of creatures for the benefit of one or both of them. Kyu's have been known to form this bond with people, because though it does seem possible for them to live without a rider inside them, their wellbeing is greatly improved by the company of a person. The dangerous thing is, that what begins as something optional for the person, ends up as something essential. Once attached to the kyu in this way for a time the person cannot live without the kyu, nor the kyu without its rider.'

'So what happens? How can a person benefit a kyu? Or a kyu benefit a person? I mean, apart from being a really awesome way to get around.'

'It's my understanding that the kyu gain warmth and companionship, and a free massage inside its chest, while the rider, like Scott, gains strength and energy from the kyu's call, but the call of the kyu is such an intense thing that it changes the rider's own body, so it becomes something the rider cannot live without.'

'Like a drug?'

'I hadn't thought about it like that, but I suppose so.'

'So Scott can't go away from Kyu, not at all?'

'Not for very long.'

'But he saved her life, they saved each other's life.'

'Yes, and now they're stuck together.'

'I didn't know that.'

'Not many do.'

'But Kyu has such a beautiful call.'

'Yes, but there are many places the kyu are feared almost as much as the Mrukai, because it is not always so. Some say the kyu can kill a man with its cry if it wants to.'

'Wow. I've got a lot to learn!'

'You're doing well darling. So what do you think, are we almost done?'

'Yes, I guess we are,' Melissa said, touching the carvings on the kyu bone one last time as she thought. 'Where do we go from here?'

'The rest of the silver city awaits!' Astrid took Melissa across the shoulders, 'come on.'

CHAPTER 24:

John, this is Melissa.

The TnTv crew had filmed what they could of Rorona in the time they had. All were weary, having worked hard to fill the days and nights with shooting back to back locations, and now they just waited for John Mark to arrive before they left for Satsuan. Most had fallen asleep, the cabin of the Blue Moon was quiet and still. Tarku wasn't asleep though, he was sitting on the stairs fixing one of Weston's radios that had got too much red dust in it. He was wondering how he'd handle being on the same ship as the man who had loved and wed his own dearest friend Syraveia. John Mark wouldn't have known her as Syra of course, he knew her when she was an ambassador for Shorakai, Amiana Lailae Arin.

Weston wasn't sleeping either. He hadn't told the crew that the executives at TnTv had just about demanded that he take the Blue Moon and this crew to Tamashan to cover the story of this war, if it was a war, as no other station anywhere had a team that could or would go, and everyone wanted to know what was happening so there was big dibs for the station that could get the story. Weston wasn't sure he'd have come if he'd known before they started out, the south was tricky enough without the added unknowns of the breaking war in Tamashan, but he wasn't about to turn around now after so much planning and pain, and besides which, even if he had wanted to turn back, the big guns at TnTv would have something to say about it, not that he cared about that, but still, it was a consideration. Though Weston did agree that the war itself should be covered, and if the execs were right and no-one else was covering it, which was almost certain because really who would be that reckless, and Weston knew what that meant, it meant more exclusives for TnTv, which equalled added bonuses for him and the team. He could buy Astrid off Q Corp even sooner, and that was a pleasing thought.

It was quite late in the night, when Weston was suddenly in rapturous exclamations that woke everyone, he had spotted John Mark disembarking from the massive freighter Trilogy and making his way towards the Blue Moon.

'Well, I'll be on my way then,' Jem yawned.

'Jem, you're booked till Satsuan, you don't have to go yet.'

'Why stay? I'll see ya's.'

They farewelled him, and Jem strode away to find another berth. Tarku screwed the radio back together and threw it in with the others, then took his seat, while Weston fretted by the door, rubbing his hands.

When John reached the Blue Moon he was not the solemn man Scott had met back on P12. They met John Mark the old soldier, longing to go, to begin, coming on board with all his gear and with energy. Weston welcomed him, shaking his hand vigorously, 'It's so good to have you on board John.'

The big man nodded, 'It's good to be here.'

'John, good to see you again, you might not remember me,' Hardan held out his hand.

'Captain Hardan!' John shook his hand warmly, 'No more cataleptic co-pilots I hope!'

'Thankfully not, no. Here, I'll stow these downstairs for you,' Hardan took John's larger bags to the cargo hold.

'Right so,' Weston buzzed, 'everyone, this, you must have gathered by now is Mr John Mark, he's going to be our guide from now on. I'm certain you will prove to be invaluable John.'

'Well, I don't know about that,' John laughed, 'but I'll do my best.'

'Right so, ah, meet the rest of the team John,' Weston directed him, 'This lovely lady is one of my accomplished crew, Astrid.'

'Pleased to meet you John,' she smiled, 'it really is an honour to have you coming along with us.'

'No, no, the honour is mine,' he replied.

'And ah, this is Tarku,' Weston continued, 'a renowned photographer in his own right.'

John shook his hand, 'I've seen your name in the documentary credits, I believe you were responsible for filming the life in the salt hills out from Shorakai?'

'Yep, that was Tarku,' Weston praised.

'An incredible feat,' John said, weighing Tarku's countenance as he spoke, but Tarku made no response.

'Come on, last person for you to meet,' Weston urged. John had to swallow to stop his heart bursting out. This was the girl Scott had told him about, this was the girl he'd seen in the footage from Shorakai, this was the girl that might be his daughter. The slimmest of hopes, the chance that fate had at last been kind. John tried not to stare at her, he had been trying not to the whole time he had been on board so far.

'John,' Weston introduced, in complete oblivion to all their new guide was feeling, 'this is Melissa.'

'Melissa,' John repeated, as a gentle smile warmed his face.

Part 2: The Last Guide

CHAPTER 25:

I am no soldier, Kyu.

The tuna were feeding voraciously in their enormous sea-bound tanks completely unaware that another conflict had begun in some far distant corner of the world. Workers toiled along the far reaching jetties, repairing, feeding and cleaning. Divers worked below the surface, checking the equipment after the last quake. Along the shore the daily column of algae gatherers could be seen walking with their large sifting nets from the bloom site back into the villages, to spend the heat of the day sheltered at the base of Oconia's low mountains, protected and cool, after stretching and draping their collection on the stones to gather at the end of the day - the uses these people had found for the otherwise destructive plant were astounding.

To this place, our traveller and his way had arrived some days ago. Kyu had created quite a stir when they arrived in the small community. She had been here before many times but the people never ceased to be amazed by the giant creature. She followed Scott wherever he went, drifting high in the sky above him or near about, casting a great shadow onto the ground below. She was larger than most ships, and endowed with a skin that seemed impervious to hazardous atmospheric conditions. She especially liked it when Scott was near the sea, as she could converse with the porpoises that swam below her. But in the days since the tremor, Kyu had allowed herself to be harnessed and with her strength and Scott's guidance, they had helped in the recovery effort here on Oconia.

With the exception of Shorakai, Oconia held the largest expanse of ocean anywhere on earth, but even so, it was split into a series of lakes. If it was a clear day and you had an exceptionally good eye, or a telescope, you could see from one side of the largest lake to the other. Most of the ocean had fallen away and turned to steam as the earth had begun to splinter. But that was a long time ago, and to everyone alive in the present time the story of the collapse is like a myth, for this is the way they have always known the world and it was hard to imagine a place so different to what they knew. But even so, a watchful eye was kept on the water levels of the lakes, and a careful plan ensured the vegetation and the shape of the hills surrounding was maintained, as these things were known to keep the land of Oconia protected almost with its own micro-climate.

Today, Scott Thomas and Kyu were worn out from their work helping to restore things to normal after the last great shift, one little tremor can cause so much damage. Scott sat and leant against a packing shed, looking out across the sea, clad only in cargos and boots, and that cotton scarf about his neck. Kyu rested on a far ridge as well, tossing around in the sand as she stretched and relaxed, and snorted happily.

This week Scott was on the tuna farm, in another few weeks he would start two months work translating for the Salamondan embassy, if the earth still existed then, he thought. He was savouring the last of the sun's warmth, the air was cooler as the evening came, but the bricks radiated the sun's heat still and was wonderful upon his tired back.

One of the managers of the farm came and sat beside him, offering him a smoke.

'No thanks,' Scott declined.

The other lit the cigarette and surveyed the afternoon as well. 'She's worked harder than any of us today,' the man said, motioning to Kyu.

'I'll say.'

'Would've taken weeks of manoeuvring without her help. Does she need anything? I'd like to show her our appreciation in some way, if we can.'

'She does have a taste for seaweed.'

'Seaweed?'

'Yes, I used to think she didn't eat anything except whatever swarming insects strayed into her mouth, but I have since found she does divert from our path if she's found seaweed. There's several streams in the wastes where it still grows.'

'I'll see if I can rustle any,' he breathed out, but sat there long in satisfied weariness.

The sun was setting in pink and red and gold. The odd boat drifted silently at its moorings, a few stray gulls sought shelter on the weather beacon at the end of the jetty.

'Better get the tuna fed I suppose,' Scott got up at last. He took a bucket, walking out along the jetty that stretched endlessly out into the ocean, tossing feed into the large tanks.

Kyu came close again, bringing her nose right down to him and snorting.

'What is it?' he rubbed her. She snorted again and nudged him gently. 'What?!' Kyu sighed a short sigh, but followed by a siren, quiet and long. 'You want to go?' Scott said. Kyu cried again, and flew towards the south-west, before flying back around and nudging him again.

'We came here like you wanted, do you really want to go again so soon?'

She sighed.

'You don't want to wait just a few weeks like we planned?'

She snorted.

'Can you give me two weeks?' Scott tried to bargain, 'Then we can be on our way again. Wherever you want I promise.'

She sighed again, but this time it was a sigh that caused him to stumble and hold onto the nearest railing. 'Hey, you don't do that with me Kyu, come on, what's got into you?! I'm not your puppet, we're friends! I can't just come and go all the time, I've got to make a living somehow you know!'

Kyu snorted and flew off to the other side of the sea.

'You talk to it?' queried the man who worked nearby, doing some repairs, 'does it understand you?'

'As clearly as you comprehend me. Yes, you understand me don't you girl?' And you can hear me all the way over there I know you can.' Her cry reverberated across the sea, but she was still angry with him.

'And do you understand that?'

'Some, but I'm always learning,' Scott replied, 'see how she's moving, she wants to be going somewhere. Where do you want to go Kyu?' Scott yelled across to her, his tanned arms outstretched and questioning. 'It's perfect here, don't you want to stay?'

She came close again suddenly, and again she called out in that dreamy underwater way, but this time she put her nose to his head as she cried, and for a moment Kyu held Scott in her world, and the notes of her song became light in his mind, like an echo-sounding of what she wanted him to see, the strokes of light condensed and became clear. Bombs fell, guns fired, a battle raged in the sky. Scott stumbled and fell back onto the boards of the jetty.

The other man went to Scott as he struggled to breathe. 'Tamashan!' Scott gasped, 'that was Tamashan?! I saw the tower! The port! Why do you want to go there Kyu! Of all the places, why there?' Scott yelled up, but she did not reply, just withdrew again over the ocean.

'What'd she say?' the man asked.

'I think she wants to go to Tamashan, why would she want to go to Tamashan?' Scott said to himself, stunned and puzzled.

'No, you don't want to be going there,' the man said matter-of-factly as he kept working with his resin, 'not at this moment in time.'

Scott despaired, 'My thoughts exactly.'

Scott pulled off the heavy work boots then sank wearily to the dinner table with the other workers. He put his head in his hands, of all the unfathomable things why did she want to go to Tamashan! Why now when it was so very dangerous?

'Here,' the manager placed the meal in front of Scott, 'eat up while it's hot.'

Scott tried to eat, he was hungry but his concern over Kyu's mood weighed heavier. Someone put the evening news on. The presenters really didn't have much more information about the conflict than they had already been over time and time again. They were essentially reporting on a lack of information, about being unable to contact anyone in Tamashan, or receive even the smallest report of what was going on, and Delevi would not be drawn to comment. Tamashan was dear to Scott, and it hurt to think the generous people there were in any way in distress. He sat there long in thought.

For several days the rift remained between the kyu and its rider, both were troubled, both were hurt. Scott couldn't understand her reasons, couldn't understand why she had gone so far to hurt him physically. Kyu moped too, also ashamed that she had done such a thing, but yearning to go.

One day Scott went and bought supplies at a little old store down the bay a bit, checking off the list of things he and Kyu would need for a long flight. They had not spoken, not since Scott had made it quite clear that he did not wish to go to Tamashan with the war there. Now he realised that all along he had trusted Kyu and never had she been wrong or led him into a situation that they could not get out of, and so he lugged all the gear right out to the end of the jetty and fell to his knees, looking up at Kyu as she came to meet him.

Scott spread out his arms, 'I am no soldier Kyu and I don't know what you expect of me, but I will go with you if you still want me to.'

The great creature again put her nose gently to his head, and cried to him. Scott breathed her music in like a tonic, and breathed out relief. Then Kyu let out a sad yet joyful sigh and rolled and dived through the air as if she were no more than a young pup and then she neared him again, awaiting him. He loaded all his belongings and equipment in and then jumped in himself, then Kyu closed the small opening. She let out another siren as she headed out of Oconia's calm atmosphere and began the long journey toward Tamashan.

The tiny island of Soamé

Kyu took her favourite route, seemingly in the wrong direction as it was up towards Shorakai, but then she flew across via the lift of the south-west gulf-stream, through the great forests they call Peacefire. Forests of overgrown doe-weed, as the northerners call it, growing up out of the wastes, though its names are far more elegant and noble in other tongues. How it lived out here, so tall like trees, was a mystery, a wonder and a symbol of hope. Its golden-olive fronds brushed Kyu as she glided through their canopy. She called out in ecstasy and sighed to Scott, telling him every detail of its beauty, playing like a sea otter, in and out of the branches, munching on its rich leaves as she went. Scott lay comfortable and blissful in the cartilaginous framework of her chest.

It requires a great deal of trust to lie like this in a Kyu, and travel for hours and even days at a time, not seeing where you were going, your own activities lit only by the faint, warm luminescence of her exposed cartilage. There was also a very great trust on the part of the kyu, to trust another being that much to let it inside its very frame where it would be capable of doing great damage. Scott stirred himself after a while and set to giving Kyu a massage. A rub inside the chest was almost a necessity for a kyu on long flights. Many other creatures lived unseen and untouched along this sward of peace where Kyu flew, strange and beautiful things not seen anywhere else on earth. It was with a sad heart that Kyu came to the other side of the forests and kept on.

After a while Kyu sang to Scott, a barely audible, low song. It was calming and his heart beat slowed down and further down, and without realising what Kyu was doing Scott was soon deeply asleep, then Kyu changed her path completely, heading back towards the south-east. Something had made her turn. She bypassed Satsuan and Rorona, and went further, fast and deep.

Many hours later Kyu came to the tiny island of Soamé. She relaxed her pace and let her chest open up so Scott could enjoy the flight in. He watched the world grow suddenly closer and closer beneath them, and was surprised and worried that it was not Satsuan or Rorona he saw below them but this little isle of Soamé. For Soamé was not on the direct path to Tamashan, indeed, although the little isle was very well in itself it was on the way to a part of the south no self-respecting nomad would take himself, considering the present circumstances, for it was on the way to Delevi and Vahrna, and east of here was the Architenebrae.

'You are pushing the boundaries here Kyu, why are we in Soamé?'

Kyu sensed Scott's amazement and distress and she sang to him again.

'You want me to see my father is that it?'

She didn't answer. 'Well, I might as well, seeing as we're here,' he said, rubbing the wall of her throat there where he sat, 'when you're ready to go let me know.'

Soamé was perhaps one of the smallest populated islands in the entire world. and on a person per square metre survey it would be the most heavily populated, but it thrived. It was always a lively place, full of interesting characters. Long before the north islands had even become known it had been a major port of call, and the air around it was surprisingly less polluted than elsewhere, though the same couldn't be said of the few square miles of earth that it was. But it wasn't just population and pollution that was of concern on Soamé. If one cared to look one would have seen that much of the rim of the tiny island was held up by giant props, networks of bolted structures that reached down into the fog to the unliveable wastes below, structures that were continually being checked and reinforced by the authorities in an effort to prevent the collapse of their beloved isle.

But one thing you will notice despite all this, is that the people are on the most part happy and cheerful. The spirit of the Soaméans has always been extremely effervescent. They are much like imps out of fairy tales, at least, that's what they reminded Scott of. The cheeky, rascally character who means well but causes a little drama, accidental catastrophes. They have tear-drop shaped faces, and are quite short, and many of them, Scott had discovered, had different variations of colour blindness, particularly when it came to changing currency. That is, it was easy for the Soaméans to pick out the tourists, and swindle them appropriately.

The children of Soamé ran out from the apartments, alleys and rooftops where they played and hurried up to the over-belt, getting as close as they could to see Kyu, gasping as her large shadow drew over them. Many other ships were flying every which way, big and small, passengers and cargo, and all so different. But who cared to watch a ship? Ships were there any day and every day, but a kyu was indeed a rare sight. Even adults stopped their work to see her. She came low and Scott jumped out with his pack. The children managed to get through all the fences and crowd around him, making his way slow as they were eager to ask him questions and beg him for treats and spare coinage. Kyu remained there for a bit, letting the little hands touch her throat.

After escaping the crowd Scott set off with a purpose, heading to the buildings of government where his father was sure to be ensconced. But on arriving he was informed the hour was late and all staff had left for the day. He checked his watch and realised his mistake, Soamé did have an unusually early end to their working day, so he promptly turned towards his father's rented apartment. He tried the bell, but there was no response. Knocked, tried to peer in the windows. No one. He sat and waited outside for over half an hour but no one came. He sighed, and went to find the manager.

'Ah, master Scott,' a friendly old man greeted him as he entered the dusty little room. This room had been hard to find, being cramped and poorly signed and sitting in the obscurity of the haze at ground level. 'Come in, come in.'

'I wasn't sure you'd remember me,' Scott grinned.

'Not remember you!' the old man chuckled, 'the tall north boy who has to bend to fit through my doorway, of course I remember you. So what have you been up to? Travelling as usual I suppose?'

'Yes.'

'Ah if I was young like you, but then, I have always loved this place. So, tell me what you've been up to.'

'Oh, this and that, I'm actually just on my way through, but thought I'd stop in.'

'That's good of you, I'm glad you did. I suppose you'd like to take your things while you're here too?'

'Things?'

'Your father left them, said he'd already exceeded his baggage limit and couldn't take them with him, so you'd just have to sort it all out yourself when you came around to it.'

'I was actually going to ask you where he was, I've just been up to the apartment, it's all shut up. So he's not here?'

'No,' the old man shook his head, 'didn't you know? He was re-assigned to Tamashan.'

'No!?'

'I'm sorry to be the one to tell you, I thought you would have known.'

'Tamashan,' Scott repeated, and rubbed his head. 'How long ago?'

'He's been gone not even two weeks.'

'Did he get there? I mean, would he be there now? Or do you think this supposed war would have already begun? Could he be stranded on Satsuan do you think?'

'I don't know, we played a game of chess and he told me he was going, I don't know any details.'

'Tamashan!'

'He said your government thought he was getting too old to be out here and so they were sending him there to be more comfortable. He thought it would be better, because out here he is doing all the work by himself, but there he would at least get a secretary because there are always northerners coming and going, but he also was regretting having to go.'

'I hope he was delayed and didn't make it to Tamashan before this conflict broke out!'

'As do I master Scott, as do I. Now, why don't you have a seat there and I'll find the things he left for you, there was a stack of books.'

Scott waited while the old man searched for his things.

'Here they are,' the old man lifted the heavy pile of books and put them on the table. 'I hope you don't mind I had a bit of a read of some. Your father says you scavenged these from remnants of past cities out in the wastes?'

'Yes, these are reproductions of some ancient texts I discovered. It keeps me busy when there's no other work. The dealers in Corrio can't get enough, they say people are longing for this stuff, any way to escape the current reality, to laugh and cry at the way things were.'

'It is incredible.'

'But it's not an easy process, it's costly and tedious work - to find books preserved enough to pull apart, artisans skilled enough to do the pulling and the reproduction, and translators of these lost and ancient writings. It takes a great deal of time and patience, that's why they're here,' Scott laughed, 'I left them with some experts and left them to it. They must have finished and left the results with my father, I'm eager to read them myself.'

'The world is so very different in these books master Scott, proof that the world was once glorious, and oceans and seas and all things green taken for granted,' the old man shook his head, 'I did not realise how different it was.'

'You will notice one thing though,' Scott said, 'the sky may have been blue but they still fought over the same things.'

'Unfortunately you're right there. Oh, there was also this in what he left for you.' The old man handed Scott a digital tablet.

'Ah, that will be the digital copies. Always best to have a back up. Thank you for keeping these for me, I am much obliged.'

'My pleasure. Now are you coming to the festival tonight?'

'Which festival is that?'

'Oh I don't know! Shortest day? Longest day? Middlemost day? Something about the something,' the old man coughed and hit his chest before continuing, 'I don't think anyone really knows, and I say what does that matter! I think the calendar makers keep inventing the holidays so we'll all forget that we're going to fall off the face of the earth tomorrow, or the next day, or the day after that. There'll be dancing and food and all sorts of things. And, my little niece will be playing the hano-imo. You remember her, last time you were here you told her the humorous anecdotes of your father's time on Rorona and now she has told them to half of Soamé I'm sure. You must tell us more of these tales. Will you come? Say that you will,' he coughed again, 'Sorry, do excuse me, keep getting too much dust in the windpipes. Of course we'll understand if you're keen to be on your way.'

'I was planning to leave when I'd seen the old man, and with this news I should certainly go without too much delay.'

'Ah, of course, I understand,' the old manager was obviously rather sad about that, so Scott changed his tone.

'But it would only be a few hours wouldn't it, and I do need to eat,' Scott encouraged. 'If Kyu will agree I shall stay for a little while, and I'll try to think of a good story to tell.'

'It would be good to have you.'

'Thank you Mr Ornlo. Do you think I could leave some of these books with you? I don't think I should take them all with me now, but I'll take a few, and I'll take the digital copies of course.'

'It would be my pleasure to keep them for you.'

'I won't hold you to it. If something happened and you had to sell them that would be alright too, but if you'd enjoy them feel free to keep them and share them around.'

That evening the festivities began and Scott was pulled this way and that, laughing with the children, having a drink with the old chaps, reminiscing with other travellers, and finally getting up to tell the story he had promised to tell.

'I am not one who often gets up to tell stories, but it seems that whenever I come to Soamé our good Mr Ornlo there will not let me escape without telling a tale. So by request, here I am.' There was a small applause, then he began.

'I wondered what story I would share with you, and I had decided on another, but I've changed my mind because recently I have been reminded of another story which likely many of you have heard, but not my telling of it. It happened when I was just a boy, on Rorona. I do apologise in advance to those of you who do not enjoy sentimentality. You will have guessed of course, that I am going to share with you my account of how Amiana, the ambassador of Shorakai, met the northern soldier, John Mark.'

Many of the group now picked up their heads to listen.

'One day, when John and the crew were giving our ship a going over, covered in grease and sand and sweat, painted with the red dust of that place as we all were, she turned up. You see, the Shorakaian ship was beside ours, and she had come, I believe, to thank her crew and tell them that the talks had been extended so they would not need to be ready for some days. She had turned to go, but she came towards us, out of curiosity maybe, I don't know. I remember she wore this flowing garment of blue that did not even appear to be a cloth, but a living and moving breath that wrapped about her and seemed more part of her than my own skin feels to me. She was elegant and stately, though John would say, like a child at the same time. All the crew stopped what they were doing as she came, at the sight of her compelling manner and beauty. John went to her to ask what help we could be.

'At first she didn't seem to really notice him, or any of us. She walked towards us, running her hand along part of our ship, as though she knew the ship, as though it meant something. I remember how her eyes lit up and she smiled then, as she asked John 'Beyu Nordan?' John nodded, 'North Island States' he said, and gave her our names, lastly he put his hand on his chest 'John Mark,' and he bowed slightly to her, as the crew of her ship did and because, as an envoy, she should be respected in every way. The crew laughed at him, and I also as I was with them. He said to me later that her eyes swam in her fresh face, searching him, as she put her arm across her chest and she spoke her name. I shall never forget how it sounded coming from her lips. No northerner can reproduce their language but we try. Our best effort at her name is Amiana. I'm sure she had so much more she wanted to say then, but something stopped her, and she walked away.

'After that meeting, John started trying to converse with the crew of her ship as well, they were generally good natured, though a little wary of us as most were at the time, as we northerners were still somewhat of a novelty and untried. It was a day or two later John ventured into the town, which for crewmen was almost illegal during the talks. But he just had to see her didn't he, and he dragged me along with him so he'd have a good excuse if he were stopped, I being the northern ambassador's son. I was glad to go with him. It was a sight I'll never forget, a place totally different to anything we knew then. Out there at the port, in that seemingly desolate place, what we had seen was only a glimpse of Rorona, it was like coming to the north islands and landing in the middle of the desert and thinking that was what all the terrain was like. It was definitely harsher than the environment at home, well it seemed that way to me, but it was not all like that. We could see the silver city from the port, but it was no more than an illusion until we were within it. In the middle of the city there was a building that stood out amongst the rest, to me at the time it seemed like a brighter silver beacon out of all the rusting spires, and red sand habitations, like an immense polished spearhead thrown by some great force causing it to pierce the crust of the earth and now it sat shining in all its magnificence. This is where the talks were being held, in this phenomenal feat of architecture. Whether it was constructed from the first or converted from a great ship which had plunged to the earth - it was grand. It stood high, and as we found out it also was built deep into the ground – perhaps it had been a great meteor which had been transformed – I never have found out, but if you've been to Rorona you know the building of which I speak, the building in which the conference hall lies.'

There were many nods throughout the listening group.

'No one seemed to notice as we walked through its levels. People were going every which way about their own business. Broushas's walked along with their sad eyes diverted, quietly chanting their monotone prayers. Roronan officials rushed about everywhere. At last we saw a member of the Shorakaian attaché and followed him at a distance for some time through the labyrinth of corridors. As he descended, the halls and archways became not like the crisp white and blue-grey architecture we'd seen above but gradually moved into older corridors carved into the red earth. Down here the Shorakaian disappeared. We found ourselves alone, I would have been glad of that save for the fact that we were now completely lost in a place we should not even have been. As we walked hesitantly along there came a voice behind us. It was her of course, the beautiful Shorakaian. 'JohnMark.' She always said his name quickly together as if it were one word. He was stunned, speechless, not that it would have done him any good if he could have said anything. He had been looking for her, perhaps just to glimpse her, and here she was, she had found him. He had never thought of what he would say or do. She motioned for us to follow, we did. She led us into their rooms. For a moment there was an argument between her and another of her number, but she won of course and sat us down on large cushions and poured us iced tea, though she took none herself. For a short time nothing passed between us, till John couldn't keep quiet 'Lady Amiana, I'm sorry to intrude, I did not mean to put you in this position, I just wanted to see you again,' he said.

'Minayun JohnMark, minayun,' she whispered and touched his lips. We had a small meal together. I found it funny as a boy, how they just sat there and watched each other eating and drinking. I think they both forgot that I was there. I listened as he tried to explain our lives and homes to her, and she to us. But they usually just gave up and laughed. We got the impression that she had a meeting to get to so we stood and I could see John trying to think what he should do. He took the eagle pin off his uniform from the shirt collar and pinned it to her sash. I shall never know what she would have done next for another one of them entered the room and called her hastily away before ushering us out without acknowledging us, if that is possible. So we were again alone in that place and it took some time to find our way back to the ship.

'The other of the crew did not believe a word John said about dining with the ambassador and when I confirmed his story they only laughed and said that he must have put me up to it. Even we, who were so new to the international community knew that Shorakai was a big deal. They are respected and revered like no other country, and so too their ambassador, so the crew would not believe us. That is, until Amiana herself came out again two days later. John happened to be asleep at the time. She came up to us and simply said 'JohnMark?' We told her he was sleeping but she just kept saying JohnMark, JohnMark... so the crew let her on board and then she understood what we had been saying. I don't know what she did but we all heard him shout. He was, as you may guess, most surprised to be woken up by a strange girl that he happened to be in love with, and all the crew laughing at him. He told me later he was so amazed that this veritable angel had come to see him. 'Yun JohnMark' she took his hand, lead him past the whooping crew; he was still half dazed. She got him onto some kind of transport buggy thing that hovered over the ground effortlessly and before I knew it they were gone. John was completely in shock when he returned, in a good way that is. The driver had got them into the city, right back to that beacon. And we pressed him to tell us everything. She'd taken his hand and pulled him after her, turning around now and then to repeat what she had said on the ship – 'come John Mark, come'. They entered the beacon and made their way until they came to the place that was just one great room, rather empty at the time but for a few cleaners. She led him into the centre of the room. He told us there was so much to take in - intricate details on the floor, filigree patterns that went every which way, like a piece of art, and yet he believed every facet of it had some meaning or purpose for those in Rauron are not a people that usually place considerable effort in decoration. Yet even with so much to look at he could not look away from Amiana for long I am sure, so I am afraid he gave us no more detail about the building, but he was definitely in awe and completely overwhelmed. She pulled him round to look at her directly, and told him to speak. Then in a moment he realised that she had spoken and he had understood. Those of you who have heard anything much of Rorona will know of the translation capabilities of that hall. That's where she'd taken him. That's why she ran out to get him.'

'Time is a thing we do not have much of JohnMark, they will come here for talking very soon,' she said.

'They must have said so much in such a short time, for all I know is that their conversation ended with her asking him, if she could convince the others in her company, to please return with her to Shorakai. So the next week when the talks had ended he packed his things and was ready to go if she would come for him. The crew, and myself, and my father, were amazed that he was prepared to go to a totally foreign place for this love that had sprung up and flourished within two weeks. But we could see why he loved her. She was fine, delicate, lovely and yet strong both in body and psyche. He went with her, under the questioning watch of the company of Shorakai. And that's where my part in his story ends.'

'Tell the rest, Scott,' Mr Ornlo spoke up, 'I know there's more.'

'The rest is a sad tale,' Scott excused, 'and today is a day for celebration.'

'Please tell us,' Mr Ornlo's niece added her voice. Scott looked around. Many in the small crowd were nodding, interested to hear the rest.

'Well, I saw Mr Mark not long ago,' Scott told them. 'He was alone, working on an outpost in the north. You see, within a year of meeting Amiana they were married, they had a child, a daughter, but within another year Amiana had been assassinated while away, as you may have heard if you were around at the time, and later their daughter was abducted from John's workplace. He searched for her, but it's been so long I think he's given up. For his sake, I will ask you to keep your eyes open, look out for each other, and also if you see a girl, who would be 21 this year, who would be part northern, part Shorakaian, ask her of her history, for John, ask her just in case she could be his lost girl.'

'We will Scott,' Mr Ornlo nodded, as did many in the crowd.

'I give you his thanks,' Scott said.

After the tale, Scott sat back down with the small group of other travellers. Under the glow of many lanterns, and amid the dimming noise of the celebrations they chatted casually about the state of things.

'Has anyone heard news of Tamashan?' Scott asked them. 'I have to go in that direction and to be honest I'm quite apprehensive.'

The travellers agreed, but the answers were all that no-one knew anything more, and they were all sticking well clear.

'At least you're not headed to Delevi,' another said. 'My company is sending me there, drew the short straw, all the other reps are going to lovely places like Satsuan, or the north.'

'Have you seen pictures of the sovereign?' another said.

'Which one? Delevian? Iviqal Viyal?'

'Yes Viyal, the guy's mad, he has these two giant blue stones actually set into his face, right on his cheek bones.'

'Midnight lazuli. I heard he collects them,' said another.

'I've seen Sovereign Viyal up close,' a boy in the group spoke up, 'the stones are shaped like ovals, and when he closes his eyes it's like the stones are another set of eyes that keep watching.'

'That's whacked!' said another.

'It's strange, but the stones are not the only thing he collects,' the boy continued, 'you should see the rooms in the palace, he collects stones, there are so many, and also plants, he has many gardens, and he also collects interesting creatures, and also people.'

'He collects people?'

'Yes, he has a slave from every city he visits, he keeps them and looks upon them like treasures, and the further they have come from and the more endangered their race, the more highly he prizes them - some in his collection are the last of their people, as the places they have come from have since fallen. Because of him, the collecting of rare peoples has become a thing of competition amongst the wealthy on Delevi and Vahrna.'

'I don't recall that he's been to the north,' Scott put in, 'just as well, as there's no slave trade there,'

'There's no slave trade in de norde?' the boy said, seeming surprised by the fact.

'Well, nothing legal, but of course it still goes on.'

'You're right though, I don't think I've seen a nordaner in his collection, but I believe I heard he was scheduled to make his first visit to the north soon as well. So maybe he will have one after that.'

'Unless he calls it off so that he doesn't have to answer questions about what he's doing attacking Tamashan,' said another.

'He doesn't care what anyone thinks of him,' the boy spoke up again.

'How do you know so much?' the other travellers asked the boy.

'I worked in the palace,' he said simply,

'So do you know why Delevi attacked Tamashan?'

'No,' the boy looked at his drink and said nothing more after that.

Many conversations rounded, but Scott eventually made his excuses to the group and made his way back to the over-belt where he could meet up with Kyu, but even as tired as he was Scott was alert enough to realise he was being followed. It was one of the other travellers from the group tonight, the boy who had tried to remain inconspicuous throughout the evening after his first and last foray into the conversation, though he had obviously been very eager to listen to the discussion of the other travellers.

Scott turned and confronted the boy after a while, waiting until they were in a place where the boy couldn't duck away.

'What are you after kid?' Scott said.

The boy looked down a moment shyly, dismayed that he had been found out and that there was nowhere he could run.

'Come on,' Scott laughed, 'if you were wanting to pick my pockets it's not going to happen alright, besides, you won't find anything much, I travel pretty light.'

'No I wasn't going to do that Mister,' the boy shook his head, angry at the suggestion.

'What was it then? If you want a cigarette, I don't smoke, if you want money, I've got none to spare.'

The boy didn't want to say but it came out at last, 'I just need a ride, I heard you say you're going towards Tamashan and I have to get to Rorona, I just thought maybe I'd follow you and try to stow on your ship, that's all.'

Scott grinned. Poor kid, he didn't know what he was in for. 'You were going to stow on my ship?'

'Yes.'

'Have you seen my ship?' Scott chuckled.

'No.'

'I see. What are your plans boy?' Scott asked in a friendly way, though trying to gauge the character of the young man, 'What was your business here on Soamé? Why do you have to get to Rorona?'

'I have no business here,' the boy replied, 'it's where my ride ended and I haven't been able to find another yet to get me to Rorona. I really need to get to Rorona.'

'Well, if you really need a ride, I might be able to take you,' Scott offered, 'it's not too far out of my way.'

'Really?! I had been going to see if I could hitch with the Soamé courier company but they keep delaying, it seems the rifts are very temperamental lately, so if it's possible,' the young man seemed a little uncertain, hesitant, but said, 'that'd be great.'

'Well, I'm not certain it's possible yet, but I'll ask the pilot and see. I don't think it will be a problem.'

'Are you going through to Salamonde then?' the boy asked, 'because if you are I know it's a little bit out of the way for you but I could do some cleaning or something to pay my part towards the fuel.'

'No, I had been planning to go to Salamonde but not anymore.'

'Oh, so where are you headed?' the boy asked.

'Ah, Tamashan, actually.'

'What?! You're not serious?'

'My ride wants to go there, so I'm going there, plus there's the fact that my father's probably there and might be caught up in all of this, which would explain why my ride was so eager for me to go, I will have to make my apologies to her. But there you are, seems I should have trusted her from the beginning.'

The boy was confused, 'Your ride?'

'Oh, forgot to say, I'm Scott,' the tall blonde held out his hand and shook the young man's, 'Scott Thomas.'

'Sovarlay,' the boy gave his name, but still did not understand what was going on. His look of confusion softened the kyu rider.

'Sorry, you don't have to come with me, but if you'd like a ride in a kyu, and if she agrees, then you're most welcome.'

'A kyu!' Sovarlay exclaimed, at once fearful and amazed. 'You mean the kyu I saw this afternoon was yours! It's huge!'

'She's not mine kid, I'm hers. Wait on, I'll ask her if it's ok,' Scott looked up into the darkness, 'hey Kyu, do you want to take Sovarlay to Rorona on our way?'

At that moment a call came from Kyu, so soft and searching, others may not have noticed more than if it were a westerly wind, or the slow wail of a truck's brakes on a distant highway, but Scott listened and followed her cry as it settled on the boy and searched him, the boy rubbed his arms and shivered as his hair stood on end.

Kyu sighed in agreement but she relayed to Scott the image of what she saw. Under the hat, the short hair, the daggy shirt and cargos - this was no boy, this was unmistakably a young woman, disguised.

'That's interesting,' Scott whispered, somewhat bemused, 'are you sure Kyu?' Kyu sighed again. Scott saw her again, but he also saw the knife hidden in her belt and the cheap pistol tucked into her bag, with a few spare bullets. 'You're sure it's alright to go via Rorona?' Scott looked up and asked Kyu yet again, as now he was having doubts himself, but Kyu affirmed. 'Alright then, well,' Scott turned to this would-be passenger, 'Kyu says it's ok, so are you coming?'

'I want to come, but aren't kyus temperamental? What if it takes a disliking to me? I have heard others speak terrified of them.'

'Well, she can sense fear like a dog.'

'Legend in Delevi says their siren can split the bones inside of you.'

'It could be true, like I said, you don't have to come, but the offer's there if you're not afraid, and if you've nothing to hide, you've no reason to be afraid.'

'I've nothing to hide,' Sovarlay was quick to reply.

'Good,' Scott smiled, 'now, tell me why you really have to get to Rorona?'

Sovarlay studied Scott a moment, then answered, 'There will be a television crew on Rorona, I have to see them.'

'I'm sure there are television crews here on Soamé.'

'No, it has to be this one. I've just come from Corrio -'

'Corrio? As in the north?' Scott raised his eyebrows.

'Yes. I saw on the TV before I left that this team from one of their stations was heading to Rorona next.'

'Weston Alamo's team?'

'I don't know all their names.'

'Why do you need to see a television crew? Why that one?'

The girl in disguise weighed Scott with her eyes again, then looked aside, 'That is my business.'

'Fair enough. What if we miss them on Rorona?'

'Then I will follow where they go. I have to find them.'

'Alright then. So it's settled. We're taking you to Rorona. Come on.'

CHAPTER 26:

My name is Sjyntani

Scott came to Kyu, and Kyu lowered gently so he could reach her. He climbed inside, hauling his amazed and uncertain passenger after him. As Kyu made her way out of Soamé and headed for Rorona Scott made sure his passenger was comfortable, then lay back and put his head down for a little while.

Sometime later Scott got up to go and give Kyu a rub, he smiled, remembering the reactions of the Soaméans as he'd told the story tonight. He thought more about his passenger, the boy, who wasn't a boy, but a girl, brave and alone. He looked around for her, under the few blankets and around the pillars of Kyu's cartilage. Kyu sighed, telling Scott where she was. Scott smiled, and soon peered around a certain pillar behind which she sat, head on her knees and tears in her eyes. She looked up at him, quickly trying to neaten her hair and reaffix her hat.

'I can't sleep,' she said, a touch bitterly, but sincerely as she tried to wipe her face, 'my heart troubles me, this creature searches my soul.'

'Yeah,' Scott knelt down, 'that can happen. Listen, are you hungry? I've got some fruit and some random bits and pieces, if you are.'

'No,' she sniffed, 'I'm not hungry, I am too guilty to be hungry. I should have told you, I do have something to hide.'

'Oh? Surely it can't be that bad?'

'It is!'

'It's ok,' Scott laughed, 'I know.'

She pulled back, 'What do you know?'

Scott shrugged, 'You're a girl, right?'

Her sorrow turned to indignation, 'What! How can you know that? Am I not a good actor? But I can fool everyone!'

'No, you're a great actor. I didn't figure it out, Kyu told me.'

'She can do that?'

'Yes.'

'Oh. Well, I have a knife and I can use it, so don't come any closer!'

'Hey, I know, I know you've got a gun in your bag too, but it's alright, I don't want anything from you,' Scott held up his hands and tried to calm her, 'I haven't come near you all this time, surely that proves something to you.'

'When did you know?'

'I knew before I pulled you up.'

'Oh. Why didn't you say something?'

'I didn't want you to feel like you feel now. I'm sorry, but I'm not the one hiding things. I think a little thanks and maybe a little explanation would be nice, not a knife in my face.'

'Don't be angry with me, it's safer for me, it's not safe to travel alone, but safer, a little, for a boy than a girl. I just walk along like I belong to someone ahead and no one pays any notice of a boy, usually, but if I am a girl this is more dangerous, the moment I appear like a stray, I have problems if I'm a girl.'

163

'I understand.'

'I'm not that young either,' she spoke now with some force, 'I'm not like 13, I'm more than 20. Not naive, not innocent either, so don't be thinking I don't know myself nor men, nor about the world. I know a lot.'

'Probably more than I do,' Scott nodded.

'Agreed.'

Scott grinned to himself at her way, but continued politely, 'So, is Sovarlay your real name?'

'No.'

'What is your name?'

She turned away, hot tears coming back to her eyes, but only a few that she quickly wiped off on her sleeve. 'I never cry like this! I must be tired,' she yelled at herself, but her voice was still strong and even accusing, 'It must be your Kyu, she's cruel to tell me to you. Why do you have to know! I don't even know you! How can I even trust that you will take me to Rorona now?'

'Have I done wrong by you yet?'

'No.'

'So, what harm can I do you by knowing your name?'

She was silent.

'Alright, I don't want to press you, but it would be nice to know. After all, you do know my name, and where I come from, and where I'm going.'

She sniffed, then looked back at him, she held her hand to her chest, 'Na mei ne Sjyntani.'

'Sjyntani?' Scott shook his head, wondering why she was hesitant to tell him that. 'That's a beautiful name,' he encouraged.

She scoffed, 'Don't tell me that I have a beautiful name or that I'm pretty or lovely; if you're easy with your compliments I will not trust you. Besides, it's not a nice name really, if you think so you don't know the meaning.'

'Oh?' Scott was trying hard to keep a straight face at her endearing frankness.

'Have you been to Flythsyge?'

'Only for the briefest moment, have you?'

'That's the first place I can remember that I knew the name of, and what I remember is them always bargaining, bargaining. You know what they say?'

Scott shook his head.

'All my life, this is what they say when they talk about me, *'es jynala-tani en talle'*. You know that? You understand? They said it so many times they got tired and lazy and so they just started saying Sjyntani.'

'The young girl is for sale,' Scott understood. 'I'm so sorry, I'm a bit thick sometimes. I could call you something else if you like, I could keep calling you Sovarlay?'

'Sovarlay? It's a boy's name. If I am dressed like a boy and you see me in some place where there are other people and need to call my attention Sovarlay is good, but otherwise Sjyntani is my name, I will keep it for now. I'm sorry I deceived you, you have only been kind to me. And now your kyu makes my heart ashamed, but it was not safe for me.'

'No, I understand. Listen, Sjyntani, you don't have to worry about Kyu, she searches everyone, and you don't have to worry about me, alright, I know how to be a gentleman.'

'Gentleman! Bah!' she scoffed, 'I have found gentlemen to be the worst of them all, for they have many foul thoughts behind their pretty faces.'

'Alright, what would you have me be to you?' Scott ask her sincerely, 'How can I make you feel safe till we get to Rorona?'

'How far is Rorona?'

'A few hours, maybe.'

She thought, then her face lit up, 'Do you play chess?'

'I do,' Scott answered her, but then corrected, 'Well I did, but I haven't for a while.'

'Teach me. They play chess in the palace on Delevi and I watched, but it was not my place to play.'

'I don't have a set here.'

'But you have things. We can make a set.'

'Alright,' Scott laughed, 'I'll teach you chess.'

Scott drew the grid of the board on Kyu's skin, where he touched the lines lit with a twinkling bluish luminescence, and he found hazelnuts for the pawns, and some of the other players they used other small food items and some they used shells left over from Scott's time on Oconia. Scott explained the pieces, but Sjyntani seemed to know a great deal already.

'Sjyntani, what did you do in the palace?' Scott asked, trying to be friendly as they played.

'I thought chess was a silent game,' she scolded Scott, 'no one speaks when they play on Delevi.'

'Perhaps I don't take my game as seriously,' Scott smiled.

Sjyntani studied the board and made a move, but she answered Scott's question, 'I didn't do much. Some work.'

'Were you an employee? An aide to the staff?'

'I can't tell you. You might get in trouble, or you might get me in trouble.'

'Sjyntani, from what you said on Soamé, you must have been close to the sovereign.' Scott moved his pawn forwards. 'Were you - did he buy you? Did the sovereign buy you? Were you one of his slaves? One of his treasures, as you put it?'

Sjyntani studied the board, then looked at Scott. Her pixie-like face, with her deep, ocean-green eyes, looking up at him. He knew he had guessed right, but she just answered, 'Can we play?'

'How did you escape?' he pressed her, his concern and interest in the little waif growing with everything more he knew.

'I didn't say anything to you, you assume much,' Sjyntani tried to hold the issue aside and made another move, but Scott would not be dissuaded.

'But I'm right aren't I?'

'What do you want me to say?' she said, with some anger in her voice, 'I don't know you well enough to tell you the truth. You want me to feel safe till we get to Rorona. Teach me this game.'

Scott grinned, 'The way you're playing so far I think you know more than you're letting on.'

'This piece I don't understand.'

'That's the rook,' Scott explained, 'side to side or up and down but no diagonal moves.'

'But that seems too simple,' she complained, 'and I want to move to that square.'

They played for quite a while, eating the nuts that they won as pieces off the board.

'So you go to Tamashan to find your father?' Sjyntani asked.

'Yes, well, Satsuan first, hopefully I find him at the embassy there and don't have to go further.'

'He must be a good man. I don't know my father. I liked the story you told on Soamé, of that man John Mark who searched for his daughter for so many years. What does your father do?'

'He's an ambassador, embassy official or anything they need him to be really. He's gone between the southern postings as long as I can remember.'

'What of your mother?'

'She went everywhere with him. She was gorgeous cute, sounds funny to say that about your mother I know, but she was. She endeared everyone we met to our north island ways, and made it so easy for my father to do his job. She schooled me as we travelled, a very smart and wise lady, with a great sense of humour.'

'But she is not with your father now?'

'No, she died some years ago. She'd always been too delicate for this earth.'

'I'm sorry. I never knew my father or mother. I would like to pretend that they were like your parents, or like John Mark, but I don't think they were,' Sjyntani opened up. 'The first trader I remember told me he got me from a merchant who told him that he got me off my parents for buying them one meal. Who would do that Scott? Who would sell their daughter for a meal?'

'Desperate people, but it might not be true. Maybe the trader was just wanting to wear you down, make your spirit low so you'd be easier to manage.'

'I was never easy to manage,' Sjyntani grinned, but grew sad again at once, 'but I have been told those words all my life. That they sold me so they could fill their bellies. I never believed it, but I wish I could know my mother and father, what they were like, where they were from, why they sent me alone into the world.'

'Do you have any clues? Where do you think you're from?'

'The first auction I remember was in Flythsyge, so I had thought that I must have been born somewhere in the Arc, but I was probably close to six years old then, and I felt different, not like the people there, because everyone passing would stare at me. The other girls said it was because I was too pretty, but I don't think so, I think I was just different.'

'Six years. So you could have been brought from anywhere. Was the trader from Flythsyge?'

'I don't know, probably.'

'Sjyntani, how did you get out of it? How are you here?'

'Do you know Delevi at all? The capital Novocas? The city rises, the great museum, the parliament and residence of the sovereign?'

'A little, I was there once when I was younger.'

'Then you know it is a great city, and that they are strong people.'

'Indeed.'

'Scott, I have been bought and sold, bought and sold all my life, never for use, always for profit, you understand, always someone thinking they could get more for me than they had paid, and they were always right. I grew up changing hands continually, each buyer wealthier than the last, more proper than the last, each one trying to break my temper, and who I was, trying to improve me and make me into something else for re-sale. So I learnt many languages, I gained an education as good as any, I learnt the rules of courts and thrones -'

'But not of chess,' Scott moved, taking one of her pieces off the makeshift board.

'But not chess,' she smiled.

'Sorry, you were saying -'

'When I saw the sovereign's palace in Novocas, I knew it would be my journey's end, that I would be bought and sold no more, and so it was. Do you know the most surprising thing?'

'What's that?'

'I was relieved, relieved that I would be bought and sold no more.'

'I can understand that.'

'I haven't told anyone any of this. It feels strange just to say it out loud.'

'How long has it been since you escaped?'

'It can't even be two weeks, I don't know, it's a blur.'

'So recently, you must be all to pieces!'

'But I didn't escape, the sovereign sent me away.'

'What?! What happened?'

Sjyntani sighed, held her mouth a moment, and looked to the side as she fought back what might have been tears, and at last she unburdened herself to Scott's ready ears, 'It's my fault. The war on Tamashan, it's my fault.'

'What do you mean?! How, how can you possibly think you're responsible for it?'

She kept her composure as best she could as she continued, 'All was not as I thought it would be once I was bought. My relief soon became anguish. It was not the sovereign that bought me, it was the viceroy, Sona P'Lalo, but I was not for her collection. Her staff kept me in an isolated room for months, they were unkind, rough, but it was different to the kind of roughness I was used to, it was quieter, and not so much visible, and with clever words that made me more afraid of them than I ever had been afraid of the traders with whips and blades. All the time in that place they were teaching me some final things before I was to be presented to the sovereign.' Sjyntani swallowed, then continued. 'I already had a good knowledge of the language of Delevi from my previous owners, and almost every country in the south, but not what they wanted. They made me to learn the language of Shorakai, which I knew some well, but not fluently, and they taught me what it was to be from Shorakai, and how I was to act. They repeated to me that I was from that place, until I was convinced, and they made me learn the culture and history, the name of every governor since the last empress right up to Viléla, and they brought clothing and trinkets traditional to Shorakai and dressed me in them. When they thought I was ready, all the staff completely changed, I felt like the empress Syratreya myself, I never thought I could ever feel like that, all the staff of the viceroy, serving me! Making me into this perfect gift, ready to present to the sovereign.'

'There is something very Shorakaian about you,' Scott observed, 'they obviously saw that too.'

'You should see me when I'm not in disguise!' she laughed, 'and my hair, it was long then, very beautiful,' she added wistfully, 'but I had to cut it off for my disguise.'

'So they gave you to the sovereign?'

'Yes. I was presented to Iviqal Viyal, the viceroy said something to him, it was high Delevian which I am not proficient, but I believe she said, "in honour of your 38th year on the throne of Delevi, the people of Vahrna, and I, your viceroy, present you with this gift. Here is the one you've been wanting for so long, a rare Shorakaian for your collection at last." But I was a pawn in her game Scott, like in this chess I see them play. I didn't see it then,' she shook her head, 'I didn't see it till it was too late.'

'What do you mean? How were you a pawn in her game?'

'From the first minute I was his, the sovereign almost forgot his duty. He would take me to the gardens and just sit there, watching me, or showing me his collection of nearly extinct plants. Sometimes he would have me read to him, even proposed ordinances I would read him, he would watch the windows and get lost in his thoughts as I read. I know he is feared across the world, that people say he is hard and ruthless, but I had never known such kindness as he showed me. I think almost like a father, but different.' Her look soured at a thought she did not speak, and tears welled. Scott took her hand and held it firmly for just a moment. She continued, 'The more he was with me, the more decisions he left to his viceroy. She used me worse than he,' Sjyntani said with pain, 'she used me to weaken Sovereign Viyal, to distract him. I can't know for certain, but I believe it was she who planned this war on Tamashan, not him.'

'P'Lalo? Not Viyal?'

'I think so.'

'But he would have to give the order to his generals, they would not act just on her say so, surely?'

'She would bring him papers and he would sign them without a glance at what they were about, she or her aide would explain the content of the document and he would sign, just like that. I know the war wasn't his decision because even the same day we heard what had happened, before we had heard, there was another large tremor across Delevi, he watched the city, he watched as some mortar crumbled even from the palace tower, and he turned to me, and you know what he said? He said "not for much longer will the world have to fear our people. We are a terrible people, finally judged. The earth will consume us before too long, and so be it." And then he turned to me, and he said, "but not you, you must return to Shorakai, so at least you will have further days than I, and some hope of surviving this end." How could I let him believe any longer? That I was not as he assumed I was? I told him the truth, as I have told you, the truth that I do not know what land is my home, that it was all show, pressed upon me by viceroy P'Lalo, and I was too afraid to do otherwise. When I had said the words it seemed he knew at once there would be more that Sona P'Lalo had planned, more trouble that would come from my distraction and it came so soon, the news of the assault Delevian warships had begun on Tamashan. He upended his room and sent me from his sight, and soon I heard the feet of his guard come to my room. I thought he would have me strung up outside the law courts to face a slow death in shame, but he didn't. A ticket arrived for me, one way to Shorakai, with documents, passport, everything I would ever need to prove that I was Shorakaian.'

'Incredible, I would never have seen Viyal the way that you describe.'

'No one would. He would not let me see him after that. So I took the ticket, but I switched flights in the chaos at Soamé, and headed to the north instead.'

'To find the media crew.'

'No, to find a certain one of the crew who may be able to help me set things right. I cannot but think that if I had realised sooner what was happening, if I had not done what the viceroy said, then maybe this war with Tamashan would not have begun.'

'You can't know that.'

'I can be fairly certain. All those people Scott, all those people on Tamashan. I can't forgive myself. And Sovereign Viyal cannot deny it was his doing, how could any king admit not having his government and military in command?'

'What is P'Lalo's purpose? Do you know?'

'No, I don't know why she would do this.'

'So who is this one in the crew from TnTv? How do you think they can help?'

'I don't want to say, because you would probably try to convince me not to do as I must. And besides, they might refuse.'

'How did you find out about this person?'

'The sovereign taught me much as he showed me through his museum. He has a collection most terrible, of things that are to be feared, but things he boasts that the Delevian have conquered, many things are there, from the smallest disease you can see only through a microscope, to creatures larger than any I have ever seen, apart from Kyu, somehow preserved and entombed behind glass for observers to examine whenever they wish. He showed me some things in that place I did not expect to see, and he told me something then that he still feared. And if he holds this fear, then so would his soldiers and the rest of Delevi, and so would Vahrna. What he said reminded me of a rumour I had heard years ago. I am following that rumour, I know it is not much to hold to, but I've got no other option.'

'You might be surprised to know that I am acquainted with several members of that crew, if we're talking about the same crew, and of those I know I can't see how any of them could help in this situation more than to take your story and put it on film to show the world.'

'I don't want to be on film.'

'Then you better be careful going to this crew, Weston Alamo records just about everything he can.'

'I don't go to see that man, I go to see another. I will be careful, I know I have to be.'

'So it's not Weston, and I don't think it would be the captain?'

'Stop guessing, I'm not answering,' she scolded, but grinned at the same time, 'look I have your king checkmate, I think.'

'What?! How did you do that?'

'See, I am a good distraction, am I not?'

'You know, you remind me of someone.'

'I do?'

'This is the second time in just a few weeks, when never before. You remind me of John Mark's wife, Amiana, you know, you really do.'

'Do I? The lady in your story?'

Scott laughed, 'Yes, and she was cheeky funny like you too. Maybe you're his daughter, it wouldn't surprise me at all you know.'

'But I couldn't be, could I?'

'You're the right age, the right look, the right history. Although how you got out here would be good to find out.'

'I like the idea that I'd have a father like that,' she smiled, 'strong, and relentless in his search, and not one who sold me just for a meal.'

'I wouldn't want you to get your hopes up Sjyntani, but I thought I should say, and also because I've stopped believing in coincidences since being with Kyu. I don't think our meeting was a chance, it couldn't be.'

'And that would mean I would actually be Shorakaian? Or partly, at least.'

'Yes, it would.'

Sjyntani smiled, liking that thought very much.

CHAPTER 27:

Leaving the sculptured silver city

The engineer's daughter would have been 21 this year. John examined Melissa. Little Melissa. Pale tan-olive skin, brown hair, hazel eyes. She was around the right age. She had some of the right characteristics. Could she be his lost girl? John studied her, trying to see something in her, trying to see something of his wife, anything. Something of himself, anything.

'I saw the section you presented on Shorakai, that was ah,' John's heart was beating too fast, 'that was, ah, really well done, in the gardens there.'

'She's my newest photojournalist John,' Weston bragged, 'I have a good feeling about her, she will accomplish great things.'

Melissa blushed. John wished so desperately to find a trace of the girl he remembered, the girl he had hoped for, but without the costume of Shorakai, without the make-up, here in the indelicate light of the ship's cabin, he wasn't sure. He couldn't be sure. He didn't feel anything.

'I'm sure she will,' John agreed.

'If you can all take a seat,' Hardan called out as he headed to the cockpit, 'you can keep talking after we're on our way.'

'That's the spirit Hardan,' Weston rallied, 'let's keep on.'

Hardan took the little ship smoothly out of the port of Rorona, leaving the sculptured silver city below, and heading into the dark, on the way to Satsuan.

All was quiet as they flew out from Rorona. John rubbed his creased brow and wiped the dust from his eyes. When the flying reached the steady height the crew unbuckled and turned to talk to each other again, Tarku went to get himself some tea. As Weston rattled on nearby him John watched Melissa, watched her as she spoke and laughed with Astrid, and from time to time as all of them shared some pointless discussion. But the more he watched and the more they spoke, the more John felt as though the cup of his hope, which had been filling up though he'd tried to stop the flow, was now emptying rapidly. Melissa. John began to believe that she couldn't be his daughter, that she was just like any other young northern girl. John shook his head, inwardly cursing himself for being an old fool. He'd followed a ghost like he always had, the ghost of hope, the wish, the memory of blue sky, when now as he sat here he came to the conclusion that there was nothing of reality in it. A small huff, almost a laugh, escaped John as he came to this conclusion.

'You right John?' Weston asked, as he noticed John's shoulders sink.

'Ah, just a little weary,' John smiled.

'If you need something to eat you're most welcome to anything in the kitchen.'

'No, no, it's ah, it's been a big week that's all.'

'I feel the same,' Weston shared, but behind his light conversation, the producer too was unsettled. He was growing more and more concerned on how would he break the news to his crew - that the execs at TnTv wanted them to go

171

to Tamashan. On their itinerary they were scheduled in Satsuan for a week, no one would be expecting any change in that, but Weston only wanted to stop there to unload a few things and to pick up some other things and double check everything again before they headed to Tamashan, into danger. The producer, however, was still having a hard time finding the right words to articulate the change of plans, particularly as John hadn't come all this way on the basis of heading straight into a war zone and John made Weston nervous on the best of days. He went to speak a number of times, but stopped, and re-thought what he would say, and how he would say it. He looked at the old itinerary, at the maps. He exhaled. It wasn't a great distance to Satsuan, and from there they would head on to Tamashan, so Weston was keenly aware that he had to tell the crew soon, but he spun the balance wheel in his mind again, putting it off for as long as possible.

'Bad news West,' Hardan poked his head back into the cabin, 'there's an unexpected rift up ahead, just received a report, there's a weather system that sounds particularly nasty so I'm going to have to take a long way around to Satsuan.'

'What does that mean?'

'Maybe a two hour trip, instead of one. I suggest you all get some sleep while you can.'

'Good idea. Thanks Hardy, but are you able to come out to the cabin for a bit, I've got something I need to say to everyone.'

'Sure.'

Weston stood up and looked at every one of them. How could he say this? What would the reaction be all round? 'So,' Weston began, trying to rally his thoughts and his courage together. 'I have some news I have to share with you all.' His seriousness made them all pay closer attention. 'The thing is, well, you all heard the news about Tamashan, and you all know that Tamashan was on our itinerary but that I'd been planning an alternate route for us. Well, I have some news, and whether you think it's good or bad news is a different matter. The thing is that no one has any footage of the conflict, there's nothing, so TnTv have decided to send us there.' The crew were silent. 'Personally I am a little, well, more than a little apprehensive about it, but I also see it as a great opportunity, but, whether or not any of you want to go is another matter and I will not be holding you to anything. Each person must make their own decision about this. I'm sorry John, I feel I owe you the biggest apology, I would have let you know before you came to meet us on Rorona but it's all happened fairly quickly. If any of you wish to pull out you are welcome to find transport home when we stop on Satsuan. You will still be paid for your work up to now, and we will cover the cost of your return, and I certainly won't think the worse of you for going home.'

'Well,' Astrid laughed, 'the world might not even be here next week anyway, I'm in.'

'The same goes for me,' Hardan nodded after some thought.

'What about your family Hardan?' Weston asked, 'I mean, even I can fly this thing if I have to.'

'No, no, I signed on, I signed a contract, my family expect me to be away for a few months and they are proud of what I do. I will continue to be the pilot for the Blue Moon.' Weston patted Hardan's back, proud of his pilot, and glad of his continued company.

'Melissa?' Weston asked.

'Um,' Melissa began.

'Take your time,' John urged her, 'give full consideration to the gravity of what lies ahead.' He looked at Weston, almost pleading with him to add his voice to dissuade Melissa from going.

'What we're going into, what we'll find, it's not going to be pretty Melis, it's not something you can un-see, or undo,' Weston admitted, 'we ourselves could be captured, fired upon, killed. Do you understand that?'

'Yes, and I could die in the north too,' Melissa said quietly.

'But the manner of death would be different,' John said, 'the Delevian who now attack Tamashan are renowned for their ruthlessness. I'd gladly quit and take you back to north myself, you don't have to do this,' he almost begged, if she'd been his daughter he wouldn't want her to go.

She breathed in some courage and answered, 'Don't we owe it to the people of Tamashan to go and find out what's happened and let the rest of the world know?'

'It's war, darling. You're sure you want to do this?' Astrid added her voice, 'We might not even get there, the Vector didn't make it, it could be all for nothing.'

'I guess it could,' she shrugged her shoulders.

'And you still want to go?'

'Yes,' Melissa smiled and looked around at the rest of them, her eyes were bright, and she was calm and certain, 'there's not much for me to go back to, and I know it's only been a few weeks, but the last few weeks filming with this crew have been the best of my life,' Melissa said sincerely, 'I don't want to leave now.'

'Ok, so that's settled then,' Weston clapped his hands, 'What about you John?'

John spoke up, 'I'd like to go. I've friends on Tamashan.'

'Tarku?'

Tarku thought about it. They'd all tried to stop Melissa going, but she'd said her piece, there was nothing for it but to go as well. 'Need you ask?'

Weston grinned, 'Good man, I thought so. Right. Well, that's settled then,' he sighed, much relieved that that episode was over.

Another thread

Hardan dimmed the lights again and continued to fly the ship smoothly along. A couple of hours to catch some sleep and they were cashing in on the opportunity as they had indeed been working hard the last few days documenting Rorona. One by one the crew left the cabin for the bunks until Tarku was the only one left. As usual he sat in the back seat, now sipping his tea.

John investigated the hot drink options in the kitchen and opened every tea container sniffing the contents, finally choosing an ordinary black tea and fixing himself a cup. Then he went back to the cabin and sat opposite Tarku. 'I couldn't find your blend in the kitchen,' he began, 'it took me a little while, but I remembered that particular aroma.'

Tarku didn't afford John any attention apart from a momentary glance.

'Only one other person in the world I've met could drink what you're drinking, as strong as you're drinking it, and stay lucid,' John continued unperturbed, 'and they didn't like it, only drank it when they'd been worked up. I'm glad your drinking it now though because I know it means you're half-way sedated and I can say what I want to you and you won't lose it.'

Tarku looked at John but remained silent. He wondered if he should tell John what he knew about Melissa. He wondered if he should tell John the real history of his wife Amiana, and the real death she faced, and all the details he knew of her life in between, but in truth Tarku had half drugged himself, and it was easier not to say anything, there'd be too much explaining to do, besides, Tarku wanted a little longer to weigh the man before he told him anything.

John spoke again, 'You can keep on your sunglasses and keep up this ruse, but I know what you are.'

'Good for you,' Tarku said at last, then took another sip.

'You're an Akaia, aren't you?' John pressed on.

'I thought you said you knew.'

'Fine. No one else would have been able to stay as long as you would have had to, to film what you filmed out in the salt hills the way you filmed it, nor many of the things I saw when I researched your career - the Duanuan migration on Vahrna, the renowned section of film from the Delahar rally, you *are* an Akaia.'

'Maybe I was wearing a suit.'

'Maybe, but I doubt it, suits are inhibiting and your shots were fluid.'

'What's your point John?' Tarku asked with a hardness coming across his voice and countenance. John was aware of it but pressed on.

'Akaia can be treacherous company.'

'So can the common man,' Tarku returned.

'Listen,' John opened, 'we're going into the unknown with this conflict in Tamashan, if I'm supposed to take this team safely through I need to know the strengths and weaknesses of everyone. If you're an Akaia I need to know more.'

'I think you know enough,' Tarku said quietly but harshly. He got up and began to walk away, but John grabbed Tarku suddenly by the neck of his jacket, pulling him into a vice-like hold as he checked behind Tarku's ears, pulled his hair aside and looked closely at the back of Tarku's neck, then pushed him away.

Tarku huffed as he pulled his dishevelled attire and hair back into place and rubbed his neck, feeling more than a little harassed but never putting up any resistance.

'Apologies Tarku, I had to know if you were -'

'Tagged?' Tarku provided. 'You could've just asked, I'd have told you.'

'I wouldn't have believed you. I had to see for myself.'

'And what did you find?'

'You're not, but that doesn't really mean anything.'

'So, what else do you need to know?' an acidic edge crept into the tone of Tarku's voice, his face grew even harder, he held John's gaze, and although Tarku was by far the shorter and leaner of the two John felt there was a condensed strength within the Akaia, an almost tangible fire stirred up by this confrontation, John felt the change in the air even as Garner had felt it. 'Shall I find you a scalpel so you can start on the inside?' Tarku glared at the old soldier.

'I don't need a scalpel,' John answered him without flinching, 'you've got ridges on your spine, I haven't seen that in a long time. How old are you Tarku? You look what, 25 at a stretch, but don't give me that.'

'You won't like the answer,'

'Give it to me.'

'Add a zero and you're not even close,' Tarku confessed.

John just nodded. So, Tarku was over two hundred years old, it wasn't really specific enough for John, but that answer would do for the moment, he didn't think it wise to push Tarku any further.

'Is the interrogation over?' Tarku asked.

'For now.'

Tarku turned once more to go when John said, 'Tarku wait, thank you for taking this lightly. Sorry I put you through that, but now I know I can trust you, other Akaia might have torn me up by now.'

'So might I have, half an hour ago, don't underestimate the tea, and don't be so quick to trust me.'

John began to reply but Tarku appeared to ignore him and walked on, but John continued, 'Listen, Tarku, why do you do this? Why this charade for everyone? You can't pretend you're not what you are forever.'

Tarku stopped for a moment, 'I can try,' he said gently.

'But why the act?' John pressed, 'Why hide in this way? You must have so much to offer, and here is Weston hiring *me* as a guide! And don't give me what Governor Echlin's doing back home as an excuse either, if you're as old as you say you are and you're still not tagged you know how to evade the forces better than any.'

Tarku thought for a while with his head down, then looked up at John. 'If you think I hide from the world and from public speculation you are quite mistaken, I don't care about the opinion of men, though I cannot deny that life is easier when they do not know the truth. But the reason, since you say you need to know, is that *I* do not want to be reminded of what I am. So I'll thank you to say no more so I can forget once again, and as for being a guide, no,' Tarku shook his head, 'my life could be over at any moment, you say you need to know more, well that's what you need to know.'

'The thing is Tarku,' John was about to say more but Tarku broke, he pushed John back against the wall and stared him down.

'Let's get this clear,' Tarku threatened in a low voice so he'd not be overheard, 'I know who you are, I know what you used to do for the army - so you think you know how to deal with Akaia? Let me assure you, you have no idea how to deal with me. You need to know more? Ok, I'll tell you more, before I even left the North Islands I had to deal with a potential uprising, the government doesn't know what they're stirring up, what I had to deal with was no small thing. Akaia that never come together were coming together, they were angry, after such a long time of relative peace with the people of the North Islands, now the government had to do this, label them as dangerous, label them as treacherous. It's true, of course, and I reminded them of this, but to remind them I had to go further than I wanted to, I fought with them, and I lost my restraint for a second as I fought, even if that was the point of the exercise, and I found within myself more traits of the Mrukai than I had thought possible and it scared me like I've never been scared, do you understand? You're right to be afraid. I calmed the uprising in the north, but the strain of the task has taken its toll on me, do you understand?'

John nodded as best he could under Tarku's hold.

'And that's not all,' Tarku continued, 'apart from that I had to deal with a petty criminal and his gang, just so this crew could all leave the north safely. Do you know how hard it was, being on the edge, having to put up this facade for everyone so I don't see their fear when they look at me? And worst of all, my closest friend in all the world was hunted down and killed not that many days ago, and I am haunted by the memory, and now you are here - you who think you know Akaia, and you are tormenting me when I am at my lowest. If we're going to survive each other on this trip you need to know when to let me be,' Tarku pushed John and then let him go. It was John's turn to rub his throat.

'I understand. You have my apology,' John breathed. 'Will you take my hand Tarku?' the soldier outstretched his own in a gesture of friendship. Tarku inspected John from under his heavy eyelids. 'I don't think I'm ready to do that,' he answered sincerely.

John nodded in understanding and put his hand away. 'You have my respect in any case,' he said.

'And you have mine,' Tarku said quietly when John had walked away, back towards the bunks. But Tarku was unsettled. He hit the back of a chair with a fist, frustrated and ashamed that he had broken and said so much to the man, it was one more clear indication that he wasn't holding it together, one more indication that the end couldn't be far away for him. He didn't want to stay alone in the open front cabin or the bunks or anywhere where the engineer or anyone else could harass him any further, so he headed for the shower, locking himself in the tiny cubicle and sitting there. He understood the engineer's reasons for acting as he had, and what John had done was nothing compared to other trials Tarku had been put through, in fact Tarku felt he could trust John now as they went into the conflict on Tamashan as he would not have been able to otherwise, but trust was one thing, he didn't have to like the man, even if Syra had loved him.

CHAPTER 28:

Waiting to Dock

'Satsuan just ahead, fasten up everyone,' Hardan's voice came over the speakers. Soon all the crew were stumbling back into the front cabin.

Coming into Satsuan the ship sped in faster and smoother as the steam and cloud thinned out quickly the further they flew in. First only deep fractured columns of earth could be seen below them, great chasms that looked like what would be left if giant claws had reared up from the wastes and rent through the earth. Nothing grew at these outer extents, it was complete wasteland. Then came the desert, just like the North Islands, Arrojor, and Rorona, except these deserts were yellow sand and clay, dotted with clumps of tough gorse, and here Melissa could make out the odd nomad and herd, the isolated tent encampments. Then the city was before them, a maze of intertwined roads and buildings, the old ochre-washed, flat roofed dwellings and the new experimental, oddly shaped structures that where mostly huge, tall structures that looked like the angled beaks of golden birds breaking out of the earth and frozen in the action of heading for the sun. Amongst them all the people of Satsuan went about their business. The island was overcrowded with ships, with all the flights that had to be diverted to bypass the conflict in Tamashan. Many were in queue waiting to dock and the crew could see it was going to be another long wait before they would be through.

'How long since you've been to Satsuan John?' Astrid asked.

'Oh, five years I think,' John ran his eyes over the familiar sights. 'Looks like it's grown a bit since then, but still, it seems mostly the same.'

'You must have a lot of memories from all your times through here,' Astrid said.

'I guess I do. First time I came through was with Ambassador Thomas, the second time was with my wife, before she was my wife.' As John recalled that time, he remembered the blue of her eyes against the yellow sand, remembered her hands on his face as she smiled, the flow of her dress in the wind, the soothing of her kiss on his sandblasted lips. He touched his hand to his lips. What would she say to him now? 'Why are you going into this war?' she would probably say that. 'Well, if you're going for the right reasons then go and don't let your conscience trouble you anymore.' She would say that too. Was he going for the right reasons? He wasn't going for the money, that's certain, nor the prestige or renown that might, possibly, come out of doing a thing like this with Weston Alamo. Why was he doing it? Was it Melissa's fleeting resemblance to his wife? Scott's urging? Weston's persistence? Boredom? Frustration? The dreams? The crash of the Vector, the memory roused in his blood, the memory of those reckless days, when nothing mattered but to keep following the ghost of a trail after his stolen child, Ava. His daughter. His wife. The memory. Life had stopped being straight forward after he had met Amiana. There was no one reason for his decision to come, it had been building up, building up, he told himself, all that momentum, then he'd seen her, Melissa, with the slightest familiarity of look, it was enough to set off the spark. 'I love you,' Amiana would say, that was certain, even when she was the most angry.

'John, what is it?' Astrid asked him as he gazed blankly ahead.

'I just realised something, I didn't dream last night, I didn't dream at all,' he said. He thought about it - there had been no blue skies, no Amiana, no Ava. Just peace. What did that mean? Maybe it was the right decision to come on this expedition after all.

As they waited Astrid found one of the local stations on the cabin TV again. Asides from Rorona, Tamashan was the nearest neighbour of Satsuan, so naturally the new conflict was at the top of the headlines. The news was much the same as what they had heard already, back on Rorona before they had left, with the addition of some interviews of crews that had come through that way, but no one could tell them what had triggered the Delevian to suddenly attack the relatively peaceable island of Tamashan. There were some unconfirmed reports of large scale raids and bombings all over the island, but there was no reliable communication channel by which to talk with anyone on the ground in Tamashan. All their systems had been disabled or weren't being monitored, and the cloud over the island was such that the satellite imagery was unclear, though there did appear to be large-scale vessel movements in the area around Tamashan. This report was followed by more bad news about islands everywhere, many were continuing to tremor and crumble.

'Do you still think it's not inevitable Tarkars? That the earth will consume itself and we'll all come to nothing?' Astrid questioned him.

He seemed to think about it for a very long time, then he shrugged his shoulders.

'So, what?' Astrid pressed, 'Is that a maybe? You still think there's hope?'

'Either way, worrying about it will do no good,' he answered. But even saying that, worry was clearly evident on his face, but far from the end of the world his thoughts were on Melissa. He didn't wait for more questions but left the cabin and followed Weston towards the kitchen.

'What pre-packaged delight would you like to partake of this morning my friend,' Weston opened a door and offered Tarku a satchel.

'I'm not hungry,' Tarku shook his head, and spoke in a hushed voice to the producer. 'Weston, are you ok with the girl coming along? I mean, we don't know what we're going to find on Tamashan.'

'Is that concern I hear from you Tarku?' Weston chuckled, filling a bowl with the ingredients of the sachet then covering it with hot water.

'I guess so.'

After a moment Weston answered, 'It's her decision Tarku, she said her piece - and very well I thought.' Weston's meal was ready, so he took it in hand and returned to the cabin.

Tarku was left to look out at the city beyond, at the coming and going of ships from many different lands, wondering if he should he have left Melissa with that

Garner man in Junto-a-Mar. At least he did protect her in one sense, but how long would that have lasted? Tarku couldn't have left her there, he couldn't. He considered again whether or not he should have informed John months ago, if he had then neither he nor Melissa would be here now, but Tarku didn't know they'd be heading into a war, unstable situations, yes, but not all out war. Should he press Weston and get him to send her back to the north? Or even better, to Shorakai? She'd be safer there. No. There were too many other dangers, like what was that Vahrnan on Arrojor up to? At least there had been nothing suspicious since then, but Tarku felt he had to watch over her himself, she was Syra's daughter, and he didn't know who else he could trust. He walked back to the cabin, glanced at Melissa, still turning that button of Matthias's in her fingers like she did when she was unconsciously worried. He'd make sure to look out for her even more closely from now on.

John and Weston grew weary of the wait and pulled out a chess board as they ate breakfast. Weston was loud and boisterous, John was quiet and studied. Melissa secretly caught them on her camera - it was a fun shot of the two men hunched over the little board. Astrid commandeered the front screen and was going through some of the footage from Rorona. Tarku made no effort to join in any conversation only continued to look out the window at the city of Satsuan. He had a book on his lap and he would write or sketch in it from time to time, but was mostly in thought and disconnected from the rest of them. Melissa turned to speak to him a few times, but something about his manner made her hesitate and rethink what she would have said, and so she never spoke. It also occurred to Melissa that she couldn't remember ever seeing him without his dark glasses on, perhaps from the side, but never his full face.

'What have you got there?'

Melissa jumped as the axe fell across her stream of thoughts and caused their severed edges to recoil. It was only John Mark, trying to be friendly.

'Sorry,' John smiled, 'I didn't mean to startle you.'

'No, it's alright, my head was somewhere else,' she looked at the button in her hand that she'd been turning over and over. 'Here,' she handed it to John for his inspection, 'it's a mech-angel button, they're kind of popular with some of the bikers back home.'

'Oh, I didn't know that,' John said, amused and interested, 'why are they popular?'

'It's a sort of homage really, have you heard of the Knight Crew?'

'Ah, mm, it does sound familiar but nothing comes to mind.'

'They're a gang over our way. They pulled off the most amazing stunts, but it all started with the first raid on a Q Corp delivery which happened to be a real live machina. They thought it was going to be tech stuff they could split and resell, but the mech-angel turned out to be better for them anyway, after the first they kind of got a taste for it and they went on to liberate, so they said, several mechs.'

'Oh, that's right I do remember hearing about that.'

'They couldn't do it after a while though of course, as Q Corp really ramped up the security, well, not that it was ever easy, but the ones the Knight Crew did free helped them to pull off some pretty major heists after that.'

'You're not a biker though?'

'Oh no.'

'From a boyfriend?'

'No,' Melissa bit her lip. She had been whisked away from Matthias so quickly, but she could still see his, 'goodbye butterfly.' Goodbye. That was it, the end. He was right, he was no good for her, there had never been anything, and she knew there would never be anything, but why'd he have to tell her he loved her at all?

'Sorry Melissa, I shouldn't be asking a young girl I've just become acquainted with questions of that nature, my apologies,' he handed the silver button back to her.

'It's ok, it was just a gift from a good friend, it was important to him, so-'

'So it means a lot to you.'

'Yeah.'

'You know, I have a daughter, she would be about your age.'

'I was reading about, about you, and about what happened.'

'Oh?'

'I found a book at TnTv while I was waiting, Weston's. I haven't got very far, but I read about your daughter, I'm very sorry.'

He shook his head, 'Seems like a lifetime ago that it happened. Tell me where you're from, myself, I grew up in the Universal City, not much to tell really.'

'I ah, Junto-a-Mar.'

'Right, the city by the sea.'

'Only there isn't a sea.'

'No, I know, it's just wasteland. I've heard a bit about it, it's in a bad way isn't it?'

'It's the first barrier against the winds that come up from the divide on that side. First to get the bad rain, and then the government and the people in the capital treat us like we're worth no more than rats. The Gutter has the highest crime rate of anywhere on Corrio, and the highest mortality rate.'

'Must be a pretty tough place, but you seem okay.'

'I had friends looking out for me, we look out for each other.'

'That's a good thing to have, a group like that,' John said as he fished around in his backpack for something.

'Yeah it is, I was lucky really, in some ways leaving was the hardest thing I've ever had to do. There they were, telling me not to come back, sometimes I can't help thinking I might have been better off if I stayed. I know that's not true, but I mean, I didn't know we'd be heading into war. I'm not saying that I want to go back though, I do really want to make a go of this, I mean, I don't think I'd get another opportunity like this.'

'Here.' John handed her a fine chain, slipping the current ornament off as he did. Melissa looked at him enquiringly. 'So you don't lose the button,' he explained. Though she let him put the chain in her hand she still looked as though she didn't know what to do at receiving such a gift.

'Well it's not doing me any good. It belonged to my wife, Amiana,' John explained, 'she always wore it. I was going to give it to my daughter if I found her, but I don't think that's going to happen so you might as well have it.'

'I can't take this,' Melissa said, concerned at accepting such a precious gift.

'Yes you can, here,' John took the silver chain out of her hand and then the button and threaded it on, then clasped it around her neck. 'Much safer now,' he said, 'and always close to you.'

'Thank you.'

'My pleasure.'

'It's a beautiful ornament,' Melissa said of the silver thing John still held in his hand. 'I've never seen a design anything like it.'

'Yes, she loved it,' John looked again at the pendant, 'she said it reminded her of a place she missed, though she would never tell me where.' There was a small silence. John cleared his throat.

Tarku noticed it, and recognised it as a chain he had bought with Syra, the ornament was a charm she'd had made after making him sit still for an age while she'd traced one section of his tattoo, while he'd gone on about all the reasons she shouldn't want to copy it. It was strange now, by choice she'd taken and carried a part of him with her, but by force now all her designs were a part of his own tattoo, now etched upon his skin and into his soul. He looked away, the memory of Syra was painful. He clenched his jaw, holding back the tears defiantly. The pain was so raw, her death replayed again and it tore like a mortal wound upon him!

He must have made some sound, some small choke or exhalation, because John and Melissa looked at him, but the sound, and the way Tarku had turned away and the look on his face seemed like disdain to them, but of course they could not see his eyes behind his sunglasses, nor the tears in them.

'Don't like sentiment, Tarku?' John asked. Tarku didn't reply, it took everything he had to hold himself together.

'Maybe you will find her yet,' Melissa encouraged John.

'Maybe,' John smiled, but answered, 'but that is too much to hope for.'

Just then Hardan poked his head into the cabin, 'We'll be in port soon, seeing as we're not staying they're getting us into a temporary spot sooner, we won't have long on the ground West so be ready to do what you've got to do.'

Weston got the necessary paperwork together and went below to prepare the cargo that he had to dispatch. It was nearing mid-morning when Hardan was finally able to pull the Blue Moon up at the international docking port.

'Best everyone stays here,' Weston directed, 'we really don't have long. Tarku, I could use a hand with the deliveries.' The two descended to the cargo hold, letting down the ramp and heading off to dispatch packages and pick a few others up. Hardan set to refuelling and doing another quick flight check.

Astrid flicked the screens back to the local TV as she finished her work. It was the end of another news bulletin and there were further reports regarding the recent ruling of the North Islands on the Akaia. It seems other countries were following the outcome with interest, especially those where Akaia were an issue. There had been some trouble in the north since the last report, but still nothing major.

'John, do you know much about Akaia?' Melissa asked, 'We were having a debate when the ruling first went through. I asked Weston and the others what they thought about it but it seemed, well I'm still confused, and I read that you had something to do with Akaia when you were a soldier. What do you think about what's happening?'

John saw Tarku and Weston's progress across the port. John knew to some degree, and he more than most, how dangerous Akaia like Tarku could be. Even in the short time he'd served in the armed forces he had seen too much of their destructive capabilities, and history had shown they were to be feared. Everyone who knew the record of the north islands knew about their role in the ending the long war years. You didn't want one for an enemy. But John had also loved an Akaia, one who had skilfully hidden her marks from the world, like Tarku. John was perhaps the most qualified man in the world to answer questions on the issue.

'Well, I suppose I know a bit,' he said at last, 'I don't have an opinion about the ruling though. It's one of those things where nothing the government could do would be right.'

'Really?'

'And besides which, they've practically been doing the same without the ruling for years, so in reality not that much will change except to give the community an excuse to behave even more badly towards the Akaia, so in that sense I don't like the ruling. But Akaia can cause a lot of damage, both to themselves and others, so there is reason for what the government is doing.'

'Jem said they're not human anymore?'

'Jem?'

'The guide you replaced.'

'Oh.'

'Is that true?'

'No,' John thought of his Amiana, her beauty, her cheek, her sincerity. 'I wouldn't go that far.'

'Oh,' Astrid joined in, 'I have a question for you John. What's the connection between the Akaia and the Mrukai? I've looked into it and all I can find are rumours and unconfirmed reports, not actual scientific facts.'

'What are the rumours?'

'That Akaia are brought into existence and used by the Mrukai for their own ends.'

'Yes.'

'You're saying that's true? That the legends about Mrukai are real?' Astrid asked, now becoming more interested in gleaning what knowledge she could from

John. Maybe she could understand what was worrying Tarku and be of some help to him.

'Well, you can take or leave the legends, but yes, the Mrukai are very real,' John nodded with some sadness, 'and yes, they are responsible for making the Akaia what they are.' He wished their conversation hadn't come to this place, but he saw the questions full on the faces of Melissa and Astrid, and he wasn't going to limit what he explained.

'So mrukai are real?' Melissa was still catching on, full of amazement.

'Yes.'

'No way! Really?' Melissa seemed at once excited and scared, 'have you seen them?'

John nodded, 'When you've travelled as far and wide as I have, you see a great many things. I would never have believed such things, but I have seen them with my own eyes, and many others have too.'

'I believe the general consensus is that mrukai live below the fragments of the earth's crust, being creatures that thrive on heat and sulphur,' Astrid said, trying to clarify things, 'creatures that very little or nothing was known about before the collapse.'

'Yes,' John nodded, 'but when the deeds of our forefather's led the earth to crumble away beneath them, the mrukai, so the stories say, came out to see what had caused this terrible destruction. We had disturbed the hornets' nest, so to speak. They were no longer indifferent to mankind but hostile towards us, and with reason. We can see how different our world became, but I imagine their world also was now exposed and forever altered. And so, for hundreds of years at the beginning of the new world sporadic conflicts erupted between these creatures and mankind. There was much the survivors in the new colonies lost against the mrukai at that time. But over the years a strange phenomena began, there is record of this in the museum in Parahn, the mrukai were seen less and less, but a new threat emerged, men with something of the fire of the mrukai within them. At first these men were thought to bring the mrukai, like foretokens they would be seen in an area which would later suffer an attack, but as time went on the reverse became true - where an Akaia was amongst a population it was less likely for the people to be bothered by the Mrukai. The same could be said of our cities now, there are many Akaia, but Mrukai have been seen only rarely. However, despite this observation the negative reputation of the Akaia persists, even though the Mrukai rarely harass the people and have barely been seen in the last thousand years, the old tales of the time when they did in great numbers still linger, and the Akaia themselves are volatile, but even so I believe that the little trouble the Akaia give us is worth the protection they afford against the Mrukai.'

'So the Akaia keep the Mrukai away?' Melissa asked.

'I think they have more than one purpose, but that would seem to be one of them. One Akaia I knew told me that she believed Mrukai were essentially blind - being creatures from within the earth sight above ground wouldn't be something they had, but they have other senses that we know nothing about, and somehow, once they've marked an individual in an area, this allows them to see something of that part of the world. Almost like a map with areas marked out that are inhabited, areas to avoid, and so avoid conflict. Think of this, many Akaia, all over the world, each with a marking that's different from place to place, the mrukai are smart, they have made these plans and carried them out with no help from us, even though they have had many setbacks - many infants found with the mark of the akaia have been killed or abandoned as soon as it is realised what they are, and even though the akaia that survive are not given an easy path, and even though most akaia cannot sustain what lies within them for long years. Even against all that, even without being able to communicate with us, the mrukai have succeeded in practically ending the conflict between us. Many have tried to figure out what the markings mean, but as yet none have been able to. Perhaps with access to the mark of every Akaia there might be a way to understand, but that's impossible.'

'What are the mrukai like?' Melissa asked, genuinely absorbed in John's information and wanting to know more.

'Well, what I saw was dark and almost indistinguishable from a shadow, a beast that seemed to emit endless ashes from its form as it moved. Some sightings have described Mrukai as being not much more than the size of a man, but the one I saw was huge, with wings of the darkest leather and a thorny skin. There was nothing appealing about it except that it seemed refined, less like a monster as they are often described, more like a creature with as much depth of thought as myself. But I always find it hard to visualize again what I saw, because the thing is if you see a Mrukai you don't hang around to find out what it wants.'

'I heard they were like a fabled salamander, or dragon almost,' Astrid added.

'Yes,' John nodded, 'there are many rumours, some have them as a folktale demon, with an indefinable body comprised of ash. True or not, peoples repeated tales have endowed these Mrukai with a voice that cannot speak in words but in scarcely heard rumours that penetrate, that feel as though a scream alone from one of these creatures could splinter your bones from the fingernails to the spine and skull, and a hollow breath that could suck the very air out of your lungs, and an unseen presence that could cause the mind to boil with fear, but I think perhaps it is fear itself that brings about these symptoms.' John paused, realising he had probably just said too much, but he loved being able to share his knowledge with Melissa, and enjoyed her enthusiasm and interest. As he gathered in his mind the words to follow on with, he was surprised at the voice he heard next.

'They're like fire,' Tarku said, having come back in silently. 'But in this world something as pure as they are cannot exist, to them our world is cold, and their bodies continually form a coating to protect itself, this is what you see, the black, like soot and ash breaking up and falling away from them constantly. To my sight the Mrukai are both flame and shadow, somehow held in a frame that is at once real, yet intangible and untouchable as smoke.'

John caught the bitterness in Tarku's voice. He got the impression that Tarku didn't care much for the Mrukai, but still, surprisingly, his other words about them were said with an element of respect.

'You've seen them too Tarku?' Melissa asked.

His mouth grew grim, 'Many times, unfortunately.'

The crew were silent for a moment, then Melissa got back to her questions.

'So how do the mrukai mark the Akaia? How does it change them?'

John swallowed. Could he go on without offending Tarku? There was no harm in Melissa knowing really. 'Along with the tattoo, when the Mrukai mark a child they transfer part of what they are, the fire and shadow, as Tarku put it, that makes the creatures what they are. That's what makes the Akaia so different from the rest of us, that's what gives them their ability to heal, their strength, as well as, well, other things, less desirable things.'

'Like what?'

'Ah, well, things that make them more like the Mrukai, and less like the rest of us.'

'How do the Mrukai do it? I mean, if they're hardly ever seen?'

'Sound,' John said, 'A mrukai's call is a powerful thing.'

'Like the kyu?' Melissa asked.

'Far more acute,' Tarku explained.

'But there's not really that many Akaia though are there?' Melissa continued her questions.

'No, there are very few, and most don't live very long either,' John answered. 'On the North Islands when new Akaia are found they are monitored by the authorities, but they usually lose their reason as they become adults, most often they head into the surrounding wastes and are never seen again. If they stay in the north it usually ends with the individuals being institutionalised or in the worst cases executed by the government before they can do any damage, but this system has been in place less than a hundred years, and it's not easy.'

'Why?'

'They're stronger and faster, they simply cannot be contained as ordinary people can.'

'No, I mean, why do they lose their reason? Do you mean they, what, go insane?'

Tarku spoke up again, 'What do you expect? They belong neither to the world of men or the world of the Mrukai, they are harassed by man and Mrukai alike, and as the fire and shadow placed within them struggles to live contained in such a finite human body, a body that is at once being strengthened yet deconstructed, it is a crazed inside that can now no longer tolerate the air up here, that fears but longs for the fire beyond the wastes but cannot have it without gaining death as well, and with a mind that half the time knows not if it is a man or something to be feared by men, sanity is naturally hard to hold on to.'

Tarku found everyone in the cabin staring at him, surprised by his answer and its length and comprehensiveness, and its passion. He cleared his throat. 'I'm sorry,' he said, now composed again, 'I need some air.'

Tarku got up and walked out of the cabin. He left the ship and went out to the edge of the raised dock, with the view of the great expanse of desert stretching out before him for miles and miles, lit up here and there with the fires of the nomads, darkening rapidly as storm clouds grew across the sky, having followed behind them since just out from Rorona. The wind running up from the desert before the storm was warm and salty. He wondered if the descendants of his old friend Bacasn still lived out there. Bacasn had taught him all he knew of photography, about the patience required to wait for the perfect shot, the healing qualities of being still, and a great deal about friendship. It had been hard to remain so young and impenetrable while his mentor grew old and succumbed to the decay of this accursed earth, until death took him and Tarku helped his sons and daughters to bury him, then left them to their grief. So many people had died while he had lived on, too many people.

Melissa thought Tarku was just being his usual, strange, cold self, and turned back to John, very interested in this subject. 'So,' she continued, 'Weston said I probably had seen an Akaia and just not realised it, how do you recognise them? The only thing I can pick up from the ones I've seen on the TV is that sometimes their eyes are different, and if you can see a mark, that's all.'

'Yes, well,' John shifted in his seat uncomfortably, 'several ways. As you noticed, most have visible markings and many have eyes that don't seem quite right, ah,' he shook his head, thinking, 'they might be stronger, or heal quickly as I said. In the past some have even been said to possess quite pronounced characteristics of the Mrukai, protrusions of stone at their joints, blood that crystallizes when it's exposed to the air - almost like scales, some in legend were even said to have wings like the Mrukai, though I'm fairly certain that's an exaggeration. Asides from that, I can't think right now.' John got up, 'I've just thought of something I've got to check with Tarku.'

Melissa sighed and gazed out at the goings on of the port of Satsuan.

'I shouldn't have put the news on, sorry darling, all that stuff about the end of the world again,' Astrid apologised, noticing Melissa seemed slightly distressed, 'like Tarku said, I wouldn't let it get you down, it's just the way things are.'

'Oh, no, it's not that, the world is always ending,' Melissa smiled half-heartedly.

'What is it then?'

'Nothing.'

'Come on, I might be able to do something about it, what's the matter?'

'No, it's stupid, it's just Tarku, he gets to me, you know.'

'In what way?' Astrid asked.

'Well, how he spoke to me just now, and other times. I shouldn't have said anything, it's nothing really, I just feel like he looks down at me because I'm from The Gutter or something. I know I don't have a good education but I mean, I'm not that un-knowledgeable am I?'

'No darling.'

'I only ask so many questions about things because I want to understand. But I can't shake it, it's just a feeling, it's stupid I know, so don't worry about it, I'll get over it. It just makes me feel so insecure, makes me lose my confidence around him, you know.'

'I'm absolutely certain he doesn't look down on you darling,' Astrid patted Melissa's knee firmly, 'I don't think you've got anything to worry about with Tarku.'

'Do you think?'

'Yep. That feeling will disappear once you get to know him.'

'But that's impossible, he's, he's like ice most of the time.'

'Exactly,' Astrid grinned, 'time and warmth, and he'll melt.'

'You think so?'

'I know so,' Astrid laughed, then continued seriously, 'when people get to be like that, so shut off, sometimes it's because they feel too much, not because they don't feel at all. And I'm not sure because he's never said, but I think he comes from somewhere just as bad or worse than the gutter, so you needn't be concerned on that head.'

'Really? Where do you think he's from?'

'Well, if you ask him he says Parahn City, Parahn, but if you were abroad you'd probably say Universal City, Corrio, wouldn't you, because it's easier than saying that you live in Junto-a-Mar which is a city on the outskirts of the cluster metropolis that is the Universal City.'

'That's right.'

Astrid laughed, 'You like him don't you?'

'What?' Melissa was confused, even shocked by the suggestion, and shook her head determinedly, 'no! I could never like someone like him.'

'Like what?'

'Well I don't understand why he says some of the things he says, and he hardly ever smiles.'

Astrid felt she should at least explain Tarku to some degree, 'You should know darling, he does have reason for what he says and how he is,' she said, then smiled, 'but come on, I think you need a distraction. Do you play cards?'

'Of course, you don't grow up in The Gutter without learning a trick or two.'

~

John climbed down the stairs of the Blue Moon and then headed across the dock to where Tarku stood facing the desert. Tarku stared at John a moment then looked back out. John leaned on the railing. 'Hey sorry about all that.'

Tarku didn't say anything.

'You know,' John continued honestly, 'situations like that wouldn't happen if you just told them who you were.'

'You mean, what I am.'

'No, I mean who you are, your heritage falls within that.'

'My heritage?' Tarku laughed, 'my kind, more like. Do you think you know who I am?'

'I know more than they do,' John nodded towards the ship. 'Listen Tarku, my time on the task force, it's not something I'm proud of, just something that had to be done and we had to do it.'

Tarku changed the topic in obvious fashion, 'A good friend of mine used to live out there.'

'Really? What, a Suan nomad?'

'Yes, that was before Satsuan sunk this far. The weather would be terrible out there now.'

'I'll say.'

Tarku sighed, 'You know John -'

'What?'

'You asked me a question before, I couldn't tell you exactly as I didn't really know, but I've figured it out. The answer is five centuries, three decades, six years, and a day.'

It took a moment for it to sink in. John nodded, then a grin stole his serious look, 'Happy birthday for yesterday.'

Tarku laughed, 'Thanks.'

'No way!' John shook his head.

'What?'

'No way! That's unbelievable! You're serious aren't you. I was going to guess fifty, or seventy, you said more than 200 and I thought, ok, maybe that's possible, but five-hundred!' John cursed, 'Are there any other Akaia as old as you?'

'I don't know. I don't think so,' Tarku thought of Syra, 'not anymore.'

'Five hundred years! It's incredible! You know by the look of you I could be your father. As a friendly move I shall share some reciprocal information with you, I'm forty-five.'

'You look at least fifty.'

'Oh thanks.'

'Well, what do you expect? The entire population has been aging faster in the past few decades. That is of course with the exception of Akaia, and the Shorakaian, but even they have not been entirely spared. And on top of that you can't have exactly taken the easiest route in life.'

'No, that's true, I haven't,' John agreed.

'So, John, what led you to join this expedition? Weston's been going on about how hard it was to persuade you to be the guide. You had a sudden change of mind?'

'Not really, I think deep down there'd been an unrest growing inside me, a combination of events, you know. There were several things, and even after my decision things happened that kept me to my resolve. You would have heard about the Vector?'

'No?'

'The Vector brought the news of the breaking war, that really shook me, and brought a lot of other factors together.'

'How so?'

'I don't know, I think simply because it came from Tamashan.' John cleaned underneath his little fingernail with his thumbnail. 'Do you know I've been searching for my daughter for the last 20 years?'

'Yes, I'd heard,' Tarku answered.

'Well, the thing that really made my mind up to come was that I thought I saw her.' John laughed, 'Would you believe I thought-' John stopped himself, couldn't quite bring himself to trust Tarku enough to tell him he thought Melissa might have been his daughter. 'The last thing I saw of my daughter, those twenty years ago, was her formula bottle, half empty, lying on the greasy surface of the dock. It would have been underneath a Vahrnan ship that had reportedly been heading to Tamashan.'

'If you did see your daughter how would you know her after all this time?'

'I don't know, I hope I'd feel something, and maybe see something in her of Amiana or myself. I've got a picture too, of what she might look like today, it's taking the baby photos and what Amiana and I look like into account, but it's only a rough idea.'

'Can I see it?'

'Sure.' John's big fingers fumbled with the papers in his chest pocket and pulled out the hypothetical likeness.

'She's beautiful John.'

'Thank you.'

'You don't think, the nose, it kind of looks like-' Tarku thought, 'no, I don't know.'

'What?'

'Nothing.'

'You think you know someone who looks like this?'

'No, not really. Just ever so slightly.'

'Who?'

'Melissa,' Tarku said simply.

'This Melissa? Little Melissa?'

'Yes.'

'I don't see it,' John took the photo back and scrutinized it. 'No, I don't see it Tarku. Well, at first I thought- you know, I thought that too, but no, not now.'

'Well. It is more probable that she isn't your daughter, all things considered, but if we make it back to the North, or even to Shorakai, I suggest you tell her what you momentarily thought and get some tests done to see if she is your daughter, there's no harm in that,' Tarku encouraged.

'I suppose you're right,' John said, 'but another thing is that Melissa's from Corrio, from Junto-a-Mar, whereas my gut reckoned all along my daughter wasn't in the North Islands anymore, but somewhere in the south.'

'Did the Shorakaian help you search John? I mean, your wife was an important person wasn't she?'

'She was an ambassador, but the only help I got from Shorakai was the assurance that they were doing everything they could. But I didn't see any action, from my point of view it seemed that once Amiana was out of the picture I was an embarrassment, just a lowly former soldier of what was then seen as the distant and less than significant north, that's the impression I got. Sometimes I wondered if they even thought that I might have had something to do with Amiana's assassination. I couldn't get work on Shorakai, my skills didn't have much use there, and their laws, the way they do things, it was difficult, I had to return to the North. Everything was spun, I couldn't care for myself, let alone my little girl. I think they blame me for losing her as well.'

'John, can I ask you a favour?'

'Sure.'

'See that ship, the Vahrnan vessel?'

'Yes.'

'Take good notice of it. They were on Arrojor too, watching us.'

'You're not just being paranoid?'

'I don't think so.'

'Well, if they follow us to Tamashan you'll definitely be right.'

'You two get back over here, we're going,' Weston yelled. A moment later Weston walked onto the ship followed by Tarku and John. 'Ready to go everyone?' he called, 'Sorry we can't stay Melis,' Weston said as he passed, 'you'd like to explore Satsuan I'm sure but we don't have the time right now. Hardan,' he tapped the cockpit door then opened it, 'Are we ready to go?'

'All set.'

'Bring your coffee and your pastry out into the cabin, I want to hold a little meeting before we head off.'

'Righto.'

Weston stood at the front of the cabin, looking from one to the other of the crew. 'Astrid I want you to film this. You right?'

'Yep, all set,' she replied, initiating the ship's inbuilt cabin camera to film everyone.

Weston knew this moment would soon be seen by millions back home if they made it to Tamashan and were able to send back any film, indeed, it would be seen all around the world.

'I ah, I want to thank you all for coming on this expedition,' he began, 'for daring to venture into this unknown and potentially volatile situation to show the reality of what is happening on Tamashan to the world. I know you will all do what you do best as representatives of TnTv and of the North Islands. You have all been selected for this trip because you are the best at what you do. Orin Hardan, for accepting the task of taking us into this situation and getting us out again, there is no man I'd rather have as Captain.' Weston gave him a little salute, then continued, 'John Mark, for being our guide in little known places and unknown situations there is no better person, I thank you for coming. Tarku, for your astounding photographic captures and your knowledge also, I am thrilled to have you on board. Astrid, for your dedication and skill, I could not do without you, and Melissa, for the new style I see developing in your photographic impressionism, I welcome you and look forward to seeing your work. I am proud to be in the company of you all, and I am overwhelmed that what we set out to do has been overtaken by a new objective, no longer are we just exploring and documenting the southern islands. Now we have something of far greater importance to do, what no one has yet been able to do, discover the state of things on Tamashan.'

CHAPTER 29:

Weston won't be happy.

The atmosphere the crew of TnTv passed through on route from Satsuan to Tamashan was like being inside a warm sunset that didn't fade but was in every direction an enveloping haze like a wash of deep and brilliant warm tones of an artist's watercolours. Ahead of the Blue Moon somewhere in that red afternoon lay Tamashan, the country that had been out of communication with the rest of the world for many days. They had quite a way to go, as Tamashan was far in the west, but the flight was easy and gentle. It seems the Pireomerai, the fiery plains far below them in the deep rifts between here and their destination, were quiet today, as if plotting. Astrid and John chatted quietly, occasionally Melissa, and once or twice even Tarku said something. Once Tarku even asked them all if they would like tea or coffee, and quietly explained the merits of several different teas to the inexperienced Melissa, and to her surprise he even got up and made it all for them. He took so long, like it was an art, and indeed it was a perfect cup he made. Tarku sipped his tea long and slowly, completely the opposite of Weston who drank his down in a few noisy gulps.

'Should I give Hardan a break?' asked John.

'You can ask him I suppose, he might appreciate it but he likes his job so he might decline your offer,' Weston shrugged.

John poked his head into the cockpit. 'How's things Hardan? Need to swap yet?'

'No I'll be good for a while still.'

'Good good. Well, call me when you need me,' John said, but before turning out of the cockpit he noticed the radar monitor. 'Hold-up Hardan, what are those?'

'I was just wondering that myself,' Hardan agreed with a yawn, 'looks like ships, but I've put a call out and there's been no reply. We're heading into an area not the best for signal relay though, could be they haven't heard the call, but the Blue Moon is equipped with some powerful transmitters so that's unlikely.'

'How far out are we from Tamashan?'

Hardan checked the route, 'I'd say an hour and a half.'

'Too far out to be a Delevian patrol then.'

'I'd say so.'

'And the ships are in formation, so not likely to be private local vessels.'

'What are you thinking? Marauders?'

'First thought that crossed my mind.'

'But what would marauders be doing out here?' Weston questioned from behind. 'There'd be no traffic to speak of to make it a profitable exercise for such a fleet, surely?'

'There might be ships trying to escape the conflict coming this way,' John explained, 'and with the Tamashani unable to maintain their patrols because of this conflict there's nothing to stop them. That's how they think, knock them while they're down.'

'The vultures!' Weston cursed, 'scavenging from those not yet dead! Are you sure John?'

'Well, that's got to be ships on the radar, and my guess would be they're marauders.'

'No wonder we've heard nothing from Tamashan, even if people get through the Delevian assault, they've got to deal with pirates!' Weston swore again.

'I've been heading to avoid them,' Hardan said in his usual casual manner, 'but the radar shows several ships spread out wide across the route.'

'Definitely marauders,' John nodded.

'What do you think? Turn back? Keep going?' Weston asked.

'I've outwitted many before,' said Hardan.

'That many? We've got to turn back Hardan,' John urged.

Hardan took a deep breath, 'Weston won't be happy.'

'No, I'm not happy,' Weston grumbled.

'I'm sure you'd rather not be dead West,' John said. 'I suggest we turn back.'

'Can't we go higher or, I don't know, the Blue Moon can take more than most ships, surely we can avoid them.'

'I wouldn't like to risk it, this lot look very organised.'

'Is there another way around?'

'Hardan's heading along the line, doesn't look like there's a break.'

'Fellas,' Hardan gulped, 'we got company behind, they came up so fast I didn't see, must have been idle in the rift below, now they're right on us.'

'How many?'

'Two, no three ships.'

'They're herding us,' John sighed. 'Marauders in this airspace! I never thought it would come to this. Weston, where are the guns?'

'Rear cabin.'

'Right. West, Tarku, with me,' John directed. 'Hardan, get above them and stay above them. I'm counting on you, they'll want to board us so just keep above them no matter what.'

Weston and Tarku followed John back. Tarku opened the hidden gun compartment in an inner wall of the ship. John quickly glanced over the cache. 'Let's hope that's enough.'

'There's more in the hold downstairs, plenty of rounds too.'

'How many of you are good with weapons?' John asked Tarku.

'Everyone except the girl. Well, West and Hardy are a bit inexperienced compared to you or I but they know how to shoot, and I've never seen Astrid miss.'

'Right, Weston, get on the ship's gun after you get yourself and everyone else armed, and make sure everyone's in protective gear in case the hull is breached and we're exposed to any toxins.'

Weston got to it without question. John pulled on a protective suit, the elements here weren't as bad as they were in the divide near the north islands, but they were still destructive and no one wanted to take any chances, and who knew if the marauders had gas canisters at their disposal. Tarku pulled on a suit too, and when John gave him a questioning glance Tarku said, 'I can take a lot but I still get hurt, and it's not as fun as it might seem.'

'Where's the safest place on the ship?'

'Probably the bathroom, it's away from any windows and the walls are thick.'

Astrid came to them to see what the plan was, 'I'll make sure Melissa has a weapon she can use then get her to the bathroom and tell her to stay there,' she offered, taking weapons for Melissa and herself then going to it.

'These guns are well and good if they're close enough to board us,' John said to Tarku, 'but there's nothing big enough for what I'm thinking of, not against the gear we have to assume they've got.'

'You know we wouldn't be allowed at most ports if they found we had anything bigger.'

'True. Still, it means we're going to need you if we're going to get out of this alive,' John admitted, and he wasn't joking. 'You're going to have to do the work Tarku. I hope you're as mad as I think you are.'

'That almost sounds like a compliment!'

'Do you understand my plan?' John asked.

'Yeah, I think so.'

'Your vagueness is instilling me with confidence.'

'I know what has to be done.' Tarku laughed, cracking his knuckles as he prepared, then checking the knife in his boot and the bullets in his gun.

'We on Hardan?' John tested the radio.

'Good to go John. We're above a ship now, they'll be close enough to fire on us soon, so whatever your plan is you better hurry.'

'They won't shoot us down yet if they want loot, we've got time Hardan,' John reassured.

Opening the rear doors Tarku and John stepped into the airlock. John harnessed himself to the inbuilt rig and nodded for Tarku to open the outer doors. Together they looked down into the swirling cloud below them. The faint outline of a ship could be seen coming higher as they sped along. Then they could see the marauders, geared up and ready at two separate gun turrets along their ship's roof, but holding their fire as yet. Hardan received a call from the marauders stating they had the Blue Moon surrounded and seeking surrender in return for no loss of life.

'Pull ahead of them now Hardan!' John yelled. Hardan pushed the Blue Moon and made the speed to gain on the ship below. 'You ready Tarku? Take the turrets out then we can get closer, I'll cover you if I can,' John yelled above the noise and the wind. Tarku grinned and pulled down the mask, then jumped down into that swirling mess. At once he was flung back with the speed but landed perfectly on the ship below, hanging on, fighting his way into the first turret, then using it against the other gun before the marauders could use it against him, then disabling it permanently. For a moment he was cornered there by the hand guns of the marauders, but then Tarku fought his way inside with the skill and knowledge John had been counting on, the five-hundred years of fight and observation at his disposal, along with other traits of his kind.

Soon Tarku had made it back to the engine room on the marauder ship, and the engines were seen to spark. John yelled to Hardan to slow and lower again. The old soldier let himself down on the wire and was there to clip Tarku on, leaving the exploding wreck to fall below them. The rest of the crew watched from the cabin in awe.

'Get back in the bathroom!' Astrid yelled at Melissa, 'keep your head down darling, this isn't over yet!'

'Only a few more to go and we're done,' John laughed as Astrid helped Tarku and himself back on board. They fell to the floor of the rear cabin and tried to catch their breath. 'Hey, Tarku you're shot!'

Tarku lifted the mask for a moment, breathed, looking at his body. Indeed there was blood swelling across the protective suit. 'You sound surprised?' Tarku laughed, 'of course I'm shot. Did you expect me to take on a whole ship without injury?' He hawked up some blood and spat it out. 'Don't worry, it'll stop bleeding soon enough.'

'You sure you're ok?' Astrid asked.

'Let's do this thing,' Tarku nodded.

'You're keen,' John laughed.

'I haven't had this much fun in weeks,' Tarku admitted.

'So you like the edge?' John asked.

'I like the challenge,' Tarku grinned.

'They're still converging on us John,' Hardan radioed back, 'one's coming alongside now, and one's trying to get above us, and the main group's still ahead.'

'Stay out of range and get higher again,' John urged, then stepped out again with Tarku. They looked at the ship coming closer, this time it was far to the side and not below, and the ship matched Hardan's move if he tried to go higher.

'They'll be on us in a second,' John yelled, 'if you're going to jump Tarku, you've got to jump now,'

'I won't make that distance,' Tarku shook his head, 'there's no way, I almost lost grip on the ship last time and that was a simple fall. We've got to get to the guns and just do our best to keep them back.'

'You could make it,' Astrid put in her word, 'it's a simple mathematical equation when it comes down to it - wind speed, ship speed, height, distance, drag - but it would have to be just at the right time.'

Tarku weighed the distance, looking out along the wing. 'I cannot simply run along the wing to gain the momentum I would need. Not while we're at this speed!'

'You won't need to run, you just need to jump, I'm not talking about the right wing, I'm talking about the left. If you're out there Hardan can spin the ship and you'll be thrown, catapulted right to them.'

'You're sure?' he questioned Astrid.

'Absolutely,' she was serious.

'Well, you score it with Hardan, I'll get out on the wing. Don't mourn me if I don't make it.' Tarku checked the bullet wound quickly, it was certainly starting to heal. He spat a last mouthful of blood out and wiped the blood from his chin then made his way out of the hatch. He slipped down the ship while holding tight to the grip-lines used for maintenance. The way along the wing was most difficult, he held tight and edged along until he was as far out as possible. This one was tricky. At speed every angle and every timing had to be right. Hardan pulled into place and Astrid instructed him on the exact speed and time the manoeuvre had to be made. All set Hardan quickly spun the Blue Moon and Tarku was flung right towards the marauder ship as Astrid had predicted. None of the crew could see how he could have made the jump but he did, and now clung to the side of the second marauder ship. The marauders were more prepared this time after partially seeing and hearing their other ship go down, and they waited by the hatch with guns ready, some even leaning out the door and firing back at Tarku. Hardan pulled closer so John could cover him, but to complicate matters the third of the pursuing ships came above the Blue Moon now. Weston operated the inbuilt gun, and Astrid opened the emergency hatch in the ceiling and joined in the fire on the craft that was seeking to invade them. Her accuracy was perfect, she and Weston disabled the turret on the underside of the ship and with a few deft shots even took out marauders as they began to descend on wires to board the Blue Moon, and finally, as the ship drew closer she identified the merest flaw in the vessel's make and shot full clean through and hit their pilot, causing the vessel to veer aside, tossing some of the crew from the open doors to fall away into the hazed depths of the rift below.

'Roof's clear,' Astrid called through.

'Get closer to the other ship,' John yelled to Hardan, 'our boy's in a jam.'

Hardan manoeuvred the Blue Moon accordingly and Astrid made her way to the rear doors again. She and John drew the attention of the marauders on the big guns that were in Tarku's way, but they couldn't get close enough.

'Hardan, take us higher again, I'll make the jump,' Astrid said.

'Astrid?' Weston stopped her.

'I know what I'm doing,' she smiled.

Hardan managed to gain the height needed and Astrid made the jump. She fired as she fell, enabling Tarku to fight forward and get inside at last. Astrid had soon taken out the final turret but seconds later the marauder ship veered higher, erratically, and though Hardan tried to follow he dared not go too close for fear of endangering their own ship.

'Where are they, where are they!' Weston and John peered through the steam and cloud.

There was a long silence, John repeatedly trying to get Tarku or Astrid on the radio. Then suddenly the marauder ship was beside the Blue Moon again, and the radio came through.

'Come on, we'll give you guys an escort!' Astrid called over.

'They're ok,' Weston breathed, much relieved.

John looked across to the marauder ship, behind the blood spattered window of the cockpit, Tarku saluted.

'Any injuries over there?' John radioed.

'Are you asking about us or the marauders?' Tarku joked.

'Is he alright?' Weston looked across at his photojournalist.

'Sure is,' John laughed.

'The line of marauders looks to be breaking up, should we go for it?' Astrid radioed.

'Yeah, I think now we're two ships they'll leave us be, we're so close they could catch us if we turned now anyway,' John replied.

They sped up and made for the gap in the line of marauder ships, holding their breath, keeping an eye on the radar.

'Looks like we're through,' Hardan put over the speakers at last. There was a collective sigh, but then Hardan spoke again, 'Hold on, I spoke too soon.' Another craft was upon them.

'Whoa! Where'd that come from!' yelled Weston. For no sooner had Hardan spoken when they felt a blast hit the Blue Moon, and then another and although Hardan dodged, a spatter of lead tore down the ship's side. The craft attacking them was fast as they come, seen and gone in an instant, leaving only an enveloping thunder in its wake, and coming back around to fire again. This time Hardan was ready and the attackers only managed minor damage, but the Blue Moon was hit and Hardan confessed to Weston, 'We're going to have to take her down West, there's nothing for it, or we'll crash down anyway.'

'Will we make Tamashan?'

'No, but we'll make the inner wastes surrounding the isle, we have to.'

'But they'll follow us there won't they?! They'll pillage us! Isn't that what they want us to do?!'

'What other choice do we have? Even if we could make Mon Karo, we don't know if it would make a difference, we don't know the state of things there. At least in the wastes there's some cover in the steam drifts.'

'You guys look like you took a shot,' Astrid radioed. 'Did you see the wing markings? That wasn't a marauder.'

'I didn't see anything, it was too fast,' Weston remarked.

'Exactly, it was a Delevian fighter,' Astrid advised.

'Oh great!' Weston held his head, 'We haven't even started to cover the war and we're getting shot at! Is it coming back Hardan?'

'I missed it last time, I don't know, it's too quick.'

'We've got to go down as if we really were crashing, then they'll leave us alone,' John advised, now taking a seat beside the pilot and strapping in. 'Are you up for it Hardan?'

'Absolutely,' Hardan tightened his seatbelt and took a deep breath, 'you all better get seated and strapped in and hold on for dear life. This is going to get ugly.'

John, Weston and Melissa were all seated very quickly, and Hardan began the fall. Smoke was already streaming from the Blue Moon's wing-cheats so it did indeed appear the ship was going down. Stomachs rose into throats and heads spun as Hardan coiled the ship in a descending spiral. Once more the Delevian fighter flew over, but it didn't fire, it sent a targeted electro-magnetic pulse to make sure the job was finished and then kept on back towards Tamashan-main. Hardan really did lose control of the Blue Moon's system after that pulse, as they hurtled forwards through the cloud, but again the design triumphed as he was able to pull up the manual controls and at last managed to pull out of the spin.

The marauder ship was caught in the pulse too. Astrid fell. The pulse had disrupted her own system. Tarku caught her as she collapsed, tears of blood coming from under her right eye and a tiny streak from her ear.

'Machina!' Tarku gasped, 'Astrid, what do I do? How do I help you?' She was in no state to answer, and there was no time, the ship was going down. Tarku found himself trying to regain control of the ship but unlike the Blue Moon there seemed to be no backup or manual system to get the ship back in hand. He couldn't find a way. Tarku turned to Astrid for help, but Astrid remained in a state of shock. After trying for too long, without success, the Akaia took the Machina in his arms and tried to make his way to the lower hatch as the ship hurtled towards Tamashan's outer wasteland, cutting through the walls of ever thickening cloud.

The Blue Moon reached the wastes and also gained the cover of that cloud, but though they flew steadily along, they were flying blind. Without the sensors they'd have to land entirely by sight, which was practically nil.

'No!' Weston gasped as they saw the glow of an explosion ahead, the marauder ship going down.

'At least it gives us an indication of how close we are to the ground,' John commented, 'they'll be alright Weston, they have to be.'

'I hope you're right.'

Hardan pulled their speed right back and waited for any sign of the ground, and soon the sand and rock was glimpsed and he took them down. It was not the gentlest landing of Hardan's career, but the Blue Moon lowered at last. The few last centimetres were the most jolting, but all the crew were glad to be on the ground, and they breathed relief. Hardan turned the engines off at once.

'Can I get a hand John, quickly,' Hardan stood up and kept about his business. 'I know we need to find Tarku and Astrid but we've got to make a quick check and make sure there's no fires or sparks or we'll end up as bad as that marauder ship and we won't be going anywhere. I expect we'll have some work to do. I'll do an interior sweep and check the engine room, you can do the checks outside.'

Eager to get to the crash site, Weston already had his mask on and medical kit on his back. He let down the door, ready to go. 'You two do what you've got to do, I'll go after them.'

'Can I do anything?' Melissa asked of Weston. He shook his head. 'I'll come with you,' she said. He didn't stop her.

They could still see the glow of the aftermath of the crash in the distance as they trudged down the steps and began across the wastes towards the wreck. The masks and the atmosphere made conversation difficult, and Weston's pace was such, even over this difficult terrain, that Melissa struggled to keep up with him.

CHAPTER 30:

Drink the tea.

Having made sure there was no imminent fire danger Hardan was deep in concentration, he had the tools out to fix a damaged connection in the engine. 'Anything I can do here Hardan?' John asked, as he put down the empty extinguisher and rags and wiped his gloves of the soot and sediment.

'Ah, not specially. This shouldn't take too long, I'm just trying to get the main engines up again, wouldn't want to be stuck out here if the back-up fails. All good out there?' Hardan asked.

'Well, the ship's not about to burst into flames if that's what you mean, but there's a lot of damage.'

'Any sign of the others yet?'

'No, and they should have been back by now if everything was alright. Will you be right with the ship if I go after them?'

'Yes, hopefully this will be fixed soon, then I'll be able to fly closer if need be.'

John took a moment to consider if he had everything he might need - rope, water, torch, another mask. He grabbed himself some extra ammunition and medical supplies and went out.

The old soldier followed the slight impressions in the sand as he went, the footprints of Weston and Melissa. They headed south-west as expected, ever further away from the Blue Moon and the besieged population of Tamashan and towards the downed marauder ship. John tried not to think the worst, but even apart from the crash, even if they had survived the explosion, there was a reason that nothing existed out here, a reason the Tamashani stayed well clear of these wastes, and it wasn't just the toxicity. Compared to some other outlands these were low level toxic, but they were devoid of the touch of human life even now, when there was a battle in the city, when it may have been a place to run to. John knew that out here there were threats living under the sand.

He trudged on. Some ground was rocky, or crumbling soil, but mostly it was sand. Sometimes John thought he was on their path, other times he doubted, but at last he made it to the wreck of the marauder ship. It was a charred and twisted hulk. Some bodies lay nearby it in similar state but none were Astrid or Tarku, and there was no sign of Weston or Melissa. He yelled out but no answer came. Then he saw it was as he feared - the ship had come down on the edge of a sand hill which became a wide and shallow cone-shaped fall away, a trap he'd heard of first in his time in the military, a trap known as a sift. The only way to identify a sift, apart from the shape, which was usually a perfect circle - but even that was hard to see given it's width, was to observe that it was clean. Any inhabited sift is perfectly clean. Devoid of vegetation, rock, animal, or litter. It's just a circle of sand in a smooth and gradual decline towards its centre, allowing for things that cross its surface to be identified and pinpointed exactly. John tossed a stone into the near decline. Within a minute or so the stone was pulled under by an unseen creature lying in wait under the sand and the surface left perfect once more. These trappers were the Tuxra, another creature that wasn't known prior to the collapse. Where there was one, there would be others. If any of the crew had mistakenly crossed one of these sifts, they would be gone already. John knew he had to be very careful just how he went on, walking back towards the Blue Moon now, but along a different line, hoping he would find the others.

Finally the faintest murmur came to John's ears, sounding further back to the east. He went that way through the low haze, then spotted an outline, just a vague darker area on the sand. He checked the shape of the sand as he went forward, careful that he was not heading too close to any sift. As John neared he yelled and ran forwards, it was Tarku, Tarku keeping Astrid's head out of the low swept sand. John knelt to them. It was apparent from the blood upon Tarku's own skin and across the sand around him, along with the state of his clothes and the awkward position he was in, that he had sustained some serious injuries in the fight and following escape from the speeding craft as it came down, even though his body didn't seem much injured now, apart from some obvious breaks. John put his pack under Tarku's head, lifting it from the sand. The Akaia was breathing, he was coming round further. Tarku tried to speak, but John shook his head to stop him, to let him know he didn't have to try.

'You landed ok John?' Tarku managed to ask, 'everyone's ok?'

'Yes, as far as I know,' John replied. He gently took the weight of Astrid from Tarku, lying her comfortably aside and resting her head in the shelter of his jacket. She seemed not to have sustained any serious injury but John recognised the pattern of blood from her eye and ear, and her incoherent state. He came to the same realisation as Tarku.

'She's a mech?' he said, quite amazed. 'Did you know?'

'No, not until now.'

'What happened? Was it the pulse did this?'

'Yes. When the pulse went over she fell, the ship's controls locked, even the doors wouldn't open. I mustn't have got out quite soon enough,' Tarku recalled trying to escape the speeding craft as it went down, the controls and all the electrics being frozen, he had at the last minute managed to pry open a door and jump free, Astrid in his hold. He coughed and tried to get up but John pushed him back.

'Take it easy,' John urged, 'you're in no state to move yet.'

'I'm sorry, I should be getting up, I know we have to get out of this place.'

'You're alive, that'll do,' John said. 'May I?' John asked permission from Tarku to help him. Tarku nodded. John re-adjusted a broken bone for the Akaia, and popped his dislocated shoulder back in. Tarku stifled several yells at the pain of it, but soon John was done. Then the guide asked the pressing question, 'Tarku, have Weston and Melissa come this way?'

'I haven't seen them, but I believe I've been in and out till just now. You've got to keep looking for them,' Tarku urged, 'I'll be fine, leave Astrid here with me, I'll make my way as I can.'

John thought about it, then nodded. 'I'll leave you a weapon,' John handed him a pistol along with a flare and stood to go. 'Hardan's back at the ship,' John pointed the direction. 'Make your way if you can, otherwise I'll be back for you after I've found Weston and Melissa.'

There were several times under that low haze that John thought he may have come upon another sift and threw a stone to test the sand. So far he was glad to find himself mistaken. He called and called again. 'Weston! Melissa!' His voice found no echo - just went out and disappeared into the emptiness so he kept on until at last there was a reply.

'John, we're over here!' Melissa yelled.

'Kept talking. I'll find my way to you!' John called back.

'I have a bone to pick with you John for sending my best photojournalist on that mad charge,' Weston's voice came through now, 'seriously, what if he isn't ok?! What if Astrid's not ok!?'

'They'll be ok,' John said, 'and so will we.' John reached them. They'd almost made it back to the Blue Moon, following a wider arc. The haze was higher here, and thin, the open sand flats around the ship were clear in sight, their figures alone in the wide desert. John was about to run forwards to them but pulled back at once. Melissa and Weston saw the action, what had John seen? Melissa took a step towards John but he yelled, 'Stop! Don't move!' She could see no danger, she didn't understand.

'Just stay still, wait,' John begged her, then radioed the ship. 'Hardan, Hardan, come in, come on Hardan, pick up the radio!'

It was a moment before the captain reached it and replied, 'Go ahead John.'

'What's the status on the repairs? Can she fly again yet?'

'Wouldn't like to try it, I've got the engine and the boosters right, but a good engine's no use without the right stuff to fly. The wings are trouble still, and the damage to the hull. I've got the electrics back online, but the system's finding errors by the second. I might need parts that we don't have.'

'Just get her to fly Hardan, even if it's just low level ok, to fly over land. I don't care if it's not quite ready, we don't have the luxury of time.'

'What's the situation out there?'

'It's Weston and Melissa, look outside.'

Hardan quickly ran up to the cabin door and looked out. Ahead he saw the scene as John saw it now. A massive sift, now moving in most definite lines, Melissa and Weston at its centre.

'I'll be there pronto,' Hardan radioed, 'hang tight.'

Melissa still hadn't fully grasped what was going on but she trusted them enough to stay where she was and not make a move. John stood where he was and waited with much angst as the Blue Moon rose, so slowly it seemed as Hardan pulled in the ramps and began across the ground. Their hearts raced further as they saw the movement in the sand grow, then the sharp, white stones, now visible as teeth lifted up and dragged with them a huge net that was the throat of just one of the giant Tuxra, one, trying to get closer than a rival and claim this meal. Melissa stumbled back as she saw it rise so close and John could take no more, she could be his daughter, she could be his Ava. The old soldier ran now, out across the sand towards the girl, between the runs of stones he knew were teeth just waiting for the time to snap closed, and they did, like a hunter's trap the mouth slammed shut only millimetres behind him, but on he ran, now pulling out his gun and firing down into the sand as he went. The bullets did no damage to the creatures but were a momentary deterrent giving him enough time to dodge past and get to them. He was right, once that first one had made the move the others came to life, they clashed against each other for the prize, their fight only half seen as they fought beneath the sand, barely above, but for a flash of teeth or horned spine or a heave of throat, throats like sieves they could move easily through the sand, picking up whatever lay upon it.

John reached them and caught Melissa up. Though shaken and overawed she was relieved at his heavy arm around her shoulders and the ringing in her ears after the loudness of his gun by her, as he and Weston shot again and again, and now he swung to sting any mouth that neared with a knife he pulled from his belt.

The Blue Moon was above them at last. Hardan threw ropes and harness down. John strapped Melissa in and clipped Weston onto the rope as well. As Hardan pulled the ship up John felt the edge of a bite, one last heave of a creature out of the sand trying to get at them, but it fell away without its prey, jarred by a succession of bullets from Tarku's gun. John looked back to see the Akaia standing on the edge of the sift. As soon as Melissa, Weston and John were safe, Hardan flew on and they picked up Tarku, who still held Astrid.

'No, no, no, no, no,' Weston muttered as he leant over his muse, as they pulled her in, the Machina20m A*id. He held her head and stroked her hair, 'Astrid, don't you quit on me!' She was awake, she held his face, but she was obviously in pain and couldn't seem to speak, her jaw only shivered with tension. It was the pulse, Weston knew, Astrid knew, the pulse had interfered with her subsystem and optics. He took Astrid up in his arms and took her to the sleeper cabin to be more comfortable.

'Are you ok?' John held Melissa a moment, the girl that could almost be his girl, and he breathed so much relief that she wasn't hurt. She was shaking so he held her yet. 'You're alright,' he assured her, 'you're alright.'

'Is Astrid ok? What happened to her?' Melissa spoke at last.

'She's a machina,' John answered, 'the pulse sent her system haywire.'

'A machina? Wow, I'd no idea. She doesn't look like a machina.'

'I didn't know either, I guess that's the idea.'

'And what were those things in the sand?'

'Tuxra,' Tarku answered as he stood up, 'another few moments and they would have pulled you under.'

'Are you ok Tarku?' she asked, noticing Tarku's bloodied figure, a look of complete astonishment and horror on her face.

'Oh, it's not as bad as it looks,' he explained, 'half of it probably isn't even mine. I'll clean up, and then I'll make everyone some tea. I think we need it.' As Tarku turned away Melissa realised he didn't have his sunglasses on, she realised she'd just seen his eyes for the first time, however briefly, and they brought up a question in her mind but no conclusion.

Hardan pulled up and landed in a sheltered spot in the relative safely of the wastes nearer Tamashan Main, then he set them all tasks about the ship, to get her back together as much as possible. The day wore out but they worked till they needed to sleep, then at last the frayed travellers slept in the still ship, its own tiny pocket of filtered air and peace. Every now and then faint stars glimmered through the clouded sky above, and the glow of the fires of war could be seen if looking towards Mon Karo, the capital of Tamashan. Melissa couldn't sleep, her tired eyes found temporary solace in that distant glow, despite the knowledge that it was war, it was the knowledge that the world was not all dead and empty like these wastes yet, people still lived and survived nearby. Her head leant against the window and she played with Matthias's button in her fingers. After these few weeks of travelling with the crew the North Islands seemed so distant. She missed them. She missed her friends, she missed the smell of the streets, the familiar streets, the cars, the simple dinners, the empty beach without a sea. The train line beyond the station where the trains no longer ran, the weeds that grew in the cracks despite everything. She looked at Tarku, who was the only other in the cabin at present, but this time he was definitely asleep, he lay across the front few seats facing the wall, completely out to it and even under a rug. Perhaps she'd never seen him asleep before in all the other times she'd thought he was sleeping. She watched the rise and fall of his ribs, and the air was so quiet she could even hear his steady breath, but every now and then she heard his breath catch, almost like there was pain in his sleep, though he slept on.

In truth the Akaia was in pain, his scars were still hot, though healed; not the scars of this last foray, but the scars of Syra's etched now in his own skin. Even as he slept the lines held him, a captive to the memories he had, and no lose thread could be found while sleeping, for him to distract himself. Such is the reason sleeping was not favoured by the Akaia, but his weary body begged him this night to sleep for a little while at least, and so he lay, but he saw into her eyes again as they killed her, he saw that blue sky of her home reflected there, he saw it fade into fire and smoke, like the end of the world, and he felt her pain within himself again. At last the hit to his psyche was hard enough to wake him from that dark place, he gasped and sat up.

'Bad dreams Tarku?' Melissa asked. Her voice was gentle, so soft to him after the vivid harshness of his pain. He was aware he wore no sunglasses and didn't know if his eyes would reveal what he was to the innocent girl, so he was sure to look down and away as he had done earlier, and pull his dark fringe even lower across his face.

'Memories,' he replied, 'that is all, butterfly.'

'I can't sleep either.'

Tarku didn't reply.

'Tarku, can I ask you something?'

'Go ahead.'

'What's in your special tea?'

Tarku chuckled, 'Did Astrid put you up to this? Or maybe John?'

'No, I was just feeling like some and wondered why. Isn't that what you gave me when I had a migraine? And what you gave us all earlier today?'

'You had the lightest infusion I could manage, but that's a good idea actually, I'll make you some. You probably feel like some because it's an all round tonic. Another will do our nerves good after what happened today.'

Tarku soon returned with the tea, he sat and closed his eyes and sipped quietly in the pleasant dark. Melissa watched him and she realised that Astrid was right, ice did melt, Tarku had shown it in glimpses, but he seemed to have a very good ability to re-freeze. She hoped he wouldn't withdraw so much again, he seemed to almost be nice when he wasn't frozen.

'Tarku, have you been in the wastes before?' she asked softly after a few quiet sips.

'Yes.'

'How do you deal with it?' she asked. 'I have lived beside the empty sea by The Gutter all my life and I knew that it was practically a waste, but it's nothing like this, I guess the wastes beyond the sea are, but I didn't realise it would be like this. Like we have seen all over on this trip, so few surviving islands amongst such vast desert and waste.'

Tarku didn't answer, only thought.

'I was trying to think how to describe it,' Melissa continued, 'how I felt as I walked out from the ship today, into the haze. It's not just the emptiness, or the desert, or the fact the just about everything is dead, except for those monsters, it was something else.'

Tarku sipped and waited for her to continue.

'It's like the further you go the heavier the weight of gravity is on your shoulders, the more it feels like there is a quicksand under you, not like really, but like your spirit is being pulled down.'

'You felt that?' his brows narrowed, concerned.

'Yes, it was horrible. It's hard to shake the feeling.'

'Drink the tea,' he encouraged.

'Tarku, why are we doing this?' she asked after another pause.

'Doing what?'

'I've just been wondering what we're doing out here? I didn't even think about it before we left, but I guess it just kind of struck me, I mean, really. There won't be anyone to see what we film if the world ends. No one will want to sit and watch what we film, or care about how wonderful it is on Shorakai or be amazed at how much the red sand gets on everything on Rorona. No one will care or want to know, not if their own world is shattering. So what are we doing out here? Why do we bother filming anything?'

'Would you prefer to do nothing?'

'No, but I wonder what purpose there is in what we're doing. It's wonderful, but meaningless, really, isn't it?'

'Doesn't the same apply to whatever it was you were doing before this?'

'I suppose, apart from the being wonderful bit,' she almost laughed.

'If you were going to die tomorrow what would you want to do?'

'I don't know, be with my friends I guess.'

'Yes. And then if you didn't die that day but you had another last day? What would you do?'

'The same.'

'Mm, this is how the world is, we are given only a day at a time, but how can you live like it's the last day every day? You can't, it becomes impractical. Life has to go on. We have to survive, so we work, we go on with the monotony, because there is no other choice. The world may end tomorrow, but the weary will still go home and turn on their television tonight seeking a light distraction for their heavy minds. And, you will have learnt by doing and living, and you will have earned something, and if the world doesn't end we will achieve on this trip what no one else has, and what we have done will be looked back upon as a very significant contribution of film to the historical archives.'

'Is that why you do this? Because you think it's important in the long term?'

Tarku laughed, 'No, I do it because I need a distraction too.'

After the special blend was drunk they both managed to sleep. Well, Melissa slept, but Tarku was as close to being asleep as he could get these days without going to a dark place, his thoughts were dulled and his heart slowed, he could close his eyes and be at peace, which was a rare change.

Weston sat with Astrid all night, fretting over her, ensuring she had everything she may need. By morning she was much recovered, but not entirely. Weston tried to get her to stay still, but now that the shock of the pulse had somewhat subsided she wouldn't lie idle but got up and went straight back to the editing room to try to debug her system. The pulse had not only shut it down, but effectively scrambled everything. She hardly knew what she was about. Apart from getting her subsystem started she couldn't get anywhere, there was a persistent glitch, leaving only a ghost of her system available, like a television that couldn't get proper reception - it wasn't good for anything.

'We just have to face it West, it's not going to happen, I'm broken, at the worst time to be broken.' She was shaking now, something so strange for him to see in her, she was always so strong. 'If I'd had the slightest warning I could have turned my subsystem off while the pulse hit us, it might have been ok. Or if we could use the transmitters I could get through to Q-corp. and get a diagnostic and reconfiguration, it might work, but we couldn't turn the transmitter's power that high or we'd attract some serious attention.'

'We'll get through this Astrid, we'll get it working again. There'll be a way.'

She shook her head, 'I don't think so. I'm just so annoyed with myself because I'm better than this, I should have anticipated the fighter, prevented all of this! Not just me, but we all almost died! That was my fault.'

'You can't expect that much of yourself, not even you could do that. Let's let it be for a while and come back to it, we're all knocked about a bit, none of us could think to fix a meal, let alone a system as complicated as yours. Maybe you do just need something to eat. Can I get you something?'

She shook her head, 'No I'm not hungry.'

'Astrid you've got to eat,' Weston worried, taking her hand and playing with her fingers, then kissing her hand. Astrid just burst into laughter, 'Now don't you get all sickly sweet on me or I'll take back my acceptance.'

Weston suddenly pulled her close and kissed her firmly, 'Better?' he asked.

'Yep,' her smile lit up and she ran her fingers through his hair, 'much better.' Then her face became serious, 'We should see if we can be of any use out there, I bet the Blue Moon needs some serious work.'

'No, you need to recover,' Weston protested, 'and I'm staying with you,'

'Don't be stupid, I'll be fine,' Astrid stood up but sat right back down again and held his shoulder, 'ok, maybe you're not so stupid.'

'Still woozy?'

'Very woozy. Can I ask you a question West? Were you worried about going to Tamashan this time?'

'What? Never! Not when I've got you. What's this past-tense business anyway? We're still going, besides we're here, I'm not turning back now.'

'But West, like this I'm not a mech,' she said, then almost yelled in her frustration, 'I can't even see out of my right eye anymore, not without the system functioning! I feel so, so inhibited, so diminished!'

'You've been off before, remember, last time we did it on purpose, we had fun.'

'That was different, I knew what I was doing, I had it under control.'

'You'll get it back under control, you will.'

'And this looks like a full on war, we haven't covered a war since we were young things.'

'I don't look that old do I?'

Astrid chuckled, 'Well, you've put on a few pounds, and you look so much less devious than you did back then Mr Alamo, without that moustache.'

'Did you like that moustache? I could grow it again.'

'No I hated it!' she laughed, but then tensed and held tighter onto Weston's shoulder.

'What's the matter?' he asked.

'Just tried it again, it's all fragments, a buzz of garbled pieces. West, if I'm not functioning I can't do my job.'

'Astrid, it's going to be alright, alright?'

'But you can't go into this conflict if I'm not a mech!'

'Can't I? Hardan reckons I'm reckless like that.'

'What are you saying? You will?'

'Well, we're here. We might as well.'

Astrid considered things then asked, 'Do you still want me to be Mrs Alamo if I'm not a mech?'

'I can't be doing a very good job being your secret love for you to ask that question. You know the answer Astrid.'

'It's just nothing seems solid anymore, the world is muffled, muted, but some things seem so razor sharp that it hurts. Everything's uncertain.'

'Welcome to humanity,' he grinned. 'Astrid, breathe, you'll get on top of this alright, just take your time.'

'Yeah, you're right, I'll get on top of this,' she repeated, but she didn't sound convinced.

'Here, let me take you back to the bunk, it might be good to lie down a while,'

'Alright.'

'What, you're agreeing with me?'

'Yes West,' she chuckled, 'just this once. I'll do another re-boot, I'll try to leave the system on so at least I might get fragments of data that may be of some use.'

'Remember the rest of us get on fine just being human, most of the time, so if you need to turn it off, just turn it off. Now, we better get going,' Weston laughed, 'if we hang here too long rumours might start! Although, I don't think anyone will be doubting how I feel about you after how I carried on when we pulled you up.'

'Good. So we can be easy about it now.'

'Yep, we can be easy. Come on, are you sure you don't want breakfast?'

'Actually, it does sound like a good idea.'

'Hardy probably has some snack to share with everyone. Probably some reconstituted frozen and defrosted confection, that still tastes absolutely delicious because of the sheer amount of chemical additives.'

'My kind of breakfast,' Astrid laughed.

'Then, I reckon Hardy will have us another good day to work on this ship, we'll get her all patched up and hopefully by tonight we can sneak closer into Tamashan, maybe we'll even get close enough to Mon Karo to get some decent film of the capital.'

'You're excited about this aren't you?' she laughed, 'we're heading into who knows what trouble and you're happy as a boy who's just made himself a slingshot.'

'Happier!' Weston admitted with a grin as they walked along to the kitchen.

CHAPTER 31:

Getting footage on Tamashan

The Tamashani were generally a social and laid-back people, boundaries and personal space were different to them. Under normal circumstances they would hug even strangers when they met, they would share gossip with you within minutes of meeting you, they would take you into their family and treat you as family, feed you full as they could and make certain your needs were met. They loved their food and they loved their community. The environment here was very tolerable, better than most in fact, and beautiful in its own way, not an extravagant or awe-inspiring beauty, but a simple beauty - hills, grass, trees, lakes, and a pleasant architecture throughout the cities despite their size. Even their high-rises seemed homely, quaint and welcoming, modern and old all jumbled together. It had been on Weston's list ever since he had begun to plan this expedition. Only, he had not expected that they would be coming here under these circumstances at all, it would never have crossed his mind, and had you proposed the possibility he would have laughed whole-heartedly and told you that the earth collapsing was more likely than war erupting on his much-loved Tamashan.

In the political sphere Tamashan was usually a passive voice when it came to matters of regional importance, they kept their own peace and didn't meddle in the affairs of other nations even when it seemed perhaps they should. But they were happy in their own peace, or had been. In recent years they had become a little more pro-active, using their good standing amongst other nations to rally support for different causes. Though no-one has yet determined if this has anything to do with this attack, still no one from Delevi has come forward with a statement, though several nations have stiffly asked for one, and still no one had been able to contact Tamashan since the strike.

That was about to change. The work on the ship had gone well and in the late morning Hardan steered the Blue Moon ever so low and slow, around the edge of the wastes then settled the ship in the outskirts of a seemingly abandoned suburb in the far south-west, as close as possible to Tamashan Main. Now the crew prepared once again to begin filming, though they were well aware of the all too near danger that awaited them out here. They could see the Delevian warships far ahead over the port at Mon Karo, they could feel from time to time the shake of the ground, not from a natural quake, but from explosions, and they could see the smoke rising from the city, smoke that was swept high and wide as the winds whipped it towards the ash clouds sent up irregularly from the Pireomerai. A brief scan outside and the crew could see no movement, no people, just empty streets.

'I think now might be a good time to send up the copter,' Weston said, rubbing his hands together in delight then opening the box he'd just placed on the table amongst their lunchtime dishes.

'The camouflaged optical terrain recorder,' Tarku observed as he ate and as Weston pulled the thing out of the box and began to unfold the contraption and secure the few clips that held it together.

'Yep, at least we won't walk into anything then,' Weston grinned.

'Although it may alert them to the fact that we're here if you're not careful,' Astrid added, 'it may even let them know our location, if they don't know we're here already.'

'They don't know, if they knew we'd be dead or in custody by now surely,' Weston remarked.

'Unless they don't think we're that important,' Hardan added, sipping his coffee.

'But they won't get our location if we don't live-stream the footage will they?' Weston asked his mech.

'We'd still be transmitting the radio signal from here, to move it around,' Astrid explained.

'What if we pre-program the route?' Weston asked.

'Then if they shoot it down not only do we not get any data, they still get our location,' Astrid pointed out.

'Someone should scout ahead then?'

'Or we set up a relay somewhere,' Astrid helped.

'That's it, alright, I'll find a spot and set up a receiver away from the ship, we can live stream to that location, then it's ok if they track it back, plus, if they shoot it down we'll have footage and they won't have us. Excellent.' Weston went straight to the back room and checked the cameras on the copter and got it transmitting to a portable set-up, then took both and prepared to go out.

'Tamashan's been waiting for a news crew for too long,' Weston breathed, 'it's now or never, are you coming Astrid? The rest of you stay close by and film what you can, but stay out of trouble, we shouldn't be too long.'

The producer and the machina ran through the empty streets, dodging from building to building, from crumbling wall to rusted fence, further away from the ship. When a fair distance had been covered Astrid found a particularly neglected building and pushed inside, setting down the interface and readying the copter for its mission. They were almost ready to launch when Astrid's shattered senses relayed to her that they were not alone here. She touched the floor and closed her eyes to try to make more sense of the feedback her system gave.

'What is it?' Weston asked her.

'People. I think there are people hiding here, under the ground.'

'Well let's find them, let's see what they can tell us.'

Weston and Astrid searched the ruins where they were, Astrid mapping the walls in her mind and finding the most likely entry point for a cellar according to comparisons of other Tamashani constructions. Soon she found the trapdoor, opening it. Many Tamashani were down here, Astrid found a gun pointed at her squarely. She put up her hands.

'Don't shoot, I'm a northerner, I'm not Delevian,' she said, 'we're press, not fighting.'

They seemed to be deliberating whether or not to shoot Astrid and Weston or to let them go.

'Close the door, you didn't see us,' they said at last.

'Wait, do you know why the Delevian came? Do you know why they're here? What their plan is?' Weston pressed.

'Mister, we were having our meal, the sirens went off but at once bombs fell and the enemy was everywhere - in the streets, in the air. We all hid, we keep hiding. We know nothing. Go from here, the danger is not past.'

The Tamashani grabbed the trapdoor and pulled it back closed.

'We should find another relay point,' Astrid said, picking up the gear.

'Yes, alright, I guess we should. I want to film them though, I want to get their stories.'

'I have the film, but it's not safe yet West, let's move.'

'Ok, ok, we'll move.'

They relocated, then again they tested the transmission and with some excitement sent the copter out. Once high it could barely be seen or heard, and when they saw the footage on the screen of what could be viewed from the little machine they already were ecstatic. A bird's eye view of this war would tell a great story.

They sent the copter out across the suburbs, back towards the east, towards the desert that most visitors crossed on the way in. They manoeuvred the copter to come back into the city from beyond and capture all, like a ship flying into port from the direction of Satsuan.

At first no signs of the conflict were apparent, but then evidences of the battle could be seen, still and silent narratives of what had passed. What seemed to be the entire fleet of Tamashan fighter craft lay destroyed. Ashen and burning hulks littered across the dunes of the Lulno desert below, amongst them only a few Delevian craft. There didn't seem to be any survivors out here, only bodies and all manner of scavengers - masked marauders pulling usable gear from the wrecks, desperate animals fighting over what meat they could get from the dead.

Slowly the copter drew closer to the city, the capital Mon Karo. The daylight shone faintly through the haze of cloud and smoke that rose up from the ground. Mon Karo had the look of a city already ruined by battle, already bombed. As the copter flew nearer fires could be seen burning unchecked in some quarters. Weston steered the copter towards the main port, closer and closer, now low over the rows of Delevian craft that were docked here. Here at last they saw some Delevian soldiers, going about their duties.

'You're game,' Astrid laughed as she watched the copter's progress. Weston grinned and went on.

The port of Mon Karo was an immense structure of many tiers that reached above the city into the sky, as big as any of the skyscrapers in the Universal City, much bigger in fact. Such a structure was needed as only small, purpose-built ships could find a place where they were allowed to land at ground level in

Tamashan Main. As Tamashan was such a popular destination each tier of the port had the capacity to house over twenty ships, the lower tiers held more than fifty ships each, and this was just the main city port. It had been a very well ordered place, each ship having a space to itself, complete with communication equipment, tools and a cleaning and repair robot that could be set to work for a small fee.

They could see now as Weston moved the copter on, that there were a few other isolated ships amongst the Delevian and Vahrnan vessels, though very few, most foreign ships would have got out of here as soon as there was any sign of unrest. Weston guided the copter to the highest of the wide lower levels, which he knew was also the level from which the Tamashani usually ran operations. The platform was partly demolished and the aftermath of a gun battle could be seen towards the central entry. The DC20 of the North Islands was on this platform too, though they could see none of the crew.

It was a few hours later as Weston pulled the copter further out again that they realised something was happening, Delevian soldiers were heading to their ships, the ships were lifting up and moving off with some urgency.

'Maybe they're leaving,' Weston suggested.

'Maybe they are.'

'They are leaving, look,' Weston pointed to the images they were seeing.

Columns of Delevian warships were soon pulling out and heading back out across the desert, away from Tamashan.

'They are leaving,' Astrid said, 'a good number of them are in any case.'

'We should stream what footage we have back to TnTv while we have the chance, if the Delevian are going, we can get this out now,' Weston said.

'Are you sure that's wise?' Astrid asked. 'We don't really know what's happening.'

'Not a question of wise or otherwise, this is more a question of opportunity and chance, and getting the story out while we can.'

'So back to the ship then?'

'Yes, back to the ship, then we get as much together as we can and transmit the package home. And prepare to make a run for it if we're intercepted.'

'Ok, let's do this.'

They hurried back to the ship and ramped up the transmitters, sending the packet out to TnTv. Astrid had hoped to link up with Q-Corp to attempt to reconfigure her subsystem at the same time but the transmission took longer than expected and she didn't think it wise to waste any more time in getting out of the area while Tamashan was still hot with hostile forces. Then Hardan moved the ship at once, temporarily back out into the wastes to hide in case there would be any repercussions from sending the footage, and turning off all devices except the air and water filtration, food chiller and a few low-lights.

Most on board had been into places such as this before, places of war. Melissa hadn't, but they were all were shocked at such immense devastation. It was silent now inside the ship.

The reaction back in the Universal City, and indeed the rest of the world who soon saw it as well, was shock, but the question still had to be answered, the question - why had the Delevian come?

CHAPTER 32:

Fire and Shadow

Alamo's crew lay low for the moment. The plan was for everyone to get a good sleep, then before dawn the next morning they would steer the Blue Moon back closer in to Mon Karo and head off on foot through the streets of Tamashan. They still wanted to find the reasons behind Delevi's actions. But it was hard to sleep again, what with the adrenalin still pumping from what they had just done, the small amount of film each had shot nearby the ship as well as all the incredible film from the copter, now sent. Despite the fact that some Delevian ships and soldiers still remained, many now appeared to be moving away from Mon Karo. Weston had danced all up and down the ship singing about the bonuses that the stunt would gain them, he was very enthusiastic. They were all excited, but eventually the crew did manage to calm and find their bunks again, to rest.

Melissa dreamed that her dear friends Kat and Matti got together. It was perfect, and she was surprised how happy she was for them. She didn't have a crush on the mechanic anymore, and she was even taking photos at their wedding. Strange really, for her friends were married down the beach opposite the girl's apartment in The Gutter, but it *was* beside the sea, a real ocean stretching out and glittering like the sea of Shorakai. It was beautiful, not littered with rubbish and fermenting waste like the reality, and there was no sign of Sir and everyone was happy. Even Jem Fisher was there, with his little family, and Astrid and Weston, and Hardan and his family, it was a supremely satisfying dream, except for the fact that in no direction she looked could Tarku be seen.

Hardan was dreaming too. Back in the sleeper cabin he slumbered with a twitch in his whiskers, and a random voiced command. 'Belay that!' Hardan muttered, 'No! To the starboard there!' and so on. He was obviously a captain that never stopped, even in his sleep.

John was sleeping, this place was a series of anxious memories and unspoken words, conversations with his wife and thoughts of his daughter, that big blue sky of Shorakai was back in his mind too. Amiana trying to say something to him in the translating room on Rauron, what was it? She was beautiful, so beautiful. Her dress was blue and flowing, her hair dark and like water over her shoulders it ran, and it caressed his face as they kissed. It was smooth and soft and had the fragrance of the seaside flowers all through it. Now her face was pale, he felt blood on his fingers, it was in her hair, now dripping down her lovely face. 'No' he said 'No, no, Amiana! Stay with me.'

She smiled at him. 'I love you but you've got to wake up now Johnny, wake up!'

There was nothing in his arms. The blue sky drew away suddenly as John was wrenched back into real life. John gasped as he found himself in the haze that was the early morning. Was that an aftershock? The ship shook as a tremor rolled across the earth, a proper tremor, soon followed by another. The air was thick. Why was the air so thick? He shook himself out of slumber and headed for the cabin. Weston was heavily asleep, John flicked a few switches on and off, no light, something was wrong. Their lights weren't working, the air filtration wasn't working. No wonder he felt so groggy. John felt the overwhelming desire just to fall back into sleep, but he grabbed a mask and breathed in the oxygen and made it to Tarku, shaking him. 'The air's gone,' he whispered, 'everyone's out.'

At once Tarku was up, as yet unaffected by the insufficient oxygen levels. He and John found the gas masks and helped the rest of the crew wake from their induced sleep, but despite all their efforts neither Weston or Hardan could be woken, they were breathing but unconscious, all they could do was hold the masks on and hope the oxygen made the difference. Astrid found the light-sticks and passed them around. It was morning already, but remained strangely dark, and it wasn't just the cloud from the fires burning in Mon Karo, it was more than that. John came back from inspecting the engines, his heart and head pounding. He shook his head.

'What's going on?' Melissa asked, as she and Astrid looked to John.

'What do you think? Is this sabotage? Are we dealing with Marauders? Soldiers?' Astrid asked John. 'I can't sense anyone around.'

'No, actually the engine's fine, the systems are going, they're just not making a difference,' John looked out the window then back at Tarku desperately. They both were becoming aware that this was no man-made circumstance. Tarku didn't say anything but he looked away and John lost the colour in his face. 'No Tarku, we have to be wrong,' John shook his head, hoping Tarku would have another explanation, but Tarku didn't need to speak, John could tell his fears were true by the Akaia's expression. Shame. Fear. Utter dismay.

'What's happening? What's out there?' Melissa asked, holding her light head.

'A shadow is coming,' Tarku told her the truth John didn't want to say. He looked out towards the desert and their eyes followed. Now they could see, a broad, condensing cloud of ash and smoke and fire drawing up from the very distant rifts and consuming the horizon even as they watched.

'Volcanic cloud,' Astrid saw, 'Maybe this is why the Delevian are moving off?'

'It may be why they disperse, but it's no volcanic cloud, not this time. It's a Mrukai,' Tarku corrected.

'Mrukai?' Astrid questioned Tarku. 'But surely it can't be? Not that!'

Neither John nor Tarku answered, they only watched the immense Mrukai in its slow progress across the wastes towards them, speechless. It truly was a folktale salamander of fire and ash. The air was sucked towards the rising dark, surely as fire consumed oxygen. They felt the ship quaver as another tremor rolled across the ground, but this was no earthquake, it was the slow pound of the footsteps of the coming Mrukai.

Astrid searched the desert beyond, 'I can't see anything but ash cloud, I can sense something but I don't trust what I see, it can't be.' She saw flashes across the landscape, and when she put those flashes together she could see the outline of the giant, and she could see that the Mrukai could easily hold the ship in its claws, its form stretched out far larger than a Kyu's. She lost her breath, in total awe and shock, now understanding what Tarku and John knew.

'The end must be getting close now,' Tarku spoke quietly as he studied it, 'It's not just any Mrukai, it's old, a giant from out of the earth's fractured core. Look, it can't even fly anymore. I wonder what it wants with me.'

'We can't outrun it, can we,' John stood there, helpless as he watched it grow ever closer.

'You can, I can't, not for long,' Tarku said, 'I will go to it, John take the ship and get out of here.'

'No Tarku, we can't leave you here, against this -' Astrid said as she went to a hidden storage cabinet and began handing out weapons.

Tarku laughed darkly, 'What do you think to do with those?'

She ignored Tarku, 'Here John,' she went to hand one to the soldier but he refused as Tarku had, shaking his head. 'Put those away, they'll do no damage to a Mrukai.'

'Go!' Tarku looked at John and made sure the man knew to heed him. Then for the first time on the trip Tarku let down the pretence of not being an Akaia. He dropped his gas mask and threw aside his dark glasses. He opened the external cabin door and prepared to jump.

'What are you going to do?' John pressed,

'If there was time I would go further from you, but there's little time, I'm sorry, I will go as far as I can. You must get away from here. I think it's here for me, don't get in its way and you should be safe. Don't try to stop it.'

'We'll come back for you Tarku.'

'I don't think that will be a good idea.'

'I am a man of my word,' John spoke seriously, 'I will come back as soon as the Mrukai is gone.'

Tarku knew John was serious so he took the gun Astrid had wanted John to take and handed it to the soldier. 'Then I give you leave to take me down. If I get through this I could be all fight and no mind. Empty it if you have to.'

John took the weapon for Tarku's sake. Tarku stood there a moment, his heart tried to build the courage to face what came, but as he turned to exit the Blue Moon the giant called, and they all saw him inhale a sharp breath, as if his body had experienced the force of some sudden and painful impact. His eyes ignited. Not even Astrid had seen his smouldering eyes before, eyes with irises as perfect grey ash, now flickering with sparks from deeper within, eyes that embodied fire and shadow, that held an intensity so unnerving. A surge of adrenalin pulsed through Melissa's body equal to that of John's yells waking her suddenly out of deep slumber and finding out a Mrukai was near the ship, as she realised what this meant. She had been close to him all this time, the entire trip, she had conversed with him, judged him, surely it couldn't be! Tarku was an Akaia?!

'Look after them John,' Tarku managed to say at last, then jumped down to the sand and headed out towards the coming Mrukai.

As John fastened his seatbelt and prepared to take the Blue Moon further away, they watched Tarku walk out into the desert closer to the massive form, that being, that great cloud all embers and ash, as it became more clearly defined. The creature seemed not to be part of this earth, a dying giant from ages past, heaving itself up from the depths and clawing the earth with the last of its strength.

They watched as their friend the Akaia, a mere speck in comparison to the giant, stopped his walk as the Mrukai reached him, as he stood before it, the bravest thing any of them had ever seen. Soon he was out of their sight, but they heard that giant call, they all heard and felt sand-paper pulled through their bones and they cringed, holding themselves against it. It was nothing like a Kyu's call. Melissa gasped at the thought of Tarku under its full force and cried because they could not help him.

The call was followed by a long and low exhalation that sent warm air circling about the dunes and even found its way into the cabin as if the walls were nothing and the ashes from the outside circled now within as well. John pulled into the first sheltered area he could, behind the barrier that bordered the outskirts of Tamashan against the wastes, and here they waited. John quickly went back to the bunks and tried to rouse Hardan and Weston again, Astrid followed him.

'Weston's breathing, his pulse is fine,' Astrid observed. They moved to Hardan.

At once Astrid was pumping Hardan's chest, breathing into his mouth to try and bring him back, he had no colour. 'John, I can't get a pulse, bring the adrenalin and defibrillator from the stowage,' Astrid directed as she keep pumping. Soon John was back and together they worked, trying to revive him.

'What's this ruckus in here?' Weston cursed as he came around, groggy. 'What are you all doing, playing games in the dark? And what was that infernal noise?' The producer bumped his head as he sat up. 'Ooh!' he cursed again, but then was suddenly very awake, his great friend didn't look so well. 'Hardy! What's happened?!'

'He's not breathing,' Astrid said as she continued the resuscitation, then she took the defibrillator and set to shock Hardan's heart to try to get back a rhythm. They tried for many long minutes, but they couldn't get him back. By the time they stopped trying to save Hardan, the lights in the cabin had flickered back on, the air quality had returned to normal, and the ashes that were the Mrukai were retreating to the far wastes and the rift beyond.

Astrid stopped her work. She shook her head. 'I'm sorry, we were too long. The oxygen didn't make a difference, Hardan's gone.'

'What?! Just like that?! Isn't there something else we can do?' urged Weston.

'I'm sorry West.'

'But there's got to be a way!' Weston urged. 'There's got to be something we can do!'

Astrid turned away and put her head in her hands for a moment.

'There's nothing you could have done Astrid,' John calmed, 'nothing, even if we had all the tools of an emergency room, nothing we can do, he was likely gone before we even knew what was happening.'

'But I should have known!' she stressed.

'No, John's right Astrid,' Weston put a hand on her shoulders. 'I didn't mean what I said that way, I just, this is, I mean, Hardan, I just woke up and he's dead.'

Melissa shuddered, feeling rather stunned and out of place. Astrid turned away. John sighed and sat down. Weston remained in a state of perplexion. To Melissa Hardan's body had completely lost the glimmer of his spirit and was now no more than a cheap imitation of Hardan. She felt she had lost another friend. She considered Hardan must now be the first of the two of the crew who, according to statistics, must die while on this assignment. And he didn't die in some dramatic or heroic way, he just died, just like that. Like a bug in a jar. Life was so fragile. She swallowed. Who would be the second one in the crew to fall? The other one in three?

'What about Tarku?' she asked.

No one answered her. Weston rubbed his forehead, distraught, 'You should've woken me up,' he said to John, 'what happened? What happened to Hardan?'

'No oxygen for too long. I tried to wake you up, but you were out for a bit too, everyone's different, Hardan didn't cope.'

'Did the filtration stop?' Weston asked but before anyone replied he answered his own question. 'but the wastes weren't that toxic where we were, we would have noticed soon enough, or the warning would have gone off, or something!'

'It was a strange thing,' John told Weston, 'it was a giant Mrukai. Its presence seemed to draw away what oxygen there was, and what energy there was running the systems.'

'What? A-a-a real live Mrukai?'

'Yes.'

'But really? A Mrukai? Near my ship!' Weston repeated.

'Yes West.'

Weston lost his words for a moment, 'I never imagined!' he cursed, 'did we film it? Were we filming it?'

No one answered his question. Astrid glared at Weston trying not to slap him. 'We just lost Hardan, Tarku's out there,' she pointed, 'probably half dead, and you're asking us if we were filming?'

'Well,' Weston shrugged, looking a little guilty, 'were you?'

Astrid slapped him.

'Wait, what did you say? Where is Tarku?'

'Come on, let's see if we can find him,' said John, 'the Mrukai looks like it's far enough away now.'

'What! You mean you can still see it?' Weston looked out the windows as John had. 'I see ashes on the horizon, is that bad? But I don't see a Mrukai.'

'As Tarku would say, lucky you,' John went forwards to the cockpit once more and headed back to where they had been overnight. There was no sign of Tarku nearby.

'Can you pick up anything?' John asked Astrid.

'No. Nothing. But my senses are still so hazy, and the wastes play interference at the best of times, I'll keep trying.'

'Weston, we better see to Hardan,' John spoke, snapping the producer out of his daze.

'Poor Hardan,' Weston sighed. 'The execs all advised against hiring an Akaia at the beginning, told me I was playing with explosives. I like the kid, he's got style, he's got skill, but now look what's happened.'

John spoke up, 'The blame for Hardan's death does not lie with Tarku.'

'Blast it!' Weston exhaled, 'of course I know that, but it's this cursed earth, everything's gone to pieces. I know it's not Tarku's fault that he is what he is, but if that boy wasn't what he was that thing would never have come here, don't you think. Hardy would still be alive.'

Astrid went to defend Tarku as well but stopped, she felt Hardan's loss too much.

'I need to say something,' John spoke seriously, 'once we deal with Hardan I'm going to go find Tarku, and I'm going to try to bring him back. So, no more of this. We've just seen more than we can understand, don't let it change us. Tarku still deserves our friendship and respect, for all I have observed of him on this journey so far is a testament to his good character. Wouldn't you all agree?' Everyone nodded. 'And besides,' John turned to Weston, 'I'm fairly certain that we'll be needing him if we're going to push further towards the capital?'

'Absolutely,' agreed Weston, but his face was troubled.

John found a sheet and covered the captain's body, bending down with Weston and lifting the heavy man. Astrid held Melissa as they passed, taking the body of dear Hardan below, to the cargo hold. Weston could hardly watch as John did what was necessary; vacuum sealing the captain's body in plastic then stowing him in the chiller beside their frozen supplies. Who knows how long it would be till they reached the North Islands again, and it was their responsibility to see him returned to his family.

'At least he's still got some apricot pastries in there with him,' Weston sighed and rubbed his whiskers. 'Goodbye dear Hardy, I shall miss your burly self and your warm heart. I shall be hard pressed to find another captain I can trust as I trust you. You have been a true friend, farewell.' Weston spoke, but he was still stunned, it had all happened so quickly, so unexpectedly. John took Weston's shoulder, then recited a pilot's prayer for Hardan.

'We could go back to the north,' John spoke seriously now to Weston, who did seem quite shaken at the whole set of events, 'with Hardan dead, and the state of the ship, and who knows how Tarku will be after this, if I can find him, and if he's alive.'

'Astrid's compromised too,' Weston said, but shook his head. 'No, Hardan wouldn't want us to go back now, I don't want to go back, and Astrid wouldn't, she hates the vault, and I don't have quite enough funds to buy her out yet. We're so close, we need to try to get some explanation for this attack and get it on film,' he said, 'then we can go home.'

Going back into the cabin, Melissa noticed Tarku's sunglasses and picked them up, putting them on his favourite seat. As she did she saw out the window, and she saw a shape in the sand beyond. Why didn't they see him before?

'It's Tarku!' she called back to the others, 'it's Tarku!' At once she lowered the stairs and ran out.

The morning was still dark and the sands swept with the rising wind and awash with ash. The giant Mrukai was so far distant, returning to the rift. Melissa soon reached Tarku and knelt down beside his body and studied him. She was scared, but she drew her courage together and felt for a pulse. Nothing. He had no breath. His chest was still. His eyes were frightening, but blank, but his was not like Hardan's body, there was still the vaguest light of life upon it and she would not despair. Melissa had watched Astrid and the others work on Hardan, so she took her own hands and began to pump Tarku's chest, gingerly giving her breath to him as Astrid had done to the captain. A tear fell from her eyelashes as she whispered, 'I'm sorry Tarku, I'm sorry I judged you, come on, you can't die, I didn't know.'

'Melissa, come away,' John called to her as he ran closer. Weston and Astrid were also making their way out to him now.

'He's not dead too is he?' Weston asked.

Melissa sat where she was on the sand by Tarku, looking to the others for direction. A little row of tears now flowed and melded together under each of Melissa's eyes and fell. Tarku wasn't waking up. She stopped the compressions.

'Melissa, come away,' John urged her again as he checked his weapon. What had Tarku said? If he survived he could be all fight. John didn't understand what was happening here, but he understood what Tarku meant - an Akaia all fight was a dangerous thing.

But Melissa stayed where she was. 'Did you all know he was an Akaia? Why didn't you tell me?' Melissa cried, almost yelled. 'Why did you let me ask so many questions? I didn't know!'

'I'm sorry,' Astrid apologised, 'I just felt it was his call if he wanted to tell you.'

'I'm so stupid, but it makes sense now, but Akaia can't just die like this can they? I mean if everything they say about them is true he can't just die!'

'No, you're right, there's life in him yet,' John assured her, 'but you've got to come away now Melissa.'

'But he's not breathing, he doesn't have a heartbeat.'

'If he's going to live he's going to live, if he's going to die than he's already dead. Come on,' John held his hand out to her to come with him, but it was then he noticed tattoos on Tarku's neck that weren't there before, and on his hand. They glimmered a little, very faintly.

'What is this?' John wondered, he looked to Tarku, then the teary eyed Melissa. 'Get back to the ship,' he told her, though he didn't wait to see her gone only quickly unzipped Tarku's jacket, then quickly unbuttoned the shirt and tore open Tarku's singlet and pushed it aside.

'What are you Tarku?' John gasped inwardly, stepping back as he saw what Tarku kept hidden so well.

'Oh wow!' Melissa whispered in wonder.

They saw Tarku's chest, that maze of patterns slightly paler than the rest of his skin. The patterns extended to every part of his skin that they could see, right up to his neck, and in places the markings seemed to be layered - some set deeper into him, and some on the surface, intricate and countless.

'No wonder he always has the zip pulled all the way up,' Weston observed.

John had to know how far it went, he took Tarku's arm and pushed up his sleeve, here too the faint pattern was visible on his wrist and arm, his entire body in fact was covered with it. 'He's not just any Akaia,' John gasped, astounded and fearful, 'I don't know what this is. Most Akaia just have one small tattoo, all individuals in the same area have a similar mark, but this is more than any I've ever seen, more than any I've read of in history. Did you know about this?' John asked Weston.

'I only know what the boy tells me, so do you think I did?' Weston answered.

Astrid just stared at Tarku, her fractured subsystem trying to make sense of the patterns upon him. She could see at once these lines were no random artwork, but just what they were she couldn't yet tell.

'So what are you all doing?' Melissa yelled at them, 'aren't you going to help him? Shouldn't we get him back on the ship at least? Aren't there those sand creatures out here?'

'I'll take his feet,' Weston bent to do so but John stopped him.

'No. I want everyone to get back to the ship. You hired me to be a guide West, I beg you, do this, don't question me, just do it. You've seen Akaia enough to know what I mean, you too Astrid, you know what he could do, get back to the ship, please!'

'Did you see that?' Astrid spoke. 'He moved.'

'Did he?'

'I'm certain. We'll go,' Astrid followed John's advice. 'Come Melissa, Tarku is coming around, he'll be alright, but we should go as John says.'

Even as Melissa finally stepped away Tarku's chest moved, he groaned. They saw the markings upon him grow even further - up his neck and out across the palm of his hand. All the lines shimmered faintly, like fire behind amber glass.

'There'll be no hiding that anymore my friend,' Weston said to Tarku, though Tarku was still out.

Finally a spluttering cough came from Tarku. Sitting up quickly, he tried to breathe air into his lungs, it was a hard effort to get the air, it was as if he still felt the rasping call of the Mrukai upon him and he tried to pull away though it wasn't there. To the crew it seemed as though he wasn't seeing them at all. John tried to talk to him, but he didn't seem to hear. The engineer knew Akaia could lose sight and sense in this world and he watched carefully as Tarku stood. The Akaia was shaky, afraid, turning around, trying to make sense of the world but tripping back into the sand. His eyes still so chilling, still seeing a place that wasn't this world. But then he became gradually more aware of his surroundings, and his predicament, as he slowly realised that these shapes he feared that he could not quite understand were in the other place, the real world, the world that was slipping away. He backed away from them.

'You gave us a fright,' Weston said, 'Tarku, are you alright?'

The world was so dim to Tarku's sight, he fought to see the world around him. Blinking, breathing. He felt the sand and tried to remember where he was, tried to place himself in the time and location of his last memory and pull himself out of the whorl of his history, of the places and times that he carried with him. What were these shapes that came towards him? People. Who were they? Who was he? He was Tarku, he was Tarku. Why were they looking at him like that? Did he know them? Why did he fear them? Should he fear them? What were their names? The big man, the other man, the woman, the girl, the girl was Melissa, yes little Melissa, that's it, and that was Weston, he knew Weston, Weston was ok, and John, yes, John Mark, Astrid, Astrid, of course, he turned from one to the other.

'Are you okay Tarkars?' Astrid asked, stepping forward. He put a hand out to stop her. Then he noticed his open shirt and jacket, looked at himself then back at those around him. They had seen everything! Everything he was and hated. He saw their faces. He saw their fear. Breathe, Tarku breathe, he told himself. They stood by, waiting to see what he would do, just staring at him, wondering what to do.

'Don't come, let me be,' he managed to whisper, then he got himself up and strode further out across the waste ground, into the haze of toxic steam and dust, towards the retreating ashes, and so shaken were the crew that they let him go.

CHAPTER 33:

Empty Cities

'Here we are,' Scott brought Sjyntani up to see the view from out the slit in Kyu's throat as they passed across the red desert and came to the port of Rorona.

'I hope the TnTv crew are here,' she said, lifting her pack onto her shoulder, again disguised totally as the boy Sovarlay. 'Thank you for the ride, say thank you to Kyu.'

'She knows,' Scott smiled, 'Listen, I'll go with you to the port authority, they may not talk to you but they'll talk to me. It will only take a moment to find out the movements of the Blue Moon if they've come through here.'

'No, it's alright, you can go on to Satsuan to find your father, don't worry about me.'

'I'm not leaving you here alone Sjyntani, my father has been around long enough to know how to take care of himself.'

'I can take care of myself.'

'I'm sure you can, but nevertheless I'm coming with you.' He lowered her to the red sand then jumped out himself. It was only a short distance from where Kyu dropped them to the port and the offices there, only a matter of metres but Scott stood still, surveying the scene before him with concern. It was quiet, even the air was too still.

'What is it? What's wrong,' Sjyntani touched his shoulder, 'Scott?'

'It's empty. Rorona is never empty. Where is everyone?'

'There are ships here, what do you mean?'

'The people, where are the people?'

Sjyntani looked around, Scott was right, there was no movement anywhere.

'Kyu, what's going on?' Scott called up. She sighed and moved, waving her wide wing almost as if pointing to the west towards the wide emptiness. Scott gazed in that direction, he could see no more than a wide haze as if a storm was brewing in the distance, but even as he watched they felt the earth shudder beneath them and he was certain that even as he looked on the haze grew more defined, and even darker.

'Let's see if anyone is below ground that can tell us what's going on,' Scott said, hurrying now, grabbing Sjyntani's arm and pulling her along behind him.

To the port centre they ran, the siren here was going off, the ships were empty just as Scott had thought from afar, the office was empty. The lifts to the underground hub weren't working, they found the stairs but heavy doors were closed and locked from inside. Scott banged, but there was no point, no one came to answer.

'What's going on?' Sjyntani asked.

'I don't know, that storm or whatever it is that's coming must be something considerably bigger than usual, Rorona doesn't shut down for anything, nor do crews leave their ships unattended, and look - the ships are all tied down, secured.'

Kyu called to him urgently.

'We've got to hurry,' Scott ran back to the port office, still pulling Sjyntani with him. He banged the door again and again but it wouldn't budge. He broke into the maintenance store, finding their tool box and running back to the office. He broke the lock and got the door open.

'First things first,' he puffed, 'where are the crew of TnTv right? Let's see if we can find the log books.'

'Here!' Sjyntani pulled up a program on a computer, all the data of arrivals and departures. 'Here, here!' she was jumping, 'the Blue moon was here a few days ago, their destination was Satsuan. That's not far! That's where you're going!'

'And we better get going without delay, this isn't any storm,' Scott said, looking at another monitor. 'It's a dirty storm, bringing ash and debris across from the Pireomerai, the volcanic western rift. We've got to get out of here!'

Sjyntani saw the screen and went white, the storm cell they could see extended beyond the screen it was so large, it would engulf Rorona city and all the desert and extents well into the wastes all around and it was coming fast.

The air that had been so still when they had arrived just minutes ago was now fresh and alive, but these playful wisps that came belied the true nature of the beast that was running towards Rorona now. Sjyntani gasped as she saw the dense clouds surging towards them, billowing ash clouds now streaked with lighting as the earth shook again below their feet.

'Kyu!' Scott called as they ran to the open ground, 'Kyu! Hurry!'

The great creature neared as close as possible to pick them up, Scott jumping in then hauling Sjyntani after. Kyu quickly rose above the weather system, though they felt her struggle like she never did, but she went higher and further, she closed her precious cargo safe inside her chest and flew on.

When they'd recovered a little Sjyntani sat up, 'Scott, will the people of Rorona be ok? They're all underground aren't they?'

'Yes, they will be safe in the pods underground.'

'Even if the earth quakes?'

'They have very clever engineers, the city underground can withstand much, and the individual pods much more. Of course, if they were hit badly nothing would be of any use, above ground or below.'

'I'd rather be above ground.'

'So would I, but not in that storm, the ash and the wind together,' Scott stopped, he'd been through a storm like that before. Kyu sang to him at the memory they shared. Sjyntani realised there was something between the Kyu and its rider that she would never understand.

'Do you think Satsuan will be ok?' she asked him. 'This storm is so big, couldn't it be there too?'

'I don't know, we can only go and see. Kyu won't go down if it's not safe.'

They were shook up from seeing the massive storm, seeing the emptiness of a city without people, that they were silent for a long time. They felt Kyu keep moving, further and further back eastwards as the storm chased them.

'I hope your father's alright,' Sjyntani said at last.

'So do I,' Scott looked up and smiled, 'and I hope you find whoever it is you're looking for.'

'Thank you.'

'Sjyntani, when we get to Satsuan, I don't know what I should do. I want to look for my father, and you will want to go after the crew from TnTv -'

'Yes.'

'But I don't feel right about letting you do this by yourself, alone.'

'I've been alone all my life.'

'I know, but -'

'I'll be alright.'

Scott sighed. 'Still, I will want to know that you've found them, that you've done what you wanted to do. We should plan to meet up somewhere after and just let each other know how we fared. No, never mind that, I'll go with you to the port again, we'll find out where the crew are, then I'll look for my father.'

'We don't even know if we can get to Satsuan yet, it might all be under that storm.'

'We'll know soon.'

It took longer than expected, maybe even a day or two. Kyu had flown high and far as the ash clouds plumed and she only now returned to their course. At last she lowered, now above the hectic urban chaos of Satsuan. They looked below as she opened the slit, and they could see the golden towers of the city rising out of sweeping low mass of remnant ash cloud. The wind was calming down, the storm moving on, and below they could see a city that had suffered under a devastating storm. Many ships from the port had been smashed into each other and into the streets and buildings, or lifted up and placed in the sands of the desert, the golden sand now awash with grey ash.

'They could be anywhere, I hope their ship isn't lost like that,' Scott said.

'Do you know what the TnTv ship looks like?' Sjyntani asked, 'I was hoping to see the name amongst the ships in dock, but I can't see it.'

'I have some idea of its make, but I didn't see it either,' he said.

Scott didn't wait for clearance or a place to land, he jumped from Kyu's throat with his charge Sjyntani, onto the top of a tall golden tower near the port. They made it to the port but the queue for enquiries was long, there were so many here wanting information and help after the storm.

'You go to your father, I will wait here,' Sjyntani said, 'if I get any help I will stay over there until you come and I will tell you what news.

'Alright, hopefully I'm not long, I'll see you soon.'

Scott had visited the North Island's embassy here on previous occasions and knew where he was going, so hurried through the crowds. Frustrated at the slow progress he found some less crowded ways and broke into a run, heading along the sand swept lanes, metre by metre his long strides took him closer to the embassy but with every step he felt a weight growing inside him, like he knew what they would say. His father was an efficient man, of course he would have made it here in time to get a flight to Tamashan. At last he reached the embassy, quickly handing over his I.D. though there was no need for the northerners were mostly all known to each other out here, and certainly Scott was known.

'My father, is he here?' he asked the girl at the desk, still puffing from his run.

'I don't know, I've been off for a few days. Let me call Kate, she'll know.'

'Thank you, thank you so much.'

'Scott, my boy!'

Scott heard the voice behind him, and his heart breathed again, 'Pa!' Scott turned and embraced his father.

'What's all this!' his father laughed, giving his tall son a pat on the back then standing him away to look at him.

'They told me on Soamé that you were assigned to Tamashan - I was so worried when I heard that, after the news about the war and everything.'

'Oh yes, terrible set of events altogether, but I'm here, I'm safe,' his father reassured. 'Yes, I was on the way to Tamashan but first I was covering for the ambassador here for a few weeks until he recovered from recent surgery, had to get a tumour removed, nasty business.'

'I'm so glad to see you safe, you can have no idea how relieved I am.'

'And I'm glad to see you my boy. You came all the way from Soamé to make sure I was alright?'

'Yes, I did.'

'Will you join me for dinner? You can tell me what you were doing on Soamé in the first place.'

'Pa, I'm not sure I can make dinner, I've left a friend at the port, I promised to make sure they were alright after I found out about you, that is, it might be ok but I've got to head back to the port now. On the other hand, maybe you can help. You'd have access to ship movements of north island vessels wouldn't you?'

'Well, mostly yes, we like to keep an eye on our people.'

'Would you have access to the arrivals and departures from the port over the last week?'

'I might, and if I don't have it I should be able to get it in hand fairly soon.'

'Genius Pa, let's do it.'

They began walking to Ambassador Thomas's temporary office, 'What's this about anyway?' his father asked.

'I met a traveller on Soamé who's in a spot, she wanted to get in touch with some of our people, don't ask me why, it's a long story, but I thought I should help, the least I can do would be to point her in the right direction.'

'I might be able to tell you without even looking at the logs, there haven't been that many ships from the north through lately.'

'The Blue Moon, with Alamo's film crew, do you remember if they've been through?'

'Why yes they came, but they didn't even disembark, continued straight on. I spoke to Weston myself, he had some supplies from home for us, you know us expats can't do without some of our home comforts.'

'Where were they headed?'

'Where do you think Scott? They're a news crew.'

Scott shook his head, he didn't understand.

'To film the war son, to try and find out what's going on.'

'No, not Tamashan?'

'Yes, I did suggest it was a foolhardy thing to do but you know Alamo.'

'Yes, I know Alamo.'

'Scott, why don't you bring this friend for dinner? I would like to meet her.'

'Oh, no Pa, it's not like that, I mean, I will see if she will come to dinner, but I, that is we, are not a couple.'

'Oh.'

'Not that I wouldn't find that an extremely pleasing circumstance, should it ever happen, but she has been through a lot Pa, I cannot ask anything of her, she just needs a friend at the moment.'

His father smiled. 'You really do like this girl, don't you?'

'I really do.'

'Then go and stop her in this folly, she cannot get to Tamashan at the moment and nor should she. Tell her that, and ask her to dinner.'

Scott found Sjyntani arguing hotly with a large Arrojori national who had apparently pushed in front of her in the queue at the port office. It was funny watching the hot headed girl in her boy's disguise almost picking a fight with the considerably taller and broader individual. Scott intercepted her, apologising to the man, 'I'm sorry sir, my little brother has a lot left to learn about manners,' he said, then pulled Sjyntani aside.

'I had it!' she accused him at first, 'why'd you do that? He had no right to push in!'

It took a moment for her to calm down enough for Scott to tell her the news. When she realised what this meant she was downcast.

'They are already in Tamashan,' she repeated.

'Come back to the embassy with me, my father insists I invite you to dinner. After that, we can talk this through.'

'What's there to talk through? I won't be able to find a ship to take me to Tamashan, and I cannot ask you to take me, can I?'

Scott didn't even see the hope in her question, the underlying desire she held for him to answer yes, even now, to say yes he would take her. But Scott almost laughed, though he was solemn, 'You can't seriously be considering following them to Tamashan? Not now Sjyntani?'

'Sovarlay,' she corrected, glancing at the people nearby them.

'Sovarlay.'

'I suppose you're right.'

Sjyntani followed Scott back to the embassy of the North Island States. Scott's father welcomed them and made his modest apartment available for their use.

'Please, please, help yourself to what refreshments you might enjoy,' he urged them, showing them the contents of his small refrigerator with a smile. 'Please, make use of the sitting room, the chairs are very comfortable, and the couch, if

226

you need a rest, as you must. I have some paperwork to do urgently, so I shall be cloistered in the study for a short time, but I promise to be back soon to see about dinner for all of us.'

'Pa, there's no need, if you're busy, I can arrange something,' Scott offered.

'Nonsense, I won't be long, I hope,' Ambassador Thomas nodded and left them.

Scott tried but couldn't draw Sjyntani to any conversation, so he lay down upon that couch as his father had suggested and closed his eyes. Sjyntani only stared at the assorted artefacts upon the walls, deep in thought.

'It's not easy being free,' she said at last, so quietly it took Scott a few moments to realise what she had said. Before he could ask what she meant she was telling him. 'You have to decide what to do for yourself, no one else makes the decision for you. Before I was always making plans for myself, thinking of what I would do if I were free. Now I am free and I don't know what to do. I have some little money left. Sovereign Viyal was very generous to me, giving me enough funds to get to Shorakai and make a start, but the flight back from the north was expensive. I don't know what I will do when the money runs out.'

'You don't have to decide anything right now,' Scott calmed, 'sit down Sjyntani, relax,'

'I can't relax.'

'You know languages, you'd make a good translator,' he encouraged.

'But who would hire me? I have no history. Besides, I'm not finished, I still have to get to Tamashan. I am free,' she thought about it, 'this is the direction I want to take, this is my decision.' She walked towards the door, 'Thank you for your help so far Scott, you have been a good friend, but I have some little funds and I will return to the port and see what pilot will take what I have to get me to Tamashan.'

'Sjyntani, no one will take you. Don't do this, please!'

Scott would have protested more, but his father emerged from his work in quite some agitation. 'The television, Scott, turn on the television! I've just had word there's news from Tamashan, Alamo's managed to get footage out!'

Sjyntani's hand fell from the door and she turned back into the room. She watched the images in horror. It was Tamashan, it was TnTv's footage of Tamashan.

'I'm far too late,' she cried, then almost yelled, 'Why did they do this!'

The images broke her, all this what she thought could have been avoided if it weren't for her. She cried out in Shorakaian, which had become the most comfortable language for her now, though also the language of her deceit, 'Why did P'Lalo make me deceive Viyal!' She turned away, angry and distressed. 'How could I ever think I could do anything! Look at what they have done!'

Ambassador Willam Thomas looked at his son with a question, trying to understand the young lady's words, grasping part of her meaning and wondering how it could make any sense.

'It wasn't your fault Sjyntani, none of this,' Scott spoke to her strongly, 'We shouldn't have let this play, you don't need to see this.' He turned off the screen. 'I'm sorry.'

'I took too long,' she spoke, in shock.

'You couldn't have done any more, Sjyntani, you travelled across half the world to try to make amends. And I don't think you did deceive Viyal, I think you are Shorakaian, and he would have seen that. It isn't your fault he chose to ignore his duties, nor is it your fault that all of this has come about. Think of the chess board. Does a pawn move the hand? No. You were only a pawn here, with no understanding of the game that was at play. We still don't know why all this has happened. Sjyntani you can't hang onto this guilt, no blame lies with you, do you understand?'

She looked away. She knew Scott's words were right, but she couldn't let it go.

'She thinks she is to blame for this?!' Scott's father said, trying to comprehend. Scott nodded.

'My dear girl,' ambassador Thomas stood and took her hand, leading her back to the couch, then sitting down with her. 'My dear girl,' he said again shaking his head and patting her hand. 'Tell me all, and I shall try to understand the chess board for you. I know a lot about international affairs, and I am also a very keen chess player.'

'It's true,' Scott affirmed. 'And what's more Sjyntani, think about this – whoever it was you wanted to talk to in Alamo's crew,' Scott gestured to the now blank television screen, 'whatever you thought they could do to stop this conflict – they're already there on Tamashan, right in the midst of it, filming it! Don't you think if there was anything they could have done, that they would have done it?'

She almost cried, 'But they say Sansahme don't feel like we do, maybe it meant nothing, but if I'd been able to ask, maybe make him understand-'

'Sansahme?'

'Yes. It was only ever the slightest chance,' she breathed in and out. 'Even if I had found him and asked him before all this happened it's likely he wouldn't have even spoken with me. I do not know him. I have no authority to ask him. Who am I? A freed slave, and he is revered amongst his people.'

'You're telling me Alamo has a Sansahme in his crew?' Scott still couldn't get past that point.

'His name is Tarku.'

'Tarku? Alamo's major?'

'You know him?' Sjyntani brightened a little.

Scott had to let her down. 'No, I only remember Alamo mentioning the name. But a Sansahme! Alamo's more reckless than I knew!' Scott shook his head. 'You're telling me you let me bring you halfway across the south to talk to an Akaia?'

She nodded.

'What help could an Akaia possibly be?!'

'I wanted to ask him to stop the war, like the Akaia did 300 years ago in the north.'

'History would tell you that's not exactly what happened,' Ambassador Thomas spoke, 'it was not a thing to want to recreate. The war was ended, but the battlefields were decimated on either side of the conflict. History would also tell you that was no ordinary Akaia.'

'Neither is Tarku, he is like that one that stopped the war, they say he is.' She saw doubt on their faces so she explained more, 'The last time I was taken through the Arc I heard his name in stories whispered amongst the Sansahme. Some of the traders hire Sansahme for protection. They call him Tarku Na Araka. There are many stories about him, you should hear what they say.'

'The despair in the Arc breeds rumours like rats - anything that gives those that must live there some hope will get clung to and whispered around. Sjyntani, you follow no more than a loose page ripped from a book of fables, you have to let this go. This war is not your fault.'

She put her eyes down but continued quietly. 'They say he is one who could call the Mrukai from where they sleep. I hoped he could. I hoped he could call them against the warships, for there is nothing else that can stand against them. I hoped he could stop it before it had really started, but I'm far too late.'

'I wish you had told me all this at the beginning, I could have saved you the trouble.'

'I would have still tried to come.'

'Warships,' Ambassador Thomas brightened, 'may I turn on the footage again? I think I might see P'Lalo's strategy.' He did turn the television back on and he sat for some time watching the running footage and nodding, saying 'yes, yes, that's it, it has to be.'

'What is?'

'Give me a moment,' Ambassador Thomas stopped the footage where it was playing and then went through some files on his own digital device, pulling up footage from previous engagements the Delevian military had made in other locations. 'You said that P'Lalo made you deceive Viyal? That she was the one behind this raid?' he asked Sjyntani.

'Yes.'

'You suspect she plays some larger game?'

'Yes, I do.'

'So we must assume then that this assault has nothing to do with Tamashan at all, but everything to do with Delevi.'

'What do you mean?'

'Well, look at this,' ambassador Thomas showed them the archive photos. 'Look, in each one, what do you see?'

'Fighter craft.'

'Whose fighter craft?'

'Delevian and Vahrnan.'

'Yes. Those two islands have worked together for years now, their societies have basically integrated. It was a triumph of the international committee's negotiations to resolve the long standing feud, especially after what happened to

Jonathan's Amiana at the beginning of those talks, although many believe that may have been the spur that meant all parties took the talks seriously.'

'And the fighter craft?' Scott brought his father back to the topic at hand. 'What's your point?'

'Yes, Delevian and Vahrnan. Now look at this new footage from Tamashan - what do you notice?'

They looked to the screen and studied the pictures that Alamo's copter had taken over the desert and towards the port in the capital Mon Karo.

'Only Delevian!' Sjyntani gasped as she realised what this meant, 'only Delevian! Oh no! I have to warn Viyal! Ambassador Thomas, can you help me to contact Delevi, I must warn them!'

'Delevi will not accept any communications, believe me, I know the government here has been trying since this all started. Delevi has cut themselves off.'

'I will go to the port, I will get transport,' Sjyntani began tucking her hair back up in her hat, preparing to be the boy again.

'You can't do this Sjyntani,' Scott shook his head. 'You said Viyal sent you away, he must have known what was happening.'

'He sent me away because I deceived him,' she maintained. 'There must be ships going that way, people don't stop needing supplies just because there's a war, someone will be taking goods surely, and the Delevian are good to pay because one thing they do have is currency.'

'You care about sovereign Viyal and Delevi this much? Vahrna has every right to want revenge on Delevi for what was done in the past! If P'Lalo is planning some assault it's none of our concern.'

'It's not about Delevi! Delevi is merely a house, like any nation, I do not care for the house, I care about the people within it, about life! Political agenda always gets in the way of the people on the street, and if I can't stop this raid on Tamashan, at least I can try to warn Sovereign Viyal about this plan and some on Delevi might be spared.'

'We don't even know if this is really what's happening! Pa, help me out here,'

Ambassador Thomas shrugged his shoulders. 'Distraction is a classical chess move. But, Scott's right my girl, it would be rash to try to get to Delevi now.'

Sjyntani was almost dissuaded from her pursuit - going back to Delevi was extreme, and if P'Lalo was really planning a strike against Delevi while a large part of its fleet was engaged on Tamashan, what could she do? Viyal might not even see her, and nobody else would. She thought it through. She would have liked to ask Scott straight out if he could ask Kyu to take her, but she couldn't ask.

'I'm going to the port,' she said, 'thank you for all your help Scott but this is where we part. Thank you for inviting me to dinner,' she hugged Scott's father, then left.

'Argh!' Scott let out a frustrated exhalation, uncommon to see from him.

'You know who she reminds me of?' his father asked.

'Who?'

'Jonathan's Amiana. She showed that sort of stubborn determination, and beauty,' Ambassador Thomas smiled at the recollection.

'She does doesn't she. I thought that too. I've got to go after her don't I Pa?'

'Do you?'

Scott embraced his father again, long, like a goodbye. 'If I don't see you for dinner you'll know she wouldn't back down and I've gone to Delevi with her, I don't think she'll let this go Pa, and I won't let her go alone.'

'Scott, you must not go.'

'Of course I'll try to dissuade her again, but I've got Kyu Pa, she'll look out for us.'

The old man shook his head, 'Even so, it's too risky.'

'So is being ambassador in half the places we lived in, you can't tell me that's not true.'

'No I can't.'

'You know how you said you felt when you met Ma? I get it now, I get it,' Scott smiled, 'Sjyntani's like that, she's just lovely, and funny, and I don't know if she feels anything for me and it doesn't matter, it's like you said about ma, you just knew you had to protect her no matter what, but at the same time she inspires you to want to do the craziest things!'

'Come here,' his father hugged him once again, now understanding exactly what Scott meant and why he was doing what he was doing.

'Thanks for being a great dad, thanks for making my childhood one grand adventure.'

'It was wasn't it.'

'And it hasn't stopped yet, I'll see you, alright, I'll see you again.'

'Look after her Scott.'

'I plan to.'

Scott ran out of the embassy and down those narrow streets and made the port. She was there already, checking the board for departures heading to Delevi, but the board was empty.

'If you're still set on it, Kyu and I will take you into Delevi,' Scott spoke.

She turned around quickly at his voice, not expecting it. She looked up from her sadness, 'You would do that for me?'

'You said lives depend on this. I don't understand how you think this will achieve anything, but I understand what you're trying to do.'

'I feel I shouldn't accept your help,' Sjyntani hesitated.

'Why's that?'

'It's not your fault, you shouldn't have to make this your problem.'

'This isn't your fault either, and don't argue with me about that, you didn't send the warships, did you? You didn't make the call, besides, I'm not making it my problem, I'm just offering you a lift,' Scott smiled.

'What about Kyu? She might not want to take me to Delevi.'

Scott looked up to the giant manta as she made her way to them, 'What is your answer Kyu, are we taking Sjyntani to Delevi?'

Her cry was long and deep, again her notes flowed through them, and broadened within them, swelling their hearts, calming their fears.

'Do you know what I think?' Scott said, remembering what Kyu had shown him back on Oconia, then how she had diverted to Soamé, and what Sjyntani had told him - of being on her way but the Soamé courier company had cancelled their flight. Scott smiled, 'I think you were Kyu's plan all along.'

CHAPTER 34:

Questions and Answers

Tarku sank to the ground and he sat there still, just as he had sat when what he was had been explained to him as a child, when the thief Eashan had told him they could use what he was, and told him that he didn't have to be afraid of being an Evaseri, as Akaia were known in Parahn at the time. But silent tears mixed with the dust and streaked his face as they had then. How much longer would this go on? How much more pain?! He had to pull himself together. He had to pull himself together for Syra's daughter, for Melissa. He had to protect her as long as he could.

It took a while for John to find him, Tarku had managed to find a particularly contaminated corner to fall into. He saw John but didn't respond. John sat beside him and waited for the Akaia to talk in his own time.

'I didn't see Hardan?' Tarku asked after the pilot, the captain, the jovial family man, but he asked almost knowing the answer, just longing to hear that it wasn't true.

'I'm sorry Tarku.'

'Did I do something?'

'No, no you didn't do anything.'

'How did he die?'

'Suffocation.'

Tarku turned his head aside.

'It's not your fault Tarku,' John tried to console him.

'But the curse is mine,' Tarku said angrily, 'and Hardan's family should not have to share in it.'

'It's not yours Tarku, Weston just put it very well, this whole world is cursed. What has happened has happened. Everything aside, there's the aftermath of war we've got to go film, and this crew is going to need you now, more than ever. Weston is adamant to go on, but I don't like our chances of getting back to the north if you're not with us.'

'Says he who was unsure about having a treacherous Akaia on board.'

'You're no ordinary Akaia.'

'I fear that with me is just as perilous as without me.'

'It's not so Tarku.'

They sat in silence for a time, then Tarku spoke up at last, 'Do you know what I said when I was six years old? I said I'd never go into the wastes like other Akaia, whatever happened. I told myself I would be stronger than them, but here I am.'

'Well technically this wasn't your choice, we parked here,' John encouraged.

'This is hardly the first time. The wastes have been my companion on many occasion.'

'Come back to the ship Tarku, you can't stay out here.'

'I can't come yet, there's still too much fire in my blood, and too many shadows in my sight.'

'Alright,' John said, but didn't leave.

'What is it John?'

'Huh?'

'The question you want to ask.'

'I have more than one,' John almost laughed.

'You wonder why I have so many markings?'

'That would be one question, yes.'

'What are your other questions?'

'You might as well answer about the tattoos, while we're on the subject.'

'You should know the answer, if there is one. You have studied Akaia.'

'No,' John shook his head, 'You are like no Akaia I've ever seen.'

'But you would have read of Akaia with more markings than usual.'

'Yes.'

'And what are we to history? We few who are marked so?' Tarku asked.

John breathed in and breathed out. He didn't answer. It wasn't without reason the Akaia were feared and that their various names persisted - soulless, destroyers, monsters; the survivors in the early colonies had known them as such, as precursors to utter devastation. 'In history,' John began, but didn't finish.

'In history,' Tarku went on, 'in what sparse records we have, we were known as guides, where we appeared whole villages were overcome by the Mrukai, destroyed,' Tarku answered his own question. 'In recent history it was an Akaia marked so who was thought to have ended the long war years, decimating armies suddenly with a simple call to the Mrukai.' Tarku stopped. John saw the soft shimmer of tears on the Akaia's rigid countenance as Tarku faced the further wastes. 'I have wondered for five-hundred years when they are going to stop, when will I be what they want? When will they use what they have made me into? You know the Mrukai see by us, we Akaia are their guideposts across this earth. Like the Kyu, the Mrukai have need of humans to survive well in this broken place. But what am I?' Tarku said, 'I don't know anymore. There are no others like me left that I know of, which makes me fear that maybe, maybe I shall be the end, their last guide. I have met the one who three hundred years ago ended the war of the mines, I have seen his marks and they were few compared to mine and yet the five islands of the north felt the shock of his single word. If his few marks brought such influence across the entire north, then what shall be achieved by mine? People fear the end will be earthquakes and tremors and volcanic eruptions, loss of clean air, a scarcity of supplies, but I fear it will be far more than that. My mother named me after the torture she suffered - the Mrukai first marked me just after my birth. I believe I would have died that day by my father's own hand if I hadn't already possessed some strength the influence of the Mrukai provides. I did not drown. I have carried their hieroglyphs since then. I fear what they will ask of me, what they will do by what I am.'

For a moment John breathed, slowly taking in all that Tarku said.

'I told you to ask a different question. Now you wish I had not spoken?'

'No.'

'You wonder if there is a way to kill me, yes? To stop whatever plan the Mrukai have?'

'No.'

'I can tell you now it would not be easy to end me. Even though I have wished for death I have not been able to come to it. It would seem the Mrukai imparted to me an instinct to fight against death as well.'

'It's not what I was thinking.'

'What then?'

'537 years. 537 years you've had to do this? Live with this! And you're still sane?'

'Debatable. And the Mrukai were incremental in the additions to my markings, little by little, bit by bit. Except Arrojor.'

'I had no idea Tarku. I cannot comprehend what you must go through every moment. I hope you will forgive my reckless introduction on our leaving Rorona.'

'It's already forgotten. What was the other question?'

John pondered whether or not to ask Tarku the other question that was at the top of his mind, but finally, considering what they were going into and that it may be the last chance they ever got to discuss it, John went ahead. 'Tarku, you knew my wife didn't you, you knew Amiana?'

Tarku turned to face him, and studied him, rather stunned. More silence.

'You did, didn't you?' John asked again, 'she was like you.'

Tarku looked aside. 'Amiana Lailae Arin, namai sarhna Syra ae,' Tarku whispered in the language of Syra's homeland, Shorakai.

'You should have this,' John took the pendant from his pocket and handed it to the boy, 'I think it might mean more to you - I saw the design on you and I've seen it nowhere else.'

Tarku studied the silver charm, his eyebrows drew together and looked at John in amazement, John had figured it out. 'No keep it,' Tarku pushed it back, 'Syra was yours so much more than she was ever mine. Give it to your daughter, just as you planned.'

'Syra was her real name you say? What do you mean?'

'She was old John. Amiana was just another alias.' Tarku thought things through himself. 'You knew she was an Akaia, one like me?'

'We were married Tarku, of course I knew.'

'She is how you know so much about us, isn't she? Not just your work for the government.'

'Yes. She told me much, though not everything. But she did not fear her fate like you seem to Tarku, she believed that there was more to everything than we could understand.'

'She believed in a blue sky,' Tarku said, 'hope where there was none to see.'

'Yes,' John nodded, smiling at the memory of his wife, 'she did. When did you know her Tarku? It must have been well before I did?'

'Not long before you met her, it would have been ten years or so before.'

'And were you close? I mean,' John paused, but Tarku could see what he wanted to ask.

'We were friends, nothing more.'

'I find that hard to believe, if she even had a pendant of your tattoo?'

'It wasn't about me. After we discovered each other's existence we tried to figure out our markings, she believed that together we carried the world, everything that is and was. She believed that part of my tattoo was an island we'd lost not long before, an island called Tanoh. The Mrukai had given me that mark around that same time. It had been a small but lovely place and she despaired its loss. As tribute she traced the map of Tanoh from me and had that pendant made to remind her not to give up.'

'Your markings are the world? The world as it was?'

'I didn't say that, I said that's what she believed - that most Akaia carry a part of the map of the earth as it is, but we - both as it is, and as it was.'

'But it makes no sense, why draw a map on a living and moving being?'

'A living and moving map for a living and moving earth. That's what she said. She wanted to find a purpose, a reason for what we are. I don't know what to believe besides the fact the earth is broken.'

'So you two were never - ?'

'Close? Yes, but we were like family, like brother and sister. She never saw me as she saw you John, believe me, and if you knew me at all you'd know I don't have a great capacity for all that in any case.'

'All what?'

'I understand concern, loyalty, failure, loss, need, anger, but love? I've never seen it, I don't know it.'

'Not many Akaia do understand it.'

'Another way the Mrukai influence our nature. But Syra understood.'

'Yes she did, to its fullest extent.'

'She needed someone who understood it too, someone who would allow her to love them and who could give in return. 15 years searching for your daughter John, I'd say she found the right man. Also, if it will make you feel any better, we had to stay apart in any case, it wasn't safe for us to be in the same place for long, the Mrukai did not like us even being in the same city and they let us know about it.'

John shook his head, 'I never could get over that, that the whole time I knew her she was still a slave to those creatures, as you clearly are too. I don't know how you do it. I don't know how she managed to live a full and normal life with me and with her work, as well as all of that.'

'Then you will forgive her that she lived even after the assassination attempt.'

'What do mean, attempt?'

'She died only last month.'

'I don't understand? What are you saying?'

'You knew she was an Akaia, but how many others knew, John? She was very careful, there was barely a soul that did. One shot through the heart wouldn't have killed her.'

'But I saw the footage,' John said, perplexed, 'the blood, she was so lifeless. I, I read the report, I was there at her funeral!'

'Yes, we bleed, we go into shock just like everyone else, you hunted us for the government, John, you know that! The difference is we can heal. After they took her away she regained her life, she wanted to return to you but because of what we are she couldn't. Just to stay alive she had to go to a far corner of the earth where neither you nor your daughter could have well survived, and so she remained dead to you, for your sake.'

'Where did she go?'

'Many places, but mainly Coeranth.'

'Coeranth is lost.'

'Is it? Maybe to you it is, but to Akaia who have been condemned, it exists.'

John wanted to push Tarku for more information about the place, but he let it be for now, instead asking, 'But she is dead now, you said?'

Tarku put his head down sadly, then showed John his shoulder, his arm. 'They gave me this not long after she was killed, can you not see her?'

John rubbed his mouth as he comprehended, 'These are her tattoos.'

'Yes, they were hers, a Mrukai came to me on Arrojor and etched them within mine, I saw her then so clearly.'

'So she's dead.'

'Yes.'

John thought it through. 'I believe you,' he said at last. 'I have dreamed of her constantly this past month and I am not a man who dreams Tarku. So I believe what you say, it's like she's found me, like she's been trying to say something to me, trying to remind me of the man I was back then.'

Tarku remained cold, 'All I saw was her death, and I know it was no dream.'

'How Tarku? How did she die the second time?'

'Be thankful you don't know, save I will tell you, at least the last was quickly, which is more than you can hope for being Akaia.'

'Was it the Mrukai?'

'I will not say, you have hot blood John, if I say you will think of nothing but revenge, when your mind must be here.'

John didn't press him, but asked, 'Did she know about our daughter? Did she know what happened back then?'

'After a time, yes, she heard, and she too searched as best she could, as did I when I found out. And John, you know she wouldn't have blamed you.'

'No, she wouldn't have,' the big man almost cried, 'but she should have, I should never have left Ava there, I should never have turned my back on Ava, not for a second.'

Tarku saw the genuine sorrow that weighed upon the big man, and not just in his face, but in his whole bearing and in the years of toil and self-negation that was apparent even in the crust of his skin and curve of his spine and shoulders. How could Tarku keep it from John any longer?

'You need to know something,' Tarku said quietly, 'I might not last much longer, I might not get another chance to tell you, so you need to know. She's your daughter John.'

'What?'

'Melissa. She's your daughter.'

'Melissa?' John shook his head, 'What are you saying?'

'I was looking for her too, Syra asked me to. It's why she's here, I had her come along so I could keep an eye on her. I know I'm not what any parent would choose to look after their child, but I did my best.'

John was speechless. Long minutes passed as he thought things through, as he rubbed his heavy jaw. 'Melissa?' he said again.

'I didn't know we'd be heading into war, I'm sorry John. I didn't know what to do, I couldn't get in touch with Syra, I didn't know if she'd want me to tell you. I didn't know if you could be trusted, or how to tell you. And I couldn't just go up to Melissa on the street and explain everything, I couldn't figure out how. I did my best John, please know that.'

'You can't be right, how do you know she's my daughter? Do you know for sure?' the big man pleaded, his brows so heavy, but his whole being longing desperately to know.

'How do I know for sure?' Tarku studied John a moment before answering. 'There's a mechanic in The Gutter that I get bikes off, and parts, you know. I was in a bad way one day, he let me crash on a sofa out the back. I was coming around when I heard her voice, it was Syra's voice, unmistakable. What I heard had a Northern accent of course, but still so much like Syra against the accents in the gutter. I thought it was just my mind playing tricks on me in the state I was in, but there was only a curtain between her and I, her silhouette on the fabric, the shape was Syra's too. I risked a glance and soon I saw I was mistaken, the girl was shorter, and the ochre tone of her skin was not as rich, but she has the same nose, the same cheeks, and more than that, the more I watched the more I knew who I had found. Melissa has a light about her, just like Syra had, she's sees blue skies, despite everything. You said it yourself, you had the same thought when you first saw Melissa, you thought she was your daughter, you thought it so strongly you quit your job and came to Rorona just to see. I asked the mechanic about her, and what he knew of her history matched up, she was brought to the gutter when she was no more than one or two. She's Syra's daughter John, she has to be your daughter, I'm certain.'

'You didn't get tests done, to be sure?' John asked.

'For myself, I didn't need to, I knew.'

'My daughter,' John breathed. All that Tarku said made sense. John knew first instincts were usually the right ones, and his first instincts were the same as Tarku's. And in all the years of his searching he'd never come close to finding any that came so close as Melissa did to fitting the description of what his daughter might be like. 'You tried to give me a hint on Satsuan didn't you? But what am I going to do?' John said, as he began to think through the implications, 'how will I tell Melissa? And how will I keep her out of this? Keep her safe?'

Tarku was silent.

'I can't can I?' John said at last. 'I can't tell her, not yet. And she's already made her choice to come, and we're already here. I wish you'd told me before we'd left Satsuan, I would have begged her even more strongly not to come.'

'I've given you my apology,' Tarku answered. 'Go back to them John, just be who Weston hired you to be.'

'My daughter,' John breathed, 'when I saw Melissa that first time I wanted so much for it to be her.'

'You don't have to search anymore John.'

They sat in silence over their thoughts for some time. At one point John exhaled deeply. 'Twenty years, and she was in the north,' he sighed as he thought through all he had done to get to this point. Finally he stood. 'Are you coming back?' John asked Tarku.

'The edge is still too close for me.'

'Well, I better go and put a stop to their worry, but you've got to pull yourself together and come back to the ship soon alright, even if you can't get rid of all the shadows in your sight,' John got up.

'What are you going to tell her?' Tarku asked John as he turned to go.

'I don't know. Nothing yet. Until we get somewhere I could get a test done, I mean - Astrid or anyone of us could do a blood test, but blood type isn't enough to prove or disprove anything, and besides I don't know if I ever knew her mother's type. Maybe Astrid could do a biometric comparison, you know, bone structure and facial features, but even then -'

'And Astrid's just gone through an EMP.'

'And there's that. I don't know if I should say anything anyway, not now, not at this time, it's too much to take on. I don't know how she'd react, I don't even know how I'd react. What if I told her and later we did the test and you were wrong?'

'Maybe when we get back to the north then, or Shorakai?'

'Yes. When we get back to the north.'

'But then you might never know, for sure,' Tarku said, 'we might never get back. I think she'd like to know what you thought John, why you came.'

'Leave it with me Tarku,' John said. 'One day, one day I'll talk to her, I'll let her know.' John turned to go, but turned back yet again. 'Wait. Tarku, you called Amiana - Syra?'

'I did.'

'No. No, my knowledge of Shorakaian history may not be adequate, but usually only those in the royal line are ever addressed as Syra, you must be mistaken.'

Tarku smiled for a long while, letting John's thoughts process. 'She was old John, almost as old as I am.'

'No, you've got to be wrong. Amiana was an ambassador, surely the authorities on Shorakai would have known if she was - *empress* - surely -'

'They don't know everything. They didn't know Amiana was Syra, and she kept it that way. Do you think they would have let a Sansahme represent them?

She didn't want to put them or herself in that situation again, and nor would she have wanted them to know who your daughter was, not until she had grown up. Namai Syra ae, John, Amiana longa namai Syraveia ae, Syraveia Nuamoi Lai-Arin, oha mo Syratreya.'

'You're saying my wife was the daughter of Syratreya? You're saying my wife was the last legitimate empress of Shorakai? Whose memorial sits in the same garden as the small plaque they placed in memory of my wife? No. She said nothing to me.' Then he laughed, 'Tarku, an empress wouldn't choose a man like me! She wouldn't even look at me! It wouldn't happen. It was stretch enough that she, as an ambassador, looked at me! It couldn't be true.'

'Believe me I would not give you this knowledge if I did not think my time was almost up, but you should know. You're right though, Amiana is not the last empress of Shorakai. Oh John,' Tarku sighed and his brows knotted as he waited for the big man to see the most significant fact yet. 'John, don't you see? Don't you see what I'm trying to tell you?!'

It took a moment, but then Tarku watched the big man sink to his knees on the sand as he came to the realisation at last.

'The empress?' John gasped, 'my Ava?'

'Syra-Ava. Yes. Melissa.'

CHAPTER 35:

Recovery and Reconnaissance

Some hours after the giant Mrukai had come and gone, and after Hardan had passed, the crew sat unspeaking, their lunchtime meals in front of them but largely untouched. No one was feeling that hungry after all that had happened. Straight from the attack of the marauders, the crash, the tense filming with the ever present threat of the Delevian soldiers discovering their presence, and then the appearance of the Mrukai, and the tremors that continued to shake the earth. It was a lot to take for anyone.

It was at this time Tarku had at last followed John's request to return to the ship, but after so long in the wastes and so far out as he had walked, so long without a suit or mask, his hair had been unevenly bleached a feathery grey, and the soft areas of his skin, his eyes, his nose, his ears, were weeping a watery blood. He didn't speak as he entered, didn't face anyone, didn't bother to shower the toxins away, didn't try to hide the markings of the Mrukai upon him, just stepped to the nearest bunk lethargically and curled up, frozen like, eyes staring at nothing, facing the wall.

The crew were still, looking at their uneaten meals. Melissa glanced from one to the other and realised no one else was going to see if Tarku was alright, so she sucked up all her courage and went to him, sitting on the bunk opposite.

'Can I get you anything?' she asked, 'Water maybe? Or your tea?'

He didn't reply. She tried to ignore the smell Tarku had brought in with him from the outside, not that she wasn't used to it, it smelt a bit like The Gutter did after the rains. Her heart was pounding, she wanted to speak to him, but was so nervous to keep going.

'I'm sorry I asked so many questions about Akaia, I feel really terrible, and stupid. I didn't know, and I'm sorry.'

Silence. Melissa was about to go but he spoke up, 'It's no consequence, and yours was not the blame,' he said, still staring at the wall.

'I ah, picked up your sunnies. I'll leave them here.' She got up and went to put them down near him. He didn't move but to turn his face away from her even more.

She noticed the signs upon him, so clearly Akaia. So clearly a creature Echlin sought to lock up and that the reports and myths told her to fear. But he was ashamed, so low in spirit, so pained. She understood him a little now. He reminded her of Kat when Kat was in deep trouble and trying to keep Melissa out of it. But as with Kyu on the roof back in the Universal City, instead of turning away from what she may have feared, what she didn't understand, she drew closer. She put down his sunglasses, then she sat on the bunk by him.

'Have you ever had a hand massage?' she asked, as if she were asking Kat. He refused to take any notice of her. 'You'll be surprised how well it works. My friend Kat showed me how it's done, I'll show you,' she continued bravely, sitting closer to him, drawing his arm over and taking his tortured hand into her own. He was too worn to protest and remained unmoved.

Melissa had no comprehension of the immensity of what Tarku was going through, but she held his hand, rubbing every part of each finger and knuckle and gently massaging every taut tendon until he relaxed, until his breathing became slow and easy, and finally he seemed to sleep. While she wondered and worried Melissa held his hand, lacing her fingers with his, like Kat had done to calm her when she was very young. Tarku was so strange, he could seem so strong and self-possessed and then so childlike and fragile like this. His hand was like a mechanic's hand, like Matthias's hands, the pores of skin and around and under his fingernails holding the dirt and grease. Melissa traced her fingers over the patterns on his hand, she had no idea what the markings meant or why they had caused him so much pain, but they were beautiful. She wondered if he could see that they were beautiful. She was almost glad to discover he was an Akaia, it explained so much. When his breathing had been easy for a while, she pulled a blanket over him and let him be.

'Is he alright?' Astrid asked her as she rejoined them.

'I think so,' Melissa answered, now continuing to try to eat what she hadn't finished before.

As Melissa ate John watched her, he watched her and thought through his last conversation with Tarku. She held her fork a certain way, she brushed her hair away from her face, she sat upright and in thought even though she was tired. He saw her kind heart in going to Tarku even though she was clearly afraid and hesitant to do so. John saw that she was like Amiana, so very much like her. Tarku was right.

'And how are you doing yourself Astrid?' John asked the machina to divert his mind away from Melissa. 'Working out any of those glitches?'

'Every day just a little bit of progress,' Astrid said, 'all my processes seem to have been affected, it's very frustrating. I've got most things running again but only intermittently, so as a machina I'm still unreliable I'm afraid.'

'I'm sure you'll get there soon,' John encouraged.

'I hope so,' Astrid smiled half-heartedly, 'Now, I'm heading for the bunks too.'

'I guess we all should take a couple of hours before we get back into it. Hopefully we'll be able to actually film something decent,' Weston said, finishing his last mouthful.

That evening Weston leant down to give Tarku a shake to get him up and let him know the plan. John stood behind for backup as Weston didn't feel up to talking to the boy alone, but it was only a blanket and pillow they found on the bunk. For a second Weston worried, but then Tarku walked past the doorway. He was showered and dressed in his trade-mark black jeans and racing boots, and he was pulling on his jacket, ready to go.

'I don't suppose anyone has any hair dye?' Tarku asked, blowing his bleached fringe out of his face forlornly as he put on his sunglasses. John and Weston looked at each other and laughed, Tarku was back.

In the cover of dark John guided the Blue Moon very slowly into central Tamashan. He was clever and got further in than Weston thought possible. In fact, he managed to gain the central business district of Mon Karo without being detected, and having done that John had enough courage to turn the lights off and head right to the port tower. They had seen in the vision from the copter that there were a few deserted foreign ships on one of the platforms, having been abandoned early in the assault. John pulled in amongst them, giving the Blue Moon the perfect camouflage.

Now as they prepared to disembark John handed out the firearms. He handed a pistol to Melissa and advised her, 'Don't use it unless you have to, remember it's always better to hide or run.' He himself tucked an extra one away as did Astrid, checking it thoroughly before slipping it into her cargos. John went to hand Tarku a gun but Tarku just looked at it.

'In my opinion journalists should not be armed then no one can lay any blame against us.'

'There might still be some Delevian patrols out there, do you want to take a chance?'

'And if you fire you're an enemy at once. I will not take a gun, besides, I don't need one.'

'Take it Tarku, for the rest of us,' John ran his eyes towards Melissa's direction and hoped Tarku would take his meaning. Begrudgingly Tarku took one and hid it somewhere in his jacket.

'Seems safe enough for the moment,' John assured, looking about the area from the vantage of the ship's windows and what data they could get from the ship's on board surveillance.

'Are all the cameras ready to roll, Astrid?' Weston asked.

'Yep. Soon as we need 'em. There's back-ups and batteries, chargers and so forth in that case there. Lenses and filters there, as well as a repair kit and cleaning gear. And I've set up a connection with the ship to store a back up of everything as we film it and then I've set a transmission in a few hours, so should anything happen they'll get the footage in the North Islands, though obviously the manual gear like Melissa's Carrelli we'll have to process later.'

'Good good,' Weston clapped his hands. 'Oh, and does everyone have their gas mask with them?'

Tarku put his hand up. 'I didn't get one,' he said with a perfectly straight face, a little mock hurt.

'Do you want one?' Weston joked, 'I can get you one if you want one kid.'

'Actually,' Tarku stopped fooling around, 'actually I will take one, after all, I'm not invincible and passing out really isn't as fun as it might seem.'

Weston laughed in surprise and held back the mask as Tarku reached out to take it, 'Since when do you care about you?'

'I don't, but I might just care about all of you, and I can't care, not if I'm dead or unconscious now can I?' Tarku snapped.

'I've never seen you this open before Tarku. It's a bit scary, but I like it.'

'Just give me the mask Weston.'

Weston did and Tarku strapped it to his low-slung waist holster with his other gear.

'What about water, everyone got water?' John checked.

'Yep. And the radios are working and everything else. Can we go already John?' Weston urged.

Now they disembarked. Their voices and footsteps seemed to echo across the silent platform. Melissa had her still camera out, attempting to capture this eerie desolation. All remained unmoved since the images of the copter had come through. There were signs of a battle on the platform. They saw bodies, Tamashani guards and officials, the wreckages, the evidence of gunfire on the structure itself. The air still held the smell of the fight, of the blood and gunpowder. They could see the glow of fires burning in parts of the city below them, but still no sign of anyone, no sounds of fighting, or guns or aircraft. No sound at all. No life at all.

'Weston, I want you and Astrid to stay with the ship for now, till I find out how we're going to proceed,' John directed. 'Tarku, Melissa, come with me.'

'What are we doing?' Melissa ran to catch up.

'Finding someone who can tell us what's been happening.'

Tapping the floor with his foot, listening for a hollowness, John found and opened a hidden door in the dock's floor, a maintenance hatch, then disappeared down into the tight passageways below. Melissa and Tarku followed. It was a maze in here, a warren of cramped corridors running in every direction to service the furthest corners of every platform, from the ground to the highest levels above. Cleaning equipment was in here, fire fighting equipment, rubbish, wires running in tight bundles followed the walls as did numerous pipes for fuel, air, gas and water.

They had made many turns when John stopped them, he signalled for Tarku to scout ahead. He and Melissa followed at a distance. The corridor they came down led to a larger one which they turned right into, towards the centre of the structure. After finding nothing Tarku shrugged his shoulders. All seemed empty still. They went on.

John was explaining to Tarku his friendship with one of the Tamashani air-traffic controllers and why he thought to find him in here, when somehow Melissa had managed to get in front, and then suddenly there was a sound of movement around the corner and Tarku grabbed her and spun her backwards quickly. There was a 'thck!' sound and he held his neck near the collarbone as blood trickled over his fingers.

'Oh dear, I am sorry,' yelled an unseen voice, 'I'm so sorry, are you alright? I fired before I looked. I heard you coming and thought you must be Delevian soldiers, but I'm so relieved to see you're not, believe me.'

After ducking and glancing about, then realising the shooter was actually friendly, Melissa rushed to steady Tarku as he reeled from the shot. John scanned ahead as out of the barely lit passage before them a Tamashani man emerged, coming out from behind a support column and making his way toward them until he stood only a metre away. He studied them intently.

'Just as well you did not have your favourite weapon on you,' John spoke to the Tamashani with a friend's ease, 'or we might all have come to our end.'

'Ha-ha! It is John Mark! My Nordan friend,' the excited Tamashani came forwards and embraced him warmly. He was pleased to see John, but they could see he was distressed as well. 'I had given up ever seeing you again. What with you stuck out on P12 watching the stars and I here still as always showing in the ships.'

'You're not doing a very good job of it D'aoda, dear friend,' John laughed.

'Ah, you can scold but I know you sent DC20 through this way, they got here just as it all started! Just to keep them from a harmless little siderolite storm! What a shock they got turning up here as the battle was heating up!'

'How is the crew, are they safe?'

'They were as safe as we are here my friend, that's the best I can say. If that is still the case I do not know.'

'Yes, I had no intelligence on the matter. It was your friend Thallo at the station who should have warned us,' John was still joking but delving for information at the same time.

'And he would have, had the Delevian not been interfering with our equipment. Ah. But John, it is good to see you.'

'My friend, tell us what has come to pass. We have not been able to make contact with anyone here on Tamashan. We have seen only a few groups that are in hiding but they are afraid and they will not speak to us. Neither have we been able to contact the Delevian authorities for an explanation. Do you know what's going on?'

'Oh a great many things have happened, but quickly, let me get some bandages,' he said much worried, 'and attend to your young friend whom I shot, regrettably, before we get into matters of such importance.'

'Do you need medical attention Tarku?' John enquired.

'Are you trying to be funny?' Tarku asked seriously. The Tamashani was wide eyed as Tarku barely even bled. He wiped the little blood there was from his neck, and it was perfect again. No signs that he had been shot at all apart from a crystalline amber shimmer in its place. D'aoda looked at John enquiringly.

'He is of the Akaia, ah, the Sa'ar you call them, or Sansahme, and is neither young, nor wounded, so let us discuss these important matters.'

'The Sa'ar? Forgive me, I assumed,' D'aoda replied, 'if only we all had such abilities Tamashan may have had a chance. But then again,' he added desolately, 'the Delevian even have weapons to fight those such as you, be careful my friend, they have weapons for everything.' He studied Tarku for a moment then went on, 'Come, come, we have some little supplies, we shall sit and drink and I will tell you what I can. Are there others of you?'

'Yes, they are with the ship.' John said. 'I'll radio them now.' John did, telling Weston and Astrid it was safe to follow.

'Good, good,' praised D'aoda, 'how many are you?'

'Two others.'

'Only two?' D'aoda was shocked. 'Not much of a resistance John. Your friend the Sa'ar we can use, but a young girl and two others,' D'aoda shook his head desolately, 'but still everyone will be a help. You must put your heads with ours and we shall figure out the best way to counter any Delevian troops that remain.'

'D'aoda,' John stopped his old friend solemnly, 'I'm sorry, my friend you misunderstand, we're not here to fight!'

'What? Then, then why are you here?'

'If it was only me that may be the case, but I have the interests of the crew in my charge, my job D'aoda, I've been hired as a guide for this TV crew.'

'A television crew? So, this is what? A travel documentary perhaps ah?' D'aoda said bitterly. 'In the ruins of what was once our glorious city? I should be your tour guide, yes? See on your left the cargo bays now a twisted waste, impossible to use, see to your right the empty docks of our fleet of guard ships, they will never return. Take a tour of our metropolis, the bones of Mon Karo, see the fatherless, the homeless, the lakes filled with the silt of our burning city. Or would you prefer the scenic route? Oh and sorry, there are no rooms left, and you'd better not stay in the open because burning ash is still falling from the sky.'

D'aoda had lost much. At once his eyes filled with tears as he could not contain his grief before them any longer, he grabbed hold of John's shoulders tightly. 'My daughter was working with me when they came,' he cried. 'I left her when the sirens went off, I ran to my post, support for those directing fighter craft. It was confusion, everyone wanted to get out of here all at once, I thought she'd be safe, being in the civilian port area, but suddenly they'd taken over everything, there were soldiers everywhere, from Delevi, from Vahrna, and even mercenaries from the Arc were rumoured to be on the outskirts, we were overcome. They would shoot those that didn't do as they asked. Last I saw they were corralling everyone who worked here into the transit lounge downstairs, but it's all empty now, at least, there are no voices, we don't know what has happened to them. But my daughter was murdered before that, I couldn't get back to her in time, my friends held me back as I heard what I believe were her final screams John. Your heart aches for a daughter you could never know, I knew my daughter, I watched her grow, I taught her everything, sacrificed everything for her, and now, just like that, they take her away from me! Forever away from me!'

'My friend,' John embraced him, his heart truly overcome with grief at his friend's loss.

'You cannot call me friend if you are not here to aid us,' D'aoda said through bitter tears, though he embraced John firmly in return.

'D'aoda I'm sorry, truly, we came to find out what happened, to go out there and take pictures, to show the people of the north and the rest of the world what's going on here. Perhaps we can get many to come to aid Tamashan.'

'It's too late, and besides, I know your people, I know the north and the rest of the world. You have too many quarrels amongst yourselves to come to our aid. I have heard that a few from Salamonde came, and a few from Satsuan and Rorona, even though Rorona has always held a perfectly neutral standpoint in everything. They were not sent by their governments of course, just individuals. They are all afraid, everyone is afraid of Delevi, everyone is afraid of sovereign Iviqal Viyal, the war is already over, we are crushed.'

'Do you know why this happened?'

The old Tamashani shook his head sadly, 'No, we are with the world in ignorance. Our government has been made mute by the Delevian, there are no channels to pass on information to us. We do not know what is happening or why, nor what to do, and those that have come to destroy us, they say no word that adds any clue. I wonder if they themselves do not know but are only following orders, ah! but that so many could do such terrible things unquestioningly I find too hard to believe. The only thing we can think of that may have sparked this is that over the last year our government has made some trade deals that affected Delevi very badly,' D'aoda said, 'and the Delevian are too used to getting what they want.'

'Bad enough to bring them to war with you?' John asked.

'One would not think so.'

'I had thought it may be the beginning of an occupation by force, Delevi taking Tamashan for their own land, but it doesn't look like that to me now I'm here.'

'No, it is not that, I am sure there would have been even more death if that had been the case. For what has happened here, the number of dead that we have seen so far is quite low.'

'So you say they turned up a few days ago and started this, no warning at all. Flattened your defences, your communications -'

'Yes, they must have been planning it for some time. There were many hundreds of craft, many thousands of soldiers. They seem to have moved on from here in Mon Karo north-west to Raijenou, but who knows what they are really doing. I cannot reach many on the ground, not even by the old ways. The few we have contacted are keeping low and so are we, there are a few of us hiding here. I have others keeping watch in different parts, we have seen no sign of the Delevian for some time, not in here, and not on the ground, but we cannot be too careful, I think this is far from over John.'

'We came to show the story,' interrupted Tarku, 'so whether or not you think it wise, I shall be going back out. We are yet to get much footage on the ground here in the city. If you would like me try to get a message to someone I would be glad to take it and return with a reply.'

'It is kind of you to offer Tarku, I thank you, but do not risk your life on my part. I have already caused you much hurt.'

'A trivial thing, I have said that I will go and I shall. You may as well send a message with me. As for risking my life, you have seen that is not easy to risk. Give me your message.'

'A truly noble spirit. I must meet these Akaia of the north.'

'I don't think you would enjoy that at all sir, besides which it is hardly possible, our government is locking them away as we speak,' Tarku replied softly and almost without emotion as he strapped on his gear, and continued immediately giving no one a chance to respond. 'I will plan to be back in two hours. John, I'll meet you back at the ship after that.'

'I'll come,' Melissa bounced up.

'Melissa wait,' John cautioned her abruptly, he had not expected her words and was caught off guard. Tarku just raised an eyebrow and waited.

'I want to go John, I'll be careful,' Melissa reassured.

'Okay, but stay close to him,' John shook his finger at Tarku to emphasise his point, then pointed back at Melissa. 'Take care of her Tarku.'

Tarku looked her over. No one could read his thoughts. He took the camera out of her hands, the old Carrelli she held constantly, she didn't dare protest. He pulled off the worn neck strap then he took a newer strap out of his own gear and attached it. He cleaned the lens and blew dust out from around the sensor, then pulled out another thing from his gear. 'Spare battery grip,' he said and clipped it in place, 'It'll give you more time.' Then he drew the strap over her head and gently lifted her chin up and nodded. With that he stalked away down another passageway following directions that D'aoda had given. Melissa followed after.

CHAPTER 36:

Taking Risks

Also keen to get to ground level and film the centre of this destruction, Weston and Astrid grabbed a lot of gear and made their way down the corridors following John, only Weston kept looking back.

'What is it?' Astrid asked.

'What?'

'Come on, what's eating you?'

'Nothing,' Weston made a blank face and shrugged his shoulders.

'Nothing? Rubbish!' Astrid laughed. 'Come on, I don't need to be fully functioning to know when you're concerned about something. It's the ship isn't it?'

Weston screwed his mouth up then winced, 'Yep.'

Astrid laughed again.

'Hey, you can't blame me for worrying,' he defended, 'it's the Blue Moon, my Blue Moon,' he added dearly, 'best little ship in the northern hemisphere. Up there, all alone, in this blasted war zone. Now if I'd known we were heading into this mess I'd have maybe got something a little more robust, or at least, something I didn't mind getting a few scratches on.'

Astrid put her arm around his shoulders for a moment. 'You know, you could always check on it by looking at the feed from the external cameras you had fitted.'

Weston snuck her a kiss, 'I knew I loved you!' he said, quickly stopping right then to pull out some equipment on which he could view the live footage. 'Oh great, would you look at that,' Weston sighed, 'there's something on the rear left lens obstructing the view.'

'I'll deal with it,' Astrid said, 'you head on.'

'I can do it.'

'No, no, I'll do it. I'll be careful West, don't worry. I just remembered there was something else I wanted to grab off the ship in any case. Tell John I won't be long. Oh, and here, you can take this too,' she deposited her case and gear into his already loaded arms, under his bemused face. 'You go on ahead, I'll catch up in a minute,' she said and ran back along the way they had come.

'No Astrid!' Weston called out but she was gone. Weston ran after her but began dropping things all over the place, stumbling over them he stopped and yelled, 'Come on, at least wait and we'll go together, no one goes anywhere alone, remember.' Silence. 'Astrid?' Weston found himself alone. He knew Astrid could take care of herself, after all, she was one of the most highly intelligent people he knew, not to mention a Machina 20m A*id that could interface with technology and sense human emotion remarkably clearly, among other things, but he still worried about her, he loved her, and she wasn't invincible, and after that e.m.p. she wasn't functioning optimally either. Weston sighed, much concerned, as he bent down to try and pull the mess into his arms again.

It didn't take long for Astrid to get back to the Blue Moon, and she hurried to remove the obstruction from the rear left camera, but then she checked the skies – as far as she could see there were no Delevian ships nearby, so she decided to take the chance, stepping inside quickly, to the back of the ship, ramping up the transmitters and setting up a secure link to Q-Corp. Soon a technician took her request.

'Code in,' he said blankly, not even bothering to look at the screen.

'2 0 Alpha Star India Delta. Would you like fries with that?'

The tech looked up, excited, 'Astrid! Hey! You never call in, I wasn't expecting you. How are you doing?'

'I don't know, that's why I'm calling in. I'm going to hook up yeah, I want you to run a remote diagnostic. I need you to be quick about it.'

'Sure, why? Do you think something's wrong,' the tech asked as he began to set the process in motion.

'Wouldn't call you if I didn't. I got hit with a pulse and everything's gone haywire.'

'Did you want to check just the processes or everything?'

'Might as well do everything while we're at it.'

'Okay, hook up, it's ready this end. So what's been going on?'

'Lots of travelling,' she said, plugging herself in. 'Have you seen the footage TnTv got on Tamashan there yet?'

'I just saw a report a few hours ago, are you saying that was you?'

'We're still here, so if I have to go unexpectedly you know why.'

'You must be taking a bit of a risk hooking up?'

'From my perspective I was taking a risk if I didn't. I'm going mad, I'm not myself without this working. Anything yet?'

'Not yet.'

'Can I possibly get another program off you when this is done as well. I need the most advanced 3d mapping software you have.'

'Alright, I'll pull it up while this is running, give me a moment.' The tech turned to another screen to find the program. 'There's a terrain predictor? That could give you an advantage.'

'No, I can analyse terrain fine with the programs I have, it's the 3d mapping I want.'

'Ok, I got it. It's set to upload once the check's complete.'

'Thank you.'

'What's it for then?'

'I can't tell you yet,' Astrid said.

'Fair enough. Ok, the check's done. Well, I can see what you mean, I'm surprised you've got anything working at all, your system is layered with corrupted data.'

'Can you fix it? I've been working on it, but it's hard when the tools I have are partially broken too.'

'I could do a complete re-install but I know you wouldn't want that because you've made so many tweaks to yourself over the years.'

'Can you run a cleaner through? Just repair the worst damage, then I can go over it more finely.'

'I'll set it up,' the tech did, 'You're going to have to go offline mode for this.'

'I know.'

'Are you ready?'

'As ever.' Astrid released her system to the control of headquarters, something she hated doing, naturally, given her mistrust of the corporation, but she had to do this. Weston may say a lot of encouraging things but she had to do her job, she felt without her subsystem she wasn't only not a mech, but less than human, as she had never in her life been without such augmentation, and without it she felt like a lost child, ill-equipped to do anything as simple as find directions on a map, let alone be part of this crew. And then there was the other puzzle her broken mind could not solve, the reason she wanted the most advanced 3d mapping program she could get. The markings on Tarku's body had stayed at the front of her mind, she was certain there was more to them, but so far there was nothing she could find in all the ways she had pulled them apart and rearranged them in her mind.

'How are you otherwise?' the tech asked her as they waited for the cleaning program to do its job.

'I've been tired, I don't know what it is,' Astrid confessed. 'I've been worrying about things I didn't used to worry about, I've been feeling like I'm not my usual self, even aside from this e.m.p., like I can't rely on myself anymore.'

'It might just be you've got past more of the psychological barriers they gave you. People worry Astrid, you know, it feels just like what you're saying. Or it might be you're just not getting enough sleep. But anyway, almost done now. Okay, now let's have a look.'

'Is everything alright? Am I okay?' Astrid asked.

'Looks good. I'll add that program for you and then you can switch back on.'

'Thank you.'

'My pleasure Astrid.'

'How's M*ko?'

'What?'

Astrid laughed, 'Don't play fool with me sonny, I know you were making eyes at her a while back, and you asked me a whole lot of questions about how I got past the psychology. So how is she?'

The tech looked down a moment, but then he grinned and looked back, 'M*ko is great Astrid, thank you.' He whispered, 'she's still got a long way to go, but we're already planning an escape.'

'You'll have to be careful, don't they have remote switches now? A simple signal could shut her down.'

'I'm a tech Astrid,' he winked, 'I think I can handle it.'

'Well good luck,' she wished him.

'To you too. It's all up and ready to go.'

She switched her subsystem back on and looked through it. 'Looks much better. Thank you. Logging off 2 0 Alpha Star India Delta.'

'Tech 7056 out. Goodbye Astrid.'

'Bye sonny.'

It was then she felt it, something wasn't right, Astrid unplugged herself and ran to the nearest window - there was a Delevian ship, still a distance away but flying towards the dock at speed, along with a number of ships even further off, but now returning.

~

John had been about to radio Weston and Astrid and ask them where they were when Weston turned up, surprised by D'aoda's weapon in his face, but quickly recognised and ushered into the group.

'Where's Astrid?' John asked.

'On her way, she wanted something else from the Moon, and she was going to clear the camera lens on the back of the ship,' Weston puffed and sat down, taking out the viewer again. 'Oh no! No,' Weston saw the view of the external cameras, 'Astrid, no! Come away! John look, there's a ship coming in towards the platform, looks to be Delevian. What should we do? I think Astrid's still there. Astrid,' Weston radioed her, 'Astrid, there's a Delevian ship coming in, get out of there quick.'

'I know, I am. There's not just one either.'

'It's not that close yet, maybe she can fly the Moon to the end of the platform there and get it inside one of the warehouses, she should be able to find one with enough room and then make her way down here another way,' Weston suggested.

'No, just leave the ship, they'll notice you if you move it now, trust me,' D'aoda said, listening to their conversation and knowing the speed with which the Delevian could be upon them. 'There's no time.'

'A friend here says to leave the ship Astrid, you'd better just follow us.'

'My poor ship,' the producer moaned, 'they better not mistreat her.'

'You've got to leave it Astrid, now,' John urged, 'just get yourself in here as quick as you can and pull down the hatch behind you.'

'Alright John, see you soon.'

'I'm going to go and meet her half way,' Weston worried, running back along the corridors.

~

Astrid hurried to shut the transmitters down, but someone was trying to get through on the ship's comm., someone from Q-corp. It could be important.

'Keep it quick,' she whispered to the young tech, 'I'm in a bit of a situation here, or I will be soon anyway, what is it? Bad news?'

'I, well, I wasn't sure before when I scanned through your report, you said to do a full analysis, but I wasn't sure so I didn't say anything, but I've done some research, and I've double checked with Harry, I know you trust Harry so I knew it would be ok,'

'Come on, out with it sonny!'

'Well, there are abnormalities in the report, issues that individually are nothing really, but if you put them together they could also be present if you were, well-'

'If I was what?'

'Infected.'

'Infected with what?' Astrid didn't understand.

'A virus, Astrid. There's been a few cases the last few weeks Harry says.'

'What kind of virus?'

'Looks like something from an activist group maybe, Harry thinks this is their style. You know they're always trying to sabotage us, they must have snuck something into our systems – it was probably in the packet we gave you, if not already in you from your time in the vault, but the vaults are on a separate network completely so I don't see how anyone could have sabotaged - but then if it is one of the techs -'

'No,' Astrid laughed, 'no, no it's not possible, is it?'

'Everyone's got a price Astrid.'

'No, I mean, how can this happen? There's too many scans, too many protocols. This is no time for jokes, I really am in a situation here.'

'I'm sorry Astrid. Harry says he thought they'd quarantined it but obviously not. I've looked over the other cases, it's not good Astrid; this one's like a tick, once it's stuck in there you got to get it out properly or you might as well not get it out, but if you leave it in, it's slow, but it will eat away your systems eventually. It might have been fortunate you were in the blast of the e.m.p, at least we know it's there now, although, that might have set it off. If it was dormant it could have been aggravated, thinking it was being attacked. Or even more likely it's corrupted too, like your system, who knows how it will progress. We have to isolate it properly - quarantine seems the best option so far.'

'Alright, thank you, I mean it, thank you very much, but I really have to go now.'

'Astrid we need to work on this!'

'I know, I know, but really, I have to go, or I won't be infected, I'll be dead.'

Astrid shut down the link and lay still and silent in the back as the Delevian ship came in and docked near the Blue Moon. But a virus? She couldn't have a virus. Not now, not in the middle of all this.

The Delevian craft was an older ship, though equally well made. Like a geometric bird that rested on the tips of its wings. Seven left the ship, five soldiers were Delevian, two were Vahrnan. They gave the Blue Moon a cursory glance but no more. They didn't seem suspicious of anything, just self assured. They headed away from the dock towards the hub and control rooms.

Astrid snuck forward and watched cautiously from a rear window, and now that her system seemed to be working she filmed footage of these soldiers and their ship until they were out of sight. Then she crept out of the Blue Moon and began inching toward the hidden hatch that led to the inner passageways, but she stopped; how could she throw away this opportunity? The Delevian ship was right here, there had to be some clue on board, something that would explain this conflict. So she started filming again, with that hidden camera in her eye. She edged nearer their ship. She couldn't see them anymore, but she put her hand to the platform surface to pick up the vibrations and by the feel of their footsteps they must now be in the lobby, which was at least 50 metres away.

She crept up to their ship and paused, everything felt alright. She tried the door on the ship, it was open. She went inside and looked around, there had to be some clue.

But somehow Astrid missed it; how could she miss that heartbeat so close - that pulse, strong and steady, a soldiers pulse, a sixth Delevian guard left with the ship, so still and silent that focussed on the others as she was she missed him there. She couldn't understand how she missed it, but to wonder and conclude that there were still glitches in her system from the e.m.p. or that the virus really was beginning to affect things. She didn't have time to react, the soldier captured her even as she set foot on the top step of their ship, and though she fought back with all determination he was solid and could not be fought off. Then he pulled her back inside, into the dimness of the strange cabin. Astrid almost escaped him here with one of her tricks but he caught her again and held her twice as firm. Then he tied her hands tightly behind her head and strung her up to a handle on the ceiling, turning her to face him.

He was like any other Delevian: tall, well built, with statuesque features, skin like white quartz, and those shallow eyes of midnight blue lazuli.

'What a pleasant surprise,' he mused in sinister whispers as he looked her over, head to feet, making a quick and accurate summation; she was from the North. 'That is, I've heard de Nordan women are, well, pleasant.'

'I've heard we bite,' she said through clenched teeth.

'I've not encountered hair so, like yours,' he played with her dreadlocks as he walked around her, 'it appears so unkempt, I don't like it, and yet I find myself strangely drawn to its fibres. Smells like, earth. I've never been close to a Nordaner,' he blinked haughtily, 'are you an average example?'

'No!' Astrid nearly spat at him but restrained herself. He was far too close to her. She couldn't guess his intent but his manner made her very uncomfortable. She swung her legs up and kicked him backwards across the floor. She tried to free her hands but he was soon up, giving her a wide berth but coming close around behind her.

'I wouldn't do that again,' he threatened with a sharp tongue, 'I could have killed you already, but,' he softened, 'I am not as ruthless as some of my compatriots, and besides, at home a northerner would be worth much more alive than dead.'

'Aren't you going to ask me who I am and what I was doing coming on board your ship?'

'I might.'

'Well I'll ask you something. Why did your people attack the Tamashani?' she challenged as he continued to examine her curiously.

'Whatever it was they must have deserved it,' he evaded.

Astrid shook her head.

'Alright I'll ask the questions you want me to ask. Who are you and why are you here? Why were you spying on us? This is not your country nor your concern and yet you risk much.' Astrid remained silent. The soldier continued, 'Everyone else has fled, leaving the Tamashani to their own defences, but you are here, why?'

Still Astrid kept silent, many things coming to mind to say, but she was unsure if it was wise to utter any of them.

'Okay, you won't say, I won't say. So, let's talk of other things. Tell me,' he continued, 'why is this earlobe, missing?'

'It was a very infected stud if you must know. Why are you here? What are you here to do? What does Delevi have against Tamashan?'

'So demanding!' he exclaimed, then whispered, 'are they all like you?' so close his breath moistened her ear and she pulled away.

'Stand back from me, let me go, I have done no wrong!' Astrid kicked out at him and struggled futilely to get free.

'A little respect lady! You think abusing me will get you somewhere?'

'Well I can't very well get on my knees and beg. Besides, I wouldn't anyway.'

'Quite true, you cannot get on your knees, but, you are wrong about one thing.'

'What's that?'

'You have done much wrong against Delevi already; trespass on our ship, a ship of his most sovereign's fleet - which is equal to trespass on sovereign land, assault of a soldier of Delevi, not to mention espionage,' he looked at her grimly, taking her chin and speaking horribly right in her face. 'You will tell me who you are, and you will tell me what you are doing here, and, you will tell me who else is here with you.'

'Can't you read my jacket sonny?' Astrid answered, 'we're media, that's all, we're journalists.'

He noticed the jacket, 'You're media. TnTv. Hmff. How many are you?'

'A few.'

'I see,' he said blankly then leaned close to her again. 'I'll tell you what to report,' he spoke in a quiet yet threatening way, 'unless you call your crew back here and leave now, you will have to report that on this day, of this year, *a few* northern journalists were detained by the Delevian army for unspecified crimes against Delevi.'

The young Delevian soldier would have said more, he was leaning over her, so close, so threatening, but Weston stood at the door and pointed his gun bravely at the soldier. 'Stop! Let her go! Let her go, or, or I'll shoot!' Weston yelled, but he was nervous, as anyone would be. He hadn't been in a situation like this for so long, and never against a Delevian. His hands were shaking. 'I said step away from her!' Weston neared, but the young soldier just looked at him haughtily.

'And what are you going to do?' the soldier sniggered and stepped towards him.

'Don't move!' Weston threatened again, his finger trembling on the trigger, but the soldier stepped even closer. Weston edged back, he didn't want to be close to this Delevian, but then the heel of his shoe caught on the rim of the top step, he tripped and the trigger was nudged too far. There was a shot and the soldier fell right there at Astrid's feet.

'Weston! What have you done! You killed him! You didn't have to kill him!'

'What? I didn't kill him! Did I? No, no, no, no, no!' Weston gulped and swallowed, 'Oh no. Oh no. No I didn't mean to do that! You saw it was an accident didn't you?! I tripped, I didn't mean this at all!'

Astrid had to remind Weston to cut her down, then she knelt by the body and tried to revive the young soldier, but it was obvious he was beyond help.

'Oh no,' Weston rubbed his whiskers, 'I, well, it's just I thought he looked like he was about to maul you, I had to do something, but not this. I didn't mean to do this, it was an accident.'

'He was just a kid really, so strange, but I don't know. He was acting it up, but I don't think he wanted to hurt me.'

'I really didn't mean to do it. I was worried about you, I was shaking, my hand was shaking, it must have been.' He looked at her helplessly with those sad-dog eyes. 'You're alright then, Astrid?'

'Yes. Yes I'm okay, I'll be fine.'

'Why didn't you come away? How did you manage to get yourself into this situation anyway? What happened?'

Astrid turned aside and looked around the ship, 'Evidence, I was looking for evidence, but there's nothing here that I can see, no clue as to why they're here,' she said. How could she tell him her current shock was not so much that she had been momentarily captured by a Delevian soldier but that her system was infected with a slow moving virus that would cause who knows what issues as it progressed. She looked at the dead soldier. She shook her head, she had to snap out of this.

'Come on Astrid,' Weston took her hand and led her down the stairs, 'come on, quickly, they'll come back, the other soldiers must have heard that shot.'

'You're right,' Astrid followed, now snapping out of it and realising what her senses were telling her. 'They're coming back.'

~

Melissa ran after Tarku. Slowly, along the flight and in their destinations, and even now as she observed him more, Melissa was changing her opinion; Tarku wasn't haughty at all, just withdrawn. Though he wasn't like her, she realised he was the only other person on this trip with whom she felt any deeper connection, which was strange because she'd thought she didn't like him, and they hadn't really spoken that much. But just like Astrid said he would, he was melting, be it ever so slowly. Melissa wished Tarku wouldn't keep himself so shut off all the time.

She caught up to him. 'Why did you get all riled back there, when D'aoda praised your people?' she asked him gently as they finally stepped out of the maintenance door after all those flights of stairs to the ground level of the dock building and began making their way through the rubble.

'They're not my people. I wasn't riled,' he answered, without emotion.

'Yes you were.' There was a pause, then Tarku looked at her with those eyes. She couldn't see them anymore, behind the glasses, but she could see them with her mind, and though the fire had left them now she could imagine it so clearly. She swallowed the awkward lump of fear that began to rise in her throat and bravely apologised, 'I'm sorry, I -'

'No,' he interrupted her softly, 'never apologise for asking questions. Everyone has an opinion, and most opinions are come to without any enquiry or consideration. All are entitled to have an opinion, as are you, and I'm one of them, one of the Akaia, part human, part who knows what – something engineered by the Mrukai. I didn't choose this, I don't want this, but this is the way it is. People have no idea what the Mrukai are, what *we* are, and we make no effort to explain anything, but you are here trying to understand before coming to your opinion, so one thing you should never do, is apologise for your questions. I might be reticent, but I respect you for that, do you understand?'

Melissa nodded. She wanted to ask him what they really were then, but instead said, 'Is it difficult that people don't understand?'

'Yes and no. Pray you never meet a Mrukai again,' he said quietly, 'the one you saw from the ship could have killed you all in a second, had it wanted to, could have killed me too, just as quickly, and I could have done nothing to stop it.'

'Didn't it want to kill you? It seemed to.'

'As it turns out, no.'

Melissa thought for another moment. 'What did it want? Was it that?' she looked hesitantly at his hand and his neck, where the new markings could be seen.

Tarku was slow to answer, he hated talk of himself, but he answered Melissa genuinely, 'Yes, it wanted to give me this,' he opened his hand momentarily.

'Must be a pretty obsessive tattooist,' she laughed, and caught Tarku grinning darkly at her humour. 'What is it?' she asked.

'What does it look like?'

'A kind of tattoo. What does it all mean? It means something, doesn't it? It's really amazingly beautiful.'

Tarku turned away. Melissa got the message, Tarku really didn't want to answer that question, but she wouldn't let him get away easily now that he was beginning to open up. 'Where are you from Tarku? You know where I'm from.'

'Parahn,' he answered.

'Where in Parahn?'

'Do you know the island?'

'No.'

'Then why ask?' he said wearily.

She shut up for a second as he filmed some more and as she stopped to focus on her job as well.

'It doesn't have a name,' he said at last, guilty for his sharp words.

'What doesn't?'

'Where I'm from, on Parahn. It was just an encampment beyond the outskirts of Parahn city, a slum built under a bridge. The bridge itself doesn't exist anymore, it was a relic that had survived since the collapse, a huge bridge, over what was then only a tiny trickle of water, and now is nothing.'

'Do you miss being there when you're not there?'

'No. Do you miss the gutter?'

'I miss my friends.'

'The few friends I had in Parahn are long dead.'

'Does it bother you? You'd be dead too if you weren't for what you are, wouldn't you? I mean, look at how you handled the marauders on the way in to Tamashan. You must love being able to do the things you can.'

'I would rather have been an ordinary man and died long ago.'

'Even death? Really? I can't believe that.'

'If you live long enough you'll understand, besides, death will come to me eventually, I am certain of that, and I fear that when it does it will be as all the deaths I should have died in the long years of my life.'

Melissa didn't know how to reply to that, and was silent for some time, thinking and taking photos of the ruined city around them. There was no life to be seen so far, no people, a few stray and terrified animals but nothing more.

'So, have I got this right,' she asked, coming back to the task at hand, 'there are two groups of people that attacked Tamashan - the Delevian and the Vahrnan?'

'That's right.'

'Even though, like John said, they are enemies themselves.'

'Yes, and no.'

'What are they like? Are they like the Tamashani?'

'No, nothing like. The Delevian are cold and proud, too proud. It's funny, so many of them I have seen with a curling lip, you know, as if they had just been made to swallow vinegar. They fear all things outside their world and over-protect their sovereignty, to their detriment.'

'What do they look like? I'm trying to remember - do the Delevian usually have a really pale complexion?'

'Yes, quite fair, even towards marble white.'

'Oh, are they the ones that are mostly bald? I saw some of them in the subway when I came in to the Universal City, I swear I almost thought they were statues until they moved, and they weren't trying to be, they were just like that.'

'Yes, that would be the Delevian.'

'And the Vahrnan? What are they like? I can't say I recall seeing a Vahrnan at all.'

'The Vahrnan are a proud people too, but they lack the egos of the Delevian. At one time in not so distant history the Vahrnan were a gentle race enslaved under the Delevian, but bit by bit the Delevian engineered the Vahrnan, altering them genetically until they were satisfied that they had slaves that could endure worse conditions than they and be put to work in the worst places on earth.'

'But they are fighting together against Tamashan?'

Tarku nodded. 'From what we have seen it is mostly Delevian, with a few Vahrnan soldiers amongst them. It may seem long ago to the current generation. Laws have changed, prejudices relaxed, and though the ties are brittle, Delevi and Vahrna are closely bound. But how the world forgot the crimes of the Delevian I do not know.'

'And what are they like, I mean, their appearance?'

'I doubt there is a single true Vahrnan left, but still, they are an extremely singular race, so unique I have heard of rich foreigners purchasing them as a peculiarity for their palaces. They are not beautiful as most would define beautiful, but they are, how can I explain,' Tarku thought a moment, 'mesmerising, in a quiet and steady way. All have the qualities that were brought into their genetic makeup by the Delevian. They are solid and tall, now standing equal to or above the height of a Tamashani. Their skin is very pale and flecked and almost transparent, but it is very tough, just as the Delevian wanted for those days on end working in the hot underground, mining ores to build Delevi. I find they lack much personality, you rarely see them smile or laugh.'

'Like you,' Melissa joked.

'No, not like me.' A curious, unreadable grin crept into the corner of Tarku's mouth as he studied her, Syra's daughter, John's daughter. Why did she have to be so unbelievably lovely? He looked away.

'I'm sorry, I was just joking,' she hoped she hadn't offended him again.

'I know,' he turned back. Then she saw it, that proper grin, though his face still held his air of melancholia, she could see he was amused, and managed to capture his expression on her camera before it disappeared. Melissa laughed, so did Tarku, just a little.

They kept on, it really was a surreal experience for Melissa, suddenly thrust into all this unknown, and now finding herself here to see the aftermath of this senseless conflict. It was silent, but for odd blasts in the distance, walking on over the rubble, through empty and broken buildings. Where they were the battle was long over and yet the smell of it all still lingered heavily around them. They came across some few bodies too, deceased citizens of Tamashan, and those that had been left for dead. They helped those who could be helped, but most they came across they could do nothing for. Tarku shielded Melissa from the worst, but there were times she could not help but turn into him and cover her face, sickened and near to tears at what she did see. He would move her along and hold her shoulders firmly until she could regain her composure. She couldn't photograph the dead up close, it seemed like a crime.

They stepped cautiously on through the rubble, staying close to the sides of buildings and the shadows. The golden-grey of rock and metal was painted with smoky black lines that ran like a creeper over everything, up the walls, along the street, through windows, up archways, along the ground, into the water of the lake. The city had been bombed, though mildly, so some of the buildings were still intact structurally, however blackened.

Every now and then a tremor would roll across the ground too, reminding them of the state of the world beyond Tamashan, and causing more of the weakened buildings to crack further and threaten to collapse.

Along their way, when the dawn began to shower more of the city with its humble light, they came across an old Tamashani woman sitting on some houseless steps. She was wrapped in a shawl, staring blankly ahead and rocking forwards and back, muttering, and holding tightly to a pot with a citrus tree in it. The streets around her were quite ruined.

'Would she speak our language?' Melissa asked Tarku, she desperately wanted to talk to her. Tarku shook his head. Melissa sat down beside her, and put her arm around the old woman's shoulders. She was silent for many minutes till she turned to Melissa and touched her face.

'Oh, dear girl,' she began to cry, tears falling over the already swollen eyes. Melissa couldn't understand her language, the native tongue of the Tamashani, but Tarku could. 'Weren't you here? Oh thank goodness you were not here when they came. They came and did this, the gas! the bombs!' Tarku interpreted from a distance as he took some video, and though Melissa tried to console her, that is all the woman could manage to say, she was so distraught Melissa eventually left her to her desolate rocking and muttering and continued on with Tarku.

'They didn't want to destroy Tamashan, nor take it,' Tarku told Melissa what he was thinking. 'These were comparatively small bombs.'

'Small bombs?!'

'Yes, for what the capabilities of Delevi's arsenal are this was very small, very targeted. Notice the kinds of buildings that are mostly left standing – ordinary dwellings, but what don't you see? I think they were targeting government buildings, business and transport hubs, communication towers, power substations, and major transport routes.'

'Why?'

'I think they wanted to cause chaos. This seems like more of a message. But still, the sense in it, the real why, remains to be seen.'

'And where are the people?'

'Still hiding in bunkers, or otherwere, like John's friend in the tower. They have watched their defences being shattered by the Delevian, so they will wait until it is safe, and the Delevian are well and truly gone. As we have seen, there are still patrols around, and more craft have returned towards the port.'

'I still don't understand how the Delevian and Vahrnan can be working together, if what you said - the Vahrnan used to be their slaves?'

'It is incredible, but it has been a long process, and recently the Delevian sovereign has even appointed a Vahrnan as leader below him.'

'That's good, isn't it, that the sovereign would elect a Vahrnan?'

'I want to believe that all will be well, but I can't but think that the Vahrnan haven't forgotten the crimes of the Delevian, that they just bide their time for the right moment, and plan for the day they know they will have their revenge, and having a Vahrnan so high in authority on Delevi makes me worry that that day may be very soon.'

Tarku thought more in silence as he set up a tripod and panned - capturing some more footage, then he and Melissa moved on to see if they could find the friend D'aoda had particularly wished to get a message to.

CHAPTER 37:

Plans Unravel

Up in the port tower, John became anxious when Weston and Astrid did not straight away return. He began making his way back towards where the Blue Moon was docked. He heard the shot, and soon the pair came rushing down the hatch and the corridor, meeting him. He could see it in their faces, hear it in their breathing – something had happened. He did not have to ask, they told it all without hesitation, pulling him on, running down the corridors and not waiting to look back to see if they were followed.

'I ah, I'm sorry John,' Astrid apologised, 'I was caught by a Delevian, I don't know what happened, I'm better than that, I know the risks, I, I don't know how it happened.'

'We better keep moving John,' Weston urged, 'there's no use beating around it, I shot a soldier.'

'You what?!'

'He's dead.'

'Dead? Weston!' John shook his head unbelieving.

'I'm sorry. What would you have me do?! I thought he was going to have his way with Astrid! I don't know how it happened but I tripped and the gun went off and he's dead.'

'I'll tell D'aoda you may have compromised them,' John sighed, 'then we'll split.'

John ran along and quickly informed his Tamashani friend of what had happened. D'aoda and the others hiding there set about leaving the place that instant.

'You should stay in this network. There are many places to hide,' D'aoda told John.

'No my friend, our job and our colleagues are out there, and besides, I don't know these tunnels like you, I would certainly lead us into a corner,' John rechecked all his weapons as he spoke, preparing for the worst.

'Then you will follow after the girl and the Sa'ar?' D'aoda asked.

'Yes, can I leave a message with you in case we miss them and your paths happen to cross?'

'Certainly, but I wish you would stay, it is still very dangerous and unpredictable out there.'

'If we don't face it out there it may come in and meet us here. I shall say goodbye D'aoda, until next time. Thank you for your directions. Come on, Astrid, Weston, have your camera's ready.'

D'aoda watched them lift their packs up and proceed down the passageway. He shook his head, said a blessing for them, then he and his people set off in another direction.

John took off, and Weston and Astrid had to pick up their pace to remain close.

'Where's the kids?' Weston puffed as he tried to keep up.

'Tarku and Melissa left a while back,' John told them, 'We'll follow on.'

'You let them go without us? Out there? You put a lot of trust in him, more than I would, even a honourable Akaia is untrustworthy simply because they're an unknown quantity.'

'So why did you make him part of your team?'

'He's a very skilled creature, couldn't do without him; besides, I've known him for years. Don't get me wrong, I trust *Tarku*, I just don't trust *Akaia*, particularly not now, not after what just happened.'

'You can't trust any Akaia, I know.' John came to another corridor and counted the ones they had passed, 'This must be the one we're meant to take. Astrid, does this direction match your reckoning?'

'Yep.'

'Alright, so we head this way. About Tarku, I know Weston, I worry too, don't think I don't. I keep telling myself that Melissa's about the same age as my Ava would have been, and thinking - would I want her out there alone with Tarku? I trust him totally, that's not the issue, but as we have seen,' John shook his head, 'he does not always belong to himself.'

'Don't you guys worry, I know he'll make sure she's safe, at any cost,' Astrid said, 'I don't know if he knows it yet, but he's deep in love with our darling.'

'You serious?' Weston questioned, 'I didn't think Tarku cared for anyone, didn't really think Akaia could care for anyone.'

'Oh no, it's unmissable,' Astrid said sincerely, but with a smile.

'No, it's not love on his part Astrid,' John said, believing he knew the Akaia better, 'he's a hard one to fathom, but I don't believe his attention is more than concern.'

'What's more worrying is that she's falling for him!' Weston added, 'for the life of me I can't see what she sees in him. I thought when she found out what he was it might cure her, but no, silly girl, she'll just end up getting hurt.'

'She was trying not to like him at the start,' Astrid laughed, 'and he helped a lot too, but lately, I don't know, something's gotta happen soon.'

'I shouldn't have let them go out alone, should I?' John screwed up his mouth at his stupidity, he wouldn't want his daughter to fall for an Akaia, as he had, but he wasn't used to having to think with a father's mindset.

The trio finally reached the ground just as Tarku and Melissa had done. They spilled out into the city, ground level, and ground zero, in all its devastation.

'We were going to meet back up there, we agreed to stay off the airwaves unless absolutely necessary, as the Delevian could listen in so,' John picked up a charred piece of timber and made some non-descript markings by the door.

'Code?' Weston asked.

John nodded, 'I think he was in the military at some point, he'll know what it means. I left a message with D'aoda too, so that's another backup if he doesn't see this.'

'Shall we get started?' Astrid asked, as always eager to be out there in the midst of it, doing her job, well, that, and taking her mind off her own uncertainties for a while.

~

D'aoda had given Tarku directions to his friend's house. Though the streets were hard to make out Tarku thought he had found the place. An old house of burgundy bricks sitting between a new complex of grey and a postal service building. It was definitely the place as there were letters, or pieces of letters, strewn everywhere.

'I don't think anyone's in,' Melissa said as she looked on stunned at the destruction and the bones that were left of the dwelling.

Tarku looked through the house. 'No one was here. They must not have been the first hit, and known what was coming. There are no bodies, that at least will be some comfort to D'aoda.'

'So they're still in hiding you think?'

'I do. They will be waiting to see what today brings. They are a patient people, already days have passed and they continue to wait. They are also a clever people, there are some groups I have seen in the dark corners, ready to move. If we had been a Delevian patrol we would have felt their blades several times already.'

'Really?'

'Yes, I have not approached them, however much Weston may appreciate the commentary, as I did not want to jeopardise their positions in the case we were being followed.'

A horrible feeling came over Melissa at Tarku's words and the way he had said them. She looked behind them, '*Are* we being followed?'

'I'm not a hundred percent sure, but I think so. Don't stop what you're doing, if we are being followed whoever they are haven't acted yet and if we change what we're doing they may feel it necessary to. We'll make our way through the streets slowly as we have been. I'll look out for a way we might vanish and return to the port tower unobserved.'

Melissa knelt on the rubble and focussed the lens into the shell of a bombed building, then set a long exposure, trying to do as Tarku had said and do what they had been doing. Tarku watched her and casually, seeing without seeming to see, the follower. The individual was still a distance away, a scout perhaps, but Tarku observed that they were definitely Delevian military. He said nothing to Melissa.

'Why do you think they picked me?' she asked, feeling once again lacking the necessary skills to be in this situation. 'I mean, you know, to come here and take photos,' she finished the shot and stood. 'You guys all have so much experience, but me, I'm just starting out, I don't even know what we're supposed to be taking photos of.'

'Take photos of what moves you. Just like you have been.' Tarku began walking forward again. 'Why did Weston pick you? You don't talk that much, haha, maybe he knew he'd have enough conversation with Astrid on board. If he hired some of the others he could have, he'd have got no silence.'

'But I didn't even meet Weston before he phoned me.'

'Well that rules that theory out. You sent a portfolio in then?'

'Yeah, well, but even before that, he said he saw my work at this exhibition we had in Junto Mar.'

'Well there's your reason, he likes your work.' Tarku bent and picked up a piece of broken mirror glass, rubbing the dirt and soot off it, checking behind them, before throwing it away.

'Yeah, but, who goes to an art exhibition in The Gutter? And it wasn't that good, and,' Melissa looked confused for a moment, 'never mind. Should we be heading back? Do you think we're still being followed?'

'We should head back. We got a few good shots hey.'

'Yeah, but it's going to be hard telling D'aoda that his friends house isn't there anymore, and that everything's so ruined. I wish I could have seen it before all this, it would have been so beautiful.'

'It was,' Tarku answered but then grabbed her suddenly and pulled her into a cavity between two leaning walls. 'Follow me, now's our chance to slip the watch.'

Together they ran along the narrow lane, ducking under curtains and balcony rails and pot plants that had spilled from the wall that was now leaning over the lane precariously. When they reached the end of the lane they ducked across another road and straight into a lane opposite.

~

Astrid, Weston and John went carefully down one of the main avenues of Mon Karo, it ran parallel to a lake, wide and calm, a lake for which the city was famous. It lay polluted now, not by the Tamashani, who revered it, but by the debris from this raid. Some of the city rises on its shore had their windows blown out and the rubble from other blasts had sent great columns and concrete blocks into the lake, and could be seen sticking up out of the water. Dust had settled across the lake too, and the silt made its former beauty but a sad remembrance. The tails of downed fighter ships stuck out of the water, and the TnTv crew wondered if the pilots were also there, buried under the water. Why would Delevi do this?!

Along with the dust and a pervasive feeling that crept and crept upon them like something intangible was dogging their tails, the crew became more and more concerned that they would not be able to film much longer, but would be caught and effectively silenced by the Delevian army. For though they had seen no sign of soldiers on the ground when they came in, they had seen two small squadrons now and had had to hide.

At one point Astrid pulled the men aside and put her finger to her lips to silence them.

'What?' Weston whispered.

'Did you hear that?' she said.

'What?'

'I think there are more soldiers close by.'

'What should we do?'

'Just wait. They'll go past soon then we can go again. But be careful, stay on the lookout, if they spot us we'll have to make a run for it.'

The ground shook with a distant blast, another fighter jet began to continue what had been started before the raid had been interrupted by the appearance of the giant Mrukai. The shattered buildings around them shook too, more glass falling from the windows and more blocks crashing and splintering across the road. They shielded themselves as best they could while it lasted, but nowhere was safe.

'We've got to get those kids and get out of here,' John said, 'we don't need more footage do we Weston? Finding out why this is happening for a television documentary isn't worth our lives.'

'I know, I know,' Weston said, 'it's pointless, but what are we supposed to do? Hey? Go back to the north and sit by the pool on Lalapahue drinking pina-coladas? I wonder how long this place has anyway? Two weeks, two months, two years and there won't even be a Tamashan or a Shorakai to worry about. But what if the world doesn't end? Or not as soon as we think. This is important. This is really important. What we film here could mean justice for your friend D'aoda and the rest of Tamashan.'

'You can film all you want, but I've got to make sure Melissa's safe. I couldn't live with myself if I didn't.'

'Wait. John, I agree, just let's be calm about this yeah. I know you're a brilliant explorer but you always got into trouble when your head got hot about something, you know it, and I'm the same, because of me we're already in trouble if the Delevian find us, so calm down, we'll do this properly, we'll figure out a plan and where the kids might be now and go there, alright?'

'Yeah. Alright,' John breathed. He hadn't meant to lose his head, but when it came to his daughter, well, he couldn't help it, even though she may not be his daughter, it was a possibility he could not dismiss, and the thought of it, of losing her again, was too much.

They decided to circle around to the city centre and then head back to the port tower, that way they would pass the house of D'aoda's friend and then, hopefully, follow the path that Melissa and Tarku would have taken to get back to the tower. However the meeting time they had set was well past, so it might be that Melissa and Tarku would have either made their way back to the place where they had originally met D'aoda, or even back to the ship, perhaps they had even come back out following the others.

They came to within sight of the port tower without being caught, they gained a view of the exit they had used. All sight of the soldiers had ceased on their way, and while in one way that was a good thing, in another way it made John quite concerned. He couldn't figure out what the Delevian plan was. As a military man the troop and ship movements he had seen made no sense. There was no sight of Melissa and Tarku.

'I hope they got your message John,' Astrid said. 'I hope they aren't making their way back to the ship, they'll be in trouble if they are; the Delevian would likely have it under watch.'

'We could radio them?' Weston said, 'I know it's dangerous, but there are so many possibilities.'

'No,' John shook his head, 'the Delevian would definitely be monitoring all frequencies.'

'So, use code. You and Tarku are smart, you'll think of something.'

Another few fighter craft flew over the city, though no bombs were dropped this time.

'The Delevian would figure out any code we transmitted, you know how clever they are, we'd just land ourselves in more trouble. I should have been more careful from the beginning. I should have insisted that you didn't transmit anything until we were on our way out of here.'

'What? Then no one might have seen anything!' Weston defended. 'We're alright John, so far, and if anything happens and we get into trouble I promise you I'll take full responsibility. It was the shot from my gun that brought us to their attention so I'll take the fall if I have to.'

'They might not give you the chance.'

'No, it was my fault,' Astrid said softly, 'you could do a report on it West, how a malfunctioning M series brought down the acclaimed Weston Alamo in the middle of a warzone on Tamashan. Give Q-Corp. some bad publicity, I wouldn't mind.'

'Astrid we're fine. John, we're fine,' Weston encouraged, 'We've been in tighter binds than this before! All of us! Now come on, we're going to go over there and we're going to find the kids. Surely D'aoda would have given them the message, we'll find him and everything will be fine.'

Weston was about to step out from behind cover but John and Astrid pulled him back just in time to avoid being in the direct path of a small blast.

'We're going to have to run for it,' John said. 'We'll get back up to the docking platform. We'll take the first functioning ship we find alright, we'll take it and we'll get out of here.'

'What about the kids?' Weston protested.

'They'll be close by, they have to be,' John insisted. 'Tarku wouldn't have gone far.'

'Ok, so we're running?' Weston breathed deeply, readying himself.

'We're running. Astrid, do you have a best route?'

Astrid touched the ground to sense the movements of the soldiers, she calculated all best outcomes and looked up, her face was readable. There were no good options, in fact, their options were all gone - it was too late. The three ran, but they heard the boots upon the ground, the shouts, the weapons load. There was no escape, they were surrounded by soldiers.

'So,' Weston smiled sadly as he put up his hands, as the guns aimed towards them, 'this looks like goodbye then.'

John laughed, but looked entirely serious. 'Just take it as it comes Weston, take it as it comes.'

~

Melissa and Tarku had found their way back to the tower and entered by the hidden maintenance door through which they had originally come. In their hurry, and in the way the landscape had changed in that time, Tarku did not see John's message. They had not gone many levels up the stairs and passageways of the platform when they couldn't go on. Several doors had been jammed shut and barricaded.

'It's no use, it won't budge, we can't go any further,' Tarku told her as he pushed against a barrier again and wondered who had put them up and why.

'Could we go out onto a platform and find another way back up?'

'Something's not right.'

'But we've got to get back Tarku, what if the others are in trouble, they might need your help.'

'They've skills enough between them. They can look after themselves,' he said as he continued to try to think of the best way to get back to the ship. 'I think these passageways must have been compromised,' he said at last.

'What should we do?' she asked, very calmly, but he could see she was growing distressed by the lines gathering between her eyebrows.

'Let me think for a moment,' Tarku sat down with his thumbs on his jaw and his fingers framing his closed eyes.

Melissa slid down the wall opposite, toying with her camera, silently catching Tarku's focussed pose. Then she started playing with the communication panel on her jacket. Scratchy voices were coming through when she pressed the button that opened the link between her and the panel on John's jacket.

'John's left his microphone on!' Tarku was surprised, and knew at once that it could only mean bad news. Then it became clearer. Melissa jumped up and sat again next to Tarku and they listened.

'What are they saying?' Melissa whispered, for they were talking in Delevian and she couldn't understand a word of it. The tone was not heartening at all, but very dire. 'They're in trouble aren't they?' she asked, all the colour now leaving her face.

It was John's voice they heard at first, Tarku understood but did not translate for their young protégé.

'I have told you that we are from the Universal City in the North Island States, we are from a television company, TnTv, we're journalists, and that is all. We don't have anything to do with this thing, we belong to neither side.' Then there was a muffled Delevian voice then John spoke again. 'Sir I fear you are being unreasonable,' a pause, a yell. Melissa and Tarku looked at each other, Melissa fearful, Tarku concerned.

'What are they saying?' Melissa asked again but Tarku hushed her.

'We could leave, we could take our ship and leave if that would please you.'

'I'm afraid none of you will be going anywhere. You are all party to the fatal shooting of one of our esteemed officers.'

'That was an accident, as I have said, entirely my fault, but an accident,' Weston pleaded.

'Don't give us your excuses. If you were Tamashani you would be shot this instant but seeing as you are from the North you will be taken to Delevi as soon as we have the rest of your crew, which shouldn't be long now. There you shall all be judged.'

'Come quickly,' Tarku grabbed her hand and ran.

'What? What did they say? The others have been caught, haven't they?'

Tarku was silent, only interested in finding the way back down and into the city with all haste, it wasn't safe in here.

'Tarku?'

'Yes, they've arrested the others.'

'Oh no, oh no, oh no, oh no!'

'Shhh,' he stopped running for a moment, held her shoulders, and looked into her eyes until she calmed down. 'It's not the end of the world, alright, not till I say so. Now come on.' He led her along the passageways and back down the way they had come.

They heard voices ahead. 'They have to be up here somewhere, they wouldn't have had time to find another way out yet.' The voices of the soldiers grew nearer. Melissa couldn't understand what was being said but she heard the voices and a rush of footsteps coming up from below with a terrifying pounding and haste that echoed around them till her head spun. At the sound of the voices below even Tarku seemed surprised and Melissa saw real fear in his face.

'We're trapped aren't we?' Melissa asked, 'they know we're here don't they? What are we going to do?'

Tarku turned around and they started going up again, and by several deviations and breaking through some partitions they managed to get back to the initial hatch that John had led them down, the hatch near the Blue Moon. Tarku peered out carefully. Too many soldiers.

'Come on, we'll see if we can get higher, I hope you're good on the stairs,' he said and they headed as fast as they could, up the ladders, along the passageways, up the stairs, around more passageways, heading higher and higher up the platform tiers, but the footsteps seemed to near them with every turn.

Tarku hoped against reason that an opportunity would present itself, a door to a platform, an abandoned ship still in working order, or even somewhere he could hide Melissa, where she'd be a hundred percent safe and he could lead their pursuers in another direction, then get back and try to save the others, get them away on a ship then come back for Melissa when the Delevian had given up. It was a sound plan in theory, but he knew it was virtually impossible.

'You're fast on the stairs,' he encouraged her.

'I haven't lived on the 11th floor of an apartment building with intermittently faulty elevators for nothing then,' she almost laughed.

Tarku and Melissa ran and ran, they tried to deviate via an internal ramp which led across to another platform, and up a secondary stairwell there, but every move they made the Delevian seemed to know, to anticipate. Only a few flights up these stairs and the pair were surprised by the sound of soldiers above them and then a canister was thrown down and fell by them, releasing its toxin around them.

'Hold your breath!' Tarku yelled, 'get your mask on.' He pulled his on then made sure Melissa was alright, but she wasn't, she was turning about, looking on the ground, searching about them. 'What are you doing? Get your mask on!'

She looked at him desperately, shaking her head, 'I can't find it,' she said, trying not to breathe, trying to see in this haze that the gas bomb also pumped out around them. 'I must have lost it somewhere. It must have come off, unclipped.' She wasn't wheezing or coughing yet, despite the gas, but she was panicking. Tarku held her, and put his own mask on her, fixing it tightly.

'Come on, you're alright, we've got to keep going.'

They couldn't go any further up these stairs, obviously, and neither could Tarku break through the barred door that led to the lower passages, but they managed to get across the ramp again to the original side, only now their pursuers were so close, from both sides now gaining upon them. Tarku's head was growing lighter from the gas, and Melissa's energy failing.

The pursuers were almost on them, they could glimpse the soldiers now and again as they ran. Tarku heard with some relief one of the officers call out a command not to fire on the girl. Even so, he doubled his fervour to get her out of this safely. He helped Melissa up as she stumbled, and ran on.

Then seemingly without reason the soldiers seemed to lose ground, and Tarku found he and Melissa had a little breathing space. But then he heard the soldiers shouting to each other in their own language; they had realised what Tarku was, that he was Akaia, or Sa'ar, as they say, and they were waiting, waiting for weapons that would be of more use against him than the ones they had, and notifying those that waited outside, ready to go to what platform their prey would exit.

Tarku stopped running, pulling Melissa into a small vertical nook opposite the ladder that was the last before the one that would lead them out onto the platform, the one he knew must lead out to the very topmost tier; there was nowhere else to go. They where metres and metres above the ground, they were tired, they had been trapped, outsmarted. They had managed to double back and circuit around and bypass the sectioned off areas but it had done them no good. They both knew it, there was no way out of this.

They tried to catch their breath in vain. Melissa pulled down the mask and looked up at Tarku. Somewhere in the chase his glasses had caught a bullet and had shattered to pieces, his face was alright now, not a scratch, his eyes a soft grey smouldering ash. She watched him as he watched the way. Her arms were tight up against his chest as they waited in this last crevice, his hands held her by the shoulders, ready to push her onward at the right moment.

'Tarku, what will the Delevian do when they catch us? Will they kill us?'

'Me, most likely they will try. You, probably not.'

'What about the others?'

He shook his head. 'I don't know.'

As her heart raced and couldn't slow down, neither could her thoughts. Thoughts of what she'd left behind, of Matthias telling her never to go back to the gutter, of Kat telling her almost the same, of getting away from Garner and the potential abuse for which she had been destined, the journey so far, the amazing sights and people. She wouldn't change it. She wouldn't change a thing, even if she was about to die. She felt Tarku's breath fall across her forehead as he tried to quiet his breath to listen for the sounds of their pursuers, they were so close. She'd tried so hard not to like him, but she couldn't deny that she did. Standing here next to him felt more comfortable than anywhere else she had ever stood. It felt right. She dared to look back at him, and before she could look away again his eyes met hers. He brushed a stray fringe from her eyes.

'Tarku I -' she began, but he put his finger to her lips, a gesture of silence, and bent his head, listening. Their pursuers were moving towards them again. Tarku almost threw Melissa up the ladder and he followed after just dodging the shots of the soldiers. They burst out of the hatch and bolted for the nearest cover, but the Delevian were waiting for them, an aircraft quickly lowered and soldiers jumped out, well armed.

~

From the ground the rest of the crew knew something was wrong.

'Look at them, they're excited about something,' Weston said bitterly as he watched the soldiers from where the three sat tied up together, awaiting transport to Delevi. 'I should have kept to the original plan, none of this chasing the war down, blast those executives! I should have stuck to my guns,' Weston shook his head. 'We still don't know why it all happened in the first place. I wonder if the kids got any clues. I can't figure it out.'

'John,' Astrid's thoughts went ahead, like Melissa's, 'what will happen to us on Delevi? I have records of reported facts, but you've been there, you've seen what they're like.'

'Well, we'll be put in prison, and await trial.'

'But we haven't done anything, well, except for West, but that was an accident, surely they'll see that.'

'I don't know, the Delevian don't like meddling foreigners, and on top of that we're witness to what's been done here, and we've broadcast it to the world. I don't think they're going to be happy.'

'Worst scenario?'

'Worst? Well, execution for Weston and I,' Astrid gasped at John's blunt assessment, 'or put to work in their penal system.'

'They wouldn't do that! Would they?'

'It's been known to happen.'

'I see, what about me? What about Melissa?'

John shook his head. In truth he was scared of what might happen.

'John?'

'I don't know, but she's young and she's pretty enough to be used as property, traded or kept, she would likely be given to serve someone on Delevi.'

Astrid sighed, she understood. 'So you don't think they'll let this go?'

'It's not likely.'

'And our government can do nothing for us?'

'No, they wouldn't dare, not against the Delevian, and Weston's the only one the powers that be would give a scratch about; I've got a record, Melissa's just a girl from the gutter and you're a mech, you're Q-Corp's problem. You think they'd try to get you back?'

'Not a chance, I'm too close to being decommissioned. What about Tarku?'

John sighed, 'You know what he is. You know what happens to Akaia on Delevi. The best he can hope for is a quick death.'

'And that's not likely, Tarku's got too much fight to go quietly.' Astrid rubbed her forehead, 'Listen, I'm sorry I got into trouble back there, I don't know what's going on with me lately, I should have seen that soldier, and I should have seen them coming.'

'You weren't to blame Astrid,' John assured her. Then a thought struck him, 'Wait, can you interface with Delevian technology?'

'I'm not designed to, but I'm working on it,' she grinned, 'it's not easy though, it could take a while, their coding is very complex.'

'Well, you just keep working on it, and let us know if you get through.'

'Oh, you'll know,' she said determinedly, but with a mischievous grin.

They stopped their conversation as some of the soldiers passed again and they listened to what they were saying. 'Warm the engines up,' one called to another standing by, 'we should have the other two soon enough.'

The mech, the producer and the engineer looked up.

~

High above, on the topmost tier of the port tower, Delevian soldiers now disembarked their craft and surrounded. Tarku looked for a way out. He didn't want to fight if he didn't have to, but Melissa was Tarku's responsibility, she was Syra's daughter and she was all that mattered to Tarku on this earth anymore. He tried to shield her behind him.

The Delevian held off firing for the moment, they didn't want to fire if their shots might endanger her, but at last a soldier saw a chance and managed to nick Tarku, and again as he stumbled. Melissa screamed and tried to hold him steady, and though the shot would have downed a man, he managed to keep standing.

One of the soldiers tried to grab Melissa as Tarku turned about, trying to cover every side. There was struggle, but the soldiers could not separate them. But then there was a yell from Tarku as one of the Delevian soldiers he'd knocked over riddled his leg with bullets, enough to cause him to stumble and lose Melissa. Then the soldiers that had followed them up from below broke through the hatch as well and quickly panned out. They fired upon Tarku and helped their fellow soldiers to secure Melissa. Their weapons were different, not electricity or bullet or wave-length pulse but something else, something unseen and terrible, something specifically designed to be used against Sa'ar. The Delevian after all were leaders in how to deal with Akaia, and they must know now that that was what he was; a mere man would have long been dead. He hadn't forgotten their skill, but he'd never had to fight them like this either. Each shot that hit him felt like a jolt that split his core in two, that seemed to force his conscious thoughts to the background as if his very soul was being forced out of his body. He'd never felt anything like this. He knew he had to give it everything and all at once if he were to survive, and if he were going to keep her safe.

There was a change. Even the atmosphere seemed to grow suddenly close around them as Tarku picked himself up again, against their belief; slowly, purposefully, and with a spark growing behind his eyes that should have been a warning. It was only a moment, but the moment felt like it had a pause on it. Everything was still and silent, then Tarku threw his shredded jacket aside and suddenly let loose. He really gave it to them, fighting like few had seen him fight before, letting himself use the skills he hated, those things that made him Akaia. He was fast, moving with his own strange form of combat, like a dancer, like a boxer, like a serpent. He yelled and tore at them and Melissa even tried to follow his lead, struggling free from her captors momentarily, and really giving them everything she had. The soldiers defended themselves until they could grab her again and hold her down till they tied her up properly.

Only six of the soldiers that fought Tarku were left standing as Melissa looked back, as she was dragged to their ship. She saw as Tarku yelled and took out two more in quick succession, but his actions were so violent she had to look away. In that moment she felt more fear at the sight of him than of the imminent unknown, as she understood now why all those things that were said about Akaia could be said. Despite all their weapons, Tarku kept at the soldiers, trying to get through them to get to her, but in a split second he saw her face as she looked back, he saw the horror written there, and in that split second hesitation, a soldier on another ship threw a gun to a soldier that was on the ground, a different gun, more powerful than those they carried with them.

'It's fully charged, take him down!' the solider called out, and one that Tarku had previously dealt a heavy blow now took aim and fired. Tarku's blood was rushing, his sight a vague and cracked haze and his head a-spin, he couldn't dodge it in time. It was sudden and horrifying, a massive blast, a shock greater than anything Tarku had ever felt. Then three more of the same shot hit his body in quick succession. He stumbled back towards the edge of the platform. He lost his senses as the blasts were so unbelievably strong they seemed to completely separate the spirit from the body, the consciousness from the mind.

The soldier stepped closer to Tarku, holding up the weapon ready to fire again.

'Now you have seen what we can do to you Sa'ar,' the soldier spoke with a snigger. 'In training we are taught that this is the best weapon against you. They say one shot is sometimes enough. You are very tough I'll give you that, but I think you're almost done.' He aimed the barrel at Tarku's chest.

In the haze that was left in Tarku's mind not much got through, but he grasped enough of the situation to know that he was done, to know that he had failed. He had failed Syra. He had failed Melissa. He had failed John and the crew. He had even failed the Mrukai. He tried to speak but words had become foreign to him, and only blood ran over his lips.

The soldier laughed, and shot again. Once more Tarku's body and spirit suffered under that blast, but more than that, every line of every marking upon him lit up at once, his eyes too, just for a second. Then his body slumped, the lines smouldered. For a moment Tarku remained conscious, but as the lines faded so did he, until there was no light upon him. As they pulled Melissa on board she saw Tarku for that last time, she saw as the Delevian put up their weapons, knowing there was no more to be done, knowing they had defeated him. Tarku became like Hardan had been, all trace of light and life left him.

'No!' Melissa gasped, as his body slowly tilted back, and then fell from the edge of the dock. She tried to pull away from her captors again, she screamed, wanting to run to the edge to see if what had just happened was really true, that Tarku had just been killed and that his body now plummeted the metres and metres to the ground. It couldn't be true. It couldn't be true!

But then as the soldiers pulled her inside the ship, even as Tarku hit the ground, it was as if the earth itself had suffered under the impact of his fall. The rifts in the distance around Tamashan shook in reply and from them arose walls of pluming ash. And not just the gulfs nearby, but the entire Pireomerai, the Great Divide, and all these rifts now breathed from their full depths, and every civilization left on the earth knew of their torment. There was not a living soul that did not hear at that moment, a collective cry from the deep. For a full minute trading ceased, the traffic stopped, no one spoke, no one moved, every eye turned to the deserts and wastes, towards those rifts and gulfs. Fear was the only thought in that minute, and after that minute there was only panic.

Captives

The Delevian craft carrying our TV crew quickly left the airspace of Tamashan. Though far below them the ends of two gulfs met, the gulf of Aliyr which surrounded Vahrna and Delevi and the tail of the Pireomerai coming down from beyond Satsuan, they did not heed the accelerated churning or the cry of the Mrukai, but only sped on. Their pride was such their consideration of these events remained minimal, and any fear they may have felt was not expressed.

Having seen to their many wounds, the soldiers who guarded the TV crew were now much more relaxed. They even laughed as one of their number pulled on Tarku's torn jacket and pretended to look trendy. 'I'd keep this, if it hadn't been worn by that creature,' the man almost spat as he said the words. 'Too bad,' the soldier took it off and threw it down at the crew. 'Let that be a lesson to you northerners, even your pet Sa'ar couldn't save you. You cannot overcome the Delevian, so help things along by not trying to.' Then the soldiers left them, locking them in the hold.

Weston, John and Astrid all turned to Melissa, they had seen a figure fall, that must have been Tarku, they had all heard the cry that went out across the earth, and they waited for her to tell them what had happened. She took his jacket into her hands. 'They killed him,' was all she said before she broke, and she could not be consoled for a long while. It was a great loss, they all felt it and felt disbelief. They let her cry. Though all their hands were bound Astrid managed to pick up the jacket and put it over Melissa's shoulders. Astrid herself clenched her jaw and raised her eyebrows in an effort not to cry. John and Weston were meditatively silent.

After some time, when they all sat in complete quiet, the small, tear strained voice of Melissa echoed around them.

'Why did you pick me for this expedition Weston? Why did you have to pick me?' She cried. She felt guilty. 'I'm the most inexperienced, the youngest, I lost my gas mask, maybe Tarku would have been more able to fight if he hadn't still had the gas in his system, if he hadn't had to protect me. Now he's dead.'

'I didn't pick you, it was Tarku,' Weston answered her question before thinking, 'well, it was my decision in the end, I guess.'

'Tarku?'

'It was his suggestion, he saw your work at the exhibition, and after I looked at your work I agreed.'

'He, but he didn't say,' then she slipped silently back into tears again.

Theirs was not the only ship now returning to Delevi. Shortly after their departure the combat and troop ships also began to pull out from around Mon Karo, Raijenou and other locations across Tamashan, only a few less would return than had come. The Tamashani had been a push over, totally unprepared for a large scale, undeclared assault. There were only a few people in the whole world who knew the reason for the attack, and they were keeping their silence. The soldiers knew their tasking, they knew their job, and they had almost completed what they had been ordered to do and now many ships were returning home, leaving the devastation they had created behind them.

John grew uncomfortable with his thoughts. He could only hope that they would get through whatever came next. He wondered how to tell Melissa what he and Tarku had discussed. What he now believed might be possible, that she could be his daughter. How much he longed to tell Melissa, to tell her of her father's love, how much he had always loved her, how much he had longed to know her. How sorry he was at all that had happened, how inadequate had been his search, and how terrible his failure now, to see ahead far enough, a mistake that had lost them Hardan and Tarku, and got the rest of them into this situation.

'Melissa,' the old soldier spoke, 'I want to tell you something.'

She picked up her head to listen, trying to wipe the tears away on her shoulder as her hands were bound like all of them were, and chained to the ship's floor.

'I want to tell you why I'm here,' he said, 'I want you to know that I saw you on the television, I saw you presenting that piece on Merouin, and when I saw you - you reminded me of my daughter, so I had to come and see you in person.'

'You agreed to be our guide because you thought Melissa might be your daughter?!' Weston exclaimed as Melissa remained silent.

'Yes,' John nodded. 'That's how it is. I don't know if what I believed is true, but Scott urged me to come, so he must have thought there was something there, and Tarku, well he believed it even more strongly than I do, that you could be my daughter.'

'I don't know what to say,' Melissa said at last.

'You don't have to say anything, I just wanted you to know,' John said, 'it might not be true, but it might be, and I don't know what we're going into, what will happen on Delevi, I just wanted you to know that if you are my daughter, know I never stopped loving you, and if you're not my daughter, I want you to know that I would have been glad if she was like you. Melissa, you've got the kindest heart, and you're braver than you realise, girl, do you know any other northern girl as young as you coming out here? Anyway, that's what I wanted to say.'

After some more silence Melissa spoke up again, 'Thank you John, for telling me, I'd be glad to think my father was like you too.'

After some time Weston spoke up. 'I wonder why we're slowing down,' he said.

'Do you know where we are?' Astrid put her head up, she had her hand spread out on the floor of the ship, trying to hack into the Delevian systems, and not concentrating on their whereabouts.

'I'd say we're getting closer to the Delevi,' John answered.

'Already?' Astrid worried. She wasn't having much luck against the Delevian coding yet.

It wasn't long and they felt the ship come to a stop.

'Delevi,' Weston shook his head. 'I had it after Salamonde on our tour of the south. If only they'd left us a camera, and a hook up, I'd film this place and get all this back to Max for editing.'

'You never stop working do you Alamo?' John said.

'Always looking for a good shoot,' Weston admitted.

'Wait, did you hear that?' Melissa looked up at a sound.

'What?'

The sound grew broader, and at last reached through to them and they all heard it. They all realised what it was.

'Kyu,' John said, 'that sounded like Kyu.'

'It certainly did,' Weston agreed.

'What would she be doing here?' John questioned.

'Hopefully she's come to rescue us,' Weston joked.

'Hopefully she has,' John was serious, 'but she sounded like she was in pain.'

'How's it going there Astrid?' Weston hoped she would have good news as they heard footsteps coming.

'No good,' she shook her head, and sighed heavily, 'I'm not equipped to deal with their technology, but I'll keep trying, whatever happens.'

'Good girl,' Weston said.

'Keep alert,' John encouraged them all, 'don't do anything reckless. Better to be separated with a chance to meet up later than blow it by doing something foolhardy too early. I'll say my goodbyes, I doubt we'll be together much longer.'

He was cut off. The door was opened into the hold, flooding it with light, so bright after the age without it, and those four left of the TnTv crew squinted to try to get a glimpse of where they were as they were taken out of the ship and pushed along various ways until they were shoved into other hands and taken on. John and Weston were taken in a different direction, they struggled to look around to keep Melissa and Astrid in their sight but they were soon gone. The two men were pushed along and then into a cell amongst a vast collection of cells, all cramped with other prisoners.

Weston stared at the big man for quite a while, trying to read him.

'Was it true what you said to her on the ship? Or were you just trying to give her some encouragement?' Weston asked John.

'It's her Weston, it has to be her.'

'I'm not usually the voice of reason, but John, she's a kid from the north.'

'Tarku agrees with me, I had my doubts, but he doesn't, and he's right, she's a lot like Amiana.'

'Man I wish I could have filmed the reunion, people eat this stuff up.'

John only glared at the producer, Melissa's beautiful young face filling his mind, the agony of all that had befallen, the fear of the unknown that lay ahead for them all. It brought back everything else he didn't want to remember, his wife's assassination, well, apparent assassination, his daughter's abduction, his years of searching. His girls were so beautiful, Amiana's smile, his daughter's face as she giggled, so small a thing in his great arms. All of these pictures melded together and sped behind his eyes.

'What are we going to do now John?' Weston sighed.

John shook his head. He didn't know.

'Come on, you always find a way, always have, and I should know, I did a doco on you.'

'We're alive West, that's enough for the moment.'

CHAPTER 38:

Her Sovereign

Kyu called and it was a painful cry. Scott and Sjyntani felt her whole being shudder after a muted thuddering, like a blast across her side.

'What's happening?!' Sjyntani cried.

'Kyu? Kyu what are you doing? Where are we?' Scott called to her, put his hand to her inner side, 'Kyu?'

The great creature called again, and was hit again, now from the other side as well. She opened the slit up just enough for them to glimpse the earth below. A clear filmy membrane still protected them from the wind and the air up here, but Sjyntani lost her breath.

'Where are we?' Scott asked.

'Heading into Novocas already,' Sjyntani looked at him, at once fearful and astounded. 'This is the outskirts of Novocas, the Delevian capital. They will bring her down Scott, they so fear the Kyu.'

'Kyu what are you doing! You should have let me know! I need to call them before you fly in!' Scott yelled as Kyu screamed again under the force of a blast along her side. 'I've got to stop this,' Scott fumbled with his portable com then found the radio frequency he needed and let the aerial out through the slit.

'Delevi control, Delevi control, this is Scott Thomas, Scott Thomas, please receive.'

There was only silence in reply. 'You speak Delevian,' Scott turned to Sjyntani, 'call them, try.'

Sjyntani took the radio and repeated the call.

'Scott Thomas this is Delevi,' the reply came at last.

'Tell them I'm with the Kyu, she will do no harm, to call off the fire please!' he told Sjyntani, she did. 'Tell them I didn't realise Kyu had ventured into their airspace, that we are only two passengers, we request safe passage over Delevi.'

There were no further blasts for the moment.

'Scott Thomas, what business brings you past Delevi?'

'Tell them I am a traveller, I pick up casual employ while I tour, with my companion,' he glanced at Sjyntani and took a chance, 'my little brother.'

Sjyntani smiled and relayed the message.

'Where do you hail from?'

'From Universal City, of the northern island of Corrio. We have come via Soamé and Satsuan.'

'Scott Thomas, safe passage granted.'

'Thank you Delevi,' Sjyntani ended the call. Scott breathed. 'Did you hear that Kyu? They will let us pass!'

They looked out over the city. Together Scott and Sjyntani surveyed the structures below them. It was breathtaking. If one thing could be said about the Delevian, they had brilliant architects, insane, but brilliant. One building stood out above the city rises, three great spires sitting on the three points of a triangle, reaching into the sky like immense silver bullets that had left the gun a split second after each other, seemingly windowless with pure clean lines, polished to a high lustre, reflecting everything, even Kyu as she flew past. This building was both home to the Sovereign and those of the palace, the parliament, when the parliament was sitting, and the courts of law, amongst other things. Open walkways ran between the columns at various heights, and from here the people on them looked like ants crawling about in their activity. It was surrounded by a greensward, and then the city ballooned out from there. But then all of that was out of sight and the next vision was before them.

They remained speechless till Kyu came to a landing platform. Kyu made a curious sound that Scott didn't know. It was a sad note, but not long, and not deep. Then she stopped moving and opened the slit fully.

'We didn't get permission to stop, I doubt they would have given it.' Scott looked out, so did Sjyntani.

'This is the international port,' Sjyntani worried.

'Kyu, can you take us to the palace? Where is the best place Sjyntani? Where can you get access to the sovereign?'

'Those bullet buildings, but they would surely shoot Kyu again, we would never get close. We will have to make the ground and try another way.'

'I suppose this is where we get off. Is this the best place Kyu?' Again that sad note. Scott turned to Sjyntani, 'Get your disguise on, and do it well. I don't understand what Kyu knows, but she wants us to get out here.'

Sjyntani hurried, tucking up her hair and putting on her hat. Collecting her few things together.

'Are you ready?' Scott asked her.

'No,' she shook her head.

'I'll be with you,' he said, and though he was just as concerned managed to say, 'Kyu always has a plan. I'm sure she has a plan.' He took Sjyntani's arms and let her down, then jumped out himself. Kyu flew on.

'The Delevian hate the Kyu,' Sjyntani said again as ships converged around Kyu, to escort her away from the city. Sjyntani was a little wobbly legged, still in awe of the flight and still overwhelmed by being back here. She knelt down on the concrete where she was.

'You don't want to be here do you?'

She shook her head. She didn't dare speak as she truly felt nauseous.

'I hope you know what you're doing Kyu,' Scott spoke to her diminishing form. Kyu sighed for a long while. 'Don't you know? Did you just perceive a little whisper of some intangible thing?' Scott saw officials heading towards them, and they didn't look impressed. 'You wouldn't have nordan papers would you?' he asked Sjyntani.

'No. Only the Shorakaian ones, and they are for a girl, not this disguise.'

'So the story is you lost your papers. I have mine, let's hope that's enough.'

Scott pulled out his Passport Internationale ready to hand to the officials. There were no queues at the international docking port here at this time, and the officials must have very little to do. A rather gnarled looking man eyed him dubiously. Scott handed him the passport.

'Welcome to Delevi,' he wheezed sourly. 'Your first visit I assume?' he asked, perusing the stamps.

'I was here once before, when I was a child.'

'I see.' He went on as he filled out some paperwork. 'You asked for passage, not entry, what is your business here?'

'I am a traveller, I pick up work where I can. If there's no work that's fine we'll leave as soon as we can. We just had some trouble with the, the Kyu, she's a temperamental creature,' Scott tried to explain. 'This is my little brother, he travels with me.'

The official only glared, then continued reading through Scott's paperwork.

'I'm afraid my little brother lost his papers. Can't keep a shirt clean that one,' Scott laughed, 'Always causing me grief.'

'I can give you three days to find work or leave Delevi. Here is a guide,' the official handed Scott a small pamphlet. 'You will find a great deal of essential information there, as well as maps, our history, philosophy,' his hand moved in a, 'and so on' kind of way and he eyed Scott distastefully.

'Thank you, ah -'

'You'll find the forms you need to apply for work at the international centre, and you can make your way into the city from there. The escort will take you.'

'Thank you, thank you very much.' Scott picked up his bag and he and Sjyntani followed after the escort.

The escort was an interesting girl who had turned up suddenly and seemed to be in somewhat of a hurry. 'Here on holiday?' the young lady asked, or rather more interrogated.

'Ah, no, not exactly, looking for a little work actually,' Scott explained again, 'while I travel.'

'Well, if you have time, there is an eye-opening exhibit currently touring, right at this moment at the Sovereign's own museum here in Novocas.'

'Oh, what's the topic?'

'The Architecture of Adversaries. The curator is very good, but this would have to be his best show yet, many have said so.'

'I have been admiring some of the buildings here on the way in, most impressive.'

'Buildings? It has nothing to do with buildings, Architecture as in design, do you understand, the design of our enemies.'

'Not exactly, no.'

'You should go and see, I can't explain it in the little time we have, but I'm certain you'll find it fascinating,' she said seriously. 'It is such a crucial exposé of the trials which have shaped Delevi and made this nation great in how we have overcome.' Scott would have laughed at the way she spoke, but he didn't want to offend, and the truth was that he was intrigued at what it was actually all about. This girl was certainly very serious.

'Thank you, I'll try to see it.'

'Good, here we are, at the centre. This is where I leave you.'

Scott spent some time filling out forms for employment, to keep up the ruse. He wasn't sure what he was supposed to be doing, but with Sjyntani's help he had applied for jobs from cleaning offices to driving instruction.

'Alright, what now?' Scott asked.

'I suggest we go see that exhibit,' Sjyntani directed.

'Really? You want to see that?'

She nodded, 'You'll see why when we get there.'

The travellers walked towards those bullet buildings. Scott checked his watch. It felt like afternoon even though it might not have been afternoon. It was hard to tell time by the light on Delevi.

'It took some getting used to,' Sjyntani said as she explained it to Scott. 'It always has the feeling of early morning or late afternoon because the whole island of Delevi has sunk by so many metres and there are a few small islands close by that have not sunk, or not by as much, and so as the sun passes over, these smaller islands steal the light leaving Delevi in a broken shade for much of the year.'

'Those mountains?' Scott observed.

'Yes, they are the islands. They call them Lapasse, Nuana and Luteni, so whichever is blocking out the sun most directly, that is the name of the time of day. Although, Nuana misses out much time because it is directly inside of Lapasse, and has sunk a fraction itself, so it receives even less light than Delevi.'

'Can't I just use my watch?'

'Sure, but local time is commonly used. You hear them all the time in the palace, saying they want this or that before Lapasse.'

'Is that a row of lights heading to Lapasse?'

'Yes. Delevi use Lapasse as a dock for big freighters, especially ones that carry cargo that needs to be quarantined. I believe much of the Sovereign's air fleet is also stationed there.'

Scott's portable com buzzed. There was a message. 'Look at that, I've got a job already!'

'What is it?'

'Would you believe, it's the dock work one, it says to meet at the central station for transport to the docks on Lapasse, first light tomorrow.'

'Did I get in?'

'Just me. You're too young Sovarlay,' Scott made fun of Sjyntani. 'What are you going to do?'

'I can look after myself.'

'We'll need to find somewhere to stay.'

'Hopefully we won't be here that long,' Sjyntani said, as they hurried on.

'Are the other islands used?'

'Yes, Luteni is the most sought after of these three isles, largely because it gets the most sun, and has a lovely aspect looking down over the sinking capital, the isle of Delevi and her diamond, Novocas. There are fewer people and buildings there, and those properties are worth more than any northerner could even dream of. At the moment Luteni is home to some of Delevi's most famous citizens,'

Sjyntani chuckled, 'though they say they don't believe in fame, nor rank.'

Scott was listening intently, trying to focus, all the while missing Kyu's stabilizing influence. The authorities here had made sure to usher her well away from the populated areas of Delevi, and ensure she remained away.

Sjyntani continued, 'Nuana is the least useable in terms of building on it or mining ores from it. It is the place where all the very sick and dying are sent. No one ever stops there.'

'Why are the sick sent out there?' Scott stared up at the little frozen looking island that was Nuana, that never received more than a whisper of direct sunlight.

'A question I asked the sovereign, he told me the alternative on Delevi was euthanasia.'

'On Corrio they have hospitals and clinics, quarantine if it's something contagious and places were the terminally ill and dying can take their time to fade out peacefully, well, that's the aim anyway, to keep them within the community and support them in their infirmity, and when the sick get well they return to their families and friends.'

'I suppose Delevi has had to make difficult choices to maintain what lifestyle the majority seek. No one ever returns from Nuana,' Sjyntani looked away from the isle and spoke quietly to Scott. 'Don't let them hear you speak like that. The sick returning to live amongst the Delevian! They would tell you your people must be very weak.'

'On the contrary, it makes us stronger.'

'I know this, but you are naïve if you think you can say things like that here and get away with it. Scott listen to me, you're questioning their systems, their systems put in place hundreds of years ago.'

'Just commenting.'

'You don't know the Delevian. There would be some that might take your life for those comments.'

'I'm sorry Sjyntani, I'll try to be more careful.'

They reached the museum, which turned out to be the first two levels of the palace and parliament, that great bullet building which they had seen from above. Now Scott understood why Sjyntani had wanted to come here first. They walked slowly up the imposing grey steps and into its mouth, as it seemed a great beast of a building.

Scott paid the fees for both of them and took the brochure that came out of the machine when he paid, they followed the directions to the exhibition. The current display, mentioned by the escort that had taken them to the international centre, was on the second floor. Scott was surprised that any museum could be so pristine and soulless. All museums he had ever known had a close and musty atmosphere that reeked of age and history, this was such a contrast, and suited to the polished metal exterior of the buildings.

As Scott ascended the stairs he felt a chill come over him, Sjyntani felt it too. 'Something is urging me to turn back. It's silly,' Scott laughed, 'it's the same way I felt as a child, afraid of what may lie in the dark.'

'It's not silly,' Sjyntani said, 'you haven't seen what's up here yet. I have, and I don't want to see it again, but it's the only way I can see to get through.'

They reached the beginning and opened up the brochure. 'Ah,' he said, 'I see. The architecture of adversaries is a history of conflict.'

'That's how it begins,' Sjyntani said. They saw a history of wars, and disasters, disease and illness, anything that had affected the life of the Delevian for the worse. It looked at it, how it happened, how it existed, how they defeated it or overcame it. All with graphic pictures, footage, war memorabilia and models, or tissue samples, sometimes even whole limbs preserved and encased for all to see. Scott shuddered, but he'd paid his money, so he'd see this thing through.

Adversary – it covered so much didn't it. Anyone or anything that was against you was an adversary. It looked at weather patterns, creatures, inventions, and of course, human enemies, other countries with which they'd fought over the years, their machines and weaponry, everything. It was supposed to be a rejoicing in the supremacy of the Delevian people, though if he'd told the truth, Scott found it a dreadful exposé of a nation's dangerous and at times cruel pride, but he went on.

There it was again, that chill down his spine, just as Scott came to a series of large black boxes lined up one after the other, high on the wall, each with a creature preserved inside. They were shadows from deep inside the fractured earth. The display told of what they had done, how they had been defeated by the Delevian. Scott knew what they called these creatures on Corrio, but he'd never actually seen them in reality, he never wanted to, never wanted to believe they were real, but now that he was here he studied them, these fabled salamanders, these Mrukai. They were not monstrous as the stories he'd heard seemed to indicate, nor were they repulsive or even ugly. They were strange, certainly; long, sinewy, with fine features that were hard to distinguish, and with a skin that seemed to repel light, they were like shadows, barely visible. But they had no life in them, these here, no fire. Perhaps the fire made them more fearsome. One case was far larger than the others. The Mrukai inside had its nearly indistinguishable wings spread and pinned out for all to see. They were massive, engulfing things and Scott felt so small standing here looking up at them. It was no wonder people called them wraiths. The fact that the Delevian had put them in boxes made them no less surreal. The notes by the case indicated that all of these had been subdued during a mining expedition deep into the earth, but not without severe loss to the people of Delevi. Scott shook his head and walked on. He could have done without seeing this exhibition. Also here were some few Sa'ar, preserved in cases. Scott didn't want to look at them, it was disturbing to think the Delevian thought it alright to do so, but Sa'ar were once ordinary people like the rest of them, it wasn't right in Scott's mind to display them like this.

'Viyal is afraid of the Sa'ar,' Sjyntani spoke as she stood and looked at them. 'he told me so when he brought me here.'

'Why, when Delevi has the weapons and knowledge to even capture and kill that giant Mrukai?'

'It's not for the reason you would think,' she said, 'Viyal told me Delevi was so proud to rid itself of the Sa'ar and the Sa'aroeya, as they name the Mrukai, but once they had that's when the scientists began to notice things going wrong, and since that time Delevi has fallen more and more into the earth, as if the Sa'ar and Sa'aroeya had held the very earth in place.'

The idea was so removed from anything Scott had before heard that his mind worked double time to think it through, along with all that it could mean. He didn't offer a reply.

'The sovereign has commissioned many studies, but he told me nothing could be proved, and few that he spoke with would lend support to the theory. He asked me my opinion, I could only say my opinion wouldn't make a difference to the truth. I can see why he made the connection, but it is hard to think that it could be true, isn't it? That our very lives could be held in the balance by these creatures that are feared so much, and persecuted.'

'Yes, it's difficult.'

'But do you know Scott,' Sjyntani shared a secret, 'the Delevian think they have defeated the Mrukai because they have weapons that seem to hurt them, but before when I have seen the shadow creatures they keep here in the glass boxes, they didn't move but I saw them watching me, they are not dead!'

'That's not comforting in the slightest.'

'Yes it is, don't you think, it just shows you that the Delevian aren't as clever as they think they are, they couldn't kill them. I wish I had not been too late to Satsuan to speak with Tarku, I wanted to ask him also if the sovereign was right, if the Mrukai do hold the islands up.' They walked on before Sjyntani spoke up again, 'You can feel them, can't you, you felt it like I did. Their presence is here.'

'Are you trying to scare me? You're doing a good job. Come on,' he urged, walking on, 'I'm here to do this thing you want to do, no other reason. We just need to do that, and get out of here.'

He made it through the rest of the exhibits without much surprise, not that they were paying too much attention to most of it, but they had to keep up the ruse, and Sjyntani had yet to explain just what her plan was to get to the Sovereign from here. But Scott stopped as they came across an historical archive picture of a family of Vahrnan slaves, it was life-size and the notes accompanying it talked about the inferiority of the Vahrnan race, what an encumbrance their tribes had been to Delevi's progress and exploration, and what the Delevian miners and scientists had done to make them useful to the mutual advancement of both of their civilizations. It was worded in such a way that made it sound as if the Vahrnan should be grateful and continue to be meek subservient creatures. Scott had to turn away. How could anyone say such things, the Vahrnans were living amongst them, right here in Novocas, and this is what they said about them, in an exhibition on enemies of Delevi! And if the brochure was right it was endorsed and recommended by their Sovereign, it was in his palace in any case, what did he want to do? Start a rebellion? He was certainly succeeding if that was the case.

'So you see how bad it is,' Sjyntani spoke after looking around to make sure they were alone, 'I don't know how they can't see how wrong it is. We're all just people. All just trying to survive. I cannot reconcile Viyal with this, but I know he is like this, I have heard him speak enough to know. It's just, he was never cruel to me, but then I was just an ornament for his palace, wasn't I, and one could hardly be cruel to an ornament - though he did throw me away, it was with the utmost care and kindness.'

'And regardless of P'Lalo's ploy he must believe, as I do, that you are Shorakaian. The Delevian do respect Shorakai from what I understand.'

'Yes they do. I heard P'Lalo say once that if Shorakai were at war even the elements, even the earth and wind and rain would be on their side. I think she would like them for allies, but not Viyal, he does not seek the favour of any nation.'

Scott half motioned to the display, 'I didn't even realise it was like this.'

Sjyntani agreed. 'Did you hear the guards we passed on the way in?'

'Yes, but you know I don't understand much of the language.'

'The prison is below the ground right here, they said it is full of dissidents and they're expecting more protests tonight.'

'Come, let's do what we have to do, and then get away from this place.'

'We're almost there,' she encouraged him on, 'there is a way I know that will lead us closer. I hope I can reach the servants quarters, from there it should be easy for me.'

Sjyntani pulled Scott along as they ran. Through a back way in the museum they had been able to navigate to a reserved function room, then on through kitchens where Sjyntani picked up aprons and hats and a food cart then Scott found himself pulled into a staff elevator, going up, and then to another reception room that was currently in use, thankfully very full and noisy. They slowed their steps and tried not stand out as they navigated through the crowd, at first with the cart, then removing the aprons and hats and leaving the room. She guided him across the central court and up a wide grey-marble staircase. On she led, and the further they went the more opulent their surroundings became, the fewer people they needed to dodge, the more Scott believed they might actually pull this off, they might actually reach the sovereign. Sjyntani knew the ways so well, both the servant's routes and the outward palace, and he could tell they were getting close.

At last Sjyntani pulled him into a room and told him all they had to do now was wait. It was a simple room, but elegant, and Sjyntani told him it belonged to a favoured older servant of Sovereign Viyal, a lady who had been the most responsible in looking after him during his childhood, and who he still allowed more access to his person than anyone else. If anyone could get them close to him, it would be her.

'I could try to go myself, but she will know where he is and what his mood is, and if he is alone or otherwise engaged,' Sjyntani explained.

'You trust her?'

'She is loyal to him. She was always lovely to me.'

The door opened at last, and the face that appeared was gentle, and lit up upon seeing Sjyntani.

'Sjyntani!' the woman whispered and ran forwards. No disguise could fool her, she hugged Sjyntani, almost in tears, 'I never thought to see you again, what happened? One day I did your hair and dressed you as his sovereign wishes, the next I did not have your hair to do nor dresses to give you! My heart was lost my Tani-Tani,' the lady hugged her again. 'I thought you had wearied his affection and lost his favour, I did not think that you ever could, and I feared for you.'

'I lost his favour yes, and much has happened, but I must see him, Jiteita, do you know where he is at the moment?'

'Will I be out of favour if I speak it to you?'

'No, this is not about me, Jiteita please, this is about Delevi, it's important.'

'Who is this?' the lady worried about Scott's presence.

'A friend, he helped me to get back here.'

'There has been much I do not understand happening in this place lately. Since you have not been seen his mood is low, he has been abrupt and cruel, but rarely do we see him at all. You should try to calm him. He sits in the far study watching the city. He would not even let me rearrange his curtains to help his view, but sent me away again. His thoughts are heavy.'

'I will see what I can do,' Sjyntani agreed and went to go.

'You can't go like that!' Jiteita scolded.

'There's no time, Jiteita, trust me.'

'If I will let you go to him, you will go well dressed. Twenty minutes Tani, and you will have your way.'

Sjyntani relented.

'But *he* cannot be here,' Jiteita eyed Scott dubiously, 'your presence I can explain to anyone, but not his, he has no place here. He must go.'

'She's right Scott,'

Scott shook his head. 'I don't want you to go,' Scott caught her arm, 'Sjyntani, your life, I can't see you walk right back to this man, not for anything. Let's go back, we'll get back to Kyu somehow.'

'I've come this far, there are good people on Delevi Scott, people like Jiteita, I will not stand by and let this happen. Get back to the museum, there's a public courtyard nearby, wait for me there. I will see Viyal, then I will come, I promise.'

Scott didn't like it, he shook his head and breathed, but could find no words to dissuade her. Jiteita and others who had now come ushered him away. The last he saw of Sjyntani she had a group of helpers swarm to her, dressing her in a weightless fabric that was bestrewn with gemstones, brushing fine gold in geometric patterns down her cheeks - the Delevian way, and adding long locks back to her short hair. The last he saw of her, was a vision of the woman in the painting, the empress of Shorakai. They closed him away and his world was now devoid of the support he needed to survive. Kyu and Sjyntani were no longer beside him, and he could do nothing for either. He felt the shock of it at once, but he struggled on, making for that courtyard, trying to do what she had asked of him.

At last they finished with her and Jiteita was happy. 'May I see him now?' Sjyntani begged, 'I must see him.'

'Of course my Tani-Tani, you are just the one he needs to see,' Jiteita nodded. She walked on and Sjyntani followed.

They passed high banners of alternating twilight blue and olive green as they walked along the grand hallway. Far ahead of them, where the hallway ended, the afternoon sky could be seen through an immense glass section, floor to ceiling, the size of which Sjyntani had never seen anywhere else. It wasn't far to the end of the hall. Her interview with the sovereign grew ever closer. Jiteita stopped and motioned for Sjyntani to go on. She came to that far door and looked back. Jiteita nodded and then walked away. Sjyntani was alone. She breathed, then stepped in.

The curtains in the study were like the banners in the hall, twilight blue and olive green, they swayed with what little breeze Sovereign Iviqal Viyal allowed into the room. Sjyntani's eyes took a moment to get used to the dim light, but she was familiar with the room, the stone furniture, the great archways. Sovereign Viyal sat there as still as his stone table, his back to it, watching the window through a slit in the curtains just as Jiteita had said. He seemed a sculptured monument, sitting in that fading glow which lightened his contours but darkened every shadow. Sjyntani swallowed. How could she approach him? But she didn't have to, he spoke.

'So, the gift my viceroy bought for me returns,' he said, though he didn't move. She couldn't speak. After some time he stood slowly and came to her. He was clothed only in a simple iron-grey dressing robe. He took her chin roughly in his hand and looked down at her. Her heart raced. There was not a person in the world who wouldn't be intimidated by him. He was tall, solidly built, and below each pale eye, as she had described to the travellers on Soamé, was an oval of deepest blue lazuli stone set upon his cheek bones. His skin was so close to hers. The delicately placed gold upon her cheeks he smeared with a careless thumb, and ran his fingers roughly through her hair. He studied her. 'My beautiful diversion,' he said, without the trace of a smile or any emotion at all, 'why did you come back?'

'Sovereign Viyal, have you seen any footage from Tamashan? There were no Vahrnan ships amongst the fleet, I feared that there may be a plan Vahrna makes against Delevi. Maybe P'Lalo-'

He put two fingers upon her lips. 'Does a toy worry for its master?' he asked her. 'I sent you to Shorakai,' he seemed verging on anger, but it was well restrained.

'I fear for Delevi,' she said.

'I know P'Lalo's plan,' Viyal said, letting her go and turning away. 'I do not think I will interfere.'

The sovereign walked back to the view, the city far below. The light was fading. His profile was proud and solemn. Without looking back at her he continued softly. 'The country I love is about to come to nothing,' he said. 'My people do not know it, but how can I tell them? It was the decisions of my fathers' before me that brought us to this place, along with the working of the earth and the passing of time. This great nation, this grand city we have built by our genius and expertise will soon come to its final end despite all our efforts - and because of them. I have considered long the question, should I warn my people? Should I mobilise the remaining fleet against what Vahrna will bring? Should I send warning to the ships that are returning? Should I give the people time to evacuate or should I let our terrible race perish?' he shook his head.

'You must mobilise the air-fleet, you must warn the people,' Sjyntani begged him, 'you can stop P'Lalo!'

'No. Our fate is sealed. Under the force of a heavy raid, Delevi will collapse, my engineers have said as much. Both our peoples will be no more, and so be it.'

'Can't you evacuate? Get the people to other islands?'

'Where would we go? Delevi has one of the largest populations, and no island will stand up long after we've fallen in any case. There would be no point.'

'The earth may last longer yet, you cannot know for sure how much time there is, Viyal, please, you're letting the guilt of your ancestors actions make the decision for all your people!' Sjyntani begged.

'It has been a long time since I held any hope for Delevi. Justice will be done. It is right that I let my people fall, and I with them. I gave you your chance, my charm, you chose to come back. If you will stay to die with us, it's your decision.'

She saw him take an object from the stone table between them, she could not see what it was in the dim light, until he removed the sheath and what light there was caught upon the blade. He held the finest stiletto in his grasp.

'P'Lalo will be on her way here, she will want to see me suffer as she tightens the vice, but I will not give her the pleasure. I'm glad I saw you again, my charm,' he said gently, 'I don't regret the days with you –'

Before he finished the sentence he slit his own throat. She didn't have time to think how to stop his hand.

'Please no, Viyal no!' Sjyntani screamed. 'No!' she was on her knees by him at once, trying to use his own robe to draw across the wound to stifle the flow of blood. 'No!' she shook, unbelieving this could happen, in complete shock.

It can't have been that long, when to her horror the door behind her opened and the lights in the room lit and flooded the scene. She knew what it would look like, a servant standing over the sovereign with blood on her hands. She found herself being pulled away from her sovereign, dragged aside as she screamed and cried. She saw P'Lalo herself rush in, and the Viceroy did seem to be sincerely distressed at what she found, she herself bent down to try to save the sovereign, but it was of no use.

'You!? What have you done?!' P'Lalo turned and shouted in Sjyntani's face. Her shock and anger seemed overwhelmingly real.

In a haze Sjyntani realised her arms were being held tightly behind her, she was being ushered away. Her world shattered all at once, she could not think a clear thought or see a clear picture, all was blur and chaos. A call from Kyu reached down to her, but it was like a final call and it wasn't for her, it reached through her, and those around her held their heads as long as it lasted. Then there was silence.

CHAPTER 39:

The Guide

The tremors that shook the earth that day were the most devastating for a long time. And the quakes weren't only in one area, nor even a few areas, but the world over shook as the thoughts of a man might shake when he clutches his heart and sinks to his knees, realising his time is almost up. The splinters of this earth were truly rusted, were truly ready to crumble, to cease their turning and let the clock finally come to a stop.

On Tamashan, now that it seemed the Delevian fighters were heading away, the people were spilling into the streets from their hiding places, there was much to do, but as D'aoda watched them go he was overcome with sadness.

'Beyrtan,' he spoke to another of their number, 'What you saw, it leaves me with a bitterness in my throat. The crew may be gone, but come with me now, we will collect the body of the noble Sa'ar and bury him with our own people.'

Beyrtan shook his head. 'The sight is grim D'aoda, I would spare you for all else you have seen. He fought a heavy battle against the soldiers, the proof is clear upon his body, and that is not all, he is completely broken, he fell from the topmost tier to the ground.'

'I have seen death enough to know the many horrors of its face, you do not need to spare me. Now come, show me where he lies.'

Beyrtan finally relented and showed the direction, 'He is atop a ventilation block, there below the tower.'

They reached the wide block of ventilation units that funnelled used air out of the underground areas of the port tower. Just as Beyrtan had said, they could see a body on top, having made quite an indentation to the louvered surface. D'aoda braced himself then pulled himself up and went across the vent structure, but he was cautious and uncertain to go closer as he saw not just the extent of damage this body had seen, but the many signs that told him this was no ordinary Sa'ar. He saw the ridges on Tarku's spine, the reach of those intricate markings across his form, and now more evidences that had surfaced during the fight, barely visible but there, and those crystalline scales that had begun forming across his wounds before his death. D'aoda knelt by the body of the Akaia. He bravely turned the face to scrutinise it properly, to make certain it was the Tarku he had met those few hours earlier. To D'aoda's surprise the faintest warmth of air condensed upon his hand.

'No!' he gasped. 'No!'

'What is it?' Beyrtan now came behind him.

'He's alive!' D'aoda exclaimed. 'We must not wait! We have to get him back to the tent where they are setting up the hospital, we have to get him help!'

'Are you sure D'aoda? His skull will be fractured, his brain no better than a smashed fruit. His ribs broken, his organs displaced, his back possibly broken - ' Beyrtan knelt. He felt for a pulse. He couldn't get one. He shook his head. But then, even as they heard another call from the Mrukai in the far distance, they saw

Tarku's chest rise and fall, just once, ever so slightly, and the faintest light flickered throughout the markings upon him. It was enough to convince Beyrtan. 'You're right, stay with him, I'll get a stretcher, I'll get more help.'

Soon more Tamashani's came and together lifted Tarku up carefully, sliding him gently onto the stretcher. D'aoda called for more hands to help the stretcher down from the vents and soon a few more had come and were carrying Tarku back to a large tent that was in the process of being set up to treat the many wounded. They bathed his skin, cleaned the wounds and wrapped them, and set what bones they could. Then sat by him when they rested from their work, little by little, trying to restore the communications and clear the debris from what had been destroyed. They did what they could, wetting cloths and bathing Tarku's forehead, but there were many others to care for too, others far less terrifying.

Tarku's eyes were moving under their lids, his face changing expression slightly, his hands moved, his muscles strained and relaxed, his chest heaved in great fitful waves. They worried over him, from time to time looking at his eyes, eyes that were on fire, that frightened any that looked upon them, eyes that would stare into them and beyond them, the sparks rimming inside the iris all aflame, disappearing into ash then igniting again. He was this way for so many hours, fighting inside himself, with himself and the part of him that was put there by the Mrukai. No Akaia had been pushed this far without losing their mind also, and it was just as well for the Tamashani that Tarku lay nearly dead from his injuries and unable to move just yet, for his mind was as much shot and tortured as his body.

Tremors continued across the earth as it continued to splinter and pull apart in its agony. Somewhere amongst the sporadic conflicts in Tarku's mind he felt the shuddering of the earth as if it were his body across which the earthquakes rolled, his body which splintered and was pulling apart, and it was agony. In clearer moments of thought he questioned why he was still alive, why the world was still here. His end had come, surely it had come. The pain was supposed to be over, he was ready to give in and let this happen, but he couldn't die. The pain just grew worse and worse.

Those watching over him found their task was to sit by him constantly now, bathing his burning skin, trying to administer what pain relief they could, but they could get nothing into him, not water, not medicine. Nothing would calm him in his delirium, and the many markings upon Tarku only seemed to intensify and increase in their flickering as if inside his skin was no longer a knitting of flesh and bone, but fire and shadow, and these lines were a window to that turbulent core.

Out of the wash of ungraspable half-thoughts of pain and fear and revenge and hopelessness that raced through Tarku's mind, one comprehensible image kept returning. It came to him again and again until it made itself clear out of the churning, so clear it made the raging confusion quieten little by little, until calm came over him.

There was a figure in his head, a woman. He wanted to reach out and touch her to see if she was real but she was too far away. She wasn't frightened of him.

'Who are you? You seem familiar,' he spoke to the woman in his mind.

'I think the question is not that, but who are you?' the lady replied calmly, but with firmness.

His mind saw himself as he believed himself now, a creature standing between life and death, light and shadow, but he could not recall anything else.

She asked again, 'Who are you?'

He shook his head, 'I don't know. I don't know who I am or what I am. What am I? What am I supposed to do? Do you know?'

'It is not for me to tell you.'

'Then why are you here?'

'To tell you that you must find out for yourself.'

'I am of the Akaia,' he said at last.

'Yes.'

'But I am not like the others.'

'No.'

'I should never have been born.'

'Is that so?'

'Yes, that much I know. Who am I? Why am I?'

'You don't know?'

'No.'

'I think you do.'

'But I don't. How did I get to this place? I can't have got to this place! I'm one of the lost, aren't I? Lost to the wastes.' His mind was going off again, his body failing. 'Kill me, please, or at least let me die! Stop pulling me apart, leave me be! I don't know where I am. Or who I am, or why I am. Where am I? Am I in the wastes?'

'It doesn't matter, just tell me who you are.'

'I am lost. I don't know. I don't know the answer.'

'Why do you hold on? Why don't you let yourself die as you have so often wished?'

'Why would I want to live?'

'Why do you?'

'I don't.'

'Are you sure?'

'Yes, all I have to do now is, is nothing, I just have to let go.'

'Yes?'

'Yes, but I can't let go. Why can't I let go? You, will you let me go?'

'Tell me your name, can you remember it?'

'No. Who are you? Tell me the answers to these questions, please, stop all this.'

'Find yourself and you will know who I am.'

'They have called me Amsgan, a monster.'

'No, you're not a monster.'

'Akaia, it's all I can think, it's all I am.'

'Is it?'

'Isn't it? It seems right, he is Akaia, of the Akaia, look at him, lock him up, it's true, that's it. But I am lost, how did I become so lost? Let me go, please.'

'No!'

'This is not me. It was not me, it is not me, I know that. But it is me now. There is no way back from here. Please let me go.'

'No. You're right. This is not who you are. You are more than what is your body, more than what is your mind. Who are you? Where is your soul? Find it!'

'But I am Akaia. Sansahme. I have no soul.'

'If you believe what people say, but they know nothing. Does it feel like your name? Think! I won't let you go till you answer me.'

He paused and thought about what it felt like. Akaia. No, it wasn't right, it might have been what he was, but it was not who he was. 'No,' he replied to this strange vision, 'but if my name is some other name, why won't you tell me?'

'You must find it, it is no use for me to tell you.'

'But I don't know it. It's important isn't it? You must tell me.'

'If I tell you, you will still be lost for it will mean nothing. If you can't find it, then I cannot help you. What is your name!' she yelled, almost in desperation, 'who are you? You must know! You must!'

Was she crying? She seemed younger than she did before, but more than that, there was something about her, something that drew upon his heart, that made him stop and think harder, for her sake.

'My name, my name,' He really tried to think, but so long he paused and nothing filled the void that called for an answer. At last he gave up, 'I don't know. I'm sorry, I'm so tired, I think I will leave you now. I don't want to know my name. I just want to go. I'm sorry, I'm going to go. I can't fight anymore.'

Even as Tarku gave up the earth shuddered in the deep places and heaved again, and around him on Tamashan those working nearby went to him, and a murmur ran through the tent that he was fading, slipping away again. But the vision would not let him go, 'No! Wait! Stay with me, don't give up, why didn't you want to die, think!'

'I can't remember, why would I want to live any more, like this, like a lost Akaia has to live, I don't want to live.'

'Why did you fight so hard? Why did you keep fighting when it hurt so badly? Why did you fight when you'd sworn yourself never to fight like that! Why did you push yourself so far beyond the point of return?'

'Why did I fight?'

'Yes, why did you?' She grew closer to him now, in his mind. He ran a hand over her face, studying it.

'You. You're Syra,' For a moment he was confused, but then suddenly it was like he couldn't breathe, he choked as realisation flooded back into his mind, and from his eyes tears welled and fell. 'Syra-Ava! ....Melissa.'

'Yes, and...'

He remembered his last view of the world - the top tier of the port tower, he saw it all in his mind - the Delevian soldiers packing Melissa into the ship and taking her away. He imagined her fear and torment, saw her enslaved and abused as the earth fell around her. Oh how death did not seem good to him anymore, and how viciously he writhed and fought against it!

'You need me - the Delevian! The earth! I -'

'You-'

'I am last of Syra, Rubeo, and Suntah! Last of Jalon and Lillia! I am the guide, the last guide!' he breathed. 'I am Tarku!'

'Yes!' she cried. 'Get up! We need your help!'

Tarku opened his eyes suddenly, choking for breath, and with every breath he managed to gasp his body began to heal even more.

'Where am I? Is anyone here?' he called as he tried to focus.

D'aoda and the others that were there at the time were startled, overjoyed and afraid all at once and they came to his side.

'You're awake!' D'aoda exclaimed, 'I had little hope for you my boy, you are so badly hurt, but be at peace, you're with us on Tamashan, amongst friends my boy, you're with friends.' The dear Tamashani took Tarku's arm despite his fear and held it with a friend's firmness as Tarku lay still and grew more aware, surveying his position. Tarku almost smiled, though he had a great burden in his eyes and shame upon his brow. He tried to speak, but his voice was hoarse and croaked with barely a whisper as though even it had been pulled towards the shadows.

'Rest my boy,' D'aoda said, 'you don't need to speak.'

Tarku held the Tamashani's arm firmly in return, and managed an interpretable speech, 'I must get to her D'aoda, tell me, where did she go?'

'Who?'

'Syra, Ava, Melissa, she was here, she was speaking to me just a moment ago.'

'Your group has long gone, no one else was here friend, just us.'

'Where are they? Melissa? John? The others?'

'The Delevian have them, they have gone.'

'They have gone?'

'Yes. Friend John and the crew were all captured, except you, and taken away. A Delevian ship left hours ago with your friends on board.'

The look that came over Tarku's face moved D'aoda's heart, a look so desolate, of a spirit weighed down with grief, and D'aoda himself found tears gathering in his eyes again at all he had lost and suffered these last few days.

'I'm afraid it is so my boy.'

Tarku lay still a while longer, as his injuries healed further, but he could not wait for long, there was too much at stake.

'Help me up,' Tarku asked the kind Tamashani, for Tarku's wounds had healed a little now and he took the man's hand and nodded. D'aoda wasn't sure the boy was ready but he did as he was asked.

Tarku sat up slowly and weakly, so conscious that his body didn't feel anymore like his own. 'I must go, thank you for your help,' he said to D'aoda.

'You may stay,' D'aoda began, then seeing the resolve on Tarku's face revised. 'Where will you go?'

'I will follow the Delevian.'

'But you can't go after them on your own.'

But Tarku would not be swayed, nor wait any longer. 'Thankyou D'aoda, and to your people.'

'I'm sorry we could do nothing for the crew,' D'aoda spoke his thoughts as they walked together. 'John was a good friend.'

'Peace D'aoda,' Tarku encouraged, 'the blame is not with you.'

'Find out for me, for us, if you can, why they did this.'

'I will,' Tarku promised, and then was gone.

The Akaia slowly climbed back up the levels of the port tower, searching amongst the ships that remained for a suitable craft. Finally Tarku reached the tier were the DC20 was docked, and nearby, still in fair condition and unadulterated by the soldiers, was the Blue Moon.

Tarku entered the ship's hold. He set the ramp to close behind him, and pulled himself up the ladder. He then went along past the bathroom, stepping quietly through the kitchen and past the bunks, then into the cabin. He looked around scanning the room, then entered the cockpit. To his surprise two Delevian soldiers were sitting at the controls, but they were cold dead. Tarku looked intently about him into the shadows of the semi-dark. There, sitting cramped in the corner was Jem Fisher, gun in hand, aiming at Tarku, afraid, and in shock.

He nodded to Tarku, hands shaking. 'There was nothing I could do, was there? There were too many of them, I wasn't even supposed to be here. I've never killed anyone, never, I've done bad things but never this, I killed them Tarku, I killed the soldiers when they came to take the ship.'

'It's alright Fisher,' Tarku tried to calm him down.

'No, no it's not, it's not alright. And you're,' he went on horrified, 'you're a-'

'Now you know how I was able to film what I filmed for the Delahar Rally,' Tarku replied. 'What are you doing here Fisher? How did you get here? Didn't we leave you back on Rorona?'

Poor Jem could hold nothing back, his world was upside down. 'I, I, I made it to Satsuan before you and I hid in one of the crates that I knew Weston had to pick up, so I could get back on board.'

'Why?'

Jem sighed, 'Well I was trying to prove myself to Weston, you know, I got to do this, I had to, you know, I thought if I could do something and prove I could be a good guide he'd hire me back.'

'So you stowed on board.'

'Yeah, worst thing I ever done! I don't know what's happened, I got tossed all over the shop and pummelled like a set of drums. Then I could hardly breathe and I almost gave up and let out that I was here but I didn't. I snuck out of the box a few times to get food and relieve myself, and grab a mask cause the air got terrible. I don't know what you guys were doing for so long in the desert, then after you all arrived here and left the ship I broke out – but Tamashan! I didn't know TnTv would send you here! Oh man! and after I'd got myself something else to eat and drink I snuck out but I couldn't figure out where everyone had gone and then those soldiers came back, so I snuck over to the other side of the platform and hid there for so long. No one came back here. I heard the soldiers, I don't know much but I heard TnTv mentioned and I knew it was bad. Then I saw you, I saw you fall. I was scared of being stuck here, and 'cause I'd seen the hatch now, what you were all using to get around without being so easily seen, so I went inside and hid, I'd my gun with me and there was no way I was going to let them take the ship, Tarku, no way, that's one thing I could do to show Weston I'm not useless. But I didn't do Hardan Tarku, Hardan is down there, I didn't do that.'

'No, that was my fault.'

'You killed Hardan?' Jem's eyes opened wide, a haze of dried tears on his terror worn face.

'No, a Mrukai killed him, but it came for me.'

'All the world is crazy Tarku,' Jem shook his head, still playing with his gun erratically. He seemed a little faint.

'Are you hurt?'

'I'm alright,' Jem said, but looked at his other hand, covered in blood, then put the hand back over his side. Tarku bent down to take a look, it was only a small wound but it was deep and blood had flowed freely, and Fisher had left it unattended as he had sat here all these hours in shock. And though he still pointed the gun vaguely at Tarku, Tarku found some supplies and bandaged the wound securely.

'You're alright Fisher, come on, get up,' Tarku offered his hand.

Jem studied it, it was not the hand of a man. He studied Tarku. The flickering fire that lay behind the ash, behind his eyes, behind his every tattoo. His whole being seemed somehow changed, as though he belonged to the shadows now, even his voice, like the Mrukai, like he was partly in another world and only half here, yet he still seemed the same, the same Tarku. Finally Fisher put his gun away and took Tarku's hand, Tarku pulled him up. 'Get yourself cleaned up, have a hot drink, you'll feel better.'

'What about them?' Fisher looked at the dead soldiers.

'I'll deal with them.'

'Then what?'

'I'm going to Delevi,' Tarku said.

'Delevi?!' Jem's eyebrows shot up.

'Yes.'

'Why Delevi?'

'Save the crew.'

'I know you don't think much of me Tarku, but, can I come? This is going to be big isn't it? I mean, like, big.'

Tarku thought about it. 'If you want to come, you can, so long as if I tell you to do something you do it.'

Fisher nodded then did what Tarku had suggested and headed off to get cleaned up as Tarku took the bodies away. Then crouching awkwardly in the captain's chair, with his injuries still bothering him, Tarku took control of the vessel and steered it out of the dock. Jem took the seat beside him and strapped in. Before Tarku set the course for Delevi, he lifted the ship to the highest level of the docks, jumping out momentarily and picking up the old Carrelli camera that Melissa had lost during her struggle. It was battered, but Tarku was sure he could set it right. Then he climbed back on board, and they were away.

~

'Do you have family Tarku?' Jem asked, thinking of his own girl, who'd left him.

'No.'

'What you mean like no-one? Not even a fling to go back to? Or a child somewhere?'

'No.'

'I got a child.'

'Really?'

'Worst thing I did, leaving her. I'm the worst sort of man there is Tarku. No good, good for nothing, all about me, you know.'

'So what are you going to do about it?'

'Well, I've been thinking, all this time, I been thinking I got to go back to her, I got to get back to the north after this expedition's done and I got to make sure my girls are alright, be the man, you know. I never wanted to be a father, never thought that I could have ever had a part in creating something so beautiful, that's one reason I left, really, someone like me would surely mess up something so innocent and beautiful as that baby girl. But I really do love her Tarku, I really do, and I'm sure I can do something for her, I mean I'll have some funds after this trip, if that's all my girl wants from me, that's what I'll give her, but I hope she'll allow me to do more.'

'You'll make good of it Jem,' Tarku encouraged.

The silvery exterior of the Blue Moon was reflecting the clouds of golden steam that rose from the Gulf of Aliyr. Tarku steered her slowly and expertly in and around its treacherous currents. Fisher gasped time and again as they just missed being caught, he was still in shock from all that had befallen.

'I could never have been a guide, not down here,' Jem admitted, 'I've travelled sure, but in the safe and usual places. This is like another planet entirely, this is.'

Every now and then they would see another ship ahead, only briefly before it disappeared into the cloud and gloaming again. The tail end of the battleships were returning to Delevi, now coming through the same way as Tarku, and a strange thing was happening, a war had begun right here. They glimpsed Vahrnan ships now, deliberately turning in the way of the Delevian ships, forcing them to become entrenched in the Gulf's drifts and firing upon them. Delevian were firing back at the Vahrnan when they realised what was going on, but it was too late, and none of these last ships made it through but for the Vahrnan ships that kept on to Delevi, as though they knew nothing of it.

Eventually the Blue Moon came to the end of the most dangerous section of the journey in terms of geography, and now the rest of the flight had to be navigated, the course had to be set, and Tarku's mind surveyed the time and distance with impatience.

Part 3: The Empress of Shorakai

CHAPTER 40:

Ava

Hours and hours had passed and still John and Weston remained in the prison of those awaiting judgement. They had managed to pull themselves together somewhat and passed the hours with jokes, stories and plans of escape. Being able to move their limbs again was a small and happy freedom in itself, if standing room was free to move, that is. They also began to get to know the others in the cell. A young freckle-eyed Delevian and his Vahrnan friends became talkative and cheery when they discovered they were with an old hand like John and easy going type like Weston.

'So what are you lot doing in here?' John asked.

'Unlawful protest,' said one.

'Is there such a thing as a lawful protest?' said another and they sniggered. 'Show us one and we'd protest lawfully!'

It had been just the right moment to be put in prison, if there was ever a right moment, for what with so many of the youth of Delevi being incarcerated for their protestations the place was full, the result was that there was a backlog of offenders awaiting prosecution, hence, John and Weston would not be facing court for perhaps a few more days.

'Not meaning any offence,' John began, 'but it's hard for me to believe that a Delevian would risk his skin for any cause but that of the nationhood of Delevi, let alone one which might, and perhaps is, splitting it. How is it that your group has become so, so impassioned, as it were? What were you protesting about?'

'The Vahrnan are our friends, we don't care if our grandfather's fought each other, we want the Vahrnan to have the same rights as us. History has proven that the Delevian have a lot to answer for, there needs to be an apology. Many of us have been able to study internationally now, we have seen how the government and social structure works in other lands and we want to change the prevailing culture of this place and make progress like we see in other nations, were different peoples are treated equally, or at least there is an effort to do so.'

'I am amazed, and so happy to hear such words coming from the mouth of a Delevian,' John said, 'and please don't take offence but I thought I would never hear anything like it. However you will still find prejudice in other nations.'

'But at least that prejudice is not written in law, it is a man's individual choice, on Delevi prejudice is expected and praised in so many levels of our society, not always written, but still law.'

'But our protest might have been too little, too late,' another Vahrnan spoke up.

'Why do you say that?' Weston asked, 'it sounds like you did a great job to me, getting the government all riled. Great job.'

'No, some have taken it to the next level, they want change to happen quickly, after so long they are tired of waiting,' he hung his head.

'What, are they planning violent protests or something?'

'Worse,' the fellow prisoners said, but would offer no more. Guards came and took the next lot off for trial and the whole place fell under a heavy air of contemplation.

In the quiet that followed, between the soft chattering of the group, they heard a difficult and uneven breathing, it spoke to them subconsciously as being somewhat familiar before they could really tell what it was. John turned to the nearest boy, 'Who is that? Are they alright?'

'That would be the other northerner,' he answered.

'What northerner?'

'Been here a little while now, he came before you,' the boys moved aside as John and Weston moved towards the noise. 'Better be careful though, he won't let no-one touch him.'

'Oh no, it's our Scott!' Weston exclaimed, 'What's wrong with him?' They bent down quickly beside Scott, he was white and sweating, cold and shivering, his eyes glassy and his face in a hopeless dream.

'Scott, Scott, it's John, West's here too. We're here, talk to me.'

'What's wrong with him? Besides that, what's he doing here? Last I heard he was going to be fishing blasted Tuna!' Weston cursed. 'Is he sick? Or did those brutes pound him to near death? He's sick isn't he?'

'How long has he been like this?' John asked those around, particularly the young lad who was watching over him.

'Most of the time he's been here,' he replied.

John talked to Scott, tried to get something out of him, he mentioned Kyu and Scott held tighter to his arm.

'They're killing her,' he said through his teeth, then turned away keeping to his pain.

Weston rubbed his whiskers. 'Is it true then, what they say, that the Kyu rider dies if the Kyu dies? Will he die? Surely he won't, he's down to earth, he knows life goes on.'

'But he's been with her for years now, even learnt to understand her language.'

'But she's just a great animal!'

'Have you felt her cry through your own skin Weston?'

'Yeah, but -'

'If he lost her it would be like losing the very pulse in his veins.'

'But he could just be sick?'

'Could be, but I doubt it, and even so, there's no hope for him here.'

Even as they worried over Scott, there was another commotion, as the guards brought yet another prisoner down. That in itself wasn't irregular, but everyone looked up now as they heard what others were yelling out. It was a servant from the sovereign's courts, a finely arrayed young woman, still with the gold and gemstones upon her.

'Hey Princess!' some whistled from the cells while others hooted. But then it became obvious to all here that this was far more serious, as they saw the still glistening blood across her garments and her arms. A hushed murmur ran through the crowded cells as the girl was rough handled, she struggled against the guards that held her, but she was thrown down, and held down, as the guards prepared the floor and checked over their tools.

'This is no internment, this is an execution!' Weston gasped.

The young woman cried, she turned her face away from the guards. John saw her, and he knew her at once. He felt his heart fall straight out of him and shatter on that stone floor as he saw the same innocent, helpless, lovely blue-green eyes that looked at him every day from the photograph. Regardless of anything Tarku had said, here he saw his daughter and his Amiana so wholly reflected in this girl's face and shape and skin, and spirit.

'Ava!' he gasped, and held the bars tightly, he shook the bars furiously. 'No, no, no! Ava!' he yelled. How could he help her? Weston saw the resemblance too as he realised John's words, this girl was Shorakaian, she must certainly be Amiana's daughter, and no one else. The guards stood her up, preparing to tie her to the stone lashing post, but she wouldn't stop fighting. Some of the prisoners urged her to keep up her fight, and she was completely aware of the situation she was in and her desperation made her fight all the harder. The guards managed to tie her up at last and they lined up, as one lifted their weapon to fire, but right at that moment Vahrna openly began its assault against Delevi with all sincerity, and even down in the prison they felt the thundering of the bombs as they fell and struck buildings across the city. The guards put up their guns and ran out at the siren, leaving her tied where she was.

For a second Sjyntani stood trembling, then she began to look around her, trying to find a way to free herself. Many shouted suggestions, also willing her to break free and hoping she might secure their freedom also, but after a while she gave up and knelt to the floor, her hands still strung up, but tired to keep standing anymore. Another thundering shuddered across the ground.

'Ava,' John spoke to her now. 'Ava, don't give up!'

She leant her head against the stone and looked towards him, she was so weary and she despaired not only at her own predicament but at everything that had come to pass, events that all her efforts had failed to stop. Her anguish was profound as she took all these things upon herself, she had felt the responsibility to prevent all of this, and was now feeling the wretchedness of having failed. At last she found enough voice to speak, 'Why do you call me Ava?' she asked John, 'I don't know you, I don't know that name.'

John swallowed, he gazed at her, taking in every fine detail of her whole being. He answered her with the truth, 'Because you're my daughter, you have to be.'

She couldn't speak for a moment, but then spoke her thought. 'But you are a northerner?'

'I am, but your mother wasn't. Your mother was an ambassador from Shorakai. I've a thousand things to ask you, a thousand things to tell you.'

She looked up, some little energy returning to her at hearing those words. 'You are John Mark?' she asked him, remembering the story.

'Yes.'

Just then there was a groan at the back of the cell, behind the crowd as Scott tried to get up and crawl through all their feet toward the front. 'Sjyntani?' Scott barely whispered. Weston leant down to him. 'Is that Sjyntani?' Scott grabbed Weston's arm and pleaded to know. The crowd in the cell parted as they could, so he could see her and she him. At once she was up and pulled on the binds, but he could barely try to stand up.

'Scott!?' she cried, 'Scott what happened?'

'I didn't get to the courtyard,' he managed to say. 'What about you? Did you see Viyal?'

'Viyal is dead,' she said, 'Delevi will fall. We have to get out of here.'

'Easy said, not easy done,' Weston said to himself.

As she looked properly around she recognised the producer. 'You are Weston Alamo.'

'She knows me!' Weston grinned, 'yes I'm Alamo.'

'I searched for your crew. I went all the way to Satsuan, but there I saw your footage from Tamashan. I was too late. Is Tarku here with you as well?' she looked behind them.

'No, Tarku was killed.'

'Then he can't help us either, nor Delevi.'

'No.'

She yelled again, a desperate cry as her attention was back to Scott, he was slipping away, she noticed his expression soften, his muscles relax. His eyes rolled back as his mind returned to the white-gold beaches of Shorakai with Kyu playing under the sunset. The bleak outlook of weathered feet upon this cold stone he did not see anymore, though he shivered and closed his eyes again. He did not feel the old soldier shake his body, nor the producer yelling in his ear, nor the gentle Vahrnan protester who took his own jacket off and gave it to him to keep him warm.

'No, you can't go!' Sjyntani yelled, as warm tears welled in her eyes, as she struggled with the bonds until her wrists were truly raw. 'Please, just stay, Scott, you cannot go! Help him! Help him, please!' she begged them, hoping with all hope that the fragile cord with which he held onto life did not fray any further.

'We've done everything we can,' John tried to assure her. He leant to Scott's chest and listened. 'He's still breathing.'

Tears flowed now much more freely till she steadied herself and just sat there with her head on the stone.

20M A*id

'I wish I'd have died instead of Tarku,' Melissa's soft words filled the silence.

'Don't say that,' Astrid tried to encourage, 'he wouldn't want you to feel that way.'

'But he'd be of much more use in this situation than I,' Melissa grieved, 'why did he choose me? Why did he recommend me to Weston? I'm not even that good of a photographer, really, compared to the rest of you.'

'You're a fine photographer, there's light in what you do,' Astrid replied, while trying to keep concentrating on the most important task at hand - getting them out of here, and trying not to think about the bug that was in her own system; it hadn't caused any noticeable issues yet, hopefully it would stay that way.

The room was empty apart from the machina and the mouse, and only dimly lit. The soldiers had passed them to guards that had left them here without a word, and they remained alone.

'Do you think Tarku meant me to find his camera?' Melissa asked after some consideration.

'I don't know.'

'Because if he was at the exhibition then he must have been to the gutter before, and you said that the Carrelli used to be his camera, and he's into motorbikes and Matthias has the best. Maybe he was there, maybe he left the camera there.'

'Melissa, I don't know.'

A while later a giant Salamondan, who was obviously a servant by his raiment, came and pulled them along.

'Don't try to run, I don't want to have cause to hurt you,' he said in his deep voice, as he led them on through the lesser hallways and finally into the servants quarters, pushing them inside. The door closed and locked behind them. Melissa had thought of trying to pickpocket a key, but there were no keys being used, only technology, and besides which, her bound hands would have made it practically impossible.

The room was long and wide, and filled with the mattresses and day to day chattels of the lesser palace servants. A young, timid girl walked up to them and bent to unchain them, as carefully and gently as if the chains were glass that may splinter and hurt them. Her deep brown eyes watched them under the wisps of her eyelashes, indeed the whole room was full of servants, watching them. A few there stood to greet them, but most just looked on. There was so many here, from so many if the disparate isles. Delevian, Vahrnan, Salamondan, Soaméan, Satsuanese, Roronan, Arrojorian, Oconian, Tanohan, Archivey, Ristan, and many from other lost isles.

'You must be very thirsty,' the girl sat them down on a low bench-bed. 'I shall get you some water.'

A curious young Vahrnan girl came and sat next to Melissa, lifting her finger to Melissa's cheeks, to her skin and the bruises and scrapes that were still raw from the scuffle.

'Where are you from?' the girl asked.

'The Universal City, on the Northern Island of Corrio,' Astrid answered for both of them, with a touch of patriotism.

'We haven't seen northerners here before,' another said. 'How did you come to be here?'

'Long story,' Astrid began, 'but I can't tell it now, we have to get out of this place because our friends are in trouble.'

'You can't get out of here,' the girl laughed and pointed to the door. 'We are the least of the servants here, we are locked in, we only go out when we are asked to go out.'

'Indeed,' Astrid agreed. 'But I am not you, and we shall be going out as soon we possibly can.' Once again the machina put her hand upon the door which locked them in, and closed her eyes.

'What are you doing?' asked the girl.

'Trying to get us out of here darling.'

'Are you praying?' the girl asked, watching Astrid very intently. Astrid smiled.

'I will pray too,' the girl sat opposite Astrid, also putting her hand up to the door and closing her eyes.

The other girl came back with water for Melissa and Astrid and salves to apply to Melissa's hurts. They both drank eagerly. Melissa was also able to wash her face, the girl unnecessarily assisting her, but the feeling of that freshness could never have felt so good.

From time to time Astrid talked quietly to the friendly Vahrnan girl about the technology on Delevi, and language and the systems in this building. She gleaned a lot of information but wasn't sure it would be enough to help her get them free, but she had more knowledge now than before, so set at it with renewed hope. The other worry of course was that she was infected, she knew that worry would have to wait, but it couldn't be helped that it came to mind quite often to disrupt her concentration, and make her doubt her functionality and wonder if she would be able to pull this off, or if all her effort would be in vain.

The isle of Delevi is positioned such that it is usually not hot like other places, nor is it terribly cold, but it is covered in what seems an eternal deep cool. To the Delevian it is the perfect temperature. The warmth here was provided by the steam that emanates from the planet's core, directly, and indirectly as the Delevian use the steam to power their cities, having harnessed several underground vents. Thankfully for the servants, the Sovereign's excesses extended to their chambers and though the stone walls were cool to the touch, the floor had vents pass through it, and so all the rooms were pleasantly warm.

Melissa had hardly let her eyelids fall, only to be startled horribly as the guard came for her, that giant Salamondan again. He took her away, and her struggling only tightened his grasp. After Melissa was taken Astrid closed her eyes and held her hand up firmly against the door lock device with renewed energy. It should be simple enough to crack, to make inroads into the Delevian systems, but their language was so complex and their coding so different! She concentrated ever so hard, and she whispered, 'Oh Melissa darling! Hold on!'

After so long of nothing else, and after the Vahrnan assault had started, just as John and the others in the cells had felt it, Astrid's hand, shaking from exhaustion on the door lock of the lesser servants quarters, finally fell as the door magically slid open.

'Yes!' she yelled, 'wooohoo! There. I'm not such a useless mech after all. I'm coming darling Melis, just you hold on, I'm coming.'

Astrid was followed out by some of the other braver servants who dispersed in every direction, as she went down the corridors towards the security hub. She didn't have to get too close, just close enough. She reached out her hand again, against the wall near where the main systems were. It was easy now she'd figured out their coding. One, two, three, and she was inside their defences. Four, five, six. Guards were given random signals.

Seven, eight. Astrid laughed, the prison doors where John and Weston were, were opened. Now to find Melissa. Astrid tried, but the system could tell her nothing of her whereabouts.

Astrid ran on to try and group up with Weston and John. The freed slaves and the freed prisoners looked after themselves, though some still sat there in shock, not knowing what to do.

Melis

Melissa was taken to a completely different place, she couldn't figure out if they had gone up or down or left or right, she was all confused. She was given to yet another guard who pulled her roughly forwards. She tried to take note of where she was, to notice the widening hallways, that they went up the stairs not down, past windows with views of the vast city below.

The guard kicked open another door and threw her inside. 'Jiteita!' the guard yelled, 'old lady! The son would have a rare gift such as his father had. Make it so. I will wait.'

'Cadeim? No, he has no respect for his father nor his father's respect for those in this house!'

'Even so, I will wait. I suggest you mellow her, she's struggling too much for Cadeim's liking.'

'But the air raid?!'

'He does not heed it.'

Melissa couldn't understand what was said, but she could see the distress on the older woman's face. Nevertheless the old lady hurried. She approached Melissa. She must be a servant also. Someone came and gave the old lady a glass which she then gave to Melissa to drink.

'My name is Jiteita,' the lady told her, holding Melissa's shoulder a moment to calm her. 'What is your name sweet girl?'

Name. Melissa knew that word. 'Melis,' Melissa could hardly speak it, for her fear of what was coming. She could see around her the same things she knew too well, the same pretty things like Kat would use to dress up and make herself up to go to the top house. Melissa dropped the glass as she heard Kat in her head scolding her for her stupidity, as she felt her will growing dull.

'Melis, that is pretty,' Jiteita smiled sadly.

Melissa couldn't breathe. 'No,' she cried, 'No, no, no -'

'Hush now child,' Jiteita soothed.

In a haze Melissa felt the hands of many come and dress her and her skin and hair, even as they had dressed Sjyntani. Quickly she was ready. The guard took her on and ushered her into the same room in which Sjyntani had so recently witnessed the sovereign's own suicide. The door closed behind her. The lights were still bright and she gasped as she saw the body of Iviqal Viyal, still lying there beside his stone table, ungraciously left as he had fallen.

'I asked them to leave him here, there is no point to take him away, we will all fall soon enough.' A man stepped forward. Again Melissa could not understand a word that was said, but she looked up and she could tell at once that this man must be related to the man on the floor. She could not piece together what was happening here. Nothing made sense, and the growing fog in her head made it worse. The man walked closer to her. He had a glass in his hand, and was sipping from the glass now and again. 'My father, I'm glad he's here to see you. The last piece he needed for his collection was one from the distant north. He never got there to collect one of you, but fate brought one of you to him after all.'

She understood that word. North. 'Yes, north,' she said, though she stepped away.

He looked at the body of his father. 'Some say he was a great man. Do you know, I used to think I was better than him, because sometime in my younger years he started giving me everything I would ask for, but now I realise that he had given up on me, just like he had given up on Delevi. But where are my manners? Please, take a seat,' the son motioned as he turned off the bright lights and left the room with only the sliver of moonlight from between the curtains. She hesitated, but he asked her again, taking her arm and pulling out the chair, directing her to it, so she did as he asked.

'I hope you have not been mistreated? I hope you have not been too uncomfortable,' he asked, maintaining an air of politeness despite his likely intent.

'I don't understand you, I can't speak Delevian,' she trembled.

He put a hand to his shoulder, 'I am Cadeim Viyal, if you do not know who I am. Viyal's eldest, and only, legitimate son.' He sighed and stepped back. 'So now I become Sovereign Viyal. The title sits ill with me. I have no care to run a government my father himself abandoned. I will tell you what all the advisers have told me and maybe you will understand why I no longer care. It appears the Vahrnan have disabled our defence shield from within, we have also just received news that they have destroyed half our regular and battle ships on the way back from Tamashan, no doubt covertly, some even during the battle there. The home fleet has been deployed in response but Vahrna has control of the base on Lapasse. On the ground it's too early to say, there have been minor riots between the loyal Delevian and Pro Vahrnan for weeks, but as yet there are no Vahrnan troops on the ground. We have our reserve force ready to take action at the word. Though it may be that many of the resident Vahrnan received prior warning and have already left the city. My father's own viceroy is thought to be behind it all! Has anyone been able to locate her since his death? No. There are unconfirmed reports that suggest she is directing the assault from our base on Lapasse.' The new sovereign laughed. 'She must know what such a strike will do to Delevi! She must be devastated that my father is not alive to see all her meticulous plans unfold. She is too much like us. We have made the Vahrnan too much like us.'

Melissa looked up at him as he spoke. He was a fairly young man, though older than her and probably older than Matthias. He was built on a large scale, and with the shadow plays in the room he seemed to tower over her so incredibly. She knew there would be no hope of fighting him if she had to fight, and she also knew what fight she had was fading quickly. Her head was empty, fear and whatever she had been given to drink was making it harder and harder to think clearly. Different place, same story, as Kat would say. This must be what it felt like to be one of Garner's girls, to be under the hand of a monster. Kat had been in this position, Melissa knew she had, though she had never spoken of it directly. Melissa knew she had to get out of here. She saw the high curtains, she saw the breeze that moved them. So she stood up and walked to the balcony. Cadeim didn't stop her, he just sat there watching her.

'Novocas is a grand city is it not?' he said.

She looked over the edge. They were incredibly high, as high as the height from which Tarku had fallen, or even higher. There was no way of escape out here.

'Do you know how lovely you are?' he said, still sitting there admiring her. 'No wonder my father gave his last months to one like you and ignored everything else.'

He was not lying. In the light on the balcony the soft gold designs they had brushed from the edge of her eyes and down her cheeks, and what they had powdered through her hair, and all the bestrewn gemstones glittered and heightened her own loveliness. Even the dress she wore, that weightless white-ashen garment, perfected the scene for the new sovereign of Delevi.

'If I could I would capture you just like this and set you on the wall so I could watch you forever. It is a shame that everything turns to dust.'

She shivered. Though the fabric felt so fine and soft, it was cold to Melissa, and its low cut back encrusted with jewels made it even colder. It increased her insecurity, and she wished so intensely for her old cargos and her boots. Such comfort they gave could never be found in a dress such as this insubstantial thing, and she longed to be held like Tarku had held her in that space before the soldiers had come, for in that moment, even though she knew it couldn't last, she had felt completely safe. She cried at the memory of his fall. She looked over the balcony rail again and pondered the height. Oh! her head was so hazy. She wished the next balcony was closer, she would try to get there but what if she fell? Tarku did not seem to think death would be so bad, but what about the time before it? The fall? The time it might take to die, the pain, and what was after it? What was after death? Again she looked into the darkness of the room. She knew he was there, happy to watch her, as he waited for the drugs to take their full effect. She wouldn't wait. She had to try. She climbed up and stood on top of the railing, wobbling unsteadily. At once Cadeim was there and pulling her back down. She stumbled back onto the stone, 'Don't touch me!' Melissa tried to push him away, but he loomed over her, fingering her gold-flecked hair. She felt his hand running over her neck, his waxen skull and cold eyes reflecting the moon's light. Her heart flinched as he pulled her closer, but her head couldn't make her arms resist him anymore.

Out of the blasts and horns and sirens that echoed through the night, a whistling suddenly grew close and the new Delevian sovereign jumped in his skin as he looked to the sky, as without warning the wall beside them was torn apart as another run of bombs drummed the city of Novocas. Vahrnan battleships were drawing in on the central city now, crude hulks converted from old mining machinery they had siphoned from the sites on Vahrna. Of the Delevian fleet returning from Tamashan - those of the craft that had not already been intercepted by Vahrnan fighters on route over the gulf of Aliyr - were now taken over by the few Vahrnan soldiers of each crew. The old scores were being settled.

The pinnacle of another of the bullet buildings was blasted away before their eyes, its fragments falling to the city streets below and splintering into other nearby buildings. In the distraction Melissa made a feeble attempt to crawl away but Cadeim quickly recovered from the shock and grabbed her selfishly, dragging her back into the room, the jewels of the garment tearing at the fabric and her skin under his iron grasp. He pushed her down, he didn't care if the city fell around him, knowing it was bound to of natural causes soon enough anyway.

Fear tore at Melissa, pulling at her heart, making it pump till it felt like her body was nothing but one great pulse, and that her skin could hardly contain the pressure of it. She was frantic, her eyes searching hopelessly for a way out, for some hope of freedom. She saw the glint of the stiletto on the ground by the dead sovereign, but she could not reach it.

CHAPTER 41:

The way in and the way out

As the camouflaging steam of the gulf of Aliyr came to an end, and in the chaos of the Vahrnan attack, Tarku pulled into the blind spot of a massive fleet ship, the last ship going back to Delevi, and he held his position cleverly. As they approached the limits of the populated regions, Jem looked down in awe.

'How will we find them Tarku? How will we find them in this place?'

'I don't know.'

It was obvious that the city was in chaos. The bombing was evident and continuing at intervals, prominent and important buildings where on fire below them. When they drew closer it was clear there were groups fighting in the streets and riots and looting and all manner of crazed activity. Some ships could be seen fleeing Delevi as well, trying to dodge the fight that was happening overhead between the Delevian and Vahrnan warships, and the bombs that the Vahrnan were releasing on the doomed island.

The fleet ship they were following was drawn into a fray so Tarku quickly dodged away, heading for the capital, Novocas, but something caught his attention in the distance, on the far side of Delevi and it made him change his course. Though he barely heard an audible cry, he felt the faintest resonance reach his skin. Kyu. She was in terrible distress, but she was still alive. At once Tarku knew what he would do.

'It's a Kyu,' Jem gasped as he now saw what lay ahead as well. She was chained and had been silenced by the Delevian before the assault had begun.

'Take the controls,' Tarku urged the wayward guide, 'Keep her high and steady as we are.'

'What? Tarku? What are you doing? Don't leave me the controls!'

'You can do it Jem, there's something I've got to do.'

'What do you have to do?'

'Make myself a pair of wings,' he explained as he left the cockpit. 'It's too dangerous to get the ship down to her there, and I cannot risk the fall.'

'You want to get close to it?!' Jem was shocked, 'why on earth would you want to do that?'

'We've got to free the Kyu, she will be able to find the crew for us, wherever they are on Delevi, if they're still alive.'

The Akaia went through the crates in the hold, finding what materials he could use - plastic, nylon, cording, tape. He looked the stash over. It wasn't going to be enough. He stood in the hold, closing his eyes and going over the design of the Blue Moon - he knew it like his own skin, every quirk and curve of its design, in every section of its build, seen and unseen. Soon he knew just what sections he would pull out, and what parts of its frame and fit-out he would use, and he set to it. The panels that walled the ceiling in the cabin came down and he tore off the fabric that backed them, and light piping he pulled from within the walls. He wasted no time to second-guess his plan, but quickly cut a shape, placed the piping, and stitched all together with staples, and then used a heat gun to seal off sections and tighten the construction, hoping it would hold.

As they came to the rocky hills where Kyu was chained Tarku prepared to jump down to her.

'What do you want me to do Tarku? Tell me what you want me to do after you're down?'

'Do a large loop beyond the mountains and head back, hopefully I'll be done by then. Stay safe.'

'Take a radio Tarku, please, I can't do this on my own.' Jem handed Tarku a small earpiece which Tarku obligingly fit into his ear. He nodded to Jem, then went down and lowered the ramp, jumping out. He sped down to Kyu, coming to her, flying just above her, like the smallest remora along her great form. He flew so close to Kyu's skin and sped along till he found the terrible hooks lodged in her flesh, that held her captive. He pulled in his temporary wings and landed upon her back, working his way to each chain and hook, manoeuvring and cutting the many barbs out, and though it hurt her she was so relieved to have them removed. Then Tarku ran further down her back and after a long struggle managed to free her of the trailing chains.

There was an understanding between Tarku and Kyu, both of them had a long history of which they'd slipped in and out of throughout the years, both of them were creatures that had no place in this world, he and she, creatures that would become legend, then myth, if the world survived these last tremors, both creatures that did not expect to live, but expected to give everything they had and were for those they cared about, and those that would never know of their sacrifice. That was enough to bind them closer than kin. Tarku put his hand upon her skin and made his silent wish as Kyu's first faint call ran over him. There was no speech between them, but they knew, and they both knew what had to be done now. Tarku held on as Kyu heaved up her great form, it took all of her effort, but she did it. Then she called out across Delevi, searching for her rider, and searching for Tarku's Melissa. At once she made for Novocas.

'I'm behind you Tarku, all the way,' Jem radioed, following Kyu. 'You should know though, I think this is it for Delevi, there's fire and ash in the rifts out there, on the edges, I could see it. I think we better hurry.'

'They're waiting for me to give up,' Tarku said to himself, 'but I'm not giving up, not yet.'

Fisher gasped often, as Tarku and Kyu and he himself in the Blue Moon had to dodge the war all around them - bombs and ships and falling debris, Kyu stayed high, and above most of the conflict, and Jem stayed as near to her as he could. They got safely as far as central Novocas. Kyu called to Tarku, pinpointing Melissa for him, there, high up in the silver bullet, and then Kyu called down to her own rider, she felt his distress, the wretched state he had come to without her, it mirrored her own weak condition. But she called and kept calling, and even as Astrid had broken through the door and released the locks where

John and Weston were held, so Kyu called and the binds that held Sjyntani were shattered.

As Kyu was almost low enough now for Tarku to jump again, he radioed Fisher. 'Take the ship down, get to an open area, there's a field just beyond the palace and parliament buildings. Stay inside the ship. I could be a few minutes, or I could be a few hours.'

'What if someone tries to take the ship? I can use a gun, but I'm not that good Tarku, besides I don't think I can guide this thing through that mess!'

'Once you're down, keep your gun by your side and be ready to show the way to the crew, be ready to help them in.'

'Alright.'

'You can do it Fisher,' Tarku encouraged, 'Kyu will help, she'll try to keep the way clear.'

'Good luck Tarku.'

'I'll need it,' Tarku grimaced. Kyu was close now, but she was hesitant to go lower, so it was still going to be a difficult manoeuvre. He ran down her wing, jumping from her, and flying down into the heart of Novocas, impossibly through the chaos, to the palace of the sovereign.

Jem slapped his own face and tried to focus as he followed with the Blue Moon, 'Come on Fisher, you can do this.'

Tarku flew straight on, so fast and so small compared to the immense city below him and the great warships above. There was only one thing that mattered to him, only one thing in all this anarchy, the hope that had held him together these last months, Syra's daughter, the girl who was still so innocent despite the brokenness she had seen in her short life. He sped towards that bullet building, that huge tri-pointed architectural vision in the city centre, that was almost the city itself, with the prison linked to it below ground, the parliament and law and judicial chambers all there as well, and the palace high up. Tarku flew straight towards the place Kyu directed, but he was hit by a projectile and pushed off course. Instead of reaching the balcony he aimed for, he was thrown to the centre, down between its spires, and he crashed through the glass roof of the sovereign's conservatory, and such was the force behind Tarku that he crashed through its glass floor as well, and into the grand hall. He picked himself up slowly, shaking the shock of the fall and the glass and debris from himself and trying to get his bearings. Where was she? The south tower. He threw the shattered wings aside and ran on, he climbed up to the high arches along the corridors and continued his run up here, unobserved and unhindered by those fleeing the building below.

~

Sjyntani ran to Scott at once as her bonds were broken, and the prison doors opened. She knelt to him and held him as he breathed in Kyu's music and began to recover from their separation, but though he heard her, the strength of their bond didn't seem as strong as before. The prison emptied and soon they were left alone, just Sjyntani and her faithful Scott, with John Mark and Weston Alamo standing over them. In the strange, light and yet heavy headedness that always follows tears, Sjyntani thought her head was pounding then suddenly realized it was not so, it was Scott, the one who had been so kind to her without reason, his life beating its rhythm again, she felt the strength of his heart beat and she knew he would be alright. Scott looked around him, looked hazily at Sjyntani as the girl smiled down at him, her tears shimmering with the remnant gold dust. Sjyntani's chest heaved with happiness at the sight of Scott's breath and the life that was flooding back into his cheeks. Scott reached up and touched her ochre cheeks, wiping away the tears, and studied those richest teal eyes he had ever seen.

'John,' Scott managed to say, 'this is Sjyntani. I think she's your daughter.'

'So do I,' John breathed. 'She is the image of Amiana.'

'It doesn't matter whose image I bear,' she spoke up, 'we have to leave this place, everything else can wait.'

'She's right,' Weston worried, watching the crumbling corners and cracks appearing in the building around them, which worsened with every blast they felt. 'But, we have another problem, we still have to find Astrid and Melissa. I'm not going anywhere without them.'

'I'm glad to hear that,' Astrid laughed as she now ran down the stairs

'Astrid! Astrid!' Weston's broad smile lit up. He ran to her and embraced her. 'Where's Melissa?'

'I don't know, I can't find her. What happened to you guys? I was so worried.'

'You were worried?! We were just held here in the prison, what about you and Melissa? What happened?'

'They've taken her away, I don't know where. I thought I'd find you guys then we could find her together. It's most likely she's back in the palace tower somewhere, but I can't see her anywhere on the security footage, she's disappeared.'

Another bomb rocked the building and they all reached for something to hold on to. Then Astrid continued, 'The next thing is to find the guard that took her but he's a big fellow and I'll need back up, if I can even find him, I wouldn't be surprised he's already fled, so many have.'

'Right, lead the way.'

'JohnMark,' Sjyntani stopped him sadly, 'We cannot go with you, Scott is not strong enough to run, I must try to get him to Kyu.'

John was torn, he didn't want to lose her now, not now, but Melissa also needed their help, and he had begun to care about that dear girl as his own daughter too. Sjyntani could see his fears and tried to calm them, 'I know there is much you want to say to me, and there is so very much I want to ask you, but you must find this Melissa, Kyu will do what she can for Scott and I.'

'I can't leave you Ava,' John despaired, 'I can't lose you again.'

'John, it's alright, stay with them,' Weston reassured, 'Astrid and I will find Melissa.'

'No, you won't get through alone, not into the palace,' John stressed.

'You haven't read her spec sheet have you?' Weston tried to laugh. He turned to his muse, 'can you get us into the armoury?'

Astrid grinned.

'There you go,' he nodded to John, 'we'll be fine.'

Before John could make a decision Weston and Astrid had taken weapons from the few remaining in the guards store and ran on, 'I hope you're recording all of this,' Weston laughed as they dodged yet another skirmish.

She winked at him. 'And do you know what else?' she grinned.

'What else?'

'Someone has the Blue Moon here, and you know how I set it to send everything we had back to the north if we didn't get back?'

'I'd forgotten that, but yeah.'

'The transmitters are still on.'

'You mean they're getting all of this? All of this will be transmitting back to the north?'

'You bet it is.'

'No doubt about it, we'll have enough to buy your freedom now for certain.'

'You won't believe who's flying the ship,' Astrid smiled.

'Not the Delevian?'

'No, we've got our way out of here if he makes it down.'

'Who?'

'Jem.' Astrid told him, then stopped to search the Delevian system for the guard again.

'Jem?! You're kidding?!'

'Come on,' Astrid pulled Weston along, 'I've got a location for the guard.'

~

Sjyntani and John helped Scott as he guided them on according to Kyu's directions. They came to a place near the central court, ground level, down the palace's wide steps, ahead across paved walkways, through gazebos with hanging lanterns and on until they reached they sovereign's own gardens, and there upon a pristine lawn was a little ship, a battered little ship, but it was a northern build. 'The Blue Moon,' John smiled as he saw it.

'Kyu wants us to go to it, she won't come down,' Scott directed.

'No, I don't blame her, it's a mess out there son,' John said, 'easier for her to guide us out from high up than come down to us, I imagine.'

'I think she's hurt badly too,' Scott told them.

'We can make it from here if you want to go after the others,' Sjyntani spoke to the man who might be her father.

As John went to go Scott yelled out and pointed, 'Kyu says Melissa's up there.'

~

In the palace's now empty kitchen, the Salamondan servant Astrid and Weston were searching for sat at ease. When they broke in they saw him at once, the giant, with a table of food before him, but only a tiny fruit in his fingers. He lifted his head at their intrusion and they were surprised to see no malice or defence in him at all, only a tear in his eyes as he showed them the fruit.

'An apricot,' he said, 'the last fruit of the last season this earth will ever see. It is an incomprehensible madness that rules humankind; to be at war when the world they war for is falling beneath them, but that is humankind for you, that is what is happening.'

'Where is she!?' Astrid demanded. He knew who she meant.

'Not here,' he shrugged.

'Where?'

'How do I know?' he said slowly, 'I gave her to another guard to take up to the sovereign's personal servants, my place has never been up there. It doesn't matter anyway, we'll all be dead in a little while.'

'Just tell us where she could be, please,' Astrid begged.

'Most likely she is on the top floor,' he sighed.

'I've searched the footage up there, she's not there,' Astrid pressed.

'Would you mind very much if I tried a tiny piece of that apricot?' Weston dared to ask.

The giant took a knife and cut a section, handing it to the producer.

'Thanks,' Weston breathed, 'This is the real thing, this is for you Hardan,' he said, then savoured the delicate taste of the fruit upon his tongue. 'What's your name?' he asked the giant.

'Ragan,' he replied.

'So, what's the best way to get to the top level?'

'Weston, you're wasting your time, she's not up there,' Astrid said.

'So what do you suggest?' Weston replied.

'The servants who work up there say the top level isn't the top level,' the giant supplied.

'Of course, a secure floor, no external surveillance!' Astrid understood.

'Thank you, Ragan,' said Weston as Ragan nodded and finished the apricot.

'Come on,' Astrid pulled him along.

John caught up to them just after this as well, he puffed, 'I don't know how it got here, but the Blue Moon's in the central courtyard, the kids are boarding as we speak, so now we just have to find Melissa, Scott says Kyu's located her up the top,'

'So we just discovered.'

Weston, Astrid and John went passage after passage, stairway after stairway, on Astrid's direction. The great columns towered into the hazy dark above them, great archways that shook and yet stayed strong with every hit of the Vahrnan raid. They came to the hallway, the wide hallway with those great banners, now billowing as wind rushed through from the shattered glass wall far ahead. They passed some few guards along the way, guards already dead, but only recently;

their bodies were still warm and blood still ebbed from their wounds. The crew were relieved they didn't have to fight the guards, but it made them all the more apprehensive about what might lie ahead. They checked doors as they went, Astrid using her senses to search each room for Melissa's particular pulse.

'Come on darling, come on! Where are you!' Astrid was frustrated, keenly aware that their Melissa needed them. She kept trying and at last she called out. 'She's up ahead! Come on, hurry!'

Even as they ran for the farthest doorway there was a scream, splitting the air, loud and clear it rang out, but it was soon gone and their ears rang in the intense silence that followed. It was not the scream of a girl, but that of a man, but even so the friends looked to each other in fear that by the time they got to her it would be too late for their Melissa also. But they reached the door and the door was not locked, even as John went to push the stone it began to slide open from within.

What faint moonlight there was in the hallway lit only the merest few feet of the darkness within that room, and the sliver of light from the window beyond showed John only an uncertain silhouette of a shape which soon diffused into the general shadow. But then they saw the ember behind the ashes in his eyes and the flicker that ran under the linework across his body. Astrid sensed Tarku's presence, though she was sure she had to be wrong, and began to blame the lingering bugs in her system, but then he spoke.

'She's drugged, but thankfully no more than that,' came his voice, though it was a voice jagged and hazy, even as his form now appeared. He carried her gently out of the dimness and out of that place.

'Tarku?!' they collectively gasped, 'we thought you dead.'

'Not quite.'

They saw the glints of Delevian blood upon him, even across his face. John still hadn't completely lowered his gun. They were obviously shocked at his appearance now. Astrid had to put her hand on him, over the lines of his tattoo, working her way around him, running a hand down his ridged spine, meditatively taking in his form, it was the only way she could believe what she was seeing was real, that it was really Tarku standing here with their precious Melis in his arms.

'Oh boy, we thought we'd lost ya,' Astrid gave him a rough hug from the side, then patted Melissa's head, 'Poor kid, thank goodness you reached her before anything too terrible happened.'

'Do you think she'll be alright?' Tarku asked the machina.

'Yes, she'll be alright.'

'And you Astrid, are you alright?' Tarku asked her, sensing some pain in the lines of her face.

'I will be,' she answered, not saying more but Tarku read that there was a great deal worrying her.

Weston made no comments about Tarku's body and did not hover around him, but stood there for a moment in casual observation. 'Glad to see you're, well, I wouldn't say alive boy, but at least you're not dead. We really might need you if we're going to make it away from Delevi. How did you get here anyways, was it you who saved my ship? Astrid says Jem's on board.'

Tarku grinned momentarily, 'You'll have to thank Fisher for the Blue Moon's safety.'

'Fisher?'

'Mm.'

'But, what? How?'

'He took out two Delevian soldiers.'

Weston changed his opinion of Fisher at once, 'I love that kid!' he gushed, 'I knew I hired him for a reason!'

'Weston, here, take Melissa, take her,' Tarku begged them, 'take her back to Shorakai, that is the safest place for all of you in the time that is to come.'

'Tarku, what are you saying? You're coming with us,' Weston urged.

'No, I cannot.'

'Come Tarku,' Astrid added her voice.

'No, I won't make it far, and even so, I don't want her to see me like this, if I could help it I'd none of you have to see me this way. I am for the wastes, my sight is slipping, what sanity I have is temporary, let her believe that I am dead.'

'Tarku, you are not as changed as you think,' John encouraged.

'Aren't I?' Tarku looked to John's hand, still holding his gun, finger ready on the trigger.

John frowned guiltily, 'Just habit,' he explained, then put his gun away.

'Please take her,' Tarku tried to hand Melissa to them, but though she was still unaware, still in that induced, hazy nightmare in her head, her eyes closed, knowing she was safe now but oblivious to everything else, and she refused to let go of Tarku. Though she probably didn't have the awareness to even know it was him, she clung to him so tightly, afraid of letting go and being alone again, afraid of being left to her previous terror. Tarku held her tight to calm her down again, 'It's alright butterfly, you're going to be alright,' he whispered to her.

'You've got to come with us Tarku,' Astrid pressed again, 'it's a long way between here and Shorakai.'

He thought about it. 'Alright. I will hold on as long as I can, I will come with you until we are away from Delevi. If I can I will go with you to Shorakai, but I doubt I will make it that far.'

'Tarku,' John spoke sincerely to the Akaia as they began back along the hallway, 'she couldn't be in better hands.'

'I second that,' Astrid said. 'There's something else you should know before we get to the ship Tarku.'

'It's alright, Jem already checked with me about our two extra passengers. I knew Kyu's Scott must be here somewhere, and Jem tells me there's a girl who appears to be from Shorakai.'

'She's Ava, the other girl, she has to be,' John told him.

'What do you mean?'

'They're very similar, Melissa and her, but this other girl - I'm not asking you to believe me, I'm just warning you of what you'll see.'

'You can't be right, if Melissa's not,' Tarku stopped speaking, his head whirling too much to grasp a word to speak, too many thoughts and questions flooding his tortured mind all at once. 'Let's just get out of here.'

Once they reached the lower levels of the buildings it was harder to go on, there were small skirmishes still going on amongst various parties and many people still trying to flee as the earth shook. At last the group made it out of the building and then through the royal gardens and finally to the field beyond. Debris still fell and missiles were still being fired but the targets were not out here in the field. Fisher did as Tarku had told him and as they ran toward the area Jem saw them and came out to help them.

'I never thought I'd be glad to see you,' Weston said, patting Fisher firmly on the back and grinning his widest, bristly stubbled grin as he stepped on board. 'Well done lad, you might make a guide after all.'

By the time the group had all settled down Tarku had tucked Melissa safely into a bunk and run up to the cockpit. 'Everyone in?' he yelled, looking ahead and refusing to look at the girl John was so sure was Ava, he couldn't let himself do that yet.

'All in,' confirmed Astrid.

'Take a seat, and strap in,' he commanded everyone, 'Fisher, with me.'

Tarku took the pilot's chair and Fisher beside him.

'Wow, flying with the master again,' Fisher said, nervous and excited as he clipped his buckle. 'So, D'Avero, Savah, and an Akaia, who else are you Tarku?'

'Too many men. I hope you've been watching and learning Fisher,' Tarku instructed as he lifted the Blue Moon up off the ground with all speed, 'I won't have much more time to teach you.'

'Only the whole trip from Tamashan watching and learning,' Fisher said, 'but I'll never compare to you.'

'Neither have you had five-hundred years,' Tarku was grim, but he turned to Fisher and spoke honestly, 'I couldn't see it at first, but you're alright Jem, there's a good man somewhere in there.'

'Thanks for the second chance,' Jem thanked him.

Then they were away, Jem Fisher, Tarku, Astrid, Weston Alamo, John Mark, Sjyntani, Scott Thomas, and Melissa, leaving Novocas behind. Kyu sang as the Blue Moon flew, she cleared the path before them, and once high Tarku pulled into her slipstream, and they continued away from the island of Delevi.

CHAPTER 42:

The fraying thread

'So we're heading for Shorakai,' Scott confirmed.

'Yes, that's the plan,' Weston nodded.

'Kyu will accompany us,' he said, even as to assure himself.

'Glad to have her.'

'Thanks for taking us with you,' Scott said.

'Wouldn't have it any other way.'

Astrid let Weston take one of her hands as they sat and recovered, all were so out of breath, so wanting to talk, full of questions of each other, but just waiting while the ship took off and drew away from Delevi. Astrid put her other hand to the wall and used her sense to check on Melissa. There was a static creeping into Astrid's senses, a haze, but she could still feel enough to know Melissa was sleeping still, and comfortable. Astrid smiled, they'd got through it. She'd got through it. Now, after finally being able to stop long enough to catch her breath, Astrid set her system to begin a deep scan for that virus and what fragments of it might be littered throughout her core and functions. After another little while the kind machina got up and made sure all were bandaged up where necessary and alright otherwise. Then finally, when the madness in their hearts had stopped pounding so hard they began to talk.

'So, ah, Scott calls you Sjyntani?' John spoke up at last.

She smiled, 'Yes, but say the name, say the name you spoke to me before.'

'Ava.'

'Do you really believe I am your daughter?'

John nodded.

'You really do look like Amiana,' Weston commented. 'Hang on, there should be a picture of her somewhere, Melissa had that book, where is that book?' Weston rummaged around and found it, then showed the image of Amiana to her.

'Oh, but she is so beautiful!' Sjyntani laughed, then became serious, 'but this book – this book is about you?' she saw, and looked to John.

'Unfortunately yes,' John smiled.

'No, this is very good, I can read all about you, if I can learn to read Northern! How wonderful!' then she turned to Weston, 'is this your book? May I have it? It would be so dear to me, to have this.'

'I think Melissa's finished it, so go ahead, it's yours,' Weston's generous spirit prevailed, and how could it not? This was history in the making, the re-uniting of a long lost daughter with her esteemed father. 'Are you getting this?' he whispered to Astrid. She gave him a knowing grin. Of course she was filming it, she was a journalist, with a kind heart yes, but when it came to the news she was almost as ruthless as Weston. She wasn't live streaming it though, just bouncing it to the on-board hard-drives for the moment, so they could edit it later.

317

'My Father,' Sjyntani said with a delighted smile out of the momentary silence, she looked around at the crew. 'Do you really think it so? You all seem very certain?'

They nodded.

'My Father,' she said again, 'I've never been able to say that before, knowing who it might mean.'

'My daughter,' John held her hand, 'I want you to know that I have loved you from the moment I knew of you, both your mother and I, we never stopped thinking of you.'

'Maybe that is why I never gave up. I saw so many others give up, but not me. I always wondered why. Maybe it was that I knew this love, somehow I knew, even though I did not realise what it was.'

John was so happy to hear her words.

'So I might be your Ava,' she repeated the name, accepting all that they said, 'Ava. What does it mean?'

'Life,' John told her.

'This is a good name I think. What would you call me?' she asked Scott.

'I will call you whatever name you want me to call you,' he smiled.

'Can I still be Sjyntani?' she asked Scott and John, 'for now at least, until we can be one-hundred percent certain. It is comfortable to me.'

'Of course,' John nodded.

'Tell me of my mother, was she wonderful?'

'There is more to your mother than I could tell, so much more. I knew her only a couple of years. She was the most beautiful woman I have met, her inner spark, she just shone. She was an ambassador for Shorakai, and I the ship's engineer for the ambassador of the North Islands, Scott's father.'

'That's right, Scott told me, we met his father on our way through Satsuan, he is such a dear man!' she turned to Scott all smiles, amazed, 'everything is connected! Keep going,' she pressed John, 'I want to know everything.'

'Well, your mother -'

'Say her name, Scott did say it, you did too, but say it to me again,'

'Amiana, although, that's not her only name, I didn't know that until recently. Tarku could tell you more.'

'Tarku?'

Even the others looked at John curiously here, Weston, Astrid, and Scott, all wondering how Tarku could know more about the Shorakaian ambassador than John himself.

'But that's a whole other story,' John dismissed. 'Your mother was so strong, and passionate, she was-' John paused.

'What?'

'Well, she had more than her share of trouble, put it that way, but she did her job, and she was a mother and a wife, everything and more, and she died doing what she thought right.'

'I would have loved to have known her.'

'Yes, I wish you could have, I often wish I could go back and undo everything, make all of this right.'

'But it's alright now, we're together,' she smiled, 'and that is very good.'

After a while, as father and daughter talked, Weston and Astrid snuck away to the kitchen, while Scott fell asleep on Sjyntani's shoulder, his torture had been great, and all was still not yet right as Kyu remained ahead, and he could not go to her. From her shoulder Sjyntani lowered his head to her lap and held him, curling his faded blonde hair in her fingers.

'How did you come to know Scott?' John asked her.

She smiled. 'It was on Soamé, he offered me a lift.'

'That's our Scott for you, he's one of the good guys,' John told her.

She stroked Scott's hair, 'I know. Don't worry, I won't let him go,' she promised her father, 'I will protect him always. I think he's very beautiful,' she whispered.

'I heard that,' Scott sleepily looked up at her and smiled, laughing. 'I think handsome is the word you're looking for.'

She laughed too, 'No, I mean inside. You're beautiful inside.'

'Oh, so I am a gentleman after all?'

'Bah! No,' Sjyntani protested, 'you are beautiful.'

'There's no arguing with her John,' Scott chuckled, closing his eyes again.

Sjyntani turned to her father, 'Tell me more about you,' she begged him, 'I want to know everything about you and my mother.'

'Where do I start?' John smiled, though there were difficult memories to go with the good.

John told her the little things he loved about Amiana, he told her some of the things that he had been through on his search to find her, their Ava, and in return she told him where she had travelled as she had been bought and sold over the years. It seems that many times their paths had been so very, very close, indeed he must have only just missed her the last time he had been through Flythsyge.

As Jem left the cockpit to make use of the facilities, Tarku brought up the vision from the cabin camera and zoomed in on the girl who John was certain was Ava. There could be no doubt that she looked to be from Shorakai and that she was strikingly similar in appearance to Syra. When Jem returned Tarku asked him his opinion.

'Who do you think she looks like?'

'I don't know. Do you mean who else on the ship or who else in the world? Because if you mean on the ship then she's sorta like Melissa, but only sorta, I think it's the nose, but if you mean world, then there was this sweet deal I met one time - she has the same eyes, man, totally the same.'

'What about on Shorakai? Does she remind you of anyone we saw there?'

'I don't think so particularly, I mean there's a lot of the generic similarities, or well, I guess there's something familiar, just give me a sec it might come to me,' Jem said.

Tarku froze the image as Sjyntani faced a certain way, trying to accept what John had.

Suddenly Jem sat up, 'I got it! She's like the last photograph that the lady showed us on the way to the governor's dinner!'

'You're sure?'

'Yeah, it's so obvious now I've remembered it. Why Tarku? What's this about?'

'John's daughter.'

'Yeah I heard them talking about that. So they reckon it's her?'

'They do.'

'You're not so sure though, are you? That's why the questions.'

'If she's John's daughter then I'm wrong about something else. It's never easy to accept being wrong.'

'True that. So what are you going to do?'

'Try to accept it.'

Regardless of what the answer was in this case, Tarku knew he wouldn't last the journey back to Shorakai, but there was something he could do for Sjyntani, Melissa and all of them, to make sure they made it back. He opened a secure transmission to his friend Keersi at the port office on Shorakai, sending him the pictures of Sjyntani, and the message, *...request escort... ...we have the empress... ...en route from Delevi...* If that didn't get the attention of the authorities on Shorakai, nothing would.

'The Empress?' Jem questioned, 'what's that about? Are you pulling some kind of bluff Tarku?'

'Let me know if they reply,' Tarku asked, 'and Jem, keep recording that front cabin camera footage, with sound. You'll see why soon enough.'

Tarku stood and left the cockpit, the eager faces of John and Sjyntani looked to him as he passed them, Sjyntani even stood and began saying something but he just said in a rough voice, 'I'll speak with you soon,' then went on to the sleeper cabin.

He sat opposite the bunk where Melissa lay asleep. He sat watching her for a long while. She was peaceful now, as the drugs were wearing off. Tears rolled down his cheeks as he watched her breathing. He had been so certain. Who was she if she wasn't Syra's daughter? Did it matter? He gently pushed her fringe out of her face again, but he was so afraid to touch her with his hands that they shook. Afraid to even breathe near her, she was so lovely. He knew he didn't have much time, he could hardly breathe the air in here – it was too good, and he so close to losing the battle he had been fighting for so long, so close to being for the wastes, so close to giving in. He knew what he had to do, he knew he had to go, but he wanted to make sure that she was safe, then he would go with an easier heart. He had to try and see her to Shorakai, but he didn't think he could. He couldn't face the end if it was uncertain that she would survive. He hoped Shorakai got the message. She seemed to become uneasy again as she momentarily slipped back into her nightmare, so he pulled the blanket tighter around her, and pressed her hand gently. 'You'll be safe soon butterfly, not long now.'

Then Tarku went back to the cabin to have the conversation that needed to be had. He sat opposite Sjyntani, next to John. 'Your name is Sjyntani?' he asked.

She was taken aback by his abruptness but answered him, 'Yes, my name is Sjyntani.'

He studied her face, the face so like Syra's. It was like he was looking at Syra before everything happened. Syra back in time. Syra without any signs of the Akaia upon her.

He reached out to touch her face to try to understand. 'Are you real?'

'Yes,' Sjyntani answered.

'You can't be real.'

'I was looking for you, Tarku,' Sjyntani continued before he had gathered his next words, 'I went all the way across the earth to find you, but I was always too late.'

'Why would you look for me?' he asked her, staring at her so piercingly. Sjyntani gulped, but continued bravely.

'Could you stop them fighting on Delevi? Would you if you could? They have made terrible mistakes but they don't deserve to fall, and Delevi will fall if you do nothing; they will destroy each other, and the earth on which they stand!' Her pleas were impassioned. 'Could you, Tarku? Could you call the Mrukai? Could they stop this? Please, I heard the rumour amongst the Sansahme - they say all you have to do is speak the word and the Mrukai will come like they did in the north, ending the war.'

'You don't know what you ask,' Tarku replied at last.

'But surely-' Sjyntani pressed but Tarku cut her off.

'You would seek to end one horror by using another? You have the right heart, but you sought the wrong answer, I am not the answer here, believe me. If you use the war in the north as your reference - Antalla and West Fall lost many of their own, the Mrukai were indiscriminate. You're looking for some good outcome in a situation where no option was good,' Tarku strained. 'You sought out a weapon to stop a war, that is not what I am. I am not here to influence the outcomes of wars.'

'But the stories are true, I wasn't chasing a lie was I? Please Tarku -'

Tarku slumped back into the seat, his face full of despair, 'The Sansahme who say what they say - did you speak to them? Did they tell you what the outcome would be? Did they tell you what they hope for? I'll tell you what they hope for - they hope I will call the Mrukai because they believe that then the end will come and their lives will be over - lives they have lived in constant persecution and agony. And all those that have been against them, that have made an already difficult life even more unbearable, all of them, their lives will be over too. That's what they want of me Sjyntani, to end it all.'

She couldn't speak. Tarku continued.

'This is bigger than Delevi. The world is at its end. If you want to do something, there is one hope left. They still have hope on Shorakai, they still have hope that one in the royal line will return and have some sway over the way things will be at the end, but it is not me. I will get you as close as I can to Shorakai and that will be that. And then Sjyntani, you're going to have to do something for all of us. You have sought help for other nations when there is a nation that seeks an answer that could be you. Sjyntani, Shorakai waits for an empress, they have waited for five-hundred years. There is a chance that you could be their empress.'

All were silent, waiting for Tarku to explain. Scott started to pay very close attention to Tarku's words now, as did Weston and Astrid who had come back into the cabin upon first hearing Tarku's voice.

'If you're John's daughter, which they all seem to think you are, then your mother was Amiana, a woman I came to know earlier in her life - as John will confirm for you, she was Akaia, like me.'

'She was, she hid it well,' John nodded.

'Before any of you tell me that Akaia are not able to have children, I will tell you that she was as surprised as anyone, and overjoyed, when she realised she was to have a child, and even more so when she realised the full implications of this birth. She could never take her rightful place in her society, she accepted this because she knew as well as I that what we are renders us undependable at best, but a child would mean she had not failed her people. John's wife Amiana was Syraveia, the daughter of Syratreya, and so if you are her daughter,' he repeated, 'you are Syra-Ava, and you will surely be the next Empress of Shorakai.'

Sjyntani couldn't speak.

'And if all that is true, then not only would you be their hope, but my hope, for everyone here. Because if I fail I fear everything will fall with me, and I will fail - the only doubt is how long I will hold, but at least I know that you will be there, and at least something of earth may be saved, if anything can be.' Tarku then stood and walked back to the cockpit.

'Did you get that?' he asked Fisher.

'Yep, recording the whole time.'

'Send it through to Shorakai,' Tarku said, then closed his eyes, trying to keep it together, 'Hopefully that will answer their questions.'

~

'Ah, Tarku,' Jem spoke up after a while, 'we might have a problem.'

Tarku saw the radar and called John in at once. It was chaotic, with so many ships fleeing Delevi, but Jem had noticed a pattern. Even then Kyu called out. They had just left the very outskirts of the gulf, now ahead three larger vessels were standing still, smaller vessels were going to and from them, and ships that neared the area would soon veer away.

'We know what they are,' John pronounced gravely, as they flew ever closer.

'What is it?' Sjyntani asked.

'Marauders, again.'

'Oh no!' she gasped, horrified.

'What are we going to do? How are we going to get past them?' Jem worried.

'Maybe Kyu can push through, they shouldn't bother her, we should be alright,' Scott hoped.

'John,' Tarku spoke up, 'take the front with Fisher, no matter what happens just keep flying, go straight through their blockade, just keep going, I'll see you on the other side.'

'What are you doing?'

'I won't take any chances, they might see that Kyu's hurt, and then she would be another prize for them to plunder. I won't let her do this alone, besides,' Tarku said, 'I need some air. Just get me above her,' he directed.

'Kyu!' Scott spoke to her, quickly following Tarku out to the rear door, the others watched too, looking out in awe and wonder as Jem guided the Blue Moon above the great creature, so close they could make out the fine texture of her skin.

'I thought I'd lost you before, I can't lose you again, don't do anything crazy ok,' Scott called down to her. Her cry rang out across the sky and all around and through the very fibres of their bodies, warming them, and she spoke to her rider, but Scott did not feel it with the same intensity he was used to. Scott's emotions were written on his face, he wished he could do something for her.

'Not everything they did to her is visible,' Tarku explained to him. 'I think they tried to contain her with some kind of shock. I have felt the same. She will take time to recover and be her normal self again.'

Scott nodded, he understood. 'She tells me you saved her?' he turned to Tarku, surprised and thankful all at once.

'Kyu and I will go ahead to clear the way as much as possible. See you soon,' Tarku said, checking his weapons, then diving out, falling to Kyu, gripping her, then jumping into the lift created by the curved fins which extended out from her head at the front, effectively flying forwards with her.

'How is he doing that? How is Tarku flying with her?' Weston asked Astrid as they watched the great creature pull ahead.

'I have no idea,' Astrid said.

'What? I thought you'd say, oh West - it's a simple mathematical equation when it comes down to it.'

'Well it is, but you don't really want me to go into it do you?'

'No, not really,' Weston laughed. 'Can you do that Scott?'

'No,' he shook his head, 'I'll have to get Tarku to teach me how!' For a moment Scott was in awe as he saw Kyu and Tarku dance, almost jealous, as they seemed to possess a bond greater than he and Kyu had ever shared, but at the same time he was relieved, for if Kyu was like this with the Akaia, then the Akaia must be trustworthy beyond a doubt.

'Strap in again everyone, this might get hairy,' Fisher warned.

'You know what you're doing?' John asked him.

'Yep,' Fisher said, 'go and keep going. No stopping or turning, no matter what!'

John came up and took the co-pilot chair, giving Fisher a pat on the back.

'If you need me to take over lad, just say,' John said kindly.

'No, no I can do this. I can do this.' Fisher readied himself, cracked his knuckles, sat up straight and said, 'If I don't get the chance to tell you later, it's an honour to fly with you Mr Mark. Right, here we go.'

Fisher lifted the speed, he had been watching how Tarku flew the Moon and he copied the master, and the ship sped forward ever faster, keeping up behind Tarku and the great Kyu.

As they came closer to the fray Kyu veered right and over the top of the nearest and most central of the pirates' base ships. These ships were far larger than those they had encountered on route to Tamashan, and they had to play it exactly right. The ship was an old one, half was an open deck, where at least twenty pirates stood wearing protective suits against the harsh elements. From the deck smaller craft also came and went, rallying out to capture and raid the ships that sped away from the conflict on Delevi. The three large vessels also had gun stations above and below, usually hidden under crates or behind panels – they would have appeared as innocent cargo ships before they had let loose. The pirates had certainly noticed the giant manta coming towards them, but as soon as Tarku spotted the most likely leader of the rabble Kyu flew over and she cried out, a near crippling cry, they even heard it back on the Blue Moon, it made them shudder and momentarily disrupted the radar, but Tarku was used to cries far worse and it had little effect on him. Kyu's cry rang over the pirate crew and they could do no more than stop and cower, bending low over themselves and holding their heads, their ears, their hearts, as all quaked with the bone-splitting, artery-shattering noise.

'Don't go too close old girl!' Tarku yelled out, fearing for her safety with the large guns below. Quickly he jumped down to the deck, he didn't stop moving, disabling the safety bolts on the big guns and turning them down to the boards on which they stood, crippling the ship at once. By the time the effects of Kyu's cry wore off, even as the crew lifted their weapons to the Akaia, Tarku dived from the prow, pulling a knife from his boot and throwing it back, silencing whatever command the pirate captain was about to give.

Kyu let out another war cry, stunning everything that lived and breathed in the area as she quickly spun underneath Tarku, lifting him high upon her back, away from the base ship, even as the Blue Moon sped past and on through the chaos.

But there was more trouble yet before they could get away, some of the posse in the scattered fleet came after them, and Tarku found himself looking back, ready to cover their tail, but Jem held the Blue Moon steady and fast, just as Tarku had shown him, and Kyu sped on, and soon they had left the pirates behind them.

They were passing through the emptiness, Soamé was now just beyond the horizon to the east, but right here there was nothing but them and the little ship ahead. Tarku breathed. He lay close to Kyu, taking a moment, letting her carry him along. He looked at his hands, as she sped on, hands so changed from those he knew as his own, but he noticed now as the wind rushed over them, as the decaying air ran over him that he no longer bled as much from its damage, but the skin just turned to ash which then fell away as the skin healed. And within the fine lines of the markings that covered his body he could see the fire and shadow within himself, it flickered now and then, he noticed, even as the fire flickered down in the deep, like the molten rock that churned up from the core. What with that, and the ash constantly forming and falling from him, black soot and white ash, breaking up and swirling around him, as smoke, he felt more akin to the Mrukai than ever.

'Kyu, whatever happens get them back to Shorakai,' Tarku said as they neared the Blue Moon finally, then he kissed the great creature in goodbye. 'Take care my friend.'

Kyu called out and those in the Blue Moon looked out to see her go beside them, then off, flying ahead once again.

'Is the boy back with us?' Weston asked, as he could not see Tarku with Kyu any longer.

'Back cabin door,' Astrid said.

The old crew went to help him in, John, Astrid and Weston. As he came through the airlock and back into the protected atmosphere of the ship it quickly became uncomfortable to breathe the filtered air, and with every breath Tarku realised his vision was also growing dim. He tried to disguise it, to tell himself he could do this, that he could make it through, he could watch over them a little longer. He forced himself to walk through to the cockpit.

'Has Shorakai replied?' he begged to know.

'No, no response,' Jem told him the truth.

Tarku wiped his forehead, and turning back into the cabin he collapsed. He began shivering now, like a child with fever; though he was burning up inside, the world was growing too cold. John knelt to him, as the others stood back and worried. The old soldier could see the boy was falling away, losing his fight to stay in the world and not let it slip into a mere shadow. Tarku's eyes turned to John, piercing him then recognising him, at once grabbing John's arm tightly, holding onto it as if onto the hand of one that could pull him up from falling off a precipice. John held Tarku's wrist firmly in return.

'I got you,' John said, 'you're alright.'

Tarku stopped John from saying anything more. 'Please John, let me go now,' Tarku winced, and tried to sit up, 'I need some air, quickly.'

John knew what he meant, he didn't mean oxygen, he meant the hot smog outside with its high concentrations of carbon dioxide, methane and nitrogen sulphide. Even the fact that he was openly asking for help was proof enough of the seriousness of the situation. John and Weston dragged him into the airlock. As soon as they had stepped back inside and knew the door had regained its tight seal they pressed the release for the outer door to open and let in its mix of gases that would both damage and heal Tarku to a small degree.

John ran back to the cockpit and told Jem to steer into the deeper haze for Tarku's benefit. He ran back to Weston's side and they watched Tarku in agony through the thick window between them. Tarku regained his composure to a small degree as he breathed, but the markings on his body were beginning to burn through, through his skin, even through his clothing.

'What's happening Tarku?' John asked through the intercom.

'I don't know, but I know I've got to go.'

'Wait Tarku, where are you going to go?! You can barely stand!'

'I'll take my chances,' Tarku struggled.

'But Tarku! '

'I've no choice John, I can feel myself slipping away, I cannot go on with you, this is my fate. Promise me you'll look after her John, even if I've been wrong all this time and Melissa's not your daughter, promise me!'

'I will Tarku, I will do all in my power to protect her and provide for her.'

'We all will,' Weston and Astrid assured.

There was a commotion in the cockpit as Fisher shouted and tripped over in his hurry to get them the news.

'They've replied, Shorakai have replied! They're sending an escort!'

Astrid quickly passed the news on to Tarku.

'Ships from Shorakai?' Tarku looked up at them and repeated, hope on his face.

'Yes,' John answered, 'they're on their way!'

Fisher's excited voice came again, 'A commander is talking to Scott right now, they're not far away!'

Tarku breathed in relief. A little peace came to his face and the smallest hint of a smile. He didn't have to hold on any longer, Melissa, Sjyntani, they would all be safe now, they would be safe at last.

'Tarku are you sure there's nothing I can do?' John took a risk and opened the doors, going out to him. He knelt beside Tarku, sure the Akaia was near to the end, near to losing awareness. Without warning Tarku pulled the engineer's pistol from its holster, putting it in John's hands and holding John's aim at his own temple.

'Do it John, end this for me,' Tarku begged him, 'please.'

'No, Tarku, I won't do that.'

'Please, empty it!' Tarku begged John to kill him, trying to get John to pull the trigger or fight him, 'Who do you think killed Amiana the first time?! It was me!'

'Don't do this Tarku,' John pleaded. 'Don't!'

'Come on! Shoot me! I killed her John.'

'No,' John shook his head, refusing to believe and refusing to shoot.

'She asked me to do it. She asked me so she wouldn't have to leave you, so you would never have to see her like this! Who do you think got her out of the crypt afterwards?! Take your revenge John, just pull the trigger.'

John cocked the trigger, but then uncocked it.

'Who do you think took her to Coeranth? Who left her there?'

'No, Tarku, I won't,' John remained firm.

'Why do you think I went to Vahrna, I wanted to die for what I'd done,' Tarku despaired, 'but I didn't die.'

'I won't do it Tarku. Likely it wouldn't work anyway, and besides, you warned me you'd fight me if I ever tried, and I don't want to fight you, I know I'd lose.'

'I have to get off this ship,' Tarku spoke quietly, calmer now, letting John take the gun away. 'No argument will change my mind.'

John knew there was no point arguing with the Akaia anymore. 'One thing, Tarku, then I'll let you go. Who is Melissa? Both Melissa and Sjyntani are so alike to Syra, but I was only searching for one daughter, and Sjyntani is so much Amiana, but there's also something indefinable about Melissa, about her character and her spirit. Who is she?' John asked.

'I don't know, maybe the answer lies on Shorakai, or maybe I just needed a reason to stay alive, maybe I just saw what I needed to see.' His voice trailed off. He sank to the floor. The others still inside stepped closer to the glass. Tarku was crouched, faced away from them, with his head in his hands. The truth was he didn't want them to see that there were tears in his eyes. The gases in this ruined atmosphere swirled around his head, and stray ashes, pale and almost like snow, frayed from his tortured skin and into that playful air. But on top of every pain he felt in his physical body he felt one thing more than all – all his life he had fought this, every single day for a hundred and eighty-nine thousand days had been a battle. He'd controlled it, he'd suffocated it till it was nearly nothing and now it was suffocating him and he could do so little to fight against it, now it had a hold, a hold so strong Tarku knew his fight was lost. But he had to hold on, he had to hold on till he had the strength to go to the wastes and there face his end. The tears that fell were also for Melissa, he'd never meant for this to happen. He was only supposed to watch over her, even before she knew of his existence, when he had finally found her that day in Junto Mar, when he thought he had finally found Syra's daughter as she'd asked him to. Had he fallen for her even then? When he had left the camera in her way, when he had subtly guided her for these few years without her knowing and led her to place her work in the exhibition. When he had shown her work to Weston to give her a way out, a way out where she'd never need know it was by his hand, and because of her mother. Now he had lost all he was, but now she was safe.

'We'll take you lower, at least we can do that for you,' John said determinedly, and that's what he did, stepping inside and yelling the direction to Jem.

At first the ground could not be seen beneath the thick covering of red and grey cloud that swept across it, but at last they reached solid ground.

'Don't forget who you are Tarku, no matter what happens, don't forget,' John Mark pressed him. He longed to open the doors again and say a proper goodbye – hold the boy, tell him he didn't have to be ashamed of what he was, that he should be proud of all he had achieved and who he was, shake his hand and let him know how he felt, but the ship's computer detected the atmosphere and John knew he shouldn't go out there without gear and there was no time to get into it, as Tarku turned and faced them now. Neither Astrid, John nor Weston would ever cease to be haunted by his expression – so anguished, so full of fear and pain, and determination.

'Forget me,' he said.

'No, Tarku – ' they all cried, but he was gone. He jumped from the ship. They ran to a window where they might catch a glimpse of him, but then they heard Melissa's voice behind them, with a question on her lips.

'Tarku? I heard you say Tarku like you were talking to him?' she said hazily, she had just woken up properly after her ordeal. 'But he's dead. Didn't he die on Tamashan? Is he alive?' She looked at them all, gradually comprehending the sadness on their faces. 'Is he here?' She suddenly felt weak and nauseas as the words she'd overheard became clearer and she saw that covered glance of Weston's towards the window. Astrid caught her as she tried to run to the window, but she wasn't strong enough to fight Melissa's spirit and she didn't have the heart to stop her. Melissa glimpsed the figure below, but he soon disappeared into the wash of cloud, as ashes into ashes.

She looked at their faces one by one in sorrowful wonder. 'That's Tarku?'

'Yes.'

'He's alive!'

'Yes darling, he's alive,' Astrid finally answered her.

'If you can call that alive,' Weston said to himself.

'But what happened to him?'

'He is an Akaia as you know, a guide, but near the end,' John answered.

'Akaia become like that?' she asked, still dazed, and hopelessly wide eyed.

'No never like that, never so completely, never so,' Astrid could not find the words.

'Like a Mrukai,' said Weston.

'Now come darling, you just go back to sleep,' Astrid said, almost in tears herself, 'when you're ready we'll explain anything you want explaining.'

'But I don't want to sleep,' she said, 'I want Tarku,' her eyes began to tear up further as she gazed out to the last place she'd seen him. She turned back to Astrid, to John and Weston, and said, 'He's not coming back, is he?'

'No darling, he's not.'

Melissa sobbed the painful cry of the twice despairing heart. She was still so weak, she almost collapsed again where she stood, but Astrid caught her and embraced her, stifling the sobs of the inconsolable girl in her kind embrace. The poor thing had been so traumatised on Delevi, she had been through so much since leaving the relative safety of the north. 'Come on, let's get you into your own things again, you'll feel better.'

Astrid took Melissa back into the bunk room and helped her out of the thin Delevian dress. The machina then packed the gown safely away for Melissa; though she probably wouldn't want to see it again, those gems could buy a great deal, if the world didn't end. Then as Melissa still seemed to be in a strange half-awake dream, Astrid led her to the kitchen and sat her up, urging her to take some food. Melissa took a little warm soup, but had continued to dream all the while, kind of aware that Scott was on board, and Fisher and John and Weston and another girl who she didn't know, but not really taking it in. So Astrid urged her back to the sleeper cabin and wrapped her under a soft blanket again.

Scott, Sjyntani and Fisher had kept out of the way, but they had so many questions about what had happened with Tarku. Jem offered to continue to take the pilot seat and John agreed with thanks.

Weston took a seat near the cockpit and sighed, 'You might not make a guide Jem, but you might make a pilot after all.'

'I've been reckoning I shouldn't have begged you to come on this trip West, the world's all gone to pieces.'

'Aye, and not just about us either, but the entire earth had lost its sanity, its integrity, its faithful existence.'

'Nothing is as it was,' Astrid agreed.

Jem flew as the rest sat there silent. Who could talk of idle things after what had just transpired. But as John thought of Melissa, wondering what he could possibly do for her, he remembered the pendant that used to belong to Amiana, that piece of Tarku's tattoo, and put it in a pouch in Melissa's bag.

CHAPTER 43:

Dance with me, my darling.

Weston was looking a fraction dejected as he and Astrid sat over a reconstituted snack in the kitchen.

'What's the matter?' Astrid asked him.

'Just thinking about Hardan. Well, Hardan, and the trip in general, everything I wanted to achieve, but haven't. We didn't even get to Salamonde. Anyway, how's the,' he gestured to her head, 'how's the thing going?'

'Oh, the effects of the e.m.p. started to settle down not long after I hooked up on Tamashan,' she covered. She still hadn't told him about the slow but aggressive virus she was attempting to locate and isolate, without much success. She could see fractures in her system starting, glitches different to those the e.m.p. had caused - these fractures were less of a blurring or distorting, but a gradual erosion, or evaporation, like dry air may empty a lake, or an ocean, given enough time.

'Good, good,' he sipped.

'It's good John found his daughter though, so maybe it wasn't a bad diversion after all,' Astrid reminded. 'Not to mention all the film we've got.'

'Not to mention that,' Weston agreed. 'This is nice, isn't it? Everything's calm at last,' he breathed, then asked, 'Would you mind very much if we broke protocol?'

'What protocol?' she feigned ignorance.

'No show of affection in public.'

She laughed, 'Didn't we give up on that protocol days ago?'

Weston leant over the table and kissed her. He sat back down and they were silent for a moment. Then he burst into a chuckle.

'What?' she laughed.

'I hope you weren't filming that!'

She just winked, then yelped in amusement and ran, as he jumped up in disbelief.

'You weren't! We've got some serious editing to do!' he yelled and raced her to the back cabin.

'Settle down kids,' Jem laughed as they almost knocked him over as he came into the kitchen to get a snack for himself.

Once they'd settled down Weston and Astrid sat in the back, editing still. To his gleeful satisfaction Weston even managed to get a live link up with TnTv headquarters back in the Universal City, and now he sat chatting with a familiar voice as they went through the film. It seems things were not that great in the north islands either, most of the staff had left to go and be with their families for the last few days the earth may survive. They who could afford it were out stocking up on supplies, including defensive weaponry, and gas masks, protective suits, water and air filtration systems, generators, and fuel, lots of fuel.

'So what are you still doing at the tower then?' Weston asked his colleague.

'Well, someone's got to hold the fort, besides,' the man laughed, 'when else am I going to get to play golf on the executives floor?'

'Good point.'

'But I wish you were back here, it's kind of hectic between holes, and we could definitely use some more eyes before the final cuts go up. Things have been going live with barely a look over, there's so much to put up and for once no one can say we're sensationalising anything. The world's ending, how much more intense can you get!'

'I hear you. Hopefully I'll be there within the week.'

'Within the week no one will be here – haven't you seen the latest footage from the core module under the city?'

'No.'

'The place is baked down there, fractures are appearing everywhere, it's only a matter of moments Alamo, then like old Mt Calligo this whole place is going to fall.'

'Can you send me the footage from the core?'

'Sure, I can give the co-ordinates to pick up the live feed if you like.'

'Yeah, send it through.'

'On its way.'

'Thanks Max, I better leave you to it for a bit, I'll get back to you again soon though alright, take care.'

'You too old man.' They shut the connection.

'Mind if I hook up?' Astrid asked the producer.

'Go ahead, don't know why you'd want to though.'

'Until you purchase me I'm still the property of Q-Corp. It's my duty to call in,' Astrid covered, but really she just wanted the tech to run another diagnostic. She took the headphones for privacy.

'Code in please,' said the tech, but then he recognised the specifications and the face.

'Astrid! How are you doing? I haven't heard for so long I was getting worried that you were, well, we saw the TV, things were getting a bit crazy were you were.'

'No, I'm not dead yet,' Astrid laughed.

'Are you alright?'

'No, not really, can you run the, the thing again, see if anything's changed.'

'Diagnostic?'

'Yeah, thorough as you can.'

'Sure, just relax, I'll set it going. Was the program I found for you last time helpful? I found a different one I could have possibly got for you, but couldn't get in touch with you by then.'

'Oh the 3d mapping software? I haven't had a chance to use it, maybe now I'll get some time. Anyway, what's the news at Q-Corp?' she asked him as she waited.

'You don't want to know the news Astrid, things aren't good. The place is shutting down.'

'Because of the bug?'

'No, well, maybe that had some impact, but it's not just that.'

Astrid thought as much by his voice and his face. 'How many mechs will be affected?' she asked.

'Well, it's hard to say, what with everything that's been happening, and so many hired out, and –'

'Just tell me, I can handle it, how many?'

'You're supposed to be relaxed or we'll have to do the diagnostic again.'

'How many?'

'Well, if you include mechs who are out –'

'How many Sonny?'

'All of you.'

'What?'

'Even M*ko, Astrid, every mech we still have contact with will be affected.'

'What does that mean?'

'It means Q-Corp. is over, they're going to be shutting everything down, sending us all home. We all heard this morning that the boss topped himself last night. It's the way things are. No one wants to face what's coming. Besides which, the stocks have fallen so far this week, nothing's worth anything.'

'And my diagnostic, is it done? What does it show?'

'What do you want it to show? It doesn't really matter does it? It won't matter in a few days, nothing will. I'll tell you whatever you want to hear.'

'Just tell me. How bad is it?'

He confirmed what she thought. 'I'm sorry Astrid,' he said. 'You're system's overrun. This thing's insidious, gets in everywhere you can't see it and before you know it–'

'You can't be right, run it again,' she begged him, 'please.'

'Astrid I don't need to run it again. You already knew the answer didn't you? You can see it for yourself, you don't need me to run this test. We were too long to get to it, and even if we had got to it sooner this thing doesn't like being seen.'

'Can't we run the cleaner, quarantine it? I haven't been able to, but surely–'

'Harry says it's broken through everything they've tried, eventually. I mean, if we had time - but there's no time, we need time, so much, and the best place for you would be the vault, it would give us a bit of breathing room, but you can't come back here, you don't know how crazy things are here.'

'What if you did a complete re-install? A complete wipe and restart, everything, all the systems.'

'Astrid, you can't - you can't want me to do that! Besides, I don't think that would work on an M series like you, the base on which your subsystem is built is where this thing hides, and that would still be there no matter how many cleans and re-installs we tried.

'So that's it then?'

'Seems like it.'

'How long do I have before this thing shuts everything down?'

'I don't know, but think about it this way, it may be that you have longer than the earth in any case. Best thing you can do if this thing progresses too far is turn your system off, and never turn it on again. You'll be fine without it Astrid, others wouldn't, but you would.'

Astrid didn't speak. She was upset. She couldn't understand why, she was just a mech, just a piece of equipment that was always going to be obsolete eventually anyway. But she was upset, all she relied upon, all that was so much a part of her identity, was going to be taken away.

'Astrid, wait there,' the tech went off screen then came back, holding some papers. 'Do you know what these are?' he asked her. They were the hard copies of Q-Corp.'s manufacture and ownership of herself, Machina 20M A*id. 'There's something I can do for you at least,' the young tech grinned, tearing them up and throwing the shreds over his shoulder. 'And I'm erasing your files on the computer as we speak. You're on your own now Astrid, for as long as you've got left to live. Forget about Q-Corp, none of this matters anymore. You're free.'

'Say it again, the last part.' Astrid asked him, pulling out the headphones and calling Weston back so he could hear.

'You're free.'

'Thanks sonny! Take care, now go look after your M*ko!' Astrid said.

'Was just about to when your call came through, goodbye Astrid.'

The machina was torn between happiness and devastation as she cut off the connection. 'He just tore up my certificate – I'm free West!'

Weston Alamo's great big smile widened even more, and he caught up Astrid in his arms. 'That's the best news I've ever heard, and I've heard a lot of news,' he kissed her quickly.

'You're not sad that you can't be the one to buy me anymore?'

'Oh, I'm sure we can find other ways to spend that money, like, we could buy a decent apartment, or we could cruise the lakes of Lalapahue for the rest of our lives,' Weston listed enthusiastically, but then grew subdued, 'or anything,' he said, 'but why are you crying?'

'I love you Weston Alamo,' Astrid cried, holding his face, rubbing her fingers over his whiskers.

'Astrid, ay, but there's no need to cry about it, is there?' Weston's mouth smiled but his eyebrows were concerned. 'Is there?'

Astrid just put her face to his neck and held him, standing there with him. 'I won't be a mech much longer West, there won't be any mechs, anywhere, after this,' she whispered. 'It's a virus. Every function Q Corp put in me, it's all being eaten away, and there's nothing we can do about it.'

'Oh Astrid!' he said, his eyebrows pulled together as he came to understand what she meant. He held her a moment, then he smiled gently. 'Dance with me, my darling,' he said, forgetting the film and the expedition and the falling world and everything for the moment, this moment, when his Astrid needed him. She gazed into him, he smiled at her and brushed away the tears with his thumb, then together they slow danced around the little room. 'It's probably just as well,' he whispered.

'Why would you say that?' she asked him.

'Well, maybe then I'll be able to surprise you,' he grinned. Then he pulled out the little stone box and showed her the ring again. 'Will you take it now?'

She smiled, a tear fell as she laughed and put it on. 'Yes.'

CHAPTER 44:

Their Hope

Far below the Blue Moon the earth shuddered, and all the earth over. Below the precarious islands, below the clouds and the sunken wastes, it was as though the earth itself groaned to be done, to have this over, to crumble, splinter up and drift out into the forgetful expanse of space. The tremors rolled around the earth, shaking the mountains. New fault lines appeared and the remaining islands teetered so precariously. Those living, who were used to quakes and violent storms, who were used to report after report of new tragedies, of hearing of lost islands and loss of life too high to imagine, even for them, who had grown up in this climate, life stopped. No one could believe the end was now come, finally, after year after year of prediction and disbelief.

Jem watched that world below them. He had to get back to the north, he had to make it right with his girls, but they had to reach Shorakai first. He rubbed his eyes and looked ahead. He rubbed his eyes again, sure he could not be seeing what he was seeing. He checked the radar. It was true.

'There are ships across the horizon!' Jem yelled out in excitement, 'all across, a whole fleet come out from Shorakai!'

'They're a long way from home!' John exclaimed.

'They must have come at speed as soon as they got Tarku's message!' Jem cried.

The Blue Moon flew on, Fisher guiding the ship towards the Shorakaian fleet. Soon they were within the fleet, embraced, as it were, and safe. As everyone returned to the front cabin Melissa also joined them.

'Here darling, come sit by me,' Astrid called her and put an arm around her as she did.

'Are we going back to Shorakai?' Melissa asked.

'Yes, it won't be long now and we'll be there.'

'I am nervous to get there, but excited too,' Sjyntani opened, 'I've never been there.'

'You'll like it, it's just like they say, like it's been pulled out of a story book,' Melissa replied quietly.

'Has anyone introduced you to Sjyntani, Melissa?' John said, 'she was travelling with Scott, we picked them up on Delevi.'

'It's good to see you again Shortie,' Scott welcomed.

'Scott! How are you here?! I thought I only imagined you, I thought I only imagined Kyu's cry! Is she still nearby?'

'Yes, just above us,' Scott smiled.

Melissa breathed in, happy in that knowledge. Though her head still felt murky, she rested in the present peace upon the ship. After a time she noticed the book of Weston's sitting beside Sjyntani. Melissa looked at her properly, and as her mind tried to make sense of things she realised who she was looking at.

'Are you - are you John's daughter?' she asked, 'you're like the picture in the book. Is she your daughter John?'

'We think so,' John answered, 'and I certainly hope so,' he smiled.

Then she noticed the fabric and the remnant of shimmer upon Sjyntani's skin. 'Your dress,' Melissa said, 'Were you taken up to that man too?'

'I went to see the sovereign, but thankfully all that is behind us now.'

'Yes, don't you let any of that worry you any more darling,' Astrid urged, kissing Melissa's head. 'It's all over.'

'Shorakai!' John breathed as Jem steered the ship. At last they had reached the island favoured above all others. The anomaly. The home of Syra. It would have brought such relief to Tarku's heart to know they had all arrived safely. They drew into that haven, guided in with the fleet, every other vessel making way for them. All those waiting to gain access, all those official vessels and security that guarded the outer borders, all the ships seemed to pull aside and watch the progress of the little ship, and the fleet, into Shorakai main. Jem flew on proudly as everyone crowded closer to better view the city as they came in.

'Is this real?' Sjyntani whispered, standing at the window now. 'You're right, this is nothing like I imagined, even from the pictures!'

Scott put his arm across her shoulders. 'It's your home.'

'My home.'

'Your nation.'

'How could I have imagined anything so beautiful! This is so much more than what I understood, so much more.' Sjyntani held Scott's hand, she would not let go in her happy trepidation.

As they grew closer John took the co-pilot seat by Fisher to assist with the approach and landing if needed, but he continued, along with the crew, to tell Sjyntani more wonderful things about Shorakai, and point out landmarks as they flew further in. But while the crew gazed at the view below and around them, Melissa looked out without really seeing it, only remembering brief catches of what had happened - of the last moments on Tamashan, of the corridors on Delevi, of the drug and what followed - the man, the beginning of the raid, of being rescued, then Tarku being enveloped in the haze. As the rest watched the nearing city, Melissa saw her own reflection in the glass as a tear ran down her face. She saw only a gutter-mouse, she saw an ordinary girl with no history and no future, only mediocre skills, in her own opinion, and an insufficient education. She wondered why Tarku had picked her. She wondered what she was doing out here, but wiped the tear away before anyone noticed.

They flew further in, past the international docks, past the commercial port, past the military stations where the majority of the fleet pulled in. Onwards still, until the guide-ship ahead began to slow, signalling the Blue Moon to follow and land behind. The beloved little ship, with its smooth lines and its silvery hull discoloured and damaged from their escapes and journeys was reflected in the glass and water of the buildings around them.

'Alright, I'll agree with Hardan. It is a beautiful little ship,' Weston said, then wiped his nose, as if a tear might run if he didn't.

They continued on and within very short minutes they came to land. Down they went, following the guide-ship, all the way into central Rinau, landing there on the roof of a grand and beautiful building. It was so good not to be running, not to have to worry about their lives, or weapons firing around them. The calm was blessed. The air was still, but the sky, that sky that had been one singular blanket, as cloudless blue as there had been, was now staggering to hold against the encroachment of the burnt horizons, and all the wide waters surrounding the cities were restless.

'Well, here we are,' John said, then prepared to disembark along with the rest of the crew.

As soon as Jem turned off the engines, their ship was surrounded. At first the captain of the guide ship and his crew came, but they did not attempt to talk, only stood at a distance and watched on as other officials came forward.

'You know where they've brought us Scott?' asked John.

'This is the where the parliament sits isn't it?'

'I believe it is. Amiana brought me here once, she said it used to be the palace.'

'Talk about royal treatment!' Weston joked as he and Astrid began down the stairs, followed by John and Jem and then Melissa, Scott, and lastly Sjyntani. Then officials of Shorakai came forward with Governor Asmara with them.

'You must be exhausted after your ordeal, if you will all follow me,' the governor spoke, but said no more, leading on.

The crew found themselves ushered into a self-contained apartment, a dining room already laid with food, and ample bedrooms ready to receive the weary travellers - complete with a change of clothes and other essential items.

'We have much to discuss, but we will leave such speech until tomorrow,' Asmara told them, 'for tonight, please take your rest.'

'Are you sure you want to wait until tomorrow?' Jem spoke up, 'have you seen the place out there? The fire in the rifts? It's ready to splinter ma'am, we might not have tomorrow.'

Asmara was not used to being addressed so casually but she smiled, 'Tomorrow will be soon enough,' she said quietly, then left them.

Weston broke the stunned silence by pouring himself a drink, biting into a fruit and making a remark about the adequacy of the lodgings. After a while all had found themselves a seat and were encouraged by the simple, homely food and surroundings, and the weariness and tension of the last days began to fall away from their shoulders.

'If John is my father, and Amiana is my mother, and Amiana is Syra,' Sjyntani still tried to think it through.

'Do you think that you might not be his daughter?' Scott asked, 'Is that what's difficult? Because if you doubt it I don't think you should, you are so much like her, you should see the picture of Amiana that is hanging in the parliament building here.'

'No, it's not hard to believe about being John's daughter,' Sjyntani said simply, 'it's hard to believe about being an empress. How is it possible? The last empress died so long ago, and Amiana only around twenty years ago.'

'Amiana, Syra, was old, I think nearly five hundred years, like Tarku,' John answered.

'Did you know that when you married her John?' Weston asked out of interest.

'No,' he shook his head.

'Did I miss something?' Melissa asked, 'what about John's wife being the empress? I thought she was ambassador?'

'That's right, but she should have been the empress a long time ago, and they think Sjyntani is the heir,' Jem answered, 'crazy hey.'

'I have learnt so much of my mother, so much,' Sjyntani said, 'but if all of it is true I don't know what I will do. The Shorakaian believe their regents can speak with the elements, do they not? And I cannot. They will surely be seeking a saviour and I am not their saviour, and I cannot presume to be, even if I am her daughter and heir. If they think I am what Tarku and you all say, if they ask me - my mind runs ahead - to even think it seems so, so, not right, but if they were to ask me to take the crown, I will tell them I cannot.'

'Why?' Melissa asked gently, remembering the words of the governor's aide as she had led them through the corridors of the building of parliament, she remembered the story. 'Maybe they just need hope.'

'But what if I'm not this daughter after all?'

'I suppose it will all become clear tomorrow,' Weston said.

'You're right, I should not think so far ahead, I must wait to see what comes,' Sjyntani nodded.

Melissa sat back, having finished what she could eat, and being so tired. 'I have no history,' she shared, 'it's just me.'

'No family?' Sjyntani asked.

Melissa shook her head.

'I did not think I had family either, then suddenly, all of this! That's why it is even more appealing to want to believe that I am John's daughter, and to hope that it is true! But even this crew is like family, don't you think? You have all been very kind.'

Melissa smiled. In a way this was the most like a family she'd ever known. But Kat and Sophia had been family too, and she missed them. The crew continued to talk as they ate together, until one by one after dinner they found the room meant for them, and slept.

In her dreams, to her surprise, Melissa found herself back in the north, again at the wedding of Matthias and Kat. Weston and Astrid were there, and Jem and his family. The sea was there again, a beautiful sea right there where it should be in Junto Mar. Again she found herself looking for Tarku, and found him sitting in the shade of a doorway, camera slung idle by his side, as it so often was, and the most curious of smiles on his face as he noticed her. He looked away and she followed his gaze and John was there, and side by side with him, in his embrace, stood a beautiful lady, the lady from the book, from the photograph on Shorakai. She beckoned Melissa to her, at once turning with Melissa to face a mirror, back in the costumer's on Shorakai. Amiana looked no longer like the ambassador, but like the warrior-empress Syratreya, and Melissa looked at herself, now in the traditional dress of Shorakai, but she too had changed, to be more like Amiana, and she became afraid and she looked back to Tarku for reassurance, but Tarku was walking away with his head down, back into the desert wastes. She looked back to John and John saw her trouble, 'You can't save him Melissa,' John said, 'no one can.'

She turned back to the desert, 'Tarku!' she called out, but then found herself awake.

'Bad dreams Butterfly?' the Akaia spoke from a dark corner, sipping his tea. She was still dreaming. She woke herself up properly and the corner was empty. Melissa got up and stood at the doorway of her room. All was quiet. With all that had happened and was happening she felt overwhelmed to a point of numbness. But she couldn't do it, she didn't care what they'd say, she couldn't stay here. She remembered Matthias at the station, 'Don't come back here Melis, not unless you're prepared to die here.' Prepared to die. She realised that was it. She was prepared to die. She left the apartment, the halls, and made her way up to the roof of the building. At one point she was stopped by some guards, but when they had checked out who she was they let her pass. 'I needed a walk, I can't sleep,' she told them as she went by. Then she began to run back to the ship as she grew firmer in her resolve.

She reached the Blue Moon and climbed on board but she was not the only one here, she bumped into Jem.

'Jem? What are you doing here?'

'I could asked you the same question.'

'I asked first.'

'I asked second,' he shrugged his shoulders, 'if you must know I was getting my toothbrush. I'm not fussy about much, but I am fussy about that, I can't sleep if my teeth aren't clean. Now, your turn.'

'Does it matter?'

'I guess not, I was just asking. Crazy day hey.'

'Yes.'

'You should go back inside Melis, remember what West said, no going alone anywhere.'

Her eyes almost pleaded with him, 'I'm not staying here, don't ask me to.'

Jem shrugged his shoulders, 'I'm not going to make you stay. If you don't like being treated to the best of everything, I'm not going to argue with you. I might think you're a bit nutty but I won't argue.'

'Good, because I'm not staying,' she said. She grabbed her bag, the only bag of stuff she possessed in all the world, for a moment she paused as she found the fixed camera Tarku had left by her bunk, she put it in her bag and turned to go again but Jem stopped her.

'What are you doing Melis? Really?'

'Going.'

'Where?' he pressed.

She wouldn't answer.

'Melis, something's up, what's up?'

She looked away, looked down, then back at him, 'You won't tell them will you?'

'Sure, I won't tell if you won't,' Jem began to pack his own things quickly. Melissa observed and of course realised he was up to something as well.

'What are you doing? You're not going too are you?' she asked.

Jem grinned at her question. 'I'm heading back to the north, if I can find a ship. You know I've got my girls there. I suppose you could come if you wanted, maybe we could combo a ride, or steal the moon together.' She shook her head. He went to say something else, hesitated, but then decided to and asked again, 'So, what are you doing Melis?'

She thought over her answer, thinking Jem would surely stop her if she told him the truth. 'I'm not needed here, I don't want to be here.'

'You've got some plan in mind Melis, I can see it. You can tell me what you got going through your head, you can go through it with me if you like. You seem, well, a bit scared.'

'I am scared.'

'Why? Where are you going Melis?'

She didn't want to answer as she didn't want to be dissuaded from her decision, but at last replied, 'To find Tarku.'

Jem was shocked, 'Nah, nah, nah, don't do it. He's dead already for sure, you saw the place, it ain't pretty, and even if you do get there there's miles and miles of charred desert and emptiness out there, you'd never find him.'

'I've got to try.'

'And you can't breathe the air, not for long without gear.'

'So I'll wear a mask.'

'You'd need a whole bodysuit Melis, and even if you did find him and he's alive, what do you expect? You didn't see him did you, before he jumped, you didn't see him? I saw him, the world is becoming cold to him, like it is to the Mrukai, he's burning up, you can't save him Melis, it's impossible, you probably can't even get near him!'

'I don't care, the world will probably end before I find him anyway, but I've got to try,' she cried, 'if the world's going to end and we're all going to die anyway, I might as well.'

'I guess if you look at it that way, you're not so crazy. But here, sit down, you've got to see what you'll be up against if you find him, I'll find the camera feed from the cabin and the rear door and you can see for yourself.'

'I don't want to see,' she cried.

'You've got to. Before you do something this crazy you've got to understand your decision. How were you going to go anyway?'

'I was thinking of taking the Blue Moon,' she said. Jem laughed, and Melissa defended, 'but I was going to ask Kyu first, to see if she would take me.'

'The Kyu?! You're kidding? You heard the thing as we passed the pirates, the Kyu's wild Melis!'

'I don't think she is, I think she's lovely.'

'And taking the ship? That's out of the question – could you even fly it?'

'I'm not completely ignorant! I'd figure it out.'

'And what if you came to really bad weather, as is likely in the current state of the place, could you handle the ship then?'

Melissa just shrugged her shoulders.

'Well, brace yourself,' Jem said, as he found the footage and played it on the screen in the forward cabin. Apart from that glimpse when Tarku had jumped, Melissa hadn't seen Tarku since Tamashan, since he had been a whole and complete person, his face handsome in a way, his eyes sincere, his momentary smile a source of happiness, his pale tattoos and what he was only a side-issue, mostly unseen and unknown, but this! Jem was right, she had no idea, she was not prepared for this. She did not sob, but she turned away from the screen and from Jem, hiding her face.

'I'm sorry Melis, but you had to know. You had to see.'

'But how can that happen?' she asked, not of Jem, but generally.

'How can a man become like that, I know.'

'No, how does he think we could possibly forget him?'

'There was a thing between you two wasn't there?'

'A thing? No.'

'Oh yes there was, didn't you see it? He was so hot for you it was eating him up not to show it, you know his eyes strayed to you when you weren't watching, couldn't look at you straight for more than a second; and you, you're no better. That's why you think you've got to go and find him, isn't it?'

'No, there was nothing.'

'No?'

'Nothing spoken.'

'But unspoken?'

Melissa recalled ways Tarku had looked at her, things he had said, even the harsh way he had told her off that time on Arrojor for going off alone – even behind those words was the concern of someone who cared for her more than she even cared for herself.

'Don't do it Melis, if you don't want to stay here come with me back to Corrio.'

'No I have to do this.'

'But you've seen him – '

'Yes, thank you, now I know what I'm in for if I find him.'

'Don't do it Melis. You can't want to go ahead with this?'

'You won't talk me out of it Jem.'

'Alright, alright,' he relented, 'You ask the Kyu, and I'll find you some gear you'll need to take for the terrain down there.'

'Thank you Jem!' Melissa ran to the door and down the steps, but she didn't have to go further, Kyu was right there, flying low in the sky as if she knew. 'Kyu!' Melissa gushed, 'I know that you and Scott are a team, but would you take me to where we left Tarku? I wouldn't expect you to wait for me, you could come straight back.'

Kyu did not immediately reply, it seemed even she had doubts as to the wisdom of Melissa's wish. Melissa hung her head, of course it was a silly idea to even think that Kyu would do such a thing. 'It's alright,' Melissa said, 'I'll find another way.'

Kyu cried out, stopping Melissa where she stood, then the great creature came lower and lower until Kyu gently surround Melissa with her forward fins, then uttered the smallest and gentlest cry. The notes ran through Melissa's body, through all her flesh and bone, from head to toe and back again to Kyu. Kyu had read her most deeply and Melissa shook from being under such an examination, but then Kyu snuffed, and called softly again, soothingly, and moved forward, moving so the opening at her underside was over Melissa.

Jem ran down from the Blue Moon with the gear he'd found, 'I guess you're really going then.'

'Yes,' Melissa said nervously, 'thanks for this.'

'Yeah, there's a suit to protect you against air toxicity and acid and heat, and a mask too, and some other bits – and um, water and, and some sachets of food to keep you going.'

'You thought of everything. Thank you Jem,' Melissa hugged him, 'but what about you? How will you get back to the north?'

'Don't worry about me, I can handle myself.'

'I better hurry, the others will try to stop me if they discover I'm gone.'

'I can't stop you, can I?' Jem asked, clearly worried for her.

'No, you can give me a leg up though,' Melissa smiled.

He did, hoisting her up to Kyu.

'Goodbye,' he said, handing the extra gear up to her, 'good luck.'

Melissa thanked Jem and waved goodbye. Even she was finding it hard to believe she was actually doing this. Kyu called out again, and with that, closed the opening and flew with all speed, out of the safety of Shorakai and towards the turmoil of the restless wastes.

Scott woke at Kyu's call but only partially, as if in a dream, and he did not stir, such was his weariness. The others slept on too as they had not slept these last days, but now they could, being safe, and well fed. Jem sat in the ship for a long time wondering what to do, he wanted to take the ship but couldn't bring himself to steal something so much as that, and he also knew the divide between here and the north was best handled by two pilots. He checked with the port, but there were no departures for the north tonight, so he went back to the rooms the crew had been provided and lay down, to wait for morning.

~

As morning came to Shorakai, those travellers awoke to find further provisions upon the dining table. As they ate and Melissa did not join them Astrid checked on her.

'She's not here,' Astrid gasped as she sensed, at the same time she noticed Jem grow decidedly more interested in his food, and his heart rate grow a little faster. 'Jem? Jem where is she?'

'I don't know nothing,' he defended.

'That's a lie,' Astrid challenged.

'No, it's the truth,' he mumbled, 'if you take the grammar into account.'

'Come on, where is she?'

'I don't really know,' Jem evaded, shrugging his shoulders. He didn't know where either, he had a vague idea of the vicinity, but he didn't know what the place was called or if Tarku would still be near where they had left him, and Fisher didn't want to tell them part of truth he did know for it would be too hard for them to hear, and also he'd promised Melissa. 'Alright, alright,' Jem confessed, 'I went up to the ship to get my toothbrush, and I saw Melissa climb right up to the Kyu and then Kyu flew off.'

None could speak as they tried to make sense of that information. Scott ran to a window to check Jem's information. He was right though, Scott couldn't see Kyu. He called to her, but her call did not return to him. 'Why would Kyu do this?' Scott asked, much distraught.

'I don't know, she's your animal,' Jem said.

'You didn't think to wake us up?' Weston berated him.

'I'm sorry, I guess I was half asleep, I didn't think it through.'

'But they'll come back, won't they?' Sjyntani tried to assure.

'If we knew where she was going we could go after her,' John pressed, but Jem kept his promise.

'She had her bag with her, she's a smart kid, and she's with Kyu,' Jem tried to calm them. 'You guys seem to trust Kyu, right?'

'But why would she go? Where would she go?' John asked.

'I don't know what her plan is!' Jem stressed, 'anyway, besides what anyone else is doing I thought I might head back to the north and see if I can do right by my girls. Are we heading back there West? Can I take the Moon or should I see if I can find a ride at the port?'

'Can you take the ship?!' Weston exclaimed. 'What? No Jem! You can't take the ship!'

'Leave it till after this meeting,' Astrid told him, 'then there might be others of us who want to go back.'

'Alright, I'll give it an hour, after that if you lot are still playing games I'm going to the port.'

'Do you want to go back?' Weston asked his muse in surprise.

'Well, cruising Lalapahue is at the top of your bucket list,' she said.

'Pina Coladas,' Weston dreamed.

'And we do have to get Hardan back to Emma.'

'Yes, there's Hardan to look after, of course.'

Before they could discuss the situation regarding Melissa or any future plans further the door opened and an official came in.

'Jonathan Mark, the governor would have a word with you.'

'Of course,' John swallowed and followed the man.

Soon the old soldier was in a room overlooking the city and the canals. Asmara waited there for him. She nodded to the official and they were alone. The governor seemed troubled. She held her hands together in front of her and looked across her beloved Shorakai.

'There is something I must tell you John, something that will be difficult for you to hear.'

John waited for her to continue.

'The child you believed to be your child, was not.'

'What do you mean? Sjyntani's not my daughter?'

'What I am telling you, is that Amiana's child died at birth.'

'No, we had a daughter - our daughter.'

'John, we have looked into it, into the claims this Tarku made. We desired to give due consideration and diligent examination to what was said, and this has come out. I'm sorry, but I'm afraid what Tarku says cannot be true. Believe me I am sorry. My people have spent this night meticulously going over every detail, to give you a thorough explanation, and to be sure - but this Sjyntani, as you call her, she does not possess the genetic markers that would be evident if she was *your* child.'

'But how then, who was my girl? Who was the babe I held in my arms? Why didn't Amiana say something to me?'

'That I cannot answer, and we can never know for sure who your daughter is as we have nothing to compare for you.'

'I should have been there at the birth! They wouldn't let me in to see Amiana for so long! There were complications, they said.'

'Yes. The nurse attending wrote a full account on the records before she filed them away. I have now read these notes for myself. It would seem that upon hearing that her baby wasn't breathing Amiana became extremely distraught. The nurse could see that it would truly break the young woman to lose the baby, and so for Amiana's sake the nurse found another babe, one who needed a family, one she could give you. The nurse did find a child, an only survivor from a refugee ship that had been brought in only moments before. The child was underweight but otherwise well, and showing a complexion and features that would suit a child of mixed heritage between the north and us, and so the nurse gave her to Amiana and told her to look after the child and Amiana did, she took it for her own at once and never wavered.'

'This is the truth?' John asked her.

'It is. The nurse recorded that she and Amiana buried your child in the hospital grounds, under a young white wisteria tree. We have checked and there is a tree of that age in the gardens near the maternity wing.'

'I wish she'd told me. It would have been alright. I was looking forward to having a child but, she mustn't have wanted to let me down, but she wouldn't have let me down. I wish I'd known, maybe I could have loved her more -' John gasped, but shook his head, 'can I see it? Can I see the tree?'

There was much more that needed to be discussed, but Governor Asmara agreed to this father's request. 'Alright, follow me.'

They did not speak all the way there, as the boatman steered them to the hospital stairs. It wasn't far, and soon John Mark found himself kneeling under that white tree, weeping. Taking a moment to try and understand everything. 'So she was here all along. My daughter.'

'She was.'

John kissed his big fingers then touched them to the tree. 'I loved you, baby girl,' he whispered, then stood again now, turning once more to the governor. 'But who is the girl I loved as my daughter that first year? Who is the girl that has been my life for the last twenty years?'

'I cannot tell you, that information was not in the nurse's notes, but I can tell you she would not be a descendent of the royal line, not by blood.'

'Shorakai knew this back then and let me search the earth for this girl, who wasn't even my blood?'

'No John, those in authority didn't know; but would it have made a difference to you, really?'

'No,' John realised, 'no of course not, I loved that baby girl, she was our daughter.'

'That's what I thought.'

'Did Shorakai know Amiana was Syraveia?'

'No, not until yesterday when this message came through. I wish we had known, maybe we could have done more for her too. I cannot begin to imagine what hardships she would have had to face for all those years.'

'She never wanted help from Shorakai,' he said, 'that I knew. Though her thoughts were always on doing everything she could for this place.'

'John, it is hard news I have given you, and I'm sorry to do that. I'm sorry to be the one to tell you Sjyntani isn't your daughter, after all this time you have searched, it must be a hard thing to hear.'

'It's, yes, and no, I've always been following ghosts,' he almost laughed, keeping brave, 'but what will I tell Sjyntani? And the crew? They fully expect something to come out of this - we all thought Sjyntani – you saw her, she looks so much like Amiana.'

'Yes John, she does, because she is.'

'What do you mean?'

'John, did you know Amiana's crypt was empty?'

'Yes, yes I did, Tarku said she didn't die, but had to go - '

'Then at least that is one less difficult thing I need to break to you, it certainly came as a shock to us, but still for you the next thing I have to tell you must be as hard to hear as the first. Our tests reveal that Sjyntani's dna is identical to dna we were able to extract from the crypt where Amiana was laid to rest.'

'Wait. What are you saying? What does that mean?'

'They are genetically identical. She is a copy, John.'

'A clone?'

'Yes.'

'You can't be right, no, her eyes - her eyes aren't the same colour as Amiana's,'

'That is easily explained - I am told environmental factors can influence eye colour to some degree.'

'But how can you be sure of all this?'

'As soon as we saw the footage we knew the resemblance was too strong to be coincidence. My team followed up many possibilities. We couldn't know until you were here and a sample taken from the girl, but it is so. Sjyntani's dna is a perfect match of Amiana's, and both show the markers of royal heritage.'

John was speechless.

'How Sjyntani came to be here is a separate question to how she came into existence, but at least the latter I believe we can answer. We must assume that Amiana herself resorted to this in the hope that someone with her heritage, but without the mark of the Sansahme would give hope back to Shorakai. My team inform me that on the way to the talks at which she was assassinated that there is a record that Amiana diverted from her course, she diverted to the Arc. We know there were unscrupulous operators out there who would have done this, for a fee, and such an amount did leave her accounts that day. Maybe she knew what was coming, that she would die, and with her any hope for us.'

'She should have told me, should have told someone – '

'John, she was truly a regent, she would not give you these concerns to bear as well as the care of your own child. Officials here at the time received a package, we think now it must have been from her. My predecessor, with whom I have been talking through all of this, remembers it clearly. No name was given as to the sender, but it was believed to be genuine – a package that detailed the existence of a child with the markers of royal heritage, and the place to find the child at a future time, but when our people turned up at the time and place given, there was nothing. The best laid plans have a tendency to come asunder, in this world. It would seem while you were chasing after your daughter John, we were chasing a ghost of our own. But perhaps Sjyntani is the one we were supposed to find back then.'

'I am beginning to realise there is much I didn't know about Amiana.'

'As are we.'

'What does this mean for Sjyntani? For Shorakai?'

'We are not sure.'

'So what do we do? What do we tell her?'

'The small council that are aware of this circumstance have debated since the early hours this morning, when we received the results of these investigations.

They continue to debate. There are many factors to consider. We don't know Sjyntani. It would be a large burden for her – to suddenly carry with her the hope of a nation, and perhaps, the world. We cannot know if she has the strength, but on the other hand do you deprive a people of hope, when perhaps, hope is right here.'

'What do you do?' John repeated.

After some time in more thought John looked up with another question on his face - 'But Tarku, before Sjyntani turned up Tarku was so sure that Melissa was my daughter, he believed it with all he was, so definitely, I could see that seeing Sjyntani really shook him. How do you explain that? He knew more than all of us, he knew Amiana better than I did, in some ways. How can he be mistaken?'

'Perhaps he wasn't, or at least, not about everything. Perhaps Melissa is your daughter, the refugee.'

'Is there any way to find out? Would there be records at the hospital?'

'No, there would be nothing to compare of the child that was given to you.'

John looked discouraged. 'And Melissa is gone too.'

'Gone?'

'In the night, with Kyu, she didn't say a word, just went.'

'I'm sorry to hear that.'

'Yes. I can't understand why she went.' John sighed, 'I promised Tarku I would take care of her, but already I have failed, and I don't know how to go after her, we cannot know where Kyu has gone or how far.'

'I will alert our fleet to keep watch for the Kyu. If anything is seen on their routes we will know.'

'Thank you,' John said. Then it came to him, 'Wait - I have some things of Ava's, I take them with me everywhere - a wrap, a pacifier, um, I have an envelope with a lock of hair, and a little toy.'

'Do you have anything of Melissa's to compare?'

'I'm sure we could find something on the ship.'

'I will ask them to run some tests for you Mr Mark.'

'You will?'

'Yes.'

'Thank you.'

'Do not hope, John Mark, not yet. They may not be able to extract any information from these things, and even then, we cannot know what the answer will be.'

'And we still must decide what to say to Sjyntani.'

'Yes, and to the people of Shorakai. I had been thinking to leave things as they are, to let Sjyntani find out for herself if she is a child of the water, and so empress of Shorakai. I believe if she is meant to be, she will be, regardless of anything we do. So it was for our ancestors, they did not ask for the river's aid, they did not know they could, but when it was required, the river and the boy did speak, and our people were saved. But on the other hand, my greatest reason for wanting to find someone in the royal line was not only that they might be able to speak with the river, but even just to give our people hope, so they do not live in despair as the end comes, and because of this, I sway towards telling her she is the Empress, because she is.'

'But then you would have to tell her that she was my daughter?'

'No, we could tell her the truth.'

'Do you think that wise? I think that if we tell her she is a copy of my wife it would be hard news, for Scott too - being in the strange situation of falling in love with the clone of my wife. It would complicate things for all of us. And Sjyntani, she was so ready to believe herself my daughter, to gain a father, a family heritage, a place in everything, and I was so ready for her to be my daughter. But if you tell her what you have told me, who is Sjyntani but a product of science?'

'Actually, Sjyntani is still a product of a great love,' Asmara corrected, 'Amiana suffered a great deal, yet she did this for us. I think she was an incredible woman, and one I would have loved to have known.'

'She was incredible.' John shook his head. 'I can see her telling me that it is always better to start with the truth, that you cannot build a city or a relationship on a lie. It's just - this is hard.'

'It is.'

'I want Sjyntani to know I'm still here for her, that she'll still my daughter, in my mind, regardless.'

Asmara breathed. 'I will put everything to the few in the core council who are aware of the facts and await their advice. I think the action in this case will never be clear. We must make a choice and proceed, and hope that we have chosen right.'

John nodded.

'If you will return to your companions and wait there, I hope we will not be long in our discussions.'

'What will I tell them?'

'That I will speak with you all soon. I will send also my people to collect those items of Melissa's and your Ava, perhaps by tomorrow you'll know the truth.'

'Thank you.'

~

As John spoke with Asmara, so the others conversed over their breakfast. When he returned and didn't have anything to tell them they continued in silent thought. At last they were beckoned again, and all were led to a more official room, where Governor Asmara sat in the company of her close council.

'Come inside, come inside,' she beckoned them kindly. They all followed and took seats across from the council. 'I hope you are all well rested,' the governor spoke. 'Most of you will know who I am, but for those that don't, my name is Asmara Viléla, I am the leader of Shorakai. There is much to say and not enough time to say it, so I will say only what is essential. To answer the most pressing question,' she turned to Sjyntani, 'You my child, are our Syra-Ava, after Syraveia, next of Syratreya, and heir to the throne of Shorakai.'

Scott turned to Sjyntani, a grin so wide upon his face. 'It's a beautiful name Sjyntani, Syra-Ava, the closest literal translation would be 'the plains around the palace', but its meaning is really, 'the protection of our city'.'

'So I am your daughter?' she turned to John.

'No Sjyntani, but you are the rightful empress.'

'But surely I am not - I cannot be,' Sjyntani shook her head, great distress upon her face, 'I don't know Shorakai-'

'So go out into the cities, get to know it, see the people, Sjyntani,' Asmara herself almost begged, begged the girl to believe. 'Now is not the time to hesitate or question, plans must be made, Shorakai must prepare for the end. You are our Syra-Ava. We won't evade the issue, or come to it circuitously, but I lay before you this fact; the world is about to tear itself apart, without help it will fall. It is fact, it is not fiction. Many come here thinking that we will not fall, but I tell you, as my staff tell those that come - we have as little chance of survival as any other nation, but now it is a lie for we have one thing that they do not, we have hope, we have you!' She smiled desperately at Sjyntani, 'Say you will stand with us.'

Sjyntani was about to refuse again, but she looked at the governor, at the others in the council who waited with as much hope written on their faces as on the governor's.

'What you would have me do and say?' Sjyntani answered, overwhelmed but sincere.

Asmara took her hand. 'Come with me. You will need to get ready. Today you shall be crowned.'

Sjyntani turned back, uncertain to go ahead to be introduced to the extended council. John put his hands on her shoulders, and smiled at her proudly. 'I wouldn't blame you if you walked away,' he said, 'but Shorakai needs you now.'

'But I am not an empress, I don't know how to be, and I cannot do as they say in the myths I have been made to know - I cannot converse with the river, I have no history with Shorakai, no connection, not in my memory.'

'It doesn't matter. All you have to do is be here, and you will bring comfort to so many as the end comes.'

'Only if the council are happy after this interview. I am sure they would not hand a rod and crown to one they do not know.'

'But they need prove nothing, your dna proves that you are a descendant of the first leaders, who served their people right here, who served with their lives and all their strength.'

Sjyntani was quiet a moment, before speaking up again. 'So, Sona P'Lalo's people were telling the truth, it wasn't a lie, I am of Shorakai.' She turned to Asmara, 'but I do not need to wear a crown or have a title to speak with the river, do I? If indeed I can.'

'Our first sovereign did not wish to be crowned either,' Asmara told her, 'it would seem it is the mark of our greatest leaders, only out of a true sense of service do they take their place.'

'And I have not a good history to bring,' Sjyntani spoke again.

'Our first sovereign was young and not of any standing when the river first spoke to him.'

'I do not wish to be empress, but I do wish to be here, I want to do what I can, even if it is only to give hope. How can I refuse? I have no other response against what is being asked of me, save that I am afraid, but fear is no excuse.'

'You are the bravest girl I know,' Scott encouraged. 'Half way around the world by yourself, through so many unknowns. I know you can do this Sjyntani, but whatever you decide, I'm with you.'

'As am I,' John assured.

'We all are,' added Governor Asmara, 'we do not ask you to do this alone.'

Sjyntani took Asmara's hand at last, and they entered the council hall.

The extended council soon gave all agreement to the plans for Sjyntani, that is, Syra-Ava, to be introduced to the people of Shorakai without delay. So as the news was broadcast and ferried throughout the canals to all the peoples of Shorakai, Sjyntani was prepared - dressed and robed and then crowned in a simple ceremony inside the parliament. Then she was taken by gondola along a central canal, to be presented to the people.

Large crowds had assembled on the walkways along the canal's length, and in balconies of buildings overlooking. Sjyntani gazed around and up at their many faces, so many, from the courtyards across the squares, filling the gardens, and on other gondolas and boats upon the water, so many came out. People young and old, and from all walks of life. Sjyntani expected a sombre mood, an uncertain people, but it was the opposite, there was hope here, there was acceptance, trust, and faith. The people cheered for her, 'Hail Syra-Ava,' they shouted. These people were her people now, and she felt the burden so heavily. She took a deep breath, then turned to Asmara.

'What do I do?' Sjyntani begged.

'You're doing well,' Asmara smiled. 'Look at them, though the world shakes, their hearts will be at rest for these final hours, because you are here, and you are a reminder that the river has always been with Shorakai.'

CHAPTER 45:

The Earth

On Tamashan the people lost all hope, their devastated island shuddered violently and they saw no reason to try and rebuild anymore, but sat down together in the open places and watched the angry sky churn, and the plumes erupt ever more from the rifts around them.

On Soamé the activity of the bright little folk had also ceased, and they sat in small groups talking and praying, eating and drinking, but in a subdued and despondent manner far from their usual rollicking ways. The grand overbelt they had created to house their ever increasing population was cracked and splintered, sitting precariously above the city; it would no doubt collapse if there were more violent tremors. Another few tremors, another shift in the air currents and the whole little isle would be lost. It had always been a precarious existence. And where would they all go if they could? Where in the world was safe? Not even Shorakai was stable anymore and they knew it, and besides, they had heard that Shorakai could take no more refugees.

On Arrojor the grey slate trembled on the high peaks, they splintered and avalanched. Many sheltered around the few lakes that were left, but nowhere was safe. On Rorona and Satsuan they sheltered again underground when the fierce sky threatened, but even here they were still afraid as they could feel the heaving of the earth and feared to be trapped within it.

On Delevi the battle still raged between the sovereign army and the force of the radical Vahrnan. It raged with such ferocity as the enmity built up over all the years between these two parties was released – they cared not that the earth was groaning and shattering beneath them, but fought on, destroying each other and their cities.

In the North Island States the Akaia who restlessly paced in their enforced detention lifted their heads, aware something was happening. In the streets the arcades were empty, the shops sold out or looted out, everyone in their own sanctuary, or glued to the screen, watching TnTv who was still broadcasting every new detail they could get of the impending end, or sitting in groups in the open spaces to avoid being crushed by possible falling skyscrapers.

Carlo sat at the counter in his cafe with a shotgun and bottle and glass, and read his favourite recipe book. Kat sat on the bed in her 11th floor apartment and watched the ominous clouds coming across the waste and the desert. Matthias hung out of the bars in his cell and longed to be free. The guards had gone, leaving the prison abandoned with all men still interned. Serace Garner had been deserted by his cronies and sat toying with his pistol and pondering the benefits of choosing his own end with a quick death over waiting for what would come. The machinas still in development at Q-Corp. and Eterna Tower were terminated. Those in stasis were left behind, they would last as long as the generators ran, and then they too would fail. The staff, the techs and doctors had walked away, those left in charge saw no other way, the mechs here, for the majority, were not like Astrid, they were like robots, really like machines; they did what they were asked without question, analysis yes, but no sense of self. They could not simply be freed, and nor could they be supported here any longer, there was no capacity and no will to save the operation. The mechs in the field were abandoned, but Astrid's young tech had escaped with M*ko, and they were now on P12, sitting in the old observatory, eating popcorn as they faced the great divide - with front row seats to the end of the world.

On Shorakai Sjyntani stood alone at the edge of the city. She had asked for the refugees on the far side of the sea to be rescued and brought into the city before the encroaching ash clouds reached them, but the government would have done so even if she hadn't said anything, Sjyntani was sure of that, the government had plans and strategies in place and she was best well out of their way. All they asked of her was that she would be here, but she wanted to do more. She had walked through the city, trying to know this place she had never been to before. Many waved to her as she went, recognising her at once and she would wave and walk on. The people showed respect to her and didn't approach her without being beckoned, and she was glad of that, for she had no answers to their possible questions.

Sjyntani had talked briefly with John Mark, but he had no solution for her, he couldn't even tell her what he thought Syraveia would do, and Scott only replied to follow her heart. So she'd followed the central canal as far as she could, the canal whose path was supposedly a mirror of the path the river in their history had coursed, the mighty river who had spoken, rather than stay silent and watch its people suffer. Now as Sjyntani stood and looked out across the ocean, out towards those far salt hills, out towards the coming storms that forebode the end, she sank to her knees.

'How do I do this? They say you are a mighty river, they say I may speak to you and be heard. What can I do against this coming storm, against this trembling earth?'

There was no reply. She continued, 'What good is it being Syra-Ava, Empress of Shorakai, if all I am is a token, no more than a lie, what good is it to have a title if the people who hope in that title will be lost?' she cried as if to the mighty river, 'They are your people, they always have been and always will be. Protect them as they say you did in the past, please, I can do nothing.' Sjyntani wept as she knelt on the last stone pier, but as she wept those coming clouds condensed across the last of the sky, above the city, above her. She shivered as the sky disappeared, and was so near to despair, but then she realised – it was starting to rain. She didn't know what it meant, if it meant anything, but she'd always felt hope in the rain.

~

While Sjyntani had been getting to know her role, the others had returned to the rooms set aside for them.

'Are you alright John?' Astrid asked.

'I hardly know,' he replied, running his hand over his head and letting out a great sigh. 'Sjyntani is safe, but how are we going to find Melissa?' John still worried, 'Why did she go? Where would she go?'

'She'll be alright,' Jem tried to console the old soldier, 'I expect she'll come back soon enough.'

'Jem's right John,' Scott added, 'Kyu wouldn't have taken her anywhere without good reason. Like Jem says, she must be alright.'

'Well, I'll be on my way then,' Jem got up. 'Would anyone mind very much if I took the Blue Moon?'

'Are you joking?' Weston admonished, 'Didn't I just tell you -'

'Man's got to try his luck sometimes. And besides, you all look pretty much like staying here, so it won't hurt no one if I take it.'

'Going to make amends with your girl and your little one?' Astrid asked him.

'That's the plan.'

'Good on you Jem, I'm proud of you,' Astrid said. 'Actually West,' Astrid turned to the producer, 'let's go with Jem, let's go back home.'

'What? It's safer here.'

Astrid shook her head, 'No-where's safe.'

'You really want to go back to the North Islands?'

'Well, we've got Sjyntani being crowned on film, we've got the crowds, we don't need to stay. Besides, if the world's ending we better decide pretty quickly what we're going to do with all those bonuses.'

'Yeah, we got a lot of those didn't we?' Weston grinned, 'Well, alright, let's go. Who's coming?'

'I bags flying!' Jem hurried up to get on board.

John and Scott decided to stay behind, packing their things and then saying farewell to the others. It was a subdued farewell, no one knew if they would ever see each other again. With John and Scott watching on, the ramp closed up and the Blue Moon took off, making its way quickly out of the city centre, over the lanes of the port of Rinau, then off, speeding towards the north.

As Fisher flew along the rain began, and the further they went, the heavier the rain became. None of them had been through such heavy rain before, not for so long either, it continued for the hours of their journey and now they were almost home, with just the great divide to navigate. The way was surprisingly easy, the hazardous drafts seemed less tricksy, the pull on the vessel much less. The storms in the deep couldn't even be seen for the steam and fog caused by the downpour.

'I might call Emma,' Weston spoke up out of the silence as they reached the end of the divide. 'She should know we're coming before we turn up with Hardan.' He went to make the call. Soon he was back.

'All ok?' Astrid asked.

'It wasn't easy but she seemed to know what I was going to tell her. She's the sweetest lady, Hardan's Emma,' Weston sighed.

After a time Weston spoke up again. He'd been down the back and now turned on the front screen. 'I want you to see something amazing, it might just be the last time we get to see it.'

'What is it?' Astrid asked.

'The earth,' Weston said and sat back to watch the video montage of clips he'd quickly pieced together of this amazing place. They were all high shots, looking down at wide expanses of the earth's surface, videos from copters, weather balloons and the odd one from further up.

'Oh wow!' Astrid gasped, 'oh wow!'

'Astrid? I knew you'd like it, but I wasn't expecting that reaction.'

'No, not the video! Tarku! The marks on Tarku! That's it! That's got to be it!'

'I don't follow.'

'I've been trying to figure out what his markings meant. Something was telling me they're important. They're cartographic marks! That has to be it.'

'I still don't follow. Are you saying Tarku's a map?'

'Wait, wait.' Quickly she pulled up the program and used it to layer every angle she had of Tarku's tattoos on top of the most current world map she had. 'No there's too much detail,' she said, trying to piece things together.

'What about other Akaia?' Weston tried to help.

'I'm unpacking archived data now. I'm going to figure this out, I'm going to figure this out if it's the last thing I do before I shut my system down!' she determined. She processed as many shots of the tattoos on other Akaia as she could, layering their details as well. Moving them around the world map. She was silent for a while as she pushed her besieged system hard, trying to find a solution, trying multiple theories, working as fast as she could in case she would break. Finally a solution came. As suddenly as it did Astrid literally fell back. 'Oh wow!' Astrid gasped again, almost laughing and breathing in and out trying to still her adrenalin at what she had just seen.

'What is it?' Weston asked eagerly.

'When the marks upon individual Akaia from across the earth are put together, it's like a puzzle board that when aligned correctly makes a map of the earth as it is, and the lines on Tarku are the same, but they aren't the only ones, there are two plans. He carries a record of the earth as it is, but underneath that, if you take away the marks that are also carried by other Akaia, you're left with something else, barely visible, look,' Astrid brought up the picture on the screen, 'from his heart - do you see the lines?'

'Yes, I see them.'

'All that underneath, if I'm right, that's the earth as it was,' Astrid almost whispered.

'What does that mean?'

'I don't know, but it's beautiful. Look,' again Astrid sent what she saw to the screen in the cabin, she took the hidden lines off Tarku and layered them across the current map of the earth.

'Ha! Would you look at that,' Weston shook his head.

'It's the memory of blue sky, Weston, look,' Astrid pointed out, 'the memory of the landscape, of the rivers, the core. The detail is almost infinite. See the mountain ranges of the north, the ocean Aramah, the Panyanae, the cliffs near P12, the miles and miles of coastline, it's all here!'

'I see it,' Weston breathed, 'but if the Mrukai are responsible for this -'

'Then they are architects, builders, and they have spent lifetimes redrafting what we lost. Suddenly I no longer fear them, but I fear to hope - maybe this isn't the end?!'

'But Tarku is dead, surely, and even if he's not, what good is that map? It's hidden under centuries of - of a broken earth. Don't hope Astrid. The world has shown Tarku nothing but hatred, fear and at best indifference, that map is buried, just like the earth's past, just like the Akaia's humanity, it's lost, it was lost a long time ago.'

Astrid breathed and took a step back and the pictures on screen crumbled away then disappeared as the virus destroyed her ability to link with the ship's system, and kept moving through these last few functions and programs she had left.

'That's it for me too,' she said. Weston couldn't tell if she was in pain, but he was sure it hurt her, whether she hurt physically or not. 'I'm shutting everything down. Are you ready, I'll just be human now West.'

He took her hand as she closed down every element of her cybernetic subsystem. 'You've got me Astrid, always will.'

She nodded, then it was done. She let out a long exhalation.

'You ok?'

'Yeah, yeah, I'll be ok.'

'Astrid, I don't know much about these things, but you can get new hard drives for computers right? So maybe we can find that young tech of yours when we get back, that is, if you wanted to, and get this all sorted out.'

'Doubtful West.'

'Well, the world might end, but if it doesn't - don't you think?'

'I guess there's a chance he could find a fix, eventually.'

'Well, if you want your system back, and there's a chance you can get it, I'm all in. We'll get this sorted Astrid, alright.'

'Alright,' she brightened a little, then even grinned, 'what about new optics? Can we spend a little of those bonuses on the latest Optika lens? I'd get some awesome film with that piece of gear.'

Weston laughed, 'Promise her the moon and she asks for the stars too!'

CHAPTER 46:

The thread breaks.

At first Tarku walked further and further into the wastes, toward the splintering veins of the earth, but his body was still vulnerable, his strength still had limits, and though with all his will he pushed forwards, as further away from any civilisation as he could, the elements prevented his progress. Hard upon the ash-swept terrain of this far sunken desert he toiled, under these swirling clouds, through sand that stretched as far as could be seen north, east, south and west, blown high into the wind and heaped deep enough to hide cities under its all enveloping blanket. He searched this vista with dismay as he lost all bearing and sense of direction. The sand rasped at Tarku's skin, stuck in and itched, pierced his eyes time and time again and came out in gluey drips from his tear ducts. Sand settled in his hair and in his clothes, filled his nose, sat upon his lips and dried them out. He sat for a time and hoped for the elements to relent, but the hours wore on so long he refused to sit still any longer. The sand, the wind, the weight of everything, it beat upon him, beat him down, he got up so many times only to fall. He must find a way to keep going, to hang on as long as he could but his body felt not his own, he ached in every corner of bone, muscle, tendon and soul, and after hours and hours more of pressing on Tarku gave up, again sinking to the sand in this desperate hourglass.

At the beginning he thought of Syra and Melissa, of other friends and homes, but Tarku felt closer now to the Mrukai than to any man. A step more, a desperate crawl, but the sand and ash was encompassing in its fury. Tarku held against it until his eyes were blasted blind, till all his sight could distinguish was light and dark, until his ears were rasped and deafened so that though the winds still howled, to him they were silent. He tried to stand, to go on, but even his inner-self was pulled by the gusts, shot through by the sand, his spirit was exhausted and his body worn out. Again Tarku sank to his knees in the sand. This was as far as he could go. This was as much as he could take. Then out of the ashes ahead a Mrukai leant towards him, ashes forming and falling from its stony face, its skin black and cracking like burnt bark, and fire glowing within, between the cracks on its skin. All Tarku could see was the glow, the pure and beautiful form of the Mrukai that lay under the damaged skin this broken earth had caused, and he feared them no more.

'Do what you will,' he whispered, 'do what you will, I am done.' The Mrukai lowered its giant nose to Tarku's form. A rumbling sounded deep inside its throat, a low-pitched remark, almost a respect paid to the dying Akaia. That rumbling was repeated by others across the furthest reaches, as all the Mrukai paid respect but willed him not to die yet. But he fell, and the sand began to blow over his body.

Into the midst of the Mrukai a Kyu's call filtered – after hours of flight and searching Kyu had finally found the place where they had last seen Tarku disappearing into the ash drafts, and followed her instincts towards the deeper wastes – and was now here. The giant creature had echo-sounded again and again all the way, coming to this place, these sunken wastes. Kyu flew low over the land. So desolate and empty it seemed, but again she called and waited for her music to come back to her. The Mrukai replied, they were not partners but neither were they enemies to the Kyu. They conversed long and Melissa could hear the back and forward of these giants of the sky and of the deep, it was a heart-pulling music, a desperate discussion between them that made all music she had ever heard before seem shallow and inadequate.

After the Mrukai withdrew to a far distance, to give Kyu and Melissa space, once more Kyu called down to trace the lost Akaia, and a faint feedback returned. Kyu made a certain sound and Melissa had no doubt that Tarku was here. She pulled on the protective suit and checked her pack, strapping it on, ready to jump, pacing, kneeling down near the opening, toes tapping inside her boots as she waited nervously.

Finally Kyu cried as she pinpointed Tarku's position precisely. Her cry again let Melissa know she was onto something and Melissa tried not to hope too much. Kyu neared the piled sand which half buried Tarku and let Melissa out. Melissa fixed her mask on tightly as she looked around, but she did not know where to look. Kyu helped her, putting her great nose to the sand and gently humming until the sand moved. Melissa ran to the place with all desperation, unconcerned by all else, she did not even look around her as she hurried to the little piece of Tarku which was not buried. Melissa's heart beat crazily, here was Tarku and no doubt it was him. Was he dead? Was she too late?

'Tarku, it's Melissa, can you hear me?' she worked to remove the sand and soon uncovered him. 'Tarku?' she brushed the sand from his face. He seemed dead. His eyes were open and unseeing, but she checked, and he still breathed, his heart still pumped, and the markings upon him still burned. He moved, coughed. He seemed to become aware that he was not alone and drew away suddenly and quite violently, his movement knocked her back.

Melissa got up and stepped away, afraid. 'Tarku, it's me, it's Melissa.'

He looked up, his hand ahead of him as if to defend himself, he looked right into her, but didn't see her. She didn't move. He sank to his knees. He seemed exhausted, confused, broken. She understood that he was blinded, she could see that a fever raged inside him. It was eating him, spirit, body, and mind. He was lost. He was like Jem had warned her, but she persisted.

'Tarku? Can't you see me?' she began, she stepped closer, Tarku seemed to get more wary in defence, though he still remained on his knees, Melissa stopped. 'Tarku, it's me, it's Melissa. Please hear me.' She stepped closer again, little by little. Tarku was aware he was not alone, but what was near he could not tell. If it was of the earth or of his fears, he could not tell. He heard no sound, no sight, only touch and pain. He felt the approach, but he didn't strike out this time, only moved his head a bit to the side trying to sense what he could. As he breathed in, considering the air, noticing the gentle movement, the familiar fragrance, his fractured mind grasped some sense of the truth. His heart leapt and sank in the same moment, and he turned his face away. Not his Melissa, not here.

Melissa knelt down and touched his hand nervously, he took her fingers firmly in response. At this encouraging sign Melissa fell to him and embraced him, crying now with such intensity from all the pent up anxiety and dread, and now she had found him. She didn't know if he could speak, as even in the last footage she had seen of him on the ship it was obvious it was difficult for him. Tarku felt her weeping, felt the sobs as her body shook, and he embraced her in return, held her completely tight until she calmed, until he calmed too and accepted her presence here.

'What are you doing here?' he managed to whisper, though all his shock and surprise and distress at the fact was surely conveyed.

She understood that he could not hear her if she spoke so she just touched his face and put her fingers between his. How Melissa longed to speak to him, to help him through this.

'Come out of the shadows Tarku,' she said, holding his face, 'see me, hear me,' she whispered to him, 'I'm not going anywhere. I'm not going to let you die without telling you that I love you, so you must come back.'

'You have to go, this will only get worse, and I will die, one way or another.'

'Did you hear me?' she asked, growing excited and hopeful, 'Tarku, did you hear me? Come on.'

After no response she went to take her hands away, but before she did Tarku placed his own over hers. 'No, don't let go, not yet,' he begged. It was like Melissa had pulled him back to the world just a fraction.

'Can you hear me Tarku?'

There was a pause to his reply, as if he really had to listen and take time to understand, like a delay on a long distance phone line, but he did reply. 'I can hear a whisper on the other side of the storm.'

'Can you see me now?'

Again the pause, then the reply. 'You're a definite light in an indefinite fog,' he said.

'I'm here Tarku, I'm right here, I'm not letting you go, alright, I'm not going anywhere.'

'Didn't I tell you to keep your distance if you saw an Akaia?' he chided, half with humour, half with pain, and though she could see he was anguished that she was here, she could see just as clearly that he wanted her to stay.

'I thought you died on Tamashan,' Melissa said.

'In many ways I did.'

'I thought I wouldn't find you,' she told him. 'They say you saved me on Delevi, but I don't remember much.'

'I'm sorry Melis.'

'For what?'

'That I took so long, that I was not myself, that I didn't see enough to act earlier. That I let you come on the trip at all, and into war, and -'

'No,' she stopped him going further, 'don't blame yourself for anything. It was my choice to carry on into Tamashan, my choice alone. And on Delevi I remember the fear leaving me and feeling safe, I remember thinking it strange that the city could be collapsing around me but I still felt so safe, and I've never felt safe, not in my life. You didn't fail Tarku, you have nothing to be sorry for.'

'How did you get here?' he asked, again despairing that she was here, 'Are the others with you?'

'No, they are still on Shorakai, I snuck away. It was Kyu, I asked her to bring me, she found you.'

'So I did hear her.' He looked up at another cry from the giant creature, she was keeping nearby. 'You should go from here, this is no place for you,' Tarku urged. 'Go and live your life, for however long you've left to live.'

'No, there is no way I will leave you this time. You asked me once what I would want to do if I only had one day left.'

'I did.'

'The answer is here, I'd want to be right here.'

'Next to a dying man?'

'Next to you, Tarku. You told me we are only given a day at a time, but you have held my days haven't you? Each day as it came, each step you directed.'

'Your steps were your own, I merely drew arrows on your road. Some you followed, some you didn't even see.'

'You got me out of there, away from Garner, away from the gutter. Why Tarku, why me?'

'You will have to go Melis, please, you can't stay here. I'm sorry, but this is the end of my time, I've got no more trying, no more holding on left in me, you're supposed to be on Shorakai.' Tarku ended simply. But Melissa was not going, she kept on, she had so much to ask him and say to him, and she knew this was the only time she'd ever have.

'How long have you looked out for me Tarku? Because you have been, haven't you? You let me think it was Weston found my work, all along, even when I asked you, but Weston said it was you that found it, at the Expo de Arms. And the camera, even before we knew it was you who was coming on the trip Astrid knew my camera, it's your camera, your own Carrelli, you gave it to me didn't you? Not that it matters now, but I can't understand. Why me?'

'You were never meant to know.'

'But why?'

'Because you didn't know me. I couldn't just walk up to you on the street and tell you that I thought you were the Empress of Shorakai.'

'What?!'

'I wanted to remain as distant from you as I could, but still watch over you. I thought you were Amiana's daughter, she was a good friend of mine, a long time ago, before she was Amiana, before she married John, ten years or so before you were born.' Tarku had to take a deep breath to keep speaking, he spoke quietly and quickly, trying to say all the words that should be said while he still could. 'I had lost all contact with her, then several years ago I got a message from her, telling me of the disappearance of her daughter, and of her inability to search herself. I found you after a while, I thought you were her, I saw the way it was for you in Junto Mar, I had to get you out but it took me a while to figure out how. After several other attempts to get you out without your knowledge I had the idea and left the camera in your way, it was sort of an accident, but it worked. You've got such a creative intuition it just worked, and what's Garner going to suspect in an old camera? I used one of my companies to run and sponsor the Expo, hoping that you would submit something. I made sure the advertising for submissions was aimed at you, hoping you'd put something in, and you did. I asked Matthias to make sure you did too, and make sure you put a decent price on the things you submitted.'

'Matthias knew?'

'Yes, do you think he and Kat would have really let you go alone?'

'You were at Matthias's, and I never saw you?'

'I did not want to be seen,' Tarku explained, and continued, 'He agreed to help you get out, he knows me from way back and what I am, he's often helped me get spare parts, or help an Akaia on the run out of the city, even if it just meant giving them an Avero at my expense so they could ride out and die in their own way.'

'So then you told Weston about my work.'

'Yes, after your submissions were accepted and put on display I phoned West, and he agreed your work was good, agreed to take you on. I wasn't sure it was the best of my ideas but at least this way you were out and I could look out for you most of the time. I didn't know this would happen so fast after that, I didn't know we'd head into war, I didn't know the Mrukai would come as they did. I'm so sorry, it would have been better for you if I'd left you where you were, if I'd have just kept an eye on Garner. I didn't know I'd bring you to the end of the world, I didn't mean – '

'It's alright, Tarku, you have shown me the world in these last weeks, a world so amazing, so scary, but so beautiful. I have seen more than I ever thought possible.'

'You've got to go Melis, can't you see I'm dying, there's no point being here.'

'No,' she begged him, 'Please Tarku, please hold on.'

'Didn't I tell you, we are only given a day at a time, any day could be the last day. My day is today.'

'No, hold on Tarku, please hold on, even just one more day. I will live, and I will, Tarku, for another day, if that is all that's left, but it will be another day that I can know you, and I want to know you. Please Tarku,' she sobbed, 'look at me. I'm real, I'm here. It's not a lie. I love you.'

Tarku gasped as she embraced him, his heart so anguished to know of her love, but to know that his time was almost up, and at the truth of her words it was as if a shockwave had ruptured inside him, a force so strong it shook him in every corner of his being. He struggled to speak. 'Melissa, I would give you the rest of your life if I could,' he held her face, his own a picture of grief, 'but if you could, tell me I don't have to hold on anymore. Tell me it doesn't matter if the world falls. Tell me you'll go with Kyu away from me, as far away from me as you can go.'

'But I need you, Tarku, I need you,' she pulled him back and held him tight.

'No, Melissa, you're strong, you're just like an empress of Shorakai, regardless of what the truth may be.'

'No, I'm just a girl from The Gutter, from Junto Mar.'

'This isn't about blood Melissa, it's about your spirit, you have courage and determination and compassion, and all of this madness, the world, it barely touches you. You're innocent. Don't you see? In all of the darkness you're a light, you hope when there's no hope to be seen, you make me smile - me!' and he did smile, through his anguish, as that rare gloss so seldom seen in the hard eyes of Akaia glinted now and spilled down his cheek in a steady stream. 'You were supposed to be safe on Shorakai, and here you are, seeing something of worth in a man who has been told all his life that he is less than a man, trying to save me, who can't be saved. Melissa, my fate was sealed the day I was born.'

'No, it's not true, I'd still be there in Junto Mar if it weren't for you. Don't go Tarku,' she tried to keep him with her, but at that moment rain started to fall, large droplets heavy with the pollution from the air. It began sparsely but then multiplied. The trembling of the ground was increasing all around them, and Melissa couldn't be sure, but she thought she may have heard a Mrukai call in the distance even as Tarku turned his head up and seemed to be searching the sky for something, seemed to become lost again, for she spoke but he didn't hear, even though she held him firmly, even though she pulled him close.

Melissa thought for a long time as she stood with him, as she watched those droplets turn to steam as they ran down his many markings, as the lines upon him also grew further - up towards his eyes, but something was happening - the secondary lines deeper within him further ignited, from amber, to blue, to white hot, running up from his heart, fighting to overtake the original lines in reach and intensity. She knew he spoke the truth, it was his end. Finally she spoke up again. 'Tarku, Tarku, can I say goodbye? At least let me say goodbye.'

He came back to her, for this moment aware of her presence again, trying to keep her in focus. She leant her head upon his, then she took her courage, pulling off her mask despite the risks, tiptoeing up and kissing him. It was a simple, sublime kiss. For a long moment he was speechless, then he managed, 'That's the last thing I expected, Butterfly.'

'I love you Tarku. If you need to let go, then let go. I can't ask you to keep hurting.'

He gave her one last hesitant smile as he touched her hair, 'You kept me alive these last months, Melis, you don't know it, but you have, you gave me something to live for,' he told her. There was silence. Tarku held her. He kissed her forehead. 'You must go,' Tarku said.

'No,' Melissa sobbed.

'Thank you,' he said, 'Without you I couldn't do this.'

'Do what?'

'Face the end.' He pulled her mask back across her face and secured it, then stepped away from her, and now their interlude was over the world grew back around them, so terrible around them. The ground they stood upon was shaking and seemed itself to be sinking even further, and the winds were strong against them, the air itself almost sucked away, leaving their bodies feeling as if in a vacuum, pressure hard upon them. The rain grew in intensity, but even more terrifying was that the Mrukai could really be heard, their splintering cries reaching up from the deep rifts, even as the rifts themselves fractured further, splitting the ground rapidly towards them.

'Go,' Tarku urged with the last of himself, 'Go from here, go with Kyu,' he insisted, and even as he spoke the great manta appeared. Kyu flew down again and Tarku lifted Melissa up, almost threw her, with desperate urgency, as a rift reached closer to them. As soon as she was in she turned back, reaching down for Tarku, 'Take my hand Tarku, please, take my hand!'

He only shook his head as Kyu sped away, and the last Melissa saw was Tarku being swallowed in debris as the wastes shattered beneath and all around them. She let a painful cry escape as the safety of Kyu's chest cocooned her from it all.

CHAPTER 47:

The City by the Sea.

The trembling and shaking of the earth seemed to stop, to pause as it took a breath in, as the plans that Tarku held were reviewed by the Mrukai. For centuries the map of the broken earth had held the dominant place upon him, their representative and guide, but the actions of one girl had changed Tarku, bringing the hope of blue-sky to the surface, and now the Mrukai knew there was still hope for the people of earth, that there was something here worth saving.

The information Tarku carried, every piece of knowledge that the Mrukai had collected and mapped upon him, was disseminated through to all of their kind, into the core and into the arteries of the earth. That shockwave that Tarku had felt now spread across the earth, a remembrance of the pulse and life that had once been. Then the quakes began to increase with renewed fury and vigour, all people believing now that this was indeed the end, not knowing that below them the earth came together. Mountains were growing where they once had collapsed, the islands that were fracturing and moving away were now pulled back, and empty oceans devoid of water and life were being readied to receive the rain that continued to come and the flow from seas below.

Astrid was right. Syra had been right. It couldn't yet be seen but the islands of the north, Corrio, Antalla, West Fall, Parahn, and El Canna, were no longer islands but joined again. And from The Urchin, P12, that great divide was closing, the massive split in the earth decreasing rapidly as the ground rose also and the rusting splinters pulled together. All the islands everywhere were now connected by open land, as clouds continued to grow together above, steam condensing into thick blankets. The rain fell hard and full and long, raining and raining like it hadn't rained in decades. It was ever by ever more encompassing, washing all the dust and toxins and festering rot away, washing it from the streets and the wastes, washing it out into the new openness, and down into the last of the closing chasms, then locking it away, and still the rain continued on. Then the waters from inside the earth came up, meeting with the oceans of Oconia and Shorakai, filling the low lakes in the mountains of Arrojor, replenishing streams and rivers that had long been dry.

The battle that raged on Delevi ceased as the combatants saw the change, in complete amazement, as the islands shook violently and instead of falling away they moved together, rising up together as the earth beneath pushed up. Delevi itself rising up to re-join with Nuana, Lapasse and Luteni, and the deserts and wastes long since lost to the deep returned around the islands, vast lands thought forever lost. Their weapons fell from their hands, and all watched, astounded.

The Blue Moon was in the air, flying in haste towards the Universal City. Weston, Jem, and Astrid could not believe what they were seeing below as the steam and the toxic airs dispersed and the new earth could be seen below them, mountains where there had never been mountains in their lifetime.

Weston got in touch with Max back at TnTv. He was still there, completely exhausted, but with a ready laugh. Weston forwarded to him the live images of the earth below, which Max streamed right out to the world, so now any who still had reception and still cared to watch could see – the earth was re-forming, not collapsing.

People who sat inside looked outside to see, others came out when they realised the rain was alright, that it did not now carry with it the sting or sourness that it had. And the streets became full of dancing and just standing still, gazing up at the rain, letting it flow over them and refresh them, as it refreshed the earth.

Many people still did not realise what was happening, that this was another beginning, not the end of the world, and they still moaned and wailed and many decided it was time to take their own lives before the earth took them. And so they lay there with glassen eyes that could not see that the rain from the clouds coming now across the wastes met with a surging of waters beneath, they did not know that it was not the end. Soon the lands were full and the rivers full of life, and the oceans reformed too, surging up to beaches that had not seen the sea for so many hundreds of years.

The water was rising, and Shorakai in a low area, and of course, rumoured to have been once a city under the Panyanae Ocean. Far from the end they had feared, they now feared the water they had revered for so long. But Sjyntani continued to stand at the edge of Shorakai as the rain came down, but she wasn't afraid anymore, she laughed as she held out her hands and let herself be immersed in the deluge. There was a rhythm in the rain, a soothing music also repeated in the surge and flow of the sea that surrounded and rose, but Sjyntani let her worries go, and the seas rose around Shorakai, but their city was not consumed - where Sjyntani stood at the edge of Shorakai, the sea came no further. Shorakai was protected in its own hemisphere as the water rose around it, as the waters lifted the ships which waited to dock, taking them up and out of view until Shorakai was completely under the rising ocean.

~

Kyu flew high, and she took her time. 'Where are we going Kyu?' Melissa asked.

Kyu sighed, Melissa understood, Kyu was taking her home. She didn't know where home was anymore, but she trusted Kyu. Soon Kyu opened up and let her see where they were going. Kyu flew ahead of a rising tide, a tide fast on its way to the outskirts of Corrio, running towards the gutter, Junto Mar. Kyu called out as she flew in, a goodbye to Melissa, and as soon as Melissa jumped out Kyu turned away and back towards the south.

Melissa stood on the beach stunned and still as she watched Kyu leave, as she whispered her heartfelt thankyou and goodbye, then watched the flood coming towards the city, the tide surging towards her. She was motionless, only put out a hand to touch the spray of the waves as they surged right up to where she stood, but no further, receding then flowing up again more gently the next time. She could smell the ocean so full and salty and fresh in her nose, she was surprised at the wonderful smell. She would never have imagined the sea would be like this.

The Gutter was the city by the sea once again, and many made their way to look, to go and touch the water. Soon the beach filled with people, people in awe at this happening. No one here had ever seen the sea. Many ran and played together now in the water like young children, not knowing quite what to do in the waves, but loving it and laughing.

Melissa looked around, all wonder, hardly believing what she saw - the transformation, the old run down city of the gutter, and the tin shacks of the slum further down, was now beside the most beautiful beach and ocean she had ever imagined. Now everyone from the Universal City, which lay inland now, would want to live here. It was so hard to believe this was real. That all of this was real. As the most glorious sunset fell over the suburb her tears fell to the swirling ocean. She touched the water, her hand gliding about through the smooth and restful waves. She thought she heard Kyu call in the distance again and looked out, but couldn't see her.

Apart from seeing the sea, and the prospect of seeing her friends again, Melissa wasn't sure about how she felt being back here. Kyu must know what she was doing, surely, Kyu must have known how desperately she longed to see her dearest friend Kat and tell her everything, and let her tears come freely in Kat's sure company. Melissa was scared of the prospect of meeting Sir, and she sat here for hours, gathering the courage to make the short walk up the street to the old apartments. She waited so long the water grew dark and glimmering under the rising moon, it was so beautiful - the sky was clear as it had never been, and there were truly stars in the gutter. At last she had enough courage.

Melissa didn't want to see anyone else, and she wanted to avoid Sir, if he happened to be there, so she managed to pull down the fire escape and made her way up to the old 11th floor apartment, in the hope that Kat would still be there. The window was open, a thin, fraying curtain flowing out gently in the breeze. Melissa tapped on the window, 'Hey Kat it's just me,' she said quietly, then jumped inside.

'Hey? What! Melis!?' was the exclamation from Kat as she saw a figure enter and then began to realise who it was. 'It is you?! Girl you're back?' Kat jumped out of bed and ran to her dear friend, embracing her so warmly, so long. 'How'd you get here? What you are doing here?'

'Kyu brought me back here.'

'You can fly in that thing? You crazy girl? Are you saying you've been here all afternoon and you're just coming to say hi now, what you been doing?'

Melissa was about to answer when she became aware that Kat had company.

Kat cried, 'Oh Melis! I'm so sorry!'

Melissa was about to ask why when the sheet on the bed moved and Matti's head appeared. He rubbed his head sleepily, 'Hey Kiddo,' he greeted, but was shame faced at once.

'Melis, I'm sorry,' Kat repeated, 'I didn't never ever think you'd be coming back.'

'No, no it's perfect, it's perfect,' Melissa said, with a sincere smile, and then she laughed, 'I knew you guys would be great together, it's alright, really, I'll go.'

'No, don't you dare go Babe,' Kat insisted as Matthias got up and sat on the bed. 'You sure you're not cut about this?'

'No, no, of course.'

'Come on, at least slap my face,' Kat insisted, 'or get angry, or throw something at Matti, come on, I'll feel better if you do. Matti will too, won't you Matti?'

'Yeah, I sure will,' he agreed, though sleep was still heavy on him.

Melissa shook her head. 'No, really I'm happy, I'm serious. I dreamed you two got together, I dreamed it twice. You just have to stay together now, and get married down on the beach, a proper beach wedding like, you know, and I'll take pictures, and there'll be cake and-'

'Here, give us another hug,' Kat pulled her in again. 'We just got Matti out of prison, he's been in there since you left. It's an epic long time for nothing.'

'Really? That's crazy, I had no idea!' Melissa apologised, 'I'm sorry Matti, I didn't know my going would cause any of you trouble, not like that.'

'Kat got the worst of it as I hear,' Matthias said.

'Oh, Kat! No!'

'Yeah it's been a ride,' Kat said, but she was smiling at seeing her little friend again. 'But I'd do it all again you know. I mean, come on, I got to see you on the TV.'

'Oh I missed you Kat.'

'Look at you now,' Kat gushed, teary, 'I thought you looked older, the couple of times we saw you on the flicker but you're just the same. Got to tell you, Garner's dead. Matti went up to give him what for, but he was already dead, so it's okay to stay now, if you were thinking of staying.'

'I think I might stay, at least for a little while, if that's ok,' Melissa said, smiling, with tears of happiness and sadness rolling out all at once as she hugged her dear friend again.

'And it's real good cause we got an apartment overlooking the sea now,' Kat continued excited, looking out again to the view.

Melissa followed her gaze, 'It's so beautiful, everything.'

'Yeah, it is,' Kat replied, but she could see there was something wrong. 'But it's all good Melis. What's these tears for? I thought you were just happy?'

Melissa shook her head, all her emotion getting the better of her now.

'I told you you've got to throw something.'

'No,' Melissa sobbed, 'it's not that.'

'How's this babe? What's the matter? You want to tell me? Either way I'm right here babe, I'm right here.'

'I can't explain what happened, everything that happened,' Melissa said. When she was unable to say any more in her grief, and only bit her lip, Kat knew something was really wrong. She nodded to Matthias then took Melissa's hand.

'Come out here in the air,' she pulled Melissa back out to the fire stairs and sat her down. 'Somebody died didn't they? Somebody in the crew you went with? I can see it. They died and you feel it something terrible.'

Melissa nodded, so Kat held her tight as the waves continued, as the sound of the ebb and flow reached up to them. Kat rocked her, and after a while Melissa calmed they sat there together, looking out at the sea, watching and listening to its soothing rhythm.

'I'd found someone Kat, or rather, he'd found me, so I don't have a crush on Matti anymore, so it's ok, I really am glad that you're together,' Melissa spoke again, before burying her head in Kat's hair again, Kat patting her back gently.

'Now I understand,' Kat said.

The night grew, and the sea became dark with it, invisible but still heard and felt, and if she looked hard Melissa could still just make out the horizon, and the glimmer of the sea, all the way out there. She felt numb, dead, blank inside, like all her motivation and will and desires had all left her. She wanted something, anything to pull her away from this state of mind, she didn't feel she could do it herself, but at the same time just longed to remain like this, just empty, just breathing with this ocean. She wondered what had become of the others. Of Astrid, Weston, John, Jem, Scott and Sjyntani. She wondered what had become of the all the lands to which they'd travelled, of Arrojor, Rorona, Satsuan, Tamashan, Delevi, and Shorakai. Would she see any of them again? See any of those places again?

'Ssh,' Kat stroked her little friend's hair as the tears returned once more. 'Ssh. It's going to be alright, alright, this here's not the end of everything. This here's just the beginning.'

CHAPTER 48:

A New Expedition

The Blue Moon pulled into the 30th floor dock of TnTv tower, which miraculously was still standing. Weston was in a great hurry.

'Go make sure your girls are alright Jem, then I want you back here as soon as possible.'

'What? Why?' Jem was confused.

'Well we're going to need a good pilot,' Weston said.

'Are you serious?' Jem smiled.

'Of course I'm serious. You've seen what we've seen coming in, we've got to get back out there filming.'

'What happened to cruising Lalapahue and spending your bonuses?' Astrid laughed.

'Oh this is better than that,' Weston grinned, 'what do you say Astrid? Another world tour?'

'Sounds good to me.'

'We just need to give Hardan a good send-off, get some repairs done on the little ship, and make sure we've got enough supplies, check all the gear, make sure TnTv will keep up their end, and we're set.'

'Right, so I have about two to three weeks do you think?' Jem asked.

'Something like that. We'll keep in contact,' Weston said.

'We'll need to find some photographers too,' Astrid added, 'and a guide.'

'I don't really want to think about that,' Weston sniffed as her words brought their losses back to him.

'Melissa might turn up,' Astrid encouraged.

'And if there's any way we can get to Shorakai now we might find John I suppose,' he added.

'The Moon should be able to get to Shorakai even if they're underwater now, I mean, once she's been fixed up,' Jem said before he left. 'Think about it, it handled the water well the first time we were there. I know we didn't try going under, but she's built to take the divide so water-proof's got to be feasible, and if Tarku designed her, which I reckon he did, then he'd have made it so.'

'You're probably right, I don't know if I want to see Shorakai though, if it's been lost in all this the sight would be too hard to bear.'

~

But Shorakai was not lost. Sjyntani stood in the humble palace looking out at the city, the dome of water all around. The air itself seemed to glisten and rainbow, but the sky was now no more than a sparkling in the water, so far above.

'The people are waiting,' Scott reminded her. 'I know you don't like it, but you must let them give their thanks.'

'It wasn't me Scott, I know it wasn't. I am certain that the river would have been with them whether I was here or not. I will not take the credit for it.'

'But to the people here you were their hope Sjyntani - their representative, to speak for them, and you did speak, didn't you?'

'I did.'

Scott sat down, obviously weary, and Sjyntani went to him, 'I'm sorry there is no word of Kyu, or if the others are safe.'

He shook his head. 'My duty is to you, Empress,' he took her hand, 'now and always. Kyu put our paths together for a reason, she knew you would be my compass if she was gone.'

It was at that moment they heard Kyu's familiar call, and then they saw the great creature break through the water and into the dome, flying into Shorakai with all haste, coming fast towards the city, calling out for assistance. Many ran to her as she flew in, as she paused above them, tipping her nose low and opening her forward fins to reveal a body she held there.

Kyu had caught him at the last. After Tarku's body had seemed to disappear into light, after all the etchings that had been upon him, that had incandesced within him, the collected knowledge of everything that was and had existed, of how the earth had been, the living map. After the rebuilding came to its completion, as the last of the rifts closed up and the remaining Mrukai gave one last call, then dived within. After they no longer needed Tarku, and after every last tattoo upon him faded back to the colour of his skin, after the rain and the ashes, and all the elements had caught him, had wore at him, etching away at him, as a sculptor might shape a block of stone, and after his body was stripped of every feature that distinguished him as an Akaia, all the damages of his five-hundred years. After he had been swallowed, unconscious, into the rising waters. As the earth grew still again, as the wind and the rain eased, that's when Kyu had found him.

The people here took him to their hospital. Sjyntani, John, Scott, Keersi the official and his wife Mila, even Asmara and others, took shifts to stay by his side, for many weeks.

At last there was a twitch in a muscle, a movement in Tarku's fingers.

'Hey old man,' Tarku whispered as the outline of John came into his sight.

John almost jumped at hearing the voice. He looked up from the book he was reading. 'Who are you calling old?' he laughed.

Tarku looked around him, confused. He saw the view out the window, which only added to his confusion. 'Oh wow,' he got up and stumbled to the window, despite John urging him to stay still. The sight was too much to stay still. 'What did I miss?' Tarku asked.

'Kyu brought you here. We're underwater now Tarkars, the whole of Shorakai, but we're safe. Of the rest of the world, I don't know, but we hear it's all new.' He paused, then added, 'Scott tells us that Kyu assures him Melissa is safe, back in the north.'

'The world is still here,' Tarku said, almost disbelieving, 'I'm still here. I don't understand.' His legs became unsteady under him, he grabbed the window sill but John was ready and held him, helping him to keep standing.

'You just take it easy Tarku. You're not like you were.'

'What do you mean?'

'Akaia don't exist anymore, no one is marked, and I have a feeling the Mrukai will soon only be legend also.'

Tarku looked at his arms, the skin, unmarked. He looked at his reflection in the glass. He was overcome. 'Let me sit down, John, let me sit down.'

John helped him back to the bed. Tarku had to breathe for some time before he could speak. But before he spoke he laughed, he was so happy.

'What?' John queried, 'what's funny?'

Tarku smiled, 'Have you ever looked at yourself and seen someone different than who you were expecting to see? Someone you didn't think you were, or ever could be?'

'Not really.'

'For the first time in my life I have seen the real me, John, the man as I am without a tag, without the marks of a broken earth, for the first time I see myself, without fear. Is Kyu still here?'

'No, she left again not long after she brought you. She was always a wild creature Tarku, I'm sure we haven't seen the last of her but Scott tells us she's gone exploring the new seas, looking for others of her own.'

'Then I will need a ship,' he determined, 'to get me home.'

'If you're thinking of going to find Melissa, there's no need. The Blue Moon turned up here a couple of days ago, Weston and Astrid and Jem. When they heard the news about Melissa they turned right back to go and find her. They plan to return, they want me to join them to be the guide on their expedition to document the new world. We didn't tell them about you, we weren't sure if you'd pull through, but I'm sure Weston would want you on board, he hasn't hired any extra crew yet, couldn't bring himself to. You rest up, I'll give you some peace, I'll get some rest myself and let the others know you're alright at last.'

'Wait John, don't tell them yet, I think I still need some space, I would be overwhelmed if everyone came.'

'Ok, I'll leave it till tomorrow, rest well.'

'Where are you staying?'

'In the palace, of course, Sjyntani wouldn't have it any other way.'

'Sjyntani - so she is? John, she is your daughter?'

'No, not exactly. It certainly feels like she's my daughter, but she's not.'

'But she's empress? How is this?'

'She's,' John had to tell Tarku, how could he not, 'she's Syra's identical.'

'She is Syra. Ha. I told Syra I didn't think it was a good idea, she'd thought about it long before she'd met you, I never thought she'd actually do it, but she must have done it, made a copy. Does Sjyntani know?'

'Yes, she does. It was so hard to tell her, but she took it well. I didn't want to tell her, I wanted her to believe she had a father, I wanted to be here for her through this, and to be honest, I wanted to be of some use. She's like my daughter, even if she's not. But after talking with Asmara, we concluded she should know.'

'I understand,' Tarku said, 'what about Melissa?'

'I'll tell her the truth, when she comes back.'

'And what's that?'

John smiled. 'That there's a chance that she really is my daughter, the one I lost. The one Amiana adopted without my knowledge, after our own baby died.'

'That's what happened?'

'It is. Shorakai says we can't be sure, they couldn't find any viable dna on the things I had of my Ava, but Melissa has the right eyes Tarku, they're not quite as bright as I recall, but I know eyes change as children get older.'

Tarku nodded. 'She does have the right eyes, and the nose, like in the picture.'

'She does.'

Then Tarku almost yelled as he moved a little and bumped the needle of the drip that was in him, causing a little blood to run, but then he laughed, 'I might need a father too John, I don't think I'm indestructible anymore. I might need someone to pull me back in line from time to time.'

John chuckled, 'Nah, Melissa will do that.'

'You think so?'

'Of course she will. I'll see you tomorrow Tarku.'

Not too long after John had gone, as Tarku watched the view out the window, he saw the familiar little ship gain the port. The evening was settling in, so the view was dim, but he was sure it had to be them. He made himself get up and slipped the needle out. He pulled on some clothes, then quick as he could navigated the corridors and out into the streets. He watched the sky. The ship was out of sight. He had to sit down many times, or hold a wall to steady himself, but he had a good idea where they would be heading and bit by bit he made his way to the central gardens, to the port where they had been given a berth on their first way through. Sure enough, the Blue Moon was there, her panelling and paint all renewed, and a tribute along her side - 'Orin Hardan 2282-2319'.

Tarku paused to catch his breath, he had been so long to get here, on his unsteady legs, but he saw her now, walking away from the ship into the tranquil gardens. 'Melis,' he called, but even his voice was still weak, and she didn't hear. He boarded a gondola and directed the oarsman to follow on, he would try to catch her up on the other side.

She had walked a long way, from the central gardens all the way until they saw her cross the bridge to the gardens of Merouin. He disembarked. At last she stopped and he caught her up. He was nervous to speak to her, like a young man just learning about love, but she paused here at the small memorial to Amiana, and he took the chance.

'Can't sleep, Melissa?' he asked her. She gasped and turned at once. There was a curious smile on his face, a beautiful smile - the product of mixed apprehension and happiness. Tarku was not as she remembered, he had no tattoos upon him now, no mark or scar or any feature to suggest what he had been. All trace of the Akaia had left him, and here he was as she had once imagined, as she had once thought he would be behind his act. He was young as her, his hair was cut short now, but was as black as she'd first seen it, and there was no pain on his face. He was as an unmarked man, whole and free of all the weight he had carried for so long.

'Tarku!' Melissa ran to him and held him. She cried, she could hardly be happier than this.

'Butterfly,' he finally whispered, and pulled back to looked at her, 'what are these tears?'

'I thought you were gone forever,' she sobbed.

'So did I.'

So long they embraced, silent, just breathing in relief, just breathing in this moment.

'Can I lean on you Melis,' Tarku asked after a while, already exhausted from his effort to catch up to her, 'just a bit, actually I think I need to sit down.'

She helped him, steadily sitting down with him, onto the grass by the memorial. Then they leaned back upon the stone, watching the glinting of the water high above, like watching the stars.

'Did you know I might be John's daughter after all?' Melissa spoke again, 'That's what he said just now.'

'Yes, it's possible.'

'I knew it when I saw his face, when he saw me he was so happy, and he gushed it all out, he couldn't help it. I didn't know it would feel like that, to have a father that cared about you that much.' She seemed to wipe her eyes again as she smiled, 'But he says we can't know for sure.'

'That's right.'

'He said Sjyntani asked him if he would be her honorary father, which of course he would, so he said now it's like he has three daughters. His baby under the white wisteria, Sjyntani, and me. And if I am his adopted daughter, then I was a refugee of mixed heritage, I could be from anywhere.'

'You could be.'

'Have you seen it Tarku?' her eyes lit up as she asked him, 'Have you seen how it is out there? The world is amazing! Astrid says it's because of you, they don't know you're alive, you should hear how they talk about you, Weston's been talking about doing a documentary on you and everything.'

'Is he? Well I'll have to put a stop to that,' Tarku laughed, but then grew serious as he looked up and around them. 'Melis, do you know none of this would have been if it weren't for you?'

'What do you mean?'

'You were the key. Syra was right, there was hope. It wasn't a big or grand idea, it was simple thing. You saw what no one else could see, something of worth in me, even though I was so broken, even despite everything. I couldn't see it until you did, but because you did you moved heaven and earth Butterfly.'

She didn't know what to say.

'I don't know what it's like out there, why it's amazing, but it wasn't my doing, it was you, your heart.' He took her hand, looking at it, trying to find the words he wanted to say next, but the right words wouldn't come to him.

'I'm sorry,' Melissa said at last, with the trace of a grin.

'For what?'

'That you have to live even more years, because of me. I remember you said you rather have died long ago.'

'No, don't be sorry,' Tarku laughed, 'that was all just prologue, whatever we do now, this is life.'

~

When the Blue Moon left Shorakai a few days later, with Weston, John, Astrid, Jem, Melissa and Tarku, the others watched for John and Tarku's reactions as the ship broke out of the ocean's waves and into the sky. It was the first time the two had seen it. Their eyes opened wide as they looked up and around, from horizon to horizon, at the huge sky. Tarku's eyes were still grey, but no longer were they clouded and stormy, but clear and bright, and reflecting that blue, blue sky, as he gazed in complete amazement. No longer a memory, no longer just a hope in Syra's eyes, no longer a map hidden deep upon his skin, but here, so vivid and real. Melissa stood beside them at the window, her hazel green eyes also watching.

'You filming this?' Weston nudged Astrid, the machina grinned and winked.

'Come on everyone,' Weston broke the silence after a time, 'let's get breakfast.'

'Melissa, wait,' Tarku held her back as the others went on, 'wait, I never did say it, I didn't think I'd ever be able to, and I never thought it right that I should.'

'It's ok.'

'No, I,' he swallowed, looked at her hands again, then back at her straight, 'I love you.'

'I know,' she said simply, smiling. 'I think I've known for a while.'

'I've known since our first stop on Shorakai,' Astrid laughed.

'I kinda suspected since Arrojor,' Jem added.

'Tamashan,' Weston said.

'Delevi,' John added thoughtfully.

Tarku and Melissa had to laugh.

'So Sonny,' Astrid turned to Jem, 'how's your girl and your little one? You talked to them today?'

'Yes, good, they're good.'

'So you getting married now or what?'

'Already happened,' Jem laughed.

'You were quick. Where's your ring then?' she cajoled.

'Hey, you think we had time to get any metal for her finger? Have you seen the place? And I weren't going to let her wear a piece of shrapnel, come on, I'm waiting till the proper jeweller opens up again, she understands.'

'So what's she wearing now?'

'A piece of string.'

'Oh Jem,' Astrid shook her head in mocking jest.

'Yeah, so what about you? You and Weston hitched yet?'

'Consider this expedition our extended honey-moon,' Weston grinned.

'Is it something about this ship?' Jem shook his head later, as he saw Tarku and Melissa, heads together, hand in hand like school kids, but asleep, as they sat in the back seat on route to their next adventure. He turned to John, 'This, my friend, is going to be a very long trip. Do you know any good pranks? They're perfect pickings, look at them,' he laughed.

John chuckled, 'Leave them be Jem, leave them be. The boy might not be invincible anymore but he's still the best fighter you'll ever see, and besides, he's likely got a longer prank list, he'd get you back good and proper.'

'Are you saying I'm not up to the challenge?'

'I'm saying you'll get beat.'

'Alright then, not today, but I'll think of something to make this flight interesting.'

'What, the view's not good enough?' Weston laughed.

'It is something isn't it,' Jem agreed as they flew on.

John just smiled. Twenty years ago he had set out to find his daughter. He would never have dreamed that he would spend fifteen years searching, five years waiting, and then end up here, with a baby at peace on Shorakai, and two grown up daughters any father would be proud of. He'd set the truth before them, and their response had been the same; nothing would please them more than to call him father. Already Sjyntani had asked if he would return to Shorakai when a wedding date had been arranged, to give her away, the answer was yes of course, it would be his great privilege and honour. He was sure Tarku and Melissa wouldn't be far behind. Jem was almost a son now too. It seems John's family had grown somewhat bigger all at once. John's grin broadened even further at the thought.

An Epilogue :

Have you seen a real blue sky? Not just blue, but wide as the eye can see blue, and deep, eternally deep. A vista at once calm and still, but free and full of dreams, so open, but somehow undeniably certain, and as much a part of the fullness of existence as breathing. This is such a sky. This is a sky full of promise, a blessed mantle covering a reclaimed landscape. The earth is new again - in its first turbulent throes.

Those few fragile islands of life that survived the reconstruction now send out their surveyors and explorers, and one intrepid media crew begins an expedition hoping to document these new territories, because the world is still hungry for stories, as always.

You don't need to be an expert to know more wars will be fought, more discoveries made, more fortunes won and lost. That men will be as they always are, despite the generous earth. They will go on as they have gone on, they will make the same mistakes their fathers made, but at least now they have another few thousand years grace.

P.P.S

Weston took out the Gerning award that year, of course, and Melissa's sincere photographs of the crew, photographs she'd taken covertly at significant moments along their expedition, were the basis for the latest book put out by TnTv's print media.

'This one's my favourite one,' Melissa turned to a page as she proudly showed Tarku the new book in her hands.

'I didn't know you'd taken that,' he laughed. 'I was smiling, you'd made me smile.'

'You're still smiling.'

'Same reason, Butterfly.'

www.ingramcontent.com/pod-product-compliance
Lightning Source LLC
Chambersburg PA
CBHW030551260626
47157CB00006B/2272